WAS SHE
OR
WASN'T SHE?

"But I don't look the way I used to."

"Don't be ridiculous. You obviously aren't a restoree," Harlan said sharply. Sara felt tension return to his body. "There isn't a mark on you."

"That's just it . . . there isn't. I've lost three scars. I had a long gash on my arm where I . . ."

Her voice trailed off as she saw his face. The mixture of horror, distaste, disbelief, anger—and, strangely, hatred— stunned her.
Now she knew something was really wrong . . . but she didn't know how bad things had become!

"*Restoree* is SF at its best . . ."
—KLIATT

RESTOREE

Anne McCaffrey

A Del Rey Book

BALLANTINE BOOKS • NEW YORK

To
"My Favorite Relations"
G. N. McElroy

A Del Rey Book
Published by Ballantine Books

ISBN 0-345-30279-6

Manufactured in the United States of America

First Edition: September 1967
Eighth Printing: November 1982

Cover art by The Brothers Hildebrandt

CHAPTER ONE

THE ONLY WARNING OF DANGER I had was a disgusting wave of dead sea-creature stench. For a moment, it overwhelmed the humid, baked-pavement smell that permeated the relatively cooler air of Central Park that hot July evening. One minute I was turning off the pathway to the Zoo in search of a spot that might have a breeze from the lake and the next I was fainting with terror.

I have one other impression of that final second before all horror overcame me: of a huge dirigible-shaped form looming lightless. I remember that only because I thought to myself that someone was going to catch hell for flying so low over the city. Then the black bulk of the thing seemed to compress the stinking air through my skull, robbing me of breath and sanity with its aura of alien terror.

Of the next long interlude, which I am informed was a period of withdrawal from a reality too disrupting to contemplate, I remember only isolated incoherencies. It is composed of horrifying fragments, do-si-do-ing in a random partnering of all nightmare symbols, tinted with unlikely colors, accompanied by fetid odors, by intense heat and shivering cold and worst of all, nerve-memories of excruciating pain. I remember, and forget as quickly as possible, dismembered pieces of the human body; the pattern of severed blood vessels, sawn bones, the patterns of the fine lines on wrinkled skin. And throat-searing screams. And a voice, dinning into the ears of my mind, repeating with endless, stomach-churning patience, collections of syllables I strained desperately to sort into comprehensible phrases.

Red, yellow, blue beads rolled, parabolically, evading a needle and its umbilical string. A spoon dipped into a blue bowl, into a red bowl; a spoon dipped into a red bowl, into a blue bowl, until my body was forced into the mold of a spoon and itself was dipped into the bowl, my greatly enlarged mouth the bowl of that spoon. Plaits of human hair swayed toward oddly shaped sheets of pale white leather. The gentle voice with the iron insistence of the dedicated droned on and on until each repetition seemed to trampoline into the gray matter of my mind.

Then, after eons of this inescapable routine, I began to clutch at snatches seen normally and rationally; a face on a sea of white which stretched limitlessly beyond my blinkered perception. I would be aware of bending over this face. I kept trying to make the face resemble someone I knew: one of the junior account men who invaded the source library of the advertising agency where I worked; one of the anonymous faces on the buses I rode from my 48th Street cold-water flat.

At other times, I would find a tray of food held in front of me and associate myself as the carrier. This troubled me even more because of all things, I hated serving food. In college I had paid for my board working as a waitress and sometimes a cook in private families, resenting the necessary exigencies of a junior female member of a large family. It seemed to me my earliest recollections were of setting or clearing the table and serving food. But the feeling of the entire scene here had an alien quality to it, despite the fact my coherent vision was limited. The tray and dishes had a different touch and the smell of the food was unfamiliar.

The next identifiable sensation was that of the warmth of sun on my shoulders and the caress of wind, of green light in my eyes. I heard screams that can only be heard and not described, but they might have been from earlier sections of the nightmare. I had the feeling on my hands of the slippery softness of soapy water. Then the face on the vast expanse of white would reappear. I gradually became aware of an unfailing order in the procedure of my dreams. Face, food, water, sunshine, face, food, water, dark. The repetition was endless and I was passive to it, prompted by the droning voice, no longer gentle, but equally insistent.

Slowly, not just that face on a sea of white but

peripheral details took form and coherency. The face would belong to a man, an ugly man with vacant eyes, black hair, sallow pitted skin. The fact that he bore not one morsel of resemblance to any of my brothers or any of the overbright young men at the agency gave me distinct pleasure. His face was on a pillow which was on a bed of hospital height. And always I was in the position of looking down, not being on a level, with him. Had he been bending over me, I might just have been alarmed that all the tales of rampant white slavery in New York City drilled into me by my provincial parents were indeed true. My first conscious query was why was I not the patient since, obviously, something was very wrong with me.

The mere sensation of sun warmth gradually expanded to include oddly shaped trees with willowy, waving fronds, and with the feel of the wind was the cool fragrance of floral odors.

The ground no longer hovered somewhere beyond my comprehension but was suddenly squarely under my feet. I was standing on a walk, bordered with blooms I never remembered seeing before. The trays I carried contained individual colored dishes with foods that smelled appetizingly and I fed them to the face in the sea of white.

I cannot judge the length of this semiconscious state. I was a passive observer, comparing the anomalies with personal recollections and finding no parallels. I was, however, not the least bit alarmed by all that, which should have alarmed me, as I am normally very curious, in a discreet way.

I do know that the transition into full consciousness was brutally abrupt. As if the focus of my mind, so long blurred, had suddenly been returned to balance. As if a kaleidoscope had astonishingly settled into a familiar design instead of random, meaningless patterns.

Out of the jumble, my grateful eyes reviewed an entire panorama of sloping bluish lawns, felicitously set with flowering shrubs and populated by couples strolling casually down the paths. Each woman wore a gown the exact cut and color of the blue one I wore. Each man had a blue tunic and a coat gruesomely reminiscent of a straitjacket. Beyond the bluish swath, lay little cottages of white stone, with wide windows, barred by white columns at narrow regular intervals. Directly in front of my face was a shimmering opacity I recognized, by some agency, as a fence and dangerous to me.

I was not, however, one of a couple. I was in a group of eight people, strolling the walks, and the other seven were men. Only one, the man directly to my left, wore the strange jacket.

A voice, issuing from the left side of the man in the jacket, spoke an irritating combination of comprehensible words and jumbled syllables.

"And so . . . he is as well as can be expected. Certainly his physical appearance has improved. Notice the firm tone to his flesh, the clear color of his complexion."

"Then you do have hopes?" asked an urgent, wistful younger voice. Its owner I could see without noticeably turning my head. He was a young man, tall and slender, with a sensitive, pale-gold tired face dominated by deeply circled eyes. He was dressed in a simple but rich fashion. His concerned attention was on the man whose harness controls I now found myself holding.

"Hopes, yes . . . [another incomprehensible spate of words. It seemed to me I was hearing another language in which I could not yet think] . . . we have had so few successes with this sort of. . . . Our skill does not include mental breakdowns . . . the strains and concerns of affairs in your behalf and for his country . . . but you may be sure we are taking the very best care of him until that time. Monsorlit's . . ."

This was not the reassurance the young man wanted. He sighed resignedly, placing a gentle hand on my charge's shoulder. It was the lightest of gestures, but it stopped the man stolidly in his tracks. In the vacuousness of the face, there was no comprehension of the action, no reaction, no sign whatever of intelligence.

"Harlan, Harlan," the youth cried in bitter distress, his eyes brimming with tears, "how could this have happened to *you?*"

"Come, Sir Ferrill," commanded a stern voice with no vestige of sympathy in its hardness. "You know that emotional stress can bring about another one of your attacks. You have little enough strength as it is."

The speaker fetched round in my sight. Immediately I saw his face, I disliked him. I considered myself scarcely a proper judge in this newly rational state of mind, but the instinct to hate him was as sharp as the fleshy face of the man was bland. His eyes, close together on either side of a large nose, were disturbingly cold, calculating and wary. His full sensuous lips sealed tightly over his teeth and his heavy jaw was implacable. His heavyset figure was ponderous, not just fleshy or muscular but unwieldy.

"Your solicitude for my health is touching, Gorlot, but I will judge which emotions I can afford," snapped the young man with such regality the implacable man demurred.

The youth continued to speak, ignoring this Gorlot.

"Since that is his condition, I must leave Harlan here," he said to a corpulent, moon-faced individual who bowed with oily obsequity at each phrase. "But ... if I am not informed the moment an improvement is noticed ..." and the youth left the threat in mid-air with the authority of one who is used to complete obedience.

The unctuous man bowed again to the back of the youth who turned and walked with brisk steps down another path. The smile on the fat man's face did not indicate obedience to the injunction. Nor did the knowing look this Gorlot exchanged with him. The others in the party walked into my line of vision and followed the youth and Gorlot.

When they were out of hearing, the fat man turned to me with a sneer and snapped a command, "To the house," and I, obviously from some well-rehearsed practice in that dim past from which I had so recently emerged, turned myself and my charge around and took a path toward a little cottage among the trees.

At the door stood an armed attendant, a brutish, coarse-looking person who spoke as we approached but spoke as one who knows he isn't heard.

"Back in your cage, most high, noble and exalted Regent." He threw open the door he had just unlocked. With a brutal shove he pushed my charge into the house. With an equally brutal and obscene caress, he pushed me inside and snapped the door lock.

The patient lay crumpled over the chair into which he had been pushed. I wondered how I would be able to get him to his feet, for he was tall and big-boned. But, as I put one hand under his arm, he took it as a signal and almost unaided got to his feet. His shins were bleeding slightly, but there was no sign of expression in the vacant eyes.

"Poor man," I muttered to myself, "which of us has been the madder?"

"Take off harness," blared a voice from the ceiling, startling me breathless. I spotted the grillwork that housed the speaker. "Take off harness," the voice repeated, slowly, distinctly, as to a child or . . . a childlike mind.

I did as I was told.

"Take off harness," the voice repeated four more times even as I had completed the task. "If I've said that once, I've said it a million times," the voice grumbled in a lower and more normal tone.

"You'd gripe in a priest's cave, you would," came a half-muffled reply. "By the Seven Brothers, you won't find me complaining. This life suits me fine. Plenty of food, nothing much to do except lock doors and . . . unlock any pretty legs I want."

"You like that, you Milbait," was the sneering reply.

"Ahhh, that's your main problem in life, Balon, you have to have a struggle to please you. Not me."

"Who do you think you are, telling me what my problem is? Monsorlit?" Balon growled. His voice altered again as he issued another command. "Seat patient."

I scuffled with the chair, picked it up, half pushing the man into it.

"Get tray at wall slot. Get tray at wall slot."

I located the wall slot and the tray on which were two sets of dishes, one red and one blue.

"Feed patient blue food. Feed patient blue food."

My patient ate with a half-animal intensity, snapping at each bite as the spoon touched his lips, gulping it down half-chewed.

"Eat red food. Eat red food," was the next order. "Damned if I care if the dummies eat or not. They give me Milshivers."

"You'd care all right if you had to feed all of Gleto's drugged prizes yourself. Then I'd never hear the end of your blasting. Your trouble is, you don't know a prime cave when you see it. Me, I like it fine. Those dummies do all our work. This is better pay than patrolling, too. Not that I'd patrol with the half-blown reliners they call squadron leaders these days. And not with a war on Tane. Who wants hand-to-hand combat? And it's better than running illegals. You can never tell nowadays when Gorlot's going to have to make more commitments and who wants to end up with a needle? Or tied to the local Mil Rock?"

"Balon," shouted a new voice in the background I recognized as Gleto's. "You've been at Lamar again. Leave him alone. Just luck I looked in at him on my way to greet Ferrill. You keep your hands off him."

"If you knew what the Milrouser had done to me, you wouldn't . . ." began the grumbler passionately.

"I don't care if he blocked your cave," Gleto said angrily, "you cut him up once more and you'll join him."

"Eat red food. Eat red food," Balon snarled into the speaker system.

There were no more incidental remarks over the speaker that day, but it was a constant source of odd, vulgar dialogues between much the same personnel during the next week.

Although I never understood their topical references until much later, my understanding of the language increased immensely . . . if limited to a very rough vernacular. I knew there was a war going on between these people and the inhabitants of another planet, Tane. I knew that the army unit, the Patrol, was considered to be run by incompetents and that the casualties were high. That there was a sudden epidemic of insanity that caused the guards no end of secret amusement.

I had been told by Balon to return the tray after I had eaten the red food. I was then told to be seated in the other chair of the room without any further commands for what seemed a long time. My private meditations were uninterrupted until the green sun had sunk from sight and a twin-moonlit night well darkened.

As the greening twilight increased to the point of low visibility, I was briefly startled to see the lights in the four corners of the room come on. It was not overly bright for me to assume that a central agency turned on all the functions of the cottage, remotely controlling the order of the days with no need for personal contact. This isolation was merciful to me as I sorted out truth from fancy in newly regained sanity.

Perhaps, on another day, if I hadn't heard the coarse interchange, I might have innocently announced my rationality. The wise decision to remain silent was strengthened each day by the grotesque conversations I overheard. It was lucky, too, that there was not a single diversion in that barely furnished room so that my activity, outside of the care of my patient, was restricted to looking out the window or sitting looking at my vacant-eyed companion. Any other industry would have immediately communicated my change to the guard on his random rounds.

I learned early that the speaker system was two-way. A chance, overloud comment on my part fetched the guard instantly. To him I presented the same vacant stare that inhabited the face of my charge. He looked at me suspiciously, caressed me in a vulgar fashion that shocked me motionless and departed with a shrug of his shoulders. After that I lived with another dread, that one of them might select me for his pleasure.

It was a good thing, too, that there was no visual check installed in the cottage or I should have been apprehended the very next morning of my rationality as I stood in front of the window and made my most amazing discovery.

For the body I inhabited bore few resemblances to the one I distinctly remembered possessing. It was the same height, same chestnut hair, but it was a slim, graceful figure I saw, not my former awkward self. And my skin was a warm golden color. All over. In contour my face was similar, but now my blue eyes stared at, to me, a totally transformed face. My incredulous fingers softly caressed the new, marvelously congruous nose. No longer was I crucified by that horrible hooked monstrosity bequeathed me with hereditary injustice from some New England zealot. This new nose, all golden, fine-grained skin, was straight, short and charming. I stroked it, reveling in the tactile sensation that proved it was really part of me and there was no more of it than I could see in the window reflection. How many, many agonies that horrid nose had given me. How often I had railed at the injustice of parents who produced child after indiscriminate child and had no money to provide more than the basic needs and none to remedy cruel genetic jokes.

Had they been at least sympathetic, I would not have left home. But they couldn't even understand why I wanted to save money for plastic surgery. Only Jewish girls felt it necessary to have nose bobs. The fact that I looked Semitic with such a nose didn't bear on that problem.

"You are as God made you, Sara, and you've much to commend you to any decent self-respecting man."

"But nothing to commend myself to *me*," I remembered saying, "and I don't see any decent self-respecting men pounding a path to my door."

They couldn't argue that, certainly, for not even my brothers could be blackmailed or pressured into getting me dates. But they could and did argue against my going to New York although I had a written job offer, a good one with an advertising firm, confirmed and secured.

"Why the library right here in Seaford has offered you a very nice position," my father had argued.

"Seaford? I might as well rot in the end of the world," I had cried. "I'm twenty-one and I'm leaving home. If I cook another meal for anyone, it'll be for myself and not for six field-hand appetites that don't know decent food from pigs' swill." I had glared at my brothers, busy shoveling food into their mouths. "If I iron anything, it'll be my own clothing, not shirts and shirts and shirts."

"The girl's ill," my mother had declared as if this explained my unexpected outburst.

"All that education," my father had retorted sourly. He had resented my insistence on college, to the point where I had had to work constantly to support myself: making ends meet only because library majors got state support.

"I'm not ill. I'm sick, but not of education. I'm sick of Seaford and everyone in it."

"But everyone knows you here, hon," Seth, the brother next oldest to me, said soothingly. He alone came nearest to appreciating my despair. He had needed glasses desperately as a young boy and his now permanently damaged eyes were weak, watering and subject to continual inflammations.

"And *no one* wants me," I had cried from the bitterness of my soul. "At twenty-one, I have never even had a date."

"I'm leaving, Mother," I had repeated quietly and to end conversation had started to clear the table. And I did leave, taking my suitcase from the back porch on my way out the kitchen door to catch the night bus to Wilmington and the train to New York City.

But now, here on some strange planet, God only knows how many light-years from Seaford, Delaware, I had my new nose. I giggled. If I ever got back home, I could use my savings for a trip to Europe. Only I was abroad already.

I stroked my nose again and then the smooth, golden-skinned arms where a dark hairy growth had once added to the list of my physical embarrassments.

Further examination proved that three prominent scars, the rewards of trying to play tomboy to my older brothers, were gone from my body. Of my disfiguring marks, only the double gash on my right instep where I had stepped on a bottle wading remained. But the corns on my toes from shoes too short for growing feet were gone.

I was utterly delighted, mystified and grateful to, if appalled by, the strange agency that had caused this transformation. I was all my most glowing dreams had once evoked. Not beautiful but pretty, healthy looking with my golden tan (only it wasn't a tan, I discovered), properly curved—and precious little advantage could I see of it, locked in one room with a mindless idiot.

The air of danger and despair that hung over the pleasant gardens and bare cottages could not be mistaken. When outsiders walked among us, the guards were tensely alert. The lack of treatments of any kind, the tenor of the conversations I overheard on the loudspeakers, contrasted strangely with the luxurious surroundings and the physical appearance girls and patients were made to maintain. The other women who paraded with their charges were pretty, perfect in their prettiness with almost frightening similarity. Their expressions were only slightly more intelligent than those of their patients. A case of the dolt caring for the idiotic in a moronic paradise.

I learned the reason for the simple harness that had to be strapped on my man before each promenade in the garden. A small, needled vial containing a tan, viscous fluid was aimed at the right arm through the padding that kept both arms bound to the sides. A jerk on the reins exerted a pressure that drove the needle into the arm.

I saw one man run berserk, yelling, dragging the girl who, in her stupidity, still clutched the reins. He halted abruptly, screaming in agony, and dropped rigid to the ground. The performance thoroughly frightened me and I regarded the big man I cared for with alarm. I knew of no such precautions should a seizure overtake a patient in the cottage. One night, though, I did hear the sudden crescendo of hysterical laughter, shrieks and a final shrill cry from a neighboring cottage. I did see the limp, bloody figure of a girl carried out. Another pretty, blue-robed woman took her place by the next exercise hour, vacantly parading her glassy-eyed charge. I took to staring at my ugly man at all times, hoping to forestall such an occurrence in my cottage. I knew every line on his face, every pitted scar, every twitch of his muscles. At one point, I started with every deep breath he took.

My patient received his first professional visit eight days

after my recovery. Three men came in; a white-coated technician pushed in a small treatment cart and immediately left; the fat-faced man called Gleto came in and a man whose appearance was an odd contrast to Gleto's.

Gleto ordered me to stand in one corner and vacantly I moved after what I considered an appropriate time for moronic comprehension. I stood, however, so that I could see everything that went on and the third man held my attention most.

He was not tall, just my height, and carried himself stiffly erect. His movements were all as precise as a Scots guardsman, no motion was wasted. His skin seemed to be drawn tightly across his skull and each straight black hair on his head was precisely combed into place. His nose was high-bridged and thin; his lips were thin, his eyes of a nondescript shade were penetrating and intense, set deeply into his skull. There was no expression on his face nor were there any lines that indicated he had ever had any expression. A colder personality I never met nor a more impressive one. In dress, manner, color, motion, speech, he was a machine of efficiency, not a human being.

He made a rapid and thorough examination of the patient, skimming the first page of the stiff chart on the treatment wagon without missing a word. Looking up, he said:

"I see no need whatever of increasing the dosage now. The injection every two weeks plus the oral amounts in his food are ample to subdue his personality," and he implied that his valuable time had been wasted.

"I'm taking no chances," Gleto replied accusingly, "and you haven't been here in two months. You know how powerful Harlan is physically," and the heavy, fat eyelids flickered with unctuous insolence, "since it took three injections to hold him under the first week."

The cold man looked at Gleto. "And you will no doubt recall from whose laboratories cerol originated and who is most familiar with its properties. I am no more eager for his recovery than you. It would interrupt my research at a time when success is a matter of weeks away." The thin, precise eyebrows raised imperceptibly and the cold man reached for the chart again, flipping over a few rigid sheets before his thin finger jabbed at a notation.

With no expression he now indicated displeasure.

"Where is the weekly absorption count? If you are stupid enough to ignore the simple precaution of an absorption count, naturally you are stupid enough to sit quivering with fright that Harlan might recover. I thought I had made the necessity of those checks adequately clear to your technicians."

Gleto attempted to pass this off.

"Do not evade the issue, Gleto," came the implacable voice. "The absorption count has not been taken for four weeks. One is to be taken immediately and retaken every other week. When I have perfected a simple check, I do not intend to waste time coming here just to remind you to use it."

"I don't have the technicians to . . ."

"What about that . . . fellow outside?"

Gleto snorted at the suggestion.

"I thought so. You've spent only enough of your wealth to maintain an outward appearance of efficiency and shiver in your bed at night because your avarice prevents you from hiring sufficient personnel to run this *place* properly."

Gleto looked at him suspiciously and then twisted his lip into a sneer.

"You don't fool me, Monsorlit; absorption rates, ha! That's just an excuse to get more of your dummies off your hands."

Monsorlit turned his eyes from the chart he had started to reread to gaze at the fat man. The room became still, broken only by the breathing of the patient, until the sneer left Gleto's face and he began to shift his bulk restlessly.

"Your assessment of the situation is erroneous and I mistakenly credited you with more medical acumen than you possess. And I correct your term 'dummy' to 'mental defective.' " Monsorlit's voice without changing pitch gave the effect of a shouted disgust for Gleto. "Since your perception is limited by its effect on your cash pouch, I will send, with my compliments, a repossessed technician who can perform this simple but necessary test. He will come each fifth day. I will have one ready for such tasks in four weeks. In the meantime," Monsorlit took a lancet and ampul and deftly took a blood sample from the ugly man.

Gleto recovered his poise and affected a knowing smile. "Your generosity, indeed," he scoffed.

"The technician's instructions will be limited to Harlan, as he is the only one with whom I am concerned," Monsorlit continued, taking up a filled syringe, testing it and then plunging it into the patient's vein. The man's body became rigid with muscular tension, quivered as if trying to release itself from the grip of the drug and finally relaxed. Sweat beaded his brow and rolled unheeded to the pillow.

"If he's here, why can't he do Trenor's nine as well," Gleto insisted angrily.

Monsorlit stood up, wiped his hands precisely with an antiseptic solution.

"As I said, my only concern is Harlan. If you wish to hire the services of the technician for the others, you may check with the business director for the rates."

Gleto's face turned an apoplectic purple and he controlled himself with effort.

"That's how you market your dummies. Oh, you're clever, Monsorlit, but one day . . ."

Monsorlit eyed him dispassionately.

"One day my techniques will replace this . . . this," his gesture indicated the gardens and cottages, "unprofessional arrangement. There will be no need for it. Men may come to my hospital, broken in body or mind, and leave whole and sane."

Gleto's little eyes widened with a touch of horror.

"They aren't dummies then; you've been restoring again. That's your deal with Gorlot. I thought your safe-from-Milness had taken a tumble." Gleto laughed derisively now. "How long do you think it'll be before Council finds out! And gasses you and your vegetables!" Gleto stopped with a sudden thought and gasped, looking at me in terror. "Is this one a restoree? Are all these dummies restorees? Are you unloading the dead-alive on me?" he screeched, advancing on Monsorlit.

"Does she act like a restoree?" the physician asked calmly. "No, she acts exactly as she is, a moron from my Mental Defectives Clinic, repossessed through shock techniques of enough intelligence to perform the monotonous and routine duties of your establishment just as others from my Clinic pick fruits and vegetables in the farmlands of Motlina and South Cant. Don't think you're the only miser to take advantage of this type of limited perception personnel in these times of worker rebellions and rising prices. And don't think you do me a favor when you use them. The only favor is to your fat self and your fattening purse." Monsorlit accurately judged the fat man's capacity for insult and took up another subject.

"The technician will be sent here for Harlan's absorption rates and, because of his limited intelligence, will be unable to grasp the necessity for performing any other tests. Trenor will, for all his imperfections, take a jaundiced view toward your neglect of his nine reluctant patients. The decision is up to you and I believe your loss would be the greatest."

Monsorlit left the room, motioning to the technician to collect the cart.

Gleto stared after the precise figure, pouting angrily, and when the technician nervously tipped over several bottles on the table, his fat fist clubbed the man viciously. Satisfied, he hitched his tunic into a more comfortable crease over his shoulders and stalked out. I stood staring in front of me while the cart was wheeled out and for some minutes after the lock snapped into place. The tension of the scene between Gleto and Monsorlit was cold and heavy in the room and I was cold and scared.

THE UGLY MAN WHOM THEY called Harlan lay twitching occasionally. I had considered it misfortune enough that he should have fallen over the edge of sanity in the prime of life. Now I knew him to be an unwilling drugged victim of some scheme, my pity was tinged with outraged righteousness. I looked more closely at the face, hoping to find in it some vestige of intelligence I had missed, some reassurance of personality to fit in with the entirely different role in which he was cast.

His gray eyes, their pupils dilated to the edge of the iris, stared with their customary vacuity at the ceiling. I saw now that the ugly face did have an innate strength and that immobility did not rob his long, heavily boned frame of its look of power. I wondered if a vibrant personality overcame the basic ugliness of features. Perhaps a smile. I fashioned one on the lax lips, but it was too much a mockery for me to judge the spontaneous effect.

I had noticed during my care of him the scars on his person: the new tissues were smooth, no gaping pulls to indicate stitches, not even on the raggedy gash across one cheek. The tip of one index finger was missing. He was a battered and bedamned fellow.

As I pitied him, I pitied myself, for my sympathy now tied me to him more effectively than any possible dedication to a mental cripple. I was stung with an impulse to batter down the door and run, run, run away from the fear, the implications of evil, the vulgarity of the guards and the massive frustrating boredom. I wanted to leave all this unfamiliarity, and somehow, although logic indicated I was nowhere near my own world, find my way home.

After I had settled him for the night, it occurred to me that if he were sane, he could help. And perhaps, he could be made sane. Monsorlit had spoken of doses in his food.

If I could withhold his food long enough, he might partially recover, at least enough to help me.

There was one drawback. If I didn't feed him, his hunger would betray me. And I would go hungry if I fed him all my food. I decided, in the final analysis, that I had no choice but to try this idea. I certainly didn't know the planet and he did.

The next morning I fed him most of my food, and just a little of his own, eating the remainder of mine and some of his to sustain me. I felt strangely disoriented all day and had difficulty in forcing myself to move. The next day this feeling had increased so noticeably that I ate none of his food and gave him none. I got very hungry.

By the fifth day, I was ravenous and he was so restless during the night I had to block the speaker grill with a pillow. He was hungry, too, and bit savagely at the spoon, so that I gave him even the little I had reserved for myself, eating only enough of the blue food to stop the roaring within me.

That night, he spoke in his sleep and I lay rigid with terror that the pillow had not sufficiently muffled the sound. Every moment I expected the guard to come striding in.

During breakfast on the sixth day, his eyes blinked and he tried desperately to focus them. He was struggling so hard, mouthing sounds in an effort to speak, that I was torn between the desire to hear and the necessity of keeping him quiet.

Such hope as swelled in my heart for his return to sanity was rudely disappointed during our morning walk. He did not seem to grasp my furtive, whispered explanations. His eyes still blinking furiously to focus were as vacuous as ever. At dinner, he ate more normally, chewing with intense concentration. The night was a continual struggle for me, against the sleep I desperately craved, against his moaning which I had to muffle against my shoulder. The next morning, he actually seemed to see me and I smiled encouragingly, hopefully, patting his hand reassuringly. The witlessness had left his expression and he looked at me, deeply puzzled, struggling to form a question when the guard walked in on one of his sporadic visits. Rigid with horror, I stared at the man I had almost rescued, my one chance to leave this horrible place suddenly torn from me as success was so near.

The guard barely glanced at me. Furiously he jerked his finger at the red bowls and then, shouting a litany of "Blue bowl for the patient. Blue bowl for the patient," he struck me again and again with his whip. I shrieked in pain and fear and cringed back from the flailing whip, trying to climb under the bed, away from the searing lash.

"This imbecile piece of idiocy is color-blind all of a sudden," he yelled at the loudspeaker. "Blue bowl for the patient. Blue bowl for the patient," he shouted, emphasizing his phrases with lashes for me until his rage was spent and I lay weeping, sore and bleeding, half under the bed.

Gleto arrived in minutes and examined the patient, giving him an injection and watching as I was made to feed Harlan from the blue bowls. Gleto added his blows to my painful back, grinning sadistically at my yelps. I cowered back against the wall as far from him as I could get.

"What bowl do you feed the patient from?" he demanded, advancing on me. "Red bowl?"

I shook my head violently.

"Blue bowl?"

I nodded violently.

"Blue bowl, blue bowl, blue, blue, blue," he roared, punctuating each word with an open-handed slap on whatever part of my twisting body it met.

"Blue, blue, blue," I shrieked back, covering my face with my arms and keeping my back to the wall.

"That'll take care of her," Gleto grunted with satisfaction and, to my weeping relief, he and the guard left.

Although some of the weals on my back and legs were bleeding, a warm soaking in the shower was all the treatment I had. That night, uncomfortable to the point where no position gave me relief or the solace of sleep, I lay awake. Several times, Harlan's heavy limbs overlapped me and made me cry out involuntarily. The speaker chortled back with delight at my discomfort. I resolved not to give them additional satisfaction and stifled my moans.

Mulling over my "bravery," I realized that I had actually escaped very lightly. The guards and Gleto were so secure in their assumption of my idiocy, they never once had questioned a deliberate attempt on my part to feed the prisoner the wrong food. They also assumed that I had made the mistake only once. They had not examined Harlan closely, but the administration of the drug had drawn him back into his witlessness. No technician, though, had come to take an absorption count. I had not yet lost my chance to escape nor to free Harlan from his stupor.

I was not lucky enough to continue my experiment with Harlan as immediately as I had resolved. A guard was present at every feeding for the next four days. Four longer days I never endured, filled with constant cuffs that added new bruises to barely healed ones and new obscenities to a list my limited experience had never wildly imagined.

As soon as I was sure they had decided I had learned my lesson, I started again. Nothing could have induced me to acquiesce now. That brief, if interrupted, respite from the drugged food contributed to Harlan's quicker recovery. By the fourth day, he responded to my insistent urgings for silence. On the fifth day, he spoke for the first time on the morning walk. I saw the deliberate effort he made to keep his voice low. It was difficult for him to enunciate. He had to repeat the simplest phrase with frustrating ineptness.

"They beat you," he managed to say finally, his eyes focusing on the bruises on my face and arms. I clutched at him and nearly wept for the unexpected comfort of his first rational words. A deep feeling of gratitude, joy, respect and love flooded me. I had been too long denied a normal society. The bruises abruptly lost their aches and I straightened shoulders I had curved against the tenderness of my back.

"How long?" he struggled to say, "am I here?"

"I don't know. I have no way of telling."

The approach of the guard curtailed conversation for a while.

"Way escape?"

"I don't know."

"You must," he insisted.

I steered him toward the menacing opacity of the force screen fence and he nodded imperceptibly in understanding.

"There has to be a way," he asserted. "The date?" and I could only shake my head as his look reproached me for my ignorance. He couldn't know I had never been taught to tell the time of his world nor understand the names of days and months.

We were herded back to the cottage and the guard, while I shuddered apprehensively, kicked Harlan into the room as he always did. I ducked by as quickly as I could as much to escape the lascivious touch of the guard as to caution Harlan against violence and warn him about the ceiling speaker. He was staring at it as I hurried to him, his lips moving, his eyes snapping as the therapy of anger cleared his mind of the last hold of the drug.

He examined his jacket with care and discovered the needle and its paralytic fluid. With bare nails we managed to pry it out of the stiff fabric. He held it in his hand thoughtfully for the prize it was, looking speculatively at the door. He grinned suddenly, not at all nicely, and secreted the vial in the belt of his loose tunic.

I indicated that we would have to sit down, would have to follow the orders of the speaker assiduously, pantomined the pillow over the grillwork and nighttime. He nodded comprehension, sighing with impatience.

So we sat, facing each other. He looked above my head, deep in thought, his big hands flexing and stroking the arm of the chair as we waited.

Now his face was alive with the spirit of him, he was no longer an ugly person. His deep-set eyes sparkled and his mobile face showed some of the changes within him his thoughts provoked. Occasionally he would glance at me, curiously, smiling to reassure me. Once or twice, after some thought struck him, he inhaled as if to speak, caught himself and compressed his lips impatiently.

The arrival of dinner was a very welcome diversion. He reached for the blue bowl and I all but snatched it out of his hands. I hurriedly dumped it in the commode and showed him that it could not be eaten.

With a quizzical expression he regarded the one small portion of dinner that remained, shrugged his shoulders and divided it in two. Bowing with mock ceremony, he handed me my spoon with a flourish that made me want to laugh. We ate slowly to make our stomachs think they were being fed. I have since looked back on that bizarre first meal with Harlan as one of the happiest moments of my life.

To have found a friend, again, to be companionable with another human!

The next day, at lunchtime, we had an awful moment. As Harlan was about to dump the blue bowl with obvious relish, I heard the lock turn. Harlan needed no prompting to assume a stupid expression. I began, slowly, to feed him from the blue bowl. The guard watched this performance, fingering his whip. I trusted he interpreted my trembling as fear of a beating rather than terror at discovery. He left and the lock clicked us into privacy.

Harlan rose swiftly and, by the simple expedient of thrusting a finger down his throat, expelled the drugged food.

That first night, lying beside him on our mutual bed after the muffling pillow had been crammed against the grillwork was another of my special memories. I was keenly aware of his warm strength beside me. Before I had had no thoughts at all about the propriety of sleeping next to an inert moron, but a vibrant personality rested beside me now and I was acutely conscious of myself and him.

Harlan recovered control of his tongue, but he was puzzled at my own still-halting speech and my inability to understand parts of his questions.

His perplexity made me nervous in a half-fearful way as if by the mere accident of not speaking clearly, I had committed some wrong. Defensively and with some involved explanations of my presence, I managed to make it clear that I knew I came from another solar system. His doubt was so apparent that I sketched the Sun and its planets by fingernail into the bedsheet. It held the impression long enough for him to grasp my meaning.

Immediately his expression became wary and veiled. He strained to see me clearly in the moonlight and shook his head impatiently at the limitations of that glow. We were lying side by side when he suddenly leaned away from his close inspection. He took my hands in his, stroking my wrists with hard thumbs. He sat up and did the same thing to my ankles, then my hairline. His confusion persisted and, against my soundless protest, he turned back my dress to run light, impersonal fingers over the rest of my body as though I had been someone dead. This reassured whatever worried him. But his body remained tense and his expression was no longer as open and friendly as before.

He asked me almost too casually how I got here.

"I don't know. But you do believe me . . . that I'm not from this world?"

He shrugged.

"My sun has nine planets, my world only one moon; my sun is golden, not green," I persisted urgently. "And the reason I have trouble understanding you is that you speak so fast and use words I don't know. It isn't because I'm stupid . . . or insane."

His withdrawal made me frantic that I might lose the precious companionship I had so recently won. He must understand me so he would take me with him. I could see he had every intention of escaping as soon as he could. I had no doubts he would succeed or die in the attempt. Death to me was preferable to the alternative of remaining in this ghastly place.

"I can't remember how I got here," I wailed softly. "I just don't know. I was walking in a park at night on my own planet and something big and black hovered over me. The rest is all mixed up in the most horrible, horrible nightmares."

"Describe them," he demanded in a cold, tight voice that scared me.

The words rolled out. The weight of the grotesque scenes and experiences, walled up in my subconscious, poured out, as if voicing them would erase the remembered horror and terror. I don't recall what I did say and what I couldn't bring myself to say until I realized that I was trembling violently and he was holding me close against him. At first, I thought he was trying to muffle my voice, but then I heard his voice soft with low reassurances and his hands were very gentle.

"Be quiet now. I do believe you. I do. There's only one way you could have got here. No, no. I don't doubt now a thing you've said. But that you are sane and . . . well, it's a miracle."

There was incredulous wonder in his tone. He looked at me again, excitedly. The only thing I cared about was that he was no longer withdrawn and cold, and that he did believe me.

"You know how I got here?"

"Let's say," he demurred candidly, "I know how you must have got to this solar system. But how you reached Lothar and this place, I can't even hazard a guess. The only possible explanation . . ."

"You mean your people have interstellar travel and brought me here as a slave," I interrupted, thinking with a sudden rush of hope that I would be able to get back to Earth. Though what Earth held for me was too mundane after this experience.

He hesitated, considering his next words. Then, settling me into a comfortable position against his shoulder, his lips above my ear, he explained.

"My people didn't bring you here. I'm reasonably sure of that. We do have interstellar travel, but I cannot believe my race has penetrated to your section of space. Before I took so conveniently ill," and his voice was sardonic, "no new exploration was contemplated." He snorted with remembered exasperation. "I am reasonably sure, however, that your planet has been invaded by the curse, and paradoxically, the salvation of our Lothar. We call them the Mil. They're a race of cellular giants which have had interstellar flight since the beginning of our recorded history, some two thousand years ago. To be precise, they *are* the beginning of our recorded history. We are, bluntly, their cattle, their fodder. That's all right, take it easy," he said reassuringly.

His similes forced me to admit to myself what I had desperately tried to hide; that the disassembled pieces of anatomy that twisted and turned through my nightmares were horrifyingly like the joints on hooks in a meat market.

"They have periodically raided this system for centuries. When we finally penetrated one of their depots here on Lothar, [I realized he was using the historic 'we'] we began the long struggle to free ourselves and our planet of this terrible scourge. We turned their own weapons on them and then had to learn how to use them properly and repair them. Kind of progress in reverse. Now, we have not only been able to keep them off Lothar, but also out of this immediate sector of space. Our losses are still heavy in every encounter, as it is difficult to best an enemy with armaments similar to your own. Our big advantage is our own physical structure. However, rarely do any of our ships and patrolmen fall victims of the Mil.

"I don't know how far they range, but I suppose we have forced them to find new sources of supply. Your planet, for one. Easy now. I forget it's difficult for you to accept such a terrible fate for your people. We've lived with it all our lives."

"But, if these . . ."

"Mil, although at one time we called them 'God,'" Harlan remarked, grimly humorous.

". . . these Mil captured me on a raid on Earth, how did I get here? On your planet?"

Harlan frowned. "I would like to believe that our Patrol intercepted the ship you were on and captured it. But . . ." and he stopped as if he could see the fallacies in the theory and they disturbed him. "It must be way past Eclipse; or is it? If it is, I've been here a long time.

Haven't you got *any* idea of how long you've been here?"

"I can only recall the last few weeks clearly. Yet it seems as if I've been here forever. I guess I was in shock or something," I ended lamely. "I certainly was surprised to find I was a nurse for someone else."

"All the more reason to get out of here as soon as possible. My head is clear now and my reflexes feel normal. It's been like swimming through sand. Still," and he looked at me speculatively again, shaking his head, "I don't understand how you managed to remain . . ." he hesitated and supplied another word, ". . . untouched."

"Untouched? Oh, but I don't look the way I used to," I assured him, my hand rubbing my nose.

"Don't be ridiculous. You obviously aren't a restoree," he said sharply. I felt tension return to his body and coldness to his voice. "There isn't a mark on you."

"No, that's just it. There isn't," I replied. "I've lost three scars," and I pointed to the areas involved, "and someone took pity on my . . ." my hand touching my nose.

"Scars? Missing?" he interrupted in a hoarse whisper.

"Yes," I prattled on. "I had a long gash on my arm where I got caught on a picket fence . . ." and my voice trailed off as I saw his face. The mixture of horror, distaste, disbelief, anger and, strangely, hatred, stunned me.

He grabbed my wrists in an angry grip and rubbed them, tracing the junction of hand and arm with fingers that hurt with their prodding. He felt around my ears, pulling my hair back roughly.

"What's the matter?" I pleaded, my delight congealing.

He shook his head, hard, as someone whose neck muscles have contracted spasmodically.

"I don't know, Sara. It's just hard to believe," he replied enigmatically. "Yet you would not have been able to think things through the way you have if . . . We've got to get out of here. We have got to get out!" he said passionately.

With a fluid stride, he crossed the room and yanked the pillow from the grill. He settled back in the bed, patting my arm reassuringly, as if he realized how worried I was by his reactions.

It was a long time before sleep came to either of us. I remember feeling his fingers on my wrist again just as I drifted into unconsciousness.

DURING HIS SLEEPLESSNESS, HARLAN HAD made the only plan of escape our mutual limited knowledge of the asylum afforded. To pass the force screen, we must overpower the guard in the cottage by means of the drug vial we had pried from the straitjacket. Harlan would wear the uniform, I would daub myself with blood, Harlan having assured me that the blood would be donated by the guard. We would try to pass out the gate of this section of the asylum as if I had been attacked by my patient. From there on, we must improvise. If it came to sheer strength, the powerfully built Harlan would prevail. However, neither of us could foresee what preparation might have been made for escapes.

We also had no choice. Each day might bring the arrival of the technician to take Harlan's absorption rate and we were too sure of the results of that test. I also couldn't tell when the next intravenous injection would be administered. With it, I would have to start all over again, denying Harlan the drugged food, waiting for his return to sanity.

Whatever qualms or fears I might have normally entertained were overruled. Harlan's anxiety and frustration intensified my own desire to be out of this mad place. And, too, not once did Harlan intimate he felt he had a better chance of escaping by himself although I was sure he did. He had included my release in his calculations and brushed aside my one half-hearted attempt at sacrifice.

Every day Harlan's recovery had been jeopardized by the random appearances of the guard. This one day, when we were nervously primed for our escape, he was conspicuous by his absence. Harlan had to exert a tremendous control over his impatience and I was constantly forced to remind him during the exercise period to stop charging up the paths, to school his expression into the proper witlessness. He endured these corrections far better than I should have. All in all, by evening both our tempers were frayed by the unrewarded waiting.

As soon as the lights were out, Harlan, releasing some of his frustration in the action, rammed the pillow against the speaker and began to pace around the room in a frenzied way.

His pacing grew as unendurable to me as a fingernail scraped across slate.

"Last night," I began hesitantly, not knowing what I wanted to say but knowing that any conversation was better than this taut silence, "last night, I told you who I was and how I got here. Who are you besides Harlan and how did you get in here? Who drugged you? Why?"

He paused in mid-stride, frowning as my questions brought him out of his thoughts. He gave a sort of snort, smiled and, after another moment's silence, began to talk. He had a pleasant voice when he kept it low, but it had the burr of the military bark and a metallic quality. Gradually, as he talked, he stopped pacing, and then sat down, watching me as he spoke with a disconcerting attention.

"You certainly do deserve some explanations, if only for all the meals you gave up," he said, gripping my shoulder as a gesture of his continued gratitude.

"Before I came here, I was Regent of this planet for my eldest brother's son, Ferrill."

"I thought the guard had called you Regent, but it didn't make any sense then."

Harlan grimaced. "That guard . . . It's the custom here on Lothar for the Commander of the Perimeter Patrol to assume the duties of Regent if the heir to the Warlordship is underage when he becomes a candidate."

"Why couldn't you be Warlord if you were brother to the . . ."

"No, that doesn't follow," Harlan replied blandly. "I should say, Fathor was my half-brother. We had the same father, but Fathor's mother was the first wife and his progeny inherit. Besides, I've other plans for my time once Ferrill is of age. Like finding your planet. I like finding new planets. I like exploring." A boyish grin lit his features. "I've had luck in that direction already. Found two new ones, fraternal planets around the star we call Tane, my fourth year on Patrol."

I gathered this involved more than just searching a section of space until you found stars with satellites. I murmured proper things, only he frowned.

"They've been more trouble than they're worth . . . almost," he continued. "The inhabitants are humanoid, but the gentlest, dumbest people imaginable. They make some of our associates here look like Council members. They've got two of the most beautiful planets, crawling with game animals; Lothar doesn't have too many anymore. Their oceans are full of edible fish; their lands, which the Tanes don't even bother to cultivate, would support millions of us. They've got mineral resources that make the mind swim when you think how many ships, instruments and fuel it means in terms of our fight against the Mil. And those innocent creatures roam from one place to another like pleasant dreamers."

"Haven't the Mil bothered them?"

"Evidently not. They don't have even an elementary sense of caution or suspicion. They would have fled from our expeditionary ships if they had encountered the Mil. Most of our fleet has been recruited from or designed after Mil ships."

"Why are the Tanes trouble then? Can't you just colonize or mine or . . ."

Harlan leaned forward, balancing his elbows on knees and slapping one palm into the other to emphasize a statement. Or, which was disconcerting, he would point his tipless finger at me.

"I don't know about your world, but here on Lothar we're crowded. So crowded that every inch of land is either cultivated or catacombed with mines, cities and factories. We run to big families, sort of law of supply and demand. But the Mil don't harvest us anymore, so every new child crowds his family that much more. There aren't enough jobs to go around nowadays nor is there enough food as there used to be. We don't need so many men in active Patrol, but yet we have to train every young man against the day we're big enough and strong enough to follow the Mil back to their own planet and wipe them off its face."

"So," I interrupted, "everyone who isn't well off wants a share of one of the Tane planets and to hell with the Tanes."

He nodded agreement. "Only it isn't just those that aren't well situated. It's the big landowners, the big industrialists and the big scientists who want priority and mean to get it. And they've got all kinds of reasons."

"I'll bet," and I refrained from giving him a brief account of the American Indian. "And I imagine no one cares what happens to the Tane."

My perspicacity pleased him.

"Council had accepted a plan to allow colonization first for farmers, because our crying need is food. But farmers are conservative and those younger sons, willing to go, those without patrons in Council, are being intimidated or beaten up unless they belong to a certain guild. And the people who lead that guild will buy up the land once the farmers settle on it and that will be the end of individual agricultural expansion. Or, take the small mining outfits. Only a few have dared to apply for permission to work the Tanes. Why? They've found their homes ruined, their credit is suddenly destroyed, or their equipment is wrecked just before takeoff."

"But surely you're trying to find out who's behind it?"

"It is one group," Harlan said wearily. "I'd found that much out before this happened to me. There is one man, or a few men, who were guiding the attacks on my colonists. But what baffles me is: why? I mean, for what reason. You see, Lothar has always had just one purpose since we first shook off the yoke of superstition and managed to repel the Mil from landing on our planet. We mean to destroy the Mil completely. Our whole psychology, our whole history, has been directed toward that aim."

"Perhaps after ... how long did you say ... two thousand years, this purpose is wearing a little thin," I suggested with the Crusades in mind.

"It couldn't," he said without qualification. "Not when the Mil are always so close." He frowned. "You see, actually it's only in the last one hundred and fifty years that we've kept them entirely away from our planet. And we couldn't have done that without Ertoi and Glan."

"Who?"

"Inhabitants of another nearby star. You can see them from here," he said blandly. He pointed out the window to a pulsating red blink that was the primary of the system.

"Ertoi and Glan take care of that entire section of space. We've been able to push our Perimeter Patrol four light-years beyond our own system. Since then, we have adequate protection against a concerted attack. The first time," he said with justifiable pride, "we lost all but two ships of our entire combined fleets, but no Mil landed on our three planets."

"Well, who do you think is the traitor?"

"My second-in-command, a fellow by the name of Gorlot." Harlan's eyes narrowed speculatively. "I'm not sure. It couldn't be that . . . No. They know we're not ready to go after the Mil yet unless that new weapon . . ." and he trailed off tantalizingly. "This Gorlot's a throwback. Uncivilized. He lives only for battle and he's a master strategist. Pulled off some extraordinary maneuvers three Eclipses ago. That's why I seconded his appointment when Gartly retired. But he's no good as a peacetime officer and the Perimeter has been very peaceful. He belongs back in the days of the first Harlan with the Seventeen Sons when it was all we could do to find caves deep enough to escape the Mil. He'd be the proper man to send out to the Mil but . . . That hothead forgets that no Lotharian has the guts," he threw in, "besides himself, because he did it one day on a wager, to walk into a Mil ship until it's been completely decontaminated. The smell of those things is enough to set a tough squadron leader raving. Until the Alliance with Ertoi and Glan, we had to wait until the Mil decomposed inside their ships before we could refit them. Fortunately, the Ertoi and Glan aren't hampered by such childish terrors.

"I wonder," and Harlan drew back into his thoughts for a long time. His conclusions did not settle his mind, for he growled with impatience and resumed his pacing, cursing Gorlot, cursing his own stupidity for falling into the trap of the asylum.

"I've got to get out of here and back to Lothara," he cried in a groan, clenching and unclenching his fists behind his back as he paced.

CHAPTER FOUR

SLEEP THAT NIGHT WAS NOT restful. It was peopled with formless obscenities and charged with fear and anger, frustration and hopelessness. I was alone in the bed when I awoke. Startled I turned in panic and saw with relief that Harlan was up and pacing, his face black with worry and fatigue.

At breakfast there were none of the pleasant panto-mimes we affected about the division and consumption of our scanty ration. Harlan ate quickly, glowering.

The walk in the garden that morning was sheer relief. The four bare walls of the cottage had grown smaller with every passing minute. Harlan had draped his jacket loose-ly on him so that a strong outward pressure would free him. We had agreed to delay returning to our cottage until the guard was forced to round us up. This assured us of a chance of overcoming him once we got to the cottage. So we dawdled at the far end of the grounds on the outside paths following the line of the force screen. We were at the high end, midway between two posts when it hap-pened.

One of the patients went berserk. He threw himself at the screen, dragging his unwilling companion with him. Together they went up into a torch of blue flame, burning fast and hotly with only the echo of screams of unutter-able agony to mark their death.

Even as I stared with paralyzed horror at these human torches, Harlan had reacted to the opportunity. Flinging off the jacket, he grabbed me by the shoulder and together we hurtled into the faltering screen. I thought I, too, would be consumed in flame. The pain and shock that coursed through my body was too intense for me even to scream a protest. Then, once past the weakened barrier, only an endurable ache and burning sensation remained. The burning was quite legitimate because our clothing had been reduced in an instant to scorched tatters. Even the heavily padded jacket was singed brown. Harlan, however, gave me no time to pause and take stock. Grabbing my hand, he pulled me through the land moat around the force screen and into the grain field with its high waving grasses.

"Have you no idea, Sara, where this asylum is?"

"None," I cried, feeling the pull of the sharp grass tendrils against my sensitized flesh. The fence had always blotted out the environs of the asylum.

"Farm, farm, farm," Harlan panted. He was tall enough to see over the rolling fields that stretched out in all directions from the institution. He glanced up at the sun, squinting, but it was too near the zenith to be much help. He halted briefly, sniffing the slight breeze.

"Sea!" he declared and abruptly turned off to the right, guiding me with a firm hand under my elbow.

"Can't we just find a road? It would lead us somewhere," I gasped, struggling to keep my feet under me at the pace he set.

"Road!" he flung at me contemptuously and trotted up the rise in front of us. He kept glancing back over his shoulder. I didn't dare look back. It was all I could do to keep up with him.

We ran through the fields until I had such a grabbing in my side, I could not run farther. He sensed, rather than inquired, about my condition and let me collapse in the shelter of the tall grain at the next rise. Keeping himself sheltered by the grain, he looked out in all directions, again sniffing the breeze.

"We may have a little time before we'll be turned up missing, Sara," he said, dropping down beside me. "They'll have their hands full, rounding up the patients. They may not even take a head count right away. They've gotten lax and overconfident. However, the situation of the asylum itself, located right in the middle of farmlands, makes an air search ridiculously easy." He stopped and grabbed up a handful of straw. "Of course. We've got part of our camouflage right here." He laughed and started stuffing straw into his tunic so that the stalks stuck straight up behind his back and out across his shoulders. I followed his lead and, when my tunic parted over one shoulder, plastered myself hastily with the soft moist earth.

"Good girl," Harlan said and smeared his own skin with dirt where it showed whitely through. We looked like scarecrows after a week's rain when we had finished.

"Now, we will make for the sea. The moment you hear any noise at all, drop flat in the furrows," and he pointed out the cultivation ridges. "The grain is tall enough and thick enough that we may not be visible when they're going to look for running figures. And, they won't expect me to make for the sea," he added cryptically.

He held out his hand to me and, taking a deep breath, I rose and we started out again.

We had scarcely gone the length of that field when I heard something other than our laboring breath. Before I could react on my own, my face was in the dirt, Harlan's body overlapping mine.

Had the searchers been on foot, passing near us, I'm certain the sound of my heart would have given us away. The chirrop, chirrrop of a plane car neared, passed over us, retreated and cautiously we rose, checking to make sure another was not hovering. Running low we made it to the top of the next field. Even I could see that the land was sloping down gradually. The smell of the sea, tart and crisp, was strong enough for me to scent as I held my sweating face up to cool in the wind.

I'm not sure I was grateful for the times we had to lie face down in the moist black soil, waiting till the searchers passed over us. I got my wind back each time, true, but the terror of waiting, unable to risk a glance above, was more breath-snatching than the exertion of flight. Six times we dropped, each time a little nearer to where the land dropped off to the sea. And then, there was the sea before us, a hundred feet down the high straight precipice on which we stood.

My courage sank, for here, at the cliff edge, which seemed to curve for miles in each direction, the fields of tall grain ended. Fifty yards between sea and field was covered with only low straggling bush, inadequate cover for us walking strawstacks.

Harlan caught my despairing appraisal and squeezed my hand reassuringly.

"There are ways down to the beaches."

"And then what?" I gasped, indicating the pounding surf.

"The tide will be going out soon and we can go swiftly on the sand, taking cover under the cliffs if necessary. Much better for us. Come, now we strike northeast. These cliffs tell me exactly where we are."

But he didn't bother to tell me, either because he knew it wouldn't matter or because he forgot I wouldn't know. As it happened, we were in South Cant.

He had held on to the padded jacket all through our flight in the fields. Now, as he removed the straw from his own clothes, he realized my nakedness. Ripping off two of the dangling tapes with which to secure his tattered tunic round his waist, he gave me the jacket. Quickly I threw it on, tying the remains of my dress around my waist.

"Good, the dirt is still useful," he grinned and, taking my hand, we set off again.

Harlan was too good a leader to tire us both to the point where we would be unable to make a final dash. We rested at intervals and a bit longer when we chanced on a stream not far from where we made our descent to the sea beach. As he had predicted, by the time we did find a way down, the tide was retreating from the bronze sands. The cool strand was refreshing to our weary feet.

My flimsy sandals, adequate for treading garden paths, gave way all too quickly on the abrasive surface of the beach. Walking on the damp coarse sands turned into torture for me once the sandals gave out and the soft skin on my feet was abraded with each step. I was wondering how long I could continue this way when I was brought up sharply against Harlan's rigid body. There was no need for him to caution me to silence. I could see the boat as it stood out from the cove we faced. I could see the men as they clustered around their fire, hear their voices as they argued. Worst of all, I could smell the food they were cooking for their supper. Now hunger overruled the other discomforts and the fact that I had missed what lunch there was to eat made the lack of dinner torture.

Harlan pulled me back into the sheltering shadows of the cliff. Had we continued on much farther, even the gathering darkness would not have hidden us from a chance look by the fishermen.

"Can you swim?" and when I nodded, "To that?" he asked, pointing to the boat.

"Yes," I agreed although I was not the least bit confident. I was so tired and my feet hurt and my stomach ached and I was very annoyed with everything for going so wrong so long. I didn't consider how extremely lucky we had been so far. At least not with the smell of food in my nostrils after a prolonged fast. I comforted myself with the thought that I wouldn't have to *walk* to the boat.

I didn't count on the icy water nor the sting of salt in the multitude of scratches and abrasions that scored my body. Nor did Harlan allow me time to ease into the water as I preferred doing on family outings at Rehoboth. Harlan pulled me inexorably deeper.

"Don't swim overarm yet," he hissed at me and a wave caught me full face. His arms supported me while I coughed the water out. "You can swim?" he asked.

"Yes, yes," I assured him, stung by his skepticism and I struck out toward the boat with a vigorous breaststroke.

As if he still doubted my ability, Harlan matched his pace to mine, only he guided me out to sea, rather than on an oblique line toward the boat from the shore. I caught his purpose, to approach the boat from the seaside, although it added many yards to the original distance.

If the sea stung my cuts, its coldness supplied me with a false feeling of exhilaration. I tried to speed up, to prove to Harlan I was competent, but he warned me not to extend myself. He was right, of course, because as we turned toward the boat finally, my weariness returned doubled. It was so difficult to get my arms out of the water, hard to keep my legs moving.

"Sara, not far now," Harlan's voice said encouragingly. His face was a white blob over my right shoulder as I swam and ahead of us the boat was a solid blackness, its single mast silhouetted against the dying light of the twilight sky. Thrashing frantically, I lunged at the stern line, missing, going under, writhing upward, grabbing out in panic. Harlan's hand found mine and guided it to the security of the rope.

"Rest," he whispered and cautiously swam round the boat. I could hear him, a barely discernible rippling, as I gulped for breath.

"No one aboard," he confirmed. "But they took the smallboat ashore." For some reason this disappointed him. "Oh, well, in that case it'll take them a long time to spread the alarm."

"Maybe they'd be friendly," I hazarded, looking up at the sheer slippery side of the ship and wondering how I was ever going to make it into the cockpit.

Harlan answered my suggestion with a snort. He lunged up out of the water, caught at the gunwale, his body a whiteness against the dark boat. He got both hands secured and then I heard him inhale as he gathered his strength to pull himself up.

How selfish can you get, I derided myself, he's just as hungry, just as tired, just as sore as you are and worried to boot.

I heard him swear softly, a note of pain in his voice. I could hear him padding somewhere on board and then his face appeared above me.

"Grab this," he whispered and a heavy soft rope dangled in my face.

I looped it around my wrists, thankful I shouldn't have to make the climb unaided. Kicking myself out of the water, I felt Harlan pull me. As soon as I could reach the side, I grabbed for it, resolved to use as little of Harlan's energy as possible. Once safely on board, I felt drained of any power to move and I was numb with the chill of the cool evening.

"Here, get this on," he urged and pressed a handful of clothing on me. The garments smelled of sweat, stale and sour, and were sticky with salt. But I struggled into an old sweater and found it covered me halfway to the knees. I rolled up the sleeves and wished it covered me to the ankles.

"I suppose it's too much to ask if you've sailed a boat," Harlan said in a low voice.

"Yes, but only as a crew member, long ago."

He gripped my shoulder with rough gratitude. "You never cease to supply my need."

I struggled to a sitting position, wondering what he meant exactly, and looked around. As nearly as I could gauge in the light, the boat was about thirty-five feet long, sloop-rigged, the sail now neatly furled on the boom, the jibsail not even out. The boat was obviously a workship; I could see piles of nets and woven baskets. There seemed to be a small cabin and it was here that Harlan had found sweaters.

"It's a shame but I've got to cut the anchor. Too much time and noise to lift it out of the water," Harlan told me. I could see the gleam of a knife blade in his hand.

"It'll save time if I cut and you hoist the sail," I told him and taking the knife, crept forward. My hands seemed strengthless as I sawed away at the heavy anchor line, thankful it wasn't chain. I heard Harlan heaving at the sail and it seemed like noise enough to rouse the dead. It did rouse the men on the beach. I sawed faster.

"Hurry, Sara," I heard Harlan call and wondered why he still kept his voice low if the men had heard the creak of the sail.

I felt the line and there was only one strand still uncut. Frantically, I hacked away and, just as I felt the pull of the ship against the wind in its sail, the anchor line parted.

"Grab the tiller and head for the sea," Harlan cried, still struggling to lift the cumbersome sail. I guess in the dim light it was difficult to see what he was doing. And he was tired, but he made heavy work with the sheet.

Tripping over deck-stored gear, I scrambled astern and found the unfamiliar tiller handle.

If for only this one adventure, my tomboy days paid rich dividends. I had run with Harlan, swum with him and now I was able to crew for him. And, undoubtedly I

cautioned myself with the memory of sour disappoint-
ments, when the Yacht Club Dance on this world came
round, it wouldn't be Sara who was waltzed by the ship's
captain.

Harlan was cursing as he tried to make fast the sheet. I
caught at the trailing line as the boom threatened to knock
him overboard. I trimmed sail and steered for the open
sea.

The men on shore now had realized what had happened
and were shouting threats across the water as Harlan
joined me.

"It's another miracle that you can sail," he muttered to
me. "I can't."

"You can't?" I gasped, appalled at the situation. "Why
not?" I demanded, as the responsibility now resting on me
became apparent to my tired brain. He couldn't possibly
imagine that I could sail this bloody boat on an unknown
sea to a port I'd never seen.

"Too busy," he grinned. "You're doing all right."

That explained his ambiguous comments and his awkwardness with the sail.

"Now, yes," I practically screamed at him, "but if you
knew you couldn't sail, why in heaven's name did you
steal the boat?"

"I'd've figured it out, but I'm glad you already know
how," he repeated complacently.

The volume of his audacity was frightening.

"That's comforting to know," I said acidly. "Sailing an
open sea is easy even for an idiot Regent. And I imagine
you probably would have figured it out before you piled
up on a beach or reefs. At least you have the advantage, I
assume, of some familiarity with the coastline of this
world. I don't. I don't *know* your goddamned world!"

"My what world?" he asked as I had interjected an
English cussword.

"What do you want me to do now?" I cried, tears of
fear, frustration and fatigue starting down my face.

"Steer for the open sea," he said blandly.

"And then what? I don't even know how big your seas
are, what the tides are like! You've got two bloody moons

to complicate that minor detail of sailing. How do you expect me to . . ."

He put his arm around me, settling down beside me. His very presence and magnificent self-confidence helped calm my hysteria.

"The Finger Sea on which we sail," he began calmly, "is deep, no reefs or shoals except along the eastern edge. We will sail due east across it toward Astolla. It will probably take all night, so we would face the reefs in daylight when nothing is as overwhelming as it is at night. I do know navigation, Sara. And since you can handle the mechanics of sailing, we'll be all right. My purpose in heading east is to reach the home of an old friend of mine." He chuckled to himself. "We fought so the last time we met, I'm sure no one will think to check at Gartly's for me."

"If you fought, why would he welcome you?" I demanded, worrying not so much about what happened when we arrived as to how we would manage to arrive in the first place.

"Gartly is part of my loyal opposition, that's all. He has no love for Gorlot at all or any of that cave. None at all," and Harlan mused on some private memories, his face sober.

The wind freshened and the ship moved at a willing clip. The wind was also cold and I began to shiver.

"First, there must be some food aboard. I could eat a brant," Harlan said. "And there had better be more clothing, too."

He found both. The coarse bread and strong cheese filled my stomach and with rough cloth pants to keep me warm, my fearfulness dissipated. The ship was simple to handle, even for one person, the lines being winched astern so a lone steersman could handle the sheets from the cockpit on a long haul.

"How long a sail is it?" I asked Harlan when he settled down beside me again after another thorough prowl about the ship.

He shrugged.

"I have only a spaceman's idea of distance. A mere half hour or so by planecar."

I groaned. "I wish you really knew what you had let us in for," I said, depression overwhelming me.

"I do what I must," he said sternly. "And I must get to Gartly."

No apologies was I ever to get from Harlan. And naturally I found myself accepting his inexorable logic that we would get where we wanted to go, novices though we were, because we *had* to.

The sheer audacity of his idea was what saved us, I think, from discovery. For we sailed all that night with a good stiff following breeze. Harlan insisted on taking a trick to allow me to rest although I was reluctant to leave a complete tyro in charge of the ship. He assured me that if the wind would change—my one worry because sailing with a good following wind is child's play—he would wake me. He kept his word, waking me at dawn when the breeze dropped off. He also pointed with smug complacency at the distant outline of mountains on the horizon.

He had used a hand line and caught us breakfast. Once I had mastered the cooking stove, we ate hot food until we were stuffed. With land at least in sight and a full stomach for only the second time in several weeks, my depression disappeared.

"We were farther up the coast than I thought," he remarked. "Let's get close enough so I can figure out where we are."

I shook my head over his blithe unconcern. He laughed at me and then peered at the rising sun.

"That is," he amended, "if we get any wind."

"That'll be a long paddle," I remarked, trying not to be too sour.

"Pessimist," he teased. "Yesterday at this time, we were securely locked up in Gleto's amusing retreat with not a chance in a hundred of getting out. You make the most of the opportunities the gods grant and you'll win out," Harlan said with fine good humor. "Did I not have you as a nurse? Did you not have the wit to understand what was being done to me? Can you say that we have not succeeded in escaping?"

"Those men had all night to get somewhere to report their ship stolen," I reminded him.

"True enough," he replied, unruffled. "But they don't know *who* stole. One man? Several? There are plenty of bandsmen prowling. Nor, if they were simple fishermen, are they likely to give wind of it to Gorlot's people. I had meant to take the smallboat which they might easily believe had been improperly tied. But . . ." and he shrugged. "But this gets me closer quicker to help. Then, too, how long will it take Gleto to summon up enough courage to inform Gorlot I'm missing?" he chuckled nastily.

"He'll delay as long as he can," I replied, feeling a little reassured by that one fact.

"And, as it is known I have never sailed, the last place anyone will look for Harlan is on the sea."

"It's going to be a long row," I repeated, looking anxiously at the limp sail and the glassy water.

"We can while the time away," he suggested in such an altered tone of voice I glanced around sharply at him.

Before I had realized what he had in mind, he had pulled me into his arms. Startled and completely surprised, I clutched involuntarily at his shoulders for balance and was being kissed expertly and thoroughly. What thoughts my emotions gave room for were chaotic. I was as split into the various facets of my personality as if I had been literally blown apart.

The girl with the beaknose had never been kissed except as a party joke or absentmindedly by departing brothers. The unwanted girl who had stolen longing looks at shamelessly necking couples in Central Park had no firsthand experience with returning a kiss. His forceful invasion of my lips met neither resistance nor response. The stranger, by some crazy agency dumped on a strange planet, could and did not want to antagonize her one friend. And the sister who had overheard her brothers' candid comments on girls was all too certain the direction such beginnings would take. And I, all of me, didn't want him to stop kissing because of the way my heart pounded and my body ached for the feeling of his hands. Yet I didn't know what to do.

I could sense the change almost as soon as it began. Harlan lifted his head and looked at me slightly puzzled.

"And what's wrong with me?" he asked.

I realized he was asking me if *he* were the cause of my inability to respond.

"Nothing, it's just . . ."

"Don't they kiss on your planet?" he asked with a boyish incredulity.

"Yes, but I never did," I said inanely, my hand going to my nose.

That did it. I could see his face change again, that closing-out look I hated. Although I was still in his arms, against his chest, he had withdrawn.

"Please, Harlan, don't go away from me like that," I pleaded.

His look softened and he took my hand, his thumb absently rubbing my wrist.

"Then you are untouched?" he asked kindly, as if this were not exactly a privileged state on his world.

I could only nod, knowing I must be blushing at his frankness. I was torn with a horrifyingly unmaidenlike desire to encourage him, even if I didn't know how to go about it at all.

He chuckled at some inner thought and hugged me with affection but no passion, kissing me gently on the eyes.

"Then, my dear Sara, this is neither the time nor the place if such beginnings are to be auspicious. We both smell to the high heaven and . . ."

A sudden flapping, creaking, caught both our attentions and we hastily disengaged to duck as the untended boom, moved by the rising wind, missed knocking us overboard by a hair's breadth.

"Yes, this is neither the time nor the place," Harlan repeated, laughing boyishly as he lunged for the trailing line and I grabbed the swinging tiller.

Again I was torn by opposing desires: relief that I had been saved rude wakenings, and frustration because I had been aroused. I *wanted* Harlan. And when again would I be in a position alone with him when there was opportunity and time?

"Damn the wind," I muttered to myself as I eased the ship about.

The purple smudge on the horizon deepened into the green of treed slopes, fringed with boiling surf. I pointed out the inhospitable coastline.

"We can't land in that, Harlan," I protested.

"Let's sail southerly. The land breaks into the delta of the Astolla River past this range. Only we want to land before we get to Astolla itself." He squinted at the mountains. "Gartly lives above Astolla and that will be the hardest part of the trip."

He didn't qualify his comment, so I didn't realize then he meant that the danger of being encountered by someone who would recognize him was greater. I took him to mean the mountains and I groaned.

He turned to me, laughing. "All uphill, Sara, all uphill. Only," he noticed my feet, bruised and raw, "we'll have to do something about them."

"And this," I added, distastefully indicating my overlong sweater.

He rummaged in the cabin and came up with additional ill-smelling garments. Finding a bucket and a line, he heaved it overboard and to my amused astonishment, he started to sluice the clothing up and down in the clean seawater. He wrung them out neatly and spread them to dry on the deck.

"Our hosts were probably good fishermen but incredibly dirty," he commented when he had finished. "They'll dry quickly. Shall I take a turn?"

"I'm fine," I assured him and then I still was, what with the recent sleep and enough food and his approval.

He went forward and I saw him heave the bucket overboard again. This time it was himself he washed. I tried to keep the sail between me and glimpses of his strong golden body. It had been one thing to tend him as a moron, another to consider him as a lover.

I should not presume on his friendship later, I promised

myself. He was of too much consequence for someone like me and I'd be more than a fool to think I meant anything to him.

We sailed on for a long while, well into the sunny morning, until I was lethargic with the sun, hungry again and very tired. I was mesmerized by the masthead and the jibsprit which I kept pointed toward the ever nearing shore line. I was lost in fatigue and musings when suddenly Harlan's hand dropped to my shoulder.

Startled, I gasped and flinched as though I'd been struck.

"Is my touch offensive?" he asked, frowning.

"No, no," I hastily assured him. "I was worlds away."

He knelt down beside me and I noticed his bare chest was red with sun.

"You've got a burn."

"So have you," he retorted and I saw he had put on clean dry pants. He thrust a handful of dry clothing toward me. "These were the smallest and may fit better. Go on forward and wash some of the mud off, Sara."

I hesitated as I rose, as much from weariness and being in one position so long, as from the knowledge the sail did not conceal much from a determined watcher.

"If I look, I won't tell," he taunted, grinning wickedly.

Grabbing the clothes from him, I turned on my heel with as much dignity as I could and made my way to the bow. The pail was there and some soft, linenlike sheeting that he must have used as toweling. Traces remained of mud stains that hadn't come out with just a seawater rinsing.

It was very heartening to remove that filthy old sweater. And better still to get the rest of the mud off my body. My face stung in the salt bath, but when I was clean and dressed again, I did feel better. With decided pleasure I kicked the rags of my asylum tunic overboard and watched them sink below the surface.

"Now," said Harlan as I returned to the cockpit, "we must give you a plausible account of your existence in case you meet some awkward questioning. Gartly was my second-in-command and is an honorable man, but you, my dear Searcher," and his phrase puzzled me, "require some explanation, even to the most loyal comrade."

"Why not the truth?"

"Sara," and he turned my face so I looked at him fully, "you have no idea how you got to this planet?" When I shook my head negatively, he continued, "Then until I do find out, or you remember, the mere fact that you are *not* of this planet is very dangerous. As soon as I can, I shall start some adroit inquiries, but for you to come out and admit to an extraplanetary origin would mean your death without further explanation to you or from you."

"It'd be much easier to tell the truth. Then it wouldn't matter how many things I didn't know," I said plaintively.

His look silenced me. "I have taken that into consideration. I'd prefer to be able to send you up to my estates in North Lothar, but I may not be able to do that right away. Of course, the less you have to say about your past the better, but Gartly's of the Old Beliefs, and clan and cavesite mean much to him. Now listen. Jurasse is the next largest city to Lothara. It's northwest of the Finger Sea, deep in the mountains. Your father . . . what was your father's name? Steven? No, make him Stane, a better Lotharan name. Your father Stane was a mining engineer. I'll put you on a professional level, my dear lady," and he grinned at me, "and as there are several hundred thousand miners and engineers in and out of Jurasse, there's scant way of checking."

"But he must have gone to college or university," I said.

"Un-i-ver-sity?" Harlan asked, puzzled.

"Advanced schooling, training in his specialty," I qualified.

Harlan shook his head quickly. "No. One learns on the job here. Stane is a fairly common name and we'll make you of Estril clan and Odern cavesite."

"What is the significance of clans and cavesites?" I asked grimly.

Harlan exhaled his breath and looked at me. Then he covered my hands with his big strong one. "I'll explain all that later. In the meantime, it is only important for you to know a clan name; the Estrils are conservative but known for their intense loyalty to their leaders, and the Odern is such an enormous old cave, hundreds of clans could refuge here."

"All right. Estril and Odern. Jurasse, next largest city, mining, northwest."

"Good girl. Your father died in a mine accident that happened just . . . well, I *don't* know how long ago now, but it happened in the Tenth Month of the Single Eclipse. Just memorize it, Sara, no explanations. The same earth fault destroyed blocks of apartment buildings. So you can have lived at the sign of the Horns and no one will be able to run an accurate or quick check. Your important relative is your mother. What was your mother's name?"

"I wish you'd stop saying 'was.' For all I know, they are very much alive," I snapped.

"Not as far as you're concerned on Lothar," Harlan said with patient firmness.

"Maria."

"Make it Mara of the Thort clan, that's a South Cant group. Farmlands had some bad plague about thirty years ago, . . . how old are you, Sara?"

"Twenty-four."

He smiled and started to say something, changing his subject even as he opened his mouth to speak. "Fine. Then all but your mother died in that plague, so you have no maternal family to worry about. This happens often enough and as the Clan Head may always be approached, no one is ever really orphaned. Between Jurasse and South Cant your accent can be accounted for. South Cant slurs and Jurasse is throaty."

"Mara of the Thorts from South Cant. No cavesite?"

"South Cant was not settled until caves were no longer a necessity."

"Where did I meet you?" I asked.

Harlan stared off into space, rubbing his mouth with his hand.

"That's the hard one, Sara. Particularly since I don't

know how long it's been since I was first drugged nor how or when you might have been brought here."

"Might there have been a group of old loyal cavemen who have fallen out with Gorlot and were suspicious of your collapse?"

"It's possible. Let me think on this. Once I get to Gartly, I can catch up on recent happenings. Then I'll fill in a logical background.

"Now," he said more briskly, "the last part of our journey presents the greatest hazard of discovery. If we are taken into custody, you can insist on silence until you have talked to a Clan Officer."

Earth-type spy stories and atrocities crowded into my mind.

"Won't they just kill me to keep me quiet and have done?"

"Kill a potential mother?" he demanded, his eyes flashing. "Unheard of." He looked at me. "Do they kill women who can bear children on your world?" he asked with trenchant scorn for such a wasteful culture.

I nodded slowly.

"Not on Lothar. Women are too important, even to Gorlot. No, your life is safe." He emphasized 'life.' "And I have made my claim on you already. Is that agreeable to you?"

His eyes locked with mine in an expression that warmed me to the pit of my stomach. I could only nod mutely. His hand again covered mine as he continued. "However, should I be taken and you can escape, no, no ... it is possible. And, Sara, you are to run if I tell you. Promise me that!" Again I nodded until his hand ceased his painful grip as he got my grudging consent. "All right, I am taken and you are free. Get to Lothara itself and to the 'Place of the Birds.' Ask for Jokan. Tell him, and only him, all that has happened. He is my brother."

"And how do I get there? Fly?"

"That's the quickest way," he said, taking me literally. "Oh. No money." He shook his head, gritted his teeth and swore with an eloquence that beggared what I had heard from the guards.

"We'll do it together, somehow, Sara. We've come this far in our search because my Sara can sail, and think and act," and he grinned at the face I made at him. "If we can win through to Gartly, we'll have money, a planecar and help. Then we can make further plans. The important thing is to make it to Gartly."

The way the surf broke so savagely against the shore line, even that modest ambition seemed unlikely. We were sailing a close-hauled tack now, and farther down the coast, I could see the mountains falling away to a plain. And at the farthest point, the glint of buildings in the sun.

"Let's beach the boat as soon as we can," Harlan urged, scanning the shore.

I glared at him.

"Pick your spot, pal."

"It's easy to see I spent my youth exploring the wrong planets," Harlan growled to himself as we sailed on and on.

I had noticed other sails, standing out to sea.

"Any chance they might be investigating us?" I asked him. He shook his head impatiently. I glanced out at the shore line anxiously and sighed.

"I haven't been to this part of Astolla in years, but it seems to me there *is* a beach. Gartly's one form of relaxation is fishing and . . ."

"Look," I cried, half-rising from the cockpit.

Directly ahead of us, half hidden by the sail's spread, was a planecar. Harlan catapulted into the cabin.

"You there in the fisherboat, " a voice, magnified artificially, roared down at me. The hovering craft swung round the ship. All I could think was they'd been able to see Harlan hiding in the cabin. "From where are you bound?"

"And what business is it of yours?" I demanded evasively, cursing because that was another thing Harlan had not bothered to brief me on.

"Answer when you're spoken to, woman," I was told rudely and I doubted Harlan's surety that women are not maltreated on Lothar.

"Come back when I can answer, you idiot," I said, throwing over the tiller on an unnecessary tack which made me obviously too busy with sheet and line to answer. It also cut off the plane's view of the cabin.

"Are you alone?" they persisted.

"Son of a Seventeenth Son, yes," I screamed at the top of my lungs, remembering a mild oath from the guards' dialogues.

The boom, swinging free, completely covered the cabin hatch although the plane was hovering suspiciously low on my stern. The ship had lost all way, sail flapping. I glanced up at the planecar as it swung forward. I saw the military uniforms on the occupants. I could even see the faces of the men and I didn't like them.

"You Milrousers, go bother someone else. I'm too busy. Get off my back," I yelled, shaking a fist at them.

The boat rolled in the surf and another look to port confirmed that my ruse was putting me in peril. Hastily I trimmed the sail and tried to get sea room between me and the jagged rocks of the shore. That I was in trouble now was too apparent to the airborne nuisances. The plane roared off with a speed startling to one used to wallowing helicopters.

"Harlan, get up here on the double," I called once the plane was safely away. "Harlan," for the tide had seized the boat, carrying us farther and farther inshore. "HARLAN!" I screamed just as the boat struck a submerged rock I had not even a moment's warning to avoid.

Harlan came on board just as the boom swung about and, as I rose in horror, it swept us both off the deck and into the sea.

I came up gasping, the heavy seaman's clothing weighing me down. But Harlan came up, too, not far from me.

"Are you all right?"

"I'm mad, clear through," I screamed at him. "Of all the stupid things to have happen . . ."

"Don't waste energy, swim," Harlan ordered as the little fishing boat, unguided, was lifted by the surge of the tide and cracked down onto the rocks. Planks, splinters, tackle, debris of all sort went flying in every direction as we swam out of the way. A flying piece of deck hit me heavily on the shoulder, but the thick sweater protected me enough so that all I got was the terrible initial buffet. Harlan disentangled himself from fouled line and we both struck out away from the flotsam on the water.

"I'm sorry," I told Harlan, swimming at my shoulder.

"I wouldn't be," he said good-naturedly. "It'll probably be easier to get ashore swimming than sailing."

We were about a hundred yards from the rocky beach and I could see that the haphazard rocks, a menace to a boat, were wide enough for a man's body to pass between them. One only had to hold one's course through them to make it safely in. Still, the tidal pull was now very strong and if we were smacked against one of those rocks, it'd be too bad. It was nervous business and we swept awfully close to the rough-skinned boulders. The uneven footing when we reached shallower water was worse going than the actual passage of the reef rocks. The footing was slippery and the tide tore at my feet. I slipped several times and then went completely down, skinning one leg so badly that Harlan had to support me the last five yards.

Quickly, when he saw the bleeding, he picked me up in his arms and carried me up the sand to the edge of the woods. He slit the trouser leg, baring the nasty gash the length of my shin. My whole leg ached from the jar of my fall as well as the lacerations. I felt very very tired.

"We must get farther into the woods before the plane-car comes back. The wreck will be noticed," Harlan said.

"Leave me here," I pleaded with him after one glance at the thick underbrush. "I'm so tired. I'll only slow you down."

"My dear lady, I have no intention of leaving you," he said angrily.

He tore the sleeve from my sweater and bandaged my leg. He was about to pick me up despite my protests when he froze, his eyes on the shore a little to the right of us.

I whirled and saw a figure sauntering along the rocky

beach, fishing gear draped all over him. The young man stopped when he saw us and then hurried forward.

"Can you give me a hand, stranger?" Harlan called. "We've lost our sloop and my lady is hurt."

I thought that his audacity would win out over the odds again. The young man was almost to us when he stopped short, his mouth open in surprised shock, his body dropping to a crouch as recognition dawned on him.

"Harlan?" he cried, half questioning, half stating the incredible fact.

It was too much for me and for the only time in my life I fainted.

CHAPTER FIVE

SOMETHING WAS BURNING MY THROAT and my leg was on fire and someone was choking me and I struck out wildly.

"Sara, Sara, it's all right," I heard Harlan say. Opening my eyes, I saw first trees all around us, then Harlan and then the concerned face of the young man from the beach. "We're safe, Sara. This is Cire, the youngest son of my old commandant, Gartly. It's all right."

"You're sure?" I asked stupidly, looking at Cire who seemed to me far too young to be as much help as Harlan's cheerful reassurance implied.

"Here, drink this." He held the metal bottle for me and it was more of the stimulant that had burned my throat. It was powerful and spread feeling through my arms and stomach, down to my vitals and my aching leg. I looked down and this had been bandaged with something white and far more comforting in appearance than the sleeve of my sweater. Cire's fishing jacket was wrapped around me, warm and far cleaner than anything else I had on.

"I don't want any more of that," I assured Harlan as he lifted the bottle to my lips again.

Harlan chuckled. "Patrol issue is noted for potency."

"How long have I been out? Of all the silly things to do."

"Yes, very silly of you," Harlan agreed amiably. Then both he and Cire laughed at my expression of shock. "That's better."

He got up.

"Now, Sara, we've got to move on. The planecar did come back and saw the wreck. What'll happen now I don't know. Cire says there's been no mention of my escape, so that planecar may only have been a routine flight. But the boat's registry number may come ashore with the wreckage. Then there'll surely be inquiries made.

58

Cire and I covered our tracks up from the beach to make them think there were no survivors . . . or survivor. But I want to get out of Astolla entirely by the time an official investigation of the wreck is made."

I struggled to my feet.

"You don't like it, but it'll help," he added proffering the bottle. I looked at him and then at Cire and reluctantly steeled myself for another long swig.

"I'll be drunk in no time," I gasped.

"You'll be walking it off," Harlan retorted.

I'm not exactly sure "walk" is what I did. Harlan made me take considerable quantities of that brew once he felt me shivering through Cire's jacket. I remember not too clearly the events following the first long climb from the shore. I remember putting one foot in front of the other and talking about it. I remember complaining because I wanted to sit down and no one would let me. I remember being carried and then I remember fighting with someone because they wanted to put me on a planecar and I knew that was not right and I shouldn't get on a planecar and I couldn't get away from Them. The last thing I do remember is Harlan's voice, angry and arguing.

"By the Deep Cave, she's exhausted, that's all. Naturally she's talking gibberish. Here, give her to me a minute."

Someone was shaking me by the shoulders and I kept trying to get free. Then Harlan kissed me and I managed to focus on his face and realized he was the one holding me.

"Sara, Sara, *listen* to me. We're safe, we made it to Gartly's. Go to sleep now. It's all right to sleep now."

"Well, why didn't someone say so?" I remember saying bad-temperedly. I heard Harlan laugh and then I slid down, gratefully, into dark softness and warmth.

For me, time resumed after my legs stopped moving even in my dreams. I awoke in a comfortable bed in a pleasantly sunlit room with an indescribably appetizing odor tantalizing me. I sat right up in bed and looked around, trying to place my surroundings. The wide bed had had another occupant from the dents in the pillows beside mine. I decided I had better ignore speculations in that direction for the moment.

It might even be a female Gartly, I told myself, having remembered Harlan's final words to me. This pleasant blue room with its heavy wooden furnishings was the antithesis of the institutional asylum cottage.

A long soft gray robe was draped on the chair nearest the bed which turned my attention on the nightdress I wore. To my relief, it was utilitarian but feminine. Whatever was cooking made me ravenous. I put on the robe and looking around for a bathroom, stumbled over Harlan's fisher clothes.

"That settles that," I told myself, both irritated and pleased.

The delicious odor was irresistible and I hurried through the necessary, noticing in passing the mirror that I had picked up a nice tan, and that I had lost my eyebrows and singed my hair slightly shorter in passing the force screen barrier.

As I opened the bedroom door, I walked out into a hall, half open to the large room on the level below. Four men were sitting around a table cluttered with the debris of a meal. They had been talking solemnly and their voices died as first one, then another man became aware of my presence on the balcony. The oldest, gray-grizzled man glowered up at me fiercely and started to rise to his feet. I was about to take refuge in the bedroom when Harlan, laden with a plate of food and a mug, backed through a swinging door from the side of the house.

"Hi there, don't run, Sara," he laughed. "Come on down." He noticed Gartly's expression. "Gartly frowns to hide a tender heart and Jessl," he added, nodding to the man he was passing on his way to the table, "frowns from unfamiliarity with the light of day." He set his dishes down and, going to the foot of the stairs, waited for me to descend. He squeezed my hand reassuringly and led me to the table.

He was an entirely different person in his joviality, in the obvious affection toward two of the men, Jokan and Jessl. The Harlan I had known in the hospital, tense, frustrated, pensive, the apparently unconcerned Harlan of the sailboat, had transformed into this admirable stranger with whom I was not at ease.

The four men rose gravely in turn as Harlan introduced us, bowing formally, each bow as different as the character of the man. Gartly gave me a peremptory bow, his mind obviously on the business interrupted by my appearance. His blueing eyes passed over my face with the light dismissal of an older man for any younger person.

Jokan, and I remembered he was Harlan's brother, was nondescript in appearance, totally different from his brother. But his eyes, a sparklingly clear blue in his rough tanned face, had a vitality that detracted from the commonplaceness of his features. His bow was leisurely as he measured my face, my body, my legs and looking again into my eyes, his lips echoed the greeting in his brilliant eyes.

Jessl, a stocky, chesty man in his late thirties, was less courtly, checking me off in his mental catalogue as woman; intelligence unknown; and unnecessary. But it was he who held out my chair.

Cire smiled warmly at me. He resembled his father in face and outstripped him in size by half a foot but with undeveloped breadth. His bow was jerky, unpracticed, and he flushed boyishly, yanked out of the fascinating world of men to which he had so recently been admitted, by the arrival of a woman his senior in years.

"How's your leg this morning?" he asked considerately.

"I didn't even remember," I laughed, kicking my leg from the full robe.

"That's because you've slept nearly two days," Harlan laughed. "Cire, I appoint you chief server to the exiled court of Harlan and hope I left enough in the pot to fill a very generous plate for Sara. I've had five servings, my dear lady," and I heard Jokan draw his breath in sharply and Jessl turned around to look at me queerly, but Harlan continued briskly, "so I'm the guilty one if there isn't enough. You should, by rights, be even hungrier than I," and his lighthearted grin included an intimate reference to my abstinence for his sake.

Cire showed no reluctance to assume his honorary rank and went to get me food. Harlan took up the conversation he had left to refill his plate.

"Hindsight, my friends, is of no use to us. We could sit here until the Mil come again before that would solve our problem. Don't think for a minute I haven't run from the caves of Jurasse to the Barren Plains for believing myself inviolate just because I was Regent. I've succeeded in making an absolute fool of myself and unless I'm careful about the next move, I shall compound that impression and lose any chance whatever of regaining the Regency.

"I've had a lot of good luck, lately," his hand touched mine in illustration, "and we'll hope it holds until Stannall can reinforce it. You're sure, Jokan, no one knows of your trip to Astolla?"

"I made the decision myself on the way to Jurasse and circled the Finger Sea," Jokan reassured him. He kept looking at me, however, not his brother.

Harlan regarded the meat on his fork speculatively, then carefully set the piece aside, leaning back in his chair.

"Now, Jessl has not been closely connected with me. Gartly and I had that quarrel about sector assignments," and Harlan's eyes twinkled at Gartly who harrumphed righteously. "They won't think of checking on any of you first. We've got to get Council in session to revoke Gorlot's temporary Regency. Ferrill can do it if we can reach him."

Jokan and Gartly immediately jumped in to elaborate on the young Warlord's rapid physical decline. No one had been allowed to see him recently, even such old friends as Gartly and his uncle, Jokan. Gorlot intercepted every attempt.

"I did get a few words with Maxil," Jokan added, "before that Milbait Samoth came breathing down my neck. I shall take great delight in kicking that fattail into so tight an orbit he's eating . . ."

"Jo," snapped Harlan, indicating me. Jokan glared at me for the curtailment of his invective.

I hadn't been paying too close attention because Cire had brought me the stew. I was eating with unladylike speed.

"Well," Jokan continued, "I was in the public gardens . . ."

"You were? How?" Jessl exclaimed.

"Moved in with the sightseers. Lothara's full of Eclipsers, so . . ."

"Eclipse will be tomorrow night," Harlan said, startled.

"That's the answer!" Jokan exclaimed.

"Don't be absurd," Harlan mocked him. "I couldn't get within ten feet of the palace wing in any disguise. With a discreet alarm out for me that would be the most closely watched place on the entire planet."

"*You* don't need to go," Jokan grinned, looking at the faces of his friends to see if they had guessed his intention.

"You certainly aren't planning to send Jessl in? Or Cire, or old gray-head here?" Harlan jibed and stopped, turning as they all did, to look at me. Surprised, I nearly choked on a much too generous mouthful. Jokan's grin broadened and he laughed with the gathering momentum of relief and delight.

"Me? Don't be ridiculous," I managed to say over my food. "I wouldn't even know . . ."

Gartly stood up abruptly, "Are you mad? This little country girl? We need someone like Maritha . . ."

"Who is so unknown at court," mocked Jokan. "Maritha would never do. Her fondness for Harlan is well known."

"It isn't her fondness, Jo, that would worry me," Harlan remarked wryly. "It's the fact that it was at her table I collapsed under such suspicious circumstances."

This deflated Gartly into a semishock, for he sat down immediately, his face rather pale and tight.

"I gather that was never made public," Harlan continued quietly. "But Sara can't go."

"Sara's perfect," Jokan went on enthusiastically, winking at me. "We can think up some absolutely idiotic quest for her."

"Quest?" I asked.

"With that face, she could pass into Gorlot's very room."

"It is not in Gorlot's room that we want her," Gartly grumbled primly, eyeing me with distaste.

My appetite deserted me.

"Aha," Jokan crowed gleefully at Gartly's expense, "beauty has the key to any room."

"Now, wait a minute," I demanded, rising. Harlan put a big hand on my shoulder and gently, but firmly, reseated me.

"Sara can't go. She has risked enough already," he said with quiet authority.

"What's the matter with you, Harlan," Jokan demanded, leaping to his feet, his eyes flashing his irritation. "It's got to be her. It's so simple a ruse it can't possibly fail. All Eclipsers have the right into the palace on that night."

"There has to be someone else," I insisted, now that Harlan was backing me.

"There is no one else we can reach in the short time we have. And it may be shorter than we know," Jokan insisted, turning to glare at his brother. "Ferrill may be almost completely broken down now, Maxil was worried sick. And we know it's not his constitution that's weak, it's drugs he's been fed. You know what drugs can do, Harlan. We've got to reach him and save his life. Or is that no longer of primary importance in your life, Harlan?"

Harlan was on his feet, the chair crashing to the floor behind him, as he faced his brother, stung, angry, silent.

"Stop it," I cried, pushing them apart. "I'll go, Harlan. I've hazarded this much already. Why not all?" I turned to Jokan once I saw the bunched muscles relax in Harlan's neck and he ceased to crouch as though about to spring. "Jokan, it's as Gartly says. I'm a little country girl. I've never even been to Lothara. But if you'll tell me exactly what I have to do, I'll do my best to do it."

Jokan's eyes gleamed down at me and he bowed ceremoniously to me.

"I like the country you're from, Lady Sara, if it breeds courage like yours," he said.

Involuntarily I turned for reassurance to Harlan. Did Jokan know of my origin? Harlan had said I might tell him if anything went wrong. Had Harlan already done so? Harlan's imperceptible nod indicated it was merely Jokan's curious choice of words. He gripped my arm at the elbow.

"There *is* more at stake, Sara, than just Ferrill's life," Harlan said persuasively as he pushed me gently back into my chair. "Which, any indication to the contrary, means a great deal to me," he added acidly to Jokan who shrugged. "Something very peculiar is happening on Tane if Jessl's report is as accurate as they always are."

Jokan's eyebrows went up in mockery. "What's peculiar about a war?"

Harlan ignored him. "It's absurd to maintain that the Tanes would have initiative enough to revolt. Those people are no more capable of taking a life or planning a cohesive rebellion like this than a restoree." Harlan's eyes flickered briefly as if he regretted making such a comparison. His hesitation allowed Jokan to get in another dig.

"You're prejudiced on behalf of your little protégées, Harlan. You haven't seen the damage these 'uninitiative' people of yours have been doing. Ferrill's the real urgency."

Harlan turned angrily on Jokan. "It's not prejudice, Jokan, and you should know me better. So drop that attitude. This supposed uprising masks another purpose. Just as my all too timely collapse and Ferrill's suddenly failing health are indications of a Millishly well-laid plan of far-reaching proportions. What I cannot understand is Stannall's lack of suspicion. Surely he of all people must realize something's drastically wrong. I cannot conceive him selling out to Gorlot or whoever is behind this treachery. But one thing I'm sure of, Lothar stands in great peril . . . of Gorlot getting complete authority, if he hasn't already; the truth behind the Tane farce and the loss of a brilliant ruler if Ferrill should have to be replaced."

"He'll be replaced, even if he gets off with his life," Jokan said dully. "He's a ruin already."

Harlan snapped an angry denial, but there was no support from the others. He turned back to me with a hint of the desperation I knew so well.

"Sara, I don't think you'd be in any danger. The idea is so simple, the time so accommodating. It has to be you."

In his eyes were his concern and his fear and a desperate plea. His hand, warm on mine, gripped me reassuringly.

"I hope you know what I'm doing," I said anxiously.

"You know Ferrill, don't you?" Jokan put in, impatiently. "All you have to do is tell him that Harlan is sane and have him convene an emergency session of Council. I assume," he began acidly, "Gorlot has started no antivirility campaigns on Ferrill."

Harlan shot him a surprised questioning look which Jokan waved aside, but Jessl and Gartly snorted derisively so his reference was known to them.

"Stannall," Jokan continued, "will then be able to do what else is necessary . . . if *he's* still with us. He ought to have far less love for Gorlot than we."

"There's no other way to get to Ferrill?" I asked plaintively.

"Our faces are known. Yours is not. In the guise of say, the Searcher," Jokan improvised and I remembered that Harlan had called me his Searcher, "you can gain entrance into the public garden. Slip into the palace wing and up to Ferrill's room."

"No," Harlan disagreed on the last detail hastily. "You said Trenor was sleeping with him to prevent another one of these so-called attacks?"

"Yes."

"Well, Ferrill will have to attend the Starhall festivities, won't he?"

"If he can walk."

"Then Sara will have a far better cover in that crowd than trying to find her way to Ferrill's rooms."

"It's all very well to make her a Searcher, provided you

can find a costume at this late date," Gartly grumbled, "but how are we to get into Lothara at all? Had that entered your glib plans?"

Harlan and Jokan exchanged glances.

"I do have the planecar," Cire suggested. "And I'm not too well known."

"She can fly in herself," Jokan said easily.

I grabbed at Harlan's arm. Sail I could, fly no.

"I don't fly," I blurted out.

"What?" Jokan looked at me startled.

"Never needed to. Lived in Jurasse," I mumbled and then looked frantically at Harlan for support.

"The one girl out of how many thousands who never learned to fly when she reached legal age," Jokan said exasperated.

And Harlan wanted *me* to go right into the middle of the palace. I'd last three steps inside the gardens and make another inadvertent mistake.

"I'd be glad to escort her," Cire repeated and then blushed, "if Harlan permits?"

"I permit all right, but I just wish there were some way we could all get into Lothara."

"As well wish you had a map to the Mil's system," Jessl snapped gloomily.

"If she's to get into the palace wing at all," Gartly put in, "she can go in no shoddy affair. It must be a rich gown or she'd be turned away."

"That can be obtained in town," Harlan remarked easily, dismissing this objection. Gartly stalked out of the room, his face reflecting pain and anger.

Harlan watched him leave, shrugged and turned to rummage on a table for a slate of waxy substance and a pointed stylus. Sitting next to me, he rapidly sketched in a small plan of the giant structure that was the capitol building, war office and palace of Lothar. Except that it resembled an unrimmed, unevenly spoked wheel, its function put me in mind of the Pentagon and the unreality of this adventure bore down on me again. I had no chance for speculation because Harlan demanded my complete attention as he described my route.

One wing of the enormous building was devoted exclusively to the quarters of the Warlord's family, intimates and servants. Between the spokes were extensive gardens. Only the ones adjacent to the palace wing were fenced in and guarded. Into one of these gardens I must gain entrance. While Jokan and Jessl listened absently to what was common knowledge, Harlan explained in detail what I would have to know.

"Get to the point, get to the point," Jokan urged impatiently once.

"Sara has never been to Lothara before and it's easy to become confused in the dark of the double Eclipse. We can't afford any mistakes," Harlan replied calmly and proceeded with my orientation. Jokan contented himself by noisily foraging in the kitchen.

Once I was in the garden, I was to make my way to any one of the ground-floor balconies, enter the room it adjoined and let myself into the corridor. The personnel of the lowest floor changed so constantly I was unlikely to be questioned. Minor courtiers would undoubtedly all be dancing attendance on their sponsors in the Starhall. I would follow the corridor to the Hub which was the Starhall on the fourth level. I would endeavor to get close enough to Ferrill to give him my message. Once that was accomplished, I would merely retrace my steps and join Jokan at the "Place of Birds." Any passenger cab would speed me there over the confusion of the celebrating. If, however, I did not see Ferrill and my presence was being noticed, I was to come back to the apartment and they would try something else.

I had to agree to the plan's simplicity, but I could not help worry that any plan undergoes revision in performance.

"If you find yourself in any trouble, Sara," Harlan remarked reading my mind, "give them one of your beautiful smiles and I doubt their minds will remain on the question."

"Oh, nonsense," I snapped.

Jokan and Jessl grinned knowingly to my further embarrassment.

"What will her quest be?" asked Jessl.

"Well, to get her into the gardens in case there is extra guard on duty, she can ask for a leaf of the Burning Shame plant. That's near the palace wing," Jokan suggested. "Once in the palace, she can say she needs a token from Ferrill to prove she has been claimed. She needs immunity against a priest she doesn't like. I've seen that one used often enough to know it's accepted." Jokan's grin to Harlan and Jessl made me suspect that ruse had a double meaning I couldn't understand.

There were too many cryptic remarks passed and references that puzzled me. Had I known then what Ferrill told me much later I doubt I would ever have consented to be a Searcher. My ignorance of the true story served me well, I admit, and I'm sure Harlan's neglect in telling me was intentional. The Searcher was an historically documented lady of good clan who had become separated from her lover during a Mil raid. She refused to believe he had been taken, and wandered over the planet, looking for him, constantly in danger of being captured either by a priest who coveted her or by the Mil. She would reward those who sheltered her with jewels. Eventually the priest caught up with her. In the joyous festival interpretation, the girl who played the Searcher very often suggested to a male friend that he be the priest to whom she surrendered herself after a token chase. Morals were totally different on Lothar. Female continence over a prolonged period was unfavorably viewed since women were expected to bear as many children as possible to replace a population constantly lost to the Mil or the exigencies of Patrol. Family continuity stemmed from the distaff side with the notable exception of the Warlordship.

"Let's hope," Jokan leered humorously, clearing his face when he caught Harlan's expression, "there aren't other priests along the way who want to claim her."

"That is why her costume is important," Gartly growled as he reentered the room, carrying a wooden box with stiff tenderness. He laid it on the table and with slow hands uncovered it, looking at the contents for a long moment before he stepped back for us to see. Jokan and Harlan exchanged glances and Harlan gripped the old man's shoulder in unspoken gratitude. He later told me the costume had belonged to Gartly's beloved wife.

I saw only the tissue-fragile fabric, deep greens and golds, the heavy ornate jewels, the intricately strapped sandals and the voluminous folds of the glossy emerald-green cloak.

"Why, it's the most beautiful thing I've ever seen," I gasped, touching the dress lightly as if it might fall to pieces.

Gartly grumbled something under his breath and then left the room with quick steps.

I suppose our concentration on the plans to enter the palace and Gartly's unexpected, touching offer had engrossed us. The sound of a knock on the door, at any rate, came like the knell of terror. We all whirled to the door as if it had become dangerous. Cire looked expectantly at Harlan who motioned him to answer even as Harlan edged quickly back to the kitchen.

"Who knocks?" asked Cire with scarcely a quiver in his young voice.

"Sinnall, Cire," and before Cire could answer, the door swung open.

If Sinnall had waited but an instant more before entering, Harlan would have reached the safety of the kitchen. As it was, he was directly in Sinnall's vision and his hand dropped from the door to his knife belt.

"Is it really Harlan?" Sinnall gasped. He didn't wait for confirmation but snapped to attention, saluting smartly. "Second Leader Sinnall, sir, reporting."

I could feel the tension leave the room as if swept out by a brisk wind. Cire, laughing nervously, threw an arm around the young officer.

"I appreciate the gesture, Second," Harlan said with a grin, returning the salute, "even though I am no longer acting as Regent." He beckoned to Sinnall to join the group around the table.

"My father served with you in Quadrant Five, sir," he remarked gravely, coming forward. "He was Nallis, First Prime."

Harlan grinned. "I recall it as being the other way round," he remarked and was rewarded by Sinnall's tentative smile.

"I can see now why there is an emergency at Lothar," Sinnall said, and held out to Harlan a tiny slate.

Harlan glanced at it, his eyebrows raising in surprise. With a burst of relieved laughter, he passed it to Jokan.

"My luck is holding," he practically crowed. "Sinnall, as a loyal officer in this sleepy uneventful little community, has been ordered to bring a loyal picked section to Lothara on special duty."

"Why should that change plans?" Jessl asked, reaching for the slate from Jokan.

"Because our orders are to report not later than noon tomorrow at Central Barracks for assignment. I can think of no better place for Harlan at the moment than right in the midst of the men trying to keep him out of Lothara."

"That'll get us all in," Jokan said, grinning broadly.

"Anyone know of your orders?" asked Harlan.

"I only got them an hour ago," Sinnall replied, "and I wanted to press Cire into section duty. I know *he's* loyal."

"To you and Ferrill, that's what Sinnall means," Cire interjected, his face intense with pride in his friend.

"Yes, sir," Sinnall replied earnestly. "I know what happens to officers who complain about the new Regent and the odd things that are happening. That's why I'm here," and he grimaced in such a way that I realized his present post was a form of military exile.

"Well, your orders do specify a 'loyal' section," Harlan said with a mirthless laugh, "but they do not state to whom, do they?"

Sinnall, relaxing even more in Harlan's presence, began to grin broadly.

"No, sir. And if I can find uniforms to fit, I'm going to volunteer all of you here as 'loyal.' "

"Room to stow my lady on the trip?" asked Harlan.

My relief that he had undoubtedly abandoned the original idea now that Sinnall's presence indicated Harlan would, after all, be able to get into Lothara, was short-lived.

Sinnall considered me with surprise. "Why, I think so."

"I hope so. I don't wish to leave her behind," Harlan remarked. "And Jokan, not you. You take yourself and your planecar and plan an accident in the Jurassan Hills. You've got to have a reason for returning to Lothara, completely unconnected with me. Gartly, Cire, Jessl and I will be the section. You wait for Sara at your place. Even if you are watched, Sara is unknown and your philandering is legend."

Jokan objected strenuously to being excluded but was finally convinced he could not be in the section.

"Why don't I just take Sara with me now? I'd better use tonight to cover my return and give me time for an accident. I could then take her on to Lothara."

Harlan shook his head. "No, Sara stays with me."

"Brother, I'm not about to . . ."

"She stays. I have my reasons," he reasserted so firmly that Jokan shrugged and pressed no further.

What remained of the day was spent in getting uniforms and making what alterations we could to get a reasonable fit. Not even the largest issue jacket accommodated Harlan's breadth of shoulder. The cuffs were halfway up his arm and, even when I had let down the sleeve all I could, it hung unmilitarily high above his big hand. Sinnall decided that regulation issue would be too skimpy for Harlan's frame in any event and the discrepancies would pass as back-country inefficiencies. The assorted ages and sizes of the four men identified them as provincials. Gartly, with darkened hair and a day's growth of beard, would not resemble the correct old soldier.

Cire sprinkled a white powder in Harlan's dark hair and with the lack of eyebrows (his, too, had been singed in the barrier crossing), an unmilitary shamble and slouched shoulders, he looked amazingly unlike himself. He even demonstrated the witless expression he could assume whenever necessary.

Hunger and fatigue vied for first place in my attention

by late evening and, when someone remembered to get some dinner, I could barely eat for weariness.

"Sara, you're barely rested," Harlan said with concern. "It's just as well she doesn't have to be Searcher tomorrow. She'd fall asleep," he laughed gently.

"I still think it's a good plan," Jessl grumbled.

"Sinnall's orders give us a better opportunity. I prefer to take my own risks," Harlan said to silence him. He helped me rise and escorted me up the stairs. "I'll be right back," he assured Gartly and Jessl who looked after us knowingly.

My face must have been burning when I got into the privacy of the room. I heard Harlan closing the door, but all I could see was the big double bed. All I really wanted was to sleep. And certainly if the boat was neither time nor place, neither was this with those men downstairs. My expression must have shown my thoughts, for Harlan took one look at my face and chuckled.

He took off my robe and led me to the bed, tucking me in.

"Sleep, dear my lady, is what you need right now," he said softly. "And I am relieved you do not need to go to the palace. That was too dangerous. Too dangerous, though Jokan's reasoning was good. He does not know, Sara. Sleep."

I did.

HARLAN WOKE ME, GENTLY SHAKING my shoulder. At first, the sight of a stranger in uniform bending over me was frightening until I recognized Harlan through the powdered hair.

"Fool you?" he grinned.

"Scared me witless," I grinned back, casting a glance at the dented pillow beside me.

"Well?" he dared me, "there are only three bedrooms here and I want it plain how matters stand between us. Remember, dear my lady, on this planet it is considered an honor to share the Regent's bed."

"I don't want to be in Gorlot's bed," I smirked at him wickedly.

"Neatly said," he said respectfully, but still grinning. "Now rise and dress or I'll make something more of that," and he indicated the bed. "After all, Sara, we slept together like innocent babes for who knows how long?"

Realizing myself topped, I gestured him out of the room. It took me a little while to figure out the closures on the green gown. I heartily wished for the simplicity of the zipper. Strange how easily I assumed in a mental leap that Earth would be able to supply Lothar with zippers when I could hardly understand the spatial distances between the two planets. Paper would be a boon, too, I continued in my mental perambulations, instead of the cumbersome Babylonique slates. I was just picking up the cloak when Harlan knocked again. I opened the door to him, the heavy jewelry clinking, tinkling with my movement. Harlan looked at me with a wondering expression on his face. He stepped quickly in the room, closing the door behind him.

"Didn't I put it on right?" I asked with a pang of doubt. "I know it took the longest time. I had to figure things out. Oh, for the lowly zipper."

Harlan began to smile, slowly.

"You are very different as the Searcher, dear my lady," he said slowly.

Pleased with the sincerity of his admiration, I pivoted on my toes, only to find myself locked in his arms, his face and eyes unbelievably stern.

"Are you still the girl who starved herself for me? The girl who sailed me to safety? Or are you . . ."

"Harlan, we've a long trip," Jessl yelled from below.

Harlan's tone had become almost savage, his arms around me tight and cruel.

"I'm still Sara, no matter what I wear," I whispered, startled.

"Sara . . . who?"

"Sara of the Estril, Odern Cave, Jurasse," I whispered, scared.

"We're coming," Harlan roared, turning his head briefly toward the door.

I thought he would release me but, holding me more tightly still, he bent his head and kissed me with rough and demanding lips. I seemed to sink inside him, held up only by his arms, knowing only the reality of his bruising mouth.

"HARLAN," Jessl bellowed and we both heard his steps on the wooden staircase.

"A map of how to get to Jokan's, from the Barracks' airfield," Harlan said hurriedly in a low voice, thrusting a tiny slate in my hand. "Anyone else would know. It's not far."

He opened the door just as Jessl reached it. It was now Jessl's turn to stare at me.

"Well, well." He looked nervously at Harlan. "That's what kept you."

With as much dignity as I could muster because I was still trembling, I gave both men a haughty look and swept out of the room.

Gartly was sitting facing the stair as we descended and he sprang to his feet, knocking the stool over. His face was completely expressionless. At first, I thought he must be equally struck speechless by my transformation. He turned without a word and left the house. I stared after him, hurt.

"The costume was his wife's," Harlan remarked gently. "She, too, was lovely."

Young Sinnall appeared in the door and bowed low. As we left the house, Cire came round the side of the house, and he too bowed.

"A lot better than stolen fishermen's clothes, hmm?" I said.

"That is the truth," Cire said, his eyes wide.

"Hey, where's my breakfast?" I demanded, stopping dead on the path outside the front door.

"Here," laughed Harlan, holding up a metal bottle and a small package, cloth wrapped. "I'll never let you starve again," he remarked, cocking an eyebrow at me.

"Will you two stop that and let's get off the ground?" Jessl snapped, irritably. "It's a three-hour trip from this cave-forsaken stretch of soil."

Laughing, I followed them down to the landing circle where the waiting official planecar idled its rotors. Sinnall had rigged a seat of sorts for me in the luggage area, apologizing profusely for the cramped accommodations. Cire announced that he would take the uncomfortable seat until such time as we encountered official traffic. Consequently I saw a great deal of such landmarks as the immense pit quarries of South Motlina, for Cire had been alone in Gartly's house near Astolla and had taken us south, away from prying inquiries about the wrecked boat. I saw the oil fields of Wingar and finally the city of Astolla itself and the delta we had nearly landed on. Northward into the mountains of Lothar the ship climbed.

I realized that Lothar had been lucky in several respects: a common enemy to unite it early in its history and the geographical accident which linked its two largest land masses from the north pole to the sixty-sixth parallel. At this point the continents split and rapidly separated east and west, leaving a green ocean between their land legs, dotted with several large islands and driblets of isles in the southern hemisphere. The eastern continent, over which we flew, was more mountainous and larger, the western one, a vast rolling plain ringed with bluffs and precipices, periodically penetrated by navigable rivers and deep lagoons. The western sea was shallow, spiked with tiny islands, deepening finally into a great crevasse of several thousand square miles before the sprawling arm and exaggerated peninsular fist of the eastern continent pouted seaward.

Used as I was to the ribbons of roads seen from the air on Earth, it struck me that Lothar had leapt from primitive wheels to a form of jet plane, thanks to the accommodating Mil. The only roads were foot trails, since most transportation, even by the poorer farmers, was done by air. Land was too valuable to be used up in wasteful roads when the whole sky was open for travel. During the trip I was constantly amazed by the gigantic craft that carried freight and the almost fragile vehicles that transported a single passenger: hummingbirds and vultures.

I missed, however, what I had hoped most to see: an airborne view of Lothara. The excessive number of aircars above Lothara, official and civil, flying at distressing proximity, necessitated my retreat behind the curtain. Sinnall answered and satisfied several official summonses before he made the turn into a pattern at the Central Barracks landing field. Here again, we unexpectedly encountered another touch of the fabulous streak of luck Harlan enjoyed.

The one unsettled detail was how I was to make my way from the Barracks airstrip to the city proper without detection. Sinnall had suggested that I remain hidden until nighttime, which meant a long stretch of hours, waiting behind the hot cloth.

I had my directions tucked in the top of my dress and was startled when our planecar was waved off an obviously overcrowded field and directed to an auxiliary civil field.

"As soon as there is no one around, you can just jump out," Jessl remarked to me through the curtain.

"Get an aircab to Place of Birds, Sara," Harlan suggested and passed in a small bag of coins.

I held it gingerly in my hand, acidly commenting to myself that it did me a great deal of good. I had absolutely no idea which coin of this realm meant how much. Just another little oversight. I would be so glad to get to Jokan's. I presumed there would be food in his larder, and I was hungry again. Once on the field, it seemed we took forever parking and three times Sinnall gave someone his orders to read and I heard each member of the unofficial section grumble out his name and a batch of numbers. Harlan, I remember, gave the name of Landar, in a stupidly high-pitched voice that almost got me giggling.

Finally, I heard Sinnall give the order to debark.

Harlan thrust his head back of the curtains.

"Gold coins are worth more, the larger the better. Silver, the larger, are alloy-mixed and worth less. Take care, dear my lady," he whispered and cupping my head with one large hand, kissed me on the lips with sweet speed. I heard him deliberately bumbling out of the planecar and then the retreating cadence calls.

I slipped into the front of the ship and looked cautiously over the windowsills. There was much coming and going on the field and many women among the men. Reassured I climbed out of the planecar. It was easy to guess which way was the entrance by following the direction of the crowd of brightly costumed Eclipsers. I strode forward confidently.

"Are you claimed, lady?" a male voice asked in my ear and whirling, startled, I saw a medium-tall man smiling hopefully at me.

"Yes, I most certainly am," I said and turning, left him standing there.

Two more offers by not as promising companions made me hover close to a large party of mixed revelers until I reached the gates. The women were allowed to pass quickly, but each man was forced to show identification and every tall man was drawn aside. The hunt was on for someone answering Harlan's description.

The novelty of being accosted by admiring males wore off before I got to the next busy street. There were plenty of planecars, but they were all aloft and I had no idea

how one signaled them. I suppose I should have asked
someone, but I had been so long away from people, all
sorts and sizes of people, that faces and forms were entertaining to me. Not so entertaining were shadowy figures at
the edge of the masses of revelers: blowsy drunken creatures, beggars with hideous purple scars, whining their
pleas. The section bordering the airfield was obviously
poor and I followed the flow of the crowd toward the
center of the city. Gradually the poor buildings gave way
to pleasanter areas of spiraling walks, connecting fluted
colonnaded buildings in muted colors. Guards were sta-
tioned at crossroads and they constantly stopped the taller
male figures in any group. I smiled to myself at the secret
joke that Harlan had entered in an official car and been
welcomed royally.

I came, finally, into the Great Bazaar, an enormous
square with a central park, comprised of successively
larger squares of shops, one outside the other, like the top
view of a child's nest of blocks. Only the stores were
staggered so that, through the separating alleys, one
caught enticing glimpses of other treasures. I wandered
through the crowds, wide-eyed at the fascinating stores,
trying to imagine the purpose of this or that; trying on in
my mind the gorgeous dresses. I decided that the jewels I
wore were better than many on display and my dress more
becoming.

Thirsty, I stopped at a beverage stand of which there
were many, some with the air of permanence, some obviously holiday-rigged.

When the counterman looked expectantly for my order,
I realized I couldn't ask for lemonade or Coke. For a
moment I could only stare at him idiotically.

Suddenly, hands covered my eyes. Frantic, I grabbed at
them.

"Guess who?" an eager young voice whispered in my
ear.

Thinking it was only an Eclipse game, I relaxed.

"I'm not good at guessing-games," I replied finally.

The hands dropped as if my skin had burned them.

"I beg, I beg your pardon, lady," a stammering voice apologized.

I turned and looked up a long expanse of white over-shirt before I came to the boyish face. There was a shocked surprise in his eyes and an appeal for understanding the boy did not expect to find. He was about sixteen, I guessed, and his frame had shot up before he could accumulate the flesh to cover it. It gave him an angular awkwardness; a bag-of-bones appearance to his clothes and an obvious inferiority. His gray eyes regarded me with an unspoken plea not to scorn him. He reminded me so of my brother, Seth . . . and someone else I couldn't place . . . but he did remind me of Seth at his gawky stage. It was this quality, this puppyish wistfulness that caught my sympathy.

"I mistook you, Lady Searcher. Really I did and I was so pleased the Lady Fara . . . I mean . . ." and he trailed off aimlessly.

Quickly I put my hand on his arm to reassure him, for he seemed about to take off into the crowd.

"No harm done. This is Eclipse, isn't it? And, truly, I am flattered to be mistaken for the Lady Fara."

A brief eagerness flared in his eyes and he looked as if he were about to smile, but his face turned unnaturally mature.

"Please, buy me a drink and think no more of it," I said quickly. "Something . . . light," I added, indicating two drunken carousers with distaste.

The smile flickered again and was replaced with a guarded expression.

"Two cornades," he said to the counterman, tossing a coin to the fellow.

"Thank you, lord, have a safe Eclipse."

The young boy handed me my drink with the polished grace of a courtier, totally out of character for his age.

It was a fruit concoction, tart and cold, and just what I had my mouth set for. We stood at one side of the crowded stand, saying nothing because I could think of nothing to say.

At the opposite end of this bazaar mall, there was a

sudden commotion, indistinguishable shouts, a startled milling of people and then a trio pushed into view. They were not very sober but not drunk enough to extenuate their obstreperous actions. The first man, a rough enormous fellow, charged with the ferocity of an angry gorilla, his long arms pushing way past those who did not move aside quickly enough. He looked from right to left, head thrust forward, bellowing at the top of his voice.

"Maxil, where is that little runt? Maxil, come here or I'll break you. Maxil? Maxil!" His two companions followed, likewise yelling for the missing Maxil, stopping people and demanding to know where this Maxil was.

I turned to my young man and found him missing from my side, just as the gorilla charged up to the stand, beckoning violently to the counterman.

"He was with this lady a moment ago," the man volunteered, not looking at me, but obviously frightened.

The lout turned on me, his liquor-heavy breath offensive, his sweating body odorous. He put his hands on my shoulders and started to shake me.

"Get your filthy hands off me, you stupid bully," I said, seething with anger at this insult. "I said, get your filthy hands off me," I repeated distinctly in the quiet that had fallen on the mall. There is some quality to righteous anger that has great strength in compelling obedience. He did remove his hands, swaying in front of me, while his thick drunken senses took in the import of what I had said.

"Who do you think you are?" the drunk asked.

"Maxil thought she was the Lady Fara," the counterman said timidly. I shot him a look I hoped would silence him completely.

"Fara? Fara here," the sot said, blinking at me, trying to see me clearly. "C'mere, Lort," he beckoned his two cronies. "Is this Fara?"

The other two peered at me, hemming me in against the counter.

"Never seen her," the one not named said. His breath was vile.

"Can't see anything here," Lort complained.

"He," and the drunk's finger jerked at the counterman, "said she was with Maxil. Everyone knows Maxil's sweet on Fara. Not that it'll do her any good." He cackled at his own wit.

Before I realized what would happen, the gorilla had thrown his cloak over my head and I was hoisted to his shoulders. I kicked, I scratched, I screamed, and then someone hit me on the head.

When I came to my senses, it took me a few minutes to recall what had last happened. My head ached and my jaw and my arms felt sticky. I think it was a concern for the beautiful dress Gartly had lent me that stung me into full consciousness.

I was sprawled on a large bed in an elegantly furnished but barren-looking room. Somewhere beyond the windows a great deal of shouting, screaming, laughing and singing was going on. I rose, carefully because of my headache, and walked to the window. Below me lay beautiful gardens, fairylands of casually riotous blooms, spilling onto the winding paths, nudging against a variety of unusual trees, enhancing stonework and sculpture. Beyond the delicate metal filigree I could see the throngs of revelers and another wing of the building.

It took very little intelligence for me to assume I was in the palace itself.

"In Gorlot's room?" I asked myself feeling very droll and wondering what I did now.

Yesterday everything had seemed very simple. This morning the plan had been foolproof. I sighed and felt like crying, but that would hurt my head more.

I did seek out the bathroom and washed my face and arms. I also dabbed at the stains I found on my lovely robes. When I heard a commotion outside, I hesitated briefly, wondering if a locked bathroom might not be preferable to what I would find in the room. I recognized one raucous laugh as belonging to the drunken gorilla and that decided me not to play the coward.

He was there, all right, propelling my young friend of the beverage stand into the room, roaring with vulgar laughter. I picked up a hairbrush I saw on the dressing table, hefting the handle, glad it was metal.

"You drunken Milrouser, how dare you," I cried, and both turned toward me.

The ghastly sick look on the boy's face enraged me as did his incredulous expression when he saw me tearing into the gorilla.

"How dare you kidnap me? This may be Eclipse, but there are limits to what is done. Get out of here, get out of here and leave us alone."

I am absolutely positive I was never so mad before in my life. Not even the time the Travis boys tried their dirty tricks on an innocent twelve-year-old Sara in their father's old barn. He had taken care of them with a razor strop and I took care of this oaf with a metal hairbrush.

If he had been sober, I should never have succeeded, but he and his two cohorts were definitely drink-fuddled and their reactions, for they did swing out to hit me, too slow for me. They howled when the metal brush contacted their arms and faces, and they backed out of the bedroom. I didn't have to chase them across the living room. I stood in the bedroom doorway and threw whatever came to hand. As soon as they had exited into the hall beyond, I raced over to the outside door and slammed it shut, swinging a heavy bolt in place.

The boy, Maxil, for I was sure it was he, stood, open-mouthed with admiration, looking at me.

I mastered the trembling in my body, got back my breath and grabbed an applelike fruit from a bowl on the table by the door.

"Who was that?" I asked the boy who had started to come over to me, his eyes still shining with his respect.

He stopped at my question and pointed inanely at the door. "You didn't know that was Samoth?"

"Samoth? No, why should I? I've never had the misfortune to meet him before." I took a huge bite out of the applefruit. It occurred to me that I would probably never not be hungry again. Most of my waking time for the last few days had been consumed by eating something.

"Wait'll I get that counterman," I continued wrathfully. "Just wait. D'you realize he tattled on you to that oaf?"

"I guessed he'd have to," Maxil said softly, sadly, looking down at his feet.

"Why?" I asked angrily. "Is everyone in this city scared of a trio of drunken bullies?"

Maxil found his ornate sandal very interesting.

"They have reason to be. You must come from out of the city," he added, looking up at me quickly and then away.

"Jurasse," I replied. "They thought I was the Lady Fara."

He looked up guiltily, flushing. "The counterman overheard us, I guess. I'm awfully sorry. It was my mistaking you for the Lady Fara that got you into all this trouble and now you'll . . ." his chin quivered and he turned away abruptly, striding to the window, his whole figure sunk with dejection.

"Now I'll what?" I urged, trying to keep my impatience out of my voice.

"I can't say it. But it is just horrible you've been dragged here like this. Samoth and the others'll be back and they'll . . . they'll . . ." he turned toward me again, his face blotched with an effort to keep back tears.

"They'll what, Maxil?" I said, going to him in my distress at his conflict.

"They'll say . . . I'm . . . impotent," and with that final dragged-out word he turned back to the windows, a pathetic young man.

"Well, of all the despicable, nasty-minded, indecent, incredible things," I said, beginning softly and ending with full vent to my indignation.

The echo of another scene came faintly to my ears and I recalled how I had helplessly overheard my four older brothers taunting Seth because he had been unable to "make it" with one of the town tarts. Even at fourteen I had known how cruel and inhibiting such taunting was. I had been completely unable to help Seth, but in his name I could try to help this boy.

I took Maxil by the hand and pulled him over the low couch.

"Well, are you?" I asked him point-blank.

He flushed. "Well, I have," he said tentatively. "But not when they're around."

"I should hope not. There *are* some things in this world that should be done at the proper time and place, in privacy." And then I, too, was blushing furiously. All I could think of was my unfortunate borrowing of one of Harlan's phrases and the circumstances under which he had said it.

"Aw, now don't say you haven't heard what they're saying about me?" Maxil said, his face still not quite resigned to tears. "Gorlot's got it all planned. As soon as he kills Ferrill off, he'll have me denounced as unmanly and put that fat-assed gut-stuffer Fernan in as Warlord-elect."

"Kills Ferrill?" I gasped.

"He's so sick and it's *not* his constitution. The Harlan clan is *not* weakening," Maxil exclaimed with pathetic emphasis.

"No, it's not Ferrill's constitution. He's been drugged."

"That's what I've been trying to . . ." Maxil gasped and turned to look at me with startled eyes, "how did you know?"

"I know. And further, they drugged Harlan, too."

Maxil stared at me. He looked at the bolted door. Nervously, he got up and went to the living-room balcony, opening the door and looking out suspiciously, before coming back to sit beside me again.

"I told myself that must have been what happened," he said in a hoarse whisper. "Are you sure it's true?"

"I'm positive. And furthermore," I continued, "he's no longer drugged. He's free and he's in this city."

Maxil stared at me as if he thought I had gone mad or he wasn't hearing properly. He blinked rapidly at me, swallowed his Adam's apple bobbing just like Seth's did when he was nervous.

"If you're just saying this," he growled in a tight, angry

voice, "if you're just saying this ... to ... to ... I can still use my authority to ..."

I put my hand on his arm, catching his eyes and holding his attention.

"Maxil, I'm telling you the truth."

Gradually his face changed as he realized I meant what I said. Hope, concern and then despair crossed his face. Groaning, he turned from me, again lost in apathy.

"It's too late," he said sadly. "It's just too late. And besides," he turned back to me again, his eyes sparkling with anger and a sternness incongruous with his youth, "you shouldn't go around *saying* that where just *any*one could hear you." He gestured wildly, at the balcony, and the bedroom and the hall door, as if overgrown ears would come leaping out of the stonework to us.

"I'm saying it to you."

"How do you know Gorlot doesn't have me under control?" he argued violently.

I found myself speaking softer and softer in an unconscious effort to tone him down.

"Well, I doubt he does if he makes such degrading assertions about you. Besides, Jokan said you were terribly worried about Ferrill. You said you hated Samoth. Well, if Harlan gets the Regency back, you get rid of Samoth. All I've got to do is to get to Ferrill and tell him what's happened and have him convene the Council."

Maxil regarded me as if I had lost my senses.

"That's all you have to do. Get to Ferrill and tell him to convene the Council," he repeated as if reasoning with an idiot. "That's all!" Again the broad dramatic gestures.

"I'm in the palace, aren't I? Ferrill lives here, doesn't he?"

It had occurred to me, suddenly, and I felt rather dense it took me so long to wake up to the opportunity, that I *was* in the palace and I might just as well put into effect Plan A.

"And Ferrill will have to appear in the Starhall tonight if he can walk," I rattled on. "And I presume you can get into the Starhall?"

"Yes," Maxil agreed, paying strict attention to me now.

"Yes, I can, and he *has* to appear." He stopped, dazed, and then his face lit up, his shoulders straightened and his chin jerked forward. The frightened, humiliated boy disappeared and the young man stood in his place.

"Do you realize what you've said?" Maxil asked me. "Do you *realize?*"

"I gather you're relieved," I said drolly.

"Relieved, *relieved,* RELIEVED!" he chorused dramatically. "I feel alive for the first time in twelve months. Nearly a whole year!" he assured me, hooking his fingers in his belt and striding up and down the floor.

"In that case, is there any way you can get me some dinner?" I asked as my stomach impolitely made noises.

"Dinner? Certainly. *Certainly,*" he said expansively. He went to the door, shot the bolt free, and swung the door open. "Guard," he said with a swagger in his voice. "I want dinner for two in my rooms."

I got a glimpse of the startled face of the guard who saluted sloppily just as Maxil swung the door closed again.

"I'd bolt the door again, if I were you. I'm not sure I want to tangle with Samoth when he's cold sober," I remarked.

Maxil was not so overconfident as to forget his conditioned response to Samoth in a half-hour's time. Indecision showed in his face.

"Look, my friend," I said seriously, "I'm glad the news of Harlan relieves you, but let's not overdo it until we can get word to Ferrill and start things rolling to get Gorlot and Samoth out of power."

"Oh," Maxil said breezily, "Samoth was dead drunk. He'll go annoy some of the ladies before he comes back here. And then he'll come in with a whole bunch of his clan and tease me. But he won't be back till he's sober. And by *that* time, we'll be gone!" Maxil's eyes flashed with determination. Then he pivoted toward me again.

"Just where *is* Harlan?"

"To tell the honest truth, I don't know. And maybe I'd better not tell you anymore than I already have."

"But . . ." Maxil urged, not to be denied reassurance,

". . . how did you know he was drugged? I mean, how did you get him . . . out . . ."

The timid knock at the door interrupted him. He looked at me, eyes scared.

"Dinner," I whispered to him and then, with sudden inspiration, nestled against his side, twining one of his long arms around my shoulders.

"Come," Maxil said, his voice not quite breaking, his arm crushing my shoulders as he awkwardly returned my embrace.

I must say he made a convincing show of someone inconveniently interrupted. A single man entered, a mousy fellow, clad in a green apron. He bowed nervously.

"What did you wish for dinner, Lord Maxil?"

"Storner, I want a *nice* dinner. What had you in mind, Lady . . ." and he stopped, realizing he didn't know my name.

"My name is Sara, darling," I said, pouting plaintively. "Had you forgotten, after . . ." and I trailed off. I thought Maxil would explode with laughter. Fortunately his face was turned from the waiter. "And I'm just famished. All I want is food."

"Two of the best . . . whatever you're serving Gorlot," and Maxil spat the name out. From the expression on Stoner's face, he had missed nothing I intended to imply. Nor Maxil's contempt of the Regent pro-tem. Whatever the waiter's opinion, he kept his face blank as he bowed out, promising dinner in a very few minutes.

"Say," Maxil breathed, his eyes wide with admiration. "Did you know what you were doing?"

I grinned at him, bouncing up off the sofa.

"I hope it's all over the palace, real soon," I grinned.

"Gee, you're wonderful," Maxil said sincerely. "I wish I . . . I mean, you've . . . just . . ." he was trying to get something out.

"The Lady Fara?" I asked delicately and was answered by his blush. "Oh, she's your girl."

"She's *my* dear lady," Maxil stated firmly. "At least," he added, "she would be. Stannall wouldn't object, I know. But Gorlot's not convened Council on the flimsy excuse that the Tane crisis takes all his time and it is a time for the Warlord, not the Peace Councils."

The subject agitated Maxil and he began his restless pacing up and down. The resemblance struck me and I realized he was much like a bad copy, a smaller-scale Harlan, unfinished, unmolded, untempered. But the resemblance to his uncle was there.

"The Lady Fara is Stannall's daughter?"

"Everyone knows that," he countered, looking at me.

"I don't. But then, I'm a little country girl," I added hastily.

"Well, you certainly don't look like it," Maxil said with unexpected sophistication. "As a matter of fact, you *do* look like *my* Lady Fara." He had his uncle's disconcerting way with the possessive pronoun. "Same height. Same coloring. And we'd planned to be priest," he fingered his white robes, "and Searcher this Eclipse. That is, before Harlan had his so-called collapse. Oh, she'd've had to wait, but we had an understanding," he ended with stubborn insistence.

"Won't Stannall be here tonight? I mean, as Councilman."

Maxil shrugged. "I don't know. He might be. When I saw you in the bazaar, and thought for just one split second you might really by *my* Lady Fara . . ." and he left the sentence hanging. "But I'm glad it was you after all," he said with a very engaging grin.

In spite of all the cruelty he had been subjected to, in spite of worrying, Maxil was a thoroughly nice youngster.

"There's not a damn thing wrong with the Harlan clan," I remarked succinctly and then smiled for fear Maxil might take me wrong.

Another knock at the door ushered in our dinner, a welcome diversion for several reasons.

"Storner," Maxil said imperiously after our table had been placed before us and the waiter made ready to withdraw, "when is the Warlord, my brother, due at the Starhall?"

"The rumor is he will not come," Storner said with a blank face.

"I'm not interested in the rumor," Maxil snapped. "What has his physician said?" Maxil's tone showed his opinion of that gentleman.

"By the tenth hour, my Lord Maxil," Storner replied in so colorless a voice it was insolent.

"Oh, marvelous. I promised to get a token from Ferrill," I giggled. "To protect me from a priest I know," I said, coyly walking my fingers up Maxil's arm.

Maxil waved Storner out of the room and we continued to make stupid faces at each other until we heard the door close. Maxil covered his mouth to smother his laughter, doubling up with boyish glee.

I waited a moment, then the smell of the dinner, steaming in its metal dishes, overcame my manners.

"Laugh all you want. I'm hungry," I announced and started to heap my plate with food.

"I've never seen a woman eat so much in my life. You pregnant?" he asked suspiciously.

"What a thing to ask!" I exclaimed, nearly choking.

"Aren't you claimed?"

There was that word again. "Not exactly," I said loftily. "I've an understanding, though."

"Oh," he grunted, mollified.

My sanitarium diet had not prepared me for such gourmandizing as this and I ate steadily while Maxil talked. He talked as if it were going out of style. I realized what terrible tension he must have been under. As well as the dramatic enthusiasms and passionate opinions of adolescence that not even Samoth's tender attentions had completely subdued, Maxil had a keen insight. His humor, often with a bitter edge to it, was wry and delightful. As long as I could keep eating, I would be able to let him carry the burden of conversation. I was distressingly aware of my all too limited acquaintance with the general framework of life on Lothar. Its everyday banalities, like Joe Dimaggio, hot dogs, Fourth of July and hammer murders, were beyond my comprehension.

I gathered that the "bandsmen" were not orchestra

players but groups of hijackers, burglars or highwaymen, terrorizing unpatrolled regions, resorting to senseless outrages of destruction in property and human life. I had to deduce that such crimes, common enough on earth, had been completely unheard of on Lothar. A step more brings the conclusion that the lawless element usually stayed in the Patrol where it had an outlet for its energies. The decreased need for active patrollers had left too many potential criminals idle. But I was surprised that Maxil had the same conclusion to make.

I learned that insanity, also a rarity on Lothar, was plotting a dreadful, steep upward curve of incidence in medical science. There was no Freud, no Jung, not even a good common-sense minister to instruct and analyze. There was no organized religion of any kind on Lothar. There was only the centuries' old dedication to the absolute and complete destruction of the Mil. This was not enough for the younger generations of Lotharians who had had little direct contact with this ageless menace. They wanted considerably more out of life than freedom from fear and the stringent safeguards evolved by ancestors buried hundreds of years ago.

Perhaps, I thought, Harlan was wrong about not seeking out the Mil now. Certainly that would absorb the restless elements. Once Lothar had laid the scourge to rest, she could progress more normally. Normally? Was my Earth any more normal with its constant, useless international bickerings? At least Lothar had a mighty purpose and pursued it relentlessly, valorously.

As we finished the sweet fruit of our final course, I made a particularly noticeable blunder.

"Sometimes you act as if you didn't know what I was talking about," Maxil commented, frowning. "And you've got the oddest way of talking. Where do you come from?"

"Jurasse. My mother was from South Cant. I guess that's why I have an odd way of speaking. Mother always said Jurassans murder . . . [I was about to say the King's English] . . . human speech."

"They certainly do," Maxil agreed, pushing back the

table. He belched without apologizing and I wondered if this were customary or adolescent. I cleared my throat instead.

We had grown accustomed to the noisy crowds outside the gardens. Now suddenly a roar of angry voices drew our attention to the windows. Maxil strode over, beckoning me.

"Another protest on the Tane wars," he remarked, pointing out banners being dipped and glided above the heads of the crowd.

"Damn the Tane wars," Maxil growled. "That's all anyone talks of."

"It masks some other purpose," I said remembering Harlan's fears.

"I'll just bet it does. And you know why that war's a farce?" Maxil demanded. "Because Gorlot's men command the patrol now. Men," he sneered, "like Samoth. *All*, even the emergency session of Council Gorlot calls, they're all *his* men. He hasn't missed a trick. Not one."

"Yes," I contradicted him, "one. Harlan's escape."

"That doesn't do any good unless Harlan can appear *sane* before the Council and *prove* it. And I'll bet Gorlot can think of a way to prove Harlan is as mad as ever."

"I doubt it. Because Harlan never was mad."

"I know it. You know it," he said gloomily.

"Sitting here won't do any good. Seeing Ferrill will. Let's go. It must be near time now," I said, standing up. Maxil's depression was contagious.

CHAPTER SEVEN

THE STARHALL WAS THE FINAL beauty in the flawlessness of the palace wheel. The vast dome-ceilinged room accommodated the throngs of people without seeming in the least crowded, without being noisy. The constellations that shone from the darkened ceiling changed perceptibly as the planet itself turned round its primary. The mocking lights glittered on hundreds of maskers who danced, drank and sported in the gigantic room. I had never seen such a magnificent crowd, nor felt so dwarfed by a walled structure. Maxil and I paused, by mutual consent, in one of the five soaring archways that gave on to the Hall proper, watching the fantastic revelry.

"Where's Ferrill?" I asked.

Maxil shrugged. "It's not yet tenth hour. He may not come in until the Eclipse." He pointed to the ceiling where facsimiles of the two satellites closed the gap that separated them and their rendezvous with their sun. "It's a frightfully noisy night for him. Not like other times. Oh, we had lots of guests but ..." His inference was directed at quality not quantity. "See that blond girl over there by the second archway. The one in the purple overdress? That's my sister, Kalina." He grimaced with distaste. "She's drunk and she's got enough face paint on for a Clan Mother. And the other blonde, the one on the couch under Ifeaus (a constellation, I later learned), that's Cherez. She's only thirteen. It's bad enough for Kalina to be here acting that way. She's already claimed. But for Cherez!"

A servant approached with a tray and paused in front of us. Maxil peered into the ornate metal goblets, snorted and waved the man away.

"Gorlot's serving delinade," he gritted out.

"What's that?" I asked without thinking.

"An aphrodisiac. Don't you know *any*thing?"

93

I was spared the necessity of replying by the change of expression that came over Maxil. It was a combination of fear, hatred, disgust and expectation.

"Where's Samoth?" a cold voice said behind my back and I didn't need to wait until I was roughly turned toward the speaker to know it was Gorlot.

"You aren't the Lady Fara," Gorlot said, staring at me.

"Samoth got drunk," Maxil said quickly, taking my arm and trying to move away.

"You are not to leave your tutor. Especially not to pick up prostitutes. As if they would do you any good," Gorlot snapped. "Go find him."

"He's supposed to nursemaid me, not me him," Maxil replied with a show of more spirit than Gorlot evidently expected from him.

"I see," he drawled enigmatically and flicked a hand at the guard behind us. "Take this trollop out."

"Immediately," a feminine voice seconded beyond Gorlot. A woman, elegantly dressed in a yellow Searcher's costume joined the temporary Regent. "I gave explicit orders that I was to be the only Searcher here," she said vindictively. Her eyes narrowed suddenly as she noticed the flash of my jewels in the starlight. She peered more closely at the fabric and cut of my gown. Its rich green made her costume too glaring a yellow by contrast. "Who is she?"

"Lady Sara, the Lady Maritha and, of course, the Lord Regent Gorlot," Maxil said with cold politeness.

"Lady Sara, indeed," Maritha sneered and snapping her fingers at a passing traybearer, took an unladylike gulp of a fresh goblet.

"Lady Sara, indeed," I replied calmly, bowing as graciously as I could, to make her rudeness more apparent. My palms were sweating.

A gleam flickered in Gorlot's eyes as he noticed the exchange. He looked from Maritha's studied blond beauty to me.

"The blond Searcher and the brunet. An interesting contrast. The Searcher has always been my favorite mask, particularly so when I complement it," Gorlot drawled, indicating his white priest's robes.

"You make a truly authentic priest," I murmured, not meaning flattery but smiling up at him from under demurely downcast eyes.

"Get her out of here," Maritha snapped to the guard, her eyes flashing angrily. "Impertinent wretch," and she tossed off the rest of her drink.

Gorlot, to my surprise, canceled that order with a flick of his hand.

"We cannot be so ungracious to Maxil's Searcher," he said as Maritha glared first at me, then at him. She had sense enough to be quiet. "However, every Searcher knows the priest who will claim her, doesn't she?" and his cold eyes flicked once more up and down my body.

Gartly's apparently prophetic words rang in my ears: "It isn't in Gorlot's room we want her."

I took Maxil's arm, more for support against my nervousness, and pulled him forward, away from Gorlot. The backward glance I shot him he could interpret any way he chose. I merely wanted to be sure he wasn't following me.

I was not the only one shaken by the encounter. Maxil's arm trembled beneath my hand. He kept his back straight and his step measured as we walked into the dancers. And there was more pride and confidence in his bearing than there had been since I met him.

The dancers and revelers parted around us to catch us up in their whirling numbers. A fear, deeper, more intense than the momentary shock of the episode with Gorlot, engulfed me in choking terror. The pressing bodies suddenly seemed to compress me in on myself. The various limbs that brushed against mine felt wet or cold and I grabbed at Maxil with both hands. He took one look at my face and brushed rudely past the maskers to get me on the safe, uncrowded sidelines.

I stammered my thanks, unable to explain my ghastly claustrophobia, clutching at Maxil as the only reality in the whole huge room.

He urged me to a brightly decorated buffet table where

tall crystal columns sparkled with liquids. Culinary masterpieces were desecrated to slide down palates dulled by drink. Maxil indicated an almost full dispenser of cornade. We were served by a haughty man who gave the impression of losing dignity by presenting so mild a brew. I gulped down the tart beverage and its cold sweetness reassured me out of my sudden nightmare. I was recovering enough of my senses to see the surprise on the servant's face as he was required to serve another goblet of cornade.

"Greetings, Maxil," said a voice whose cheeriness was another touch with reality.

Maxil's face lit up first, then flushed. I turned, hopeful of seeing Ferrill but barely able to cover my dismay when Maxil grabbed the arm of a well-groomed, wise-faced older man.

"Stannall," he cried eagerly.

"The Lady Sara, is it not? I noticed you passing inspection at the door," and the First Councilman bowed deeply, his shrewd eyes not leaving my face. "Do I congratulate, Maxil?" he asked.

"No, no," Maxil said hastily. "Isn't *my* Lady Fara here?"

"*Your* Lady Fara?" Stannall repeated, lightly questioning the possessive pronoun. "No, Fara is not here," Stannall continued before Maxil had a chance to say anything. Stannall turned a disapproving face toward the shrieking revelry beyond us.

"I mean, is she in Lothara at all?" Maxil persisted hopefully.

"Yes," Stannall said, unbending enough to reassure the boy.

"I'm just filling in for the evening," I felt constrained to say when I caught Stannall's austere expression.

"Rather to the discomfiture of the Lady Maritha," Stannall observed.

"Gorlot called Sara a trollop," Maxil exploded.

Stannall held up a quieting hand. "Evidently the ... ah ... Lady Maritha did, too. She chooses to forget she no longer wheedles Harlan but placates Gorlot."

Maxil and I exchanged glances. I couldn't decide whether to say any more to Stannall or not.

"Have you seen my brother . . . Ferrill, Sir Stannall?" Maxil asked anxiously.

Stannall dropped his pose of urbanity and became deeply troubled.

"I have, indeed, and . . ."

"Where is he?" Maxil interrupted breathlessly.

Stannall ignored the discourtesy and nodded toward a far doorway where two figures stood watching the revelry. I could not see distinctly, but I thought I recognized the taller figure as Ferrill by his stance. Maxil was about to make a straight-line plunge through the dancers for his brother, but I twitched his robe and held him back. Actually, my thought was not caution but a return of the tongue-drying fear that had struck me when we had first gone into that weaving mob. We watched as Ferrill, slowly, almost as if movement were effort, stepped down into the crowd and was swallowed up.

"I can wait for my token," I said with forced gaiety, turning to Stannall. "I need one from the Warlord against a priest I don't like."

"There is no known token for one priest I can name," Stannall remarked calmly, adding in a lower voice that Maxil didn't hear, "unless, of course, that is your purpose in being here."

I smiled at him. "Sir, it was at this priest's instigation I came and believe me, I have no intention of leaving his side this evening."

Stannall bowed and excused himself. I watched him disappear among the dancers and wondered, fleetingly, if I should have mentioned Harlan to him. Still, wasn't he powerless until Council was convened? Surely, any attempt of Harlan's to communicate with the First Councilman would be intercepted. Yet—I had been in the position to speak.

And how was Harlan even to get into the palace at all? Where was he now? Did he know I wasn't at Jokan's?

Maxil touched my arm and led me with a secure grip around the fringe of the revelers, making toward the archway where Ferrill had been. We had circled halfway round the room without a sight of him when he stepped out of the crowd right in front of me.

I was appalled at the change the last few weeks had made in him. The effort I had noticed across the enormous room was tragically obvious close up. His face was very pale, the skin almost transparent. His breath came unevenly, his eyes had sunk into his head, the sockets darkened with pain and sleeplessness. His voice, no longer vibrant, as it had been at the asylum, shook nearly as much as his hands. Maxil put out a quick arm to support Ferrill as the aging young Warlord mounted two steps and joined us.

"I have been wracking my poor brains, dear Searcher," Ferrill remarked in a wheezy, rasping voice that somehow managed to retain a certain forcefulness, "to remember where I have seen you before. Not here, certainly."

"Your memory is better than Gorlot's," I replied as casually as I could, for tension again clutched at me. "But I have bettered my condition in the past few weeks."

Ferrill held up his hand as he searched his memory, Maxil anxiously watching us and the crowd simultaneously.

"It was in the company of Harlan," and I saw the frail shoulders straighten as if the very name of his uncle was a tonic. He said nothing. "I left his company this noontime at the auxiliary airfield," I continued, beginning to share Maxil's anxiety over Ferrill. "He wants you to convene the Council. He is sane. He never was mad. He was drugged just as I imagine they have been drugging you. Give me a token, anything, to explain my speaking to you. And have courage."

Ferrill's breathing became more shallow. He swallowed several times, all the while maintaining a politely attentive smile on his face. With a controlled gesture, he took a dangling medallion from his belt. I accepted it with a little curtsey.

"He may be too late," Ferrill wheezed, "even for Lothar." He descended three steps, touched Maxil's hand affectionately and moved off into the crowd.

"Gorlot saw us," Maxil said, swiftly, the hangdog expression returning to his face.

To cover my own fear, I smiled inanely and laughed as if Maxil had amused me. I searched the crowd frantically for sight of Stannall, for a doorway with the fewest guards, for some reprieve from the man implacably bearing down on us. Maxil whirled me away among a sudden knot of drunken prancers, back toward the beverage table where we had last seen Stannall. The fear of Gorlot met my claustrophobia in a brief struggle for supremacy and the fear of Gorlot won.

But Gorlot never reached us because a shriek of horror pierced the noise and music. Shouts of "The Warlord. . . . He fell" followed. The entire vast hall was silent for a horrified minute. Then Gorlot's voice called cold orders for Trenor, for a stretcher.

We watched, clutching at each other for comfort at this catastrophe as the limp body of Ferrill was carried away.

"I've got to get out of here now, Maxil," I cried. But as we turned to look, all the doorways were blocked by guards with weapons held at the ready.

"Stannall then," I hissed. Maxil craned over the heads around us and then pulled me roughly after him.

The First Councilman had been about to leave the hall when Maxil urgently tugged at his arm, insisting on a private word. Stannall frowned as Maxil indicated me.

"I've no time to undo your coquetry, miss," he said severely, drawing away.

"Would you class news of Harlan as coquetry?" I stated.

Stannall turned slowly back. "What's this? Explain!"

"Harlan was never mad. He's back in Lothara tonight to prove it. At Central Barracks in the section of Sinnall, son of Nallis, who is *loyal* to his Regent," and I stressed the title, not daring to continue for the press of people around us and the sudden approach of two guards.

"The Regent requests the presence of the First Councilman immediately," one guard said, saluting.

"He's *my* brother. I must come, too," Maxil pleaded.

"Only the First Councilman is required," the guard said dispassionately.

Maxil's eyes clouded and his lip trembled a moment. "But he may . . ."

"Lad," Stannall reassured him kindly, "I'll send for you," and he followed the guard.

Maxil's face wore the old, bitter mask. I tried to comfort him, but it was the appearance of his younger brother, Fernan, drunken, strutting in premature triumph, that stiffened Maxil's resolve. Looking at the youngster, his face greasy and swollen with overindulgence, I could scarcely see why anyone would choose *him* over Maxil.

Deliberately Maxil turned his back on Fernan and ignored the whispers we both heard very plainly. Gorlot had spread his fiction about Maxil with an efficient hand.

We didn't have long to wait to know why Stannall had been summoned. He, Gorlot and another man Maxil said was Trenor appeared in the archway and the maskers quieted expectantly.

"The Warlord Ferrill has been seriously taken with a heart attack. He is resting comfortably at the moment. It is the opinion of his physician that with care and rest he will recover," Gorlot's harsh news rang out into the Hall. "We have been concerned with his health for some time. It is our deep regret that his frailty will prevent him from fulfilling his promise as one of Lothar's great Warlords."

"He regrets," Maxil growled.

Someone was moving through the crowd which parted to make way. As he stepped up to Gorlot, we saw it was Fernan. Maxil winced. I saw Stannall beckoning to Maxil and gave him a prod in the ribs. Because the boy refused to let my hand go, we both made our way through the reluctantly parting throng. I gave Maxil one final push and jerked my hand free as we reached the steps. Gorlot, however, saw me and his eyes narrowed. I returned his stare with a defiance I hoped was convincing.

People began to whisper together and then someone tittered and Maxil, standing by Stannall, turned to face the Hall.

"What makes the eunuch think he can be Warlord?" some self-acknowledged wit quipped from the safety of the mass. Laughter rippled from all parts of the Hall.

"Eunuch?" I echoed angrily, rising to the first step and turning to face the direction of the voice. "Eunuch?" I repeated as the laughter died and attention was centered on me. I snorted with disgust and disbelief. "Can you know," for the wit had been a man, "better than I?"

The mutter from the assembled had an entirely different tone now, one of surprise, and Maxil added the final touch.

"Sara, not here," he pleaded, an agonized expression on his furiously blushing face.

It couldn't have been more perfect. The canary-satiated look vanished from Fernan's fat face. Gorlot's eyes narrowed to angry slits and his right hand clenched and unclenched the knife at his belt.

"In deference to the illness of Ferrill, it is my suggestion that you carry your revels to another place of enjoyment," Stannall announced quietly, motioning to the guards to step aside from the archways. "Lord Maxil," and Stannall stressed the title, "the Lady Sara, may I ask that you attend me?"

Gorlot stepped in between Stannall and us.

"As Regent, I would like to ask the Lady Sara a few questions," he almost snarled.

There was a hint of a smile on Stannall's calm face as he answered Gorlot.

"Gorlot, you were Regent to Ferrill. Your Regency, a temporary appointment in any case, has ended with your acknowledgment of Ferrill's incapacity. The Council will convene tomorrow to install the new Warlord-elect and consider the appointment of *his* Regent."

Calmly Stannall motioned us to precede him out of the Hall. I couldn't resist one backward glance and saw Fernan pulling at Gorlot's sleeve impatiently, his putty face screwed up with childish petulance.

CHAPTER EIGHT

STANNALL BRUSHED ASIDE MAXIL'S impatient questions about Ferrill. As First Councilman, Stannall had apartments on the fourth level of the palace wing. We made a silent progress down the blue, softly lit corridor, punctuated with doors and guards, past Maxil's quarters. At the door of his suite, Stannall paused, motioning the guard aside. He produced a curiously shaped rod and pressed it into the small panel in the center of the door. A low whine was audible and then the door opened inward. Lights came up immediately, exposing the graceful main room of the apartment and a filigree-framed balcony.

When the door was closed, Stannall turned to me sternly and demanded an explanation of my cryptic remarks in the Starhall. I gave him an expurgated edition of Harlan's recovery from the drug, intimating that "suspicions had existed in certain minds" over the cause of Harlan's unexpected collapse. I told him of our escape, my meeting with Maxil and my subsequent abduction. As far as I knew, Harlan was in Central Barracks in a detachment from Motlina, under the Second Leader Sinnall.

"I realize now why I was suddenly invited here for the Eclipse," Stannall mused, rubbing the side of his nose thoughtfully. "My presence has not been required much lately. Obviously Harlan could be kept from seeing me here," and he nodded toward the guarded door. "But there are other problems now to be surmounted."

He turned toward Maxil thoughtfully.

"Although . . . ah . . . *the* Lady Sara has already neatly undone much of Gorlot's plans to undermine your election," Stannall began, inclining his head graciously toward me.

"But we . . . she . . ." Maxil stammered.

Stannall frowned and looked at me for explanation.

102

"We met for the *first* time this afternoon," I said meaningfully.

"Then the boy could be . . ."

"Nonsense," I snapped, regardless of Stannall's position and age. "He doesn't think he is and he should know."

"My daughter, Fara . . ."

"You *know,* sir, Fara and I have had an understanding for just *years,*" Maxil blurted out.

Stannall regarded him with a kindly expression. "I had hoped that would develop into a constant feeling."

Maxil swallowed hurriedly. "It has. I mean, it would if you'd ever let her come back to the palace."

Stannall raised his eyebrows. "More of Gorlot's machinations clarify suddenly. Yes, of course, it wouldn't be to his advantage to have Fara at the palace. Placing you under a tutor the like of Samoth . . ." Stannall shook his head. "Believe me, I was not in favor of that appointment. But I felt at the time it was only for a little while."

"Little while!" Maxil snorted, revealing the abuse he had endured all too long.

"However," Stannall said more briskly, "we shall take care of that little detail right now. Before anything else."

He touched an ornate switch on a bare wall which slid back, revealing a complicated set of panels, desk area and closets. Flipping a series of switches, Stannall activated a vision circuit on which a picture clarified of an old man, clad in a dressing robe.

Stannall greeted the man as Cordan, explaining the Warlord's collapse and asking Cordan to contact Luccill and Mallant and bring them immediately to the palace wing to confer with Trenor.

"With Trenor?" Cordan shouted indignantly.

"Yes, Trenor," Stannall reiterated clearly. "We shall need a full report in the morning for Council. You will then insist, I repeat, insist on seeing me, no matter what the hour, to give me, as First Councilman, your opinion. I cannot overstress the urgency of this. Do you understand?"

Cordan nodded gravely and Stannall broke the connection. Maxil sighed with relief and flopped down into an armchair.

"Why didn't you tell me of Harlan's escape before you rushed off to Ferrill?" the Councilman asked me sternly. "You realize, of course, that the news was too great a strain and brought about his attack? I could have effected a convention myself, given your information."

Maxil turned a horror-stricken face to me.

"I didn't know that," I said, tears springing to my eyes.

"But, my dear girl, I *am* the First Councilman. Surely you know the prerogatives of that office."

"The Council was not in session," I argued in defense. "Harlan didn't dare get in touch with you at your holdings."

"Harlan made a poor choice as messenger, then," Stannall retorted, anger in his voice.

"I wasn't even supposed to *be* a messenger," I cried. "I just had the misfortune to tangle with Samoth and the next thing I knew I was in the palace and in Maxil's room. I thought it would *help* Ferrill to know Harlan was all right."

"Please, Sir Stannall," Maxil interposed, alarmed at my tears. "I'm the one to blame. *I* knew how *sick* Ferrill was. And I knew all about Harlan. It's my fault, not Sara's."

"Oh, my situation is absurd," I cried in my frustration. "Accusing me doesn't heal Ferrill now and it doesn't get Harlan into the palace and make him Regent again."

"He couldn't be made Regent anyway," Stannall reminded us dryly.

"Why not?" Maxil's voice cracked in dismay.

"First, he has to be proved sane. Second, the same condition I cited to Gorlot applies to Harlan. He was Regent for *Ferrill*."

"But what if I want Harlan as *my* Regent?" declared Maxil with dawning comprehension. "I'm over fifteen, so I can choose."

"That's perfectly true," Stannall replied as if he, too, had only realized this fact. He brought his hand down hard on the communicator switch, dialing quickly. He turned to me again, his eyes blinking rapidly, his lips pursing in thought. "There is no doubt of his sanity?"

"Of course not. He never was insane. He was drugged into a semblance of mental imbalance. If you are having those physicians here for Maxil, get Harlan here, too. They must be as qualified to judge Harlan's sanity as Maxil's . . . virility."

A voice declared it issued from "Central Barracks," but no picture evolved.

"This is First Councilman Stannall," and the picture came on abruptly. "I need additional sections for special duty at once. Are all assigned?"

"No, Sir Stannall, but the ones available are all provincial reinforcements called in on special assignment," the officer apologized.

"That doesn't matter. Have you any men from my province?"

"No, sir. I could recall those from duty . . ."

"That would consume too much time. What have you got?"

"Units from Motlina, South Cheer, Banta . . ."

"Motlina. Leader's name?"

"Sinnall."

"That would be Nallis' son, wouldn't it?"

"I believe so."

"Fine. Have him report by planecar to my balcony and give him clearance through all that mess out front."

It was too simple. I sat with my eyes closed in relief that Harlan would soon be here. Stannall, pursing his lips in thought, brooded over the length of his right foot. Maxil walked over to the fruit bowl on the table and chose a piece to munch.

"I wonder," Stannall mused aloud, "what else Gorlot has been busy doing."

"Harlan seemed to think the Tane uprising was covering something up," I remarked into the silence.

Stannall shook his head in disagreement. "I've checked and double-checked the reports on that from the first attack. I've interviewed some of the survivors of the first raids. Those that were paralyzed with cerol. Wicked stuff that. I suspect some connivance with Glan or Ertoi. They have always been so complacent about their role in the Alliance. It isn't natural. And then there's that treaty concerning the Tanes that Gorlot has been trying to ram through Council."

I shrugged, not having heard anything about that. The sound of Maxil's munching was infectious. I rarely needed an excuse to eat lately, so I wandered over to have another bite.

We were all expecting it, but when the whir of the planecar's approach suddenly drowned out the muted revelry beyond the gardens, we jumped to our feet, startled.

The car hovered, connected with the trelliswork of the balcony and disgorged its passengers. Stannall held up a warning hand and allowed the group to file in. The planecar was closing its slot door when the door to the hall burst open and the guards rushed in, weapons drawn. The masqueraders, acting on reflex, pulled out their own arms. The two forces glared at each other suspiciously even as Stannall's easy chuckle dissipated the sudden menace in the room.

"I'm pleased to see such alertness," he remarked to his guards with that measured calm of his.

Weapons were sheepishly replaced.

"Mark these men well, guards," Stannall continued, indicating Sinnall's section. "They'll be coming and going all night. Oh, and when the physicians Luccill, Mallant and Cordan arrive, they are to be admitted immediately. They are expected."

The guards backed out with one final suspicious glare at the newcomers.

As the door closed behind them, Harlan spotted me where I had been half hidden by Maxil.

"Sara, how did you get here?" he exclaimed, striding to me.

Stannall snorted. *"That* reaction proves he's sane," he commented almost sourly. "You've heard the news?"

Harlan, one arm around me, turned back to the First Councilman.

"Bad news needs no announcement," Harlan said heavily.

"Your emissary," and Stannall gave me a curt nod of his head, "was too literal in the discharge of her duty. In consequence she also robbed you of yours."

"Stannall, that isn't fair," Maxil interposed before I could explain anything.

"Sara, you were supposed to get to Jokan's," Harlan muttered, gripping me tightly in his concern.

"Best laid plans," I sighed. "I ended up here, talking to Ferrill after all."

Stannall frowned and went into bitter detail of the events leading up to Ferrill's heart attack.

"Sara wouldn't have known you could help us, Stannall," Harlan said firmly. "Had I even the slightest hope you would be here at Eclipse, I would have . . ."

Stannall waved off the rest of his sentence. "You realize, of course, Harlan, that your Regency also is terminated by Ferrill's incapacity?"

Harlan nodded, settling himself beside me. I sat there inanely holding the core of my fruit because I didn't see anywhere to dispose of it. Behind Stannall's back, Harlan took the core and tossed it at a seemingly bare spot in the wall. A slot opened as the core neared and closed silently behind it. Harlan's grin and the squeeze he gave my hand mitigated Stannall's scathing disapproval.

"However," Stannall continued, pacing, "young Maxil here is next in line. He claims he's ready to stand up and cry for you in front of Council."

Harlan turned to Maxil, a mixture of emotions on his face and a flurry of unspoken thoughts muddying the color of his eyes.

"With thanks for the honor, young Maxil, I'm not at all anxious to be saddled with the Regency again."

Everyone in the room turned to stare at Harlan.

"But you were . . . driving us like cavehunters to get here," Jessl stammered out.

"To save Ferrill's life, yes. It's in good hands now. And neither Gorlot nor I is Regent."

"But Harlan, you're the only one who *can* be Regent,"

Maxil cried out, his voice cracking perilously in his distress.

Harlan regarded him a moment with tolerance.

"You could certify me for good if I agreed with you, young Maxil," he said lightly. "You'll find dozens of men eager for the job. I'll give my personal recommendation that you'll be easy on the new Regent."

"This levity is uncalled for," Gartly growled disapprovingly. "There aren't dozens of men qualified for the Regent of the Warlord in these troubled times. And you know it."

"You're one, friend Gartly," Harlan pointed out. He rose. "I had been Regent for seven years," he said, directly to Stannall. "That's a slice out of a man's life. I've got other plans for the next six years while Maxil grows up," and his eyes slid enigmatically in my direction.

"For instance?" asked Stannall with an edge to his voice.

"You know my preferences well enough, Stannall," Harlan replied sharply. "You've vetoed my requests for more exploratory ships. You've overridden my insistence that we must find more allies for the final attack on the Mil homeworlds."

This seemed to be the prologue for the renewal of an old battle of more than unusual importance to both men. Stannall opened his mouth to reply and then dismissed the subject with a sharp wave of his hand.

"It does you no good to find new planets for Lothar if she is in the grip of men like Gorlot and the petty bullies of his clan. You were, as I recall it," and Stannall's voice was heavily sarcastic, "the one who initiated the colonization policy that would give the run-from-the-Mil his first chance for independent holdings . . ."

"If there were not two but eight, nine, ten planets to divide, there would be no such struggle," Harlan interposed.

Stannall snorted his contempt. "Of course, it doesn't signify that such men as Lamar, Newrit, Tellman—and I could name a dozen others—are no longer available as prospective Regents."

This was news to the others as well as Harlan.

"Yes, that surprises you, doesn't it," Stannall said with calculated scorn. "Newrit and Tellmann were killed in the Tane revolutions; Lamar and Sosit are in survivor asylums in pitiful condition. In their places we have such notable personalities as Samoth, Portale, Losin . . ."

"Bumbling incompetents," Harlan exploded. "I've kept them on the Moonbases since they aged into section leaders because they blasted well can't do much harm to raw rock."

Stannall smiled mockingly. "Yet they are now *quadrant* leaders and the only choice besides Gorlot that Maxil here would have."

Harlan glared fixedly, almost sullenly, at Stannall. "I have already done more than my duty for Lothar," he muttered.

Stannall's eyes narrowed angrily, but he controlled his face into an appearance of good humor.

"Yes, you have," he agreed. "So has Ferrill."

"I have the right to lead a private life, now," snapped Harlan, jerking himself away from Stannall and stamping over to the balcony.

"How would you lead it under the Regency of a man like Gorlot . . . or Losin?"

"Gartly qualifies. So does Jokan."

"Aye, and Gartly's willing," the old soldier spoke up sternly.

"Jokan's reputation as a philandering dabbler disqualifies him, however," Stannall pursued, "in the eyes of the conservatives as much as it enhances him in the halls of the liberals. You know where that would end: stalemate."

Harlan stopped pacing and stood, his back to all of us, staring out at the revelry beyond the palace and absorbing the quiet of the still gardens. There was resignation and tired defeat in the set of his shoulders.

I wondered in the tense silence that fell if his reference to exploration made me indirectly responsible for the outburst that had stunned the others. This change of face was unlike the dedicated man I knew. He had thought of nothing for the last weeks but to get back to Lothara, be reinstated as Regent and save both Ferrill and Lothar from Gorlot's plans. It was incredible that he would suddenly separate duty to Ferrill and duty to Lothar when he himself had given me the strongest impression that the two were indivisible in his eyes. Hadn't Stannall's revelations impressed on him that Lothar needed him more than ever before? Why did he hesitate?

"My friend," Stannall began in a subtly persuasive tone, "your return and the fact that you were really drugged into insensibility are the final pieces in a puzzle I have been meditating ten months. Does it not appear all too propitious that Gorlot should have been in Lothara at the time of your collapse when you had ordered him on Rim maneuvers? That three days after your ... illness, the Tane wars break out? That Socto, Effra and Cheret are replaced within the month, leaving Hospitals, War Supplies and Records in the control of Gorlot adherents? That petty officers with records as martinets and incompetents are suddenly promoted to quadrant leaders? That Ferrill, whose health has never been as robust as we could wish, is suddenly afflicted with a strange debilitating malady and is successfully treated only by Trenor, a relatively unknown physician from a back province in Gorlot's holding? That Maxil is shepherded, disgraced, shamed, humiliated by a bullying byblow, while Fernan is feted and cozened? That Council is left unconvened except for the emergency quota all during a long summer and that that quota is composed of those barons who have opposed your reforms? They fit in, these pieces, don't they?

"And don't think I haven't left a cave unsearched to find out what is really going on. I've seen every report from the quadrants, talked with the wounded; seen the shivering wrecks that were our most promising patrol leaders and tried to convince myself that nothing was wrong. Because there has been no discernible evidence of illicit activity.

"And then, miraculously, you return as sane and hearty

as when I saw you in the Starhall two hours before your collapse."

Stannall paused. He looked at Harlan to see what effect his disclosures were having.

"Tell me," the Councilman's facile voice changed flavor again, "have you no personal quarrel to pick with Gorlot for taking ten months out of your life? Can he shame you with the stigma of insanity and not expect to answer to you? Or are you still insane? The man who tells me his duty was done with Ferrill's deposition does not sound like the Harlan I knew ten months ago. It sounds like a drug-weakened dreamer, filled with delinade, not guts and blood."

Instead of being stung by the insults, Harlan turned wearily from the window. He looked toward me first, but his face was expressionless.

"You touch a point none of us have brought up, Stannall," he said slowly, heavily. "It is necessary *first* to prove I *am* sane, to the Council, to the planet, and to myself."

Jessl and Gartly exhaled tightly drawn breaths. Stannall allowed no expression of triumph whatever to cross his features.

"Harlan," Maxil burst out, his voice cracking again, "if you don't want to be Regent for me . . ."

Harlan crossed quickly to the boy and threw an affectionate arm across the rigidly held shoulders. "My . . . hesitation . . . has no reflection on my fondness for you, lad. Or, I should say, my lord."

"That, too, has not yet been decided," Stannall said briskly. He sat down at the desk by the communicator and pulled out slates as he continued talking. "The physicians will report here after they make their examinations of Ferrill . . ."

"There's no chance that the initial verdict can . . ." asked Harlan.

"None," was Stannall's emphatic answer. "I presume Gorlot has been merely biding his time before he brought up the matter of the lad's health officially. Perhaps he didn't expect Ferrill to collapse so completely."

"But you said he'd be all right," Maxil said anxiously.

Stannall frowned slightly at this interruption. He turned and looked at Maxil as if the boy had changed completely.

"I said he'd live. The extent of his invalidism we'll know when we receive the full medical report. At the same time they are here to see you, my lord, they can make a preliminary examination of Harlan. Undoubtedly a more extensive one will have to be made at the War Hospital Clinic at a later date." Stannall added a final mark to the slate he had been writing on and handed it to Sinnall.

"Section Leader, this must be delivered at once to Lesatin. I believe he planned to be in Lothara for the festivities, but I doubt he was invited to the palace." Stannall smiled wryly. "His sympathies have never paralleled Gorlot's interests. Once the message is delivered, consider yourself under Lesatin's orders. Try first at his town residence, Place of the Triangle Red. Someone there may be sober enough to remember where the man went.

"Gartly, I want you to contact every old patroller you know, in town or not. Jessl, get your younger friends together. I want word spread that Harlan is back, that he is sane. That he never was mad. Your group can spread the news quicker than the Mil can evacuate the city. By the way, where's that ladies' man, Jokan? I'd've thought he'd be along tonight."

"He's waiting at his place for Sara. And I think she'd better go there," Harlan said.

"On the contrary," Stannall countermanded, turning to look at me. "The young lady must spend the night in Maxil's suite."

It was Harlan's turn to frown.

"I don't see the necessity of . . ."

"You don't see, Harlan," Stannall interrupted testily, "that she is essential to counteract Gorlot's campaign to have Maxil set aside as impotent. In front of the entire Starhall, she admitted his claim on her."

Harlan turned white and stared at me.

"I did not," I cried, although I didn't understand the undercurrent between Harlan and Stannall that was directed at me. "I said nothing of the kind. And I only met the boy this afternoon at a cornade stand in the square. Then . . ."

Stannall waved me silent. "That *must* not be known," and he pinioned with his glance everyone in the room separately, exhorting unspoken compliance with this essential lie. "The *impression,*" and as his voice underlined the word, he looked squarely at Harlan and then Maxil, "must stand."

"A moment," Harlan said in a too-quiet voice. "I had a prior claim."

Stannall turned to Harlan coldly. "I cannot help your private plans for the Lady Sara. The fact remains unalterable that Lothar must remain under the impression that this girl is Maxil's lady. That voids Gorlot's scheme to have Maxil set aside in favor of Fernan. Gorlot neglected to include an element of chance in his calculations. We cannot permit his neglect to go unutilized because of private feelings or dealings. I'm certain that both Lord Maxil and the Lady Sara are aware of the circumstances in which they now find themselves and will conduct themselves accordingly."

"Sara, I'm sorry," Maxil pleaded with such adolescent embarrassment that I swallowed the words that rushed to my lips.

"There is so much at stake," I began, directing my plea to Harlan whose jaw muscles were clenched with his unspoken anger. "After all, it is an honor to be the Warlord's lady. If I ever dreamed a simple glass of cornade would lead to all this . . ." and I made an attempt at a carefree laugh. Maxil gave me a rather sickly grin of gratitude, but Harlan refused to unbend.

"With *your* permission," he grated out between his teeth at Stannall and then drew me out to the balcony. Stannall watched us leave and then beckoned to Gartly and Jessl to leave and for Sinnall and Cire to join him at the desk.

Harlan was gripping my hand painfully tight. He shut the glass balcony door and drew me into the balcony shadow.

"Sara, that gesture may cost you your life," he began.

"Don't be silly. I've braved the worst that Gorlot could do and . . ."

"Gorlot is nowhere near as deadly for you as Stannall," Harlan said in such earnest my levity failed me.

"You never come right out and explain," I wailed softly.

He shook his head irritably. "It is not a simple thing to explain. I don't understand how you came to let Maxil claim you. Surely you must realize how little you know of this planet."

"I couldn't agree more."

"Then how can you expect to play a part which calls for constant public appearances where everything you do and say will be remarked. The tiniest slip will be noticed. Sara, Sara."

He took me in his arms, pressing my head against his chest, folding me carefully but tightly against him, his lips on my forehead.

"What else could I have done? I've been as backed into a short cave as you have."

At my choice of words, he gave a little chuckle, and released me. I could see his face in the shadow, his eyes on me were tender.

"There was one chance in several thousand you'd manage to carry off what you've already done. But I'd far rather see you safely on my holdings until we find out more about how you got here. And preferably, find your world."

"Is that what you meant when you said you had other things to do with your life?"

"Yes," he said sadly. "Yes. There's more than just finding your world and helping them defend themselves against the Mil. But that's scarcely an issue to throw into the confusion of this mess."

"But *why* is my origin so dangerous?"

"It's all wrapped with the horror of restoration," he said

in a tight voice, "which I have no time to explain. But you say you've come from another planet. The only *way* you can have got from another planet that I know of is by way of a Mil ship. And traveling on a Mil ship ... well, it follows that you must be a restoree. And to almost everyone, a restoree is a horror to be exterminated at the first opportunity."

I stared at him, my throat dry.

"But I'm not horrible, am I?" I whispered, scared deep inside me by the intensity in his voice.

"Dear my lady," he said softly, framing my face with both hands, "has not half of Lothar acknowledged your loveliness?"

"But your restoree talk scares me," I said, biting back my tears. Fatigue, hand in hand with fright, seeped past the barriers excitement and novelty had created. I was desperately tired.

"I know, Sara, but I must scare you enough to make you doubly cautious. I feel so powerless to protect you."

"I'm too tired to think," I groaned, putting my hand to the place on my jaw that ached.

He opened the door and handed me back into the room.

"*My* Lady Sara is exhausted," Harlan said, issuing his challenge at Stannall.

The First Councilman looked up at Harlan for a long moment.

"Maxil, you have heard Harlan's claim."

"Yes, sir, I have," Maxil agreed somberly, rising to his feet.

"All right, both of you escort her to Maxil's apartment. Then I want *both* of you back here," Stannall said with exasperation.

Harlan, bowing slightly to me and then Maxil, gave Maxil my hand and opened the door to the hall for us.

There was no doubting the shock of surprise on the faces of the guards as they recognized Harlan on the way to Maxil's quarters. Neither Maxil nor Harlan looked right or left. Maxil palmed open his door and stood aside to let me and then Harlan pass while the startled hall guard snapped to attention, his eyes wide and rolling around to get the closest look at the Regent.

Maxil closed the door and let Harlan lead me to a bedroom, opposite the one in which Samoth had dumped me that afternoon. The lights came up immediately in the lovely room.

"How do you turn them off?" I whispered urgently to Harlan.

He pulled the door to and waved one hand over a panel of darker wood by the doorway. The lights went out. I saw the whiteness of his hand move again and the lights came up.

He stared at me fiercely.

"By all the mothers of all the clans, I should have claimed you on that boat after all. Remember, you are *my* lady."

The incredible possessiveness of his look stayed before my eyes long after he left. I realized suddenly what the formality of "claiming" and using the personal possessive pronoun must mean. I had got myself married to Harlan without even knowing it. I fell asleep trying to see all the ramifications of my paradoxical situation.

CHAPTER NINE

THE NEXT MORNING WHEN I woke, I felt rested completely and, of course, hungry. I was torn between a bath and something to eat. On the bed was a heavy green robe. I glanced at the other side of the large bed and assured myself I had been its lone occupant. I rose and belted the robe and tiptoed to the door. I peeked out into the living room, saw a clear path to the fruit on the table and started for it.

"Lady Sara, I hope I didn't wake you," and I whirled to see a young blond girl in a blue overdress, her eyes wide and anxious.

"No," I muttered.

"I am Linnana and at your service. May I draw your bath? There are gowns for your choosing and, if I may suggest it, the others will soon arrive for breakfast." She glanced at the hall door nervously, expecting an invasion momentarily.

Beyond her, I saw on the raised level at the balcony door the table set and awaiting diners. I nodded but nevertheless grabbed up an applefruit before I returned to my room. I didn't care what she thought. I was hungry.

I bathed and then allowed Linnana to show me the clothes she had mentioned. It was a mistake because there were far too many of all colors, lengths and fabrics, and a small chest of jewels as well.

"I'm just a simple country girl," I began finally as even Linnana showed impatience at my indecision. "I don't know what to choose to wear in the palace for breakfast."

She giggled. "That's easy. With your permission?"

She held up a knee-length tunic and overdress in contrasting shades of a soft rust, and took from the jewels a simple chain of gold with jadelike buttons in the links. When I had dressed, no longer worried about unfamiliar

117

closures because she took care of that, she set me down again and opened a small metal box. With a brush, she recreated eyebrows for those I lost in the force screen. She added a touch of color to my lids and a blush of paint on my lips and studied the effect. When I glimpsed myself in the mirror, my hand inadvertently went to my nose. I snatched it back into my lap for fear she would interpret the gesture.

"My pardon, Lady Sara," and she brought out powder for me.

It was a little reassuring to know that women still used such guiles on Lothar.

Evidently she felt no more was needed and followed me to the door.

When I stepped out into the room, I stopped abruptly on the threshold. Linnana had neglected to tell who had been expected for breakfast and I had not bothered to count the place settings. It would not have been so overwhelming if I had known what to expect. Over twenty men were gathered in that room, of whom I knew only Stannall, Harlan, Maxil and Jessl. Following Maxil and Harlan's example, those seated at the crowded table rose instantly. I believe I was the only one who saw Harlan prod Maxil forward to greet me.

Maxil struggled with his embarrassment as he took my hand to lead me to my place. Our flushing faces only compounded the desired impression.

A servant came quickly with the steaming chocolaty beverage which was the Lotharian equivalent of coffee. It helped clear my head, certainly; hot, tart and stimulating.

"You'll be pleased to know, Lady Sara," Harlan began formally but with a wicked twinkle in his eye, "that the Lord Maxil and I have been cleared of the various physical and mental deficiencies attributed to us. And, by the foremost physician of the world, Monsorlit."

I grabbed frantically to balance the cup in my hand before my trembling spilled the hot stuff all over me. Maxil hastily proferred a napkin and a servant materialized to mop up and produce a fresh cup. I muttered inanely about hot cups and tried to catch Harlan's eye. His remarks were addressed to the table in general and he did not look at me.

"Gorlot was ... obviously ... mistaken about Maxil," he continued blithely. A polite ripple of laughter forced a bright smile from me. There were no lascivious sidewise looks at me from the men at the table. Actually fathers were quick to urge a likely girl to become the unofficial lady of a Warlord. A child of such an alliance might well be Warlord-elect if the father died without other, more legal issue.

"The most exhaustive tests brought by Physician Monsorlit failed to show me mentally defective but he's to try his worst this afternoon in that precious Clinic of his. I am, evidently," and here Harlan's laughter was echoed by the others, "to be congratulated on my astounding return to sanity."

"Physician Monsorlit," the name rang in my brain and I couldn't believe it. Could there be two with the same name?

"Remarkable luck, that," said a man standing by the balcony, "getting one of Gorlot's own to validate your sanity."

Harlan frowned at the comment.

"I say I find it difficult to believe a man of Monsorlit's caliber is connected with Gorlot. He's too fine a scientist and physician ..."

"Not too fine a man to have dabbled in the vile practice of restoration," snapped Stannall with such massive hate and condemnation in his voice that it filled the room with tension.

I stared, amazed at the First Councilman for the passion of his denunciation.

"He was severely disciplined for that youthful attempt," a gray-headed, senatorial man remarked, "and has turned his remarkable energies toward our truly pressing problem of insanity. Look what he has achieved with that Mental Clinic of his. He's been able to train useless idiots to perform simple duties perfectly."

Stannall was not impressed.

"He has sought the proper cave in company with Gorlot."

Then why, I asked myself, did Monsorlit say Harlan was sane. Don't they realize that Monsorlit was responsible for Harlan's collapse?

"Gorlot will have difficulty now keeping Maxil from the Warlordship and Harlan from being appointed Regent," someone stated.

"I wouldn't be too sure," Stannall said sourly. "Remember, there was little Monsorlit could do when three other noted physicians were sincerely convinced of Harlan's recovery."

"Then you expect trouble tomorrow when the Council convenes?" Grayhead asked worriedly.

"Of course I do," Stannall said. "Do you think Gorlot will simply step aside because Harlan has returned unexpectedly? No, the man is incredibly cunning, else we should have suspected him long ago. How many of you doubted his report of Maxil's impotency until last night? How many of us have questioned any one of his other unusual acts? The appointment of a back-province physician for Ferrill instead of Loccan or Cordan?"

"But Trenor effected some relief for the War——the boy," another voice interposed. "There *was* a definite improvement."

"Yes, a cessation of whatever drug they used to debilitate the boy," Stannall retorted.

"Did the physicians find the residue of any such drug in Ferrill's body?" Grayhead asked.

Stannall snorted. "There are many drugs with peculiar properties, my dear Lesatin, whose traces are completely absorbed in the system within a few hours. Cordan suggests that perhaps cerol was used since Ferrill's motor system has suffered most. But that is confidential information."

"Cerol?" Lesatin exclaimed in horror, "but that's a Tane-grown drug."

And, I amended to myself, the same thing they used on Harlan.

"Then the Tanes are behind this," someone blurted out.

"No," Stannall replied with such calm assurance that the rising hysteria in that quarter was calmed. "But I have good reason to believe that the Tane Revolution masks some intention other than meets the eye."

Stannall smiled slyly at the anxious requests for explanation.

"We have already sent a ... ah ... qualified observer," and Stannall glanced quickly at Harlan with an accusatory expression, "to Tane to bring us back a firsthand report of the situation. I have not been satisfied with the all too reassuring official reports."

"Neither have I," Lesatin asserted loudly. "They've been ... ah ... em ... too vague."

Maxil muttered in my ear, "Jokan took off on his own last night. Harlan was fit to tie him to a Mil Rock. So was Stannall but not for the same reason."

"But Jokan was supposed to wait for me," I said inanely.

"That's why Harlan was mad. That Jokan!" Maxil chuckled with delight.

Stannall was continuing smoothly. "He will return as soon as he has properly assessed the problem. In the meantime, it is essential that we delve into every corner of Gorlot's administration and bring up from the depths of each cave those inconsistencies which can bring the majority of council to its senses with regard to this tyrant."

"I should think poisoning Ferrill would be sufficient," remarked a wiry, black-headed man later named to me as Estoder.

Stannall pointed a finger at him, punctuating his words, "*If* we had proof of it, which not even Cordan can find ... except by the process of eliminating other factors. Indeed, without Harlan's miraculous escape and return, we would not even be possessed of the suspicion. The action of that new drug is comparatively unknown, you realize."

"Just how did Harlan escape, if he'd been so heavily

drugged? No one's clarified that point," Lesatin remarked, pointedly staring at me.

Harlan shot me a quick encouraging smile but allowed Stannall to speak first.

"The . . . ah . . . Lady Sara," Stannall had difficulty for some reason in deciding on my title, "managed to penetrate the sanitarium and became assigned as Harlan's attendant."

"We are doubly indebted to the Lady Sara," Lesatin remarked, bowing in my direction.

Lesatin seemed to me to be the sort of person who dotes on being possessed of the fullest information on any given subject that attracts his attention. He reminded me unpleasantly of an officious junior executive at the agency library who had plagued me unnecessarily for infinite details about this or that. I steeled myself for the questions Lesatin, if he bore out the resemblance, might throw at me.

"Can it be possible to assume," Estoder spoke before Lesatin could, "that Socto, Effra and Cheret were removed from Hospitals, War Records and Supplies more by Gorlot's intervention than the normal course of events?"

"Possible, probable and entirely feasible," Stannall agreed, "and I suggest we begin our checking immediately with these offices with the thoroughness of the ancient priesthood in examining a novice."

Everyone now had a question or an opinion or a suggestion. The breakfast broke up into little groups of debaters, calling to Harlan or Stannall for approval. Men departed in pairs or singly. Finally there were only four of us left. Harlan reached for a heavy surcoat. I tried to catch his eye so I could tell him about Monsorlit's visit to the asylum. I was also afraid of being left alone with Stannall after his remark about restoration.

Harlan spared time only to grip my arm and mumble about seeing me later. As the door swung shut behind him, I felt awfully alone and vulnerable.

"Maxil," Stannall said, "I think you had better present yourself to your brother's quarters."

"Fernan?" Maxil countered, distastefully.

"No," Stannall frowned, "Ferrill. The morning's report is reassuring. The paralysis of his right side continues. But last night's examination contradicts the theory of a heart seizure. It will look well that you have been to see him. And take the Lady Sara with you. I have assigned four men as your bodyguard. Absolutely trustworthy," and the First Councilman's face relaxed into a reassuring smile for Maxil. "You two," and he flicked his eyes to me, "are not to be left unguarded for a moment. Oh, and when you've seen Ferrill, your new quarters should be ready. I'll see you at dinner, Lady Sara," and he bowed punctiliously in my direction.

"He doesn't like me, Maxil," I said when the First Councilman had left.

"Aw," Maxil shrugged it off. "He will. Harlan'll see to that and when Fara gets here," and Maxil blushed furiously, "I mean, aw," and Maxil rolled his eyes to the ceiling in adolescent embarrassment.

"I know what you mean, Maxil," I laughed, patting his arm consolingly. "It will be a great pleasure to step aside for my competition."

Maxil's face screwed up even more. "Oh, Sara."

"Oh, Maxil," I teased back, trying to reassure him.

A knock at the door disclosed Sinnall, in resplendent Palace Guard uniform, at rigid attention. Behind him I could see an equally rigid Cire and two huge guardsmen. Sober-faced and taking his new position very seriously, Sinnall saluted.

"My orders, Warlord, are to guard, guide and defend you and the Lady Sara. May I present Second-Leader Cire, and Patrolmen Farn and Regel!"

"Second-Leader Cire," Maxil said, grinning broadly at Cire's good fortune. Then he hastily cleared his throat and recalled his new position in life. "My compliments, *Group Leader,*" and his voice underlined Sinnall's double promotion, "and my thanks for your loyalty. I wish to see my brother, Ferrill."

Saluting smartly, Sinnall backed out into the hall with

his men, waiting at attention until Maxil and I started before he signaled his men to fall in behind us.

There was a vastly different atmosphere in the hallways this morning. Perhaps it was the green sunlight that flooded the hall from the skylights and balconied alcoves. Perhaps it was the crisp snapping to of the guards who saluted as we passed where last night they had insolently glanced our way. Perhaps it was the obsequious salutations of the men and women who paused to greet Maxil, openly eyeing me. Several would have engaged Maxil in conversation, but he was too nervous to give them any encouragement and, to my relief, they tactfully withdrew.

There was a marked difference in Maxil's bearing as we continued. Last night he had come close to cringing away from passers-by. Today, his shoulders were erect. He held his head high and his eyes lost their apologetic furtiveness. He was beginning to accept the fact that he was Warlord-elect; that this good fortune was his and that he could no longer expect ridicule. No longer was he Samoth's whipping boy; nor the "younger brother" of a promising Warlord, but the heir himself. And I was proud, too, to see him conducting himself in what he considered the proper manner.

Leaving our escort outside, we were immediately passed through to the inner rooms of Ferrill's suite. At the door of the bedroom, a double guard was posted to whom Maxil issued his request with new-found imperiousness. One guard excused himself and entered the darkened room. He returned immediately, holding the door respectfully for the man who entered.

Maxil's confidence disappeared instantly and he muttered a halting request. I was in no position to bolster Maxil because I was staring straight at Monsorlit. I trembled with fear and apprehension. Round and round in my mind whirled Stannall's words, and the volume of his revulsion and contempt seemed to grow with each cycle. I looked frantically around for some exit or something I could do that would remove me from Monsorlit's notice.

"Certainly you may see Ferrill, Lord Maxil," Monsorlit assented smoothly. He stood courteously aside to let the boy pass. "I must, however, caution you to keep your visit short so as not to tire him."

"He'll be all right, I mean ... that is, he's not going to die or anything, is he?" Maxil asked anxiously.

Monsorlit shook his head, smiling enigmatically. I turned toward the outer rooms.

"No, Sara, stay with me," said Maxil pleadingly.

Monsorlit turned, curious, to me.

He started to incline his head in an acknowledgment, stopped, stared puzzled for a split second and then straightened. There was nothing in his expressionless face to indicate whether he recognized me as Harlan's whilom attendant or not. I was certain it would be only a matter of time before he pulled my identity from storage in his orderly mind. Maxil saw all this, but his interpretation of Monsorlit's stare made him flush. I wrenched myself around and escaped into the darkened bedroom.

A greenish glow, pleasant, restful, fell on the book-piled desk, the panel of communications screens, shelves of souvenirs and slates that covered the inward walls of the room. Against a side wall was Ferrill's wide bed, flanked by chairs and an austere hospital table with its neat array of medicines.

"Greetings, Maxil," said a low voice from the shadowy heaps of pillows. "Come to view the departed?"

"Aw, Ferrill," Maxil groaned, dropping on to the bed.

"My lord," I heard the low hoarse chuckle, "I couldn't be more pleased at this turn of events. In all truth, it's been hard to play Warlord. No idealist, no dreamer like myself should have to come to grips with the realities of ruling a world. His heart is not sufficiently armored against sentiment and suffering for the strict impartiality essential for the domination of millions. I would soon have failed Harlan, my father's memory ... and Lothar."

The voice trailed off into a cough. Maxil, a gangling awkward shape, shook his head in denial.

"Ferrill, if I'd only known how awfully sick you were, I'd never have let Sara tell you about Harlan. Stannall says that's what made you collapse," Maxil confessed brokenly.

"Good thing she did," the sick man stoutly reassured his brother. "The only thing that saved my life, believe me, was fainting last night. Otherwise you would really be gazing on the departed."

"What do you mean?" cried Maxil aghast.

"Simply that I'm positive Trenor would have administered a lethal dose of his palliative last night. The moment Sara told me Harlan was free I could feel the prick of that final fatal needle in my arm. As it is, I'm extraordinarily lucky to come out of this with just a mild paralysis. Cerol is dangerous stuff. I'd've died a lot sooner did I not come of stout-hearted stock. That heart attack rumor is false."

"You mean, you *knew* you were being poisoned and never told anyone?" Maxil cried out.

Ferrill snorted. "Who would have believed me? 'The boy's delirious,'" he quipped in an elderly voice.

Cerol, he had said and that was what they had used on Harlan but the results were so different. On Ferrill they caused debilitation . . . on Harlan only a senseless stupor.

"Stannall believes you were poisoned."

"Certainly he believes . . . *now*. Who is that lurking in the shadows? Come here," Ferrill commanded. "Ah, the Lady Sara. My harbinger of good news. Again thanks."

"I'm relieved to know that last night's message was good news to someone," I said gratefully. "Even if Stannall objects."

"My dear girl, you ruffled his feelings. Stannall has been thwarted of late, both personally and politically. He dislikes most of all being uninformed on curious happenings. A failing of his, but it makes him an extraordinarily capable First Councilman. Almost too capable. Gorlot must have had a paragraph in his plans for him, too."

"Have you any idea what Gorlot was building up to?" I asked curiously.

"Apart from complete domination of Lothar," Ferrill said with a nasty laugh, "I have only vague suspicions."

As I looked down on the gaunt-faced man who had still been a boy a few weeks ago, it was difficult to realize that there were only four years between Maxil and Ferrill. It looked more like forty. "I suspect he gave the Tane planets away to those who have backed him. After Harlan's convenient sick-leave had been arranged, Gorlot descended on us like a Mil ship that didn't bother to orbit. Everyone had a good word for him. Took me a while to come to my senses, I want to tell you. Then it was already too late. His men were in strategic positions. The Tane war was under way and I was kept almost too sick to care. After that, patient optimism and intestinal fortitude seemed my only alternatives."

"Is Monsorlit really helping you now?" I asked, speaking my fears. "He isn't just another Trenor for you?"

Ferrill's smile was very knowing and wise. He waggled a weak finger at me.

"Don't doubt our leading authority on nervous diseases, sweet lady."

"But he's the one who was drugging Harlan in the asylum. And I know there were others in there just as unwilling as Harlan. And Trenor was their physician."

"I don't doubt it."

"And you still let Monsorlit treat you?" Maxil quavered.

"Yes. For the simple reason that *I* trust the man."

I stared at him.

"Why he is allied with Gorlot, I don't know," Ferrill continued. "He is an oblique fellow but it will be a sorry day for Lotharian medicine when he is gone."

"But . . . but . . ." I stammered.

"Monsorlit is not a proper cave-mate with Gorlot, no matter what the appearances show," Ferrill said with more vigor than you would expect from so frail a person. Then he frowned at me. "You are certain that he drugged Harlan? Monsorlit was *not* at Maritha's the night Harlan was taken ill."

"But I *saw* Monsorlit give Harlan an injection and he called it cerol. They thought I was a moronic attendant. And I know that there are nine other men in that sanitarium, drugged by Trenor, with the same stuff Monsorlit used on Harlan."

Ferrill raised a thoughtful eyebrow and pursed his lips, a gesture imitating Stannall.

"That's when you decided to help Harlan?"

I nodded. Ferrill shook his head, frowning as he tried to correlate this information with his picture of Monsorlit.

"You must retire now, my lord and lady," said the soft, respectful voice of Monsorlit.

I jumped and Maxil got to his feet, for none of us had heard the door open. I waited breathlessly for Monsorlit to denounce me. "You will tire the young patient," was all he said.

But as we passed him on the way out, his eyes glittered at me and I wished passionately I knew how much he had overheard.

Maxil turned frantically to me once the door was shut.

"We've got to tell Stannall, Sara," he said breathlessly.

I shook my head violently. At the moment I didn't know which of the two men I feared more, the physician or the statesman.

"Stannall will find out all he needs to know by himself, I'm sure. You know his opinion of Monsorlit. And if Ferrill is to recover from this poisoning, Monsorlit is undoubtedly the only man who can do it. We *can't* take away Ferrill's chance of recovery. Let's forget, right now, what we said in there. Completely."

Before he could object, I pulled him into the filled entrance room. We were greeted by queries after Ferrill's health. Twice Maxil was importuned with unveiled hints for patronage. At first I thought Maxil didn't catch them. Once we had reached the quiet of the corridor, he snorted out a bitter remark.

"You should have seen them all laughing yesterday when Samoth dragged me back with you over Varnan's shoulder."

Our guards filed behind us as Maxil led me down the corridor beyond Ferrill's suite.

"We have the rooms my father and mother had, I think. They're the only ones vacant I could use."

There were guards at that doorway, too. Sinnall received the salutes and replaced them with his own men. He then opened the door wide, stepped inside and quickly checked each of the doors leading into the reception hall. Evidently reassured no assassins or Mils lurked anywhere, Sinnall threw open both of the big doors leading into the main room of the suite.

Stannall's charming rooms seemed barren, cramped and cold in comparison with the spacious splendor of this four-balconied living room with its various levels. A wide window overlooked the riotously blooming gardens, backed by the towers of the city, magically iridescent in the green sunlight, sparkling in an incredible panorama to my alien eyes.

Linnana and a white-tuniced young man approached and both bowed.

"My Lord Maxil, I've checked Ittlo's credentials and Stannall has already approved Linnana," Sinnall said with stiff formality. "Subject, of course, to your approval."

Whatever comment Maxil may have had was drowned by an uproar outside. I had heard that bull bellow only once before, but it had been indelibly engrooved on my eardrum.

My reaction was annoyance. Maxil turned white, his shoulders resumed their slump and he crouched as if to hide. I caught him by the arm and gave him a shake. He didn't see or hear me. Sinnall expressed his annoyance actively by opening the door with an angry jerk.

"What is the meaning of this disturbance outside the Warlord's suite? Get rid of that man."

I doubt that Samoth would ever have passed the guards for all his burly strength. He was at the moment impotently raging against their crossed weapons. He quieted a moment as he saw Maxil and then began bellowing.

"I'm the Warlord's appointed guardian," he yowled.

"The Warlord's appointed guardian is the Council, not an individual," Sinnall answered with a snort at such ignorance. "Remove this nuisance," and he beckoned to two guards farther down the hallway. "Hold him in custody. The only reason he was permitted to remain free was the generosity of Lord Maxil. This has been exhausted. Off with him."

The guards promptly took over and there was a certain overzealousness to the restraints they applied. Sinnall cut off the indignant mouthings of Samoth by slamming the door. He apologized to the stupefied Maxil for the unwarranted interruption.

"Maxil," I said in a wicked way, for the boy still looked scared stiff, "think up something juicy for Samoth to do. Like decontaminating Mil ships."

Maxil's eyes began to gleam. Sinnall had difficulty retaining his official face as the boy's unguarded expressions showed his reflections on suitable vengeance.

"Maxil," I began, having wandered around the room, peering into a study, a small anonymous room, a room set aside for communication panels, three bedrooms. There wasn't a bowl of fruit in sight, but there were plenty of flowers. "Maxil, I hate to mention this but I'm hungry."

Maxil looked at me with disgust.

"I've never seen you when you weren't. Are you sure . . ."

"Maxil, order me some fruit at least," I pleaded cutting him off in midsentence because I knew perfectly well what he might be going to say.

"My apologies, my lady," Linnana said, coming forward swiftly. "A terrible oversight. I'll remedy it immediately. Ittlo!" and Linnana gestured the other attendant toward the communications room with a fluttery hand.

A knock on the door and a gentleman entered, bowing, followed by boys carrying a variety of uniforms and other masculine apparel.

"Ahem," Sinnall said discreetly behind his hand, "there will be a formal dinner, Lord Maxil. If you please . . ."

Maxil looked up at the ceiling in dramatic exasperation at such matters but went obediently into his bedroom.

We were eating a marvelous lunch when Maxil was called to the communications room for a call from Stannall.

"Council will convene tomorrow morning, Lord Max-il," Stannall said formally. "Your presence is required. The Lady Sara will hold herself in readiness to attend the convention."

"Yes, sir," Maxil agreed readily.

"I trust your quarters are satisfactory?"

"Yes, sir," Maxil agreed enthusiastically.

"You are satisfied with the personnel?"

"Indeed I am," Maxil replied, grinning broadly at Sinnall and Cire.

"Then until the dinner hour this evening, Lord Maxil," and Stannall courteously signed off.

"Formal dinner," said Maxil gloomily. "I knew Stannall would put them back in."

There was another tap at the door and one of the guards motioned to Sinnall. There was a brief conference and then Sinnall went out into the hallway, looking over his shoulder at Maxil. I moved so I could see into the hall and caught a glimpse of an anxious young face. It took me a minute to get the significance and then I turned to Maxil.

"I'll bet I got a glimpse of Fara in the hall just now."

"Fara," and Maxil's face lit up with joy. He ran to the door and yanked it open. Sinnall and the girl were deep in earnest conversation. She caught sight of Maxil, her mouth made a round O and she looked like she would burst into tears.

"Get her *in* here," I hissed at Sinnall.

Poor Fara had no opportunity to run as I was sure she wanted to. Maxil had her by one arm and Sinnall by the other. I motioned to Sinnall to close the doors to the inner hall so that just the five of us were in the main room.

"Maxil, father will be furious if he knows I'm here," she wept and then she gulped back her sobs as she came face to face with me.

Her emotions were painfully obvious. She had heard all the gossip and had been hurt by it. She had been betrayed in her love and denied sight of him by her father whose political common sense dominated his personal prefer-ences. She did look like me, even with her eyes red with her tears and with her hair disheveled. A younger, prettier, gentler, totally different girl.

What impressed me more than her delicate loveliness was Maxil's tenderness toward her. He drew her against him, one hand holding one of hers to his lips, the other arm drawing her possessively to him. There was no hint of the gawky adolescent who had clumsily tried to embrace me the previous night as we deceived the waiter. He was Romeo to his Juliet, strong and loving, tender and sure.

"Fara, I'm so glad to see you. What do you mean, your father will be furious with you? I've asked for no one else but you," Maxil was saying.

"But . . . but . . . we were sent from the palace and no one would let us come back and Father wouldn't let me come to the Starhall last night and then . . ." and she glared at me. She drew herself up to her full height, suddenly regal for all her youth.

"You heard those *rumors* about Lady Sara," I finished for her.

She swallowed hard, too proud or too hurt to answer.

"Well, Lady Fara, they are only rumors," I said. "Lord Harlan has claimed me as his lady."

Her eyes widened and she gasped, looking trustingly to Maxil for confirmation. I don't know how, but Maxil kept from blushing as he nodded solemnly to Fara.

"Now, will you stop glaring at me and sit down while we tell you the whole thing?" I suggested. "I think I can see why your father was not anxious for you and Maxil to meet right away," I added as her emotions of uncertainty, curiosity and distrust crossed her transparent little face.

By the time she left in Cire's company to dash back to her suite, we had the whole thing pretty well thrashed out. She didn't much like it, but she understood. Maxil was so relieved I thought he'd explode.

"She'll accept my claim. She'll accept," he cried, sliding down into his chair with delight. Stretched out full length, his long legs stuck out at angles, he sighed deeply and closed his eyes. Then, slamming both hands down on the chair arms, he propelled himself up with astonishing force, careening around the room. It was obvious from

Sinnall's expression he did not consider this proper behavior for a Warlord-elect.

"Leave him alone," I laughed at Sinnall. "You're only this young and in love once and I've presented a terrible complication. You must admit that."

Sinnall shook his head. "What if they give themselves away?"

"They only have to play along for a few days."

Sinnall still wasn't convinced, but at that point Linnana and Ittlo suggested it was time we dressed for dinner.

FORMAL DINNER MEANT JUST THAT, but it was a formality that very few of the main participants enjoyed. Harlan and Stannall, alone, at the head table, behaved as if they were enjoying themselves.

A portion of the Starhall had become a dining room, with a head table on the raised circular section between two of the five archways, while four long tables splayed out from it on the level below.

I don't know who was more nervous, Maxil or me. His behavior vacillated between an almost unbearable imperiousness when addressing his younger brother and sisters to adolescent sullenness when he gazed at the table where Fara sat with adult members of Council. Stannall, of course, was at the head table between Maxil's sisters. I was seated at Maxil's left, and Lesatin, the curious councilman, sat on my left. Harlan sat at the end, too far away from me for the conversation I wanted to have with him.

It was not a cheerful meal although the food was excellent. Kalina and Cherez, Maxil's two sisters, were dressed as befitted their age and station, their pretty faces much sweeter devoid of last night's excessive makeup. But they were sullen. Maxil told me that Kalina had been told she was to deny the claim of the man Gorlot had mated to her. Fernan, completely cowed by Stannall's presence and under Harlan's scrutiny, ate the sparse meal set before him. His glowering fat face with its pasty pimpled complexion was not a pleasant sight at dinner. I avoided his direction as much to keep from seeing him as to keep myself from Stannall's notice.

I must correct myself. Lesatin thoroughly enjoyed himself. He made conversation for us to agree with, commented on one course after the other. I felt terribly conspicuous and surreptitiously waited until I saw what Har-

an used as silverware. Perhaps I felt a constraint because
n Harlan's presence I was so conscious of inadvertently
tripping over my own ignorance. With Maxil or Sinnall I
could laugh off a slip or divert attention. But Harlan was
so preternaturally concerned with concealing my origin, I
was unnerved. The menace of Stannall and Monsorlit
completed the top-heavy pyramid of my anxiety.

By the time the entertainers whirled out into the center
of the huge hall, I was weary. My back ached, my stomach felt overfull and churned with odd tastes and textures.
My neck felt stiff with tension and I wondered if I could
ever relax again.

When we finally filed out of the great hall, I tried to
stay by Harlan. He gave me a warning look as he handed
me over to Maxil. I was furious and frustrated. I desperately needed a few private words with Harlan on what to
do tomorrow if the Council should actually call me. I was
forced to go to bed without that reassurance and I was
filled with worry, worry, worry.

In the alarm-clock way I had acquired since coming to
Lothar, I awoke suddenly and completely. My head still
ached, the room was unreal in its luxurious appointments
and my body felt logy and disjointed. Linnana was evidently a skilled keyhole listener because I no sooner
stretched than she appeared to announce my bath was
ready.

I chose the simplest of the rich gowns and a single
strand of contrasting beads as much to forget the extravagance of last night as to present Council with the "simple
country girl" I had styled myself in jest.

The breakfast table held a surprise for me. Jessl was at
it, chatting companionably to Sinnall, Cire and Maxil. The
boy had recovered his equilibrium this morning, it
seemed, for he rose with a spring as I entered. Jessl seated
me with a flourish and a flirt. Linnana and Ittlo bustled
about with dishes.

The mood in which I awakened could not linger with
such gay breakfast talk. Jessl insisted on a ribald recount-
ing of town gossip about Maxil and me and he was so
deft with his recital I couldn't be offended. Even Maxil,

now that he had set himself straight with Fara, laughed. The morning beverage stimulated me and unbound the knots of tension at the back of my neck.

"Sara, Harlan said not to worry about Council calling you. Today at least. We can all watch in the board room," Jessl indicated the chamber devoted to communication panels. "It's a closed circuit into this room from the Chamber. It will be a real pleasure to follow Gorlot's downfall."

"You're sure of it?" I queried hopefully.

Jessl scoffed at my unspoken doubts and leaned forward across the table in a mock conspiratorial fashion.

"The things we've uncovered about that man would make your skin curl off. Remarkable, isn't it, how the slightest breath of scandal on any public figure brings forth previously forgotten slights and errors."

"But will these things discredit him as a candidate for Regent?" I wanted to know.

"Sure, surely," Jessl agreed expansively. I wondered then if Jessl had been purposefully sent to allay Maxil's doubts or whether Jessl was an incurable optimist.

"What's the gossip about Harlan's return from insanity?"

Here Jessl did hedge. "There's a great deal of controversy about that. I only wish we had some conclusive proof that he never had been insane."

"But he never was," I insisted forcefully. "He was drugged. Gorlot and Gleto drugged him." Why I inserted Gleto's name instead of Monsorlit's, I don't know. "I heard that from Gleto's lips myself."

"Does Harlan know that?" asked Maxil anxiously.

"Of course he does," I assured him.

"Then why doesn't he have you appear before Council today?" the young Warlord fretted.

"Perhaps you are the main issue today, not Harlan's sanity," I suggested.

Jessl shook his head.

"No, Maxil's as good as confirmed right now. Stannall had an inspiration and had the physicians check Fernan over, too. The kid's heart has suffered from his overeating and he could never stand even normal acceleration. Maxil's therefore practically the only choice. But it's the Regency that's to be the heavy contest. Don't worry, lad. I mean, my lord," Jessl said with sincerity. "Harlan and Stannall know what they're doing."

I fell to mulling over exactly what I had told Harlan concerning himself in the asylum. I had mentioned Gleto and his being drugged but not Monsorlit's visit, nor one other, possibly very important fact. Yesterday I had told Ferrill that there were others held under drugs at the sanitarium. If those men all recovered as Harlan had, and told their stories, it would be definite proof, by association, that Harlan never had been insane. I tugged Jessl's arm.

"Has anyone checked into the medical histories of Gleto's other recent patients? I mean, say other squadron commanders or men of position who have also suddenly and unexpectedly gone mad."

Jessl swiveled around to look at me with dawning comprehension.

"Trenor had nine other patients at that asylum," I continued. "At least that's what Gleto said. If they could be restored to sanity the way Harlan was, wouldn't that prove that Harlan, too, had been drugged, had never been insane? And I *know* those men were drugged."

Jessl was at the communicator panel before I finished my hypothesis. The screen lit to show Stannall's crowded living room. Jessl asked Stannall to close his circuit. The background of the room blurred and only the first Councilman's face was distinct. Jessl repeated what I had told him. Stannall's face quickened with obvious interest.

"How long does it take to recover from the effects of the drug?" he asked, excited.

"About five days' abstention from the drugged food," I reluctantly advised him, knowing how important the time factor was. "But maybe there's an antidote or a stimulant."

"We can try. It would be very interesting to check this. It would implicate Trenor still further. Can you identify the patients concerned?"

I couldn't. Stannall pursed his lips over this disappointment. Then he thanked me with absentminded courtesy and the screen dimmed. Jessl came thoughtfully back to the table.

"Sinnall," he asked, "do you recall anyone going off his orbit recently?"

Maxil came up immediately with one name, a communications man at the spaceport who had run berserk all over the flying strip. Then there had been the case of a police official in the city. Jessl himself thought of two group leaders. Sinnall suggested a veteran trader on the Tane routes who had come home babbling some strange tale before he had been drugged quiet by physicians.

"What kind of a tale?" Jessl asked.

Sinnall frowned. "Oh, he made a rhyme of it, the way I heard the story." Sinnall shuddered at the memory. "Went like this:

> For a change the Mil can eat
> The gentle, juicy Tane meat.

Of course, there hasn't been a Mil raid for the last two Eclipses. And only a few Perimeter skirmishes reported."

A few skirmishes in two Eclipses: that would mean more than a year. Was I in one of those ships? Could I have been on Lothar that long? But Harlan had only been in the sanitarium ten months. And the Tane war started a week afterward. When had I been taken? Before or after? And how? Harlan could only guess that I must have been transported from Earth to Lothar in a Mil ship. How then did I get off the ship; where did I go from there for Monsorlit to change my skin and my nose? I was certain now that Monsorlit had been responsible. How did I get into the sanitarium where I should have been a patient, not an attendant?

"Sara's thinking. Maybe she knows another official for our missing four men," Jessl jibed, startling me out of my frightening contemplations.

"Me? No, I haven't followed that sort of thing. I was too busy with Harlan."

"Which reminds me to ask you," Jessl began forcefully, "where did you meet up with our Regent? Jokan doesn't remember ever meeting you, but he's been on and off Ertoi gazing into crystals. I've been underfoot and I don't remember meeting you in our closed circle," he ended with a complimentary leer.

"Which should prove to you that Harlan is pretty good at minding his own business all by himself," I hedged archly.

This would not put Jessl off. "Where do you come from, lady of mystery? Your accent is slightly southern, if anything, but your appearance is northern."

"A girl can't keep anything secret around here," I laughed.

"The lady minds her business pretty well, too," laughed Jessl in good part. "I'll bet I'll figure you out yet. That's my specialty."

Sinnall and Maxil laughed with him. But I could see he was a little piqued at my continued evasion. I hoped he wouldn't pursue the subject before I had the chance to talk with Harlan. Clan, cave and mining engineering notwithstanding, I had very little knowledge to fortify me against the determined curiosity of a friend. Or had he felt that his own would not question the girl who had restored him from the living dead?

"If you guess correctly, I'll tell you true," I promised easily.

Jessl merely smiled at me queerly and I noticed he was looking at my hands. It was all I could do to keep from jerking them into my lap. Harlan had been singularly interested in my wrists, too. Examine them as I might, I could find nothing to warrant such scrutiny.

The guard entered to say that Council was assembling.

Maxil rose with an excess of nervous energy, while Jessl, putting a reassuring hand on the boy's arm, got more casually to his feet. He guided Maxil to the door and watched him down the Hall, Sinnall and Cire flanking him.

In his unguarded face as he returned to the table, I saw the weight of Jessl's own doubts. He had been careful to hide them before the boy. The dread that had bothered me on waking returned in double measure.

Jessl and I went silently into the board room. I signaled Linnana to bring more to drink as Jessl flipped on the screen to the seething Council Hall. He yelled at Ittlo to leave off clearing the breakfast table. Then he settled himself beside me on the couch, to stare moodily at the screen.

CHAPTER ELEVEN

HAD HARLAN AND STANNALL been aware of how many people Gorlot had touched in establishing his massive plans, they would have approached the Council Hall with even more trepidation that morning. Gorlot had chosen his victims well.

I know my own sense of foreboding was lulled in the first hour of that crucial meeting. The very familiarity of a roll call for the Councilmen as they named their provinces and districts (The Council consisted of scientists, military men and landed gentry instead of the proportional representation practiced on Earth) was reassuring to me.

Stannall as First Councilman called the session to order with a few words about the gravity of the situation and a reassuring report on Ferrill's condition. If it deprived Ferrill of his birthright, at least it did not mean his death.

An ancient-looking, heavy collection of tablets was rolled to the front of the chamber right up to the raised dais where Stannall and the seven senior Councilmen were seated. (The significance of the number "seven" harked back to ancient history and the first Harlan's Seven Brothers.) An old man mumblingly read from the tablets the names of Fathor's children. At a motion from the floor, Ferrill's name was ceremoniously canceled as ineligible for the Warlordship. Maxil was named as next in line and he was asked to step forward and present his claim. All this was couched in the floweriest language, with great gestures and ceremonial pauses.

Maxil came forward, holding his tall gangling figure erect. He bowed gracefully to the eight in front of him, to the Council behind him, and presented a much bemedaled slate to the secretary. A great show was made of reading it. The legality of his birth was then formally recorded.

Stannall took over and the simplicity of the procedure of investiture was refreshing. It amused me, for it sounded so like an Earth marriage ceremony. Stannall asked if anyone present knew of any just reason why Maxil, second son of Fathor, son of Hillel, son of Clemmen, true blood and seed of Harlan the First, Defender of the People, should not be Warlord-elect in this, his sixteenth year of life.

A massive silence prevailed. I gathered that this would have been the opportunity for Gorlot to bring up Maxil's supposed impotency.

Stannall's words of formal acceptance of Maxil in the name of the Council were drowned by the roar from this august body. The entire room was on its feet, shouting the boy's name, and saluting continuously. Maxil smiling nervously accepted the acclaim with poise.

When the furor had subsided, a tense, uneasy restlessness took hold of the assemblage. Stannall motioned to Maxil to be seated on the single raised chair to the right of the eight elders.

"Since our young lord, Maxil, is under the legal age, it will be necessary for the Council to consider those men who are qualified to instruct him in the military duties of the Warlord and, with the aid and guidance of this Council, in governing and guiding this world toward its great and recognized goal, the extermination of the Mil from the skies."

Stannall consulted a slate in his hand.

"We note that Lord Maxil is over fifteen years of age and therefore considered to have reached the age of reasonable discretion. Following the custom of our laws, he has the right to agree with or disagree to our choice of Regent, and to propose, if he should have a qualified candidate, a man sympathetic to his personality and his welfare."

Jessl chortled to himself at that speech and I noticed a definite stirring among the Council members. I could not see either Harlan or Gorlot.

Stannall turned slightly toward Maxil and the boy rose as if forcibly ejected from the chair.

"I do have a choice, one acceptable to this Council since he has been Regent to my brother, Ferrill," and

Maxil's voice stumbled a little over his brother's name. "By my legal and accustomed right, I will choose Harlan, son of Hillel, son of Clemmen as my Regent, with the Council's permission."

"But the man's been mad for months," a voice from the back of the room protested quite clearly in the stunned quiet. Others chimed in with similar sentiments and a general arguing shout rose in volume. Stannall folded his arms to ride the noise a while before he called for order.

"We call Harlan, son of Hillel, son of Clemmen, before this Council."

The great doors at the opposite end of the Hall opened and Harlan marched in, looking neither left nor right. He held himself so proudly, so regally, tears of pride came to my eyes. Harlan bowed to Maxil, to the Council, to Stannall. Not all of the seven elders had had a chance to see Harlan before this appearance and he was scrutinized carefully. Stannall indicated the empty chairs drawn up on the left of the main platform and Harlan, bowing briefly, seated himself there.

"We see that the name of Harlan, son of Hillel, is on the list of those men eligible by their age, conduct and military experience to be Regent. We also call before this board the following men, their merits to be weighed before Council this day."

Stannall began to call off his list. The first three names were unfamiliar to me and at each one a Councilman arose to ceremonially remind Stannall that so-and-so had died, or was over the maximum age. The fourth name was Gorlot, son of someone—I didn't hear because the name of the implacable man echoed in my mind harshly. Gorlot strode in, his square face as still as ever, his square frame devoid of the grace and litheness that characterized Harlan. He bowed to the young lord, to the elders, to the Council and was gestured toward the waiting chairs.

Gorlot hesitated at the chair next to Harlan and then, with deliberation, left two seats empty between them. His action had the appearance of being cautionary rather than insulting. But it was a well-calculated piece of business. Jessl groaned and cursed with vehement originality.

I started again as Gartly's name was called and this gray warrior stepped forward. He was but a year under the maximum age. He took the seat next to Harlan, flicking his cape contemptuously in Gorlot's direction. I could have kissed the old grump. Jokan's name, too, was called and a mutter arose from the Council. Stannall turned to the seven with the comment that Jokan was absent on a special mission for the Council. As he was well known, his record would have to speak for him.

There were other names called, men I remembered Harlan using as examples for candidates for the Regency: men who were reported dead or in survivor asylums. I wondered if any of them were among the nine unwilling guests at Gleto's. Jessl seemed to have the same thought, for he glanced at me significantly.

At any rate, by the end of Stannall's little list, only three were seated at the left of the seven. No one doubted that the contest was between Harlan and Gorlot.

"We are fortunate indeed," Stannall began with a slight smile, "to have as candidates two men who have already had experience in the arduous position of Regent to the Warlord-elect." His bow was impartial.

"At the young lord's request, we first consider the eligibility of Harlan, son of Hillel, son of Clemmen."

A sigh ran through the Council and was echoed by me. Stannall made a sign to the secretary who nervously cleared his throat and read off in a rattling way the personal history of Harlan. I couldn't always catch his mumbling or the stilted phrases and ceremonial longhand he spoke. But it was evident that Harlan's early career as a fighting man had been brilliant, crowned with the discovery of the Tane planets as well as some daring innovations in perimeter patrol techniques.

The secretary came to the last slate of the pile before him, and his voice noticeably slowed.

"On the twenty-third day of the thirteenth moonset, Regent Harlan was stricken ill and relieved of his duties toward the Warlord until such time as his recovery was effected."

Stannall smiled slightly and there was a loud spate of excited whispering among the Councilmen. I wondered who had slipped that helpful phraseology in the document or whether it had been there all the time. Stannall raised a hand and the whispering died.

"As is customary, Council asked all candidates to present themselves to the War Hospital to be examined as to their physical ... and mental fitness. Physician Monsorlit, as head of that establishment, may we have your report on Harlan, son of Hillel."

Stannall stepped aside as Monsorlit, whom I had not previously noticed, rose from his side seat in the front row of the Council and took the center of the room. He bowed to Maxil, to the eight men, to the Council, to the three candidates. I caught myself holding my breath. Perhaps now would come the bombshell to our hopes. Monsorlit's duplicity with Gorlot was certain in my mind. He may have lulled the suspicions of others, but would he show his true self now? If restoration were such a heinous crime as I gathered it was, Monsorlit would not care to risk Gorlot's exposing him. For Gorlot certainly must have known Monsorlit was restoring people.

Monsorlit spoke well and without a plethora of confusing technical terms. He summarized being called by Stannall with the other three physicians to determine the state of Harlan's mental health.

"Even a cursory examination without benefit of special equipment proved that Harlan had recovered from the grip of mental disease that prostrated him ten months ago. You can imagine, gentlemen, how delighted and surprised my colleagues and I are. No other patient suffering from similar symptoms has recovered to such a marked degree."

I glanced at Gorlot to see what his reaction was and, in spite of the man's studied carelessness, I thought I detected a smug satisfaction to his patience.

"Naturally, such a superficial examination was not conclusive proof. Harlan himself suggested a more thorough one at the Mental Clinic." Monsorlit paused to thumb through tissue-thin metal sheets in his hand. He finally sorted one to the top. "I have here the results of our most exhaustive tests which we compared with the last physical examination of Harlan, taken shortly before his illness." Again he paused and I took another deep breath. Harlan was looking with obvious but not anxious intent at Monsorlit. Gorlot sat, showing that trace of smugness. Maxil fidgeted continually.

"There was a noticeable discrepancy between the two reports," Monsorlit continued. Gorlot's smile broadened slightly. "It was apparent that the reaction time in certain coordination tests and in the general response to spoken and written questions was shorter."

Gorlot's semi-smile disappeared and there was an agitated rustle in the Council Hall. Monsorlit had thrown his bombshell all right but not in the expected direction.

"In short, Harlan is in better general physical health today than he was eleven months ago, the time of the last full physical examination."

"What about mental health?" a voice demanded from the floor, heedless of protocol.

Monsorlit glanced unperturbed at his notes.

"My colleagues and I are in agreement. On the basis of the most exhaustive tests in our means, Harlan is both mentally and physically capable of any duties or offices required of him by Lothar."

Maxil clapped a hand to his mouth to suppress his glad shout. Others in the Council had no inhibitions about expressing their approval, but the jubilation was not as widespread as I had hoped it would be.

Gorlot was glowering now and he watched angrily as Monsorlit resumed his place, in the front row, oblivious to any censure from that direction.

Stannall stepped forward again, bowed to Harlan and held up his hand for silence.

"This is indeed good news for the entire world. I trust that you and your colleagues are already working to effect similar recoveries on others of our leaders who have fallen victim to this new scourge."

Monsorlit contented himself with bowing his head briefly in assent.

"A question, Sir Stannall," a loud voice interrupted. Our attention was directed to a portly individual in the right rear of the hall.

"You have the floor, Calariz of South Cant," said Stannall after a very brief pause.

"I recall the physician for further questions. I, and I am certain there are others of my mind, am not sufficiently reassured by this ... this glib certification to trust the tender mind of an untried youth to a man so recently mad beyond speech."

Monsorlit came forward again.

"Physician, have there been other recoveries from this form of illness?"

"Yes," replied Monsorlit blandly, to the consternation of his questioner.

"As complete as Harlan's?"

"No. As I remarked earlier, Harlan is in better condition than before his collapse. Due, no doubt, to the rest and quiet with which we find it best to surround our mentally disturbed."

"Why then, and particularly since you have been the physician in charge of Harlan's case, was not the improvement noted and reported? I believe I am correct in stating that this Council expressed a deep interest in being kept abreast of any improvement in our ... ah ... former Regent's health."

Monsorlit did not hesitate with his reply. "In such cases as we have been able to observe where an improvement has been noted, it has been either so gradual as to escape the untrained eye, or a matter of instantaneous return to normal."

"And Harlan's recovery was in which category?" prompted Calariz.

"Instantaneous," was the bland reply.

"The liar," I exclaimed.

"What else can he say?" muttered Jessl.

"Ah, very good, I'm sure," Calariz was saying. "Were you there?"

"Unfortunately, no. My time has been heavily scheduled by the weight of our rising mental disease and the supervision of casualties from the Tane war."

"Quite so." A neighbor beckoned to Calariz and had his ear for a moment. The smile on the face of the man from South Cant was not pleasant as he straightened.

"Tell me, Physician, is there any guarantee that Harlan will remain sane? I mean," and Calariz had to raise his voice to top the sudden whispered agitation, "can we be sure that say, six or seven months from now, Harlan will not collapse under the stress of the Tane war and the task of training our new Warlord?"

Jessl and I groaned together over this loaded question. Monsorlit considered carefully.

"There is no such guarantee."

Gorlot's face lost its angry blackness. Harlan appeared unmoved, but Maxil's distress was obvious. Poor boy, he saw himself with Gorlot as his Regent whether he wanted him or not. He probably pictured himself dying slowly of some poison as Ferrill nearly had.

Calariz looked around him triumphantly and sat down. Before Stannall could take the floor again, another man rose to be acknowledged.

"You know me, gentlemen, as one who has supported Sir Harlan in many of his policies and moves," this fellow began with the oily ease of one accustomed to long perorations before arriving at his point. "I have stood squarely behind him, as I did behind his brother, our late and much loved Fathor. I was the first to deplore the illness which deprived us of Harlan's brilliant leadership and I want to be one of the first to welcome him back officially to our midst. But . . . I have a serious duty. For ten long months, this fine commander and statesman has been out of touch with the struggles and trials of our daily living. He has been unaware of our internal battles with mental illness, unemployment, crime and general unrest. Can we put upon him the added burden of reassessing past months when we can't hesitate so much as a millisecond in forging strongly ahead? Can we ask him to take up again a part of our world's life that nearly deprived him of his health and personal happiness forever? That he has allowed himself to be drafted to resume the onerous duties of state is indeed a credit to his patriotism and honor. But ... my friends and worldsmen, is it fair to the man, to Harlan?"

"That old ..." and Jessl finished the epithet under his breath. "He's one we were certain was loyal to us. How did Gorlot reach him?"

I slumped down in my corner of the couch, utterly miserable. I got more depressed as the next hours were filled with debates for and against Harlan, only more were against. The text of their arguments was substantially the same: Harlan had been mad once, he could go mad again. Harlan was not sufficiently attuned to the political and social scene and this was made to seem essential. Others tempered their views with the feeling that Harlan had served his world long and well enough. Other personalities were needed. There were those who did speak out for Harlan, couching in general terms their dissatisfactions with Gorlot's Regency. But it was a negative approach where a positive one was necessary. One man used the thinnest possible veil for hints that Ferrill's health had declined rapidly and concurrently with Gorlot's Regency. He was shouted down by Calariz and the oily representative from Astolla.

Stannall finally called a halt to this verbal massacre of Harlan and turned the discussion to Gorlot's suitability. The old firebrand, Estoder, who had hinted at Ferrill's suspicious illness, rose first to cite inadequacies in Gorlot's administration and conduct of the Tane war. Calariz and the Astollan gave him little time to speak and talked loudly with their neighbors during his remarks.

"Jessl, he'll never win at this rate. What happened?" I wailed.

"It's the insanity angle. A lot of those who would follow Harlan through a Mil raid are afraid of that. Frankly, if I didn't know Harlan had been drugged, I'd be worried, too."

"Then why doesn't someone come out and say he was drugged?" I demanded. "I can prove it."

"How?"

"I was there. I saw it done. I heard Gleto talking about it. He said he was afraid Harlan could throw off the drug and he wanted to increase the dosage."

"That *isn't* proof we can substantiate, unfortunately. It's hearsay. And it would be ridiculous to stand you up against the testimony of men like Monsorlit. No, my dear. We'd have to have a physician's report that traces of the drug were actually found in Harlan's blood. We tried it, but his system had absorbed whatever they used."

"They used cerol and you know it," I reminded him sharply.

"And cerol is rapidly absorbed into the system," Jessl retorted angrily. "Besides, all we'd need to prove to them that Harlan was still unstable would be for us to come out with a statement that he'd been drugged all along. We'd be laughed off the planet. If only we had had more time and could revive one of those men at the sanitarium."

"They're setting it to a vote," Linnana cried out.

I had to watch but it was horrible to witness this defeat.

"But Maxil won't have Gorlot," I said helplessly.

"He'll have to take him," Jessl muttered.

"But they can't do that to Maxil," I insisted. "He'll be poisoned like Ferrill and what Gorlot's intended to do all along will get done and then where will Lothar be?"

The roll was being called with droning fatality to Harlan's chances. I wanted to break the connection so I wouldn't have to watch. I was halfway to my feet to shut it off when there was a commotion at the Hall doors. They burst open suddenly to a scene of struggling guards.

"I am Jokan. I have the right to enter. STANNALL!" a voice rang out above the scuffling and shouting.

"Let Jokan advance," Stannall bellowed with more power to his voice than I imagined he'd have.

Jokan ran up the aisle. He spared no time for ceremonial bowing. Catching Stannall by the arm, he spoke softly and urgently. The First Councilman's eyes widened with disbelief. He backed up, his hand reaching behind him for the support of the table. Jokan stopped speaking, his face grim. Stannall stared at him. He managed to ask a question to which Jokan only nodded slowly and gravely. You could see the effort with which Stannall drew himself erect.

"I have grave news. The gravest. I must speak of something I never thought would be said of a Lotharian. I must speak of treachery so abominable that the words gag in my throat." Stannall's voice did choke, before he gathered strength and volume and venom. "There has been no war on Tane," he declared in a tight, measured way. "And furthermore there are now no more Tane on their two silent planets. Why? Because they have been taken by the Mil."

A concerted gasp of horror rang throughout the Hall.

"How, you may well ask, did the Mil get the Tane? How did they, for that matter, penetrate so far in from our Perimeter Patrol? Because the Patrol has been withdrawn from the Tane sector.

"There is only one man who has the power to do that. I accuse Gorlot," and Stannall's finger pinioned the traitor, "of the highest, most gruesome treachery. I accuse him of the foulest . . ." and here Stannall was drowned out by the savage roar that came up from the very floor of the Hall. There was a mass stampede toward the traitor.

Jokan had leaped to Gorlot's side during Stannall's denunciation. His weapon was pointed at the man's throat. Ironically enough, it was Harlan who kept Gorlot from being torn apart alive by the hysterical Councilmen. It was Harlan who brought the mob under control and back in their seats while guards formed a tight ring around Gorlot.

It was Harlan who called squadron outposts along the Perimeter to report their positions. It was he who reassigned them and called up additional units from the spaceport to rush to unprotected areas. It was Harlan who kept his head, the man they considered unsafe to trust with their government.

But it was Stannall who recalled the business of the day long enough to insist on a re-vote which was dispatched with unanimous haste. Harlan was again Regent!

CHAPTER TWELVE

I HAD A SAMPLING OF THE general reaction to this startling news from the three people in the room with me. Linnana started to weep hysterically, throwing herself at Jessl's feet and imploring him to take her to the Vaults where she would be safe from the Mil. She evidently supposed the Mil to be on their way from Tane to Lothar although this had not even been hinted. Ittlo cursed monotonously, alternating his curses with "How did he do it? How could he do it?" This was substantially what Jessl wanted to know.

First he managed to calm Linnana by reminding her that the inner network of alarms gave them a full day's warning before the Mil could possibly land on Lothar. There was no possibility of Gorlot's tampering with those sentinels. She continued to weep quietly, falling into a little lump on a chair, until I thought to have her go with Ittlo and get quantities of the stimulating beverage. I had a feeling we'd need it.

With something to do, both Ittlo and Linnana were in better shape. The door flung open and Fara came racing in, her eyes wide in her white face.

"I had to come, I had to come. Maxil will be so upset," she pleaded with me.

Jessl and I exchanged looks. She was, of course, quite right. True, I didn't realize that tradition would require a sixteen-year-old boy to be on the flagship of the fleet that would undoubtedly meet the Mil the next time they came thundering down on Tane.

Her concern for this crisis and its effect on the boy was instinctive and creditable to the unselfishness of her devotion to him. I felt ashamed. All I had considered was the fact that Gorlot was finally exposed and Harlan vindicated.

"Help me get to him," Fara cried, looking first to me,

then to Jessl, gesturing at the pandemonium in the Council Hall.

"Harlan will bring Maxil back here, I'm sure," I said encouragingly. "And I don't think anyone could get through to him right now. Look."

Fara and Jessl turned to the hectic picture on the panel. Harlan, Stannall and Maxil were easing themselves out of the Hall, all the while directing various agitated groups of Councilmen. The comic relief was supplied by the secretary. He was trying to keep his unwieldy table of tablets from being upset in the push and shove. He kept jumping up and down on one leg, weeping in distress at the ghastly news he must record.

Ittlo's questions, "How did he do it? How could he do it?" were answered in the course of the next few violent days. But there were a lot of other questions that were never adequately answered.

The perfidy toward the gentle Tane who had so recently been reviled as expendable savages shocked Lotharians of all degrees out of their petty squabbles and united them once more in their ancient crusade against the Mil.

"How could he do it?" was answered by the blazing personal ambition of the man Gorlot, who had correctly assessed the greed of barons and patrol dissidents, seizing upon the unrest of the time to implement his scheme. There were many who had wanted the Tane planets as their own playgrounds, or for their business monopolies. They were not especially interested in having the Tane there. They gave Gorlot the support he needed in Council when he needed it, in return for his extravagant promises of large grants when his colonization reforms went through. His choices of squadron leaders were promoted through rigged military boards and the incumbents thrown out, moved up, or liquidated in one manner or another. In return for their explicit, blind obedience, Gorlot substituted in all key Perimeter positions the incompetent men who had formerly been denied promotion. The few who went along only far enough to get suspicious of Gorlot's ultimate goal or who found out inadvertently were silenced. Some ended up as mental cases, others as com-

plete paralytics doomed to a short and useless life in the
thrall of cerol, conscious but unable to blurt out the
frightful truths held locked in their brains.

Gorlot had withdrawn the Perimeter defenses on the
Tane sector, creating a funnel down which the Mil, en-
couraged by the lack of resistance, headed toward their
new prey. The routine engagements Gorlot reported during his period as Regent were actually those few Mil ships
he had had to destroy to control. Some of the men sup-
posedly in cerol shock from Tane attacks had been captured by the Mil. Frantic appeals, like the case of the
rhyming trader, had been put down to the ever-mounting
toll of mental health. I wondered how Gorlot, once the
Tanes' planets were stripped, planned to turn back the
Mil the next time they approached the funnel. Or would
the Mil know they had had all the life those two ill-fated
planets bore? Would Gorlot have risked a Mil raid on
Lothar? My private opinion was yes, he would have
dared, particularly if he could be the hero of the occasion. Perhaps he meant ultimately to discard the "weakened line" of Harlan and start a new dynasty, the vigorous
"line of Gorlot."

The real miracle in the affair was Jokan's role. He had
started back for the north and staged a realistic crash in
the mountains as planned. The men who rescued him
were patrollers on leave. They recognized Jokan as the
man who had been experimenting on Ertoi with the crystals. These crystals had enabled the Ertoi to keep the Mil
off their planets long before the Alliance. The sonic vibrations of the crystals were powerful enough to disrupt the
cellular construction of the Mil and reduce them to a
battered jelly. The Ertoi were a much older race than the
Lotharians. Thanks to the magnetic storms with which
their planet abounded they had early found a means of
defending themselves against the depredations of the
Mil.

Jokan had worked for several years on a project to
incorporate similar electromagnetic crystals on every
Lotharian ship. Laboratory tests had proved that the crystals were effective if the Mil victim could be encircled. It

was this new weapon that had given Harlan the hope that Lothar might seriously consider attacking the Mil home planet. However, there was as yet no adequate way to shield humans against the effect of the crystals. A man, because of his relatively denser cell composition, could stand a much higher frequency than the Mil. But man still suffered from the vibrations emanating from this weapon.

Jokan's patrollers mentioned that all the ships they had seen or served on recently were now equipped with the crystal resonators. There was considerable secrecy attached to these installations. Jokan was deemed the permissible exception. He had, after all, been instrumental in their development. But Jokan had not known that the installation of the crystals was so widespread. He was immediately concerned and questioned the men closely. What he learned was enough to send him back to Lothar to make his desperate and successful attempt to get to the Tane planets. He had left word at his apartment of his intentions, believing me soon to arrive safely there.

The patrollers had also told him they had been in maneuvers off Tane, using the crystals on Mil type transports, driving the ships toward Tane. There had been several of these "war games," combined with expeditions on the Tanes in which the "rebellious" Tanes were herded into cantonments to await punishment for their "offenses" against Lothar.

I don't know where Gorlot was taken immediately after the fiasco at the Council Hall because it had to be a well-kept secret. The palace was mobbed by endless throngs and deputations, screaming for possession of the traitor. Numerous attempts to invade the palace by force to seize Gorlot were repulsed.

Fara's concern for Maxil was just. He returned from the Council Hall in grim silence. He made continual appearances on the balcony overlooking the great Square, reassuring the people that the Mil were not lurking in the clouds above, ready to swoop down and depopulate Lothar. With a sternness astonishing for his relative youth, he assured them of punishment for the traitor. The only reason for a delay in dealing with Gorlot was to discover how far-reaching his plans had been. However, it became necessary late that night to bring Gorlot from his prison and show him to the frenzied mobs before they could be made to disperse.

Someone had started a rumor that he had been rescued or was going to be rescued. What group of zealots might do such a mad thing no one ever said. But Maxil showed them a Gorlot, manacled with ship-anchor chains, bruised and bloodied, quite a different man from that morning.

The enflamed people had to be satisfied with effigies of Gorlot which were burned, tortured, dismembered, tied to Mil Rocks all over the planet, thousands of times throughout the night. Vengeance was easy to accomplish by pointing fingers at those who had enjoyed Gorlot's favor during the past ten months.

Maxil proved himself a true descendant of Warlords, carrying himself with great dignity during his trying personal appearances. I appeared with him, as did Fara, Stannall, Jokan and Jessl. But I think it was Fara's presence that steadied him most. Once Stannall recognized this, at my insistence, there was no longer any problem about Fara remaining in the Warlord's suite.

I think all the arrogance and imperiousness went out of Maxil that day. The glamorous trappings, the little dignities and privileges that went with his position had been brutally torn aside to show him the ugly mechanics underneath. It was a frightening initiation into manhood.

The Regent and the First Councilman seemed to be on strings, in and out, back and forth. Jessl stayed with Maxil but apart from one public appearance with Maxil, Jokan was not in evidence. He joined us very late that night as Jessl and I sat up, listening to the disturbed sleep of the new Warlord, far too keyed up to rest ourselves. The noise from the streets was still audible. I was, as usual, eating. I'll say that for my participation in events that day: it was I who remembered that people had to eat occasionally, particularly people under stress. And I made everyone have dinner, including Stannall and Harlan.

Jessl took one look at his half-brother and did not offer

food. He poured him a full cup of a potent patrol brew. Jokan showed every minute of the forty sleepless hours of his trip to and from Tane. He was no longer the debonair man-of-the-world, playboy and wit. Jokan was too dead-tired to play any role. He had lost the last of his few illusions. Jessl and I waited as he drank, his legs sprawled out from the chair, his chin on his chest, one arm limp over the back of the chair, the other cradling the tumbler against his cheek between gulps.

"You know Jessl," he said finally, "I circled those damned planets and I quartered them. I went to every sacred grove on both Tanes. They were fenced round with forcers. Only the forcers were off and there wasn't anyone around. Used to be, there was always someone in a grove.

"And quiet? You've never been on such a quiet world. Those Tanes were always making some kind of noise, that silly croon of theirs. You always heard it. But there was always some kind of noise. I tell you, it was the weirdest thing I ever felt. And those burned-out acres where the Mil ships had landed. You could smell them. It made me sick. I was sick until I couldn't stand and crawled back to the ship on my hands and knees."

I noticed that he wasn't exaggerating. The knees of his now disheveled flying suit were torn and mud-caked.

"Jessl, if I hadn't been there," he continued, miserably, his eyes filling with tears, "I wouldn't've believed a man, a Lotharian who knows what the Mil do, who's been brought up to kill the rotting species, could conceive such a scheme." He shook his head and drained the rest of his cup, holding it out for Jessl to refill.

"Didn't you find *any* Tanes?" asked Jessl hopefully.

Jokan shook his head slowly from side to side, from side to side. "A whole race of gentle natural people who never hurt anyone, who didn't suspect treachery in others until it must have been too late. A whole race wiped out. By one man. One man."

Draining his cup again, Jokan flung it viciously against the wall. It clattered and bounced noisily onto the carpeting. Jokan sat there looking at the battered cup with narrowed eyes. Jessl reached for another tumbler, filled it and passed it over to his brother. He and I watched until Jokan drank himself into a complete stupor. Then we put him to bed.

I went to sleep in the final hours of that night, listening to the dull rumble of public frenzy which showed few signs of dying down from sheer inertia. There was no less noise than there had been the previous night with Eclipse festival going full blast. But there was a different feel in the air now ... a feeling of hate so strong it smelled, so tense it pressed against you like heavy fog and made breathing difficult.

CHAPTER THIRTEEN

WHEN I AWOKE AT MY usual hour the next morning, I felt oddly refreshed by the short sleep and curiously alert. I was up well before Linnana this morning, I thought with a grin. She didn't even appear when I drew my own bath. In a way it was a pleasure to be alone, feeling as I did, and I hummed to myself as I bathed. Gorlot had done his worst and it had backfired on him. The yoke of apprehension was lifted from the back of my neck. Somehow, to me at any rate, the Mil did not seem as terrifying as Gorlot had.

I threw on a robe and walked out onto my balcony. The gardens lay below me, trampled and battered by yesterday's surging mobs. Beyond, the city was preternaturally quiet, the way New York could be, early Sunday mornings. A sudden muted drone caught my attention and I located the sound from the trail the ship made as it needled upward into the greenish morning sky. The trail was barely thinning when another roar split the air and a second, a third, a fourth line of smoke spurted upward. I watched this exodus for some time before the knock on the door roused me.

Harlan came in and motioned to me to stay on the balcony where he joined me. There were circles under his eyes and fatigue lines drawing down the corners of his mouth. But his step was quick and his voice firm.

"Good morning to you, Regent Harlan," I said and gave him a full court curtsey.

"Very graceful," he grinned back and gave me a hand to steady my rising. "I didn't hope to find you up. But I took a chance. Jokan is far beyond wakening."

"He was very tired last night," I tendered.

"He was also very drunk," Harlan remarked, teasing me. "Hardly blame him. Wish I had the chance."

159

I could think of nothing witty or apt to say because Harlan's very masculine presence disturbed me.

He leaned against the wall, facing me, folding his arms across his chest, regarding me with disconcerting directness.

"What is all the activity at the spaceport?" I asked, nervously gesturing at the smoke trails.

Harlan didn't bother to glance over his shoulder. "Sending out replacements and technicians for the Perimeter. Have to replace nearly every man Gorlot appointed with someone competent. He did a thorough job of removing, permanently or temporarily, every able man in Patrol unsympathetic to him."

"You *are* afraid the Mil are coming back in force."

Harlan frowned at me intensely. "There is always that possibility."

"It's what everyone seems to fear."

"Well, they might. Gorlot gave the Mil a wide-open field with Tane. What's to prevent them from assuming that the entire section isn't wide open? Especially since we've always maintained such a vigil."

Harlan moved to the balcony railing, looking out over the battered gardens. Then he turned back to me, leaning against the iron support.

"Have either Jessl or Jokan been after you? About your origin?" he asked anxiously.

"Jessl calls me the lady of mystery," I laughed lightly.

Harlan frowned.

"I can't keep both of them away from you and they're curious. Look, I'll send you some vision tapes about Jurasse. You can't read Lotharian yet, I gather? Hmmm. That's too bad and there's no chance to teach you. Well, you'll have to assimilate as much from the historical and vision tapes as you can."

Harlan stared thoughtfully into space, scrubbing his chin thoughtfully. I noticed he must have just bathed, for his hair gleamed damply in the rising sun. His lean profile stood in bold relief against the green sky, emphasizing the strength in his rough features. I put that picture into a special corner of my memory for easy reference. He turned back toward me suddenly. The wry grin on his face set as he caught my absorbed expression.

"I've never thanked you, have I, Sara?" he said gently. "If you hadn't had the courage of . . ."

I shook my head to stop him.

"You forget, you were the only way I had of getting out of that ghastly place."

He reached for my right hand, raising it to his lips without taking his eyes off mine. Then he pulled me slowly toward him.

"Maxil's Fara has joined him," Harlan said with a meaningful grin. His arms held me tightly against him and his eyes compelled me to look only into his face. "Maxil is as eager to claim *his* lady as I am to claim mine."

Slowly he bent and lifted me into his arms, his eyes never leaving mine. I could feel the warmth of him through the thin fabric of his overtunic and hear the beating of his heart, fast and strong. I felt I must be only one loud, frantic pulse beat. He put me on my feet by the side of the bed, his eyes warm and intense with feeling.

"This is not a smelly fishing boat, dear my lady," he said softly as his hands unfastened my robe. "And it is much too early for anyone to be up and looking for the Regent." He shed his own tunic and I swallowed hard with nervousness. Quick concern crossed his face and he framed my head with gentle hands. "Is this body you cared for so long offensive to you?" he asked softly. "You know it so well."

"I know it well, yes, but not the man within it," I whispered.

He smiled then, a wonderful tender possessive smile.

"When the man I am is within you, you will know all of me well and I, all of you. And you will no longer be afraid of me."

My arms, of themselves, slid up around his neck and our bodies touched. I couldn't control my trembling.

"Dear my lady Sara," he said very softly, his voice rough with passion. "I'm claiming my own. *Now!*"

A long time later, I heard his soft chuckle in my ear.

"You know, you were untouched after all. Those bully boys Gleto used as guards weren't above rape."

"I know," I said in a very small whisper into his chest, "I was terrified they might have when I wasn't in possession of my senses."

He tipped my head up so I had to look him straight in the eye.

"Afraid of *me* now?" he asked gently. He wouldn't let me duck my head and he grinned at my furious blushing. "I can see you aren't and I'm glad." He kissed me quickly and settled me against him. "I'll do better by you next time, sweeting. But I can't give a guess when that'll be. This is stolen time." He sighed deeply and the lines loving had lifted briefly settled back into place.

"You look so tired, Harlan," I murmured, worried, touching the raggedy scar on his cheek.

"I feel a lot better now than I have for some time," he grinned wickedly at me and kissed my breasts. His hands tightened on me roughly. When he looked up at me, his face had changed completely. "If anything should happen to you now . . ." He sat up abruptly, his strong back to me. I could hear him slap one fist against the other palm.

One long arm reached out for the overdress he had dropped to the floor. In one fluid movement he had thrown it over him and buckled it into place. He looked down at me.

"That's why I can't stand to have you stay on here. Too many people get to see you. You've too unusual a face to be easily forgotten. Someone who knows where you were before you were made my attendant is going to remember you. But . . ." and he sighed deeply, "there's no possible chance of whisking you away to a less public place."

"Nothing will happen, Harlan. Surely someone would have come forward by now. I've been seen so much," I reassured him. "And I've been doing quite well. I've had to."

"You've recalled no memories, not even fragments that would give us a lead?"

"None I want to remember," I said, suppressing a shudder.

He bent to kiss my forehead in apology for stirring up those memories.

"By the way, we got those nine men out of Gleto's tender care," he said, sitting down beside me. He took my left hand in both his, stroking my wrist gently. "They're coming round and furthermore, we found enough cerol in Gleto's medicine room to supply an army. There wasn't much of that stuff available before the Tane wars, too new a drug, so it was obvious someone has been importing it in quantities. We'll find out who soon."

"Then you *can* prove to anyone that you never were insane in the first place. Not that it matters now."

"It still matters," Harlan assured me. "But what is more important, we should be able to learn from those nine when the Mil first got to the Tanes . . . in what force. . . ."

"Can't you get Gorlot to tell you?"

"We're working on him, too," Harlan said grimly. "We've had more success with his cronies in Records and Supplies, but they don't know the total plan."

"What about Monsorlit?" I asked hopefully. It would be nice to be rid of one menace.

Harlan looked at me questioningly.

"He drugged you, after all. And Gorlot appointed him," I argued, not understanding his reluctance to indict the physician.

"No. Monsorlit has always been in charge of the staff at War Hospital," Harlan said quickly. "Gleto has been accused," he added to pacify me. "But other than Gleto's counteraccusation there is no proof Monsorlit was involved. Gleto's such a wretched cave-blocker his word doesn't go for much."

"But mine does," I replied, trying to ignore the fear that sank like lead into the pit of my stomach.

"Look," and Harlan closed strong hard hands around my shoulders. He gave me a little shake to make me look at him. "We'll have to forget about Monsorlit's duplicity. If restoration is once brought into this, you'll be killed just as if you were any other restoree. Monsorlit must have done the restoration. He's the only one who would dare or who could do such a superb job. But how he did it and when, I am not interested in finding out. And neither, dear my lady, should you be. By the mother of us all, Sara," and he threw his hands out in an exasperated gesture as I stared at him, unconvinced, "do you *want* to be discovered?

"Monsorlit has covered all traces in this affair," and Harlan swung off the bed to pace restlessly up and down the room, "just as delicately as he covered all trace of restoration on your body."

He turned and pointed his stumpy finger at me. "If his hospital ship had once been on Tane at any time, we could accuse him of hiding treasonable information or of direct collusion with Gorlot. But he's clever. He kept his ships in orbit one hundred miles above the planet. The wounded were ferried up to him by small rocket. We can't pin a thing on him.

"There's just enough cerol in his hospitals for experimentation. And his staff is so cave-bound loyal to him they wouldn't spit unless he said to. How can we pin anything on him that would remove him as a danger to you?

"He's got Ferrill back on his feet and to top it all, he's come up with an antidote for cerolosis. That makes us grateful to him. And his clinics for mental health all over the planet have touched too many little people for us to try to defame him."

"But he drugged you," I insisted inanely.

Harlan shrugged. "I can do nothing that won't endanger you."

"What if Monsorlit remembers me?" I pleaded, desperately afraid.

Harlan dropped to my side again. "Sara, Sara, please. Go on making yourself into a Lotharian. It's safer." He smiled plaintively and kissed me tenderly. "You're one now anyway. But remember, fear of a restoree is almost as deep as fear of the Mil and to many ... you heard Stannall ... just as hideous."

I was about to say something when a gentle knock startled us.

"Just be careful, dear my lady," he whispered urgently as the door opened to admit Linnana.

CHAPTER FOURTEEN

I OFTEN FELT IN THE next few days as if I lived in the old Grand Central Station. Harlan and Stannall conducted much of their business in Maxil's living room and board room, including Maxil in all discussions. The boy would reel to bed late at night exhausted, rise the next morning and grimly plunge back into the tedious reports from Councilmen and Patrolmen, or broadcast reassuring messages to the planet. The palace seethed with feverish activity and the air was punctuated day and night by the blasts of shuttling rockets and great ships.

A full report of the death of the Tane was partially cushioned by the discovery of a lone group of sixty badly frightened, suspicious survivors.

All Patrol reserves were recalled for reexamination and assignment. The fiction that this was due only to a reshuffling following the collapse of the Gorlot Regency was not fooling many, but it kept hysteria under control. Every available ship, no matter what size, was being refitted with Jokan's electromagnetic resonators. Busy as the spaceport beyond Lothar was, Maxil assured me that the Moonbases were bedlam. Jokan spent most of his time with Ertois and Glans although I didn't get to see any of these extraplanetary allies until later. Jessl was occupied with some radical planetary defense system and appeared only once at the formal dinners that Stannall insisted be continued for public morale.

Maxil announced plans for a speeded-up colonization of one of the Tane planets. Applications from all walks and trades would be acceptable. With a wry afterthought, it was also announced that both Tane planets were being equipped with the Ertoi defense crystals to prevent a return of the Mil. I realized then that that must be what occupied Jessl, the erection of a similar last-gasp defense for Lothar itself. To have admitted this publicly would have crystalized everyone's nightmare.

My public appearances as Maxil's companion continued, but I insisted that Fara also be included. Maxil always felt more at ease with her than with me although I know he liked me. But I was eight years his senior and, as Harlan had made plain he had a prior claim, Maxil was uncomfortable when the three of us were together. With both Harlan and Maxil bringing pressure on him, Stannall finally conceded that people would be too concerned with the Mil crisis to worry about such "minor details."

However, members of the palace circle soon took advantage of the fact that Maxil had made no formal claim on me and pressed their attentions. Stannall would not, however, permit Harlan to make his formal claim public, which infuriated the Regent.

If Linnana ever mentioned finding Harlan in my room that first morning he claimed me, she never passed the information along. I was deeply grateful to her and she became very helpful in dissuading importunate suitors who tried to enter my room.

My private time I spent listening to the tapes Harlan had sent me until I felt I knew Jurrasse intimately and could tour its eighteen hills blindfolded. Fara and I went to the Great Bazaar and I listened to the talk of the crowds, shopping, watching, familiarizing myself as much as I could with Lotharian ways.

Lothar was an odd contrast of technical advances and primitive inventions. There were no land vehicles other than animal-drawn carts of the crudest type. Women baked on wood stoves while the land Patrol and the palace cooked with a form of thermal energy in gigantic ovens. There was radiant lighting, but a crude type of radiant heating. Cloth was all handloomed. There was efficient refrigeration but no canned supplies. No paper but the awkward slates or thinly extruded metal sheets for more permanent records. Widespread television existed and recording tapes but nothing approximating typewriters or printing presses. Epic poems were sung by skilled bards using stringed instruments and drums, but there were no dramas other than mummeries. Glass and high-grade plastics but no china, porcelain or clay.

My days were busy, but I waited impatiently for the few hours Harlan could spare to be with me. He would come late at night, waking me from sleep, or early in the morning as I could not break my habit of early rising. If he came at dawn, he would bring cups of beverage and fruit, teasing me about my ravenous appetite.

"When do you ever sleep?" I asked him, half anxious, half amazed at his inexhaustible vitality.

He rolled onto his side and ran a caressing hand the length of my body.

"Here and there," he answered absently. He stroked my wrist softly. "Remember, I had months of sleep in the asylum and," he added with an engaging leer, "as long as I have access to the greatest of all restoratives, I'm doing fine. When I think of the time I wasted in that asylum, the opportunities I was oblivious to . . ."

"You are absurd," I protested, laughing.

"And you are delightful, dear my lady," and we would be off again.

He never completely forgot my exposed position and my lack of background. But I became more at ease and lost my fear of self-betrayal. I was full of confidence.

The communicator panel, which was always busy, flashed on one morning just as I was rousing from a post-breakfast stupor. Harlan had been with me late that night. Jokan said the call was for me.

I recognized the speaker as Councilman Lesatin. In most courteous terms he asked me to attend a meeting in half an hour at Stannall's office beyond the Great Hall in the administration wing.

My curiosity, not my concern, was aroused. Lesatin had been a dinner partner twice and I dismissed the man as an amiable, exaggerating character. He happened to be the representative of the mining interests in Jurasse and we had chatted about my coming from there. The only question I hadn't been able to answer was what shaft my father had worked in. I had fobbed that off by confessing to a sudden lapse of memory. Very silly, I had said airily,

to forget a title I knew as well as my own clan. Lesatin
had helpfully named a few shafts and I had picked one
eagerly. He had not seemed unduly concerned with my
forgetfulness.

When I reached the office, not only Lesatin was there
but also Stannall and several other senior Councilmen
whom I knew by sight. I still had no apprehensions.

I was greeted most courteously and asked to be
seated.

"One purpose of this meeting," Stannall began in his
most formal tone of voice, "is to acquaint you with the
public approval of this Council and the citizens of Lothar
for the considerable part you played in exposing the traitor, Gorlot. Had you not suspected and been able to effect
Harlan's release, we might have discovered all too late the
perfidy planned against the entire Alliance. Our gratitude
takes this material expression," and Stannall handed me a
much decorated slate. I glanced at it with what I hoped
was intelligent comprehension and thanked them most
fervently.

"We feel we can never adequately recompense you for
the danger in which you voluntarily placed yourself."

I muttered something to cover my embarrassment.

Stannall's official countenance relaxed into as pleasant a
smile as he had ever directed to me. The other five men
beamed paternally at me. I wondered if Stannall had now
forgiven me my various sins. He had been less curt,
certainly, since Fara had joined Maxil's suite. Perhaps she
had championed me.

"We would be interested in knowing just when you first
suspected Harlan was being drugged. Also anything you
can remember that would lead to the apprehension of
other traitors."

"There's Gleto, of course, and his armed guards."

Stannall nodded and remarked that they had been in
custody for some time. "Gleto makes some odd charges,"
Stannall added absently, "which we are unable to substantiate."

"Oh?" I remarked hopefully, not at all suspicious of this
line of questioning.

"He had involved several men of prominent position whom many would like to see cleared of such basely derived suspicions," the First Councilman continued smoothly.

"I'm not sure I could give you any help. I was shut up constantly in the one cottage. I had no opportunity to overhear or see any visitors of consequence. Except when Ferrill came to see Harlan. I think that was the first inkling I had of irregularity," I said truthfully.

"Oh?"

"Ferrill asked particularly to be informed of any change in Harlan's condition, you see," I continued, goaded by Stannall's noncommittal reception. "Gorlot made a sign to Gleto and he smirked. I mean, Gorlot was plainly indicating that Gleto should not inform Ferrill if Harlan got better."

This was considered and commented on.

"Did Physician Monsorlit ever attend Harlan at the asylum in your presence?"

My throat dried up suddenly and I coughed evasively. The truth, the truth is the one thing you never stumble over. But I couldn't tell the whole truth. Not now when I saw what Stannall was after: an indictment against Monsorlit. But they all knew that Monsorlit had been the attending physician.

"Yes, he came," I admitted slowly.

"What did he do?" Stannall seemed to leap on my confirmation.

"Made a routine examination of Harlan, administered a drug and left."

"Did you have any idea what drug?" Stannall snapped.

I swallowed and claimed ignorance. Stannall stared at me with such a menacing intensity it was very difficult to act unconcerned. My throat was parched.

"Tell me," Stannall began casually, turning his back on me for a moment, fiddling with slates on his desk. "How did you obtain the position as attendant to Harlan?"

"The usual way."

"Which is through Monsorlit's Mental Defectives Clinic,

according to the records," Stannall retorted, wheeling back to me with blazing eyes.

"Well, certainly," I replied with mock amazement that he should consider this remarkable.

My admission confused him and Lesatin muttered something to one of his colleagues.

"You *admit* having gone through the Clinic?"

"Certainly," I was forced to reconfirm. "Mental Defectives Clinic" I heard my mind echoing and an icy finger twisted deep into my stomach. I fought the sudden panic. I must think clearly now. I must. I had just admitted to having been insane . . . no, no, I was seriously disturbed, that's all. It meant I would be shielding Monsorlit whom I wanted to expose. It meant, more certainly, I hadn't given the proper thought to my background story at all. No one was asking me how many hills Jurasse had nor the position of the Odern Cave Vaults nor the placement of the inner labyrinths. Nor what shaft my father had worked in.

"Why were you in the Clinic?" Lesatin asked into that chill silence. I looked at him and realized that this affable man with the insatiable curiosity was quite capable of correlating odd pieces of information into logical theory.

"I went there for help," I said slowly. "You see, I'd had several very bad experiences that upset me. Some friends thought I might get help there."

"What kind of experiences?" Lesatin urged gently.

"Remember the apartments near the sign of Horn? The ones that collapsed in the earth fault? Well, I was trapped in my room for hours before they could get me out. Then my father was one of the men who was killed in the fault. I didn't have any relatives and I never could get to see my Clan Officer. I'd have these terrible nightmares," that was true enough, "and finally, I went to the Mental Clinic."

I wondered if neurotics were acceptable in this Clinic. Certainly in terms of earth psychiatry, those two traumatic shocks were sufficient to cause a psychosis . . . if you tended to be psychotic. I looked pleadingly in each face to see the reception of my fabrication. I was relieved to see sympathy replace skepticism and suspicion.

"Then you are naturally grateful to Monsorlit for curing your ... ah ... nervousness and nightmares," Stannall suggested.

"Well, not Monsorlit, certainly. I wasn't a very unusual case and you had to be pretty bad to get his attention what with the Tane war."

This was not the answer Stannall hoped for, I knew, but it was plausible.

"Did you ever see anything ... unusual ... while you were in the Clinic undergoing treatment?" asked Stannall conversationally.

"Unusual?"

"Yes. Cases where men were perhaps completely bandaged from head to foot. Patients with scars on their wrists, ankles or necks?"

"Oh, no," I replied hastily. I knew now what he was driving at. He wanted to be able to accuse Monsorlit of restoration. And here was Stannall's proof sitting in front of him. "Oh, no, no. No restorees, only men he had repossessed," I blurted out without thinking.

"Repossessed!" and Stannall snapped the word up hungrily and turned triumphantly to the others.

"What exactly do you mean?" asked Lesatin anxiously.

"I don't exactly know," I stalled. "I mean, the other girls in the sanitarium were called 'repossessed' and some of the technicians too." I recalled the conversation Monsorlit had had with Gleto about restorees and repossessed. "I guess I mean people who have been ill mentally and he has repossessed them of their senses. People he's trained to do certain things. I guess you could almost call Harlan repossessed, except that he was never really insane."

The qualification had an effect on the Councilmen. They talked quietly among themselves.

"Perhaps we have been wrong in our suspicions," Lesatin began without his usual pomposity. "The two terms, repossessed and restored, have similar meanings. This young lady's statement bears out what we already know.

And we have certainly examined every hospital record and each patient carefully. *I* have found no evidence of restoration."

Stannall turned angrily toward Lesatin. I gathered he wished Lesatin had not been so outspoken. Lesatin shrugged off the silent reprimand.

"All we have is the word of a low Milbait like Gleto against the innumerable proofs to the contrary from unimpeachable sources," Lesatin said. "Surely, Sir Stannall, you must realize the splendid contributions Monsorlit has made toward the insidious problem of insanity . . ."

"I realize that Monsorlit, in some way, despite all oral and written proof to the contrary, aided and abetted Gorlot in his treachery. If just one, just one of those casualties had been capable of speech, we would have discovered this obscene plot. Why couldn't *one* of them speak?"

"Monsorlit received all casualties in the orbital hospital ship. There was ample opportunity for someone like Trenor, who has admitted his complicity, to silence them effectively with cerol," Lesatin pointed out.

"Can't you help us?" Stannall said fiercely to me, his eyes blazing with a fanatical hate. *"Won't* you help us?" His intensity startled me so that nothing could have made me speak out. I comprehended too well the logic behind Harlan's advice to forget Monsorlit's part in his incarceration.

Stannall advanced on me, to my growing terror, for the mild-mannered First Councilman was as one possessed, his face gray with emotion, his wiry body trembling with rage.

Harlan burst in the door. At sight of him, I cried out in relief. Harlan's entrance was explosive, not casual. The news he blurted out with no preamble cleared the room of all other interests.

"The Mil are coming," he cried in a tight voice. Striding to the communicator wall, he snapped on the picture to a scene of complete confusion. A gasping older man in uniform was shrieking out his message.

"The Mil! THE MIL ARE COMING!"

"Report position, report position," Harlan said in a

controlled voice, forcing comprehension through the man's hysterical repetition of his ghastly message. I could see the squadron commander, for I realized this was a ship's signal room, gulping for control. The slate he held in his hand shook violently, but his voice lowered.

"I beg to report," he gasped, seizing on the inanities of protocol to reassure himself, "infiltration past the first ring. Twenty-three Mil ships, fifteen Star class, five Planet, with three attendant satellite trailers. Moving directly Taneward at equatorial intersection."

"Twenty-three," Stannall murmured incredulously. "The largest force in three centuries. And moving toward Tane."

"Spur infiltrations?" Harlan demanded, his voice metallic with command.

"No, sir. Just the direct route unless . . ." and the squadron commander's hand shook more noticeably, "they break off later."

"What is their pace rate and interception potential for supreme task force?"

"Base is working on it now, sir," a shadow voice put in.

"Proceed with Prime Action, and, Commander, are *all* your ships equipped with the new electromagnetic crystals?"

"Yes, sir, they are, sir. But we've had no test runs."

"No matter. Maintain surveillance but under no circumstances, repeat, under no circumstances, attempt standard delaying tactics. My respects to you and your squadron, Commander. You will receive additional orders shortly."

The picture faded as Harlan punched another dial. Before the picture had been fully established, I heard a piercing wail outside, the eerie panther-cry of a warning siren. Stannall and the others left the room, walking stiffly as people in the midst of a horrible dream. I heard Harlan's voice, calm, unhurried, the unusual metallic burr of command adding its harsh note, as he announced to the planet total, immediate mobilization and complete civilian evacuation.

I listened stunned through this electrifying broadcast.

Then he switched with unhurried sureness to the vast globular room I identified as the Moonbase Headquarters of the Patrol. Here also was the unfumbling dispatch of trained men reacting to an emergency that had been theory for three generations and was now, unexpectedly, grim actuality.

I saw Gartly and Jessl among the men in the Moonbase and, for the first time, representatives of the Alliance planets, Ertoi and Glan. The former were as humanoid as a saurian species can appear, complete with gills and scaled armor. The second, the Glan, were willowy skeletons with three digits and an opposing thumb. Their bodies were covered with a fine down, their faces, long and narrow, were sensitive. Their apparently ineffectual bodies were deceptive for the Glan were structurally twice as strong as Lotharians and equal to their scaly space neighbors, the Ertois.

From them, Harlan received the news that their entire force was speeding toward the penetration point. I thought this was excellent cooperation until I saw the spatial tank and realized that their relative position had a great deal to do with such all-out collaboration. Spatially speaking, they were above and beyond Tane and Lothar but only as the apex of an isosceles triangle is above and beyond its base points. It was to their advantage to deflect any further penetration of the Mil at Tane or Lothar, for the angle of the Mil advance made the triangle two-dimensional and therefore Ertoi and Glan were not galactically far from Lothar.

The Alliance contingent, however, had the farthest to come and there remained the calculation of experts to determine if it were better to wait for their reinforcing navy before joining battle or whether to attempt it with only the Lotharian fleet. That decision ultimately rested with Harlan as Regent and, in this emergency, the de facto Warlord.

The decisive figures were not to be completed for several hours and Harlan signed off with the advice that he would presently board his command ship. All further communications were to be forwarded there. He made one more call and I saw the startled boy-scared face of Maxil. He was being dressed in a shipsuit by a grim Jokan.

"It is my duty to inform my lord," Harlan began formally, "that Lothar is in gravest danger. I must now assume all rights, responsibilities and privileges. Will you accompany me on board the flagship?"

"What do I say?" Maxil asked, his voice steady.

Harlan gave him a reassuring grin.

"You acknowledge the danger, relinquish to me your rights and responsibilities and say you'll join me. You're a little young for this, lad, but I don't think you'd want to miss it. And, if you're feeling scared, you're not alone. I'll see you in half an hour. Now, please let me speak to Jokan."

Maxil nodded and stepped aside.

"Jokan, you'll take Sara along with Ferrill to the Vaults. Stannall and the Council will be assembling there presently. I've got the power so they can't object to any emergency measure I propose. Space help us if Maxil and I go down together. I'm ordering you alternate Regent this time," and he snorted at his behindsight.

"Now wait a minute, Harlan, I'm going with you . . ." Jokan objected, his eyes flashing angrily.

"No, Jokan. You can't," Harlan said with absolute finality. "It could be more important to Lothar's future to have you alive if something goes wrong with our attack plan. I haven't more time to explain now. Jo, you know I wouldn't ask it if I didn't have to."

Jokan glared helplessly, searching for an argument strong enough to sway his brother.

"Jokan, I count on you. I can't trust anyone else," Harlan repeated, his voice tight with the desperate urgency of his appeal.

Jokan set his teeth and bowed his head once in stiff resignation.

"Where's Sara?" Harlan asked.

"Here," I reminded him.

Harlan whirled around and stared at me fiercely for a moment. I didn't know whether to be amused or hurt he had forgotten I was there.

"Jokan, I call you to witness that I claim the Lady Sara to be *my* lady," he said formally, drawing me by the hand into the range of the vision screen.

"I accept the claim of Harlan, son of Hillel," I said proudly and Harlan kissed my hand formally. Even now his thumb paused over my wrist.

"Jokan, I'll give Sara the alternate commission of Regency. And Jo, if something should happen, guard Sara. If I don't come back, she has something very important to tell you. Now get Maxil off to the spaceport. I'll meet the boy there."

He flicked the panel to one more station, ordering his planecar brought to the balcony of the office in twenty minutes. Turning away from the set, he looked at me with such avid hunger in his face I had to turn my eyes away from his naked desire.

When I looked up at the slam of a drawer, I saw he was swiftly styling a slate. I sat down and watched him as he wrote, thinking with a sense of despair that this might be the last time I ever saw him. I memorized his face so that my mind would be able to recall the image faithfully should I never see the original again. It was difficult to reconcile the fierce and gentle lover I knew best with this grim warrior, urgently writing last-minute instructions for the safety of a world he might never walk again. He finished one slate quickly, tossing it aside with a clatter to clear space for the next. This, too, he wrote quickly. The third one, however, did not come as readily and he frowned as he wrote, blended out, and restyled. He punctuated this final message noisily and flipped a protecting film over it which he sealed. He gathered the three together and then stood up.

He came toward me and I rose to meet him. I had lead in my stomach and I needed iron in my thighs which did not seem strong enough to support me as I stood. In a few moments he would go out the balcony windows and . . .

He put his strong fingers on my shoulders and gave me a little shake to make me concentrate on what he had to say. His face had softened its grim expression and his eyes wandered lovingly over my face.

"If I don't come back . . . but I will," he reassured me quickly as I gasped at his fatalism, "give the third slate to Ferrill. To no one else. Ferrill is the only one who would be able to help and stand up to Stannall. Jokan can guard you because I have pledged him to it, but only Ferrill can help against Stannall. Stay with those two as long as I'm gone and watch that quick tongue of yours."

"Harlan . . ."

He gave me another little shake to hush.

"If I were a soldier on your world and going to battle . . . but maybe your world doesn't have wars . . . pretend, anyway. How . . . Oh Sara," and he pulled me into his arms, holding me tightly. "I have known you such a short, little time."

I threw my arms around his neck, choking back a sob.

"Not with a tear, Sara," he reprimanded me gently. "Surely not with tears?"

"No, not with tears," I denied, crying, lifting my lips to his kiss.

I clung to him desperately, for the passion that his slightest caress evoked in me welled up to meet his. Abruptly he took his mouth from mine and held my head fiercely against his shoulder, burying his lips in my hair.

Slowly he released me, holding my hands gently as I struggled to hold back my tears.

"Honor my claim to you, dear my lady."

A horn blasted outside and I saw the hovering aircar. I felt his hands pressing mine around the slates and, through my tears, saw him stride out to the balcony and into the car. I watched until I could no longer see it over the arc of the palace gardens.

My head ached with the pressure of stifled grief and my body from the stimulus of his caresses. I would always associate the mingled odors of car-fuel, fresh slate wax and mid-morning musty heat with that scene.

CHAPTER FIFTEEN

I CARRIED THE SLATES, holding them stiffly in both hands just as Harlan had placed them there. I walked down corridors that were obstacle courses of hustling men and equipment. There was no panic, just urgent dispatch. No hysterics, only grim determination. But I was oblivious. Their haste, their muttered apologies bounced off the numb shell of my exterior.

I don't think I had quite accepted the fact that Harlan really cared for me. I accepted the fact that he was grateful to me; that he found me useful in sailing a ship; that he liked to be seen with me; that he liked to go to bed with me, but not that his emotions were involved. I knew he was concerned for my safety, but I had irrationally connected that with the fact that only I could recognize my own home planet in space and Harlan keenly wanted more allies to help overthrow the Mil. It was just difficult for me to assimilate the knowledge I was Harlan's lady, me, Sara Fulton, late of Seaford, Delaware and New York City.

It seemed an age before I reached Maxil's suite where a pacing Jokan waited. He looked at me sardonically, the muscles along his jaw working. I handed him the slates and he glared down at them as if they, too, were enemies in the alliance to keep him planet-bound when all his soul wanted to be in space with the fleet. He handed one slate back to me brusquely.

"That one's for Ferrill, not me," he said with no courtesy. He scanned one quickly and placed it in his belt. The other he read, his frown deepening. He glanced at me twice during the reading and then sat down. His anger drained out of him and a hopeless impatience took its place.

"Oh, sit down, Lady Sara. I won't eat you," he said kindly, seeing me still standing in the same spot.

179

I sat down and promptly burst into tears, gulping out apologies as I sobbed. He leaned over and roughly patted my shoulder, muttering reassurances. When I didn't stop, he fetched a drink and made me get it down.

"Patrol issue," I choked.

"Of course, we're pretty lucky," he said with no prelude. "Harlan's the most brilliant commander we've ever had. We're better prepared for this sort of thing than ever before in our history. Never thought there would be a Prime again, but we've got it and there's no panic. It's not as if the Mil were able to swoop down on us with no forewarning the way they used to. It could be a lot worse, you know. We could have Gorlot as our Regent and I bet we might just as well skin ourselves if he were. But he isn't. It's Harlan and he'll save our skins if anyone can. Because, my dear brother's lady, right now we can annihilate the Mil in the sky."

It was not the words he said but the way he said them that stopped my senseless weeping; I looked up at him in amazement because there was triumph in his voice; a certainty that exceeded the trivial phrases of his verbal assurance.

"I hope so," said a wry voice from the doorway. We both turned to see Ferrill there, supported by two men. "I'm being conducted to the Vaults," he said, indicating the escort with amusement. "Coming?"

Ferrill's smile, oddly mocking, made his old-man's face younger.

"There's really no need for me to be bulwarked by all the ingenuity of the Vaults. The Mil wouldn't bother a wreck like me," Ferrill continued amiably. "I gather," and his face grimaced ruefully at Jokan, "Harlan has made you stay behind to guard the sacred persons of the Warlord's progeny. You've worked as hard for this contingency as he. Pity you can't witness it. But *I'm* glad it's you that's here!" Ferrill's sincerity reached Jokan through his bitterness.

"It is my honor, sir," he replied in a neutral voice, but the bow he made the ex-Warlord was deep and respectful.

Jokan indicated I was to precede him to the Hall. I hesitated at the doorway so that Ferrill might precede me as I felt his due. He bowed slightly and I continued. We made our way to the down-shaft through hurrying people who stopped and stepped aside respectfully to let Ferrill's party pass.

"Nuisance to be sent scurrying down so early," Ferrill commented as we reached the shaft. "Nothing will happen for a day or so."

"True," Jokan conceded, "but they have activated the spatial tank below and set up the remote connections there rather than in the Council Hall. It's more reassuring to the general public to vault themselves anyway. Too much has happened to unsettle them. They fancy themselves more Tanes, I'm told."

"Hmm. That's reasonable," Ferrill replied thoughtfully.

When we reached the cellars of the palace, we passed a six-foot-thick section of wall that would swing up into place, closing off the entrance to the Vaults beneath the palace. Huge guards saluted as we passed this impenetrable lock.

We walked down a short corridor to an enormous, low-ceilinged room where partitions blocked off working, resting and eating areas. The busy occupants spared Ferrill a grave smile or bow. The next corridor was doubly sealed by more six-foot sections. The precautions were so formidable I wondered what kind of attack armament the Mil mounted which could penetrate such fortifications. Maybe the effect of the doors was more psychological than necessary.

"I haven't been in the Vaults in years," Ferrill remarked. "I often wondered who dusted them and how frequently."

Jokan gave a mirthless snort at such a fancy while I surprised myself with a genuine laugh at such drollery.

We paused before a final heavy door and were admitted by guards into the innermost section, the retreat of the Council and the Warlord's family.

The huge room, which appeared to be as large as

Starhall, was dominated by a spherical tank some ten feet in diameter. I did not have the chance to examine it because Stannall approached us from one of the cubicles beyond. He bowed gravely to Ferrill, glanced at me curiously and clasped Jokan's arm in welcome.

"Sir Ferrill, your quarters are prepared in Room Seven. I regret you must share them with your attendants and your brother Fernan but . . ."

Ferrill shrugged off the inconvenience and excused himself. He rested more heavily on his helpers although he had moved along the public corridors with a semblance of vigor.

"I had not expected the Lady Sara," Stannall said severely.

"Lord Harlan has claimed the Lady Sara in my presence," Jokan said bluntly. "I have, here, an alternate commission of Regency," and Jokan handed over the slates to Stannall, "as well as Harlan's official record of claim and acceptance."

The First Councilman glanced quickly through both, scowling at me again with intense irritation.

"Very well," Stannall acknowledged sourly.

"You mean my appointment as Regent," Jokan said pointedly.

"No, of course not. I approve of that heartily." He looked up, conscious of Jokan's stare. I had not exactly expected Jokan to come to my defense, particularly against Stannall, so his attitude was very reassuring. "My congratulations, Lady Sara. I know the Lady Fara will be glad to see you."

"Did Maxil . . ." Jokan began.

"Fara accepted the honor," Stannall said quickly.

"Congratulations all around then," Jokan said with a wry smile.

"Maxil claimed Fara?" I repeated, hoping that at least one area of irritation might be erased between Stannall and me.

"Thank the mother of us all for that," Jokan muttered. "Room Four?" he asked and when Stannall nodded, he drew me off to the side where I saw numbered doors, closed against the noise of the main room.

"There is much for me to order, Lady Sara," Jokan said, opening the door for me.

"And I am tired."

A droning voice muttering unintelligible syllables in a room beyond penetrated my sleep and woke me, startled, in an unfamiliar darkness. Frightened, I lay still until the mounds of deeper shadow became distinguishable as Fara, Linnana and two empty beds.

The drone continued and I had been so startled on awakening that my ability to sleep was gone. I rose and stumbled across to the bathroom.

The lights of the main hall and the muted conversations that blended under the theme of the droning voice were a shock after the dim quiet of the sleeping room. I stood in the doorway, looking over the bustle for Jokan or Ferrill. Stannall was standing in front of the cubicle that was his office, his slight body slumped with weariness. While he talked to a Councilman, his eyes were fixed on the space tank and the measured tread of the blips within it. There were few in the room who did not glance frequently at the tank, frequently and apprehensively.

I located the drone as issuing from one of the twelve big screens at the top of the room. A communications man was talking, calling off sector units and parsec figures. In turn, clerks noted down these figures at tables that circled the screen and tank area. From the other big hall messengers came and went, officials in patrol uniform or Council robes met and conversed quietly in the linking corridor. Their voices were pitched lower than that continuous drone.

Jokan came striding down the corridor and up to Stannall. Ferrill, walking slowly from Stannall's office, joined them. The Councilman who had been talking to Stannall bowed and moved away. Jokan was arguing and Stannall was objecting, shaking his head dubiously. Ferrill added a sentence and Stannall regarded the ex-Warlord with a long scowl. The three of them moved over to the tank and Jokan pointed, scribing a circle with his hands and indicating its position in the spatial reference. A messenger came up and handed Jokan a slate. This had a bearing on his argument because he pointed out several lines for Stannall to read. The First Councilman shrugged, shook his head again. When Ferrill added his comment, Stannall lifted both arms in a gesture of exasperation. Jokan bowed formally and went to the main communication screen, one that looked in on the giant refitted Mil ship that was Harlan's command vessel.

My attention was abruptly diverted from Jokan by a touch on my arm. To my concern, I saw Monsorlit standing beside me, regarding me with a cold impersonal interest tinged with some private amusement.

"Lady Sara," he said, making a mockery of the title with a flick of his eyes, "for a moron, you've made remarkable conquests. I've reread your dossier and find it fascinating."

"Moron? I'm no moron," I said with all the disdain I could muster. I turned from him, but his hand, as cold as his expression and as strong as his personality, closed round my wrist.

"As I was saying, I have examined your history and I find it differs considerably from the public version of your origin."

"Against Harlan's word, what can you prove?" I demanded.

He smiled blandly, his eyes wandering over my face and body with clinical dispassion.

"Against Harlan's word, I have the facts and witnesses. Facts that would prove extremely interesting to the First Councilman, to young Maxil. And, certainly to Harlan himself, unless you are more of an innocent than you appear."

"I don't know what you mean," I gasped, trying to twist my hand free.

He looked down at my wrist, holding it up and stroking it with his thumb. Then he glanced suggestively into my face. I had no strength to hide the shock that gesture gave me.

The smile which was no smile cut across his thin face.

"You are unique, Lady Sara. Absolutely unique and as a serious scientist, I cannot allow the originality to go unremarked. I intend to have you back in the Clinic and I give you warning. You may come of your own free will, explaining your request to your protector any way you wish. Or, I will force you to come, by edict of the Council. I doubt you like that alternative."

"Physician," said Ferrill's soft voice at my side. Monsorlit looked up and bowed to the invalid.

"Do not overexert yourself in this excitement, Sir Ferrill," Monsorlit advised sternly.

"Exert myself? Oh, not likely. I have accepted the role of passive observer. That requires no exertion at all."

So saying, Ferrill neatly turned me away from Monsorlit and guided me toward an unused table in the dining area. He motioned me to sit and gave an order for hot drinks to the servant who appeared.

"Why does Monsorlit terrify you?" he asked quietly, his eyes slightly narrowed.

"He's . . . he's so cold," I blurted out, still trembling with the shock of the encounter.

Ferrill's eyebrows raised questioningly but, at this moment, the waiter returned. I drank hastily, the comfort of the warm beverage dissipating my inner chill. When I raised my eyes over my cup, Ferrill was regarding me with curious intentness. He reached over and lifted my right hand, turned it over and rubbed one finger across my wrist. I jerked my hand away and sat staring at Ferrill in a sort of helpless horror.

Ferrill smiled to himself and then included me in that smile.

"Lady Sara," he began with a rueful grin, "for the short time you have been in our circle, you have managed to elicit an amazing amount of talk. You succeed in antagonizing one of the most powerful men on the planet for some obscure reason and you stand in petrified terror before our leading scientist. You appear out of nowhere in Maxil's keeping, deliver me from evil, and now I understand that our noble Regent, who has kept remote from all permanent entanglements, has claimed you as his lady." He shook his head in mock consternation. "I can dismiss a good ninety percent of the talk about you as the fabrications of envy. I have a good idea of the basis for the antagonism, but I am at a complete loss to explain the terror."

I did not trust myself to answer him. Instead, I pulled out the slate Harlan had given me for him and thrust it across the table. Ferrill took it with a brief glance at the outer inscription and shoved it into his belt.

"Surely it's not restoration that makes you fear Monsorlit. The punishment is the same for the operator as the victim."

I looked nervously around to reassure myself no one could overhear us.

"As I told Monsorlit," Ferrill continued, "I am merely an interested bystander. I consider myself qualified to make all kinds of deep, penetrating observations which, to project my new image, I like to think are acute and perceptive. I have had much time for passive reflection, you know.

"Monsorlit is a great artist, a genius in his field. He is interested in achieving perfection, to which I say 'well done.' But he must have allowed himself to be carried away with his zeal, if he can be said ever to be carried away by anything." Ferrill's grin was a bit malicious. "For he neglected one axiom of nature . . . which prohibits her from duplicating anything . . . even two sides of the same face." He stopped and, narrowing his eyes, stared keenly at me. Pointing negligently to my wrists, he continued, "He was exceptionally deft in disguising the graft joints. I gather he has done a great deal of work on that crucial spot. But he made your features too symmetrical. If a mirror were handy, I could easily prove that both sides of your face are the same, except for your eyes. The left one droops a trifle at the outside edge. I wonder if that irked him in his search for perfection," and Ferrill chuckled. "However, if he had been able to change that, I do believe he would have ruined the total effect. That slight imper-

ection gives your face a touch of humanity it would
otherwise lack."

I wasn't sure I understood all he˙was talking about. His
one was so light, so conversational, that his disclosures
vere robbed of their gravity.

"Still," and he frowned thoughtfully, "I doubt anyone
ias the time for the close scrutiny my conclusions require.
And, since Monsorlit has conveniently done away with the
one weak spot, the one detectable, unmistakable weakness
n a total restoration, what do you have to fear?

"I should say he has proved his point. And Monsorlit
doesn't care for the approbation of the multitude as long
is he has satisfied his own curiosity. As you know, he has
always maintained that restoration itself did not cause
mental vegetation. As he expresses it," and Ferrill evident-
y did not agree completely with the theory, "it is our
ancient fear and superstition that breaks the mind. He
says we had so many centuries of passive acceptance of
death under the godlike Mil that a man unconsciously
wills himself to die when he is captured, whether his body
dies or not."

His words began to make some reassuring sense to me
and I started to relax. After all, Harlan had said that
Ferrill was the only one who would or could understand
and help me. Had he guessed that Ferrill knew I had been
restored? At least, Ferrill did not regard me with horror
and revulsion. I sipped my cup and the warm liquid ran
down my throat, spreading its comfort to my fingers.

"That's better," Ferrill said with a grin. I realized he
had been talking as much to put me at ease as to tell me
of his theories.

"I gather," he continued, smiling, "Monsorlit's new
techniques of shock treatments worked on you to bring
you out of the mental death. You certainly are a far cry
from the ghastly parodies that gave restoration its death
sentence. I shall suggest to Harlan that he repeal that law
quietly if you're the result of the latest techniques of
restoration. Or should I say 'repossession'?" Ferrill's smile
mocked the semantic hairsplitting. "So you see, you don't
have anything to fear from Monsorlit. Anything."

"But I do," I protested. "He wants me to go back to that horrible Clinic of his. He said he'd *make* me if I didn't come willingly."

"He can do nothing to you," Ferrill said blithely. "For one thing . . . well, Harlan knows you've been restored, doesn't he? Well, *he* won't permit it."

"But . . . if Harlan doesn't . . ." I stammered and couldn't finish the sentence.

Ferrill tapped his chest with a thin finger. "Then *I* won't let you go back. Oh, I may be a frail invalid, my dear, but I am still Ferrill," he announced, his voice ringing.

"I'm so terribly sorry . . ." I began but Ferrill waggled an admonishing finger to silence me.

"At the risk of repetition, I owe you my life, Lady Sara, or whatever is left of it. Besides, I wouldn't be very good at that sort of thing," and his gesture indicated the spatial tank. "Now, Maxil, as is the habit of younger brothers, has always been a scrapper. You never saw a boy keener on spaceships. Right now, if he isn't free-fall sick, he's having the time of his life. By the way, there's Harlan on the screen now."

I rose hastily, peering over the obstructing partition for the best view of Harlan. I ignored Ferrill's chuckle.

Harlan was addressing his remarks to Stannall, Jokan and the elder Councilmen, continuing an argument that must have been going on for several minutes.

"Sir," said Harlan, stressing the title as one whose patience is also stressed, "I *know* it hasn't been tried before. But neither have we had the equipment or the emergency. I insist, and so do my commanders, that the gamble is worth the game. We are fortunate that so many of our ships were equipped with the electromagnetic crystals during my disability. We may thank Gorlot for that at least," and Harlan permitted himself a wry smile at the shocked distaste occasioned by his remark.

"That is enough to make me distrust that innovation completely," Stannall said stiffly, looking for agreement among his fellow Councilmen. Several of them sided with him by their nods of disapproval.

"You forget, sir," Jokan put in, defending a system he
ad developed, "that it was Harlan's innovation, a de-
elopment of war research under my guidance. And you
rget that it was Fathor who thought the Ertoi planetary
efense mechanism might be adapted to shipborne arma-
ent. Gorlot was at least strategist enough to recognize its
alue as a weapon when no one else considered it more
han a toy."

"Sir Harlan," expostulated Lesatin pompously, "a deci-
ion of this magnitude cannot be made in so off-hand a
nanner."

"By my Clan Mother," Harlan exploded, "your own
ommittee of specialists approved the installation of the
nagnetos two years ago, Lesatin. Why all this time-
onsuming chatter? I've not asked for your decision. I've
lready made it for you. I'm telling you what I'm going to
o. The battle plan remains as I have outlined it."

"The responsibility," Stannall said forcefully, "of the
eople lies on our shoulders, too, not yours alone. Your
isregard of time-proved successful action . . ."

"Time-proved in the jetwash," snapped Harlan impa-
iently, "life-wasting, you mean. The resonant phenom-
non produced by the electromagnets can crush the Mil
vith greater personnel safety, less risk and loss of ships
nd lives than any improvement in our battle tactics since
ve refitted the first Star-class ship. By all that lies in the
tars, I will use the resonant barrage if we have to form
efore Lothar itself.

"What you grandly ignore, good sirs, in your preference
or these time-proved orthodox methods is the plain and
imple fact that we've never had such a concentration of
Mil against us. You ignore the recorded facts that it takes
he concerted action and an eighty-five percent casualty of
wenty ships to disable . . . with luck . . . a Star-class
vessel. We have *fifteen* out there in the black speeding
oward our puny four Stars. And whether we form before
_othar or at the first circle of defense, the casualties from
/our 'time-proved tactics' will be the same."

Jokan had been writing furiously on a slate. He passed
he results to the most disturbed Councilmen. They

grouped around him, their voices rising in the excitement
his figures aroused. Harlan glanced down at the confusion, at first with annoyance, until he saw the change of
attitude in these skeptics.

"We are approaching communication limit. If I don't
come back, you can skin me in effigy. If I do, it will be as
a victorious commander and we'll debate the ethics involved. In the meantime, Jokan has as many answers as I
since he's been in charge of the project. You have the
benefit of his talents and I do not. Jokan, jet it into their
thick heads, will you?" Harlan urged. "I'll beam you at
zero hour and, unless you like the noise, you'd better cut
the sound on all screens," he warned.

"You technicians got the spatial coordinates now?" he
asked the clerks in the banks around the tank. They raised
right hands in reply. Harlan's eyes left the immediate
foreground and scanned the space above the Councilmen's
heads. I made myself as tall as I could in the hope he
might be looking for me, but the expression on his face,
set, cold, tired, did not change. The picture began to
waver. Harlan looked off to his right in the control room,
then back to the Councilmen.

"We're at the limits, sirs. My respects to you all," and
the picture dissolved into blurs.

The droning voice had ended, too. The big room was
strangely silent for what seemed a long, long time. As if
everyone found the quiet unbearable, everyone began to
talk at once. The Councilmen turned on Jokan with intense expressions and garrulous queries. Messengers began
to move back and forth around the room. I sat down,
confused by all the discussion and disheartened by its
tone. Ferrill appeared disinterested and I drew some courage from his attitude.

"What was that all about?" I asked, abandoning any
pretense of knowledge.

My request did not surprise Ferrill. He leaned forward,
planting his forearms on the table comfortably as he enlightened me.

"The Ertois are workers of crystal and quartzite. They
had developed a primitive form of energy, electricity, they

alled it, long before the Mil descended on them. Our
orce screens are an adaption of their electricity. They
iscovered, by what freak chance I don't remember, that
he Mil cannot stand electrical currents or sonic vibra-
ons. They ringed their planet with gigantic electromag-
etos, activating them in case of Mil attack. The metal of
he Mil ships became a conductor and the Mil were
lectrocuted. Now, we had to figure a way to adapt this
rinciple to use in space. Sound doesn't travel in the
acuum, of course, but regulate the frequency of the
lectromagnetic radiation and you produce a resonant
henomenon in the ship hulls that literally tears the Mil
ell from cell. Ironically, though the Mil are much larger
han we, they are easy victims to a weapon that we can
ndure.

"My father was very interested in this application of
esonators. You see, we've never had an offensive weapon.
hat's why our casualties have always been so high. The
nly advantage we have had over the Mil in battle has
een our ability to take higher accelerations and make
harper maneuvers. It's a pretty slim advantage.

"This project has been going on for several decades. It's
een expensive and was discontinued when Fathor died.
ouncil had an attack of conservatism and the Mil were
uiet on the Rim. Harlan reinstated the project under
okan who is one of our few creative geniuses.

"The reason our skeptics have been so upset is that they
ave never seen what the resonators can do to a simulated
Mil protoplasm. I have seen it and, granted it was under
deal laboratory conditions, the results were incredible."
His eyes narrowed. "There is a minor theory going
round, which I am inclined to support, that Gorlot used
he resonators to herd the Mil into Tane. It's the only way
e could have managed to control their direction."

"Why didn't Harlan mention that?" I asked. "Didn't he
now?"

Ferrill shrugged. "Where the Mil are concerned, logic is
ometimes useless. Particularly right now. Look what's
appened. The Mil have actually been allowed past the
erimeter. They have been allowed to wipe out an entire

race. For seventy-five years, they haven't been able to penetrate the Rim defenses for more than a few parsecs.

"Our ancestors were used to the menace of the Mil in their skies. As accustomed as one is able to get to such a thought. But we aren't. Stannall may be our leading Councilman and a very intelligent fellow, but the mere thought of the possibility of the Mil coming back into Lotharian skies turns him into a quivering mass of ancient fears and superstition. And Harlan has just blithely assured him that he will wait to reform before Lothar itself in order to test this new weapon!"

"Why does he have to wait?" I asked confused.

"Because, Lady Sara," Ferrill explained patiently, "the beam attenuates with distance, losing its strength. The maximum effect is gained at close quarters—spatially speaking—from an encirclement, so that each resonator is equidistant from the target, setting up the resonating phenomenon at maximum efficiency."

"If they can't encircle?" I asked, perceiving some of the dread with which Stannall and the others received Harlan's gamble.

"The usual tactics, only we will have a ringside seat," and Ferrill gestured heavenward.

"What *are* the usual tactics?" I insisted.

Ferrill regarded me seriously for a moment.

"You really don't know, do you?" he remarked with amazement. "We have discovered only two ways to dispose of a Mil ship. Both are dangerous to the attacker because we lack an offensive weapon other than speed and maneuverability. We must either knock out their control room, which means a close-range assault with nucleonic weapons that match theirs, or we must make a direct hit on their fuel source. The first is preferable because it leaves us a new recruit for our fleet . . . after decontamination, of course. The second method blows up the ship."

"You heard Harlan mention eighty-five percent casualties, didn't you?" Ferrill continued and I nodded. "He means just that. There are only four Star-class cruisers in our fleet, eighty-five planet weight and forty satellite variety plus about fifty rider suicide ships. Figure out your eighty-five percent against a force of twenty-three Mil ships, *fifteen* of them Star-class and you can see why Harlan is going to gamble on our new offensive weapon."

My mental arithmetic was not up to estimating the odds, but eight-five percent was obviously a Pyrrhic victory.

"Back in my great-grandfather's day, we once had a force against us of one Star-class, four planet and a satellite. We had, at the time, eighty ships. Nine returned. We disabled two planet-types and the satellite. That was the biggest force we have ever attacked until now. The Mil usually send a group of planets and satellites. With their consistent losses in this area of the Great Starry Wheel, you'd think the Mil would have left us alone long ago."

"You mean some of their ships still get through?"

Ferrill looked startled. "No! We destroy enough so that they retreat. But there is always a terrific loss of life for us.

"To knock out the control room, a suicide rider with nine men must approach to maximum penetration range of the nuclear missiles. That's about one hundred land miles. That's too close to a Mil, believe me. The ships are nothing but speed and one long cannon. Their success depends jointly on the skill and diversionary tactics of the pilot and the accuracy of the gunner. Very often, the suiciders are crushed by the impact of their own blast. All too often, the Mil gunners get the range first. And sometimes," and Ferrill shuddered, "the riders are grappled and pulled inboard. Even if we do disable the Mil ship, those men are lost."

"Why?" I asked without thinking.

Ferrill clicked his tongue at me. "One, if the men haven't as yet been touched, they've gone mad by the time we reach them. Two, if they have been skinned, Council's edict about restoration makes euthanasia imperative."

"Skinned," he had said. I had been "skinned," alive! I fought the rising nausea and the shaking that gripped my diaphragm.

"I'll wager that's why!" Ferrill said with a note of triumph in his voice.

"Why what?" I managed to say, pushing to the back of my mind his last words.

"Why Monsorlit tied in with Gorlot"; and he leaned forward so that our conversation could not be overheard. "Gorlot knew some ships and men would fall into Mil hands. He had to have someone make perfect restorations on the victims so they would seem to be no more than Tane casualties. And Monsorlit went one step better. He pulled those restorees out of shock so there could be no suspicion whatever of the men having been Mil victims. To prove his point, Monsorlit would take a far greater risk."

"I'll tell Harlan you're trying to dishonor his claim," said Jokan's voice behind me.

Ferrill grinned up at his uncle with a deprecating laugh. Jokan pulled up a chair and signaled a server.

"Did you manage to reassure the skeptics?" Ferrill demanded with an affectation of disinterest.

Jokan shrugged expressively and threw the slate he carried toward Ferrill who cocked his head sideways to read the slate without having to pick it up.

"The odds *are* favorable," he said with some surprise. "Even if a trifle close to home. Don't they see that?"

"What they see is the space tank and the proximity of the Mil to Lothar," Jokan scoffed. "I believe the older one gets the more the fears and superstitions we should have abandoned centuries ago cloud the thinking."

"Don't they realize that the older one gets the less valuable he becomes to the Mil?" Ferrill pointed out cold-bloodedly. "No fat. No meat. No smooth hide."

Jokan did not hide his distaste of Ferrill's observation.

"I'm not concerned," he said stiffly. Then grinned as he added, "But then, I'm under the largest pile of reinforced rock and metal on the planet. I also remind myself what the resonators can do to the Mil . . ."

"Under ideal laboratory conditions," Ferrill inserted maliciously.

"Under ideal laboratory conditions," Jokan assented without rancor, "which Harlan, with the reinforcement of the Ertoi and Glan, can reproduce."

"If the Ertoi and Glan arrive in time," Ferrill amended.

Jokan's eyes sparkled angrily. "Are you through qualifying the odds against us?"

Ferrill flashed a look at Jokan but thought better of what he was about to say and hitched one shoulder negligently.

"I'm realistic, my dear uncle. Also I find an element of humor in the situation."

Jokan snorted with disgust at this observation.

"Your humor was never so warped before, my dear nephew."

"Nor was my life," Ferrill added quietly, then added too brightly, "Monsorlit has been frightening Harlan's Sara."

"Ha. He's in no position to frighten anyone. Stannall's after him again. Monsorlit had best look to his own defense. And you have the strongest protection, Lady Sara," Jokan said stoutly.

He had finished his quick meal as we talked and now rose.

"You two can exchange insults, if you wish," he said as he glanced at the large time dial above the space tank, "but there are precisely eight hours and thirty-two seconds before encirclement and I intend to use it in sleeping. I relinquish our mutual ward into your safekeeping, Ferrill." He bowed to the ex-Warlord and then to me, with a touch of his old insouciance, and departed.

"He's sure about Stannall being after Monsorlit?" I asked hopefully.

Ferrill shrugged. "Stannall has been after Monsorlit for years. Never did know why. Some old quarrel. Stannall has a capacity for grudges that is astonishing."

"Didn't I hear Jokan call you nephew?" I asked after a pause.

"He is, after all, my uncle."

"Well, why isn't he a candidate for Warlord, instead of Maxil?"

"He and Harlan are only half-brothers to my father, Fathor. But you should remember that only my father's line can inherit under the old laws. If Fathor had died without issue, and he certainly waited long enough to claim his lady, it would have been different. It's a pity, too, because Jokan shows the real Harlan strain."

"Doesn't Harlan?" I demanded, piqued.

Ferrill chuckled and I realized his omission had been intentional. "Obviously. But Harlan's real mission in life is to find more and more new planets. The Tane success went to his head. He's got jet-itch. Besides he's got nowhere near the deviousness of Jokan."

"Then," I demanded, confused by the intricacies of Lotharian governmental structure, "why wasn't Jokan made Regent instead of Harlan?"

Patiently Ferrill explained that Harlan had been a Perimeter Commander. Jokan had never reached that rank nor intended to. Unfortunately, such military experience was the prime requisite for the Regency.

"Is that how Gorlot got in instead of Jokan when Harlan was drugged?"

"Naturally," Ferrill assented, his eyes glittering angrily. "The system has too many faults and this affair should make it obvious to the Council that a revision of the old laws must be made. We are too hampered by age-old superstition and pre-Perimeter contingencies." He snorted derisively. "It's absurd to assume that only a direct descendant of the original Harlan can lead us to victory over the Mil. It's ridiculous to bind the genius of modern military tactics to planet-bound traditions. Just like that argument over there!" and he indicated the group of Councilmen arguing vehemently around the space tank.

"Would they really censure Harlan for disregarding them?"

"How can they?" Ferrill scoffed. "At the moment, he *is* Warlord. That's why he was picked as Regent, in the event of a military emergency an inexperienced stripling could not handle. His plan is law: it's just typical of Harlan to wish to have Stannall's agreement. It *is* preferable to

have the First Councilman agree with you if you are
Regent or Warlord."

He rose abruptly.

"Jokan's suggestion is contagious. We've hours yet before the crucial test of Harlan's revolutionary tactics. Sleep
passes time admirably. But first, join me for a glance at
the tank?"

Ferrill and I stood a little removed from the others. He
rightly assumed I needed an explanation. The science
behind the tank's projection he did not bother to expati-
ate. Its physical presence, however, was awesome enough.
It was composed of an amber, transparent liquid or gas
with no apparent material enclosing its circumference. It
stood ten feet high and wide in the center of the room it
dominated. A coil of wires at its foot was the sole connection to the machines and computers that formed a
semicircle at its base. Beyond them, built obliquely from
the ceiling, were the now blank screens. Only one panel on
the boards below the screens was active, the master panel
to which each ship in action was hooked. If the light
which identified the ship went out, the ship had been
destroyed. The technician could also tell by the color
variation and pulsations the extent, in theory, of damage
to any given vessel. At the computers the clerks were still
busy. In all the room, no one's eyes stayed long away
from the mesmeric quality of the slowly moving masses in
the tank.

Guardedly Ferrill indicated Lothar, a green ball in the
approximate center of the tank. Above and beyond were
Ertoi in blue and Glan's yellow. Below and away from the
other three systems was the red of the two Tane planets.

From Ertoi and Glan, lancing downward and bypassing
Lothar were the light points of the Alliance ships, speeding to their rendezvous with Lothar's fleet. Beyond Ertoi
and Glan, I saw eight tiny points of light at regular
intervals; far, far apart. Ferrill said they were the skeletal
Perimeter Patrol that would be all Glan would have to
defend it from the Mil if they broke through. Ertoi relied
still on its sonic barrier.

"Why doesn't Glan have it, too?" I asked, thinking that would have freed eight more ships.

"They never considered it necessary with the protection the Alliance has afforded them up till now."

Speeding out from Lothar and converging from other points around the remaining quadrants of the tank was the fleet, moving not as swiftly as the Alliance ships but as inexorably. From the bottom of the tank, approaching with what I thought appalling comparative speed were the invading lights of the Mil. The alarm of the Councilmen was no longer a verbal fear that Jokan's assurances and Ferrill's amused air could dispel. It took no technician to estimate how near to Lothar that battle would take place. And the Mil's ominous approach was aimed at the equator of the seemingly doomed Tanes.

"Would the Mil land on one of the Tane?" I asked.

Ferrill shook his head in a quick negative response.

"The Mil would never land with such a force approaching them. They could be blown off a planet and our casualties would be light. We overused those tactics a few centuries ago. No. They'll meet Harlan in space. They're pretty contemptuous of us in space, you know. I doubt they'll remain so long."

We watched, as others did, in hypnotized silence as the blinking lights made their almost imperceptible way. Finally, Ferrill touched my arm lightly and we both retired to our sleeping quarters.

CHAPTER SIXTEEN

A GENTLE TICKLING ON MY FEET roused me. The room was lit and I could see Ferrill grinning mischievously as he gave my foot one last brush.

"I used to wake Cherez like that and she'd throw a fit," he grinned. "I thought you'd like to be in on the fun. Harlan's brave gamble is about to start."

I scrambled out of the cot, took time to dash cold water in my eyes and comb back my hair before joining Ferrill. I wouldn't have needed Ferrill's comment to know that the climax was at hand. The entire room watched the screen, some standing on chairs or desks for better views of the all-important spatial tank. The computers were silent. Conversation was limited to terse low whispers. The tension, fear and apprehension in the main room was like a physical blow after the sleeping quarters. Ferrill had paused at the threshold and we both drifted through the watchers until we found Jokan. He was standing behind Stannall and Lesatin. Jokan looked around irritably as I brushed against him to make way for Ferrill. He gave us the sketchiest of acknowledgments before turning back to the tank.

I had to make myself look at the sphere. Its story dried up the saliva in my mouth. I was certain the pounding of my heart would be audible.

Tane had been bypassed. Empty space separated the straggling Lotharian space fleet from the home planet. The blips of light that were our defenders resembled a tiny crystal string of beads thrown casually on a jeweler's velvet around a pendant of twenty-three bright diamonds in random pattern. The beads circumscribed no circle; one end, the Ertoi and Glan contingent being too far out to complete even the roughest circular formation. Ferrill's groan was not noted by anyone.

At first I wondered why the Mil would let themselves

199

be even so loosely encircled. Then I remembered that the Mil in space would wreak terrible losses, so they could be arrogant about our puny trap. I watched the beads, still loose, but slowly, slowly perfecting their circle. They drifted at the same time with such snail slowness toward Lothar. Ertoi and Glan became stationary, being uppermost to Lothar; below and beyond it, I could see the barely larger blips that were the four Star-class Lothar battlewagons in their major compass-point positions. The pendant moved inexorably and the rear quadrants moved still closer, the uneven beads gradually, gradually settling into a rough circle.

I had been so fascinated with the fleet movement that I had not noticed the movements of the Mil pendant. Once a mass of light, it now began to lose its compactness and to string out into a rough line.

Jokan groaned and twisted his tense body in an unconscious effort to bunch the Mil ships back into their former position. Stannall covered his face for a moment, with a shaking hand. When he turned to Jokan, I was aghast at the exhaustion and hopelessness of his expression.

"That maneuver, doesn't it decrease the effectiveness of the resonant barrage?" he asked, hoping to hear the contrary.

"It depends, sir, it all depends."

"On what?" Stannall demanded fiercely.

"On how much our men can stand of the backlash from the electromagnetos that generate the resonance. If we can saturate the Mil ships with enough force, their belated dispersal means nothing." Jokan clenched his jaws grimly. "I *wish* we had had time to develop effective shielding for the power-bleed. At the moment," he continued in answer to Stannall, "we can be sure of this section being completely paralyzed," and his finger stabbed at the center of the Mil pendant. "Partial disability on either end and, with luck, our normal tactics can take care of the rest."

"If they string out farther?" Stannall dragged the words from his mouth.

"The decrease in total disability is proportional. Individual engagements increase."

Stannall's expression was desperate and his lips, thinned by fatigue to white lines, closed obdurately over his teeth.

We waited. Glances at the time dial were more frequent. It lacked but a few moments of the hour set for the barrage. Jokan was counting off nervously to himself and someone else on the other side of the room counted out loud. I was not the only one to mouth the seconds in concert.

Zero hour!

The tank remained unchanged. I don't know what I expected to happen. How much of a time lag there was between the ships and the tank I didn't know but the next moments or minutes seemed eternities.

A new voice broke the stillness. Glancing up I saw that a patroller was standing before the master panel that checked the condition of the ships. His voice, dispassionate and measured, brought us no consolation.

"No casualties. Two minutes and no casualties. All ships functioning. Three minutes and no casualties."

No casualties, my brain echoed. What an odd war. Bloodless, remotely fought, remotely observed. Would death, too, seem remote to the dying? Fear, however, was not remote. It laid lavish hands on everyone in that room, on everyone, I was sure, on those ships and on the planet of Lothar.

"No casualties," the drone continued.

The intervals between his litany lengthened and suddenly, unable to watch the unchanged picture longer, Stannall whirled on Jokan.

"Nothing has happened. How long does it take?" he cried in tense, strident tones that echoed through the fear-filled room with piercing audibility. Someone started to sob and stopped, choking the sound back.

"The maximum vibrations for the Mil should build in no less than six minutes," Jokan said tonelessly. "The beam is played across the ship for maximum effect. We count on the fact that the Mil cannot initiate evasive tactics at high acceleration speeds as we can. The longer they remain within the effective range of the beam, the quicker the resultant destructive resonance is reached."

Someone was counting the seconds again. Still the formation of the ships, all the ships, remained the same, a circle of beads tightening slowly around the menacing gaggle of Mil ships. The man had counted to ten minutes past the zero hour before a voice, in the anguish of waiting, shrieked for him to stop. The circle of beads tightened, drifting ever upward toward the system of Lothar.

"It isn't working, that's what's wrong," a beefy Councilman snapped, his voice trembling. "That puny electricity doesn't work. Fathor stopped that research. He must have had a reason. They don't work, that's what, and we'll all . . ."

"All ships functioning," the official voice, calm and deliberate, broke in. "No casualties."

"Look, look," someone cried, gesticulating toward the tank.

The string of beads was breaking up, splitting into smaller circles, driving for the ends of the Mil line.

"They're using the suicide ships now. The resonators didn't work at all. We're lost. The Mil will be here," a man beyond Stannall blubbered.

Stannall strode to his side in three swift paces and, although the fellow was younger and heavier, the First Councilman fetched him four sharp cracks across the face and turned defiantly to face the room.

"If the Mil should come, we will be ready with the courage and fortitude which have brought us so far along the road to freedom from their awful raiding. Let no one else forget his valiant heritage."

"One suicide ship casualty," the announcer droned. "All others functioning."

On the tank, a small expanding glow appeared and then one bead blinked out. One light obediently darkened on the master panel. But the tank also told another story. The midsection of the Mil line proceeded unharried by the ships which concentrated their efforts on the ends. The tiniest blips flashed in with unbelievable speed compared with the lumbering efforts of others. The upper end reflected a brief glow and the announcer tallied another casualty.

"They're attacking only the ends," someone cried in dismay. "The rest are coming straight at us."

"NO!" shouted Jokan, his voice ringing with triumph. He sprang to the side of the spatial tank. "The midsection is totally disabled. The resonators did their work. Look, would that big a detachment allow the others to be attacked without firing? See, here, here and here, our positions would be vulnerable to their range and yet there are no casualties. I tell you, that weapon works. It does. It does! And see, there's one of the lead Mil ships going up."

One of the larger Mil lights at the head of the line flared and died. The announcer gave us no death notice for a defender.

"See what Harlan is doing," Jokan continued excitedly. "We have plenty of time to disable the far end. He's tried two passes with the riders to the foremost Mil and is blasting them out of the sky. That means they must be partially disabled. No Mil will set down on Lothar!" His words rang through the big room and set off a cheering, shouting, weeping roar of hysterical relief. Jokan, grinning so broadly his face seemed to split, tears in his eyes, looked around, thrilled at the sight of hope where despair had so long enervated morale.

I, too, was caught up in the emotional backlash, weeping not so much with the relief of salvation as with the knowledge that Harlan would return, in honor and unharmed. The fear of the others did not touch me as deeply, I suppose, because I had not lived with fear of the Mil all my life. Vicariously I was caught up in that joyous hysteria until I noticed Stannall. He was clutching wildly at his chest. His face was gray, his lips blue, his breath shallow, eyes pain-filled and he grabbed wildly at me in his weakness.

Glancing around for someone else to help me, I was even grateful to Monsorlit who must have seen Stannall's seizure from across the room. The physician was fumbling in his belt as he pushed through the milling, shouting, jumping men. He reached us, jammed a hypodermic needle into Stannall's arm and smoothly reinforced my grip around the First Councilman.

Jokan, aware of Stannall's distress, pushed through and lifted Stannall easily into his arms. Bawling for passage, he carried the ailing Councilman to his sleeping room. Monsorlit ordered me to get his instruments from Room 12 and I ran with no respect for dignities.

When I returned with the case, Stannall was pillowed into a sitting position. Although he was sweating profusely, his breath came with less effort. Monsorlit grabbed the bag I opened and seized a stethoscopic device. Jokan was joined by Ferrill now. Monsorlit's examination relieved him, for he gave a barely audible sigh and reached with less haste for his bag. He picked a vial carefully, filled a new needle and administered the medication.

"Good sir," Monsorlit said in such low tones only I could hear, "there are too few of your fiber for us to be deprived of you. This time you will have to listen to me."

He rose from the bedside and, as he turned, I caught the flickering of the only expression I ever saw on Monsorlit's face. It was the more astonishing to me, this combination of fear, relief, worry and compassion, since there was no doubt of Stannall's trenchant disapproval of Monsorlit. The physician glanced at me briefly, his features composed in their usual coldness. He passed me and motioned all of us out to the corridor.

Ferrill and Jokan, instantly the door closed, demanded the diagnosis with impatient concern.

"A heart attack," Monsorlit said dispassionately, replacing his stethoscope with care, rearranging a vial or two precisely before closing the bag. "Natural enough with such intense strain and inadequate rest. I've administered a sedative that should keep him asleep for many hours. He must be kept absolutely quiet for the next weeks and complete bedrest is indicated for the next few months. Or, we shall have to elect a new First Councilman. I believe Cordan is his personal physician. He should attend our

Council Leader immediately. To reassure all of us." Monsorlit permitted himself the vaguest of wry grins at his afterthought.

"But Stannall's presence is . . ." Jokan began, gesturing toward the tank.

". . . is required in his bed and asleep," Monsorlit finished with bland authority. "I do not care what duties he leaves unfinished. There are certainly enough qualified men to make decisions until Harlan returns. Unless, of course, you wish to commit Stannall to the Eternal Flame tomorrow?"

With that, Monsorlit turned on his heel and walked away.

By now the jubilation had subsided sufficiently for the drone of the announcer to be heard. The score of casualties had mounted, but only nine lights were out on the master panel. Two flickered weakly, eight pulsed, but the strength of the light indicated only minor damage. Jokan, after a glance at the picture in the tank, strode across the room to the knot of anxious Councilmen. Stannall's collapse had been noted as well as the exchange between Jokan and Monsorlit.

"I think," commented Ferrill thoughtfully, "that the situation is now under the efficient control of Jokan. Will you join me for some refreshment, Lady Sara?"

"Shouldn't someone stay with Stannall?" I protested.

"Monsorlit seems to have taken that into account," Ferrill said and directed my attention to the brisk figure coming from the farthest sleeping rooms. The woman, a large, efficient-looking person, stopped at Stannall's door. She opened it with a quick practiced gesture and entered. A pair of guards simultaneously took positions on either side of the door.

There was little time for Ferrill and me to refresh ourselves. Food and drink grew cold before we could eat. Ferrill, though no longer Warlord, still had all the knowledge of his former position. He was, furthermore, privy to the confidential matters of the high position and the offices of both Regent and First Councilmen. In this emergency he set aside his affectation of disinterest and made quick, clear decisions, gave orders with an easy authority that controlled the quick-tempered and calmed the hysterical. Messengers crowded around the table, waiting turn. Councilmen opportuned and only Jokan could claim precedence. The little people, too—messengers and technicians—stopped to ask about Stannall or say something, shyly, to Ferrill.

Ferrill remained cool and detached, casual and unconcerned by the rush. At first, he answered the Councilmen's and Jokan's questions with a little self-amused smile. But gradually, I could see the grayness of fatigue conquering the slight color in his face. I urged him anxiously to rest.

"Rest? Not now, Sara. I want to know every detail of the stimulating events. I shall record them in a personal history I shall now have time to write. The firsthand impressions of an ex-Warlord about an emergency and triumph of this magnitude will certainly carry historical weight."

"If you're not careful, the only historical weight you'll carry is a fancy monument," I snapped.

He regarded me with the expression he had used so effectively on Monsorlit, but I was too concerned for him and stared him down. He changed his tactics and reassured me that he knew the limits of his strength.

"I have made no move from this table. I let everyone seek me."

"I thought you didn't care anymore. I thought you were just going to be the bystander," I goaded him.

His eyes flashed angrily. Then he smiled in recognition of my baiting. He reached for my hand and pressed it firmly.

"I *am* still the bystander, shoveling out bystandorial advice by the shipload. But I am the only one who can answer many of these questions in Stannall's absence. Jokan certainly has no practical experience as either Warlord, Regent or First Councilman, and he is all three right now."

I made one of the messengers go for Monsorlit who appeared just as Jokan also reached our table. Jokan did

ot care for Monsorlit's presence. Ferrill's smile mocked
ae for my interference.

"Ferrill is exhausted," I said before Ferrill or Jokan
ould send Monsorlit away.

"Give me a shot of something salutary," Ferrill com-
aanded the physician, proffering his thin, blue-veined
rm, daring Monsorlit as well as Jokan and me.

"All of you need stimulants to keep on at this pace,"
ae man observed quietly and issued us five tablets apiece.
An effective compound but harmless," he continued as
okan eyed the pills dubiously. "One every three hours
vill be sufficient. I do not recommend taking more than
ve. That gives you fifteen more hours of peak efficiency.
'hen no one will have trouble getting you to rest."

He moved off briskly. Ferrill took his pill down quickly
nd Jokan, shrugging, followed his lead. I waited and then
aw Ferrill watching my indecision with such amusement I
ossed it down waterless.

"I never really know what to make of him," the ex-
Varlord commented to no one in particular.

Jokan uttered a growling sound deep in his throat and
hen launched into the reason for his coming to the ta-
ole.

Monsorlit did not underestimate his potion. It did keep
ıs going for the next fifteen hours. I watched Jokan and
'errill as their eyes brightened, reddened and teared with
atigue, knowing I was no better off. Jokan took to
houting for me if he could not come to us and I became a
iaison between Jokan and Ferrill.

As I listened to conversations concerning the resump-
ion of the planet's normal activities, the hurried rear-
angements of landing facilities and refueling schedules, I
vatched the tank. Everyone did. And I, too, did not push
he announcer's assessments of the casualties from my
onscious hearing. On the tank, I saw the midsection of
he Mil fleet continue blindly on its course for nowhere
vhile Lothar picked off additional enemies. I watched as
he helpless section was set upon by a double row of our
essels, turned into a new course as Ertoi and Glan pilots
»enetrated to the control rooms and altered the courses for

the naval satellite bases and the one planetary space installation in the southern sea. Landed, decontaminated, the
ships would ultimately be refitted and recommissioned
into the Alliance force. I saw other Mil ships join this
passive group. I saw a Lothar squadron drop down and
turn toward the rim of the spatial tank, taking up Perimeter positions until it seemed that the tank was lightly
sprinkled with diamond beading on its periphery. I
watched as the main body of the fleet turned homeward,
catching and passing the convoy of cripples, pushing on
toward Lothar. Then I, too, turned my hopeful attention
to the screens, waiting for the time when the communication limit was reached and we might have a detailed
description of the victory from her triumphant commander.

Of the great navy that had set out to meet the invader,
only twelve were not returning, a statistic which brought
another wild burst of exultation. Of the twenty-three in-
vaders, once arrogant and feared, nineteen were carefully
shepherded toward exile. Never, never, I heard it shouted,
had so great a victory been achieved in the annals of
recorded history. And, to crown this feat with more glory,
fourteen of the fifteen Star-class ships had been taken.

Now we waited, as we had waited for particular moments so often these last violent days, for the screens to
reflect the images we wished most to see. So tensely was
the first ripple anticipated, a concerted gasp echoed in the
room when the picture was abruptly before us, clear and
unmuddied.

It was Maxil we saw; a Maxil as changed as only a boy
can be who has abruptly survived a brutal initiation to
manhood. His voice, harsh with fatigue and physical
strain, broke the communication silence. Harlan was
nowhere in sight.

"Men and women of Lothar, I bring you victory. I
bring home all but twelve of our valiant ships. I bring you
news of an offensive weapon against which the Mil have
been powerless. The day is not distant when we can reach
out and find the home of these vicious marauders and
destroy them forever."

But where is Harlan? I whispered to myself.

Maxil paused and licked his lips, glancing off to his right. Then he smiled and continued.

"I am not responsible for this victory. I doubt any of us would have returned today if it had not been for Harlan. He's done the impossible today. He has made the Mil fear *us*. All Lothar must recognize their debt to him."

A cheer, as loud and sincere as it was spontaneous, sprang from the throats of the watchers as Maxil pulled a reluctant Regent to his side.

I could see how tired Harlan was, his shoulders slumped down even as he tried to hold himself erect. His shipsuit was mottled with a white dust, and it was torn at the sleeve. I saw no sign of damage in the control room, but other officers coming and going in the background wore torn or burned tunics as well as bandages. But Harlan was all right.

"I don't see Sir Stannall, my lord," Harlan commented.

Maxil peered out at the crowd and frowned. Jokan stepped forward and formally bowing to the young Warlord, explained the circumstances. Jokan continued to advise what had been done, Maxil and Harlan both questioning and advising further steps.

I don't recall much of what they said. I was content to look at Harlan and know he was safe and coming back. The multiple perils that threatened were dispersing: Gorlot's perfidy, the Mil, and now Stannall was sick. He couldn't resume his deadly questioning so I needn't fear his drive for revenge on Monsorlit. I only had the physician to deal with and Harlan would never let him overwhelm me. A weary exultation filled my tired body. Even the ghastly announcement that Gorlot, chained to the Rock for the Mil as their traditional first victim should they arrive, had been hacked to pieces alive by hysterical Lotharians did not touch me.

The reprieve from fatigue granted by Monsorlit's pellets expired all at once. I was weary to the very marrow of my bones. I turned from the screen that no longer held Harlan. Ferrill had fallen forward across the table, unnoticed by anyone. I touched his hand, fearfully. It was damp with perspiration, but the slow pulse was steady in his wrist. I sat looking at him for a little while, I think. Then it occurred to me that I should get someone to take him to bed, but I didn't have the energy to open my mouth to call. So I put my head down on the table, too.

CHAPTER SEVENTEEN

I DID NOT SEE THE victorious return of Lothar's flagship. Nor did I see the triumphant parade of Maxil and Harlan back to the palace. I did not see Maxil publicly acclaim Fara as his lady from the balcony of his apartment. My presence there might not have been appreciated by the public. I did not see Harlan and that I cared about. I should have given him a proper soldier's welcome. But I was dead to the world and so were Ferrill and Jokan. Monsorlit had threatened the servants with dire vengeance if they did attempt to wake us.

What finally awoke me was, as usual, hunger. What roused me was the unfamiliarity of my surroundings. The dim room appeared to be all wrong to my sleep-dulled faculties. For one thing, the balcony was to the left of my bed instead of to the right. For another, the window hangings were a deep crimson. The furnishings, the heavy chairs and chests, were the wrong shapes and there were enormous shields on the walls, their metallic designs picking up what light there was. A gentle snuffling set me bolt upright in the bed reaching for the light panel in the headboard. The soft glow fell on Harlan's sleeping face and I immediately waved it off. Exhaustion was etched deeply on his face. He had fallen on to bed, still dressed in the torn, creased shipsuit. His right arm dangled in the air above the floor and his right leg was off the bed entirely.

I hoped he had seen me before he fell into unconsciousness, that he at least knew I was here, where I belonged. It worried me that he might have felt I slighted him by not being a part of the welcome he was certainly due.

My eyes accustomed themselves to the dim room and I looked down at the tired warrior. How often I'd looked at his sleeping figure in the asylum, wondering what he was really like. I certainly had had more of his unconscious company than was necessary. There was so much I wanted to know about this man. One day, we would both have to make time to be together when both of us were awake, in the same room, at the same time.

My hunger could no longer be denied. I eased out of the bed, a needless caution with Harlan in the depths of the deepest sleep of exhaustion. He'd wake soon, uncomfortable in that awkward position, I decided. Placing his arm across his chest, I turned him so that all of his body was supported by the bed. I removed his boots, loosened his shipsuit and covered him.

I found the bathroom and discovered that my clothes had again followed me while I played suite hopscotch around the palace wing. I dressed quickly and went out into the next room.

This was a study, deserted but apparently well-used by Harlan to judge from the clutter of slates and film cans. As I reached the door in the far wall I heard the subdued mutter of voices.

"*I* received *my* orders from Harlan himself," an irate man in patrol uniform was saying to Jokan who had placed himself between the patroller and the door to the study.

"Harlan is *not* to be wakened," Jokan was saying firmly. The Patrolman saw me at the door and tried to edge around Jokan.

"Lady Sara, is the Regent awake?"

Jokan gave me a quick high-sign.

"No, sir, he is not! Nor could anything wake him. He is completely dead to the world and will be for some hours more, I'm sure," I said with a firmness that matched Jokan's.

"My orders were definite," the poor officer kept insisting desperately.

"I'm sorry, sir," I replied unapologetically. "But I cannot feel that there is any matter so urgent that it needs the attention of an exhausted man. Surely Jokan here, who is alternate Regent . . ."

The officer was adamant.

"No, my orders are for the Regent only."

"Well, you may certainly join us while we wait," Jokan suggested amiably. He took the officer by the arm and led him, resisting all the way, to the far side of the living room.

The two Councilmen and Jessl at the breakfast table rose as I approached. Linnana came bustling in from the pantry, wreathed with smiles and looking very well pleased with herself. She greeted me effusively and set my hot cup down in front of me.

"Hungry, Sara?" Jokan said with good-natured raillery.

"I still have several weeks of eating to make up," I replied tartly. "And I don't think I ever will."

"You missed all the excitement," one of the Councilmen said.

"A matter of opinion. The Vaults were exciting enough for one lifetime. I was never so tired in my life as I was last night," I declared.

Jokan exchanged amused glances with Jessl and Linnana giggled.

"You mean the day before yesterday," Jokan corrected me.

I stared at him, suspecting him of teasing. But everyone else was grinning at my disbelief.

"I was very tired," I repeated emphatically, refusing to be annoyed. "No wonder I'm so hungry. I've missed eight meals," I exclaimed suddenly.

Even the thwarted officer joined in the laughter.

"Don't worry. There are films to be seen."

"Then when," I asked with concern, "did Harlan get to bed?"

"Approximately six hours ago," Jokan said with a nasty look at the officer who squirmed on his seat uncomfortably. "He and Maxil got in about sixteen hours ago. The rest of the fleet keeps trailing in." He continued, nodding toward the crisscrossing of plume trails in the sky. "Harlan and Maxil were touched, patted, kissed by everyone in Lothar. I'm surprised the noise didn't wake you."

"Barbarous not to let him rest sooner. He must have

been weaving for lack of sleep," I exclaimed, outraged. "Why wasn't I wakened? I'd've . . ."

"We had our orders about you, too," Jokan laughed, his eyes dancing wickedly. "From Monsorlit."

I hastily covered the initial start his name gave me.

"Did you explain to Harlan why I . . ."

"Several times," Jokan assured me dryly. Jessl snorted his disgust. "He insisted on seeing both you and Ferrill. But he woke *me* up!" Jokan looked so sour I couldn't help laughing.

If I hadn't been so shocked by the fatigue in Harlan's face, I would have taken pity on the officer during the long hours that followed. He sat stolidly, watching the door and waiting. Not all Jokan's cajoling could budge him from his post or elicit the message he brought. We finally gave up.

About noontime, Maxil came in. He looked tired still, the shadows of his grueling experience lurking in his eyes but his step was resilient. He gave me a glad smile and took both my hands in his, squeezing them affectionately.

"We missed you. Harlan was fit to be tied," he said. "Made everyone wait while he checked with Monsorlit about you and Ferrill. Oh, and Stannall, too. Did you know about Fara and me?"

"That's all I heard about the first day in the Vaults," I said.

"Yes, I guess so," and Maxil, although he looked sheepish, did not blush. We had strolled over to the balcony, apart from the others.

"That Harlan's got real nerve," Maxil said quietly, slamming one fist in the palm of the other hand, imitating his hero. "You know, he waited and waited to throw on the resonators until we were so close to Lothar even seasoned spacers were green. And then, those resonators," and Maxil gave his head a respectful shake, drawing his breath in with a hiss. "You don't expect to be able to hear again. And it's not exactly a noise . . . it's a whine inside your skull that jars your teeth loose." His eyes briefly reflected the pain he had endured. "And when it stops . . .

it's like there'll never be any noise again in the world." He shook his head and added with a smile. "But he did it and we'll never have to fear the Mil ever again.

"You know, it's funny how things work out. Gorlot had those installations made on every ship we had in service. But, if he *hadn't* used them during the Tane business, we'd've got every single ship without a casualty of our own. Every time I remember I ate in the same room, breathed the same air as that . . . that unrestored unprintable did, I get sick. *Sick.*"

His choice of adjective had the same effect on me. I tried to fasten my thoughts on Maxil's explosive maturation. For he was no longer an adolescent. He had found himself in his baptism under fire. I think Ferrill was wrong when he felt that Jokan was the only one who showed the true Harlan strain.

"Have you seen Ferrill yet?"

"Oh, yes," Maxil assured me solemnly. "I've just come from there." Then he grinned at me broadly, a touch of the boy showing. "He said you were marvelous, Sara. When Stannall collapsed, when everyone was running around cave-hunting, you were so calm and controlled."

"Ferrill gave you a description of himself, not me," I laughed, nevertheless flattered. I wondered if Ferrill might be indulging in some subtle sarcasm. "He's recovered? He had no business working under such pressure for so long. I was very worried about him."

"No. He's . . . he's . . . Ferrill," Maxil ended lamely as suitable comparison failed him. "Say, what's Talleth doing here? He looks as if he's sitting on . . . something hard."

I tried not to giggle as Maxil changed phrases midsentence.

"He keeps telling us, every hour on the hour, that he has orders to report immediately to the Regent. He has some burning message he'll only give to Harlan. And we won't wake Harlan up."

"You shouldn't," Maxil agreed. "He sent me off not long after we managed to get through the crowds to the palace. I was asleep before I could kiss Fara."

He beckoned to Talleth who, after a quick glance at the study door, rose obediently and came over.

"What's the problem, Talleth?"

"I was given a commission by Regent Harlan," Talleth began patiently. "When I had accomplished it, I was to report directly to Lord Harlan. I've been waiting for five hours and ten minutes, sir."

"When did Harlan get to bed, Sara?"

"Approximately ten hours and ten minutes ago," I replied keeping my face straight.

"He'll be up soon, then," Maxil said easily and, nodding to Talleth, indicated he could resume his post.

I thought Maxil was just saying that, so no one, except Talleth, was more surprised than I when fifteen minutes later, Harlan himself opened the door to the study.

He swept the occupants of the room with a swift glance, smiled briefly at me but held up his hand as I started to come to him. Instead, to my chagrin, he beckoned Talleth into the study and closed the door.

"Close your mouth," Maxil suggested in an aside. "I guess he really did want to see Talleth after all."

Ignoring the slight as best I could, I hastily ordered Linnana to get warm food. Maybe Harlan was annoyed with me because I had been asleep when I should have been there to greet him. Linnana interrupted my nattering by asking what she should order for the Regent's breakfast. I realized I didn't even know what Harlan liked to eat. Certainly the asylum fare was no criterion.

"Plenty of meat, he'll be hungry," I temporized.

Whatever business Talleth had with Harlan, it was brief. The officer exited, saluted Maxil respectfully, glanced at me with a worried frown and left the apartment. Harlan did not appear.

Hot food came up from the kitchens and no sign of him. It was too much for me. Trying to appear casual, I went through the empty study to the bedroom. Just as I entered, he emerged from the bathroom, buckling on a uniform overtunic.

"Harlan, are you . . . displeased with me?"

He gave a little laugh and came over to embrace me,

his face slightly damp, smelling cleanly of soap and fresh linens. "No, you please me tremendously, except when you keep my officers waiting."

He released me quickly, for I was left standing, kissless. He strode over to the big chest to one side of the study door and rummaged through a top drawer, stuffing several objects in his belt pouch.

"I'm hungry," he announced, his smile making his words an intimate reminder.

"It's hot from the kitchen," I assured him as he ushered me out to the living room.

Although he had reassured me verbally that he was not displeased with me, it seemed he was not at ease somehow. As if he held himself from me purposefully. As if there were something between us, separating us. With Jokan and Jessl, Maxil and the two Councilmen as well as the servants, it was impossible for me to pursue the subject of my unrest or set it at ease.

Harlan pulled me to the chair beside him at the table but, as he talked to the others, cheerful, rested, he never once glanced at me. He gave Jessl some instructions about putting their fastest Star-class ship in readiness for a long trip. He all but pushed Jessl through the door to get him started on the assignment.

Once Jessl had left, he turned earnestly to the two Councilmen.

"I appreciate your waiting on me like this, although I had expected to be awake long before this hour," and he shot a humorously accusing glance at me.

"I did it," Jokan interposed, taking full blame.

"I'd've preferred you returned the compliment I paid you when I got in," Harlan said so caustically Jokan looked surprised. "However, Talleth brought me word I hoped against hope he would have. For the first time, we have captured, *intact,* the Mil star maps, complete with primary notations and time symbols."

Jokan and the Councilmen exclaimed excitedly and leaned forward eagerly as Harlan continued.

"I don't say we now have the route to their homeworld. It is impossible to tell whether they were on an outward or inward orbit. The holds were barely half full," he added, dropping his voice and swallowing. I guess I wasn't the only one who looked ill. There was no longer any question in my mind what those holds carried.

"However, I believe it is important for us to retrace their route, starting from the notation that is the Tane group and working backward."

The sound of a planecar right on top of us made me glance up startled. Talleth was at the controls. He secured the craft to the landing balcony and stood waiting.

"I have a quick trip to make, gentlemen, after which I will explain myself in greater detail. If you will excuse me," and Harlan rose.

"You have to go right away?" I murmured, deeply disappointed. I was positive now there was something separating us.

"Will you come with me, Sara?" Harlan asked. There was a quality, a pleading in his voice, that I had never heard before.

"Certainly."

The fact that he wanted my company, coupled with his unsettling look, was not altogether reassuring. But, perhaps during the flight I would have time to get to the bottom of the problem.

This aim was soon thwarted completely when I realized that this plane, fast as it was, was also small. Talleth, stolidly piloting, was no farther away from me than my outstretched arm. This was scarcely the time or place for an important private discussion.

The trouble with public life, I thought bitterly, is that it *is* so damned public. If I had to put up with six years of this while Maxil grew to his majority, I would be a frustrated woman.

Harlan's unaccountable nervousness was obvious in many ways as the trip progressed. He kept up a superficially agreeable conversation, inquiring about the events after the attack, the reactions of the most skeptical Councilmen once the resonators were proved effective.

"Where are we going?" I asked as casually as I could

when our forced conversational gambits were exhausted.

"To Nawland," Harlan said crisply.

"What's that?" I persisted.

I obviously should have known because Talleth jerked his head as if to look at me, but changed his mind and kept facing the instrument panel.

"The Space Research Station," Harlan answered in a tone that brooked no further questions.

But my own terrible worries were more than I could contain, even faced with his unresponsiveness.

"Is Monsorlit there?"

Harlan looked at me, startled. "Of course not. He has absolutely nothing to do with this."

I was too relieved that Monsorlit had not made good the threat he had made in the Vaults. The fleeting impression that Harlan considered Monsorlit a lesser evil than the installation at Nawland did not occur to me until later.

A taut silence settled in the little cabin. The set of Harlan's jaw and the feeling that he had again withdrawn from me were inhibiting to the point that all I felt free to do was stare out the window at the sea.

We were flying swiftly over a long tail of islands in shallow water. In the distance, a smudge across the horizon, loomed the purple shadow of a land mass. Above it, a lance against the darkening evening sky, I saw a rocket blast off. Several miles away was another airborne plane, heading toward our mutual goal.

The sight of a fishing boat, similar to the one Harlan and I had escaped in, sent a stab of pain through me. I blinked back the tears that came to my eyes at the memories that sail evoked. Sitting in silent sorrow, I waited passively for this journey to end.

Space Research Station conjures a picture of purposeful activity, launching pads, half-erected gantries, waiting spaceships. But Talleth circled round the island, away from just such a scene, coming in across a quiet cove to an almost deserted strip of slab rock and sand. Two enormous hulls, all their airlocks open like terrible wounds to the setting sun, rested untended on the strip. A smaller rocket was parked to one side of the giant ship Talleth hovered near. Both he and Harlan peered out their side of the plane, searching for something. I noticed that Talleth's face had a greenish tinge and he was sweating profusely.

Then I noticed there were huge tubes, several feet in diameter, plugging the entrances to three of the locks. A variety of equipment, tubing and wires, was carefully stacked against the curve of the huge ship's hull, half obscured by shadow.

"Number Three," Harlan muttered savagely.

Wordlessly Talleth guided the plane down the length of the ship to an open lock, tubeless, in which stood three tall Ertoi figures, one beckoning to us.

Talleth set the plane down, the sweat pouring off his face. It hadn't seemed that the plane required that much effort to fly and the temperature was mild.

"I must ask you to come, Sara," Harlan said in a terse, hard voice. Glancing at him, I was startled to see he, too, was sweating and constantly swallowing. He opened the plane door. An awful smell overwhelmed us and I coughed wildly to clear my lungs of the stench.

I heard Talleth groan, but Harlan had a hand under my elbow and was urging me out onto the sand.

"What's that stink?" I asked, covering my nose and mouth with a fold of my tunic.

Harlan didn't answer. His face showed great distress. Relentlessly he guided me quickly up the rampway to the open lock. The three Ertois moved quietly aside to let us enter.

"This way," one of them thrummed in an incredibly deep voice.

Harlan didn't answer and now I felt his hand trembling even as his fingers took a firmer grip on my elbow. Now, I was scared, too.

"We have put samples in the nearest chamber," our guide boomed hollowly, his voice echoing and echoing down the long dim corridor. "The others have been disintegrated."

The Ertoi stopped by an oddly shaped orifice and nodded his head gravely to Harlan.

Harlan looked ghastly, the sweat pouring down his face, his jaw muscles working furiously as he swallowed. He gave every indication of someone about to be violently ill and mastering the compulsion by sheer willpower.

The moment I stepped through that orifice a scream tore from me. Only because the Ertoi and Harlan were holding me fast did I stay on my feet. I knew why Harlan looked ill. I knew what that smell was. I knew where I was. I was on a Mil ship and I had been in such a room before. I had been in such a room and what I had seen there had sent my mind reeling into the deepest shock.

"They do not look like *you,* the Ertoi say," Harlan managed to say between his teeth. "I have to make you look."

He and the Ertoi half carried me to the long high frame where several sheeted mounds lay still. One of the other Ertoi very carefully pulled back the top of the sheets and the first face was visible to me.

I didn't want to look down. But I had to. With that dread fascination horrible accidents have for you. No matter how ghastly, you have to look and assure yourself it is just as bad or worse than you have already imagined. He was Chinese or at least some Oriental ... his race didn't matter beyond the fact that he had once lived on my planet. I was propelled to the next victim and this was infinitely worse. Because it was a blond girl with the fresh misty complexion of an Englishwoman. Her hair had been shorn off close to her scalp and her face was contorted in the horrible rictus of death. There was no skin on her neck, only raw red flesh, the muscles and neck tendons exposed. I gave the covering a twitch and saw, as I instinctively knew I should but nevertheless had to confirm, that all skin had been flayed from her body. Skin, golden skin, my new golden skin. I, too, had once been flayed and ... restored with golden skin. How much skin can a human lose and live? I stood swaying, my eyes unable to leave her face until I spun away to retch in deep terrible spasms.

I knew it was Harlan who picked me up and carried me out of that charnel place, I felt skin not scales under my hands as I struck out wildly, intent only on inflicting pain on him who had led me, all unwitting, back into horror. I must have acted like a madwoman, shrieking, flailing with arms and legs. Then the pressure around me and in me was relieved as I felt the tart freshness of uncontaminated air around me and the smell was gone from my nose and throat and lungs. I was conscious of the sound of surf, the unlimited sky above me and then a sharp prick in my arm.

A scaly hand thrust an aromatic under my nose, but it only caused my stomach to heave again.

A hand, gentle for all it was scaly and hard, held my head as I vomited, stroking my streaming wet hair back from my face.

As the convulsive dry retching subsided, I became aware that I was propped against the scaly leg of one of the Ertoi. Another Ertoi was shielding my face from the brilliant sunset, his saurian face kind and compassionate as he bathed my face and hands.

Beyond my line of vision, I could hear someone else being violently ill and the thrumming voice of the third Ertoi talking quietly.

I don't know how long it took before we recovered from the experience but it was already full dark when Harlan came over to where I lay, still propped against the patient Ertoi, too weak and spent to move.

"Are they people from your planet, Sara?" Harlan asked with sad weariness.

"Yes."

And I knew why he had subjected me to that horror. I knew, too, what incredible courage it must have taken him to accompany me, knowing what he would see, knowing what he must put me through, and unwilling, despite the cost to himself, to let me go to that little death alone.

"You may proceed with orders, Ssla," Harlan murmured.

One Ertoi saluted Harlan and then me and went back

o the ship. In a minute or so I heard the chirropp, chirropp of the planecar.

Harlan managed to get into the plane himself, but the two Ertoi had to lift me in. Harlan held me in his lap, my head against his chest, both of us too exhausted to move.

Talleth took off at top speed. He, too, had had more of that stretch of Nawland than he could endure.

Whatever injection had been given me, the lassitude it produced spread through my body. Although I feared for a sleep that might be punctuated with the nightmare of revived terrors, I felt myself slipping without volition into the black velvet well of unconsciousness.

The first thought that crossed my mind on wakening was that it wasn't hunger that roused me. It was a soft light, diffused on the wall above the bed. I turned my head to see Harlan, propped up, writing quietly but quickly on a thin metal slate. It was the slip of the stylus across the metal that had penetrated my sleep.

At my movement, Harlan turned, his expression anxious and hopeful, changing quickly to a hesitant smile as our eyes met.

"You were so still. So deeply asleep . . ." he said in a low voice.

"No, I'm all right," I assured him, giving his hand a reassuring pat. He caught my hand, squeezing so tightly I gave a little cry.

He put down his writing and turned on his side toward me, his eyes still concerned.

"They have a saying on Earth," I began, trying to lighten his mood, "the criminal always returns to the scene of the crime. Then the law catches him. In this case, it was the victim who returned."

Harlan groaned and dropped his head down to the bed, hiding his face from me.

"Frankly," I continued, around the tightness in my throat, "I think it did the victim good. By all rights, I should have had horrible nightmares and I didn't."

Harlan grabbed me by the shoulders, shaking me, his face twisted with emotion.

"How can you forgive me? How can you ever forget what I have done to you? Forcing you to face that unspeakable horror?"

"Harlan," I said, *"You* went with me. It must have been ten times worse for *you*."

He stared at me blankly, as if I had lost my mind.

"You're incredible. It must have been ten times worse for me?" he repeated, shaking his head in disbelief at my words. "For me? For ME!" He gave an explosive snort of laughter and then hugged me so fiercely I cried out. "I'll never understand you. Never. Never." And he began to laugh, rocking me back and forth in his arms, laughing, I realized, in sheer relief.

"Well, it wasn't very funny," I reminded him, nonplussed at his reaction.

"No, not funny at all," and Harlan continued to laugh, softer now, with silly tears coming to his eyes.

The strained look of worry had lifted from his face when he held me off a little to look at me. His eyes and mouth held traces of his laughter, but his look was intensely proud and possessive.

He brushed my hair back from my forehead tenderly and settled me against him, my head on his chest.

"I have several things to tell you, Sara," he began in a more normal voice. "One, I was honestly afraid you would wake mad or hating me. No, don't interrupt," and he placed a finger on my lips. "I never expected you to understand why I had to subject you to that ordeal. I said be quiet," and his voice was stern, more like himself. "I had only a short time to get you there for the identification. If you remember, I told Jokan and the two Councilmen that we had discovered undamaged star maps from which we could retrace the routes of the Mil. From certain procedures we know they follow," and he swallowed suddenly, "Ssla is of the opinion that their last touchdown was at the planet from which those people came." He held me tightly as I inadvertently began to tremble again.

I took several deep breaths and nodded at him to continue, to ignore my reactions.

"The Star-class I ordered Jessl to refit will carry Jokan

and Talleth to your own world with such help as we can give." He paused and then added in a low voice, "I was going to suggest that you return with them."

"You were going to," I pushed away from his chest so I could see his face.

"I don't want you to leave, but I felt, in view of what happened yesterday, I owed you the choice. There may be someone on your world you would prefer to be with."

I turned in his arms, looking him squarely in the face. His expression was grave but gave me no indication of his thoughts.

"Are you trying to get rid of me?" I asked, amazed at the hoarseness of my own voice. "I've made a pest of myself, I know. First I tag along on that escape. You could have got away much faster by yourself."

"But I don't sail."

"And you should have left me at Gartly's. That would have made much more sense."

"True. But you'd not have encountered Maxil and got into the palace."

"Where I caused Ferrill to collapse completely."

"Which meant Council automatically convened, exactly what I hoped to effect."

"But I angered Stannall so."

"And got yourself into an untenable position as Maxil's woman." I saw a flare of anger in his eyes.

"I got myself involved with everyone!" I said, sunk in miserable reflection.

"Causing Harlan to complicate his own life unnecessarily by claiming you before anyone else dared."

"I'll unclaim you any time you want," I said wildly in my dejection.

"Do you really think I'd let you?" Harlan laughed, half frowning, half smiling. "I haven't known a moment's peace since you half starved me in that asylum. For the sake of the clan mothers, *do* you love me, Sara?"

"Yes, of course. Isn't that obvious?" I gasped, astonished. "I've been madly in love with you since you propositioned me on the boat."

His face relaxed into such an expression of tenderness and entreaty I thought my heart would stop.

"Love me, Sara!" he commanded softly. His hungry mouth claimed mine in a giving and taking that was complete fulfillment for us both, a release from the uncertainties and terrors of the past few days and a promise of richness and peace to come.

CHAPTER EIGHTEEN

"I HATE TO WAKE YOU, SARA, but Jokan's pounding at the door," said Harlan's voice in my ear. I felt a feather kiss on my eyes. I stretched with delicious languor as Harlan continued, "and I want him in here where we can be private."

"Well," I prompted agreeably.

Harlan, standing at the side of the bed, looked down at me quizzically.

"You have nothing on, dear my lady, and while he *is* my brother . . ." and Harlan threw my robe in my face. "Put it on. He's got to keep his mind on what you're *saying*." Harlan laughed at the face I made at him.

I drew the robe on and accepted the hot drink Harlan handed me before he called Jokan in.

"You *want* me in here?" Jokan asked pointedly, glaring at me. I learned later that such intimacy was unusual in Lothar where men were extremely possessive of their ladies.

Harlan indicated Jokan should close the door. Shrugging, Jokan approached the bed and took the chair Harlan pointed to.

"Well?" Jokan asked helpfully, looking from one to the other of us.

"Ssla discovered that the latest Mil victims," Harlan began quietly, sitting down on the edge of the bed beside me, one arm loosely on my shoulders, "are people very similar to us. From certain indications," I noticed Jokan also swallowed rapidly, wiped his forehead nervously, "the last planet was not far away. I want you, with Talleth as captain, to take the Star-class command ship and retrace that route, establish relations with these people and give them whatever scientific and military experience we have to share. Provided," and Harlan held up his hand, "they will agree to joining forces with us to track the Mil to their lair and destroy them."

Jokan snorted, shaking his head at the orders his brother had given him.

"Just orbit in, in a ship no different from the ones raiding them, land in the midst of the poor barbarians with their spears or swords and say, look here, *I'm* friendly."

I was conscious of Harlan's hesitation.

"Use one of the smaller rockets," I suggested and Harlan's hand pressed my arm in approval. "You'll need it to get past the satellites and to take evasive action against the nuclear missiles that, I assure you, will be launched."

"To get past what?" Jokan asked, blinking in surprise.

"The planet in question has atomic energy, has landed robot ships on the moon and orbited its nearest space neighbors."

Jokan glanced, wide-eyed, at Harlan for confirmation. Then turned his incredulous blue eyes to stare at me.

"Oh, and we already have electrical power in quantities. So once you explain the Ertoi defense mechanisms, I'm sure they can be put in place very quickly. If someone hasn't worked out an even better defense already."

Jokan made an attempt to rise from his chair and then sat back, stunned.

"I came from that planet, Jokan."

A look of horror replaced the surprise in Jokan's face and he turned to his brother with an angry accusation. At first all I could think was he was revolted by the natural conclusion that I was a restoree.

"You took Sara *with* you to Nawland yesterday?" he rasped out, his eyes flashing.

Harlan nodded slowly.

"I had to identify the victims," I said hurriedly, taut with strain for his reaction.

"But you ... you're ... not ..." and Jokan stared at me fixedly.

"Yes," I said slowly, because Jokan's good opinion mattered. "I am a restoree."

"Sara!" Harlan snapped, anxiously.

"No," I countered, watching Jokan's face as he struggled with his emotional reactions. "I think Jokan should know. I don't like to deceive *him*."

Jokan continued to scrutinize me, not masking traces of revulsion because he had them subdued quickly. He looked at me with great interest and finally, rubbing his hands slowly up and down his thighs, he began to smile at me.

"While I went into deep shock," I continued hastily, "not from restoration, but from ... what I saw, I came out of it gradually. *That's* how I met Harlan. I must have been taken to Monsorlit's Mental Defectives Clinic sometime during the early part of the Tane wars when a Mil ship was disabled, either on Tane or in space. I guess Gorlot's people thought me a Tane colonist. At any rate, there I was. When I overheard Monsorlit and Gleto talking, I realized Harlan had been drugged. And, well," I ended lamely, "you know what started happening then."

Jokan expelled all the air from his lungs in a deep sigh. He began to relax, nodding his head slowly up and down.

"Well," he said briskly, slapping his thighs, "that explains a great many things, doesn't it?"

"It should," Harlan agreed, a faint smile on his lips. I could feel he was still tensely waiting for something.

"It's very reassuring to learn, however, that your people are *not* hiding in caves," Jokan remarked in a completely different tone of voice. He rose, drawing a slate out of his belt pouch, and sitting down on the bed beside me, asked if I could draw a map of my world.

The tension left Harlan's body and I realized he had been waiting, hoping that Jokan would do something of this order, proving that my restoration did not render me physically revolting in his eyes. That he had hoped Jokan, too, could put aside the conditioned reaction toward a restoree.

"I'll be glad when you bring back paper," I muttered, struggling awkwardly with a stylus.

"What's that?" Jokan asked, sharply inquisitive.

"It is made of wood pulp combined with rags, pressed flat and thin. It can be made quickly and cheaply and is much easier to write on."

"Wood pulp, rags?" Jokan repeated. "Doesn't seem very durable. I've been using this pocket slate for years. Can you use the same piece of . . . what did you call it . . . paper . . . for years?"

"Well, no," I demurred, "but you people are backward in a lot of other things."

Both Harlan and Jokan rose up in concerted protest.

"Just because you have space travel—which you inherited, you didn't develop it—don't go looking down your noses at my world. We had to start from scratch to get off our planet. There are plenty of things on Lothar where it'd be better if you started all over again with a clean slate." I stopped, bemused by my pun. "You see," I told Jokan archly, "we gave up slates a century ago."

"All right, all right," Harlan chuckled. "Draw."

I had the general outlines sketched in when a vagrant thought came back to me.

"You know, getting you on Earth is going to be a problem," I said with concern. "You're right in that you can't just touch down. Particularly not in a Mil-design ship. You see, we have a radar network that would spot you miles up and while I don't know what the Mil may have done to the internal politics of Earth, you're sure to meet a barrage of nuclear missiles. And a Star-class is just too big to miss."

"The rider ships are not Mil-designed," Jokan suggested.

"That doesn't mean they won't be shot at."

"What kind of communication systems does your planet have? They must have some if they are experimenting in space flight," Harlan put in.

"Telstar!" I cried with sudden inspiration. "Why you'd reach every country in the world!" Then I got deflated just as quickly. "No, I wouldn't even know how you could jam it or interpose your broadcast on it."

"What is it?" Jokan prompted hopefully.

I explained as best I could and Jokan beamed at me patronizingly.

"We may still be using slate, dear sister, but in space we are completely at home. It's a simple matter to locate this Telstar of yours on *our* equipment, well out of the range of your radar screens and defensive missiles. Interfere and use its transmission for our purposes. That's an excellent idea."

"Fine," I agreed tartly, "I grant you can do it. Then what?" I demanded acidly. "No one *there* speaks Lotharian."

I couldn't help laughing at the expression on their faces.

"Now, get me a tape recorder and I will introduce you. I speak enough of our languages to get across what I mean. The point is to get you *down* to Earth and let the linguists take over from there."

"Good," Harlan put in, his face echoing his prideful pleasure in possessing me. "Sara has a curious habit of supplying our need. Did you know she can sail boats?"

"I believe you've mentioned that, Harlan," Jokan remarked with dry testiness. It was my first indication, however, that Harlan had ever mentioned me to anyone. He had seemed so concerned I shouldn't arouse any attention at all.

"You can see why she's been so important," Harlan commented.

"Because she can sail?" Jokan retorted with an innocent look.

"I'm surprised," Harlan continued, ignoring his brother, "it hasn't come up in conversation so far this morning," and he regarded me suspiciously, "but I'm hungry. And I'm going to break my fast."

"Why didn't someone say breakfast was ready?" I exclaimed sitting straight up.

Jokan jumped to his feet. "We'll all work better after eating. Less snarling at each other." And he grinned boyishly at both his brother and me.

"Jo," and Harlan stopped his brother with a hand on his shoulder, "do I need to caution you about revealing Sara's . . ."

Jokan shook his head solemnly from side to side.

"She's just infernally lucky it was you," he commented. "But I'd suggest that you in your official capacity as Regent, redirect Stannall's campaign to put Monsorlit on the Rock as a collaborator. Sara could be implicated."

"Yes, the day the Mil invaded, Stannall was trying to get me to accuse Monsorlit," I added, and fear of the cold physician, never far from my consciousness, returned. If Jokan had also noted Stannall's preoccupation, I had not misinterpreted my danger.

Harlan put an arm around my waist comfortingly. "I also know Monsorlit and, despite everything I've heard, I don't think Sara has anything to worry about from him."

"Well, I'd rather find a deep cave I didn't need than not have one when I did," Jokan remarked pointedly and, turning on his heel, started for the main room.

Harlan gave me another reassuring hug before we joined him.

There were just the three of us at breakfast this morning. A very unusual occurrence in itself, for breakfast was the hour of the patronage seekers or intense political conferences. The intimacy we three shared was therefore an unusual and unexpected respite. Because of Linnana and Harlan's servant, Shagret, we couldn't talk about Jokan's mission. And, as soon as breakfast was over, the communicator lit up. Harlan was called to meet the Councilmen in charge of Jokan's mission, so he left for his offices in the administration wing to get the necessary clearances.

Jokan and I retired to the study with closed doors and I taped a message that he would, he assured me, be able to transmit over Telstar. I started to give him a brief summary of our world history and decided it was useless to predispose him. The menace of the raiding Mil might well have consolidated and changed everything. Instead I spent the morning giving him some basic English phrases and such terms as he might need to effect a safe landing. I suggested that Cape Kennedy or the new Dallas Space Center would be able to accommodate the huge Star-class ship. I showed him these centers on my rough map, sighing at such inadequate cartography.

It was as if a cork had been pulled out of me that had damned up my Earth past. I talked and talked while Jokan listened, directing me occasionally with questions about his own areas of interest. My work as a librarian in a huge advertising agency had forced me to acquaint myself with a broad index of references, so I had a thin understanding of many facets of industry and technology. But I was painfully lacking in the details he needed or wanted so that he groaned over the tantalizing snips and snatches I held out to him. I talked until I was hoarse. Then Jokan covered up his slates and announced he was going to see what progress Harlan was making in ramming through the expedition.

Jokan was able to leave two days later, a big coup for Harlan who had indeed rammed the clearance through any opposition in Council. He attributed his success to the fact that Lesatin, thoroughly shaken by the Tane disaster and the Mil penetration, was more than willing, as Acting First Councilman, to expand the Alliance. Stannall, Harlan remarked privately to me, would have delayed until he "had given the matter mature consideration."

"However," Harlan said with a grimace, "I did have to agree to take a committee of Councilmen to the Tanes to see firsthand what has happened there." He covered my hands with his, smiling ruefully. "I'd take you along if I could . . ."

"I'm all right. How long will you be gone?"

"Two, three days, depending on how much convincing they take. And one of them is Estoder."

"I remember him from the Regency debate," I said sourly.

"So do I," Harlan remarked in a thoughtful way.

So he left and the first day I occupied myself with the mechanics of getting my Council grant in order. The much bemedaled slate Stannall had given me the day of the Mil invasion turned out to have considerably more value to me personally than a mere official propitiation. Harlan had read it to me and explained that I had been given a lifetime income from three iron-producing shafts in Jurasse. Someday I would have to inspect these but in the meantime this income was a tidy sum.

"It's enough for you to be comfortably placed if you were still unclaimed," Harlan explained, then his eyes twinkled wickedly. "It also provides that, if you die while you are unclaimed, the income devolves to your issue until they reach their majority."

I glared at him. I had a lot to figure out about the complicated marital and extramarital and post-, pre-, and ante-marital mores of this world where women are expected to produce children and no one asks who is the father.

"However, you are very much claimed and I will provide for your issue, making certain it is all mine."

I held him off for he started to wrestle me and I didn't want to be diverted quite yet from this subject.

"Are you rich, Harlan?"

"Yes, I guess so," he said. "I have the family holdings, of course, as my mother is dead. There are the prerogatives and privileges of my position. I haven't used much of my income and neither has Jokan. I had intended," and he grinned one-sidedly at me, "to finance a private expedition. However, my lady Sara," and his smile broadened, "as usual, chose to come from a very interesting planet so Lothar is the outfitter."

"Then, with that settled, I'll go out tomorrow and spend it all on my back," I declared.

"I like your back the way it is right now," Harlan murmured and he started to make love. A thrifty man, Harlan.

At any rate, while Harlan was on his way to Tane, I took my slate to his estate agent. This gentleman, one Lorith, was very polite and helpful. I was extremely pleased with myself that I made no blunders in our interview over matters I should have understood. One thing, however, I decided I must get Harlan to do immediately on his return from Tane was to teach me how to write at least my own name. Lorith would start the proceedings to

ecure the grant, but there would be many things for my
ignature in a few days.

Consequently I was not in the least apprehensive the
ext morning when Lesatin asked me to attend an in-
ormal meeting in his chambers.

I had not expected, considering the wording of his
nvitation, to see the large committee room filled with
Councilmen, including four of the Elder Seven and a
voman and seven doctors, by their overdress. I was also
urprised to see Ferrill enter. He nodded to me and sat
eside me at one end of the large room.

Lesatin was scanning the faces of the assembled when
Monsorlit entered. I glanced, apprehensive for the first
ime, at Ferrill. He smiled noncommittally and I settled
ack, reassured. As far as I could tell, Monsorlit did not
o much as glance in my direction. The woman, however,
onstantly looked at me.

"We are met today to assess accusations made against
hysician Monsorlit," Lesatin began in a formal opening
of the session. "These charges include complicity with the
rchtraitor Gorlot in the genocide of the Tanes; furnishing
drugs capable of inhibiting and demoralizing certain
officials in our government and . . ." Lesatin glanced at his
ote slate, "illicit surgery."

I pulled at Ferrill's arm nervously. Illicit surgery meant
estoration. Monsorlit was unruffled by these charges and
Ferrill only patted my hand.

Lesatin first called various hospital officials and techni-
ians who had been in charge of the victims taken off
Tane. They testified that the early wounded to arrive at
he hospital were invariably in some stage of paralytic
cerolosis. Cerol, in unadulterated form, could produce
otal paralysis of the body and its functions, resulting in
death. Complete and immediate blood transfusions would
essen its deadly effects, but too often brain and nerve
centers were affected. Monsorlit had developed a series of
cold and hot baths as shock treatments, a radical new
approach in Lotharian medical practice, to rouse the sluggish, cerolized areas. Two physicians who testified did not
entirely approve of such a rigorous course of treatment

although they admitted Monsorlit's techniques effecte
partial cures that were considered miracles. Patients wei
able to do for themselves, perform simple duties an
relieve society of the burden of their care.

Yes, it had been Monsorlit's idea to place a hospita
ship so near the Tane planets for prompter care of th
injured. No, they could not say that any of the me
appeared to have been restored. Of course, at that time, n
one looked for such evidence because no one had realize
that the Mil were in any way involved. Yes, they ha
heard Monsorlit use the expression "repossessed" ofte
One surgeon had called him to account because of th
word's unfortunate similarity with the unpopular practic
of restoration. Monsorlit had replied that the men wei
actually repossessed, repossessed of their faculties disable
by cerol.

Had Monsorlit practiced any total restorations since th
edict against it? Yes, two operations had been performe
with official sanction on burn victims in a satellite yar
fire. What were the results? A reconstruction so perfect a
to defy detection.

I found myself unconsciously stroking one wrist an
hastily clasped my hands firmly together. Looking up,
was aware of Monsorlit's eyes on me. He had caught m
gesture and smiled slightly.

I knew then that he had merely bided his time. That
had been foolish to think myself immune. I wondered
he had planned this trial to coincide with Harlan's ab
sence. I hoped desperately that someone else beside myse
could incriminate him; that his own preference for lif
would keep him from disclosing my restoration.

Lesatin continued his investigation with further que
tions about the illegal restoration.

Was it possible that total restoration could be detected
Only by a check of cell coding within a month of restora
tion and, even so, there would still be room for doubt.

Lesatin asked for an explanation of cell coding. It wa
so long and technically detailed I paid no attention.

"I fail to understand its application to restoration,
Lesatin prompted patiently.

Before restorations had been ruled illegal twenty-five years ago, intensive research had tried to perfect ways in which a total body graft could be undetected. It had been felt that the unsightly scars at wrist, ankle and neckline contributed to the revulsion caused by restorees. A high fever was induced in the patient by a virus injection for the purpose of changing the cell coding of the body so that it would accept new skin from any donor. The new skin would bond properly, assimilating and overgrowing what original epidermis remained, leaving undetectable the restoration.

Well, that explained the golden tinge to my skin, I thought. I'd wondered how they'd accomplished that.

In cases of plastic surgery, this technique was often applied with detection-defying results.

I managed to keep my hand from my nose.

Lesatin continued doggedly. Was it possible for any of the so-called Tane wounded to have been restorees? Possible, but not probable, for the men admitted to the War Hospital had been unquestionably suffering from acute cerolosis. Most were now able to take care of themselves and were employed in routine jobs. By common definition, they could not be restorees, as it was well known that a restoree was incapable of any independent action.

Crewmen on the hospital ship that Monsorlit had sent out were questioned. They gave detailed descriptions of cases they had handled. They confirmed in every way the information already given.

Lesatin paused and then asked several men how long they had worked for Monsorlit. They had, without exception, been trained by the physician, had served him since their certification and were, admittedly and vehemently, loyal to him. Lesatin dismissed them, having made a point.

From Lesatin's questioning and bland manner there was no indication whether he was out to clear Monsorlit or convict him. But I knew clearly what I would do. I would speak out against Monsorlit. I would tell them he had perfected the drug that had been used on Harlan and the others. I would tell them all I knew and remove

Monsorlit from a position in which he could threaten and terrify me.

Lesatin issued an order I didn't overhear and the side door opened to admit a chained, shrunken, groveling Gleto, flanked by two strong guards.

Lesatin turned to Monsorlit with an apologetic gesture.

"This is one of your accusers, physician," he said. "Gleto has sworn that you developed the drug, cerol, into several compounds which were used to depress Harlan, Japer, Lamar, Sosit, to name only a few. That you were completely aware of the perfidy against the Tane race and knew that the supposed casualties you handled in your hospital were victims of the skirmishes with the Mil ships. That you have actually performed illegal restorations to cover evidences of Gorlot's treachery."

Lesatin smiled deprecatingly and he was joined by the four Elders who were plainly telling Monsorlit that the source of these accusations was very suspect.

"Gleto has also gone on to insist that your personal fortune has swelled to enormous proportions. That you have secretly continued your abominable research on human beings."

Monsorlit nodded calmly. It was well known that Gleto's personal fortune had also swelled to enormous proportions. The physician arose and presented a thick pile of slates to the first Councilman at the table.

"Sealed and documented records of all my personal financial affairs," he said. "I beg pardon for such a bulky package but my income is heavily involved with my experimental work at the Mental Clinic."

Lesatin acknowledged this and motioned the Councilmen to examine the slates.

"As to the secret and abominable research on humans," Monsorlit continued, addressing the Councillors, "my colleagues will tell you that some of my work is done in secret, behind closed doors and the results are in locked files. That is the only way to protect the privacy of our patients, some of whom are well placed in life, despite their inner uncertainties. Yes, the research we have been

conducting lately might once have been called abominable, but the results have been a return to health for many.
Very often a medicine tastes abominably, but that does
not mean its efficacy is affected."

He spoke so glibly, his explanations so pat, yet nothing
he had said sounded rehearsed or insincere.

"As to my developing cerol compounds, I could scarcely deny so well publicized a fact," and Monsorlit smiled
pleasantly. "My laboratories have been aware of its effectiveness ... if properly and abstemiously used ... in
restraining mental cases, in the stimulation of certain muscular centers, in ... ways too numerous to list. It is a
remarkably versatile base for a wide range of uses. It will
be some time before we reach the end of its potentiali-
ties.

"But, as the man who invented our slates cannot control what we, centuries later, write upon them, I cannot
control the uses to which the discoveries in our laboratories have been put," and with a shrug Monsorlit resumed
his seat.

Lesatin exchanged low comments with several of the
Councillors.

"Did you, physician, at any time suspect you were
being used by Gorlot to cover up his treachery against the
Tane?"

That to me was the silliest question yet. But Monsorlit
considered it gravely before answering.

"I am not a politician, gentlemen, but a serious scientist. It was my duty under Regent Gorlot to perform such
services as he required of me in my capacity as Head
Physician of the War Hospital. If I had any doubts as to
the authenticity of the afflictions, I had little time to
pursue them due to the extreme pressure of work and the
speed with which it is necessary to treat acute cerolosis."

"Does not acute cerolosis parallel the symptoms of restoration madness in so far as the mental processes of the
patient are concerned?" snapped Lesatin.

I gasped and so did others at the sting of the question.

But it reassured me that Lesatin must be after Monsorlit.

Monsorlit pondered this question calmly.

"Yes, it does," he said deliberately, still in thought "There is an absolute paralysis of mental centers, sluggish reactions, no independent action. But, as you gentlemen are aware, the shock treatments we have used have brought the patients back to as normal a pursuit of life as possible, considering the irreparable damage done by the cerol in some cases."

There was an unfinished quality to his statement that reached me if no one else.

"You are noted for your skill in restoration, Physician Monsorlit," Lesatin continued. Monsorlit accepted the implied compliment as his just due. "Are there other surgeons today capable of such technical perfection?"

"If you mean partial restorations due to common accidents, yes. My techniques, as published in the Medical Library, are effective for partial as well as complete restorations. I could name dozens of surgeons capable of performing undetectable restorations. Partial ones, of course."

"Could Physician Trenor perform undetectable restoration?"

Everyone waited for Monsorlit's reply and again I wondered if Lesatin were for or against Monsorlit.

"It is entirely possible although I have never observed the physician in question in the operating arena."

Had it been Trenor all along and not Monsorlit? Had I been mistaken? No, no, that wasn't possible. Something vital assured me of that.

"Thank you, physician." Lesatin consulted his slate. "May I call the Lady Sara?"

I stood up nervously.

"You were Lord Harlan's attendant during his . . . stay at the asylum, weren't you?"

I confirmed this.

"Monsorlit was Harlan's physician, I believe," and Lesatin looked first at Monsorlit, who confirmed this and then at me. "Did he attend Harlan at the sanitarium?"

"Yes."

Lesatin knew this, for he was referring to slates he must have made during the inquiry Stannall conducted.

"Did you ever have occasion to suspect Harlan was being mistreated? Drugged into insensibility, rather than helped to regain his sanity?"

"Yes, I did."

"What aroused your suspicions?"

"A conversation between Gleto and ... Monsorlit," I announced, looking accusingly at the physician who merely watched.

"Really?" Lesatin appeared sincerely surprised. "Can you remember this conversation?"

"Yes, I most certainly can. Gleto had called Monsorlit to examine Harlan because he was afraid Harlan would revive from the drug."

"The drug was named?"

"Yes. Cerol. Monsorlit said that there was no need to increase the dosage. He told Gleto to have a weekly absorption rate taken and that would give an indication when more would be needed. Gleto said he didn't have the personnel and Monsorlit offered to send him a repossessed technician who could perform the test on Harlan. Monsorlit also said that Gleto had better do the same for the nine men who were Trenor's patients." My story came out in a rush because I was afraid of being interrupted and because I wanted desperately to say it before I lost my nerve.

Lesatin turned with anxious concern to the Councilmen. They whispered agitatedly among themselves.

"Why didn't you bring this conversation to light in the earlier investigation?" I was asked.

"I never got the chance. The Mil came," I defended myself.

Monsorlit's voice asked for the right to question me and permission was given him.

"How did you obtain the position as Harlan's attendant?" he asked me pleasantly.

"I was placed there from the Mental Clinic."

"Oh. You'd been a patient there?"

Watching every muscle in his controlled face, I nodded.

"How long were you a patient at the Clinic?"

"I don't remember exactly."

"Accuracy to the minute is not required. A rough estimate is all that is necessary."

"Two months," I blurted out because that number came to my mind first. It was wrong. I could see that in the gleam in Monsorlit's eyes. He drew out another bundle of slates and passed them to Lesatin.

"The Councilmen will see the documented record indicates a stay of over five months."

He's covered up here, too. All I have to do is not get rattled. He can't beat me. I'm right and he's wrong. He's dangerous. They've got to believe *me*.

"Lady Jena," and Monsorlit turned to the other woman in the room, a gray-haired, gentle-faced lady, "was the ward nurse in Lady Sara's early days with us."

"I was indeed, poor thing."

"Describe her condition."

"Sir, she couldn't speak at all. She didn't seem to understand anything. They're like that sometimes, poor dears. Especially the civilians who came to us from Tane. But it took her longer to understand even the simplest things. Her early achievement tests are just too low to be possible. I have included them in the records."

Lesatin hemmed and cleared his throat, looking at me with an expression close to anger and resentment. I saw that I had been wrong. Lesatin really wanted to clear Monsorlit and here was my incriminating testimony to confuse the issues already settled in his mind.

"The Lady Sara seems quite able to make herself understood now," one of the Elders pointed out dryly.

"Notice, however," Monsorlit said smoothly, "that odd labial twist. Notice the aspiration of the hard consonants, as if there were difficulty in controlling the speech centers."

"A personal quirk?" asked my champion.

"Possibly," Monsorlit admitted, but there was no conviction in his voice. "Lady Sara," and he spaced his syllables oddly, "what is the capital of Ertoi?"

"I don't know," I replied quickly. "Do you?" and I directed my question to one of the Councilmen. He blinked at me for my insolence.

Monsorlit laughed. "They can be very shrewd."

"Sir," Lesatin began angrily, "your line of questioning is irrelevant and offensive. Lady Sara's contribution to Lothar is great and you must be careful of your aspersions."

"She isn't careful of hers," Monsorlit answered tolerantly. "They often aren't tactful. But she is very beautiful, isn't she?" he added kindly.

I held my breath. He couldn't be going to . . .

"She has only to smile," Monsorlit continued, "and be admired. Beautiful women know that intelligence is not required of them and conduct themselves accordingly. However, the fact remains that the Lady Sara was a patient in the Mental Defectives Clinic and she *fails* to remember how long. She does not know the capital of Ertoi and there isn't one. Here, Lady Sara, write me a few lines. Write your name. Even beautiful women who have attended our Mental Clinic can write."

Monsorlit thrust a slate and stylus at me.

"I protest this preposterous treatment," I cried.

"That's a good sentence to write, isn't it?"

The slate was put in my hands. I didn't know what to do. Lesatin and the others were waiting with increasing impatience. It was such a simple thing and I couldn't do it.

"I cannot write," I said finally.

"Of course not," Monsorlit said, turning to the Councillors. "Her records show that she was incapable of learning anything except the most routine duties. How to dress herself neatly, keep clean, act cooperatively. That's why she was in a mental-home attendant's position. She can learn anything by rote. *Anything*."

"You certainly cannot insist that Lady Sara has responded to rote lessons today?" my champion asked.

"Not entirely. I most gladly admit she has improved

tremendously since she left the Clinic. She shows more promise of complete recovery than those records indicate possible. She must be allowed every opportunity to grow toward complete mental health, to restore her lost knowledge. I suggest, Councilman Lesatin, that she be returned to my Clinic to complete a recovery so auspicious."

Someone must contradict this diabolical man. I turned anxiously toward Ferrill and saw to my horror that his seat was empty. How could he leave me? Now, when I needed a friend most? I burst into tears and tried to draw back from Monsorlit as he placed a proprietary arm around my shoulders and began to lead me from the room. I resisted, but the man was unbelievably strong. He led me out a side door into a small anteroom while, in the chamber behind, the Councilmen burst into angry questions and discussion.

"You should have come of your own accord. I did not wish so public a humiliation for you," Monsorlit chided.

"You *know* I'm no defective. Harlan will be back and you'll be sorry."

"Threats. Threats. Harlan can return when he wishes, but you will go back to the Clinic and stay until my treatments bring about a full recovery."

"No! I am recovered. I don't need more treatment."

"You do. One day I'll have a complete success with my technique of restoration," and his eyes were fixed at a point above my head, "mind and body. There will be no mental blocks such as you have in the memory synapses. It will be a complete cure."

I stared at him. He didn't know either. I had always assumed he did. He thought I was a Lotharian and just didn't remember. He really believed I had been a colonist on Tane when the first Mil attack came. He had collaborated with Gorlot so he could prove, to himself if to no one else, that restoration itself did not cause the mental deterioration.

"You're mad," I cried. "And you're wrong."

The door opened wider and Lesatin and several other Councilmen entered.

"The charges against you are dismissed, Monsorlit," he said gravely. "And you have our permission to take this ... girl with you. For all our sakes I hope you do effect a complete cure for her."

"It's a pity she had been so closely connected with the young Warlord. I wondered why Harlan tolerated her."

"Harlan has always liked a pretty face. Look at Maritha. And then, too, Harlan is probably grateful."

"No, no, no," I shouted at their pitiless faces. "That isn't it!"

Monsorlit took my arm in one steel-fingered hand.

"She's done remarkably well considering her early ineptitude," he said. "I can't imagine who could have turned her against me."

"No one," I shrieked at him, trying to twist free. "I'm not defective. I can't write Lotharian because I don't even come from this planet. I came from Earth, the place those corpses on the Star-class Mil ship came from, the planet Jokan has gone to find. I'm not from Lothar. I'm from Earth," I screamed desperately, for Monsorlit was fumbling in his belt pouch and I knew what he was seeking.

"What's this about Jokan's expedition?" "Another planet?" "Who's been babbling?" The Councilmen all asked at once.

"Delusions," Monsorlit reassured them, smiling at me as he got the needle out of his pouch.

"On the contrary," a new voice said from the hall doorway. Ferrill pushed through. "On the contrary, she is telling the truth. And here is a slate, written by Harlan before he left for the Battle of Tane. It is addressed to me. Lesatin, I suggest you read it to everyone. You see, in this corner is the date, hard and fast."

Monsorlit dropped my hand as if it burned him. Even he looked his incredulous surprise at Ferrill's news. I ran to the ex-Warlord, weeping with relief, clinging to him. He put an arm around me with awkward but very reassuring gentleness.

Lesatin mumbled the phrases Harlan had written and the others peered over his shoulder. When they had read, they stared at me in complete confusion.

"How did you get here?" Lesatin roused himself to ask.

"Evidently on a Mil ship," I said cautiously. "I . . . don't really know. I was in shock. I'm here. I'm me. I'm not mentally ill."

"But those tests we were shown? Jena is a very reliable person. A woman of her background and breeding would have no reason to fabricate lies," Lesatin stopped.

"The tests were undoubtedly accurate," Ferrill suggested sensibly. "I doubt any of you could understand her language so how could you expect her to understand ours . . . particularly after having been so nearly . . . skinned alive."

Monsorlit's eyes blazed as if I had suddenly changed into another person.

"How did she get here?" Lesatin repeated, dumbfounded.

"She was brought into my base hospital along with several other cases," Monsorlit interjected smoothly, but there was a curious look of triumph in his face. "I assumed at the time she was one of the colonists who had been attacked by the Tane. There was no reason to suppose otherwise at the time. We know that Gorlot had several brushes with loaded Mil ships. Some were disabled. Undoubtedly she was on one of them."

"In what condition was she brought to you?" demanded Lesatin with fierce urgency. I clutched at Ferrill for support.

"In a state of complete shock."

"No, no. Physically," demanded the Councilman.

Monsorlit looked at Lesatin with surprise, then back at me as if comparing two pictures in his mind. "Why, much the same as she is now," he replied unhurriedly. "Much the same."

"Could she have been restored?" my old champion demanded, bluntly.

Monsorlit pursed his lips. "How could she have been? She is as rational as any of us," and to my amazement he smiled at me.

"A few moments ago, you assured us she was mentally incompetent," Lesatin reminded him, eyes narrowing.

I could see that Lesatin was not entirely sure my comments were rote lessons.

"My remarks on her apparent defectiveness are still valid," Monsorlit pointed out. "She does not read or write Lotharian. She does not know simple facts our children do. She still talks with an odd accent. But she does not know how long she was at my clinic. She most assuredly had the violent nightmares such as were recorded. She most certainly was incapable of anything but the simplest, most routine tasks. She has been in deep shock and by some miracle has survived and regained complete mental control. *When* she gained it, I do not know." He stressed the conjunction deliberately. "Therefore I can clinically doubt her recollections of a conversation such as she reported here today."

He paused to see the effect of his words. I was about to contradict him, but Ferrill shook me quickly and silenced me with a glance.

"But, gentlemen," and his voice rose above the interruptions of the others, "she presents an incontrovertible proof that I have tried for years to have recognized. That it is the capture by the Mil, not the restoration, that produces deep shock. We have completely restored burn victims and they did not go into shock. It has been our own fears that kill us. She never heard of the Mil. She went into deep shock, true, but she has recovered. I believe that any Mil victim can recover, if properly treated. Restoration has nothing to do with it. Can you realize that?" he demanded triumphantly. "*There* is your proof."

I sagged wearily against Ferrill at the end of my strength.

"As you can see by that slate," Ferrill drawled, "Harlan, our beloved Regent, has entrusted the Lady Sara to my care. She needs it right now. You will excuse us," and he led me from that room.

I remember hearing Monsorlit's voice rising above the arguments of the others as the door closed. I had been forgotten and I was glad.

CHAPTER NINETEEN

FERRILL MARSHALED ME DOWN the halls and back to my apartment without stopping for anyone.

He called Linnana to bring a stiff drink and then propelled me to my bed. He propped me up, covering me with a shaggy blanket, took the drink from a startled Linnana and shooed her out of the room.

I gulped at the stimulant gratefully, disregarding the raw bite on my throat.

"Don't leave me, Ferrill," I whispered as he turned from the bed.

"My dear aunt, not even a surprise attack by the Mil could stir me from my post," he said with complete sincerity. He brought a chair to the bedside and settled himself comfortably.

"My curiosity is boundless and you won't get rid of me until I hear everything I want to know about your fascinating recent past. Really, Sara, I consider it immensely rude of you not to have relieved my tedium these past days with this exciting disclosure. A planet, full, I hope, of other enticing females? My, my! Jokan will have fun. I do hope he returns with another extraplanetary aunt. They're much more alluring than the homegrown variety."

His absurd raillery was more effective than any tenderly delivered conciliations. The drink diffused its heartening warmth and it was ridiculous to think events would not turn my way with Ferrill putting them into their proper perspective.

The door exploded inward and I cried out, trembling all over even after I saw it was only Jessl.

"Who's been knocking caves down?" Jessl demanded, glaring fiercely at me.

"Easy," snapped Ferrill, holding up a warning hand, his eyes flashing authoritatively. "If you've come storming in here, you know as much as you should."

"The Councilmen are in panic. I thought we were to leave Monsorlit alone. And I thought news of that new planet was to be strictly confidential. What on earth possessed you ..."

"Hold your tongue, Jessl," Ferrill ordered with such force in his tone that Jessl eyed the ex-Warlord in respectful silence. "Sit down." Jessl complied.

"Now," Ferrill continued more calmly. "Sara has had good cause to be frightened of Monsorlit. Harlan, in his infinite wisdom, chose to ignore it and none of us had the facts to understand her concern. During the Alert, Monsorlit threatened her that she must return to the Clinic," Jessl started to interrupt, staring at me suspiciously. Ferrill held up an imperious hand, his eyes flashing, his pose of bored bystander forgotten. "Don't interrupt *me!* That's better.

"Even if she weren't Harlan's lady, that establishment has little to recommend it to the healthy-minded. Consequently Sara found herself placed in an untenable position at the meeting. I had no chance to warn her what it was all about because I only found out by accident Lesatin had scheduled the hearing today. I was under the impression Harlan was to preside. You are, I believe, aware of the terrible strain Sara has been under," and Ferrill's face was stern. "I sympathize with her completely. I doubt I could have maintained such control were I in a similar position, struggling to survive on her planet."

"Then what Lesatin was saying ..." Jessl stared at me anew, "you *are* from another planet?"

I nodded.

"Then what ... they say about Monsorlit doing restorations," Jessl began in a hoarse voice, his attention riveted to my face.

"... is nonsense," Ferrill said in an airy voice not echoed by the tense expression on his face. "Her planet is so close to the Tanes that she hadn't so much as a mark on her. She was, understandably so, in deep shock. Monsorlit's team discovered her and assumed she was a Tane civilian casualty. She was processed along with others through the Clinic and ended, so fortuitously as far as Lothar is concerned, as Harlan's attendant."

Ferrill's easy explanation gradually reassured Jessl who began to untense and ceased looking as if he wished he were anywhere but in the same room with me.

"But, if she were never a mental defective, then her testimony about Monsorlit's complicity is valid," Jessl said.

Ferrill shook his head in exasperation. "It is useless and wasteful to implicate Monsorlit. No one, except Stannall or Gleto, really wants to indict him. He's done too much among the little people of our world. And just as much for the rich who might want a new face. He is too well established in people's sympathies. His entire hospital staff worships the ground he touches. No real evidence can be found against him. Except Sara's testimony. And because she cannot establish when she came out of shock, Monsorlit has cleverly convinced the session that her recollection of a conversation in her recovery period is probably faulty."

"But I can establish the moment I recovered," I contradicted. "It was the day you visited Harlan with Gorlot and four other men. We were all walking in the gardens and you said 'Harlan, to see you this way.' Gorlot told you you had to keep your mind clear for the evening's work and you told him he could control your decisions but not your heart."

"You were sane then and didn't speak out?" cried Ferrill stunned.

"That was the day everything cleared up. Before it had all been so confused. But I didn't know where I was or what I was doing so I just kept quiet."

"Continue to do so," Ferrill suggested with authority.

"But," and I had another horrible thought, "if the Councilmen now know I'm from another planet, won't they wonder about restoration?"

Ferrill shrugged this suggestion off.

"Why should they? Monsorlit has testified you weren't and he should know."

"Loyalty? Statesmanship—better to say I wasn't, even though I was, from top to toe, a restoree?" I said.

"I feel certain," said Ferrill firmly, "that the incident is closed. Council has something of great moment to concern itself with . . . preparations to attack the homeworld of the Mil itself."

Jessl rose slowly, nodding his agreement with Ferrill's pronouncement.

"My apologies, Lady Sara, but I was deeply concerned," he said. He bowed respectfully to Ferrill and left.

Ferrill waited till he heard the outer door close. Then he got to his feet, smiling broadly.

"Yes, my dear Aunt Sara, Council is going to be very busy. They'll leave you alone and Monsorlit alone."

"You're sure Monsorlit will leave me alone? That I won't have to go back to that ghastly Clinic of his to prove anything more to him?"

"Yes, Sara, I'm sure. You don't have to fear Monsorlit anymore," and Ferrill grinned with his secret knowledge. "Don't you realize why?"

"No."

"The only reason he wanted you back was he thought he had failed in a complete recovery. Now that he knows you have all your old memories, now that he has proved to himself that capture by the Mil does not, in itself, produce insanity unless the victim has been taught to expect it, he doesn't need you anymore. Your case is closed as far as he's concerned. So," and he shrugged his thin shoulders, "you have nothing to fear from Monsorlit."

I stared at Ferrill as the logic of his argument dispelled the last vestiges of my apprehension. He was quite right. Monsorlit had proved his point. I didn't have to worry about returning to the Clinic. Or about my restoration.

Ferrill had pulled the draperies back from the window. The Young Moon, the faster nearer satellite, was rising in the early afternoon sky, a ghostly globe on the green horizon.

"Ironic, isn't it, Sara?" he commented into the compan-

ionable silence that had fallen. "We've finally disperse
the last shadow of our fears of the invincibility of the Mi
We can stand free of any subconscious taint of sacrileg
after two thousand years at war with ourselves and our ol
gods. Our weapons can paralyze their strong armadas. Ou
science is conquering superstition and releasing the las
captives from the thrall of the Mil just when no Lotharia
will ever have to fear being captured. Our envoy speeds t
bring us a new ally."

He looked out over the city. I threw off the blanket an
joined him.

"One of my planet's great statesmen said, at a ver
crucial time in our history, that the only thing we need t
fear is fear itself."

Ferrill looked around, pointing a finger at me.

" 'The only thing we need to fear is fear itself.' I like th
sense of that. It is very sensible, you realize from you
own recent experience with fear." Then he laughed, mock
ingly. "Of course, it doesn't make allowances for coward
like myself."

"Ferrill," I said angrily, "don't give me that nonsens
about being a bad Warlord and you're glad Maxil's got i
now because . . ."

"But I am glad," Ferrill objected strenuously. "Some
thing I can't seem to convince you, Maxil, Harlan, every
one . . . except Jokan who understands completely . . ."
and he broke off. He snorted, annoyed he had risen to m;
baiting.

He laughed and, taking my hand, led me from th
balcony.

"It's an exciting era for both our planets
Sara, and I'm going to be a part of it . . . even a bystande
can enjoy that much. But right now," and his eyes dance
as he waggled his finger at me, "I'm afraid," he chuckled
"I'm afraid I'm hungry. Aren't you?"

I burst out laughing, dispelling the last shadows of m;
weeks of fearful doubts and uncertainties.

"Have you *ever* known me when I wasn't?"

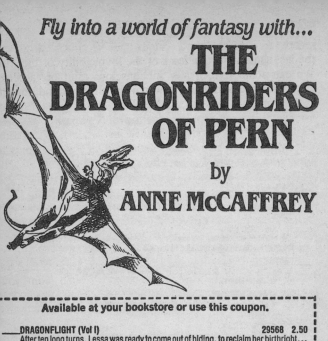

From DEL REY, the brightest science-fiction stars in the galaxy...

Life for the travelers on the Oregon Trail is hard, extremely hard.

As they traveled, they saw more and more graves as well as animal carcasses along the Trail. They also met turn-arounds nearly every day. They all told of the same dire future for the wagon train. . . .

"I'm hot," Willie said one day. "I need a drink, Martha. Please, get me a drink."

"I can't, Willie. We have to wait until we stop tonight."

"I can't wait. I'm thirsty now."

"So am I," Petey said. "My throat hurts."

"Why don't we pretend we're in a nice cool lake, swimming," Rachel said. "The water comes to our shoulders so we just lie down and start kicking our legs and stroking with our hands. Are you getting too cold, Willie?"

Willie laughed with delight at the game. "Not yet," he said. "I want to swim some more."

"All right," Rachel said. "Just be careful you don't go out to far. It might get deep."

Both boys got into the game until they forgot all about being hot and thirsty. . . .

The next afternoon the train stopped for some reason . . . . When Rachel went to see what was wrong, she found Tom Dorland talking softly to Tamara Richards. As he talked, Rachel realized a snake had bitten the woman.

VERALEE WIGGINS, author of many books, lives in Washington State with her husband. One of her novels, *Llama Lady*, was voted favorite contemporary inspirational romance by **Heartsong Presents** readers.

Books by VeraLee Wiggins

HEARTSONG PRESENTS

HP17—Llama Lady
HP33—Sweet Shelter

Don't miss out on any of our super romances. Write to us at the following address for information on our newest releases and club information.

Heartsong Presents Readers' Service
P.O. Box 719
Uhrichsville, OH 44683

Heartbreak Trail

VeraLee Wiggins

Heartsong Presents

For my most special husband in the world,
I appreciate your faithful, caring, gentle way.
Encouraging but not pushing; helping but not forcing,
And always being there, no matter what my need.
I love you more than words can say, Sweetie Pie.

ISBN 1-55748-476-7

HEARTBREAK TRAIL

one
March 1, 1859

"Papa," Rachel Butler wailed, her blue eyes flashing. As she shook her head in emphasis, tendrils of red hair fell from her neatly done braid and then curled around her plump face. "You don't seriously expect me to go all the way to Oregon! Out there, if the Indians don't get you, the wolves will. Besides I'm all registered to start Illinois College this fall. Please, Papa, take me home!"

"Ha!" Papa said. "You'll learn more in six months on the Oregon Trail than you would in four years of college."

Eighteen-year-old Rachel Butler was an only child who'd had the good life in her home in Quincy, Illinois. Nathan Butler, her father, had earned plenty of money for his family in his successful blacksmith shop.

"It'll take all summer to get to Oregon, Papa, if we don't die on the way. It's not fair to make me miss college because of your senile whim."

Tall, graying Nathan Butler, with his clear blue eyes, wide upturned lips, and straight-as-a-ramrod, trim, muscular body, looked anything but senile. Just having bought three covered wagons, he displayed undiluted excitement. No one in the world could be kinder than this man who'd always been her champion. But forcing her to go to Oregon in a covered wagon? How could he do that to her?

His soft eyes met her angry ones, unflinching. Then they crinkled into a smile. "We're going, Rachel, so why don't you decide to have fun? Don't you know we're making history? Now, go get your mother and let's find the cattle market. We need about fifteen yoke of oxen."

Rachel didn't rush going for her mama, but found her in a fancy dress shop. BOUTIQUE, ELEGANTE—INDEPENDENCE, MISSOURI, the sign above the door said. "Come on," Rachel said quietly, "Papa wants us to help him buy a million oxen."

"Why in the world would he expect us to do that?" Mama asked, hurrying to the shop's door where she almost collided with her husband who'd come seeking her.

His eyes expressed joy at seeing his two "lassies," as he called Alma and Rachel. "What would you be doing in such a fancy place just before starting on the Oregon Trail?"

Alma looked surprised. "Looking for things that won't be available in the wild country."

Nate laughed out loud. "Come on, woman, you won't need anything like those dresses where we're going. Let's go buy some oxen. Should we buy a saddle horse for each of us, too? I'd like to take some milk cows along and a few chickens. I'll bet no one has cows or chickens in Oregon yet."

In the next few days Nate bought the stock he'd suggested plus bolts of sheeting, linsey-woolsey, and denim for men's clothing. Then Nate asked to see the best walking shoes they had.

With disdain Rachel tried on the heavy high-top shoes. "I can't wear these things, Papa," she wailed. "I'd never let anyone see me in them."

"Are they comfortable?" Papa asked.

"Yes, but what good will that do if I don't wear them?"

He nodded with a small smile. "You'll wear them. We'll take three pairs," he said to the storekeeper. While Rachel fussed, he bought three pairs of shoes for Alma and three for himself.

Then Rachel didn't like the warm mittens he bought for each of them. "At least they don't have to be that ugly gray-brown color," she said. "Why can't they be bright?"

"I don't see any others," Papa said. "Wrap them up," he instructed the man.

Then they bought staples: flour, dried beans, dried apples, coffee, sides of bacon, sugar, salt, and baking powder. He bought some potatoes and fresh meat to use the first few days. He added a dutch oven for baking over the fire, some simple pots, and the cheapest of dishes and silverware.

Back at the wagons, Papa put in things he'd brought from home: books, a family Bible, a dictionary, an arithmetic text, a grammar book, some charts, maps, old letters, and diplomas of graduation.

He put some heavy blacksmithing tools into one of the wagons, the only cargo that that wagon carried. In another wagon he put a double-sized featherbed on the wagon floor for him and Alma, two comfortable chairs, plus some of the other things. Rachel's wagon contained one cozy chair, a single-sized featherbed, and the rest of the things they had to take.

"Everything's ready," Papa said, his voice ringing with excitement. "But I have one more thing to do."

Rachel watched with wonder as Papa tore the floorboards from one of the wagons, pushed in a big pouch of money, and replaced the boards. "There," he said, triumphantly, "no one would ever know there's a false floor in that wagon. Would you have known, Rachel?"

She shook her head. "Who cares about false floors anyway?"

He grinned. "You'd better care, lassie! I just put all our extra money in there. Plenty to buy everything we need to get started in Oregon. We'll be leaving in a couple of days, I hope. You know this train we're joining is all

Christian, don't you?"

Rachel shrugged. "I know, Papa. You've told me that before. But I couldn't care less. It isn't like joining a church. We'll just be traveling together for safety. We probably won't even meet the people in the other wagons."

Nate got to his feet and jumped down from the wagon. "You want me to give up on you, Rachel? Let you have a terrible time on this whole trip? Well, I just might do that." He walked over to a group of men standing around talking.

The next day, while Papa and the other men elected a train captain and decided on the rules for the wagon train, Rachel and Mama went on a last walk around town. They found a beautiful green ball gown that set off Rachel's red hair to perfection. "I must have it, Mama," Rachel said, spinning around. "You know I won't find one this perfect in Oregon. Their gowns will probably be made from flour sacks. I doubt they ever heard of satin."

Mama sighed. "I know, love, but Papa told me we can't buy anything more. He says we have to load lightly so the oxen can pull the wagons two thousand miles."

Rachel stomped her slippered foot, but took off the gown. Then the two had a long leisurely dinner at a nice restaurant and returned to the maze of wagons and people. Oxen and cows bawled, horses nickered, people yelled, and children cried. The barnyard smell didn't add much to Rachel's serenity, either.

Somehow Papa spotted them and hurried to them. "Everything's all set," he said. "We leave in the morning at sunrise."

He led them to their wagons and talked to them as he fastened a box containing five chickens to the back of Rachel's wagon. "Now we'll not only have milk, cream, and butter," he said, "but we'll have eggs to go with our bacon." He stopped talking and peered at his lassies. "Can't you be a little excited?" he asked.

Alma patted his forearm. "I'm getting excited, dear. It's going to be fun."

Rachel didn't answer.

Nate took them out for supper. "The last time we eat in a restaurant until we reach Oregon," he said as though bragging.

"How did the meeting go, dear?" Alma asked, putting a bite of dainty white bread into her mouth.

A huge smile spread across Nate's face. "Just fine," he said. "We elected Charles Ransom for captain. He'll be good. Hasn't been over the trail but he's read all he can get hold of. And we decided to use the Ten Commandments for our laws. Ransom said we'd be here the rest of our lives trying to get up as good a set of laws as the Creator gave us." He picked up his knife and fork, cut a bite from his steak, and put it into his mouth. "Oh, yes," he said after eating a few more bites, "Ransom had a bunch of copies of the Latter-day Saint's Emigrants' Guidebook, by Clayton. He said it's by far the best guidebook out so I bought one."

Rachel swallowed her bite of salad. "Who needs a guidebook, Papa? You said the trail is well marked."

Nate laid down his fork and nodded. "Yes. Well, the book doesn't just show where the trail is. It tells about things like camping spots where there's water, grass, and wood, how far we've come and still have to go. And lots of other things we'll need to know. Say, did you know some of the men are riding horses? No wagons?" He thought a second and smiled. "One's riding a cow. This oughtta be some journey, lassie."

When they returned to their wagons, Captain Ransom stood at the next wagon in line, inspecting its load. "You can't haul this much in one wagon," he told the man.

"Them's tried allays wear out their oxen and end up leavin' the stuff beside the road anyways. Better save your animals and lighten the load now."

He left that wagon and approached the Butler wagons. After looking them over, he turned to Nate. "You done good, Butler. You'll get there with as many belongings as anyone, anyways. Might even get there with all your oxen." He started to walk away, then turned back. "For identification, this here wagon train'll be called the Ransom Train."

Papa saluted. "Sounds good to me."

The captain started away but turned back again. "I notice you got a herd of cattle. Got anyone to drive them?"

"Nope. Never gave it a thought."

The grizzled man grinned. "Better give it a couple." He motioned with his thumb over his shoulder. "Some men over there are hopin' to work their way on the Trail." With that, he walked away.

As soon as the captain left, the man in the next wagon approached. "Wha'd the old windbag say to you? Thinks he's God already."

Papa looked at Rachel and winked. "He's purty good. Watchin' out for the animals and all. What you got in that wagon anyway? Seems to have set him off right good."

The man stuck his hand out to Papa. "Thurman Tate. Come'n see what you think."

Rachel followed Papa and Tate to the wagon. She peered inside at a heavy iron cookstove, a big chiffonier, and a heavy dresser. It looked heavenly to her. She'd wanted desperately to bring her beautiful piano but Papa wouldn't hear of it. "Want to kill the oxen?" he'd asked knowing how much Rachel loved animals. They'd ended up leaving the piano as well as her small dog and two cats with her grandmother.

"Ransom's right," Papa told Tate. "You'll kill your animals and lose the stuff, too. Better unload it here whilst you can get somethin' out of it."

"Never," Tate said. "My wife needs that stuff." He gazed at the oxen a moment. "Them's strong animals, ain't they?"

Nate looked the oxen over. "They're strong all right, but they have a two-thousand-mile pull ahead of them. Better give them every advantage you can." He took Rachel's arm and headed back toward his wagon. "Good luck, neighbor," he called but he got no response.

When Rachel climbed back into her wagon, she saw Papa a ways away, talking to a group of men. Probably hiring someone to herd the cattle to Oregon. She lay down on her soft featherbed, thinking. Is there any way at all we can stop Papa from this insane idea? If we really go, we'll probably all die before we get there.

The next morning, March fifteenth, men shouting, oxen bawling, and the smoke and the smell of bacon and coffee cooking awakened Rachel early. . .very early. She hustled into her clothes and climbed down from her wagon. Mama handed her a plate of pancakes, bacon, and eggs, smothered in syrup, and a cup of coffee, black and steaming.

In an hour the wagon masters had yoked the oxen and lined up the wagons in the order they'd travel; the next day, the wagon at the head of the line would move to the back. Rachel climbed into her chair in her wagon. Lots of people milled around on the ground preparing to walk. The atmosphere seemed gala, almost like a big celebration. Well, she'd see how all those silly people felt in a few days. Maybe by then they'd realize what they were getting into.

When the young man beside Rachel's oxen started them

moving, Rachel felt herself jarred, jerked, and jolted. The chickens on the back of her wagon must have felt the same way for they all started squawking.

Twenty-seven wagons, sixty people, a dozen horse riders, and one cow rider began the long ordeal.

Before an hour had passed, Rachel developed a headache as well as a painful back, bottom, and several other body parts. After a few hours, she wondered how she was going to stand such pain every day for six months. Papa had had some crazy ideas in his life, like the time he'd brought home a guitar for her knowing full well that the piano was her instrument. Well, after she got over the shock and took some guitar lessons, she found that she enjoyed it a lot. In fact, her guitar lay tucked among some bedding in her wagon.

But he'd really done it now. Mama must be in agony, too. Then she remembered Mama walking with some women from other wagons. Mama had invited her to walk with them but she wasn't about to walk. Riding was bad enough!

At nooning time Rachel sat on the tongue of the wagon while Mama cooked some potatoes and bacon for lunch. "Here you are," Mama said, cheerfully handing Rachel a heavily laden plate. "That should give you energy for the afternoon."

"Don't you start, too," Rachel growled, shoving in a bite of bacon-flavored potatoes. "Papa's ruined my life. If you switch to his side I won't have anyone left."

Mama tried to put her arm over Rachel's shoulders but Rachel shook it off. "I didn't realize there were sides," Mama said, "but we're on our way so we may as well enjoy it."

"I'm not having fun," Rachel said, "and I'm smart enough to know it. Why don't you go eat so I can at least enjoy my food?"

Rachel thought she'd never survive until evening but she did, hurting in every joint, bone, and muscle. When they stopped for the night, she gingerly climbed down and sat on the wagon's tongue again.

"Come help me with supper," Mama called. "Moving around will make your bones feel better."

Rachel refused. Sitting on the tongue she wondered how she got into this mess and how far they'd go before discovering how dumb it was. Then, hearing squawking, she remembered the poor chickens. Were they the only ones besides her who had sense enough to abhor this trip? She got some cracked corn and water for them and went back to the wagon's tongue feeling a little better.

"Come eat, Rachel," Papa called. "We have fresh butter for our hot biscuits. The churning can worked and Mama's fixed up a grand supper." Rachel still felt grumpy but ate a good meal.

The next morning, Mama awakened Rachel at dawn to eat breakfast. After she finished, she struggled back into the wagon. How could riding in a wagon possibly make a person so horribly sore? How could a bunch of people and animals possibly make so much noise? How could Papa possibly have forced her into this ridiculous pilgrimage?

As Rachel sat there feeling sorry for herself, she saw movement out of the corner of her eye and looked left. A dark-haired young girl ran up beside her wagon. A medium-sized black, gray, and white dog trotted beside her. "Come on down and walk," the girl called. "It's lots easier."

"Why should I walk?" Rachel snapped. "It wasn't my idea to come on this idiotic trek." Rachel watched the girl's shoulders slump and her run slow to a walk.

"Okay. Goodbye then," the girl called and ran ahead,

probably finding someone else to walk with her.

Rachel's conscience bothered her a little for being so rude to the girl who was just trying to be friendly. But why should she care? She couldn't walk with every inch of her hurting so badly, could she? Wondering if she could live through the rest of the afternoon, she changed her position for the five-hundredth time.

Just when she thought she'd scream in agony, she saw a man riding on the back of a small Jersey cow. He looked unstable hanging onto his belongings with one hand while trying to control the cow with the other. The cow looked as if it were about to fall down under the man's weight which was obviously too much for her.

When Rachel's wagon moved ahead of the cow, she realized the man and his cow were falling behind. She leaned forward to watch him when suddenly the cow dropped her rear end sharply. The man tumbled off backwards, his arms pinwheeling in the air. Rid of her burden, the cow took off running with the man ten feet behind her, screaming.

Rachel almost laughed until she remembered where she was and how unhappy she was. How could she even think of laughing out here on this horrendous trail? How could she endure the pain any longer?

Then the dark-haired girl appeared beside the wagon again. This time she had a small blond boy with her as well as the dog. "Come on," she called merrily, apparently having forgotten Rachel's rudeness of the morning. "It's fun to walk," she continued. "I'm walking all the way to Oregon." She giggled happily as if she were having lots of fun. She indicated her dog. "Josephine has to walk. Papa told me that before he let me bring her." She giggled again and shrugged. "So, I have to walk with her. Come on. Even my little brother will walk a lot. Maybe halfway. One reason we walk is that this trip is purely hard on the oxen. Every step we take makes it easier on them."

Rachel hated to give in. After all she couldn't think of a single reason why she should walk. She came on this trip under duress and should make it as easy on herself as possible. On the other hand, she liked animals better than people. So if it would make it easier on the oxen. . . besides, her behind was killing her.

After glancing at the dark-haired girl's cumbersome shoes, she reached into a box and pulled out a pair of her ugly new shoes and put them on. Then she climbed down as the oxen lumbered along with the wagon. No sooner had her feet touched ground than the shaggy dog, Josephine, ran and laid her big head against Rachel's side, stealing her heart. She patted the dog's dirty fur. "Nice girl," Rachel said softly. "Oh, Josephine, you're so sweet and you like me, don't you?"

The dog raised her head and looked deep into Rachel's eyes then gave her one lick on the hand. "I love your dog," Rachel heard herself say. Now why did she do that? Just because she'd climbed out of the wagon hadn't meant she wanted to be the little waif's friend.

"She likes you too," the dark-haired girl said. "She doesn't take to everyone like that. You must be a special person. I'm Martha Lawford. This is my little brother, Willie, and that's Josie you're petting."

Rachel stiffly told Martha her name.

"Oh, aren't you thrilled to get to go to Oregon?" Martha asked, excitement making her voice ring. "I'm just having so much fun already. I can tell it's going to be a good trip."

"Don't be too sure," Rachel grunted.

"But I'm not going to Oregon," Martha said, ignoring Rachel's negative comment. "We're stopping in Walla Walla Valley, in Washington Territory. That's about three hundred miles before Oregon City. Oh, Rachel, I can't wait to see it. My brother, Jackson, says it's God's Garden of Eden on earth."

"I've heard the same thing about the Willamette Valley," Rachel said. "As far as I'm concerned, Quincy, Illinois fits the description just fine."

As the girls continued talking and walking along, the man who'd been riding the cow tore past them still screeching at the cow that was no longer in sight. The girls looked at each other and burst into wild laughter. "I hope he never finds her," Rachel said. "I saw him riding her and she about collapsed under his weight. It was awful."

Rachel walked with Martha again the next day and found it much better than trying to ride. At the end of the second day of travel, the train camped on the Missouri-Kansas border. A festive air emanated from the camp.

"What's all the laughing about?" Rachel asked her mother.

"Everyone thinks we're leaving civilization," Mama said, wearing a happy smile. "I don't exactly know why as Kansas has been a U.S. territory for five years."

Nevertheless, after the meals were finished and cleaned up, someone brought out one of those new-fangled instruments called an accordion, and someone else a violin. Before long, lively music brought the plains to life. Soon, a square dance was being called and danced. Many people stood around, singing the mood-elevating songs.

"Why don't you take your guitar out there and play?" Papa asked.

Rachel wasn't about to enter into such foolishness. Why, they didn't even have a floor under their feet. Just grass and dust. What was there to sing about, anyway? She sat on her usual seat, the wagon's tongue, to wait for the crowd to settle down and to just think. One of the chickens had died that day while they traveled; the others looked bad.

Papa had said they should eat them. He might be right.

"I say, you look lonely," a young man said. "Gotta git up and work out the kinks. Wanna go out there with me?" Not waiting for an answer, he squatted on his heels near Rachel. "I'm Martha Lawford's brother, Jackson."

Why this? Didn't she have enough to put up with? The young man looked clean but his clothes had been mended in several places. Rachel jumped to her feet, elaborately dusting off her long skirt. "I'm afraid I'm tired, Mr. Lawford. If you'll excuse me, I think I'll try to get some sleep, if that's possible with all the racket around here." Then she hopped into the wagon, leaving Mr. Lawford sitting there, alone.

two

Rachel almost laughed at the man's look of surprise.

"Well, good night, Miss Butler," Jackson Lawford called into the wagon. "I'm sure we'll see each other again."

She heard him plodding across the ground. There. She'd been rude to both Martha and her brother. But what did it matter? They'd never see each other again after this summer. But already she couldn't help liking Martha a lot. Maybe she shouldn't have been rude to Jackson. She could have let him know, without being rude, that she wasn't interested. Oh well, what's done is done.

The next day, Mark Piling's wagon broke an axle. The slight, rough-sounding man with tobacco-stained teeth, was angry and used words that indicated to Rachel he'd forgotten at least temporarily that he was a Christian. No one seemed to know what to do, so Nate Butler hauled out his tools.

"Better call nooning," Nate told Charles Ransom, who was trying to calm the irate Mark Piling. "This'll take a while."

Several young men crowded around Nate, helping however they could. "Looks to me as how that axle was near broke before we started on this here trip," a tall thin man said.

They finished the job in a little less than five hours. "Thanks, fellows," Nate said. "That's the quickest I ever fixed an axle."

Mark Piling didn't thank anyone. "Sandy!" he yelled at his wife, "why aren't you in the wagon and ready to go? I notice you're always in the wagon, sick, when it's time to do a little work." He emphasized the word "sick" as though he doubted it. "Get that boy into the wagon right now. You're holding up the whole train."

The thin pale woman adjusted the baby in her arms and climbed into the wagon with no help from her husband. "Petey," she called weakly, "come on now. We're starting again." A moment later, a little boy showed up from somewhere and silently climbed into the wagon beside his mother and sister.

As the wagons began to move, Rachel, walking with Martha, Martha's little brother, Willie, and Josie, moved close to Martha. "I see everyone isn't all that pleasant on this wonderful 'Christian' wagon train."

Martha laughed quietly. "He prob'ly felt purely awful holding up the train. It's hard for some people to put others out." She grinned at Rachel. "He may truly be the nicest person we could ever meet."

Rachel grunted. Why couldn't Martha have agreed with her? Maybe she didn't like Martha so much after all. She might be a goody two shoes.

Later that afternoon Rachel noticed the man who'd been riding the cow coming toward them from the front of the train, his gray hair flying, mud and dust decorating his torn overalls. "Where's your cow?" she asked impishly.

"Ain't seen that critter for over twenty-four hours now," he ground out. "She'd better stay outa my sight, too. She might make a big barbecue for this here train."

Rachel couldn't stop pestering the man. "How come you're going the wrong way?" she asked. "It's far enough to Oregon without going backwards part way."

"I ain't dumb enough to walk all that way," he grumbled. "I'm goin' back to Independence afore I git any farther away." He jerked his head forward and, with a determined stride, started off toward the back of the train.

"I wish I could go with you," Rachel called after him

but he didn't miss a step. "Guess that means I don't get to go," she muttered.

The next day they came to a stream with a rickety bridge over it. As the first wagon, which happened to be Rachel's that day, approached the bridge, two tall Indians dressed in buckskins and moccasins came to meet the men driving the oxen. The Indians' long black hair hung in single braids down their backs.

"Twenty-five cents to cross," one of them said.

"Not me," Rachel said. "That bridge'll fall down if a wagon tries to cross."

Nate, driving the wagon behind her, came up to see what was going on. When told, he asked the Indians if the water was deep. They assured him it was. Nate pulled out seventy-five cents for his three wagons and they made it across without incident. Soon, the rest of the train crossed too, one wagon at a time.

All except Mark Piling. "I ain't gonna pay them savages nothing," he grumbled. "I'll just walk my critters across."

"Better not," Nate said. "They said the water's deep."

Piling didn't bother to answer but drove his animals to the water and began lashing them when they refused to go in. Finally, after losing several strips of hide to the whip, they gingerly stepped into the stream. When they faltered, he whipped them again until they walked into water up to their bellies. Suddenly, the wagon began to sink.

"Help!" Piling yelled.

Immediately, Nate Butler ran into the river. Upon reaching the oxen, he took hold of their yokes and pulled. "Come on," he said. "You can do it. Come on, boys, pull!" The valiant animals gave it all they had but the wagon didn't move. Several more men, in water to their waists, positioned themselves behind and beside the wagon. "This thing's goin' deeper in the mud every second," one yelled. "We'd best hurry." On the count of three, the men in the back shoved the wagon, those on the sides lifted, while four in the front pulled with the oxen. Their concerted effort unmired the wagon and it then rolled on with the men pushing and pulling with the oxen. In a little more than an hour, the wagon rolled up on the far bank, none the worse for wear. Several men dropped to the grass, gasping for breath.

"Well, I done it," Piling said. "Glad I din't help make them savages rich."

Rachel, who'd been watching the excitement from the bank with Martha, jerked to face her friend. "Did you hear what he said? And not a single man answered him. How come?"

Martha laughed a merry little tinkle. "Because this is a Christian train. Didn't you know?"

Rachel nodded her head. "I know. But what does that have to do with anything?"

"God doesn't want us all to go around saying mean things to each other. Instead, we have to forgive people like Mark Piling."

You might, Rachel thought. But I'm staying clear of that cowboy. I don't like him. I won't forgive him either.

As the wagon train continued, Martha and Rachel had only to stroll to keep up with the slow-moving oxen. Even Willie kept up with no trouble for several hours at a time. And Josie ran circles around everyone.

That day they made camp at noon so everyone could prepare for the Sabbath rest tomorrow. When Rachel fed and watered the chickens, she discovered another dead one. This trip was even harder on the chickens than on her. She felt bad to have them dying. After all they didn't ask to be stuck into a crate and hauled on the bumpy wagon. She dug a hole with Papa's shovel and buried the dead hen.

"Want to learn how to make cakes in the dutch oven?" Mama asked when Rachel returned. "It's a big pot you put over the fire, sort of like an oven. Then you put your cake pan or biscuits into it to bake."

Rachel shook her red head. "No. I don't even know how to make cakes in a real oven. And I don't care to." She walked off to find Martha. But her friend was busy doing her family's washing. Josie greeted Rachel as though she hadn't seen her for days. Rachel sat down in the grass and petted the dog for a while then wandered back to her own wagon.

When she got back, she found Mama doing their washing in cold water from the stream they camped beside. She noticed Mama looked a little tired but she didn't offer to help and Mama didn't ask.

Papa found her sitting on the ground and sat beside her. "The chickens don't look good," he said.

"No."

"They're going to die one at a time, you know."

"I know. Oh, Papa, why did we come on this foolish thing?"

"We came because it was the thing to do. Thousands have made this trip already, Rachel, and are starting new lives in Oregon. One day you'll be glad you came. But, back to the chickens. I think the kindest thing we can do is to prepare them for tomorrow's dinner."

Rachel reluctantly agreed, so that's what he did. At least the chickens were through suffering.

That night a good-looking young man went from wagon to wagon inviting everyone to an evening worship service. When the Butlers arrived, they sat on the grass along with everyone else.

Then the young man stood before the group. Rachel noticed first his broad shoulders and muscular body. Then she saw how tall he stood, well over six feet. His closely clipped dark beard and mustache complemented his longish dark hair and eyes to perfection. She'd never seen a more handsome man anywhere, not even in the big church in Quincy.

"Hello," he said loudly enough for everyone to hear. "I'm James Richards. I believe I'm the only minister on the train so I'll be taking the responsibility of keeping you close to the Lord on this hard trip. Let's begin with some singing."

With his strong baritone voice, he led them in a dozen happy hymns. Soon, nearly everyone joined and the group truly "made a joyful noise unto the Lord." Rachel enjoyed the singing and gladly joined in. Then the young minister preached a short sermon about serving the Lord no matter where you are. "Remember," the handsome young man said, "Daniel served God from the lion's den, and Shadrach, Meshach, and Abednego served from the fiery furnace. I have no doubt we'll think we're in one or the other before we finish this emigration, but we can serve the Lord no matter what's happening or where we are." He closed the meeting with another song and a prayer.

As Rachel walked away, she saw people flocking around Pastor Richards. She wouldn't have minded flocking a little herself. As she lay in her bed that night she decided the trip just possibly might not be so bad after all. Finally, she fell asleep.

Men shouting, oxen bawling, smoke from camp fires, and children crying jerked Rachel from a sound sleep at dawn the next morning. What was this, anyway? She'd expected to sleep late this morning. It was the Sabbath, wasn't it? She turned over on her feather mattress and hoped to fall asleep again, but it wasn't to be. Too many loud voices, too much clattering and banging around. Finally, she struggled from her warm nest, pulled on her clothes, and jumped to the ground to see what was happening.

"The good Lord'll be pleased if you rest with us," Captain Ransom told someone she didn't recognize. "You know the fourth commandment, don't you? Besides, the animals'll fare better with a rest day each week. This trip ain't gonna be easy. Think it over, brother. The good Lord knew what He was doin' when He made the rules for us to live by."

"Well, we're goin'," the strange man said.

"Didn't you know this was a Christian train when you joined?" Ransom asked.

"Shore, but no one said it was fanatical. Might's well save your breath, Captain. We're goin'."

After more noise and confusion, the camp became deathly still but Rachel couldn't fall back to sleep. She lay in bed nearly an hour before jumping up, wide awake.

Mama squatted beside the campfire, cooking breakfast. After greeting Rachel, she hurried to tell her news. "Six wagons left this morning. That leaves twenty-one. Think we'll make it all right?"

Rachel dropped to the ground beside Mama. "Of course. Who needs those people anyway? Who needs anyone?"

Mama smiled sweetly. "I'm sure we all need each other a lot, Rachel. What makes you so caustic this morning?"

"I don't care if everyone leaves, Mama. I really don't. But I do care that those idiots woke me at dawn on the one day I planned to sleep late. I was counting on catching up on my sleep. This is the day of rest isn't it?"

After breakfast the minister gathered his flock again and had a nice long hymn sing, then a prayer meeting in which everyone who wanted to, prayed. Then he preached a sermon about God, living within us wherever we are.

The man impressed Rachel but she disagreed with his message. "I give God credit for being smart," she told Martha as they walked back to their wagons. "And He'd never be dumb enough to come on a fool's trip like this."

Martha looked at her with twinkling eyes. "Don't you know the Lord says in His sacred Word that He'll live in us if we belong to Him. Don't you believe that, Rachel? If you do, you have to know He's with us everywhere, even out here in the prairie."

Whether God was here wasn't high on Rachel's list of things to worry about, so she didn't.

That day the entire wagon train put their food together for a giant potluck dinner. While they ate, Rachel got a chance to see most of the young people on the train. She felt delightfully surprised to learn there were many more young men than women, even though they looked and talked like yokels. If she'd gone to college she'd have had the cream of the crop from which to choose.

She discovered a skinny woman, named Tamara, was Pastor Richards's sister. Unimpressive, the mousey little thing looked like the pastor's shadow, letting him do most of her thinking for her. Rachel felt she and Tamara had nothing in common, but what did it matter? She'd probably never see her again on the Trail or later.

Soon after the meal, Pastor Richards came over to where the girls relaxed on the grass. He folded his long frame and gracefully dropped to the ground beside them.

"How's the weather down here?" he asked. "I've been noticing how comfortable you two looked all afternoon. Now I get to find out for myself."

"Oh, Pastor Richards," Rachel gushed, "I'm so glad you stopped to see us. I may never have heard a better speaker than you. And what a beautiful singing voice. How did we ever get so lucky as to have you on this wagon train?"

"Thank you," he said casually. Then he turned his attention to Martha. "How did you feel about the services?"

She thought a moment. "Well, I purely loved the singing. And I'd never get through a day if God didn't live in my heart. We need Him more out here in the wild than we ever did at home."

He nodded. "Right you are. And how are you enjoying the traveling? Haven't I seen you walking?"

"Oh, yes. My dog, Josie, and I are walking all the way. Now Rachel walks with us and it's lots more fun."

He talked to Martha a few more minutes then hopped to his feet. "So nice talking to you ladies," he said. "And I'm especially glad you're enjoying the journey so much. I'm sure we'll be meeting again. I must get back to my sister. She's shy so she depends on me a lot. Good bye."

As he walked off, Rachel felt herself getting angry. Very angry. She hopped to her feet too, and leaned over the still-sitting Martha.

"Singing is one of my very favorite things to do," she said in an exact imitation of Martha's bell-like voice. "Why didn't you just get up and hug him?" she yelled at her friend, her only friend. "How could you make those cow eyes at him when you knew I was interested in him? How could you do that to me, Martha? How could you?"

three

Martha's eyes opened wide. Then she got up. "I'm purely sorry, Rachel. I didn't know you were interested in Pastor Richards. And I didn't know I was making cow eyes at him." She stopped and giggled. "Truly, Rachel, I don't even know what cow eyes are, and besides I don't have the slightest interest in the man. Really, I don't."

Rachel felt chastened. If Martha had returned her anger she could have stayed mad. "Well," she muttered, "I'm not interested in him either. I just didn't want you making a fool of yourself."

Martha tinkled out another laugh. "Thanks, Rachel. I purely don't want to make a fool of myself."

A young girl approached them so they turned their attention to her. "Hello," she said hesitantly. "I'm Julia Tate. I bin watching you walking together havin' fun. I wondered if you'd mind if I walked with you sometime."

"We'd love to have you," Martha said instantly. "You just find us in the morning and join us."

Rachel didn't say anything but she wished Martha hadn't invited the kid. What made it worse, Martha sounded as if she had meant it. "How old are you?" Rachel asked.

"Sixteen," Julia replied. "How old are you?"

"I'm eighteen," Rachel said. "And Martha's seventeen. We've both finished high school." She hoped the girl would get the message that they were older. Then she remembered Thurman Tate. "You must be Thurman Tate's daughter," she said. "How are your oxen getting along with that horrendous load they have to pull?"

Julia looked perplexed. "All right, I guess. I don't pay

much attention to them. Were they sick or something?"

"No. Your father just refused the captain's orders to leave some heavy things in Independence."

Martha looked uncomfortable. "Well, you just come and walk with us tomorrow, Julia."

The girl left and Martha turned her attention back to Rachel. "We have to be kind to everyone," she said quietly. "Whatever we do for anyone, we're doing it for our Lord Jesus, you know."

Later that afternoon Rachel sat with her parents in their wagon, reading Scripture together, something she considered necessary but extremely boring.

"Hello," a young man's voice called from the outside. "Mr. Butler, could I talk to you a minute?"

Papa hopped to his feet, then down to the ground. Rachel sat quietly and listened.

"I just discovered we have an extra cow," the young man said, "and I don't know what to do with it."

A silence told Rachel that Papa didn't know either. All at once she remembered the man who'd been riding a cow. She jumped down beside her father. "I might know, Papa," she said. "Could we go see it?"

Sure enough, she recognized the cow as the one the man planned to ride to Oregon. "It belongs to the man who was going to Oregon on cowback," she said. "I saw him fall off her and try to catch her. I also saw him heading back to Independence on foot."

"Well," Nathan Butler said, "I guess it don't matter all that much, Ernie. Why don't you just leave her with ours for now."

The next morning, Martha and Rachel hadn't been walking an hour before Julia caught up with them. "What did you think of the preacher?" Rachel asked. "Handsome man, isn't he?"

Julia smiled shyly. "I guess. But he's too elegant for me. I like plain men better." She giggled. "But I like all men a lot."

A silly man-crazy girl! Rachel wondered how she'd put up with her all day every day. Maybe Julia would get tired and go back to her own wagon.

That afternoon a small dirty boy ran up to them from somewhere behind. "My name's Petey Piling," he said, puffing breathlessly. "Mama's sick and Papa told me to stay away so I won't bother them. Can I walk with you?"

Martha reached for his grimy hand. "Of course. You just walk right here between Willie and me. You two boys will have lots of fun together."

Ugh! Rachel bet Martha would welcome the most vile animal in the world. Why was she like that anyway? With the three big girls, the two little boys, and Josie, they had quite a group. Well, Rachel wasn't giving up her place to anyone.

The little boys started running around and yelling. Josie followed, yapping all the way. Martha acted as if she didn't hear a thing. "Can't you stop that racket?" Rachel asked.

Martha stopped talking and listened. Then she nodded. "They're all right," she said merrily. "We'll worry about them when someone starts crying."

Rachel felt like asking Martha if she planned to have any sanity left when they reached their destination, but she didn't. As she wished for some quiet, a small dirt clod hit her in the back. Spinning around she saw a look of surprise and fright on the two small faces.

"He didn't mean to hit you," Willie said. "Honest. Petey threw it at me and you just went and got in the way."

"It's all right," Martha said. "I'll brush her off. You all just go on and play." She moved to Rachel's side, brushed her off thoroughly, and finished with a few loving pats.

Only those pats kept Rachel's mouth shut and even then it wasn't easy. If she were in charge of those boys they'd be seen and not heard.

The next morning Rachel felt put out with the world in general and the extra people walking with them in particular. The boys had gotten cranky after a few miles but Martha didn't scold them. She started teaching them little songs. Afraid to say anything to Martha about the crowd she'd gathered around them, Rachel began on her favorite subject. "If God loved us even a little bit, we wouldn't be on this horrible journey."

"Not true, my friend," Martha said merrily. "God definitely wants us on this trip. There must be trappers or Indians we'll be telling about God's great love. For that matter there are people on this wagon train who don't know God. Like Mark Piling."

"If that's what we're going for I may start back right away," Rachel said. "I can think of a lot of boring things to do but that tops the list."

The boys and Julia walked with Martha and Rachel every day and no matter what they did Martha never became impatient.

One afternoon, Petey and Willie grew wilder than usual, tearing around and yelling at the top of their lungs; Josie was at their heels, adding her barking to the uproar. Just when Rachel thought she'd lose her sanity, Willie fell down. Petey fell over the top of him and into a mud puddle, thoroughly coating himself with the messy stuff.

"I can't walk in these clothes," the little boy wailed. He looked up into Martha's blue eyes. "Can I take them off, Martha? Can I?"

Martha winked at Rachel. "I'm not sure you should do that, Petey," she said. "But we'll take you to your wagon for fresh clothes. How will that be?"

Petey hung his head as though he'd rather just take off

the clothes. But he didn't say anything. Martha took his hand and also Willie's. "Come on, girls," she said to Rachel and Julia. "Let's find the Piling wagon."

Just about the time they found Petey's wagon the train stopped for the night. As they approached him, Mark Piling looked out of sorts. "Petey fell into a mud puddle," Martha said, laughing. "We brought him home for clean clothes."

Mr. Piling punched one of his oxen in the nose as he unyoked it; the ox grunted. Rachel stiffened and would have yelled at him if Martha hadn't poked her in the ribs. "I ain't got time to waste with you hoity-toity wimin," he snarled. "I'm too busy taking care of my sick wife. So go on back where you came from. How could I have clean clothes for anyone? What do you think I am, some kind of a nanny?" He turned toward the wagon. "Get down here and make a fire," he yelled into the wagon. "I'm hungry. I ain't laid in bed all day like you. Hurry up, woman!"

A moment later Sandy Piling's pale face appeared at the front of the wagon. She didn't speak to anyone but climbed down and looked around on the ground as though wondering what she could make a fire from.

"Want me to find you something to make a fire?" Martha asked.

"Get out of here before I take an whip to you!" Piling shouted, moving toward the girls. Petey, who'd been standing with Martha, flitted out of his father's way as if used to moving quickly. Rachel didn't need a second invitation. She took off like a deer, back to her own wagon.

"Wait for me," Julia yelled from somewhere behind but Rachel wasn't stopping for anyone. She put one foot in front of the other as fast as they'd go until she reached the Butler wagons where Mama squatted before a snapping campfire.

"What ever is after you, a bear?" Mama asked with a warm smile. Rachel waited until she caught her breath. "You said it just right, Mama," she finally got out. "Do you remember Mark Piling? He's the meanest man I've ever seen in my entire life. He really is. I hate him a whole lot."

"No you don't," Mama said. "You don't even know him. Tell me, what did he do to an animal?" She dumped some potatoes into bacon grease in a hot skillet. "This is the last of the potatoes until we find some to buy."

Just like Mama. She knew Rachel got upset when anyone abused an animal. But he did! "He did, Mama, but I got so mad at him later, I forgot all about it. He doubled up his fist and punched an ox in the face as hard as he could. But that's not all. He made his wife get out of the wagon to cook supper and she's real sick. Then he threatened to use a whip on us. You should have seen Petey get out of there. He's used to Mr. Piling hurting him, Mama."

Mama had stopped her meal preparations to listen to Rachel's wild story. "That's awful. What did you girls do to get him so riled up, love?" She picked up her bowl and started mixing the biscuits again.

"You know Petey walks with us all the time. Well, he fell into a puddle and wanted his clothes off really bad, so we took him to their wagon for clean clothes."

Mama had been shaping biscuits while Rachel talked. Now she put them into the dutch oven and laid it over the coals. "Sounds as if you didn't do a whole lot. The man's probably concerned about his wife. I've been hearing she's quite ill."

Strange way to show concern, Rachel thought. Well, she'd stay out of Mark Piling's way. Poor little Petey! He couldn't stay away all the time. But she could, and would.

"Would you take them some milk and cream?" Mama

asked as she poured some of each into bottles and capped them.

Rachel shook her head. "Mama! I just told you he threatened us with a whip. I'm not going over there for anything. Ever again."

"Can you stir the potatoes in a few minutes then?" Mama asked. Without waiting for an answer, she strode off toward the Piling wagon.

She returned a few minutes later, shaking her auburn head. "You're right, Rachel, he isn't very nice. But he accepted the milk and cream for his sick wife. Maybe it'll help her get well."

The next day, the train reached the Kansas River and camped at noon to prepare for the Sabbath.

Mama carried the tubs to the river and washed the family's clothes. She didn't ask Rachel to help and Rachel didn't offer. Down the river a ways, Martha worked over a scrub board; Rachel wandered over to talk to her. "How come you're doing your family's clothes?" she asked.

Martha looked up, her face red from exertion. "Oh, hello, Rachel," she said with a welcoming smile. "I'm doing the washing to help Mama. While I'm washing she's doing the baking for tomorrow. Haven't you heard that many hands make light work?"

Rachel thought about that as she wandered back to where Mama worked. When Mama looked up, her face was red from the hard work. Rachel felt a strong love tug at her heart. "Why don't you let me do that?" she asked. "You go back to camp and start the baking."

Mama looked relieved and, thanking Rachel, headed back to the wagons.

When Rachel finished an hour later, and had the clothes all hanging on the small bushes bordering the river, she ambled over to see why Martha wasn't finished yet.

"Well," Martha said. "I did finish our wash, but I'm doing the Pilings' right now."

Indignation turned Rachel's face red. "How could you be so dumb, Martha? Mr. Piling doesn't deserve to have one piece of his washing done for him."

Martha nodded, picked a little sock from the water, and scrubbed it on the board. "I know," Martha agreed. "But I'm not doing it for Mr. Piling. I'm doing it for Mrs. Piling and she purely needs all the help she can get."

On March twenty-seventh, the Sabbath, Pastor Richards preached and the women put another potluck meal together. Julia joined Martha and Rachel for the meal. When the girls had nearly finished their plates, two young men came and squatted near them in the grass. "Good afternoon," the tall skinny one said. "I'm Andy Shackleford. I hope you girls are enjoying the Sabbath rest."

"Oh, we surely are," Martha said. "And the good food. I believe I counted seven kinds of cake. God takes care of us even out here in the wild country. I'm Martha Lawford, and these are my friends, Julia Tate and Rachel Butler."

"And this is Ernie Cox. I believe he works for your father, Miss Butler."

"Oh." One of the oxen drivers, or herders. She didn't know, or care. She'd walk away from these yokels if it weren't for Martha. She couldn't do that to her special friend.

"Hello, Mr. Cox and Mr. Shackleford," Julia's young voice said. "We're glad to make yer acqu. . .acqui. . .we're glad to meet ya."

The two young men hardly gave Julia or Rachel a glance as they talked animatedly to Martha. Finally, they reluctantly left.

"I thought they'd never go," Rachel said. "I expected

any minute that you'd be inviting them to walk with us. You're way too friendly with people, you know."

Martha looked surprised. "I didn't know you could be too friendly with people, Rachel." She thought a moment and then broke into merry laughter. "Unless you make cow eyes at them."

That evening several people on the train heard strange sounds and knew for sure Indians were sneaking up on them. Captain Ransom called the people together and warned them. "Everyone better be watchin' every minute," he said. "Else you mayn't have another minute."

When Ransom finished, a young man moved in front of the people. "Hello," he said with a friendly smile. He stood over six-feet tall and looked lean but well muscled. His blondish hair hung over his ears but his closely trimmed darker beard and mustache looked dashing. "I'm Dan Barlow," he said. "I was just thinking what strange creatures we are. I wonder how many of you know that in 1825 the government took all the Indians' property and gave them Kansas for theirs. Now look what's happening," he said. "Here we are, invading their property by the thousands. I wonder what we'd do if thousands of people started taking our country from us?"

He stepped back into the crowd as quietly as he'd come.

Rachel sat up and took notice of Dan Barlow. That man makes sense, she told herself. I'm keeping my eye on him. Not too bad looking, either.

Another man stepped to the front. Middle-aged, the man looked kindly and round. "I'm George Rahn," he said. "I hope we all agree with our kind brother. I do. But I'm still afraid of the Indians so I suggest we watch carefully."

four

Rachel fell asleep that night, frightened almost to death. She knew for sure she'd wake up with a tomahawk in her skull.

But the sun shone brightly the next morning and everything looked normal. Before they finished breakfast, George Rahn came around, laughing and joking. "I've been to nearly every wagon," he said, "and everyone seems to be all right and wearing his hair this morning."

That day Willie and Petey got into more trouble than usual. Willie's father had made him a little white horse from sticks and polished it up nice and smooth. Petey wanted the horse in the worst way and tried off and on all day to take it from Willie. Both boys ended up crying many times.

Rachel wished Martha would spank them both or at least give them a sound scolding. But Martha thought up some trail games. "Let's see what those white clouds look like," she said one time. "I see a sheep."

"I see a man with white hair," Willie said. "I think it's Jesus."

"I see a big white horse," Petey said just before lunging at Willie's horse again.

Finally, Martha stopped Petey and held him by the shoulders. "Petey, it's not nice to take things from other people," she said in her kind voice. "If you'll be really good the rest of the day I'll try to get Papa to make you a horse tonight."

A sun-laden smile covered Petey's face and he didn't

cause any more trouble.

That night one of the horse riders, Stan Latham, appeared at the Butler camp just before supper. Mama was baking biscuits and stirring bacon in a skillet. "You look beautiful tonight, ma'am," he said to Mrs. Butler. "And your culinary skills must approximate your beauty. The food smells totally aromatic."

Rachel felt like vomiting. But Papa only smiled and invited the man to eat with them. Mama kept the man's plate filled.

"Did you observe my herd of twenty-one of the east's finest horses?" he asked. "I'm planning to breed the best horses in the west and earn mountains of money. I'm sure horses will be badly needed there."

"I noticed your horses," Nate said. "Good looking bunch. Lots of luck."

During the meal Stan let slip a few words that Rachel wasn't accustomed to hearing.

After he left, Rachel scolded Papa for inviting such a dirty, sloppy, loud, and uncouth man to eat with them. "You wouldn't have let me associate with his kind in Quincy," she said. "Or were you fooled with his big words?"

Nate shook his head. "Not fooled, Rachel. But the man was hungry."

The next day, Willie held two smooth wooden horses. The moment Petey joined them, he held out the new one. Petey could hardly talk over his excitement. "I don't have any other toys," he said. "I like it." Martha had to keep after the boys who only wanted to get down on the ground and play with their horses. "Come on or we'll get left behind," she called. The boys would jump up, run a ways ahead of the girls, and flop onto the ground again for another few minutes of play.

That afternoon, clouds started gathering in the sky, hiding the sun. As the hours passed, it grew darker and more threatening. "Looks like rain," Martha said. Rachel hugged herself.

"I bet a thunderstorm's coming," Julia said. "I'm skeered of lightning and thunder."

"Thunder never hurt anyone," Rachel said. "Thunder tells you the lightning missed you."

About four o'clock, the first flash streaked across the sky to the west; thunder followed a little later. In a few minutes, the flashes grew brighter and the thunder followed, quicker and louder.

Josie crept along beside Martha, obviously frightened. The cattle began lowing and the horses grew nervous. Then the rain came. At first, infrequent big drops, then they grew smaller and came faster. Within ten minutes, a cold drenching rain poured over them.

"We'd better get into the wagons," Julia said, moving toward Rachel's.

"No," Martha said. "We won't melt any more than the animals will. We shouldn't make it harder on the oxen." Julia came back and the girls walked in the downpour. Josie, obviously delighted that the loud racket had stopped, ran and jumped and spun in the rain. Soon, the girls were soaked through and their feet were wet and muddy.

Then Rachel noticed the oxen struggling to pull the wagons. The wheels sank six inches into the mud. Several wagons stopped and drivers began yelling and then using their whips. The oxen pushed hard on their yokes but the wagons didn't move. The whips sang through the air then cracked on the animals' backs. The drivers' yells grew louder, the oxen's bawling made a terrible roar, but the wagons didn't move.

Suddenly, Rachel snapped. She ran to her own driver. "Stop abusing those animals!" she screamed into his face. "Can't you see they're trying their best? The wagons are stuck too hard." She stopped long enough to take in a few breaths of wet air. "You're supposed to be Christian on this wagon train so start acting like one or I'll grab that whip and use it on you!" She ran the length of the train, screaming the same words at every driver.

By the time she'd said it twenty times the drivers began to see she was right. No matter how hard the men whipped, no matter how loud the animals bawled, they simply couldn't pull the wagons through the mire. The men unloaded the wagons in the pouring rain. With water streaming down their faces, they put branches under the wagon wheels, and pried the wagon onto the branches until they came unmired. Then struggling, the oxen moved the empty wagons. Corralling the wagons, they made camp for the night.

The rain stopped as suddenly as it began. Rachel huddled away from the wagons and cried. She couldn't help it. How could anyone mistreat animals so horribly? Blood ran from the oxen's backs. She cried for the animals, then she cried for herself. Whatever on earth was she doing in this awful place? Heartbreak Trail. That's what it was.

Hearing more bawling, she looked back where Thurman Tate still whipped his oxen. Wait! She didn't see his things beside the trail. He hadn't unloaded! She ran right to him, grabbed the whip from his surprised hands, and dashed back to Captain Ransom. "That Tate man is still whipping his animals," she puffed, "and he didn't even unload."

Ransom nodded and headed toward Tate. Rachel threw the whip as hard as she could, about eight feet, and followed the captain. "I thought we all understood we had to unload," Ransom said quietly to Tate.

Tate replied with an oath. "Ain't no one'd help me," he finally got around to saying. "I can't do it alone so them oxen'll just have to work harder." He looked at Rachel, standing a ways back. "You better get that there wild woman under control if you know what's good for her."

"I'll find someone to help you," the captain said, hurrying away. "Come on, Miss Butler," he said when he passed Rachel. "You'd better stay away from that man."

Rachel helped Mama make a fire with wet wood, then cook supper on a sizzling smoky fire. As they ate, she noticed about ten men approach Tate, unload a heavy cookstove from his wagon, a large chiffonier, and other things. Then the oxen managed to pull the wagon from the mud and into the circle.

After the Butler family finished eating, Rachel stood by the fire, drying her clothes. She and her parents dried their featherbeds and quilts, holding them before the fire, turning them every few minutes.

A young man approached the fire, one of the men who had helped Tate unload his heavy stuff. Rachel noticed several patches on his clothes and holes that needed mending. He wasn't all that clean either. "Hello," he said to Rachel. "I just wanted to tell you I'm elated to find someone brave enough to stand up for the helpless animals. I wish I'd done it, but I didn't and you did. Even a big oxen is helpless when a man starts on him and I agree it's time we considered their feelings, too. Thanks again, Miss Butler." He walked off into the night.

Rachel thought about him after she climbed into her featherbed. The man was a mess, but he cared about animals. She'd thought maybe she was the only one in the whole world who did.

The next morning the sun shone brightly and the people dried their belongings before they started. The same young men who'd unloaded Tate's wagon reloaded it. Rachel heard some of them asking Tate if he wouldn't like to leave the cookstove there to save his oxen. "Never!" he said. "Them oxen are just lazy. After getting away with what they did yesterday they'll be worse now."

The next morning Rachel grumbled to Martha about Tate and what an awful man he was. "I hate that man," Rachel said. "I really hate him. I hate Heartbreak Trail, too."

"It's hard all right," Martha said. Then she giggled. "I was purely surprised to hear you yelling at all those men. But the men may be kinder to their animals now."

"I feel just like you, Rachel," Julia said. "Those oxen feel pain just like we do and it's cruel to whip them when they can't work any harder."

For the first time ever, Rachel felt kindly toward Julia. When she thought about Julia's father, she could hardly talk to Julia. Now she knew Julia wasn't just a young copy of Tate. Come to think of it, she'd noticed that the girl's parents never checked on her or seemed to care where she was. Hmmm. Julia and Petey were somewhat alike. No one cared about either of them. She really did have something for which to be thankful. Both her mama and papa loved her dearly and would do anything in the world for her.

April third was the Sabbath and Pastor Richards led the group in singing again and preached a fitting sermon. Then, he acted as if Martha were of utmost importance to him and Rachel hated every minute of it.

The next day they'd traveled a few hours when one of the horse riders reported a large band of Indians ahead.

Captain Ransom stopped the train, calling a meeting of the men to decide if they should corral the wagons or keep going. They decided to keep going with weapons loaded and ready.

When they reached the Indians riding spotted ponies, they discovered they wore complete war outfits, including feathers, and held large bows in their hands. Rachel, her heart racing, the saliva dry in her mouth, marched with Martha, their heads high. The stench of the Indians, combined with her terror, made Rachel physically ill. It seemed as if those columns of Indians and ponies would never end but the savages looked dead ahead, never glancing in the direction of the wagon train. Someone counted 1,500 Indians.

After they passed, Rachel felt such a relief that she got silly; so did Martha and Julia. They laughed at everything and nothing. "What's funny?" Petey kept asking but the girls just laughed some more.

Day after day they traveled on. Rachel appreciated and loved Martha more every day. She still wished Julia and Petey and even Willie didn't have to be there all the time, but she grew somewhat used to them. After all, where else could they be?

Julia kept talking about a man she'd seen. "He's tall and blond," she said. "You have to see him."

"Show him to us next time you see him," Rachel said.

One afternoon, Martha acted strange, and Rachel wondered what had happened. Maybe she'd seen a man, too. The preacher acted as if Martha were the only girl on the train but she didn't seem to return the feeling. Maybe she'd seen someone else. Finally, Martha told her. "I'm purely embarrassed to tell you, but my brother Jackson shot a rabbit this morning and Mama asked me to dress it. I've never done such a thing, but I'm going to do it if it kills me."

"Why would you be embarrassed?" Rachel asked. "I've never even touched a dead animal, let alone fix it to eat."

Martha heaved a relieved sigh. "Maybe you'd like to watch me fix it," she offered as if she could use the moral support.

That evening Rachel watched but didn't help. She couldn't figure out how such a horrible looking mess could turn into something so delicious.

The next evening, as the men corralled the wagons and unyoked the oxen, Tate's animals didn't move fast enough to suit him so his whip whistled as he used it on their backs. The animals bawled as Tate yelled and whipped hide from their backs. Some nearby oxen stampeded, running over several men and into the circled wagons. When they got everything under control, they found Andy Shackleford, Dan Barlow, and another man hurt and two oxen badly cut up.

The young man who'd thanked Rachel for standing up for the oxen came with a black bag. First he checked the men and told them they had no broken bones but were badly bruised and to take it easy for a few days. Then he got some stuff out of his bag and began sewing up the oxen. Several men held the animals but the young man doing the sewing kept talking kindly to them. They seemed to understand and stood still. Rachel had never seen anyone so quietly kind to both men and animals. Different from most of the people around for sure. Come to think about it, she hadn't heard him spit out any filthy words either.

The next morning she asked Martha about the man.

"Don't you know who that was?" Martha asked. "He's Dr. Thomas Dorland, a brand new doctor. I heard someone say he's planning to make a difference in the lives of the pioneers. He's one of the horse riders."

"You mean he doesn't have a wagon?"

Martha giggled. "No wagon. Everything he has, including his medical supplies, is in that bag behind his saddle."

Rachel shook her head. "I don't understand how he can live like that." Then she thought of herself and giggled. "But I don't understand how I'm living like this either."

At dusk that evening a small group of Indians approached the wagon train. The men loaded their guns and stood watch. Rachel didn't have a gun but she watched the approaching group too, counting five ponies and five men. But when they neared the train, one looked like a woman.

A white woman at that, bareheaded with faded brown hair. When they reached the first wagon, ten men surrounded the Indians, their guns pointed at the ground. The woman jumped from her pony to the ground. "Don't look so scared," she said loudly. "We're friends." She took her pony's reins and handed them to the closest Indian. The Indians turned the ponies and headed back the way they'd come.

The woman, as big as most men, grinned. "Well? You got room for one more?"

"What's going on?" Captain Ransom asked quietly.

"Hello," the woman stuck out a hand, "I'm Deborah Petty, genuine white woman, nothing to fear."

Ransom shook her hand.

"I went mushroom picking yesterday and somehow got lost. Before I found my train, three white snakes got me. They weren't about to help me back to my train so I started screaming my head off." She laughed loudly. "Imagine how I felt when four redskins charged up. I figured we'd all lose our scalps and thought it might be worth losing mine just to see those white savages lose theirs."

"I see you're still wearing your hair," George Rahn said with a grin.

The woman laughed. "Yes and so are my captors. The Indians scared them plenty but didn't harm them. Anyway, when they saw this wagon train they brought me here and that's the story. They fed me and kept me last night, so my opinion of what color savages are has changed a bit."

Mrs. Ransom put her arms around the big woman and held her close. "You can share our wagon, Deborah. We'll work it out. But what about your train? Do you have a husband on it?"

"Naw. I'm all alone in the world. If you got room for me, one train's as good as the next." She laughed nervously. "You can see I'm plenty big. I like to work so I can earn my room and board."

As the days wore on, it seemed to Rachel that the mornings were getting colder rather than warmer. She kept putting on more clothes every morning and still froze. "I'm going to have to help more with the cooking," she told Mama, "so I can hang around the fire." She'd been helping some lately and found she didn't mind at all.

The train came to Big Blue River and found no bridge or ferry. The river wasn't wide but was about three feet deep. The men led the oxen in pulling the wagons cross and the women rode horseback. Rachel hung back almost to the last. Already freezing, she wasn't eager to get wet. Finally, Papa told her she had to go. He and Mama rode their geldings and Rachel her mare. "Tuck your dress up as the water comes up," Papa said, "and you won't get wet."

"Somebody might see me," Rachel wailed.

Papa shrugged. "Do. as you please."

Lifting her dress modestly over her knees, Rachel gritted her teeth as Ginger, her horse, stepped into the water. She leaned forward and patted the horse's sleek neck. "It'll be cold for you too, baby," she said softly. But the horse didn't seem to mind the water. After a bit Rachel decided the water would come only a little above her knees so she tried to get used to the cold. When they passed the middle, Rachel heaved a sigh. Papa said everything looks harder than it is and this hadn't been all that bad.

Just at that moment, Ginger dropped from under Rachel.

With no time to prepare, Rachel found herself in the cold water, gasping as she took in a big swallow. Burdened with all her clothes, she couldn't seem to get herself above the water.

Briefly, she heard men and women yelling, then forgot all about anyone else as she tried to swim. But she couldn't catch her breath, she just couldn't.

five

The next thing Rachel knew was that she felt herself choking and that she still couldn't pull in any breath. Opening her eyes, she found herself lying on her stomach on some grass. Then something pressed on her back and water poured into her mouth from her throat. She choked some more.

"Cough hard," a soft male voice said. "Try hard, Miss Butler. Just keep trying to breathe. You're all right now."

She didn't know who spoke and felt too tired to look. Then the pressure started on her back again and some more water came into her mouth. After a little while she could breathe though it hurt and made a raspy sound.

Then someone turned her over. She looked into the soft eyes of Dr. Dorland. He smiled at her. "You gave us a scare, but you just need to breathe and cough a while now."

Suddenly, Papa dropped to his knees beside her, gathering her to him. "My lassie," he said brokenly, "we'd have lost you if this young man hadn't pulled you out."

Young man? Rachel looked around but saw only Dr. Dorland.

"Yes," Papa said. "Dr. Dorland swam out and pulled you to safety."

"What happened?" Rachel rasped.

"Ginger stepped into a hole and went under. But you're both all right."

Dr. Dorland, who'd been on his knees beside Rachel, got to his feet. "I might as well go find my horse now if you don't need me anymore. Don't hesitate to call me if you feel anxious about anything."

Rachel tried to sit up. Papa helped her. Mama knelt down beside her and hugged her. "I love you, child," she said.

Rachel soon walked to the wagon that had been corralled with the others. She didn't feel too terrible except she still coughed some. Mama made some bean soup that went down easily. Rachel began to feel stronger.

During the night of April ninth, a cold wind arose and Rachel felt chilled right into her bones. She didn't get up for breakfast but Mama brought her some hot oatmeal with cream. It tasted better than almost anything Rachel had ever eaten in her life.

The fierce north wind forced Pastor Richards to cancel the Sabbath's preaching service and potluck dinner. People huddled in their wagons or around their fires, trying to keep warm. Papa read some Bible chapters to Mama and Rachel then said they'd pray together.

"I'm not praying," Rachel said. "If the Lord loved us even a tiny bit we wouldn't be out here in the middle of nowhere."

"That's enough, Rachel," Papa said sternly. "God didn't force you to come on the Trail. I did. You can be mad at me or yell at me or refuse to talk to me. But you're to stop blaspheming God at once. Do you understand?"

Rachel nodded, almost ashamed of her outburst. Almost.

The following week, the train crossed the Big Sandy River then the Little Sandy and followed it for several days. The weather improved; Rachel's spirits lifted, too.

One day she noticed the oxen's necks were bleeding from the pressure of the yokes. Rachel felt so sorry for the animals she went off by herself and cried again. Why did the animals suffer so for men's stupidity? Rachel wouldn't consider making the oxen pull her weight in the wagon now. Besides, she enjoyed walking with Martha. Sometimes though, she wished Martha weren't so perfect. Then she realized that that's why she loved her friend and why everyone else did, too.

One day, Willie and Petey seemed extra cranky. Every afternoon the boys took a nap in the Lawford wagon but it wasn't nooning time yet. Rachel wished it were.

Martha never lost patience with the two little boys. Never. This day she got them into a game thanking God for blessings. The boys, each trying to think of more blessings than the other, forgot to fuss. When they finally grew tired of this game, Julia got them started naming the animals God has waiting for them in heaven. The boys liked that game almost as well as Martha's and searched their minds for animals until nooning time.

The train reached the Little Blue River and traveled along it for several days. Rachel helped Mama with the cooking and cleaning up now. The green willow sticks, their only fuel, put out a pungent smoke that always got into Rachel's eyes. "Smoke follows beauty, you know," Papa said, winking at his only child. "It couldn't find anyone prettier than my two lassies."

"So how do you explain the bugs?" Rachel asked. "They get into everything, even the food we're cooking."

Mama smiled and stirred the biscuit mix. "One thing the Trail's teaching us is not to be so picky. We just have to take the bugs out of the food before we eat it."

Rachel knew that. But she hated it.

They camped early on Saturday to prepare for the Sabbath. Rachel and Martha did their families' washings then Martha washed Mrs. Piling's things. The poor woman didn't seem to be getting any better.

Mama and Rachel made several kinds of cakes with their supply of milk and cream. The cows' milk supply had dwindled but they still gave enough to share with several families.

With the warmer calmer weather they would have preaching and a potluck dinner. They made do without eggs and no one seemed to notice. They also fixed a big pot of baked beans in the dutch oven for the meal.

Rachel hated to admit it even to herself but she looked forward to the next day, especially for the chance to see Pastor Richards.

That evening, several men came to see Papa, telling him they'd dallied enough on the Sabbath and that they should all get together and tell Captain Ransom they wanted to get going.

"I wouldn't think of it," Papa said. "The oxen have sore necks, sore feet, and they're losing weight. They need the day to catch up. Trust the good Lord to know what's best, brothers."

The next morning, about the time the preaching began, Rachel saw some women carrying tubs to the river. What were they doing? Not washing on the Sabbath! Then they heard the men pounding on the wagons and saw two of them heading out with their guns.

Rachel, who couldn't care less about the Sabbath, felt shock ripple through her body. No one ever worked on the Sabbath! After sitting in shock for a while, not hearing a word Pastor Richards said, she began giggling to herself. What was she expecting? The Lord to send fire from heaven to consume the Sabbath breakers?

She turned her attention back to the preaching. The reverend was telling the people that Christ's children find ways to serve Him, even in the wilderness. The working field is still there, only smaller. She wondered if she could help Martha a little more with the children. Julia did. If they both helped, it would unburden Martha a lot.

After dinner Rachel went to the minister. "Would helping take care of children be the kind of ministering you meant?" she asked.

His smile was sincere. "It certainly would. And it would help you as much as the children's mother." Someone else crowded in to ask the man a question so Rachel went back to her seat. A lot of good that did. She got to talk to him for about two minutes.

A little later the pastor found Martha, and Rachel watched them talking and laughing together for some time. A lot more than two minutes!

"Ah, there you are," Jackson Lawford said, squatting beside Rachel. "Where you been hiding out? Did you make any of the grub I ate?"

"I'm afraid I wouldn't know," Rachel said in a cold voice. "I have better things to do than watch whose food you eat."

Jackson didn't hang around long, exactly what Rachel wanted. She wanted to be alone in case the Reverend wanted to come talk to her. But he didn't. At one point she caught Dr. Dorland watching her but when their eyes met, he turned away.

The next day they left the Little Blue River to enter the Platte River Valley, so level you could see seven miles. "Look," Petey said, "the grass is getting greener every day."

"Yes," Martha told him with a smile. "I'll bet the oxen like that, don't you?"

"Can we pick some and take it to them?" Willie asked.

"Not now," Rachel said. "The oxen are working. Why

don't you wait until almost nooning time, then pick a big bunch for them? I'll help you."

One day Jackson told Martha they were seeing antelopes but couldn't get close enough to shoot.

"Good," Rachel said. "They're too beautiful to shoot."

"You don't mean that," Jackson said. "We're all in desperate need of meat."

Rachel thought that over. Almost all the meat they'd had on the trail was dried side meat. But she still didn't want them to kill the antelope.

The next day three men rode to meet the train. When they reached the wagons, they asked Captain Ransom if the people needed meat. When assured they did, the men gave them four skinned and gutted antelopes.

"How do you happen to have all this extra meat?" Rachel heard Ransom ask the men.

"We found the herd and knew someone would need meat," they answered. "Meat's been scarce lately so we just got it while we could."

"Much obliged," Nate said. "Where you fellows headed?"

"Salt Lake City," one of the men replied.

Pastor Richards seemed to come alive at the name of the town. "You must be Mormons," he said softly.

"That we are," the last man said. "And we'd best be on our way. You folks enjoy the meat."

"I have your trail guidebook," Nate said. "In fact, most of us have a copy. I don't know how we'd have gotten along without it."

One of the men pulled a battered copy from a deep pocket. "We use it, too," he said with a pleased smile. The men saluted, turned their horses, and took off down the trail ahead of the Ransom Train.

As the train lumbered along, some stopped wagons

appeared on the Trail in front of them.

"They must be having trouble," Martha said. "I hope it isn't sickness."

But when they reached the wagons it seemed the train was having internal strife.

"Can we help you folks?" Captain Ransom asked one of the sullen looking men.

The men, having a severe disagreement, didn't even hear Ransom speaking.

Rachel, Martha, Julia, and the boys moved close enough to listen.

The men argued whether to continue or go back. "We're already out of food," someone said, "and we're not half-way yet. If we continue, we're sure to starve."

"That's your problem," a loud voice answered. "You knew it was a long way when we left. Let's go on," he said to the others gathered around. The people seemed about evenly divided in their desire to return to Independence or continue on.

After bickering another fifteen minutes, one of those who wanted to continue on turned to Ransom. "Maybe those with guts enough to go on can join your train," he said to the captain.

"You can join us if you're Christian and if you can keep up," Ransom said.

"We'll make them oxen keep up," the man said. Ransom extended his hand. The other man grasped it and they shook.

Hearing the conversation, Rachel didn't like the men. They didn't care a thing about their animals and wouldn't hesitate to mistreat them. She wished they hadn't joined the train. But they didn't treat their animals any differently than their own people treated theirs.

One day she noticed again their own oxen's raw and

bleeding necks. The animals' tongues hung from their mouths as if they didn't have strength to hold them up. Many of the animals limped badly. Rachel's heart felt as if it would break as the drivers forced them on. She ran and threw her arms around one of the bleeding necks. "I'm so sorry," she whispered, tears running dusty trails down her cheeks.

"Get out of there!" the driver yelled. "You're in the way."

Rachel dropped her arms and turned to the driver. "You don't even care about these animals!" she screamed. "I hate every one of you. You're worse than animals. Why should the animals have to suffer so much for man's stupidity?" A moment later she covered her face with her arms and moved back beside Martha.

Martha stopped walking and crushed Rachel in a big hug. "I'm sorry for them too," she whispered into Rachel's ear. "But no one knows what to do. Whether we go on or go back to Independence, we can't do it without the oxen." She pushed Rachel back so they could see each other. Tears ran in muddy streams down her face, too. "What can we do?" she whispered.

Rachel shook her head. She didn't know, but she couldn't bear what they were doing. The rest of the day all five walkers remained quiet.

On Sunday, April twenty-fourth, Rachel once again awakened to men's rough voices at dawn. Why couldn't people catch on that this was a rest day? The only day they got to sleep late. She turned over and pulled the pillow over her head. She still heard the commotion so she jumped out of her featherbed, dressed, and then dropped over the side of her wagon.

The new men had Captain Ransom surrounded. "We

didn't bargain for setting around all day," one of them said. "We gotta get going or we'll be caught in the mountains in the winter."

"I told you this is a Christian train," Ransom replied calmly. "We figure we and our animals need the rest." He motioned west with his thumb. "If you don't agree, nobody's holding you here. Just meander on down the trail."

"You tryin' to get rid of us?" one of the men bellowed.

"Nope," Ransom said. "Ain't tryin' to hold you here, neither."

"Who crowned you king and lord of everythin'?" one yelled.

Two others came at Ransom with their fists flying. Ransom barely had time to look surprised before receiving several hard blows to his face that put him on the ground, dazed.

six

Daniel Barlow, evidently hearing the fracas, came roaring into the midst of the trouble, punching both men's faces with hard staccato strikes. The two turned on Barlow who could nearly handle both. As the men pounded each other, Captain Ransom struggled to his feet. "Stop it!" he shouted, "or you'll all leave this train immediately." The fists continued flying, most ending with a low thud and groans.

Ransom thrust himself into the middle of the brawl still yelling at the top of his voice for them to stop. For some reason they all stopped and stood staring at the brave man.

Someone called Dr. Dorland who arrived soon with his little black satchel. On examining the men he found all three cut up enough to need stitches. Rachel moved up almost beside him as he cleaned the wounds and gently stitched them up, all the while talking quietly to the men. Not a word of recrimination, just fixing them the best he could. He was a real doctor, worthy of the title.

Dan Barlow thanked Dr. Dorland several times for his help; the other men said nothing. After the doctor finished, they yoked up their oxen, packed their wagons, and left the train.

The camp seemed exceptionally quiet as the remaining people built fires and prepared breakfasts.

"Wasn't Dr. Dorland wonderful?" Rachel asked her parents. "I've never seen anyone so quiet yet so kind. He's very dedicated."

Mama and Papa agreed then they all hurried to the

preaching service.

Pastor Richards spoke about doing to others as we would have them do to us. "If everyone lived that way," he said, "there would be no more trouble between people—ever." Afterwards, Rachel made it a point to tell him she appreciated his talk and how much she agreed with him. "Thank you," he said with an appreciative smile. "You have no idea how much it helps a pastor to know how his congregation feels about his sermons." By that time several people crowded around, distracting him with their silly comments. Rachel stomped off feeling rejected. She hurried home to help Mama with the food for the potluck dinner.

As usual, Martha, Julia, and Rachel ate on a quilt on their own little spot of ground. They'd barely sat down when Julia started going on about Dan Barlow.

"Wasn't that brave of him to protect Captain Ransom?" she asked. "He'd have beat them both up if the captain hadn't stopped him."

Rachel laughed at the younger girl. "I thought it was pretty dumb," she said. "One against two is never good."

Just then Dan stopped beside them. "Did I hear my name used in vain?"

"I hope not," Rachel said. "I just said two against one is bad."

"I think you were brave," Julia said. "Do you feel all right now?"

"Mind if I sit down?" he asked, settling on the ground near them. "I feel fine. That's one good doc we have. I say we're a lucky train."

"I do, too," Martha said. "We've needed a doctor several times and who knows how many more times we may yet?"

Soon Pastor Richards joined them, seating himself

beside Dan. He seemed to direct most of his comments toward Martha.

"You have quite a varied congregation," Rachel said. "Have you found out if everyone is really Christian?"

"I'm not a judge," he said. "If people say they're Christians, they are." He continued his discussion with Martha about caring for two little boys on the Trail.

As the little group talked, Rachel felt someone looking at her and raised her eyes to a group of men standing nearby. Sure enough, she met Dr. Dorland's soft gray eyes. He turned away so quickly his sun-streaked hair flipped across his face. What a kind, gentle face. But why was he watching her?

The next day, the wagon train reached Fort Kearney. Rachel had been looking forward to this because she expected a glimpse of civilization. But it wasn't to be. The frame houses of the four officers looked passable but the rest were made of sunburnedbrick. The fort, fences, and outbuildings were made from dirt cut into blocks and stacked up. They called it adobe. Fort Kearney was set up by the government to guard the Oregon Trail. Papa's Mormon guidebook said the fort was 319 miles from Independence, too far to turn back.

Fort Kearney disappointed Rachel a lot and the officers looked more like fur trappers than government men.

After passing the fort, the train reached the Platte River and followed it. Several men in rough boats tried to navigate the wide but shallow river.

"What are you doing?" Julia called as they walked past.

"Trying to catch some fish," one young man said. "We run aground fifty times each day and spend half our time on sand bars." He grinned as if he didn't mind as much as he might.

As they walked along the river, other men called to the girls and Julia always answered. "Don't you know young ladies don't talk to strange men?" Rachel scolded.

Martha laughed. "I don't think it hurts anything, Rachel. There's enough of us here to protect her. It's kind of fun to hear what they're doing, don't you think?"

A strange unearthly racket interrupted and the girls looked down the Trail toward the sound. A huge line of Indians pressed toward them, some walking, some on ponies. The Indians screamed, howled, and made war whoops that nearly broke Rachel's ear drums. Suddenly, she felt ready to run back home, on foot, all by herself.

But as they neared the Indians, she saw several men carrying a body on their shoulders. The dead man wore a complete headdress and war paint, making it look pathetically fierce. The girls laughed hysterically with relief knowing the Indians didn't mean them any harm. Besides that, the Indians were making so much noise they'd never hear the girls' talking and laughing. Finally, the Indians passed.

"I wonder if that poor man knew our Saviour," Martha wondered out loud.

Julia and Rachel burst into laughter again. "Tell me, how could he?" Rachel asked.

Martha nodded. "Probably not. That's why we're here, Rachel, to share our wonderful God with them and everyone else."

"Spare me," Rachel said. "I'm not sharing anything with anyone." But inwardly she admired Martha and envied her unwavering faith.

The next day they came to the south fork of the Platte River where they had to cross. The river was half a mile wide but very shallow. "The problem," the men explained, "is the quicksand in spots."

Making sure the animals had all they wanted to drink so they wouldn't stop during the ford, the men hooked several wagons together with eight to ten yoke of oxen for each wagon. The oxen drivers worked with their own animals while other men swam and waded, digging out the wagons as necessary.

The girls and little boys stood on the bank and watched. Andy Shackleford, Dan Barlow, Tom Dorland, Stan Latham, and Ernie Cox worked in the water.

"Who's that big fellow beside Andy?" Julia asked.

Rachel and Martha burst into laughter. "That's not a fellow," Rachel said. "That's Debbie Petty, the woman the Indians brought to the train."

"Well, she's working like a man," Julia said. "I wish I could help."

"Go ahead," Rachel said.

"No, you don't," Martha said. "Debbie's bigger and stronger than most women. You'll just be satisfied to watch. Understand?"

As they watched, the string of wagons stopped and the men flew into action, pushing, lifting, shoving, and shouting. Using a shovel, Debbie frantically pawed mud from around the sinking wagon wheels. At the same time the drivers urged the oxen to pull even harder. When the wagons began moving again, the watching people cheered loudly.

Finally, the last wagon emerged from the water and Captain Ransom called corralling.

As Rachel helped Mama fix supper, she wished Pastor Richards would come calling. He was so good looking, educated, and always clean. Come to think of it, she never saw him except on Sabbaths. She wondered where he kept himself and what he did during the week.

That night Rachel awakened in the night feeling

something on her face. She brushed her hand across it and felt bugs. Lots of bugs! Jumping from her bed in the dark she brushed over her face, arms, chest, and back. They seemed to be everywhere. She tried to sweep her bed clean with her hand but, being in the dark, she felt unsure.

After blindly cleaning herself and her bed several times, she gingerly climbed back under the covers and fell asleep almost at once. Some time later, she awakened again with bugs marching across her face. Jumping up, she went through the wild sweeping off of the bugs from the bed and herself and fell asleep again, exhausted.

Several more times the bugs, walking across her face, awakened her. Each time she fell asleep more exhausted than the last time. Finally, dawn broke and the train began to awaken.

That day everyone laughed and joked about the dor-bugs as they called them. Rachel didn't say a word but she found nothing funny about the insects, even though assured they don't bite.

"They come out of a hole in the ground," Julia said. "My dad told me they won't hurt you. They just run across your face fifty times. He says we'll get used to them and sleep right through."

Not me, Rachel thought. Never!

At least the dor-bugs came out only at night. Many other kinds of bugs swarmed over them during the whole day from dawn to dusk. Sometimes they bit, sometimes they didn't, but red welts covered most everyone's body, especially the children's bodies.

Just before serving the beans, Mama scooped the bugs from them. Even so, Rachel always had to spoon out many bugs while she ate. As she did, she remembered how she hated the Trail. Most of the time she didn't think about it anymore. Just sometimes.

At Plum Creek the horse riders spotted a single buffalo ahead, the first one they'd seen. Some of the men rode out after it and two hours later they returned, many of them with parts of the buffalo hanging over their horses.

That evening they had another of their rare celebrations with music and dancing. The people ate all the meat they could hold. The next day they jerked the rest of the meat before moving on.

As they traveled, the sand began deepening until it became hard to walk on. The oxen strained pulling the wagons, even on flat ground. Wildflowers, starting to bloom on the prairie, sent out a fragrance that brightened the day.

One day they met a wagon with four rough-looking men walking beside it. "We've been up and down this trail," they said. "It gets lots worse. The oxen won't be able to pull the wagons. You won't even be able to walk in the deep hot sand. Your oxen will all die on this trail and most of you will, too."

"Don't put too much stock in what those men said," Captain Ransom told them after the men left. "Something made them bitter."

Nevertheless, the girls, Rachel, Julia, and Martha trembled, remembering what the men had said. The little boys didn't play or fuss as usual either.

That night they camped on the north fork of the Platte River, two miles short of Ash Hollow, 504 miles from Independence, the guidebook said.

Martha and Rachel discovered an empty little cabin near the Trail. Inside they found hundreds of letters addressed to nearly everywhere in the world.

"Why would people leave them here?" Martha asked.

Rachel shook her head. "I don't know. Maybe they

thought someone would see their letter and would take it to the address on the envelope." As they looked through the envelopes, a noise outside caused them to drop to the floor.

"Shh," Rachel said. "Maybe they won't see us."

When the door creaked open and two men walked in, Rachel thought her heart would beat through her chest. But when the men's voices reached her ears, she recognized them! Andy Shackleford and Dan Barlow.

About that time Martha laughed and scrambled to her feet. "You nearly scared the daylights out of us," she said to the men.

Rachel crawled from her hiding place. "You caught us," she said. "What are you going to do with us?"

Andy laughed. "Do you know it's getting dark? We're going to see you safely back to your wagons. How's that?"

The next morning Rachel didn't waste any time telling Julia that Martha and she spent some time in a log cabin with Andy and Dan.

"How come you didn't take me?" Julia cried. "You knew I'd want to go."

"Because we didn't know we'd see them," Martha said sweetly. "We just found the cabin at the same time they did. We didn't even spend time with them. We went right back to our wagons. That's all there was to it."

That day the sand and dust grew deeper, spilling over Rachel's high-top shoes. The dust rose until it caused her eyes to burn and water; soon, they were sore and inflamed. Willie and Petey became cross and fretful. Martha, unmindful of her own discomfort, soothed the little ones the best she could.

Rachel noticed the oxen stumbling blindly along, their eyes nearly closed against the blowing dust. She ran and dipped her handkerchief into the river and tried to clean one of her ox's eyes. The ox tried to jerk its head away from her hand.

"Get out of there!" the driver yelled at her. "You tryin' to get hurt? Or just gettin' in the way?"

Rachel withdrew, knowing by now it didn't help to argue with the drivers.

The train camped early due to the dust. After Martha and Rachel finished their washings and other work, they explored and found many different kinds of flowers, including wild orchids, dainty pinkish flowers hiding in the shade of larger bushes, broken branches, or whatever.

Several kinds of butterflies flitted among the flowers— huge yellow-and-black ones, small brightly colored ones, and everything in between. As she watched the beautiful creatures fluttering through the air, Tom Dorland appeared from somewhere.

seven

"Kind of pretty, aren't they?" Tom asked quietly.

"Yes," Rachel whispered. "I love them."

Stepping a few feet away, he broke a twig and carried it to Rachel. "Here's one that's fresh out of its chrysalis. Let's watch it." He carefully transferred the yellow-and-black creature with crumpled wings to Rachel's finger where it clung. "It's a tiger swallowtail," he said. "And no, it isn't crippled. That's the way they look at first."

They didn't talk anymore as they watched it beat its wings up and down, up and down. Gradually, the wings grew fuller and less crumpled. Then, the little hooks at the bottoms of its huge wings straightened and took on many colors—pinks, blues, lavenders.

"It's beautiful," she whispered softly, holding her hand perfectly still.

"Shhhh," he whispered. "It's about ready to fly."

As they watched, it lifted its big wings one more time and fluttered into the sky. Rachel didn't want the experience to end.

She turned to the doctor. "Thank you, Dr. Dorland. That was the most beautiful thing I've ever seen in my entire life. And I'd have never seen it if you hadn't happened to be here."

"I enjoyed it, too," he said, turning away. "Thanks for sharing the moment."

After he left, Rachel lost interest in continuing her investigation. On her way back to her wagon, she brushed several metallic-looking green beetles from her clothes.

As dusk neared, sand flies and mosquitoes swarmed from the river, biting her face and hands.

On Sunday, May first, the morning wind and dust died down in the afternoon so Pastor Richards invited everyone to a hymn sing and preaching service. Rachel enjoyed watching the man who always looked as if he lived in Independence rather than on Heartbreak Trail. She didn't necessarily admit it even to herself but she enjoyed the songs, too. A few people played instruments and everyone else sang with whole hearts. Although Papa had asked several times, Rachel left her guitar in the wagon.

Pastor Richards told the people in his sermon that faith is the most important thing for a Christian. "We must spend time in the Word," he said, "and pray until our faith grows so strong it cannot fail."

Afterward, Rachel told him she agreed with him that faith was an all-important necessity to a Christian. "I work on my faith all the time," she gushed.

He gave her a brilliant smile. "Please, don't work on it," he advised. "Just spend a lot of time reading His Word and communicating with Him in prayer." As usual, people crowded between them.

Later, the people all brought their suppers together for a potluck meal. Pastor Richards joined the girls, sitting near them on the bare ground.

"I'm so glad you joined us," Rachel said eagerly. "I've been wanting to discuss a theological problem with you." She searched frantically for something she could bring up that would interest the young minister.

He held up a big hand. "No deep talks today," he said smiling to soften his words. "I'm here to relax." Then, he turned to Martha. "Still planning to walk all the way to Oregon?"

She laughed. "We all are, Rachel, Julia, and me. Even the little boys walk all the time except for when they nap."

Pastor Richards laughed with her. "How are the shoes holding up?"

Dan Barlow appeared and sat down beside Pastor Richards. "This looks like the most interesting conversation around. Mind if I join you?"

Jackson Lawford folded his long frame down beside the other men. "Needing a little protection, sis?"

Rachel sighed heavily. With so many people, Pastor Richards would never notice her. She got to her feet, her empty plate still in her hand. "If you'll excuse me, I should go check on my folks. Nice to see you all."

One more wasted Sabbath, she thought as she ambled toward her wagon. Well, maybe *Pastor Richards* would see now that she wasn't chasing him. As she thought about it she wondered if he hadn't given his best smiles to Julia today.

The next morning Rachel had nearly finished breakfast when she heard Martha screaming, "Help, someone help, quick!"

Rachel ran back to the Lawford wagon about the time a dozen other people reached the site of Martha's cries. Martha stood beside Josie, who lay on the ground.

"Papa," Martha screamed. "Josie's hurt. Really bad."

Rachel ran and knelt beside the trembling dog. Then she saw. Through Josie's torn-out stomach she saw the dog's intestines, nearly falling out. She lifted her eyes to Martha. "What happened?"

Martha couldn't answer, but shrugged.

Just then Tom Dorland appeared. "What happened?"

"She doesn't know," Rachel answered softly.

Mr. Lawford appeared with a gun in his hand. Leaning over the dog, he talked softly to her. "I'm sorry, Josie," he murmured, "but you're hurt so badly we can't fix you." He lifted the gun and Rachel turned away.

"Don't do it!" Tom Dorland said in a trembling voice. "Please don't do it, Mr. Lawford."

Mr. Lawford lowered the gun and looked into the young doctor's eyes. "Nothin' else to do," he said. "Coyotes got her. She's ripped clean apart." He raised the gun again.

"Let me try to fix her," Tom pleaded. "I don't know if I can save her and she'll have a lot of pain but she might make it."

Mr. Lawford looked at Martha. She nodded. "Yes, I want to save her, Papa. I love Josie."

"I know you do. But it's cruel to put her through the pain when she could die painlessly. She'll die anyway, you know."

Martha shot Tom a pleading look. "Please try, Dr. Dorland. Please save my dog."

The young man swallowed loudly, blinking the moisture from his eyes. "I'll do my best," he choked out. He swallowed again, squared his shoulders, and spoke. "Will someone please take Miss Lawford away for an hour? And I'll need someone else to help me."

Suddenly, Rachel wanted desperately to help Josie. "I'll do it," she said, standing straight and swallowing her tears. "I love Josie more than anyone else. . .except Martha. She'll like having me with her."

"All right," Tom said, opening his case. "We'll try to disinfect the wound with alcohol and it'll burn like fire. Can you hold her?"

Josie lay almost still while Rachel whispered into her ear and Tom poured whiskey over and around her intestines. The pitiful moans caused tears to roll down Rachel's cheeks but she kept up her soft talk and held on tightly.

"Now I'm ready to sew her up," the serious-voiced young doctor said. "How about a man taking Miss Butler's place. Rachel...Miss Butler, you help me with the stitching and keep talking to Josie. It really helps. It could make the difference whether she lives or dies."

Andy Shackleford held Josie still while Rachel held the wound closed and talked to Josie until she thought her throat would close up. "Good girl, Josie. Just lie still so the doctor can make you well. I know he's hurting you, baby, but he has to put you back together." Over and over and over.

"Well, I think we're finished," Tom finally said. "You're a fine assistant, Miss Butler." His voice still shook.

Rachel felt so weak she sat on the tongue of the wagon to catch her breath. As she rested, she heard Tom's soft voice.

"Our Dear Father in heaven," he said, barely above a whisper. "We thank You for loving each of us, as well as all Your creation. We just tried to save this special dog's life, Father. We've done the best we know how. We can sew flesh together, but we can't heal, so we're asking You. We ask in Jesus' name and thank You for hearing and answering our prayers. Amen." He turned to the waiting people. "Josie will have to ride in a wagon for some time."

The doctor walked off quietly, bag in hand. He said nothing and no one spoke to him. The enormous lump in Rachel's throat stopped her from saying anything to anyone.

Rachel's father moved to Josie's side. "She can ride in our wagon."

Mr. Lawford very gently lifted Josie up into his arms. "She'll ride in ours," he said. He laid the dog on Martha's featherbed. "Martha will have to find a new place to sleep," he said tenderly to Rachel. "She won't mind."

When Rachel's strength returned, she ran after Martha and her mother. "Josie's all right so far," she told Martha.

The next day Josie still lived and rode in the wagon. Rachel remembered how bumpy it was and wished she could help Josie somehow.

Dr. Dorland joined them for a few minutes that day. "Josie must have plenty of food now," he told Martha. "You feed her all you can spare and I'll bring her something when I can."

As they walked along the road, they saw several more graves and lots of dead animals.

Two days later, they reached the trail that led to Chimney Rock, three miles off the Trail. The train stopped so those who wanted could go see the huge rock formation up close, though it was plainly visible from the Trail.

Dan approached them on his large gelding. "Someone want to ride with me?"

"No," Rachel said with finality. "A horse is never supposed to carry more than ten percent of its own weight. That means one person per horse. We'll ride my family's three horses."

"You're right," Dan said. "But we'll be going only a little way, and we'll go slowly."

"We'll ride my family's horses," Rachel said. The three girls rode the horses, leaving the little boys with the older Lawfords.

As they neared the large Chimney Rock, Dan estimated it to be about 250 feet high, with the chimney on top measuring about 75 feet. The young people climbed up 200 feet and engraved their names in the soft stone, among the myriads of others who'd gone before.

"Look! Indians!" Andy Shackleford yelled as they

climbed down the structure. Rachel raised her eyes to see a dozen Indians, each on a spotted pony, moving toward them. No one had any weapons so they just waited.

"Maybe we should make a break for the wagons," Pastor Richards said.

"No Indians have hurt us yet," Dan said. "I doubt they'll be starting now."

When the Indians reached them, Rachel saw they were young, even younger than she. The Indians smiled and pointed to their bows and quivers of arrows. Then they motioned to the Train's young people as if pulling back bowstrings.

"They want us to shoot," Tom Dorland murmured. In a little while the red youth and white youth engaged in a shooting contest, which the experienced Indians easily won. Waving and smiling, the young Indians rode off the way they'd come.

The young people of the wagon train headed back to the wagons in good spirits, their opinions of Indians up about 500 percent. As the merry group neared the wagon train, they came upon a herd of buffalo a mile wide by the Platte River. Of one accord they all stayed back, fearing the huge animals would stampede and run over them. The buffalo ignored the people on horses, giving them a good chance to enjoy the magnificent creatures.

Later that day Tom Dorland brought Josie a small, skinned animal. "I'll try to do this often," he told Martha.

The next day they reached Scott's Bluff, 596 miles from home, with many 500-foot-tall bluffs. The crystal clear sky opened up the landscape until it looked as if you could see forever.

"The guidebook says you can see three hundred miles," Papa said.

"I'm sure I can see that far," Martha said laughing.

"What about you boys?"

"I can see all the way to Heaven," Willie said.

Petey gave Willie a big push, sending him sprawling. "No you can't. That's straight up in the sky."

Tears trickled down Willie's face, then a sob burst from his throat. Martha gathered him into her arms and carried him a while.

"You're a bad boy," Rachel said to Petey. "You made Willie cry. Don't you know he's smaller than you?"

Martha soon had Willie laughing and set him down. She dropped an arm over Petey's shoulder. "You didn't mean to hurt Willie, did you?" she asked the small boy. He leaned against her, putting his cheek on her arm.

One evening a high wind arose, bringing heavy rain. Before long the wagons were in danger of being blown over.

"Call the boys," Debbie Petty yelled and right away Tom Dorland, Dan Barlow, Andy Shackleford, George Rahn, Nate Butler, and George Lawford showed up. "Let's fasten all the wagons together," Debbie yelled into the wind.

"Good idea," Nate Butler replied. Working quickly in the wind and rain, they fastened them together so they couldn't tip over.

"Good," Tom Dorland screamed into the wind. "But that won't keep the contents dry. I guess everyone's on his own now."

Rachel's wagon leaked but it was better than being in the rain. And it felt so much better having the wagons more secure.

The next morning the sun shone brightly and wildflowers bloomed everywhere. After everyone dried the contents of their wagons, they marched onward. And saw more graves.

The train traveled among the gigantic bluffs for several days.

"At least they protect us from the wind," Rachel said to Martha while looking up at the mountainous bluffs around them.

One day as they walked, Josie whined from Martha's wagon. "She wants to walk," Martha said. "She's been begging for several days. Think she should?"

Rachel ran to the head of the wagon line to find Dr. Dorland. "Josie wants to walk," she said. "Can she?"

"For one hour," he said. "You might also tell Miss Lawford that I'm planning to take out the stitches tonight."

Mr. Lawford lifted the dog down and Josie obviously enjoyed herself though walking gingerly. Later, when Martha's father put her back into the wagon, she barked her disapproval.

That evening Tom Dorland stopped by Rachel's wagon. "Come help me take out Josie's stitches," he said. "It wouldn't be fair if I didn't ask you," he added, "as this is the fun part."

When Martha brought Josie out to Tom, the dog began trembling hard. She squatted low and her tail dropped to the ground.

Tom knelt beside her and put his arms around her, talking softly. "I hurt you badly last time, didn't I, girl? I don't blame you for being afraid." He smiled. "But I'm not going to hurt you at all this time." He raised his eyes to Rachel. "Come and hold her."

Rachel dropped to the ground and turned Josie over so her stomach was exposed. She could hardly believe how much better the dog looked. Hardly any swelling, hardly any redness, and the wound itself under the stitches looked dry and black. "It's all right," she whispered to the still-trembling dog. "We're going to be very careful with you, Josie, and make you all well." She couldn't believe the love she felt for the shaggy dog.

She talked to Josie as Tom worked swiftly but gently. "There you go," he said about two minutes later. He petted the big head. "Doesn't that feel better? Now it won't pull anymore, Josie." He lifted his head to Rachel. "Thanks, Miss Butler. Some day you're going to be a nurse." Then he got to his feet and turned to Martha, who'd been standing near, watching fearfully.

"She's just fine, Miss Lawford. Much better than I could have hoped. She's a good patient, too. Did you notice she didn't flinch once?"

Martha shook her head. "No, but I'll never be able to tell you how much Josie and I appreciate what you did. I love her so much, Dr. Dorland."

He laughed quietly. "Call me Tom. And I can see how much you love her. But don't thank me. I can't heal anyone or anything. God does His miracle every time any wound heals, no matter how small. In Josie's case it was a big miracle. God created animals, too, and He loves them even more than you do. She'd have never made it without His special care. Did you ever think of that?"

Martha's smile held a beautiful radiance. Rachel felt jealousy rise in her throat. "I didn't think of it," Martha answered, "but now that I do, I know you're right." She raised her beautiful blue eyes to the cloudless sky. "Thank You, Father. Thank You so much for loving and healing Josie. I love You."

Tom's eyes softened. "You really do, don't you?" He turned back to Rachel. "Thanks again for the help, Miss Butler." He picked up his black case and headed off among the wagons.

Martha's eyes still radiated love. "Isn't he wonderful?" she said quietly.

"Yes," Rachel agreed. "He's a good doctor." Sometimes she wished she had the faith of these two good people.

The next day they met more turnarounds, as they called the men returning from the Trail.

"There's so many dead animals ahead you won't be able to go on," one of the dirty, tattered men said. "They're in the Trail, beside the Trail, and even all through the streams. The smell makes you sick and the water'll kill you."

True to the men's word, each day rotting carcasses became more prevalent, and the smell truly made Rachel sick. She could hardly face food. One day she happened to take a look at her body and discovered that all the plumpness had disappeared. She looked hard and lean. Smiling, she decided not everything on Heartbreak Trail was bad. Not quite everything.

A few days later they crossed over the Laramie River on a shaky bridge that the Indians had made. They charged two dollars per wagon which everyone paid rather than ford the river. When the train made camp to prepare for the Sabbath, Indians swarmed everywhere, most of them dressed in white man's tattered clothing. A few wore buckskins. All wore soft moccasins.

Rachel and Martha always did their families' washings now. "Want to help me do Sandy Piling's?" Martha always asked. Rachel usually said no, but this time she took half and they finished it in another hour.

The next morning, May eighth, was the Sabbath. Pastor Richards conducted a moving hymn sing early in the morning. With his lovely voice and pleasant way of getting everyone into the spirit, the music bathed the prairie in happy and joyful sound. Rachel felt herself growing close to God and she had no intention of doing that.

Then he preached about how much God loves each person. "He loves us much more than any earthly parents ever loved their own child," he said. "God actually loves us as much as He loves His precious only Son. We know because He allowed his Son to die for our sins so we could live with Him forever."

Rachel had always heard about "God so loved the world" but she'd never really thought about how much God loved her.

At dinner time Julia, Martha, and Rachel found their own little spot to spread their blanket to enjoy the meal together. Not that there was any special food. Everyone brought beans fixed one way or another and people had made cakes or dried-apple pies the best they could. But they enjoyed relaxing together.

As the girls filled their plates, Petey ran to them. "Can I eat with you, Martha?" he asked. "I'll be good."

Martha pulled him close. "Of course you can, Petey. Do you have a dish and spoon?" He ran back after them.

When the girls returned to their blanket, they discovered another one a few feet from theirs. "Shall we go somewhere else?" Rachel asked.

"No," Martha said. "Maybe God wants us to meet some new friends today. There are many people on the train we don't know."

Dan Barlow appeared with a huge plate of food and sat down on the blanket. Rachel checked Julia's face and found excitement all over it. That girl really liked Dan.

eight

Before Dan looked in the girls' direction, Pastor Richards, Tom Dorland, and Andy Shackleford arrived with heaping plates and dropped to the blanket. "Ah," the preacher said. "Does this feel good or does this feel good?"

"It feels good," Tom said. Then his eyes happened on the girls. "Hey, fellows!" he said with excitement. "Look who followed us here." The others looked the ten feet to the girls and showed surprise, too.

A big laugh burst from Rachel's throat. "You didn't even notice our quilt, did you?"

"No," Dan said. "Was it there?" He shook his light-colored head. "No. Why don't you girls just admit you couldn't resist eating with us?"

"I admit it," Julia said, laughing too. "We put our blanket here so we could eat with you."

Dan moved over a little and patted the quilt beside him. His clear eyes drilled into Julia's. "Is that a fact? In that case, why don't you prove it. Come over here and sit with me. Please?"

Julia picked up her plate, marched over, and sat beside Dan, then smiled a "see what I did" smile at Rachel and Martha.

Half a second later Pastor Richards heaved his six-foot-plus frame to his feet, carefully lifted his overflowing plate, and headed toward the girls' blanket. At last! Rachel had been waiting a long time for this. She moved over slightly to make room for him. But he walked around the blanket and dropped to the quilt beside Martha. For a moment

Rachel thought she'd cry, but she swallowed twice and hid her disappointment. Just then Andy Shackleford dropped beside her.

"Well, here I am, odd man out," Dr. Dorland said.

Immediately, Petey got up and carefully carried his half-filled plate to the men's quilt and sat beside the doctor. "I'll be with you," Petey said. "Willie's eating with his mama and papa so I don't have anyone, either."

Tom patted Petey's shoulder. "We'll get along fine, won't we Petey? Pretty soon we'll go back and get some cake or pie."

Later in the afternoon the talk turned to God and how they could know His will for them.

"God doesn't care for any of us," Rachel said loudly. "Would a God Who cares let His people go through what's been happening to us? Not to mention the animals. How could He let the animals suffer and die when they didn't do anything to deserve it? And little kids! God doesn't care!" When she finally stopped, the silence went on forever. She wanted to demand that the preacher answer her accusations, but she refused to talk to him because he chose to sit with Martha.

Rachel had put such a pall over the group that they soon broke up and went to their separate wagons. Later that night Rachel wondered if she'd made a major mistake. A minister might want a real Christian for a good friend . . .or especially for a wife.

The next day they reached Fort Laramie, 650 miles from home, the second fort set up to guard the Oregon Trail. The fort looked nearly like Fort Kearney, big, ugly, and adobe. Beyond the fort lay a little city of neat white houses. Rachel would have liked to walk among the houses and feel a tiny bit civilized but Captain Ransom hurried them on.

As they bought provisions, the officer told Nate and others that '59 was the largest migration ever known. "Over thirteen hundred wagons have been past here already," he said, "and twelve-hundred-head of herded cattle."

When they returned to their wagons, Nate laughed. "Did you hear the man say thirteen hundred wagons are ahead of us," he said to Alma and Rachel. "And we thought we were in one of the earliest trains."

They hadn't gone far when the wagon ruts grew deeper. They'd seen deep ruts but nothing like these. Pretty soon word filtered down the wagon line that this place was called Register Cliffs and had the deepest ruts on the entire Trail. Cliffs on each side of the Trail got taller as they traveled. The wagons had to go single file because of the cliffs and the ruts soon reached the middle of the oxen's bodies.

Rachel began to feel crowded as she, Martha, Julia, Petey, and Willie walked single file beside the wagons. When Dan Barlow came along, he and Julia messed around until the others left them. Soon, Petey and Willie got cross and so did Rachel. The cliffs on each side made Rachel feel as if she were in a small world and couldn't get her breath.

"This is the worst ever," Rachel complained to Martha. "I can't stand this anymore."

"It isn't so bad," Martha answered. "It's a lot better than the deep sand. The oxen had bad trouble in that."

Rachel knew Martha was right but she didn't say it out loud. "Well, it's always too hot or too cold," she said, "and too dusty or windy. Or something else."

"But this isn't so bad," Martha insisted. "The oxen are doing all right and the temperature is comfortable."

"Why do you always have to be so perfect?" Rachel

snapped. "Do you have any idea how tiresome that gets?"

Martha crumpled a little. "No," she said in a tiny voice. "I was just trying to cheer you up. I want you to know God loves you, Rachel, and is taking care of you."

"God doesn't love me! He doesn't love you either. You just keep saying that to keep your courage up."

After a short silence Martha spoke in a tiny voice. "Do you believe there is a God, Rachel?"

That surprised Rachel a lot. She couldn't deny she believed that. She nodded.

"Do you believe the Bible is God's Word? And that it is true?"

Rachel bowed her head. "Yes," she mumbled.

Martha looked as if she'd just been given a fine gift. "If you believe the Bible's true," she said, "you have to believe God loves you. It says He loves you as much as if you were His only child. Remember Pastor Richards said God loves you more than you can love your own children. That means He loves you much more than your father and mother love you. Many times more, Rachel. Did you know He loves you so much He cries when you reject Him?"

Rachel couldn't answer Martha anymore, but her friend's words hung in her mind. God loved her more than her parents do? Papa had brought her on this long Heartbreak Trail against her wishes but she knew both her parents loved her with all their hearts. She was everything to her parents. And God loved her more than that?

That night, as she lay on her comfortable featherbed, she thought about it some more. God loved her many times more than her parents did. Martha had said that was because He loved sinlessly, a perfect love, and her folk's love was a selfish love. All human love is selfish because all have sinned.

As she lay there she felt love for Him grow in her heart until she could hardly contain it all. She felt happier than she could ever remember feeling in her whole entire life.

The next day she asked Martha some questions. "I've gone to church all my life," she said, "but I don't have any idea how to know Jesus as you do."

"It's purely easy," Martha said. "Just tell Him how much you love Him, and that you want to love Him more. Thank Him for dying to pay for everything you've ever done wrong, tell Him you want to become His child, and ask Him to forgive your sins. That's it, Rachel. That's all there is to it." Martha choked on the last two short sentences, as though she were about to burst into tears.

"Aren't you glad I want to do this?" Rachel asked.

Martha hugged Rachel. "I'm so happy I'm crying," she blubbered against Rachel's cheek. "Now, do it."

"I love You, God," Rachel cried. "I love You because You love me so much, enough to die for me. Thank You for loving me so much. Thank You for dying for my sins. Please, God, I want to belong to You! Forgive my sins and teach me how to be Your child." She stopped and sniffed. Then she coughed. "I love You, God," she sobbed.

"I love Him, too," Petey said. "Can I be His child?"

"Me too," Willie echoed. "I love Jesus, too."

Martha stopped right there in that narrow alley between the high cliffs and hugged them both. "You're both His very own little boys," she said to them. "You must always remember that, no matter what. All right?"

"Let's sing," Rachel suggested. So the little boy voices joined the girls' as familiar hymns rang out from their hearts.

The wagon train soon camped along Horseshoe Creek, not getting very far due to the ruts, cliffs, and bluffs. They found plenty of grass and water for the animals and wood for the fires.

As they traveled, they saw more and more graves as well as animal carcasses along the Trail. They also met turnarounds nearly every day. They all told of the same dire future for the wagon train.

By the time they reached the Laramie Mountains with snow on the mountain tops, the sun was scorching.

"I'm hot," Willie said one day. "I need a drink, Martha. Please, get me a drink."

"I can't, Willie. We have to wait until we stop tonight."

"I can't wait. I'm thirsty now."

"So am I," Petey said. "My throat hurts."

"Why don't we pretend we're in a nice cool lake, swimming," Rachel said. "The water comes to our shoulders so we just lie down and start kicking our legs and stroking with our hands. Are you getting too cold, Willie?"

Willie laughed with delight at the game. "Not yet," he said. "I want to swim some more."

"All right," Rachel said. "Just be careful you don't go out too far. It might get deep."

Both boys got into the game until they forgot all about being hot and thirsty.

The next day when the boys napped, Rachel wanted desperately to do something for God. "Martha," she said. "How can I let God know how much I love Him? I just want to show Him."

"You showed Him yesterday," she said. "When you took the boys swimming you showed God your love. The Bible says, if you do something nice for anyone, even the least, it's as if you did it for the Lord. So just look around. There are lots of people on the train who need help. And helping them will make you feel better than you ever have. It's really doing it for Him, Rachel."

Rachel watched but didn't see anything special she

could do.

The next afternoon the train stopped for some reason. A few minutes later, Rachel heard a woman crying loudly. When Rachel went to see what was wrong, she found Tom Dorland talking softly to Tamara Richards. As he talked, Rachel realized a snake had just bitten the woman. The doctor kept reassuring the terrified woman but he didn't do anything. Why doesn't he get to it? Rachel wondered. The woman will die if he doesn't do something.

Suddenly, Rachel had a strong feeling that she should help the preacher's sister. She walked up to them. "May I help you, doctor?" she asked.

Relief washed over his face when he looked up. "Please do," he said. "I just prayed for someone to come, and He sent you." He showed her how to loosen the tourniquet he'd placed on the woman's swollen arm. "I'll tell you when," he said. "In the meantime I have to incise the wounds. Will you hold the arm still for me?"

When they finished the grizzly job, Rachel cradled Tamara's head in her arms for a moment. "I'm sorry we hurt you," she whispered. "But now you're going to get well."

Tom thanked Rachel and told her he'd be calling on her again. "You really should be a nurse," he added with a sincere smile.

Rachel, in a rosy glow, hurried back to her wagon. Martha had been right. She felt better then she ever had.

The wagon train resumed its journey and, after a while, they came to a ferry. But, since the river didn't look deep, they decided to ford it. As they forced the animals into the river though, the animals refused to cross. After many of the animals refused several times, the people paid the money and ferried everything across—wagons, animals, and people.

"I ain't lettin' these critters tell me what to do," Mark Piling said, wielding his whip. He drove his animals into the water many times but each time they turned back. Finally, he spurred his horse into the water, too, and whipped the oxen pulling the wagon, ripping strips of flesh from their bodies. His screaming and the oxen's loud bawling got the attention of the entire wagon train who gathered on the other side of the river to watch.

"Let them go back," Nate yelled. "I'll pay your ferry, Piling. Don't force them across."

If Piling heard he didn't respond. Finally, the bleeding oxen struggled out of the water, the wagon bumping up the river bank behind them. He drove them on about thirty feet, then turned back to drive his stock across. He had one milk cow, twelve horses, and four more oxen.

Forcing them all into the water together he continued using the whip harshly on their backs. The horse he rode tried desperately to turn back too, but Piling spurred him until he screamed. This time when the animals reached the current, the cow spun a complete circle then, at the mercy of the cruel water, washed downstream, sometimes her head out of the water, sometimes her feet out. Two of the horses lost control and the river swept them away, too. When the other horses and oxen made it across, they climbed wearily out on the other side. Piling followed them on his horse, pushing it to go faster. They nearly made it to the edge when an undercurrent swept his mount's feet out from under it, spilling the man into the stream. The horse disappeared downstream in the frothy water. Piling managed to stay on top of the water but hurtled downstream until he disappeared.

"Well, so much for that," Captain Ransom said. "Who's gonna tell his woman?"

nine

No one offered to tell Sandra Piling that the river had swept her husband away.

"Shall we?" Martha whispered into Rachel's ear. "We probably know her better than anyone. . .from doing her washing."

Everything in Rachel shouted for her to get out of there before Martha talked her into doing something she'd be sorry about. "Let's go," she heard a strained voice say, then recognized it to be her own. How could she do this? She'd just caught herself thinking that it served the horrible man right. He'd caused the death of several helpless animals. Why shouldn't he die, too? She shook her head. That wasn't good thinking. God would never have her think that way. Help me, God, she prayed as she followed Martha.

The Piling wagon was only a few feet away. Maybe Mrs. Piling had heard the commotion and already knew. Rachel jumped up onto the wagon behind Martha.

"Are you all right, Mrs. Piling?" Martha asked in her soft sweet voice.

Mrs. Piling sat up in her rough bed on the floor of the wagon. "Yes. Is something wrong?"

Tears reddened Martha's eyes. She nodded and took the woman's hand. "Yes. The river just swept your husband away. I'm afraid he's gone, Mrs. Piling."

The frail woman smiled. "Thank you, dear. Now, don't worry about me. I'm all right." Rachel thought for sure she saw relief in the woman's face. No, she must have imagined it.

"Can we do anything for you?" Martha asked.

The woman thought a moment. "I'll need a little time to get organized," she said. "Do you think I can drive the oxen?"

Martha's dark head swung back and forth. "Driving's a hard job, Mrs. Piling. A sick person could never do it. The men will think of something."

"Let me try before you get anyone else. I think I can do it."

"All right. We'll camp here tonight so you can get yourself together."

As the girls hurried back to their wagons, Rachel voiced to Martha her thoughts about Mrs. Piling showing relief at her husband's death.

"Don't even think such things," Martha scolded, "let alone say them."

Captain Ransom gladly made camp. "You be sure to see what we can do for her," he told Martha and Rachel.

The two girls returned to the Piling wagon just before dark. Rachel brought some fresh milk and cream that was getting more dear every day. The cows had cut from thirty gallons a day to about six. They found Mrs. Piling up and caring for her children.

"Would you like us to take the children for tonight?" Martha asked.

The woman's eyes, looking brighter than Rachel had ever seen them, looked up from the fire she cooked over. "Oh no," she said in a strong clear voice. "We're doing just fine. We'll stay together, but thanks anyway." She handed Petey a plate of bacon and pancakes swimming in brown syrup.

As they approached their own wagons again, Rachel didn't say a word, but she'd never seen Sandy Piling look so strong and happy. She wasn't imagining it, either.

A little later Tom Dorland stopped at Rachel's wagon. "Could you go with me to see Sandra Piling?" he asked. "In her condition a blow like this could be very hard on her." Rachel kept quiet but gladly went.

Tom listened to the woman's heart and lungs and did some other things, then smiled broadly. "You're doing just fine, Mrs. Piling. Just fine. If you get anxious or feel bad, don't hesitate to call me. Please accept our condolences. We're so very sorry."

As Tom walked Rachel back to her wagon, she hoped he'd say something. Sandra's relief had been as plain as the rising sun. But he didn't mention Mrs. Piling at all.

Early the next morning Rachel took a pot of oatmeal with cream floating on it to the Piling wagon. Rachel dropped the oatmeal and nearly fainted when Mark Piling himself jumped down from the wagon and met her belligerently. "My family don't need your charity," he snapped when he saw the pot.

Rachel didn't say a word, just grabbed her empty oatmeal pot and ran for her parents' wagon. "Mama, Mama!" she called. When her mother appeared, she continued. "Mark Piling's back. Oh Mama, why couldn't he stay dead?"

"Rachel!" Mama cried in distress. "I thought you were doing so well and now this! How could you say such a thing, young lady? And are you sure he's back? That he didn't drown."

"He didn't, Mama, and he's as mean as ever." Then Rachel couldn't help it. She told her mother how happy Sandy had been when she thought her husband dead. "She got right out of bed, Mama, and she was all well."

"I've heard about situations like that, Rachel. She might be better off without him, but he doesn't have to die."

Word soon got around that Piling was alive and as nasty as ever. Rachel wanted to go see Sandra Piling to see how she was now, but her mean husband kept people away as he always had.

"Are you happy your daddy's back?" she couldn't help asking Petey that morning. The little boy hung his head and wouldn't answer.

That day they traveled in a continuous line of wagon trains; where one ended the next began. And the dust was terrible. Sometimes they couldn't see their own oxen. Everyone's eyes burned as they choked on the terrible dry stuff.

Late in the afternoon word came to Rachel that Andy Shackleford was sick, possibly with cholera. The Ransoms had taken him into their wagon.

That night there was nothing to burn but sagebrush. It burned fast, not putting out much heat, and the smell sickened Rachel's stomach.

The train stayed in camp the next day as Tom Dorland didn't think Andy should bounce around in a wagon.

That afternoon, several cows got into some quicksand by the river. Tom, Dan, Nate, George Lawford, George Rahn, Debbie Petty, and three other men ran to the scene with ropes. Tom, being the lightest, ran to the cattle and fastened them together. Then the men pulled on the ropes while Tom urged the animals to struggle. It looked as if they'd go down. Rachel wanted to run and help but she didn't. Finally, the valiant animals started to move. The men cheered and pulled harder. Within an hour they had them all out. Every one.

The next day they stayed in camp again. Andy seemed a bit better but one of Thurman Tate's oxen died. Someone discovered rabbits and sage hens in and around the sagebrush. Jackson Lawford and others went out and brought back enough for several meals for their families.

As Martha and Rachel cleaned their meat, they saw a man go hunting without a gun.

"I ain't got one," he answered when they asked him about it. "But I'll catch something anyways." He soon found a rabbit and chased it all around the camp and through sagebrush. He ran until he dropped, exhausted.

Although Martha and Rachel laughed at his antics, they gave him two cleaned sage hens.

On Sunday, May fifteenth, Rachel got to sleep later but still wasn't ready to awaken when Captain Ransom came around.

"We have to move on," he told everyone. "The cattle have eaten all the grass and they need all they can get."

"How's Andy?"

"Not good. I hate to move him but we have to care for the cattle, too."

They left the Platte for the last time and camped near Willow Springs. After supper Rachel saw Tom Dorland head for Ransom's wagon. "May I help you with Andy?" she asked.

He shook his head. "I'd rather you stayed away. I'm sure it's cholera and somehow it gets around. No need for you to chance getting it."

"What about you?"

The doctor shrugged. "Someone has to take care of him. But truthfully, there isn't much a person can do for cholera."

As Rachel walked away, she looked back and saw Tom praying over Andy. A black dread covered her. Andy might die. What a horrible thought! Andy really might die!

Later, Tom asked Rachel to help him dress Tamara

Richard's snake bite wounds. The woman looked good and her wounds were healing nicely.

The next day they saw the Sweetwater Mountains with ice and snow glistening on the peaks. When Petey and Willie complained about being too hot, Rachel showed them the cool tops of the mountains.

"The white on them is ice and snow," she said. "We'll pretend the cold is down here." She shivered and hugged her arms to her chest. "Brrrr. I'm cold," she whined. "Willie, would you run and get me a sweater, please?"

"No," Petey interrupted, thrilled with the game. "You have to be cold because you don't have a sweater."

"All right. I guess I'll get warm next summer when the sun comes out."

The sight of the cool mountaintops kept the boys cool the rest of the day.

"You're getting good with the boys," Martha told her. "You're really helping 'the least of these,' Rachel."

Rachel laughed happily. "I discovered you're right. It feels good to help and be kind to people."

One day they met a small train of four wagons. "You're going the wrong way," Julia called when they met.

The oxen driver stopped his wagon. "You're right," he called back. "We're taking seventeen children back to civilization. Indians massacred all the adults in their train and left the children."

Rachel could hardly bear to listen anymore. What was in store for them? Would they ever get to Oregon? Were the same Indians lying in wait for them?

On Sunday, May twenty-second, before the preaching service began, Dan took Julia from Martha and Rachel and found a place for them to sit. Afterward, the group put their food together as usual. The girls had barely started filling their plates when Pastor Richards came and asked Martha to eat with him.

"We'd be glad to, wouldn't we, Rachel?"

Rachel's first inclination was to stick her nose in the air and flounce away, but better sense told her this would be an opportunity to impress the minister. So, she held her tongue.

Pastor Richards gave his attention so completely to Martha he barely knew Rachel was there. "Did you like my sermon today?" he asked her.

"Oh, yes," Martha said. "I always love to hear about our Lord."

"I mean the wording, and the way I delivered it."

"Oh, dear," Martha wailed, "I listened so hard to what you said about my Jesus I forgot to notice how you said it."

"Oh. Well, did you enjoy my song leading?"

"The only thing I like better than singing to our God is praying to Him," she said with a silvery laugh.

"I see. Well, did I look presentable?"

Martha laughed heartily at that. "You always look nice, reverend. How you do it, I can't guess. Everyone else looks like a strong gale just dropped them."

He laughed in appreciation. "I thought it was a minister's duty to look presentable at all times. Do you like the way I wear my hair?"

By this time Rachel began to wonder if the pastor's charm included his good looks and nothing else. She'd never heard anyone so vain in her life. Then her conscience told her she was having a bad case of sour grapes. Maybe. Oh, but he was good looking. She felt like laughing out loud as Martha struggled for diplomatic answers to the man's inane questions.

"I don't notice hair," Martha said softly. "I notice

willing workers in an emergency, people out helping others, and I especially enjoy being with people who love to talk about our Lord."

Rachel smiled to herself when Pastor Richards had the grace to blush. Martha's words probably hurt him a lot. Everything she'd mentioned, he lacked. After gulping a few breaths of air, the minister smiled. "Well, know what I enjoy? I enjoy being with you. Know why? Because you're sweet and dear, and one hundred percent honest even if it hurts." He squirmed a moment before continuing. "Now, how about you two lovely ladies going for a little walk with me?"

"I'd like that," Martha said, "but I promised Mama I'd take care of Willie while she takes a nap."

The fine looking head turned Rachel's way. Suddenly, she didn't yearn to be with him as much as she had. But she couldn't be sure. "I'd enjoy that," she said.

They walked through the sagebrush away from the wagon train, causing several rabbits to scurry away.

"If it weren't the Sabbath I'd get you some meat," he said to Rachel.

"I'm glad it's Sabbath then," she said. "Don't you feel bad having to hurt innocent animals?"

He jerked his eyes open in surprise. "I hadn't thought about it," he said.

"You hadn't? Don't you know they get scared and feel pain just like we do? And when you shoot an animal it may leave a nest of babies to starve."

He slowed to a stroll as he considered Rachel's words. Finally, he shook his head. "No, I don't think so. They aren't smart enough to be scared and I doubt they feel much, either."

"Why do you suppose they run so fast from men?"

He looked perplexed. "I don't know." Then a smile

reached from his full lips to his dark, deep-fringed eyes. Rachel's heart nearly missed a beat as she took in the tall, extremely handsome man. "But," the minister continued, "don't confuse me with the facts, all right? You could ruin one of my greatest pleasures—eating."

By unspoken agreement they turned back toward the wagons. "How would you like to think up a subject for me to preach about next week?" he asked as they walked.

"I'd like that," she said quickly before he changed his mind. "And I have the subject already. I'd like for you to tell the people exactly how to accept our Lord Jesus' great sacrifice for us and be saved."

His dark eyebrows lifted ever so slightly. "Everyone already knows that."

"Don't be so sure. You should teach that every few months forever."

By this time, they'd reached the wagons. "Thanks for walking with me," he said. "I'll give your suggestion some thought."

Later in the afternoon, Tom came to Rachel's wagon. "I wondered if you could go with me to check Tamara Richards one more time. I'm sure she's fine but I need to be sure, for her sake as well as mine."

The woman's wounds were almost healed but she was glad to see Tom and Rachel. "My brother James doesn't stay around much," she said, "and I get lonely."

"There's someone who could really use a friend," Tom said as they walked back to the Butler wagons.

Tom didn't stop long enough to tell her how to go about the good deed he'd suggested. Rachel wondered how she could befriend Tamara Richards, or if she wanted to.

The next day they passed Alkali Lake, an evil-smelling body of water many miles long. The water had an ugly whitish cast but the hot thirsty animals tried hard to reach it. The drivers held them back as the guidebook said the water was poisonous. The many dead animals lying along the Trail reminded everyone to restrain their animals, no matter what. Graves grew more numerous each day, too. The Trail was definitely taking its toll.

Soon, they came to Independence Rock, 815 miles from Independence. The huge granite rock, 500 feet long, 200 feet wide, and 250 feet tall stood alone in the Sweetwater Valley. Rachel, Martha, and Julia all grabbed knives, planning to carve their names in the Rock but soon learned granite isn't soft like Chimney Rock had been. The many names on the rock hadn't been carved in but painted on. They gave up and ran to catch up with the train.

Later that afternoon Tom Dorland stopped the train to tell them Andy Shackleford had died. Pastor Richards spoke a few words then they buried him right in the Trail. Rachel thought that was awful, but when the wagons started running over the grave she burst into tears.

ten

"We run the wagons over the grave so animals or Indians won't recognize the grave and dig it up," Tom, who'd come up behind her, explained. "It looks awful but it's for protection."

Rachel felt black depression after Andy died. Why did the people and animals keep dying? And for nothing! Right now she hated Heartbreak Trail more than she could say.

Martha talked to her all the rest of the day. "You feel God's love for you don't you?" she asked quietly.

Rachel nodded and swiped at her running nose with the back of her hand. "I thought I did."

"Don't allow yourself to doubt His love. Not for a minute, even when hard things come. We can't hope to understand everything, but we can trust and love. Then He'll help us through. Here's something else to think about. God loves Andy more than we did. Even more than his mother and father did. Many times more, so we just have to trust Him to make good come from bad."

After some time Rachel started to feel better. She needed to feel better for the little boys' sakes anyway. She started a game with them and by the time they camped, she felt His love again. Although she felt sad for Andy she truly knew God loved and cared for him forever.

They forded the Sweetwater River the next morning. The river was cold and clear, sixty feet wide and three feet deep. The stifling hot weather tempted the girls to wade across.

"Think we can?" Martha asked in response to Rachel's suggestion.

"The book says it's three feet deep," Rachel said. "We'll have to carry the boys partway but we can do that."

All the walkers in the train ended up wading across and having a wonderful time doing it. It cooled them for several hours.

A few days later they started up the Rocky Mountains on good but steep roads. Another of Mark Piling's oxen gave out and they left it lying on the ground.

"Who's going to take care of it?" Petey asked.

Rachel shuddered. "We'll pray for God to help it get well," she told him and they did. Rachel left the ox, hoping desperately that God would heal it.

Soon the roads became insufferably dusty. As a result, everyone's eyes became inflamed and sore. Some people had goggles to wear over their eyes, others wore veils. Martha and Rachel had only linen handkerchiefs so they tied them around their faces and also the little boys' faces.

Later the same day, Rachel had an idea. "Martha!" she said, "I'm going to cover our oxen's eyes with thin handkerchiefs." But when she tried, the oxen didn't understand she was trying to help them and neither did the drivers. They yelled for her to get out of the way and not to come back, tomorrow or the next day or ever!

A few days later Thurman Tate came past the walking girls, herding a brown cow in front of him. "See what I found," he said proudly. "I can add her to my others and have a herd."

"Does it give milk?" Willie asked.

Tate laughed. "I don't know yet. The thing won't let me get close enough to find out. But I'll get her tamed and breed her in Oregon. First thing you know, I'll have a whole herd of Jerseys."

On Sunday morning, May twenty-ninth, Rachel felt the fierce winds as she lay in bed. The top of the wagon snapped so hard she feared it would tear off the wagon and the cold reached through her many quilts right to her bones. When she finally crawled out of bed, she discovered the wind had brought thick dust with it.

Mama and Rachel had a tough time getting a fire going and when it finally caught, the smoke and dust burned her throat all the way down. How could she endure this for the rest of the summer?

Before they had breakfast ready two men came to talk to Papa. "Why should we stay here?" one of them asked him. "Let's get out of this foul weather."

"I'm not the man to talk to," Papa said. "Go see Captain Ransom, but we agreed to rest on the Sabbath, you know. Maybe we should have faith that the Lord will still the storm. He can, you know."

"Yeah," the man said as they walked away. "But I ain't seen Him doin' it."

About an hour later three wagons left the circle, leaving seventeen wagons and forty-one people.

Thurman Tate came along, looking for his cow. "I guess the wind spooked her," he said. "But I'll find her. I guarantee I'll get her, dead or alive."

The wind and dust continued so strongly that the preaching services and potluck dinner were canceled. So, Rachel ate and slept; she hadn't realized how tired she'd become. Later in the day the wind and dust died down, the sky cleared, and the sun peeked through, giving the travelers a hint of the heat it could still pour onto them.

That evening Tate went looking for his cow again. "I'll get her, you just wait and see," he told Rachel's father. Later, they heard the report of a gun and figured he'd found the cow. Now at least he'd have meat. But Tate came back herding the badly limping cow. "I got her," he yelled at Nate. "Had to shoot her a little but it cooled her down."

"Papa, make him kill her quick," Rachel said, as the cow staggered along in front of Tate.

"Better kill the poor thing and get it over with," Papa called to Tate.

"I ain't killin' her yet, Butler. We'll need the meat more later."

"But that's horrible," Rachel yelled. "Can't you imagine how you'd feel if you were all shot up and someone forced you to go on walking?"

Tate laughed. "I didn't force her to run off."

That night the wind came up again. The wagon rocked until Rachel wondered if it would tip over. The top snapped loudly, almost sounding like the report of guns. Rachel finally asked God to help her sleep, and He did.

The next morning, all of them lightened their loads some more. They broke up trunks for wood and threw out extra axles, shovels, chains, and other things beside the Trail. As the drivers forced their tired oxen on, Rachel, Martha, Julia, Petey, and Willie noticed deserted wagons and carts as well as furniture lining the road. Dead animals lay on and around the castoffs.

Rachel and Martha watched Thurman Tate's oxen stumbling along. When they faltered too much he laid the whip on their backs. He'd tied the cow to the wagon and she staggered along the best she could, bawling at nearly every step.

Rachel went to find Tom Dorland as he felt sympathy for animals more than anyone she knew.

"I'll talk to him," Tom said when Rachel told him about Tate's animals. "But I doubt he'll listen. I haven't heard him listen to anyone yet."

He rode up to Tate's wagon. "Your oxen are looking bad," he said. "Want some help dumping your stuff?"

"Them oxen are all right!" Tate yelled. "Why don't you go put a bandage on your mouth?"

"How about letting me treat the cow then? I might be able to make her more comfortable. She'd heal up faster, too."

"That cow's going to be meat in a week or so, so don't worry about her. You take care of your horse and I'll take care of my livestock."

Tom kept beside the Tate wagon as it moved slowly along. "Well, if you need some help, be sure to ask." Touching his heels to his horse's side he moved ahead.

Rachel stomped along, fuming. "Did you hear that?" she asked Martha.

" 'Most everyone in the train heard it," Martha said. "Calm down, Rachel. You have to learn to accept things you can't change."

Two days later the wagon train reached South Pass. Captain Ransom called the men to a meeting. Thirty minutes later, just as Alma and Rachel had dinner ready, Nate returned with Stan Latham. After they asked God to bless the food and also them, they filled their plates.

"This is where Sublette cutoff leaves the main trail," Nate explained. "It's supposed to save four days travel but there's a fifty-mile stretch with no food or water for the animals."

Rachel turned her back on him and dipped a biscuit into her beans. "What did you decide, Papa?"

Nate grinned through a mouthful of beans. "Well, most of us decided to stay on the main trail. Our animals are gettin' thin and worn. We decided it'd be too hard on them."

"Good for you, dear," Alma said. "You made the right decision."

"But that's not the end of the story. Tate's taking the cutoff. Said he'd wait for us at the other end."

"Oh, Papa, his oxen are worse than anyone's. And you know about his cow."

"I know. But we can't tell the man what to do."

But later that night Tate fixed part of the problem himself. Rachel heard a gunshot a half-hour before Tate appeared. "Want some beef?" he asked. "Just butchered the old cow. Figured she wouldn't make it through the cutoff."

"You figured right," Nate said. "Your oxen won't make it either. Better dump the heavy stuff and still take the regular trail."

Tate said a few words that didn't harmonize too well with his Christian claims. "Do you want some beef or not?" he added.

"I suppose we could use some," Nate said after a little thought.

"Come and get it then," Tate said, marching off. "Seems like people would appreciate some meat way out here," he mumbled.

"I don't want any of his meat," Rachel said. "I won't eat it either."

Nate glanced at Alma who shook her head. "Go tell him then," he told Rachel.

She didn't have to be told twice. She took off running in the direction he'd taken. She caught him at the Lawford wagon. Dr. Dorland was there, too.

"We're not interested in eating that poor creature," Martha was telling Tate. "I don't understand how anyone could treat one of God's creatures the way you've done that cow."

Dr. Dorland took up the conversation. "Only a man with absolutely no feeling in his heart could do it. I feel for your family. But about the cow. The meat is infected from her wounds and not fit to eat. I hope no one takes any, Tate, for their sake."

"Well, forget I asked. I shoulda just eaten it all myself." He hiked on down the row of wagons, not stopping at any more.

The next day the Tates stayed to jerk the meat. "We'll still beat you by three days," he told Captain Ransom. "We'll just wait for you and rest."

"I forgot to tell you girls one more thing," Nate said when Rachel returned. "There's another cutoff being built. It won't be finished until fall but it'll cut off one hundred miles and it has more water than the Trail." He sighed. "Won't do us any good, but it'll be a godsend to next year's emigration. It's called Lander's Cutoff."

The next day the train discovered that even on the main trail water was in short supply. They found none all day, not even at their camp. The Butler herd of cows' milk had dwindled from thirty gallons a day to less than one between them all, less than a cup apiece.

The next day, about noon, they reached Green River. The drivers couldn't hold back their parched oxen who pulled the wagons into the river. They camped beside the river so the animals could get their fill of grass and water.

An Indian trading post dominated the spot beside the river. Rachel saw Pastor Richards trade some fishing lures for several pairs of soft white deerskin moccasins.

The three girls and the little boys ran around looking at the colorful flowers.

"Look, Rachel," Willie said. "What are these red things?"

Rachel looked and discovered wild strawberries.

Strawberries! Real strawberries! The girls grabbed pans and picked all they could find.

Petey looked longingly at Martha's pan filled with the red treats. "I wish I was your little boy," he said.

"You can't be my little boy because you already have a mama," Martha said, hugging him, "but you can have half of my berries. Think your mama would like that?"

Petey's brown eyes sparkled with starry sunshine. "Thank you, Martha. I love you."

Rachel gave Martha part of her berries; Martha's family, after all, had more people to feed than her family did. Still, Rachel took home enough of the juicy red fruit for each family member to have a nice dish of them.

It was too cold and windy again for preaching on Sunday, June fourth, so Rachel had a nice day of rest. In the afternoon, the wind died down and Pastor Richards came by her wagon looking as if he'd just stepped from a shower into clean, freshly pressed clothes.

"How about a walk?" he asked.

Rather than hurt him, she tucked up her hair and went. Leading her to all of the train's young women, he invited them to his own wagon.

"What a nice surprise," Tamara said. "I love company."

Pastor Richards got out the moccasins and gave each girl a pair, including Tamara.

"How beautiful," Rachel said, turning hers over and over to see every bead and thread.

"You're welcome," the pastor said. "I wanted you all to have a reason to remember me."

Rachel knew she'd remember Pastor Richards with only friendship in her heart. How could she have thought she felt more?

The next day the oxen started another long hard week.

Rachel, Martha, Julia, Petey, and Willie walked together as always. Rachel hardly noticed when it happened but now she enjoyed the boys and missed them during their nap time.

A bunch of turnarounds told them that five men had been massacred by the Indians a little ways ahead.

"I don't believe them," Martha said. "They're just trying to impress people. And scare them."

Later, they came upon five graves, side-by-side. "Well, so much for what you don't believe," Rachel told Martha. "These are the graves the men told us about."

Finally, they reached the west end of Sublette Cutoff, the road Tate had taken. Not finding Tate waiting for them, they made camp and settled down for the night. That evening, the Tates showed up, wishing they'd stayed with the group.

"We lost two more oxen," Tate said. "And a cow. We can't take our wagon on as we don't have nothin' to pull it."

"I could help you make it into a cart," Nate Butler said. "Maybe your animals could pull it that way."

"No, you aren't," Tate's wife shrilled. "I have to have the things in that wagon."

"Shut up!" Tate said. "I bin listenin' to you too long."

"Then we'll have to keep the half with the cookstove and the dressers." She glared at Nate. "Do you have any idea how much those things cost?" Then she shook her head, answering her own question. "No, I'm sure you wouldn't."

"Ma'am," Nate said, "do you have any idea how much them oxen are worth or where you'll get some more?"

"Make it into a cart," Tate said. "Don't pay no 'tention to her."

It took all that evening and the following day but by the

next day a light, sleek, two-wheeled cart was ready to go. The cookstove and dressers joined the many other items abandoned beside the road.

As the train moved the next morning, Rachel noticed the Tate items. "How can they live with themselves," she said to Martha, "when they killed and tortured several animals by forcing them to haul that stuff up and down the hills. Now it's by the Trail."

Martha shook her dark head. "What a waste of life."

As they walked and talked, Rachel got brave enough to ask Martha what she thought of Pastor Richards.

"I think he's a good man trying to work for God," Martha answered.

But Rachel wasn't satisfied. "I know he's a good man, but I want to know how you feel about him personally. You know what I mean."

Martha smiled her sweet smile. "You mean do I more than like him? Well, I'll tell you the truth. I'm purely not romantically interested in any man, anywhere." She grinned impishly. "He's all yours, Rachel. Or yours, Julia."

"I don't want him," Rachel said. "I may have thought I did once but I know better now. I simply don't want him. He's all yours, Julia."

Julia giggled. "Well, thanks. But what am I going to do with two men? For the whole trip I've liked Dan Barlow a whole lot. But if you don't like the Reverend anymore, Rachel, who is it you do like?"

eleven

Rachel almost stopped walking as she sucked in her breath. She'd always "liked" someone since she'd been in eighth grade. But who now? She picked up her pace as she thought. "Well," she finally said. "I thought I liked the Reverend just because he's so handsome and tall and clean. Especially clean."

"Did you ever notice how he stays clean?" Julia asked, her eyes twinkling. "He never does a lick of work. Never. Not a lick. I'd rather have a real man."

Rachel laughed. "I told you I discovered I don't care for Pastor Richards that way. But you've put a claim on Dan Barlow so I can't have him."

Julia laughed happily. Obviously they'd finally found a subject entirely to her liking. "I hope you can't," she said giggling, "but I'm not sure. But who do you like now, Rachel?"

Rachel swung her red head back and forth. "There isn't anyone else."

That afternoon while Petey and Willie napped, the Ransom Train caught up with another train, stopped in the Trail. As they walked past the stopped train the girls noticed people standing around in groups. One man stood between two others as if they were restraining him.

The Ransom Train stopped; Martha and Rachel hurried to watch.

"Howdy," Captain Ransom said. "We interruptin' somethin'?"

"We're havin' ourselves a little trial," a white-haired

man said. "Wanna watch?"

"Yes, please," the girls whispered to each other. None had ever seen a trial.

They soon learned that the man had stolen a horse from some Indians, who had probably stolen it from a white man. After he'd been declared guilty, the "judge" told the jury they should determine the man's punishment. About twenty minutes later the jury foreman announced that the man should be "hanged by the neck until dead."

Captain Ransom turned on his heel and rushed back to his own train. "Let's get going," he yelled.

As they walked away, Rachel saw someone hoist the criminal onto the back of a big horse. Someone else climbed into a tree and tied a rope to a low branch, dropping the other end of the rope that was then secured around the man's neck.

"What's going to happen?" Julia asked.

"Someone's going to hit that horse really hard and make him jump out from under the man and he'll be 'hanged until dead,' " George Lawford said.

The girls hurried on looking straight ahead, not caring to see what happened next.

"What if he didn't do it?" Martha asked.

"Better hope he did," Rachel said. " 'Cause he's paying for it anyway."

A few hours later they nooned at Soda Springs, nine or ten sparkling, boiling, bubbling springs of clear water. Someone discovered that by adding a little acid to the water it made a good drink. Rachel and Mama tried it. Not that good, Rachel thought, but something different.

"I'll bet it would be good in biscuits," Mama said. Papa brought a small pail of the water and never had Rachel seen Mama's biscuits rise so high. Mama put the water into jars to take with them.

A fourth of a mile farther they found Steamboat Springs with warm milky water. The train camped there and the women did their washings, the first in hot water since they left Independence. Martha and Rachel did their families' washing, then Mrs. Piling's. The woman hadn't gotten better since Mr. Piling returned from the dead. In fact, as the days passed, she seemed worse.

After the girls finished Mrs. Piling's laundry, they did the wash of several of the horse riders and for Mr. and Mrs. Pitman, an old couple who seemed to be in nearly as bad condition as the oxen. They were considerably older than the fifty-year age limit advised for the vigorous journey, but they'd insisted on coming.

Later that afternoon, as Martha and Rachel returned from doing all the washing, they met Dr. Dorland with a small bloody animal in his hand. Josie's nose twitched as she hurried to Tom.

"I got a gopher for Josie," he said. "Thought she'd be needing another one."

Martha grimaced, then reached for the horrible looking bit of flesh. But Tom drew it back.

"No need for you to touch it," he said. "I'll just give it to Josie." She gladly accepted the bloody morsel, biting it twice before swallowing it whole. Tom laughed and nodded. "I'll keep watching for food for her." He hurried away, wiping his hands on his pants as he went.

The dust continued to plague the travelers and the oxen. Not only did it get into man's and animal's eyes but it piled over the shoe tops making it extremely difficult to walk. Rachel, Martha, Julia, Petey, and Willie wore thin linen handkerchiefs over their eyes and noses.

Rachel noticed the oxen's eyes ran thick with yellowish stuff as they limped along on sore feet. After several failed attempts to help them, she'd learned that she couldn't do anything. But one day Tom Dorland happened by on his mare so she called him over.

"We have to do something for the oxen's eyes," she said. "They're just awful."

His smile faded into a solemn concerned look. "I've noticed," he said. "Not only yours, but all the oxen in the train. It's too hard on them."

"Well, what can we do about it?"

He shook his light head. "The only thing I know would be to stop traveling until the dust dies down. But as far as I can tell, it plans to fly forever."

Disappointment temporarily made Rachel forget she was a brand new Christian and that whatever she said "to the least of these" she said to Jesus.

"Are you going to just let them suffer then? Just say we can't do anything? Not get the train stopped?" Her voice grew louder as she continued. "I thought you cared, Tom Dorland, but you're just like the rest. You're not made of fit material to be a doctor!"

Tom watched her fume for another moment before he grinned. "I'm not an animal doctor," he said softly. "But I do care. I cared about Andy Shackleford, too, but I couldn't help him either." He touched his heels to his horse's sides and trotted off to the front of the line.

One evening they camped by a busy little creek of delightfully cool water where grass grew abundantly. Martha, Julia, and Rachel waded along the creek, enjoying the ice cold water on their feet.

"Look!" Julia shouted, "berries!"

Rachel climbed out of the creek in a hurry and found serviceberries growing thickly on low vines. By that time Martha had pulled herself away from the creek, too, and the girls ran back to the wagons for containers. They filled every pot and pan they could get hold of.

"What'll we do with them?" Martha asked Mrs. Lawford.

Martha's mother was sweet and round, always ready to help the young people. "Well," she said, "we can't take them with us." After thinking a moment, she clapped her hands. "I know. Why don't you make some pies, cobblers, fruit cakes, and whatever you can think up and invite the horse riders to help you eat them?"

So the girls did. Each took some berries and cooked everything she could think of with what she had to cook with. Then Julia ran to invite everyone who wanted to come. Soon, people arrived from all around the wagon circle.

"It smells good," Pastor Richards said with one more exaggerated sniff. "When do we get to eat?"

Stan Latham arrived next with his tin plate and a dirty looking fork. Tom Dorland came next, wearing a wide smile. Dan Barlow came with Tom, both looking as if they anticipated something special. Jackson Lawford trotted into the group, eagerly looking at the treats.

Then Tamara Richards came with her hand through a tall thin man's arm. She looked almost like a real person, Rachel thought. She smiled, her eyes sparkled, and she walked with energy. "I'd like you to meet my friend, Evan Mann," she said almost as if showing off a prize race horse.

"Where'd he come from?" Rachel blurted out. "I thought I'd seen everyone on the train."

"He stays with his wagon and oxen most of the time," Tamara said. She laughed quietly into the man's eyes. "He's shy, but I've been sending him some food, and my brother James shot a few ducks for him, so we got acquainted."

"Good afternoon, Evan Mann," Rachel said, extending her hand. As the man accepted and shook her hand, she recognized him. He was the man who'd tried to catch a rabbit! Rachel tried not to show her recognition and hoped that Martha wouldn't either. It could embarrass the man to be reminded of that hilarious run through the sagebrush.

Julia served Dan first, then herself. They went off somewhere to eat, leaving Rachel and Martha to serve the others. There was plenty of food for everyone who came and several had seconds. Stan Latham alone had thirds.

Pastor Richards led an inspiring collection of songs and preached his usual stirring sermon on June twelfth. Then the group ate lunch together. Rachel felt rather detached since she'd lost interest in the young minister. The silly young men running after the girls meant nothing to her anymore and she wondered how she could have been so enthralled with all of it only a few days ago.

The next morning Rachel happened to be near when the handlers yoked up the oxen for the day's travel. For the first time the oxen tried their best to avoid the yokes. But with a few strong words and two men working together, they forced the heavy yokes onto the oxen's raw necks and shoulders. When the rough wood hit their sores, the animals bawled a moment then quieted as if willing to do what must be done.

Rachel forced back the tears that tried to come into her eyes, then ran around the still-circled wagons to Captain Ransom's wagon.

"Mr. Ransom, you have to stop the wagon train so the oxen can get better," she cried.

The man rose from the box he'd been sitting on. "What's happened, Rachel? Are you all right?"

"No, I'm not. And neither are our oxen. They didn't want the yokes rubbing on their sore necks this morning. They're limping on sore feet and they're getting thinner every day. You have to help me, Captain Ransom."

He shook his thick gray hair. "You're right, girlie. Them oxen need weeks to recuperate. So do some of our people."

Rachel felt a moment's relief but the man continued on.

"Thing is, we don't have time. We're already behind our schedule. Gotta get to Oregon City afore the snow flies. We get caught in the mountains, we'll all die, animals and all." He moved to her, put his arm around her shoulders, and pulled her close. "So we gotta keep movin'. I allays tell the men to treat their animals right, though."

Rachel thanked the man for listening and stumbled back toward her own wagon. At least she knew how it was.

Two days later, just after the wagons corralled, Dan Barlow came to Rachel's wagon. "Miss Lawford," he said quietly, "your father wants you at your wagon right away." Turning his eyes to Julia, he smiled. "See you tonight." Touching his heels to his gelding, he rode ahead.

Martha looked curious. "Strange," she said. "Papa's never called me before. I hope everything's all right. Guess I'd better go find out."

"Want me to come, too?" Rachel asked, staying by Martha's side. "Maybe Julia would watch the boys until we get back."

"I'd love to," Julia said, her eyes still full of stars from her encounter with Dan. "You just go on and do whatever you need to. I'll take good care of them."

When they neared the Lawford wagon, Tom Dorland jumped to the ground and met them a few feet away. "I'm sorry to have to tell you, Miss Lawford, but your mother's sick."

Martha's face lost every semblance of color. "What is it?"

He shook his head. "I can't be sure but it looks bad." He drew in a long breath. "Could be cholera," he murmured.

"No." Martha didn't say more or move a muscle.

But Rachel drew in a long breath and bolted for the wagon, slowing only to jump into it. Mr. Lawford sat on a box near his wife who looked still and small in her featherbed. Rachel knelt by the woman and took her hand.

"Mrs. Lawford," she said. "I'm here to pray with you."

Mrs. Lawford opened her eyes. "Bless you, dear."

"Oh dear heavenly Father," Rachel began, "we thank You for Your great love for us and giving Your precious only Son to die for us. Oh, Lord, You know how Mrs. Lawford loves You and what a wonderful influence she is on everyone. Please, dear Lord, make her well right away. We all need her so badly. I pray these things in Jesus' precious name, and thank You for hearing and answering my prayer."

Rachel opened her eyes and looked down at Martha's mother, almost expecting to see her get up and start gathering sticks for the supper's fire.

But sweat ran from the woman's unusually red cheeks. She reached a hand to Rachel. "Thank you dear, for that lovely prayer. I'm sure He'll have me up in a day or so."

Rachel, on her knees, leaned down and kissed the hot cheek. "Of course He will," she whispered. "Now you sleep for a while and don't worry. We'll take good care of Willie."

"I know," the sick woman said, her eyelashes falling against her cheeks.

Rachel jumped to the ground where Martha and Tom still talked. Tom smiled at her. "Got yourself all exposed, did you?"

Rachel hadn't given that possibility a thought. Well, if

there was anything to be exposed to, she probably did. "I might have," she admitted.

"I'll be back in a couple of hours," he told Martha.

Martha didn't talk much. "We'll keep Willie tonight," Rachel said. "And I'll come over later to see what Tom says."

On being told that his mama was sick, Willie agreed to stay with Rachel. After the supper things were cleaned up and put away, Rachel hurried to the Lawford wagon. Martha met her outside and told her Tom was certain her mama had cholera.

"I'm going to help take care of her and make her well," Rachel said. "I'll be over in the morning."

The next morning Captain Ransom called a day's stop for the train to give Mrs. Lawford a chance to recover.

The woman had worsened during the night, Rachel learned when she arrived at Martha's wagon. "You go do something or rest," she told her dear friend.

Mr. Lawford sat on his wooden box in the wagon, looking heartbroken. "Don't you worry, Mr. Lawford," Rachel said. "We'll have her on her feet in no time. You just sit here and watch and listen if you want."

First she wet washrags in cold water and put them on Mrs. Lawford's hot forehead.

"That feels so good," the woman whispered. "Please, don't stop."

"I won't," she told the weak woman. "I'm going to be here and keep them on you all day."

She applied the cold compresses and read the Gospel of John to the Lawfords most of the day. Both listened quietly to every word. But, every time she stopped to cool the washrag, Mr. Lawford asked how his wife was now.

Tom came by a little later. "I don't know if you're helping her physically, but you're doing them both a world of good," he told Rachel. "As you read, you're giving them something positive to think about and the wet cloths certainly do make her feel better." He smiled a gentle smile. "Since you already got yourself exposed, I'll just say keep up the good work."

At noon Rachel stopped and made some rabbit broth from a rabbit Jackson Lawford had brought and cleaned. After giving Mr. Lawford a bowl and spooning some into Mrs. Lawford's mouth, she went back to her reading and applying the cold compresses.

"What have you been doing today?" Rachel asked when Martha finally appeared at the wagon.

"I've been doing people's washing," she said. "I had a feeling I'd be busy when washing day came so I got it done today. How's my mama?"

"I don't know," Rachel said. "She's not talking as much as she was this morning."

Rachel ran back to her own wagon just in time for supper. Willie and Julia had gathered sticks for the fire and Mama had biscuits and side meat cooking.

Willie slept in Rachel's wagon again and morning came quickly. After breakfast, Rachel hurried to the Lawford wagon again. Martha ran to meet her.

"Papa's sick, too," Martha whispered. "They're both awfully sick."

Both girls worked all day caring for Martha's parents. Both seemed too sick to listen to reading but Rachel did it anyway, just in case. Rachel cared mostly for Mrs. Lawford and Martha took care of her father. At noon, both girls fixed broth for Martha's parents.

"Papa thinks I'm Mama," Martha whispered. "Oh, Rachel, I'm afraid they aren't going to get well."

"Yes, they are," Rachel snapped. "God will make them well."

twelve

Tom Dorland came by several times that day and left looking sadder each time. One time Rachel found him kneeling beside Mrs. Lawford, his hand on her forehead, praying earnestly for her and Mr. Lawford.

That night Rachel stayed with Martha to help. Mrs.
Lawford died early in the morning. Mr. Lawford didn't
know. He died that afternoon.

Pastor Richards said a few words, prayed for Martha,
Jackson, and Willie, then they buried Mr. and Mrs.
Lawford in the Trail. The emigrants yoked up to continue on and many wagons ran over the graves, trying to
hide them from Indians and animals. And the wagon train
moved forward. Always forward. Relentlessly forward.

Jackson guided the Lawford oxen who seemed nearly
as broken as he. They could hardly walk and Jackson
could barely hold his head erect.

Martha, Rachel, Julia, Petey, and Willie walked with
Jackson. Rachel thought she couldn't bear losing the
Lawfords. They had been good to her, even when she
hadn't been all that nice to anyone.

"Why didn't God heal them?" she kept asking Martha.
"We prayed so hard. Even Tom prayed."

"We can't understand everything," Martha said, "but
just keep on trusting Him, Rachel. He knows the beginning from the end."

Those words didn't satisfy Rachel. "What's the use
praying if He doesn't answer?" she asked bitterly.

Martha remained calm. "I'm not sure. Maybe we'll go

through some horrible hardships that would have been harder for them than to die quickly and peacefully. This may have been the best way. No, I said that wrong. This was the best way. God loved them much more than we did, and He wanted the best for them even more than we did. But He knows all. And don't forget that death isn't the end, Rachel. There's a beautiful home in a beautiful world waiting for them. . .and for us. Please don't lose your faith."

As the days passed, Rachel thought about the things Martha had said. Finally, they made sense to her. She felt better and God's sweet peace returned to her heart.

One day they neared Fort Hall, 1300 miles from Independence. Abandoned wagons, household goods, and dead animals grew thicker around them. As they drew close to the large fort, Jackson called Martha to him. Rachel moved closer, too, as they walked along the dusty trail.

"Have you noticed the oxen can barely walk?" he asked.

Martha nodded. "I've noticed, Jackson. It's really sad, but what can we do?"

He gave her a long look. "They're giving out, Martha. See them stumbling? Almost blindly? They're going to die within two days. We'll have to leave them at Fort Hall. With rest and some good food they might recover. Otherwise, they're dead."

"Leave them, Martha," Rachel cried. "Give them a chance to live."

"But what will we do?" Martha asked. "We don't have extra oxen like you."

"Martha!" Jackson said. "Either we leave them and hope for the best or they're dead. They can't help us if they're dead."

"Leave them," Rachel repeated. "We have extra oxen. I'll get Papa to put some on your wagon."

So that's what they did. The fresh oxen pulled with a strength that the Lawford animals hadn't had for weeks.

The next day after they left the oxen, Jackson called Martha to him again as they walked. "I keep thinking I need to go back on the Trail and meet Aunt Mandy and Uncle Cleve," he said. "They deserve to know what happened."

"No, Jackson," Martha pleaded. "You have to care for the oxen while I watch Willie."

He walked a while then continued. "I have to, don't you see? I just have to, Martha. Someone will help you with the oxen."

Martha begged and pleaded with Jackson but couldn't change his mind.

The next morning he gathered his clothes, a little food, and climbed onto his horse. "As soon as I tell them what happened I'll come right back," he said. "I won't be gone more than a few days, so wish me well."

"I'll try," Martha said in a small voice. "But you shouldn't be doing this. The oxen are your responsibility."

"I'll tell you what I think," Rachel said. "I think you're not even a man but a big baby. Don't you think Martha hurts as much as you? And poor little Willie. How's he going to feel when you run off?"

"Sorry," Jackson mumbled. "It's something I have to do." He touched his horse's sides with his heels and took off trotting, back the way they'd come.

On Sunday, June nineteenth, the warm sunny weather lifted Rachel's spirits. And she hadn't heard a single mosquito during the night! Could it be that they were through with that plague?

Pastor Richards preached a stirring sermon on having

faith when it seems all reason for faith is gone. "Faith isn't faith," he said, "when all goes well. Faith is believing when all looks dark and your prayers don't seem to be heard. That's real faith. And our Lord will help you with this faith if you only ask."

The people shared the noon meal so they could all be together on their day of rest.

As Martha, Willie, Rachel, and Julia filled their plates, Pastor Richards approached, this time giving Rachel his attention.

"Would you lovely young ladies mind if a tired old preacher joined you for dinner?" he asked.

Before Rachel had a chance to panic, Stan Latham crowded between Pastor Richards and her.

"You look uncommonly lovely today, Miss Butler," he said in his oily smooth voice. "I'd like the privilege of sharing the meal with you."

Suddenly, she looked longingly at Pastor Richards. At least she could eat with him sitting there. She'd almost for sure throw up if the filthy Stan Latham were in sight. What could she do?

Before she answered, another oh-so-welcome voice broke the stillness—Tom Dorland.

"Oh, Miss Butler, there you are," Tom said. "I need your help right away. . .if you have time. I need to medicate a couple of bad eyes and can't do it alone."

Rachel jumped to her feet before Tom finished. "I'm ready," she said, heaving a huge sigh of relief. "Let's go."

As they walked away from the dinner, Rachel felt a stab of remorse for having left Martha at the mercy of Stan Latham. "Where is this person who needs treatment?" she asked.

Tom grinned. His eyes had a lovely glow that Rachel

hadn't seen before. Come to think of it she may have never noticed his eyes at all. The soft look must come from his close relationship with God. "Did I say it was a person?" he asked. "I had in mind treating your oxen's eyes with some boric acid. It might make them feel better."

Rachel stopped in her tracks. "What's going on, Dr. Dorland? I tried hard to get you to help those oxen and you refused. What's changed?"

They reached Rachel's wagon where Tom had stashed the medicine. "Well, I mixed up this stuff and decided to try it," he said. "If you still want to, that is." Then they took the medicine and went searching for the oxen but couldn't find them.

"They're somewhere gorging on grass," Rachel said. "Wouldn't it be better to do it while they're yoked?"

He nodded. "I think you're right." He grinned mischievously again. "So, should we go get something to eat?"

Rachel laughed and headed back toward the dinner. "Well, I'm glad you thought about the oxen and got me away from Stan Latham. I panicked when that pig showed up."

"Oh, one more thing," Tom said as they neared the crowd of people. "When we finish eating, I have to take some food to the Pitmans. If you help me, we can do it in one trip."

As they reached the rest of the people, Rachel agreed to help. Pastor Richards and Stan Latham still sat with Martha and Julia. Dan Barlow was there, too, sitting close to Julia. Tom and Rachel filled their plates and joined them. Rachel faced away from Stan Latham and pretended he wasn't there.

Later, Rachel and Tom carried a nice meal to the

Pitmans who thanked them profusely. As they walked back to Rachel's wagon, she thought about the old couple.

"Will the Pitmans get cholera and die?"

He shook his head. "We can hope and pray they won't."

When they reached Rachel's wagon, Tom seemed reluctant to leave. They talked a little about Martha, how brave she was, left all alone with Willie, the wagon, and the oxen.

The next day they traveled on. Soon, the sun became scorching.

"The dust comes over my shoes," Willie complained, "and it hurts."

"I know," Martha told him tenderly. "It comes over mine, too. Try to put your feet straight down when you step."

He couldn't so Martha carried him a while. "It's hot on my feet, too," she told the little boy. "Can you walk now?"

He walked a while then she carried him again, all the time keeping the oxen going. Petey managed to keep going on his own.

Early in the afternoon they came to Fall River which they had to ford. The deep river with steep banks looked impassible.

"How can we go across that?" Petey asked.

"I don't know," Martha said. "Shall we sit here and watch?"

Soon, they saw the men putting secure ropes around a wagon, then tying the ropes to five yoke of oxen. With men guiding both the wagon and the oxen, they let the wagon down the steep cliff. They lowered all the wagons the same way.

Then the same weary oxen pulled the wagons across the deep swift stream. The men made it as safe as possible by hooking several wagons together and doing the same with the oxen. At near dusk, the last wagon emerged from the river and Captain Ransom called corralling time.

The next morning the road turned into a big rock pile. Big rocks, little rocks, smooth rocks, sharp rocks. So many rocks that when the oxen stepped onto one it rolled onto the others, causing the weary animals to stumble and nearly fall. The girls had the same problem.

The sun beat down so hot that Rachel saw little heat waves coming off the oxen and felt herself wavering, too. She couldn't see one bush or even sagebrush anywhere to shade people or animals from the burning sun. They nooned at a place where they found a little patch of grass but it wasn't nearly large enough to satisfy the famished animals.

"Why did you stop here?" Rachel yelled at Captain Ransom. "Can't you see the animals need more food?"

"I've heard about enough out of you, young lady!" Ransom shouted back. "Just where am I supposed to find grass, anyway?"

"There must be some if you'd just look harder," Rachel yelled, then burst into tears. Why did she act so mean, anyway? Ransom had never been unkind before. She voiced her worries to Martha.

"He's doing his best," Martha said. "It's the heat that's causing people to lose control. Just ask God to help you be kind."

While Rachel and her mother fixed dinner, Rachel heard people yelling at each other from other wagons and decided Martha was right. The heat made people crazy.

Just before dinner was ready, Papa left the area and Mama asked Rachel to find him. She ran all over looking for him, finally finding him with Captain Ransom.

"I've been looking all over for you," she said much

louder than necessary. "Why do you run off just when dinner's ready?"

"I'm not your child," he yelled. "I'll go where I want whenever I want if it's all the same with you."

Rachel wheeled around to run back to the wagon and ran into Tom Dorland. "Why do you have to sneak up on me all the time?" she yelled at him. "You could at least let a person know you're coming."

He opened his mouth, closed it and remained silent a moment. "I'm sorry," he finally said. "I didn't intend to sneak up on you." His voice remained sweet and calm.

Embarrassed at being so unkind, Rachel turned her back on him and tore back to her wagon where she realized she wasn't representing God very well. No, she wasn't representing Him at all. "Please forgive me, Father," she whispered. "I'm sorry to be so terrible. I hope You won't give up on me." Immediately, she had a strong feeling that she should ask Captain Ransom, Tom Dorland, and Papa to forgive her. But she was much too hot to find all of them right now.

Each day was the same. Scorching heat, burning dust, and people yelling at each other. All except Tom and Martha. Those two stayed nice no matter what.

On June twenty-sixth, every creature needed the rest so badly and the sun stayed so hot that many didn't turn out for Pastor Richards's service or the potluck dinner afterward. Rachel attended though, so Martha wouldn't be alone. They didn't even have their plates filled when Pastor Richards joined them. Speaking especially to Rachel, he talked about his sermon, the singing, his hard-to-keep-pressed clothing, and his absent parishioners.

She tried to listen patiently, wondering how she'd ever thought he might be the man for her. About the time they finished eating, Tom, who hadn't eaten with the group, arrived with another small dead animal for Josie.

The next morning the train started early and traveled hard. Rachel thought her feet would burn up, even through her shoes. The dust on the ground burned so hot she couldn't keep her hand on it. Finally, after what seemed like forever, the train stopped to camp at Salmon Falls. Tepees, ponies, and Indians swarmed everywhere. One Indian brought a thirty-five-pound salmon to swap for old clothes. Several families traded clothes for the Indian's huge fish.

The Indian gave the fish to Papa, then looked the clothes over. He seemed pleased until he found a long rip in one shirt. With hand motions he requested a needle and thread that someone provided. Then, he sat on his heels and went to work on the tear. A few minutes later, he handed the needle back, nodding and wearing a wide smile. Rachel signed for him to hold up the shirt for her to see. Surprised, she discovered the Indian had used some skill in repairing the shirt.

The next day as they traveled, carcasses became so thick they almost blocked the Trail. The overpowering stench seemed more than the emigrants could bear. And graves became so numerous Rachel lost count.

When they stopped that evening, one of Thurman Tate's oxen dropped dead in the yoke. The other's legs gave way and it couldn't get up. The next morning the ox still couldn't get up so Tate had to leave it there. He also had to leave the cart. Several families took a few of the Tates' clothes but all their oxen were too worn-out to carry much more so the rest of the Tates' belongings were left alongside the Trail.

"I wish someone would tell that man how much misery and death his greediness has caused innocent animals,"

Rachel groused.

The train continued on all day with no grass or water for the oxen. At five o'clock that afternoon they reached the river and, in their eagerness for water, the oxen pulled the wagons into the river again.

So desperately did the animals need the nourishment that the guides went off the Trail, looking for grass. The train was stopped any time someone found grass.

The next day the train came to a good camp at Glenn's Ferry at Three Island Crossing, 1398 miles from home. As the people prepared for the Sabbath and Rachel and Martha washed clothes, Rachel told Martha they'd never see civilization again.

On Sunday, July third, people came from all around to hear the preaching and share the meal. Since no one had much food anymore, the potlucks consisted mostly of beans, biscuits, and dried apple pie. Fewer and fewer people came to the dinners.

The next morning everyone repacked and threw away anything they could live without. They'd done this so many times that Rachel wondered how there could be anything left. But more items edged the road each time. When everyone was ready, the people lined up to be ferried across the river. All except Mark Piling.

"I ain't makin' those cutthroats rich," he said. "I'll just get myself across and save the money."

"Better not," Nate Butler said. "They say the river's ruthless here."

"Who says?" Piling asked scornfully. "The men who run the ferry?"

Rachel, Martha, Julia, Petey, and Willie sat on the river bank to watch Piling ford the river.

But Mr. Piling came after Petey. "You get yourself over

to our wagon!" he bellowed at the trembling little boy. "Fergot you even had a family din't you?" As Petey skittered past his father, Piling reached out a hand and cuffed the back of Petey's head, knocking him, face first, into the dust. "Get up!" Piling yelled. "Get into that wagon and make sure the water don't get too high." Petey scrambled to his feet, tears running down his dirty face, and raced ahead of Mr. Piling to the wagon.

Piling hooked his oxen to the wagon and started them into the river. The animals balked several times and Piling rewarded them with hard lashes from the whip. Eventually, they made it to the first island. Then, with more lashing, the oxen reached the second island. They'd nearly made it across.

"It's going to be all right now," Julia breathed.

But, just as she spoke, a swift undercurrent snatched the wagon, tipping it over. Mr. Piling, who'd been in the river with the oxen, grabbed his wife as she tumbled from the wagon. Mrs. Piling held tightly to the baby but Petey whirled past them and on down the river.

thirteen

Martha screamed and bolted toward the river. Rachel caught her just in time to stop her from plunging in after Petey. Mr. Piling held on tight to his wife and baby, watching Petey spin and whirl down the river until he disappeared from sight.

A moment later, the oxen became tangled in the harness and cumbersome yoke and couldn't keep their heads above the water. One of them managed to let out a loud bawl as they careened down the river, over and under the wagon. Soon, the wagon's contents littered the surface of the river and parts of the wagon bounced on the water until they lined the far bank.

"Go get him!" Martha screamed to anyone who might be listening. "Go get Petey! He's in the river!"

No one plunged into the river, but many people ran down the banks looking for the little boy.

Rachel had to restrain Martha again. As Martha screamed and struggled, Rachel thanked God she was bigger and stronger than Martha. Rachel had never seen Martha upset before, let alone in a horrible state like this.

"You can't go into the river hoping to find Petey," Rachel said quietly. "You'd only drown yourself." Martha continued to struggle with all her strength. "Martha," Rachel said a little louder, "you have Willie to care for. Remember, Martha?"

Finally, Martha wilted in Rachel's arms, her strength gone. "They aren't going to save him," she murmured over and over and over. Finally, she quieted.

The men looked for Petey all that night and until noon the next day. Early in the afternoon Pastor Richards held a short service for Petey after which wagon train moved on.

The Rahns took in Mr. and Mrs. Piling and the baby. The Pilings had nothing left for anyone to haul. Rachel walked to a spot where she could see Mrs. Piling. She looked like a snow white dead person with no expression at all.

The train traveled five miles to a good camp at Wickahoney Creek. Rachel stayed with Martha that night. Poor confused Willie stayed with Rachel's parents. Martha, who had been so brave when her parents died, went completely to pieces now. She cried and moaned all night; in the rare moments she slept, she called out for the little boy. Rachel cradled her in her arms and held her tightly.

Pastor Richards came to Martha but she turned him away. "Rachel's taking care of me," she said. "I don't need anyone else. No one cares anyway, not even God."

Rachel, realizing their roles had been reversed, reminded Martha that God loved Petey even more than they did and that He was crying with them. "Petey'll wake up with Jesus in the most beautiful home he's ever had," she promised. "Jesus will love him and never hurt him. Mark Piling hurt Petey, Martha. Haven't you noticed how Petey kept away from his father? And how he hurt him that last day? Maybe God took Petey away from his father to protect him from more pain and suffering."

After several days of crying and listening to Rachel explain how God let this happen to save Petey from his abusive father, Martha seemed to accept Petey's death. She clung to Willie and didn't mention Petey anymore, though her white face told of her continued suffering.

"I want you to remember one thing," Rachel told Martha as they trudged along beside the oxen one day. "You gave Petey more happiness than he'd ever known. I know you did. And you taught him to love Jesus. Day after day you taught him of Jesus' love for him. That's something for you to rejoice about. We both know how much Petey loved Jesus, don't we?"

Martha smiled tremulously and nodded. "We purely do. Thank you, Rachel for being so good for me right now. You've become a real Christian."

But, inside, Rachel wasn't sure about that. She felt so furious with Piling she thought she couldn't handle having him around anymore. One day she told Martha how she felt about the man. "I wish he'd died instead of Petey!" she said. "Mrs. Piling would have been glad, too. I know she would."

Martha took her eyes from the oxen and hugged Rachel. "I know how you feel," she said. "But we can't feel that way. Remember the Lord's Prayer says God will forgive us as we forgive others. Let's ask God to help us forgive Mr. Piling. Let's pray for God to touch Mr. Piling's heart, too." So the girls prayed right then and there.

Still, Rachel couldn't stop thinking about Mr. Piling, and her thoughts weren't good.

One day Captain Ransom stopped the train when a little girl, Jennie, fell in front of a wagon and an ox walked on her. Tom Dorland sent someone after Rachel to help him.

"You have to hold her still while I pull her leg into place," he said in his kind but firm voice.

Rachel held the child, murmuring encouragement into her ear, doubting the girl heard over all her screaming.

"There," Tom said a while later. And, in the middle of a sob, the little girl stopped crying. Rachel looked up with a question in her eyes. Tom smiled. "The bone snapped into place," he explained. "I'm sorry I had to hurt you," he told the little girl. "I won't hurt you anymore." Then he instructed Rachel how to help him put the splint on the leg in the most comfortable way. An hour later they finished and Rachel felt as if she'd been running all day.

"You're the best helper I've ever had," Tom said, his eyes showing his appreciation. "You really must consider going into medicine."

Rachel laughed quietly. "I'll do that," she said. "I'll enter the first medical school I find in Oregon City." Then she thought of Piling. "May I talk to you a minute?" she asked.

"Sure. I'll carry Jennie back to her parents first. Then we can walk for a little while."

When they finally stood where no one could hear them, Rachel felt shy to be talking to Tom like this. He was so good, he probably never had a negative thought about anyone. But she'd brought him here and she would share her thoughts. "I can't stop thinking about Mr. Piling," she said softly. "I can't stand the man, Tom, and I don't think he should be allowed to stay on the train. Could you ask the captain to put him off?"

Tom looked surprised for just a second then cleared his face of expression. "I wonder if you've thought this through," he finally said. "If Ransom puts Piling off the train, his wife and baby will go, too. And those poor people have had it rough enough already, don't you think?"

True enough, Rachel hadn't intended for the wife and baby to go, but they probably would.

Tom smiled kindly at Rachel. "I understand how you feel and I suspect most of the people on the train feel the same way. But we're a Christian group, remember?"

A few days later they met four more turnarounds. "You oughta go back while you can," they said. "It's nothin' but desert fer a long ways. By then it'll be winter and you'll never git through the Blues. Them mountains is killers. They kill the oxen and people just the same."

The men from the Ransom Train huddled around the four trying to decide how much the men knew and how much they surmised. "We must be almost through the desert," Dan Barlow said. "The Mormon guidebook says—"

Suddenly, one of the turnarounds pointed a finger at Dan. "I know you," he yelled. Then he turned to the others. "You'uns know who you got on this here train? That cur's a horse thief. I seen him escape just before he got hisself hanged. 'Twas in Illinois, it was. Ran right through the crowd, grabbed the sheriff's own horse, and escaped. In broad daylight, he did. Get a rope, boys. Let's finish the job."

"Just hold on here," Captain Ransom said quietly. "This here's my son and he's been with me all his life. Never set foot in no state but Missouri. Musta been someone else. Come on, let's get this thing movin'."

"Hey," the accuser yelled, "I know that face for sure. He's the man. Get him, boys. 'Tain't right for a man to flout the law." The other three men converged on Dan who made no effort to protect himself.

Stan Latham turned to Tom Dorland and Nate Butler. "Grab your guns," Stan said. Almost instantly, a dozen men had guns, all aimed at the turnarounds.

"Turn the man loose," Nate demanded. "We don't want a war over this but you can't come in here and abduct the captain's son."

The turnarounds released Dan, backed to their horses, mounted, and galloped away, cursing loudly.

After the men were nearly out of sight, Dan turned to Ransom. "I'm the man, Captain. I stole a horse when I was nineteen, old enough to know better. I thank you all for defending me but I'm ready to pay for my crime now."

Captain Ransom shook his wiry gray hair. "The Dan Barlow on this train always pulls his weight and then some. He's had plenty of opportunities to help himself to things but never has. He's allays thinking of the other guy. No, the Dan Barlow on this train isn't a taker, but a giver." He looked around at the circle of men then back to Dan. "The Dan Barlow on this train is a genyooine born again Christian and I don't want to hear you or no one else say or even think anything foul about this here Dan. Is that clear?" No one said a word, but some flickering smiles met Ransom's stern command.

The train started to move again and, as always, Rachel and Julia walked with Martha and her borrowed oxen, helping her as they could and especially entertaining Willie, who kept asking for Petey.

"Wasn't that exciting?" Julia asked, referring to the encounter with the turnarounds.

"A little too exciting," Rachel said. "Someone could have gotten hurt."

"But isn't Dan brave? And isn't the captain wonderful? Imagine him, claiming Dan for his son."

"That was because he knows Dan's a really sincere Christian now," Martha said, "a new person in Christ. He'd never have done that if Dan was the same man who stole the horse."

"Have you decided to go on to Oregon City?" Rachel asked Martha for the millionth time.

"I purely can't," Martha said. "Jackson and my aunt and uncle and cousin will come looking for Willie and me there. And Josie, of course."

"Jackson doesn't deserve to find you," Rachel snapped. "He should spend the rest of his life looking for you." She pointed at the oxen and the wagon, then down at Willie. "Look what he left."

Martha nodded. "He shouldn't have done that. Sometimes I still get mad at him for it, but he's kin, Rachel. So are my aunt and uncle. They're all Willie and I have left."

"You have me. And I love you more than all of them put together."

Martha smiled but shook her head. "I love you, too. I'd rather go on with you, Rachel. I purely would. But I have to stop. I have to."

Later that afternoon the Trail ran so close to a ten-foot embankment beside the river there was barely room for the oxen driver to walk beside the animals.

Tom Dorland appeared on foot. "You'd better let me take the oxen for a while" he said to Martha. "If they balk just a little they'll push you right off the cliff into the river."

"These oxen are just like Josie," Martha said. "They wouldn't hurt me for anything."

Tom reached for the small walking stick Martha carried. He grinned. "Where's your whip?"

She smiled back at him. "I don't need a whip with these nice boys. Once in a while I guide them a little with the stick, but I haven't had to hurt them even once."

"Okay, I'll use the stick for a cane, all right?"

Martha heaved a sigh of relief as she fell back with Rachel, Julia, and Willie, behind the wagon. She started singing Jesus songs with Willie right away, and the girls joined in. After a while Rachel noticed a strong, clear tenor harmonizing with them—Tom.

Tom walked with the oxen until stopping time that

afternoon, then unyoked them and took them off to pasture.

Martha and Willie stayed with their wagon to eat their meal and Rachel ran back to hers where she found Mama trying to get some sagebrush to burn.

"The trouble is," Mama said, puffing from her efforts, "when it catches, it burns so quickly it puts out hardly any heat."

Between Mama and Rachel they finally got the fire going and made biscuits. By now their supplies were low, the cows had long since given up trying to make milk, so the meals grew simpler and simpler. Every now and then Papa shot a bird or rabbit and that made a big difference. The biscuits were only flour, baking powder, salt, and water. They had side meat with them and sometimes beans, but not tonight. They felt lucky to get enough heat to cook the biscuits and side meat.

"When we reach a trading post, we'll replenish our supplies," Papa said. "That shouldn't be too long."

It was even a shorter time than Papa thought. They camped about where the Owyhee River joins the Snake, three miles from Fort Boise.

On July tenth, Sunday, the group had their usual singing meeting and preaching but so many Indians, trappers, soldiers, and emigrants, came and went that it didn't feel very restful to Rachel.

The next day, about midmorning, the train reached Fort Boise. The fort was a small replica of Fort Hall, made from adobe bricks like all the other forts, but was much smaller. They traveled along the Snake River where a few patches of grass grew. The train still stopped for the grass but thankfully it wasn't quite so rare anymore. They'd seen no trees or even shrubs between Fort Hall and Fort Boise, but at least now they seemed to be through the desert.

Rachel's father bought much-needed supplies at the fort, as did others who still had money left.

As a group walked away from the fort, a whiskered old man told them to be careful about drinking cold water. "Lots of people have died from exactly that," he said.

After they'd gotten away from the man, Tom leaned toward Rachel. "I think that man is miles off. The only time we shouldn't drink water is when it's contaminated. The Good Lord gave us water for cleansing the body, inside and out, and history will prove me right."

Rachel believed him. Come to think of it, she'd probably believe anything he said.

"Let me take the oxen a while," Rachel said one day to Martha who never complained about being tired, or anything else.

"I can do it," Martha said. "They're so good it isn't very hard."

"Get out of my way," Rachel said in play. "They're my oxen and I'll lead them part time." After that Rachel led the oxen half of each day. Julia watched Willie part of the time, and Tom and Dan took a turn with the oxen several times a week.

One day they stayed in camp until two o'clock to let the cattle feed. That day they left the Snake River for the last time and before the day ended, reached Burnt River where they expected to have plenty of water and grass for the animals. They seemed to be out of the desert.

July twenty-fourth, Sunday, the train enjoyed a good rest without throngs of people running around and through their camp. Rachel truly enjoyed the uninterrupted singing and sermon that day. The minister talked again about

God's unfathomable love for us. How He loves each of us much much more than we love our children.

Rachel carried the message in her heart and felt better every time she thought about it.

The group put their food together even though it was a pitiful thing to call a potluck. Martha though, didn't come, so Rachel went looking for her.

"I couldn't come," Martha explained. "All we have to eat is Trail Bread, without most of the things that make it Trail Bread." She laughed. "It's just flour, salt, and water. But Willie eats it and so does Josie."

"Well, you come anyway," Rachel said. "I'll get Mama to fry some extra side meat for you to bring."

As the meal began, Stan Latham showed up and asked Julia Tate if he could join her for the meal. When Rachel saw the cornered look in the younger girl's eyes she thought she might grab Julia's hand and run anywhere. But Tom Dorland happened by and told Latham his horses were leaving the area. Latham hurried off to check his animals, Tom beside him.

Pastor Richards asked Rachel if he could eat with her. Rachel said of course, and called Martha to join them. Julia ate with them, too.

Later that afternoon Tom showed up and asked Rachel to help him. "I need to check Sandra Piling," he explained. "She's failed a lot on the trip."

After checking the woman over, Tom talked to Mr. Piling. "She seems to be failing quickly. You'd better keep her in bed and feed her the best food you can beg, borrow, or shoot."

"Who's gonna fix all that wonderful food if Sandra's in bed?" Mr. Piling asked.

fourteen

A look of surprise flitted across Tom's face then disappeared. "I thought you'd cook for your family," he said, "but if you can't or don't have time, I'd be glad to do it for you."

Rachel almost laughed when Tom offered to cook. But Mr. Piling didn't. "Ain't got 'nough food for you," he groused.

"Oh, I'll eat before I come," Tom said. "I won't eat your food."

Piling didn't say any more so Tom and Rachel headed back to Rachel's wagon. When they got there she turned to thank him for walking her home, and caught a strange but gentle look in his eyes.

"So," he said with a chuckle, "I caught you laughing at the thought of my cooking, didn't I?"

"I hope not," she said with a giggle of her own.

"Well, I did, and I'll have you know I can cook anything. . .as long as it's boiled potatoes. Alas, I haven't seen a potato for months."

The next morning the wagons creaked as tired oxen plodded along with sore feet and necks, almost too weak to pull the wagons. Rachel watched Martha gently urge her animals along, while hearing the sound of whips and anguished bawls, together with rough male voices yelling at their oxen. She told herself that Martha probably got more out of her animals than the cruel men did.

Vultures blackened the carcasses on and beside the Trail. As the wagon train passed, the huge birds rose into the air screaming their displeasure at having their meals interrupted, then waited impatiently nearby until the train passed and they could continue their feast.

Late in the afternoon the train came upon a man with a baby in his left arm. The other arm hung bloody and useless; blood covered his clothes, too.

"Dorland!" Captain Ransom yelled, stopping the train. "What's going on?" he asked the man.

"Well, sir, my wife died about a week ago. Two days later, two of my oxen died and the others couldn't pull the wagon, so I left them. I took my horse and four mules and started out but before long, Indians attacked and took the animals." The man grimaced. "They like horses and mules a lot better then oxen. I'm thankin' the good Lord they didn't hurt the baby."

Tom appeared about then, looking to Rachel like the most beautiful person in the entire world. The man who helped everyone. He glanced through the faces until he found her. "I'll need you," he said softly.

After Mama took the baby, Rachel helped Tom clean the man's wounds with whiskey. The brave man stiffened but didn't utter a sound. Then, she held the man's arm as Tom stitched the wound. When he finished, he looked at Rachel. "Seventy-five stitches," he said smiling. "Looks pretty neat, doesn't it?" Then she helped him put the man's arm in a sling.

The thought passed through Rachel's mind that whoever married Tom Dorland would have to share him with the world. How awful!

Then she realized his compassion had a lot to do with why she loved him. She loved Tom? Yes! She loved him! She loved Dr. Tom Dorland! All she could ever want would be to help him help the world. . .all the time . . .forever. No doubt about it, she loved this man she'd been helping all along the Trail. But, suddenly she felt shy, as if she had to get away from him.

"Are we through now?" she asked quietly.

"Yes, for now. Thanks, Rachel. You're always a big help."

"The man and his baby will be sleeping in your wagon," Papa told her when they stopped that night. "There was no other place for them. You can sleep in ours."

Rachel surprised herself and her father by not minding. She'd be just fine with her parents.

The next morning they passed through miles and miles of prairie where the grass had been burned off, leaving a black stinking mess.

"That's the Indians' way of stopping the white man," Julia said. "Dan told me the Indians are trying to starve our cattle so we'll go back where we came from."

"I wonder how far it goes," Martha said. "We thought our animals would have plenty to eat now." But the cattle went all day without grass.

That night they camped by Powder River with plenty of grass and water. As the girls inspected their campsite, they discovered the river was alive with salmon.

When they spread the news, many men brought their guns to shoot some fish for supper, a dream come true for the weary travelers. The men all tried but no one could hit the fish. Finally, Tom looked up at the watching girls and flashed a smile. Rachel's heart melted into a small puddle in her chest. But he didn't give her any special looks or seem to notice.

"I'm going to shoot under the fish," he called. "We'll see what happens." He hit the fish, pulled it out, and the men crowded around. "Just shoot a few inches under the fish," he said. The men thinned out one by one, as they each shot a couple of the large creatures and hauled them off toward home.

To go with the fish, Mama made biscuits that she'd wrapped in clay and buried in the coals. Rachel invited

Martha and Willie to enjoy the feast with them.

After they finished, Rachel took half of a fish to Tom to share with the Pilings. Trembling at the thought of meeting him, Rachel nearly turned back, but forced herself on. The Piling's needed the food.

Tom's welcoming smile showed no change. He couldn't tell that she loved him. She'd thought a sign, RACHEL'S IN LOVE WITH TOM, might be emblazoned on her forehead.

As they delivered the large piece of fish to the Pilings, all Rachel could think about was her love for Tom. Tom, who stood about five feet, nine inches tall, was slim, blond, and boyish looking and was exactly opposite from the dream man she'd carried in her mind all these years. Oh, but he was exactly her dream. She forced the personal thoughts from her mind so she could be casual with him. Mark Piling didn't even thank them for the food but Sandra did.

As they walked back to the Butler wagon, Tom told Rachel to tell Martha to thoroughly cook some salmon and feed it to Josie. Rachel cooked a large fish and took half of it to Josie, who wolfed it down as if it were half a slice of bread, her tail thrashing the air wildly. When Josie finished, she leaned against Rachel and gave her hand a few sloppy kisses. "I love you, too, Josie," Rachel whispered to the shaggy dog.

Rachel took the other half of the big fish to the Pitmans, the older couple who were doing better now. Through tears, they thanked Rachel for her thoughtfulness. Rachel walked away completely happy. Martha was right. . .nothing satisfied more than helping other people and dogs.

Back at the wagon, she stopped to relax and she realized how cold the evening had become. What a change from the burning heat they'd endured for the last few weeks.

The next day the girls found themselves walking on

rock piles again. Rocks on rocks on rocks. The oxen struggled valiantly to pull the wagons over the rough terrain and the walkers tried to keep their feet under them. Finally, the Grande Ronde Valley opened up before them, a large, lush, green valley with the river meandering through it.

On August seventh, a Sunday, the train camped at a shady, tree-covered spot along the Grande Ronde, the most perfect camping place in the world. But the valley was alive with emigrants, cattle, Indians, and ponies.

Someone said the Indians were Nez Percè and Cayuse, all friendly, well clad, and clean.

Everyone wanted to sell something, or buy or beg something. Pastor Richards gathered his flock and tried preaching but so many people and animals milling around made concentration impossible and forced him to stop. He substituted a long hymn sing that everyone enjoyed, even those coming and going.

After the service, an Indian approached Rachel, Martha, Julia, and Willie, motioning that he wanted to trade a pony. But what did he want to trade it for? He pointed at each of the girls, then the pony, who was fat, brown-and-white spotted, and pretty.

Papa came to them. "What's going on?" he asked.

"He wants to trade the pony," Rachel said, "but we can't figure what he wants to trade it for."

Looking at the Indian, Nate motioned to the pony. The Indian's eyes shifted to the girls and he pointed at Rachel, then Martha, then Julia, and back to the pony.

Nate started laughing and shook his head no. "He wants to trade it for you three girls or one of you. I'm not sure which." Nate shook his head no again, and put his arms around all three girls. "Mine," he said, pointing to the girls then himself.

The Indian nodded as if he understood, smiled a toothy grin, and walked off. Thanking Nate profusely, the girls followed him back to his wagon.

The next day they started into the Blue Mountains where thick groves of yellow pines adorned the hills, a real treat after the weeks of wallowing in the desert. But the steep hills weren't a treat for anyone, animal or man. Many of the trees carried scars from chains that the earlier emigrants used to brake the wagons on the steep descents.

The oxen began the struggle up the hills, deep moans coming from their throats, their feet so sore they stumbled on every step. Their tongues hung from the sides of their mouths and their eyes had the look of wounded animals. Every muscle of their gaunt bodies strained almost to the breaking point, trying to get the wagons up the cruel hills.

"I don't know if they can make it," Rachel said, tears streaming from her eyes.

"They'll make it," Martha choked out past her tears. "Let's pray for them."

"Dear Father in heaven, I know you love the animals more than we do," Rachel began, speaking through her tears. "I know it's a sin to force them to work so hard. But please, Father, help them do the job without injuring themselves.

"Thank you for all your mercies," Martha continued. "Could You just give them the strength to do this hard job? One more thing, Father. Please help them not to have so much pain. It's not their fault they're in such a hard place. And forgive us for abusing them. We don't know what to do. Thank You, Lord for helping us. We love You, Father. We ask these special favors in Jesus' name and thank You so much for hearing and answering our prayers."

"Amen," all their voices said together.

fifteen

Rachel watched, hoping to see the oxen pulling easier and limping less. "I think they're better, don't you?" she asked Martha.

"Yes," Martha said, "but we still have to help them all we can." She looked down at her little brother who clung tightly to her hand. "All of us must keep praying all the time. Can you do that, Willie?" The shaggy blond head nodded.

The oxen still limped and moaned as they pulled the wagon up the hill but both Rachel and Martha thought they were doing it better.

As they neared the top of the first hill, Tom rode by on his mare. Rachel's heart beat so loudly she feared he'd hear it. "When you get to the top, wait for the men to help you," he said.

"We don't need help," Martha said. "We're doing just fine."

He laughed softly. "I'm sure you are, but we're helping all the wagons down. The hills are too steep. So just wait your turn, all right?"

The girls waited at the top even though they considered it time wasted.

When the men came, they brought a huge ox dragging a tree. "All right," Dan Barlow said. "Start your wagon down. Then stop so we can hook the tree to it."

Martha obeyed instructions. "The limbs on this tree will put a hard drag on the wagon, acting as a brake so your wagon won't run over your oxen," George Rahn said. "Just hold your animals back hard. Can you do that?"

Martha nodded; Rachel wondered if she was as sure as she acted. When the men had the tree secured to the wagon, they yelled for Martha to take the oxen down easy.

Rachel could hardly take her eyes from Tom who, with several others, grabbed the top of the pine tree, holding it back. He looked so beautiful and strong and good. How could she have ever thought he was scrawny and plain and dirty?

The wagon began descending the hill with Martha beside it talking softly to the oxen. The men pulled hard on the tree and the oxen walked slowly down the steep hill. "Stop!" someone yelled. Martha stopped the oxen until the men had everything under control. They repeated these steps several more times. A half-hour later, the wagon stood firmly at the bottom and the men led their big ox down to pull the tree back up to help the next wagon down.

They repeated the process of struggling up the hill then waiting for help to get down. "At least the oxen get to rest while we wait," Martha said.

The wagon train spent the following days going up and down hills, slowly increasing the distance from Independence, slowly nearing their new home in Oregon City.

One evening, after the train corralled, the men unyoked the oxen and led them out to feed. Rachel and Martha looked around. Majestic, dark green evergreens stood against the bright blue sky, grass grew rampantly, and a clear stream bubbled past.

Dan Barlow joined the group from somewhere with a deer draped over his horse's rump. "I have another one waiting across the ravine," he said easing the deer to the ground. In half an hour he returned with the other.

Rachel and Martha, along with the other women, washed clothes in icy water; every little while, Rachel had to warm her hands in the folds of her frock. Never in her life had she been so cold. Not only her hands but her body as well. The girls washed the Pilings' clothes, the horsemen's, and the Pitmans' though Mrs. Pitman insisted she could do it herself.

That night, the train feasted on roast meat but no one mentioned singing or dancing for a good night's sleep sounded better than anything.

The next day was Sunday, August the fourteenth. The camp at the top of the mountain caught all the early sunshine to warm the people from the cold night. After everyone enjoyed a hearty breakfast of meat, Pastor Richards led the group in a long hymn sing to warm them up then preached a sermon about the glories God is preparing for those who love Him.

"It's right to appreciate the beauty God has given us here," he said. "But it's only a shadow of things to come." As he talked about beauty, several bald eagles soared overhead, a regal sight. When he finished, he held out his hands to stop the people from leaving. "We have a special treat coming up right after this service," he said, wearing his widest smile. "I hope you'll all stay for our wagon train's first marriage. My beautiful sister, Tamara Richards, a schoolteacher, is being married to Evan Mann, a beginning attorney, and a fine man. I'm going to be proud to introduce him as my brother-in-law." He looked behind the group. "They're here now," he said, reaching his hand forward. "Come to the front, please, Tamara and Evan." He performed a simple but meaningful ceremony, ending by asking the people to all join in the Lord's Prayer.

Everyone crowded around the new couple, congratulating them and wishing them the best.

The men had put a third deer on on barbecue early that morning and soon the group enjoyed still another feast of nature's bounty in honor of the new couple. The women made biscuits to go with the meat and after Tamara and Evan were served, everyone had plenty.

Watching, Rachel could tell that Tamara wasn't entirely comfortable being the main attraction. Probably couldn't wait to get back alone. . .well, alone with her new husband.

The next day the wagon train started down the hills of the Blue Mountains for the last time. Rachel felt almost happier than she ever had.

The men still helped the wagons down and the oxen still struggled as they climbed the steep hills but each descent went a little lower. Soon, they'd be down to the prairie again.

During this time, Rachel worked so hard she barely had time to think of Tom except while he helped the wagon descend. But when she fell into her bed at night she thought of him, and dreamed of him, and prayed for him. That's all she knew to do.

They reached the valley on Saturday and camped to prepare for the Sabbath again, everyone feeling festive to be on the prairie.

The next day was Sunday, August twenty-first. The people rested, feeling they'd put in a good week's work. Rachel listened to Pastor Richards's stirring sermon with interest. He preached sermons that touched her heart every time and she had to admit he was a wonderfully dedicated man. But, she loved Tom. . .she definitely loved Tom. How could she not have known it long ago? And how could she get him to notice her?

The next day, as they descended lower into the valley, they saw majestic Mount Hood, 150 miles away. Soon, they'd pass only a few miles from that rugged, snow-capped mountain.

One day they passed a Cayuse town where the Indians raised corn, potatoes, peas, and other vegetables to sell to the travelers. Nate Butler bought some corn and potatoes and others bought what they could afford.

For the next two days, they traveled on smooth level roads, enjoying the comparatively easy traveling. Martha, Rachel, Julia, and Willie laughed, sang, told stories, and played games, something they hadn't done since before Petey died.

One day, Rachel saw a lone wagon ahead and showed Martha. "Why would it be alone out here? And with no oxen?"

Martha laughed. "I can answer that," she said. "If it weren't for your good father, I'd be sitting somewhere with just my wagon, too."

When they approached, they found a young mother with three small children, sitting on the ground beside the wagon.

Captain Ransom stopped the train. "Are you all right?" he called.

She got up and hurried to him. "No," she said. "I have a husband in the wagon who's too sick to sit up."

"Where are your animals?" Ransom asked.

"We were using oxen that belonged to a wealthy man who wouldn't let any of us ride in the wagon. When my husband got sick he took his oxen and left us here with the wagon."

"I don't know what we can do," Ransom said. "We've been picking up people all the way. I think we'll have to talk." He walked past the wagons, calling the men from them.

Rachel, who made sure she got in on most everything, couldn't think of an excuse to follow the men so she stayed with Martha.

A half-hour later, Ransom returned. "We'll try to take

you folks," he said, "but we can't take the wagon. "The Rahns will take your husband and Butler said he'll crowd you and the children into one of his wagons."

Dr. Dorland wiggled a finger at Rachel, then grabbed his medical bag. Together, they checked the family over.

"Everyone seems healthy," he said, "except the father, and I'm sure he doesn't have cholera. He'll be well in a few days."

The Ransoms gathered the small amount of food they found in the wagon and put it into their own.

When the train nooned, Papa told Mama and Rachel that he'd had to leave his blacksmith tools to take in the new family.

"How awful," Rachel said. "After you've hauled them this far."

Papa smiled sweetly. "People are more important than tools, lassie. The good Lord will provide some more tools."

The next day high winds and dust hindered the travel but they reached the Umatilla River by noon. They camped to prepare for the Sabbath and also to avoid the ill weather as much as possible.

While Rachel ate dinner with Mama and Papa, he asked her to help him a little later. "There are provisions available here," he said. "But, with all the people we've been feeding and taking into our wagons, I'll need more money." He winked at Rachel. "Could you help me get it from our bank?"

For just a second, Rachel didn't understand. Then she remembered. He'd put a big pouch of money under the false floor of one of the wagons. "I'll help you, Papa. Just call me when you're ready."

After they finished their meal, Papa told Rachel they'd pull the wagon away from the others so no one would know what they were doing. When they'd moved about a hundred feet west of the train, Papa asked Rachel to watch and tell him if anyone started toward them. Then he went to work with a screwdriver and hammer.

Rachel watched the people, listening to the many screeches and squawks as Papa pulled out the nails and lifted the false floor.

"It's gone!" Nate exclaimed. "The money's not here." After a long silence, he sighed. "I must have brought over the wrong wagon," he said. "But that floor looks as if it's been torn up before."

"You said the other wagons don't have false floors, Papa."

He nodded. Then she watched as he tore off more floorboards and double-checked to make sure the bag of money hadn't slid into a dark corner. When he looked up, his eyes met hers. She'd never seen Papa so stricken. Never, not even when she'd acted so terrible about coming.

"It's gone, Rachel," he said. "Someone took it. We're just like all the others on this train. . .almost broke."

Rachel's stomach constricted until it hurt. "Maybe you're looking in the wrong wagon," she said hopefully. "Why don't we check the others?"

He nodded. "All right, but the money's gone. Someone got it while we were away from the wagons sometime or another."

Papa checked the other wagons and found they didn't have false floors. Someone had taken the money. Almost all the money they had! "It'll be a miracle if we have enough money to get to Oregon City now," he whispered hoarsely. "Let alone having any to get started there."

"You'd better tell Captain Ransom," Rachel whispered into his ear. "What are you going to tell Mama?"

Papa looked into her eyes, his still showing shock. "I'm telling her the truth, what else?" he asked. He motioned for her to follow. "Come, let's tell Ransom."

The grizzly haired and whiskered man stood in silence after Nate explained what had happened. "I don't rightly know what to do," the kind captain said. "We both know you'll never see that money again." He looked off into the blue sky. "We don't even know whether it was our own people or someone else," he mused.

"Whoever took it knew it was there," Rachel said. "We haven't been away from the wagon long at any time. Someone had to go right to the spot and get the money in a hurry."

Ransom nodded. "Right. It was a slick one. Want me to try to bluff the guilty man into giving it back? I'm afraid that kind don't bluff."

As they walked back to their wagons, Rachel felt devastated. No doubt about it, this was Heartbreak Trail. NO! Money lacked a lot of being everything. God saw the person steal the money and allowed it. Why? Maybe the person's family was starving. Maybe the Butler family would grow closer to God without money. Maybe God had some special blessing in store for them. Maybe He just allowed this to happen for no special reason. But Rachel didn't believe that for a minute. God loved her family much more than they loved each other so there was a purpose in all this. And they'd be all right.

She dropped back and walked beside Papa. "It's all right, Papa," she said softly. "God just showed me we'll be all right."

Nate reached an arm down, dropped it over her shoulder, and smiled. "Know what, lassie?" he asked. "He just showed me the same thing. He'll care for our needs."

Then it was Sunday, August thirty-first. Indians roamed back and forth, Pastor Richards started his hymn sing, and many of the Indians joined them. After the singing,

Pastor Richards preached a basic sermon about God's love and sacrifice for all.

"Thank Him for loving you so much," he told them, "and tell Him you love Him, too, and want to belong to Him. He'll come right into your heart and live with you forever."

Rachel watched the Indians and prayed for them as they listened with rapt attention.

That afternoon, when Rachel took food to the Piling family, she found Tom there. "What are you doing?" she asked.

He grinned as he turned pink. "I'm cooking," he said. "Remember I said I would?" Rachel remembered, but she hadn't taken it seriously. Setting her food down, she helped him finish the meal. Serving it onto plates, they gave one to Sandra for her and Judith, and handed one to Mr. Piling.

Piling took the food but didn't thank them for it or speak. He just glowered at them as if they'd intruded.

Rachel felt surprised when his rudeness didn't upset her. She didn't feel hurt or mad. Nothing. Just concern for Sandy and her baby. Thank You, Lord. You're changing me from a self-centered hothead into a human being. Thank You again, God. I love You.

"Does he always treat you like this?" she whispered to Tom.

Tom nodded. "He's pretty good today. Must be because you're here. Let's clean up and get out of here."

"Is Martha still going to Walla Walla Valley?" he asked on the way back.

Rachel nodded. "I can't bear it, Tom. I just can't let her go. Help me talk to her, will you?"

He grinned and nodded. "Sure. But she won't listen to me. You're her closest friend."

"I've said all the words I know. She won't listen."

Again, Rachel begged Martha to go to Oregon City but she wouldn't consider it. "My family will be looking for me," she said, her usual reply.

The next day Nate prepared to take one of his wagons to Walla Walla Valley to leave with Martha but bring back the oxen he'd lent her. "Try once more to talk her into going on with us," he told Rachel and Rachel begged her not to go. While Rachel was begging, Rachel's mother, Alma, came up. "If you go," she said in a soft loving voice, "I can't let Willie leave with you."

"He has to come with me," Martha cried. "He and Josie are all I have. He has to stay with me."

"How much food do you have?" Alma asked kindly.

"Almost none," Martha admitted. "Just a pint of flour. But my family will be in the Walla Walla Valley nearly as soon as I will."

Tom had arrived and stood beside Rachel. "We can't know that, Martha," he said. "They may not come until spring. Or not at all. We aren't even sure they ever started, are we?"

Martha stared at him with wide eyes. "They planned to come within a week after we left."

Alma wrapped Martha in her arms and held her tightly. "Please, stay with us. You might starve to death if you go."

Martha shook her dark head. "I purely have to go, Mrs. Butler. My aunt and uncle and my cousin and brother will be there. What will they do if I'm not there?"

"But they have each other," Tom said. "You're going to be all alone."

Martha looked serious. A dull red rimmed her eyes. "I have to go."

Alma nodded. "We'll give you a gallon of flour. That's all we dare let go of now that we don't have money. We're taking Willie. Either you can come after him or we'll bring him back next spring."

Martha didn't argue, but dropped her head in defeat.

Julia hugged Martha tightly but couldn't talk. Dan Barlow, standing nearby, put his arm around Julia. "Now, don't you be worrying about Miss Tate," he told Martha. "I plan to keep her safe. And happy, too. So you just take care of yourself and Josie."

Pastor Richards made a passionate plea for Martha to go on with them to Oregon City, insinuating he'd make sure she was cared for. She shook her head.

The other Butler wagons would rest at the Umatilla River until the Butlers returned. Captain Ransom hadn't decided whether the train would wait or continue on.

Right after nooning, Martha led her oxen off toward Walla Walla Valley. Rachel walked with Martha and Papa drove their oxen. The sun shone brightly, prairie grass, though half-dried, grew everywhere.

On the second day they met some Indians with lots of potatoes and wanting to trade. Nate traded one of his shirts for a dozen nice big potatoes. Before the sun set, they reached their destination, Steptoeville, in Walla Walla Valley.

As they approached, only a few, eight to be exact, rough buildings, four on each side of a Nez Percè trail, met their eyes. Several dirty tepees huddled on the north side of the trail behind the shacks.

About a quarter-mile away, past the rickety buildings, a group of even smaller and more destitute shacks sprawled, obviously deserted.

"Doesn't look much like the Garden of Eden to me," Rachel said. "Oh, Martha, I'm sorry. Please, come with us to Oregon City."

sixteen

Martha laughed shakily. "You're purely right, Rachel. It doesn't look as beautiful as I expected." Then she pointed south and east. "But look at the mountains. They're pretty enough."

Nate looked, too. "Say," he said, "I think those are the Blue Mountains. We just came over some of them."

The little group parked the wagon at the west end of the Indian trail and unyoked the oxen. A small stream to the north provided plenty of water for the animals as they began grazing on the grass.

The girls prepared a meal with the potatoes, side meat, and biscuits, a feast fit for kings, Rachel said.

On Sunday, September eleventh, Rachel and Martha decided this was the quiet Sabbath for which they had been waiting. Entirely too quiet, they agreed before the day ended. Rachel and Papa spent the entire day trying to talk Martha into going back with them but she couldn't be persuaded.

Early the next morning, Papa gave Martha two of the remaining four potatoes and yoked up the oxen. Rachel's heart hurt so badly she couldn't talk, not even to beg Martha once more to come.

As they returned the way they'd come, Rachel looked back to see Martha kneeling beside Josie, hugging the dog tightly, and waving as hard as she could.

Rachel sobbed until she could barely walk. She ended up crying all the way back. Would she ever again see her dearest friend in the world? Her friend who taught her to love and serve Jesus. Her friend who taught her how to love and be kind. Please be with Martha, she cried silently. Take good care of her, Father. She has no money and so little food. Send someone to help her right away. Oh, thank You, God. I love You so much.

When they reached the Umatilla River again, they discovered the wagon train had gone on. But two of the horse riders and Tom had waited. Now they had three wagons and about a dozen people in their group.

As Tom ran to greet Rachel, her first thought was of her eyes, red from crying. When Tom reached her, he stopped and Rachel could see the struggle in his mind. He wanted to hug her! She knew he did.

His arms moved nervously as he stepped from one foot to the other. Finally, he forced himself to settle down. "Welcome back!" he said heartily. "We missed you a lot."

Rachel swallowed. In her wildest dreams she hadn't expected Tom to show this much enthusiasm for her return. "Thank you," she said. "Your welcome makes me feel better. It hurt me so much to leave Martha in that desolate place."

Willie spotted Rachel and came running to her. "Where's Martha?" he asked, tugging on her long calico skirt. "I want Martha now."

Rachel knelt and hugged the little boy. "Martha couldn't come right now," she said, holding him close. "She asked me to take care of you until she can have you with her. She loves you a lot, Willie, and will come after you as soon as she can. Can you be happy with us until then?"

He nodded and returned her hug. Poor little boy. First, he lost his parents, then his brother, next his best friend, and now his sister. Rachel gave him an extra tight hug. She'd have to be mother, father, sister, and friend to Willie while he was with them.

The next few days Rachel tried hard to keep Willie happy. She had nothing else to do or anyone else to be with so she didn't mind. Rather, she enjoyed his company as they walked, sang Jesus songs, and played games.

The small company camped early on Saturday to prepare for the Sabbath. After Rachel and Mama did the wash for everyone, they made a pie with the last of the dried apples. "At least we'll have a decent Sabbath," Mama said.

On Sunday, September twenty-fifth, the sun shone brightly even though October would soon be upon them. The whole group ate together since the Butlers were the only ones with wagons and cooking things.

Since there was no preacher, Tom led the group in a hymn sing. The dozen people made a joyful noise unto the Lord. In fact, Rachel thought they sounded all right. After the singing, Nate read some praise chapters from Psalms.

Later, after lunch, Tom asked Rachel to walk with him. He lead her to a quiet place, overlooking the valley.

"Beautiful," Rachel said. "This looks a lot more like the Garden of Eden than where Martha is."

"You may not have seen the best of the Walla Walla Valley," he said.

She laughed softly. "I hope not. What I saw wasn't very nice. But you know what? I asked God to send someone to help her right away, and I know He did. I have His peace to assure me. It makes all the difference."

"You've changed a lot since we started on the Trail," he said quietly. "Do you realize that?"

She nodded. "Yes. That's because God found me, even on Heartbreak Trail. He's with us no matter where we go, did you know that? No matter how foolish we are or what dumb things we do, He's there to help us. Isn't that remarkable? If I were God, I wouldn't be that good."

He laughed. "You would, Rachel, because you'd be God. Perfect, long-suffering, complete love. I've learned to appreciate you a lot on this long painful trip. You've been irreplaceable, helping with my work. I can't thank you enough for that."

"I enjoyed it, Tom. A lot. You may be right, saying I should be a nurse."

"I don't want to lose you, Rachel. I want you to go on helping me."

"I will. If you stay around. I'd really enjoy that." Rachel giggled. "I purely would, as Martha would say."

Tom swallowed loudly. "I didn't exactly mean just with my medicine," he said in a choked voice. "I've loved you for a long time, Rachel. I want to marry you when we catch up with Pastor Richards. . .or another preacher."

Rachel couldn't answer. Were her dreams coming true? Out here, on Heartbreak Trail? Where she'd seen nothing but death and disaster? She tried to swallow the lump in her throat. Then she sniffled.

"Is there someone else?" he asked quietly. "Maybe back in Quincy?"

She swallowed again. And sniffed again. "No," she whimpered. "I've never loved anyone but you. Never. I've loved you for a long time, too. Why didn't you tell me sooner?"

He smiled tenderly. "Well, I noticed you the first thing. I'd never seen such beautiful hair in my life. And your eyes, Rachel. They're something to take away a man's breath. You caught my attention right away but," his eyes twinkled, "somehow I got the idea you were spoiled. And that you didn't care all that much about God. The life I have to offer a woman will be hard; I need a woman with lots of faith, one who isn't afraid to work."

Rachel laughed into his eyes. "So, I wasn't good enough for you."

He shook his sunshiny hair. "No, you just weren't right for me. But I couldn't quit watching you, and admiring you from a distance. And I ended up watching you grow."

They talked a while then ambled back to the wagons where they found Nate.

"I have something important to ask you," Tom said. Rachel could see concern in Tom's eyes.

"Well, sit here on the wagon's tongue," Nate said. "I'll do my best to give you a good answer."

Tom stood. "Rachel and I have just discovered we love each other," he began.

Alma burst into laughter. "Why didn't you ask me? I could have told you a long time ago."

Tom smiled. "Well, we learned that we've cared for each other for some time, all right." He turned his attention back to Nate. "I'm asking for your blessing, sir, as I'd like nothing more than to marry Rachel and spend my life caring for her and making her happy."

Nate jumped up from the wagon hitch he'd been sitting on and extended his hand to Tom. "Welcome, Tom," he said happily. "I can't say this is a complete surprise. Not with Alma whispering in my ear. But you're exactly like the son I never had. I'd be honored to have you marry my only daughter."

Alma rushed out and hugged Tom. "Willie, can you give Tom a hug, too?" she asked when she released him. "He's going to be even more special to us now." Willie hugged Tom, always glad to get another hug.

After everyone quieted, Tom asked Rachel to walk with him again. When they found the same quiet place, Tom pulled her into his arms. "Everyone's been hugging but us," he whispered into her hair. "I love you my flaming-haired princess and want to never be separated from you again, not even for one day." His arm gently circled her waist as he pulled her closer, tipped up her face, and kissed her parted lips ever so gently.

Rachel returned the kiss that sent tremors through her entire body. A moment later she pulled away, discovering she'd never felt so lightheaded in her life. . .or so happy. She pulled his lips back to hers. "I'm dizzy," she whispered, "but kiss me again. I love you an awful lot."

The next day they traveled on, Rachel walking with Willie. She tried to sing all the songs and play all the games Martha had. The little boy seemed happy but he clung to her with quiet desperation.

Tom came around several times each day and every night he helped Rachel clean up after the meal. Then they walked and talked and dreamed.

One day at noon they reached the mighty Columbia River. Standing on the banks of the river she'd read about, sang about, and heard about all her life, Rachel felt small and insignificant. What was she? A fly compared to this river, and even less compared to the universe God had created. How could He care about anything so small as her? Oh, but I'm glad You do, Lord. Thank You for loving me, even more than the mighty things You've made. Thank You, Lord. I love You, too."

The group nooned on the bank of the river and traded some old clothes to Indians for a huge salmon, then headed for the Deschutes River where they camped.

On October first, Rachel and Tom spent the cold and rainy day together in one of the Butler wagons with her folks, making plans and trying to keep warm.

The next day they reached The Dalles, 1820 miles from Independence, about one hundred miles from Oregon City. The Dalles was almost the climax of the journey, the place where they had to decide whether to go by boat on the river or to take the Barlow Road over the Cascade Mountains. The Cascades were said to be even steeper and more dangerous than the Blue Mountains.

Rachel felt disappointed in The Dalles. She'd hoped she'd finally reach civilization there, but the town consisted of only a few houses; she'd call them shacks.

"I know we need food," Papa said as they walked around a little, "but I have to find out how much it's going to cost us to get over the Cascades before I spend anything."

Nate, Tom, and Rachel walked down to the docks where boats constantly loaded for the trip downriver. A man, obviously a traveler, spoke to them.

"Howdy," Nate said. "We're wondering what's the best way to get to Oregon City."

The man laughed out loud. "You and everyone else," he said. "Well, I'll tell you the best way. Put everthin' you got on boats, even your livestock. 'Course, I can't afford that so I'm tearin' up my wagon, an' shippin' it and all my goods and my wimmin folks. Me and my hired man're gonna drive the cattle over Barlow Road." He shook his head, sending his wild gray hair into a worse mess than before. "By the time the cattle git here they ain't got the stren'th to walk over, let alone haul wagons over."

Nate asked how much it cost to send a wagon and goods. Satisfied by the man's response, he smiled and extended his hand. "That's just what I'm going to do, too. Sounds like a good compromise."

The man shook Nate's hand aggressively. "Best bet," he said. "But if yore gonna go over the Road, best not to even ride yore horses. I heerd of several good saddle horses not making it neither. Just lead the horses and don't push none of the stock."

Nate thanked the man again and headed for the shipping office where he booked passage for three wagons, the contents, and two women.

"I'm not going by boat, Papa," Rachel said. "Tom will take care of me if I walk. Who'll help us when the boat sinks?"

Alma seconded the motion so they all worked together to get the wagons and barrels of goods ready to ship, then planned their own trip over the Cascades.

"We can buy some food now," Nate said. "Let's find some."

Before they found any food they stumbled across an overgrown potato patch. "Looks as if no one plans to dig these spuds," Tom said. "Why don't we check on them?"

When they found the owner, he said he hadn't planned to dig them. "If you'll do the work, I'll let 'em go for five dollars a hunnert."

"I don't think we can haul them over the mountains," Alma told Nate.

"Why couldn't we divide them among all the horses?" Tom asked. "Potatoes sound good about now."

They dug two hundred pounds of the potatoes and decided they'd better stop before they had the animals loaded too heavily.

"Are we going to buy other things to eat?" Rachel asked.

Nate shook his head. "Someone might shoot something. Otherwise, we'll eat potatoes until we reach Oregon City." He gave her a quick squeeze. "Things are different for us since we lost our money, lassie."

"Potatoes will be fine," Rachel said. The others agreed so they packed the saddlebags with potatoes, a big skillet, side meat grease, dishes, and silver, and started over the mountains.

The road seemed to be mostly cleared of trees and the biggest rocks, but the ascents and descents were even steeper than those in the Blue Mountains.

"I'm so thankful the animals aren't pulling wagons," Rachel said.

"So am I," Tom, who was walking with her, said. "And I for one will try to keep anyone from pushing the animals." He looked up the hill beside the road where the trees grew so closely together that a man would have trouble walking between them. "Do you realize the first people over had to clear away trees as they went?"

Rachel prayed silently for God to help them all, people and animals, over the brutal road. Carcasses of oxen, cows, and horses lay at the edge, testifying starkly to the still unmerciful road.

"I'm thankful to God for being so good to us so far," Nate said. "Do you realize we still have all of our original animals plus the one that joined our herd?" His eyes turned soft as he looked at Rachel. "Mama and I talked last night and decided to give half our animals to you and Tom when we reach Oregon City. That's half of thirteen cows, three saddle horses, and thirty oxen."

Rachel hugged her father, then her mother. "Thank you both. That's enough for a good start. We'll take good care of them as you have."

That night Alma and Rachel fried enough potatoes to fill up all the people traveling with them. Everyone enjoyed the change the potatoes brought.

For the next two days the weather stayed warm and dry though the evenings turned downright cold. The group slept, wrapped in blankets, under the stars.

One of the young men went ahead and brought back

some rabbits to go with the fried potatoes. They all agreed they were eating like kings.

Then it clouded up and rained. Everyone got soaked and so did their blankets. Fortunately, lots of tree branches lay near the edge of the road so that night they made a roaring fire and tried to dry their clothes and blankets.

"It's hard," Rachel complained. "The fire's so hot I can't stand close enough to dry the blankets." The blankets finally dried but as soon as they put them on the ground the wet seeped into them again.

The next morning Rachel got up, sore and chilled, to help Mama cook potatoes again.

When they started walking, the road was wet and slippery; the animals picked their way carefully. The oxen and horses, shod, fared better than the loose cattle.

Tom and Rachel walked carefully, each leading a horse. Rachel felt tired before nooning time and couldn't wait for the rest. As the group struggled up the hill, Tom's horse's foot struck a slick rock and slipped, knocking Tom's feet out from under him.

Although quick, Tom couldn't catch his balance. He fell to the ground, hitting his head on a sharp stone and cutting his forehead. Blood gushed from the wound as Tom lay dazed, uncaring.

seventeen

"Grab something and shove it against the wound!" Mama yelled.

Rachel snatched the hem of her skirt, turned the worst mud inside, folded the fabric a few times, and shoved it into the jagged cut in his forehead.

Tom stirred and opened his eyes. "I'm all right," he said, evidently reading fear in the faces gathered around him. "Head wounds bleed profusely." He looked at Rachel, kneeling next to him and still pressing the hem of her skirt into the wound. "You'll have to sew it up, Rachel."

An enormous lump dropped into her stomach. She couldn't do that! She shook her head. "I'll hold my skirt against it all day but I can't sew you up. You know I can't, Tom."

He grinned, emphasizing his white face. "Sure you can. You've watched me enough times."

"I can't, Tom." How could he ask her to do something like that, anyway? He'd gone to school a long time to learn how to be a doctor. Now he expected her to be one with no training at all! Then she noticed blood oozing through the skirt she held against his head. "Are you going to bleed to death?" she whispered.

He smiled wearily. "No, I won't bleed to death. But if you don't stitch it up, I'll have a bad scar. Looking at my face will scare you so much you'll run away and refuse to marry me."

She shook her head. It finally sank into her head that

Tom couldn't sew up his own wound. None of this group knew anything about medicine. Almost for sure she knew more than any of the others after having helped Tom for the last six months. "Will you tell me what to do?" she whimpered.

A look of relief crossed his face. "Exactly," he said. "Get my bag off my horse." She did. "Now, find the pouch that says needle and thread. Put the thread through the needle just as if you were going to do some embroidery. Then, pour some of the whiskey over it."

Rachel did everything he told her, feeling shaky with all the eyes watching. After pouring whiskey over the needle and thread, she knew the next step—cleaning his wound. She held up the bottle and showed Tom.

He nodded, giving her a small smile. "I get to find out how it feels, don't I?"

She turned his head so the whiskey wouldn't run into his eyes, then slowly poured it across the wound. Watching his arm and neck muscles tighten, she knew it hurt. "I'm sorry," she whispered and touched his lips with hers before remembering the dozen people watching.

His arms reached gently around her, pulling her closer. "Thanks," he whispered against her lips. "That helped a lot." Then he lay back on the ground again sighing. "I guess I'm not very strong right now," he said. "Better get me fixed up."

"All right, Tom, but you have to help me."

With his eyes closed, he instructed her. "Close the wound with your left hand," he said almost in a whisper, "and stitch with the other. Be sure to get the thread through all the layers of the skin."

A picture appeared in Rachel's mind of Tom working on Josie, so much more horrible. She saw him bringing the skin together over the dog's intestines, pushing the

needle through the thick layer of skin, then pulling the
skin together and stitching again.

She knew exactly how to do it. But it would hurt him!
No matter, it had to be done. "All right," she said softly.
"Relax. I can do it." She followed the picture in her
mind, step by step, until she put the last stitch in and
secured the thread.

Tom hadn't said a word and barely flinched while she
worked.

"I'm all through," she said when he didn't stir. She
leaned down to his ear. "Know what happened?" she asked,
then answered her own question. "I did a perfect job,"
she said. "God showed me how to do it, step by step. In
pictures, Tom. He showed me in pictures."

Tom opened his eyes but obviously didn't share her
enthusiasm at that point. "Good girl. I knew He would."
He quieted and rested a few minutes then opened his eyes
and found Rachel again. "Know why He showed you?"
he asked.

Rachel nodded, her eyes dewy from the strain but still
thrilled with what had happened. "Because you needed
help and there wasn't anyone else."

He nodded, his eyes closed. "That, too," he agreed quietly. "But He showed you because you're walking that
close to Him now. If you weren't, you wouldn't have
heard Him."

Papa built a big fire and Mama cooked up several more
skillets of potatoes, which everyone ate with relish—
except Tom who didn't feel hungry.

"I wish you could eat," Rachel told him, sitting close.
"I'm hungrier than I've ever been in my life." She giggled.
"I didn't realize how much energy it takes to sew people
up."

By evening Tom ate like a hungry ranch hand and by

the next morning he walked as well as any of the little company.

Sunday, October ninth, was cloudy and dry but not too cold. So, Tom led the small company of believers in all the songs they could remember. When they finished, Nate read some Psalms then offered a prayer of praise and thanksgiving for caring for them on the long hard trip and bringing them safely to God's Garden of Eden on earth.

When he started to dismiss them, Rachel stopped him. "I have something to say," she said, running to the front. "I just wanted to tell you something God did for me," she said, facing the group breathlessly. "I'd helped Tom sew up several animals and people but I didn't remember how to do it. But when I started to sew Tom's wound, God showed me, step by step, how to do it. He did such a fine job that the wound is looking good already and Tom isn't in pain. It made me think of something He wants to do for us. If we'll read the Bible faithfully, He'll bring it to our minds when we need it. Isn't that fantastic?"

Several people said, "Amen" or "Yes, Lord."

Suddenly, Rachel didn't know what to say. "I guess that's all," she finally said. "I just thought it was so special I wanted to share it."

Nate Butler started them early the next morning as all were getting excited about arriving in Oregon City. No one knew exactly when it would be but they all knew it would be soon. . .very soon.

Two days later, they reached the summit. A rough sign stated the fact in black hand-painted letters, surely one of the most beautiful sights Rachel had ever seen.

That night the group celebrated with a small deer one of the men had shot. They built a spit, placing a strong green log over two crossed logs and hung the cleaned animal by its hooves until it turned brown with juices oozing out all over the carcass. The meat and potatoes made a meal they all ate with relish.

The next morning they started down the rugged mountains.

"Down is always easier than up, isn't it?" Rachel asked Tom.

He grinned. "Always," he agreed, "unless there's a wagon behind the animals trying to run over them. Then I'm not sure."

As he talked, Rachel noticed how well his forehead was healing. Not a bit of redness remained, the swelling had gone from the wound, and it looked almost insignificant. Rachel touched the spot. "How does it feel now?" she asked.

He snatched her to him. "You look beautiful, like my own healing angel, like my dearest gift from God, like my reason for living." He released her and looked into her eyes. "That was what you asked, wasn't it?"

She shook her head, laughing into his eyes. "I asked how your wound. . .you know what I asked. So tell me."

"It's all well. I've kept track of it with my fingers. It's smooth, no puffiness or drawing at the stitches. Nothing. It isn't even sore anymore." He stopped and looked to his left, then to his right. "Don't let the word get around, though. I'll lose all my patients to my associate. . .," his eyes softened as they looked into hers, "my wife," he finished. "One of these days I'll be asking my doctor to remove the stitches."

Alarm bolted through her chest, then quieted. "That's easy, isn't it?"

He nodded. "Simple as pulling a tree down a mountain." Then he laughed. "Yes, it's easy. It'll take about five minutes with no pain or strain."

Nate kept the group moving slowly, though all, even the animals, were eager to reach the bottom of the mountain. "We don't need any accidents now," he said. "So far we're all still here, man and animal alike. But just think how close we came to losing one of us. If Tom had broken a leg we'd have had to shoot him."

As they traveled, Rachel kept her eyes west. Sometime soon the mountains would drop behind them and Oregon City would spread out before them. "What do you think it'll look like?" she asked Tom. "Will it be a nice, thriving city?"

Tom shook his head. "I think it'll look pretty primitive. Some log cabins, a few rough stores. I think there'll be lots of farming and cattle but nothing you'd consider a city."

She clung to his arm. "I can't wait to get there." Her eyes rose to his. "Know why?"

He smiled, his eyes filled with love. "No, but I know why I'm eager."

"Is it so we can find a minister?" she asked softly.

"You guessed it the first time," he said with joy. "You can't know how happy I am that you didn't say you wanted some big department stores or fancy restaurants."

She laughed, a happy sound that gladdened all hearts that heard it. Her eyes twinkled with mischief. "I'm sure some great stores and restaurants would have been my first wish if someone hadn't taken all our money. Now I have to settle for you, Dr. Thomas Dorland." She laughed again. "What a letdown."

All that day they came down hills then went back up, though not as far up as down. The entire group was caught up in a sort of holiday atmosphere for their destination lay almost within their grasp and that was reason enough to be excited.

When they started the next day, Rachel knew for sure that it would be the day but no Oregon City popped into view between the mountains and they had to camp one more night on the road.

"I just checked the animals," Tom said, later that night. "They're surprisingly well considering what they've been through. No doubt they'll all make it now."

Late the next afternoon, Rachel thought the mountains were beginning to thin out. But, once again, they camped under the stars, cold but dry stars.

The next day, Rachel and Tom talked so much and so fast that someone else spotted the city before she did.

"There she is!" someone yelled at the top of his voice. "Laid out like a picture between them mountains."

The beautiful sight, plus the thrill of seeing the end of their journey, wrenched Rachel's breath from her throat. A huge valley lay beyond the craggy mountains. White frame houses, each surrounded by acres and acres of farmland, barns, and corrals looked exactly like Rachel had hoped.

Nate pulled the Mormon guidebook from his pocket. "This thing says we're one thousand, nine hundred thirty miles from Independence."

"Does it say we're five miles from our new home, the Garden of Eden?" Rachel asked.

He shook his head, joy displayed over his face. "No, but that's about it."

No one wanted to stop for nooning, so they continued on. The descent leveled out soon and the highly excited little company walked as if they'd just begun the long trek rather than ending it.

Rachel felt so much joy she didn't know if she could contain it. Here, before her, was her new home. . .her new home with her new husband. She thanked God that

He'd impressed Papa to force her to come on Heartbreak Trail.

It had taken a lot for God to get her attention. Maybe she'd have never come to know Him if she'd stayed in Quincy where everything always went right. Sometimes it takes pain to draw people to Him. Heartbreak Trail had done it for Rachel. How could she have ever gotten along for so long without her dear heavenly Father?

She'd wanted to stay in Quincy to find the cream of the crop, but God had the very very best waiting for her on the wagon train. And when she was ready, He brought Tom to her. Not when she acted like a baby, but when she grew up!

Thank You, God. Please take charge of my life forever. I love You!

A Letter To Our Readers

Dear Reader:

In order that we might better contribute to your reading
enjoyment, we would appreciate your taking a few minutes to respond to the following questions. When completed, please return to the following:

Rebecca Germany, Editor
Heartsong Presents
P.O. Box 719
Uhrichsville, Ohio 44683

1. Did you enjoy reading *Heartbreak Trail*?
   ☐ Very much. I would like to see more books
      by this author!
   ☐ Moderately
      I would have enjoyed it more if _____

   _____

2. Are you a member of *Heartsong Presents*? Yes   No
   If no, where did you purchase this book? _____

   _____

3. What influenced your decision to purchase
   this book? (Circle those that apply.)

   Cover   Back cover copy

   Title   Friends

   Publicity   Other _____

4. On a scale from 1 (poor) to 10 (superior), please rate the following elements.

    ___Heroine   ___Plot

    ___Hero   ___Inspirational theme

    ___Setting   ___Secondary characters

5. What settings would you like to see covered in *Heartsong Presents* books?

  _____

  _____

6. What are some inspirational themes you would like to see treated in future books?_____

  _____

  _____

7. Would you be interested in reading other *Heartsong Presents* titles?   Yes   No

8. Please circle your age range:

Under 18	18-24	25-34
35-45	46-55	Over 55

9. How many hours per week do you read? _____

Name _____

Occupation _____

Address _____

City _____ State _____ Zip _____

····· Hearts♥ng ·····

ROMANCE IS CHEAPER BY THE DOZEN!

Any 12 *Heartsong Presents* titles for only $26.95 *

Buy any assortment of twelve *Heartsong Presents* titles and save 25% off of the already discounted price of $2.95 each!

*plus $1.00 shipping and handling per order and sales tax where applicable.

HEARTSONG PRESENTS TITLES AVAILABLE NOW:

·········· Presents ··········

Great Inspirational Romance at a Great Price!

Heartsong Presents books are inspirational romances in contemporary and historical settings, designed to give you an enjoyable, spirit-lifting reading experience. You can choose from 76 wonderfully written titles from some of today's best authors like Colleen L. Reece, Brenda Bancroft, Janelle Jamison, and many others.

When ordering quantities less than twelve, above titles are $2.95 each.

"You act as if I'm your wife!"

One eyebrow rose in cynical query. "My dear Alyse," Aleksi said, "I have in my possession a marriage certificate stating clearly that you are. Does it bother you that I accord you a measure of husbandly affection?"

"Courteous attention I can accept," she acknowledged angrily. "But intimate contact is totally unnecessary."

His smile was peculiarly lacking in humor. "I haven't even begun being intimate."

Her eyes dilated with shock. "Don't. Please!" she added as a genuine plea to his sensitivity rather than as an afterthought.

"You sound almost afraid," he derided silkily.

Afraid I'll never be the same again, Alyse qualified silently, hating the sexual chemistry that drew her toward him like a moth to flam

W9-CHI-074

Books by Helen Bianchin

HARLEQUIN PRESENTS

751—DARK TYRANT
839—BITTER ENCORE
975—DARK ENCHANTMENT
1111—AN AWAKENING DESIRE
1240—TOUCH THE FLAME
1383—THE TIGER'S LAIR

HARLEQUIN ROMANCE

2010—BEWILDERED HAVEN
2084—AVENGING ANGEL
2175—THE HILLS OF HOME
2387—MASTER OF ULURU

HELEN BIANCHIN

the stefanos marriage

Harlequin Books

TORONTO • NEW YORK • LONDON
AMSTERDAM • PARIS • SYDNEY • HAMBURG
STOCKHOLM • ATHENS • TOKYO • MILAN

Harlequin Presents first edition January 1992
ISBN 0-373-11423-0

Original hardcover edition published in 1990
by Mills & Boon Limited

THE STEFANOS MARRIAGE

CHAPTER ONE

THE traffic was unusually heavy as Alyse eased her stylish Honda hatchback on to the Stirling highway. From this distance the many tall buildings etched against the city skyline appeared wreathed in a shimmering haze, and the sun's piercing rays reflected against the sapphire depths of the Swan River as she followed its gentle curve into the heart of Perth.

Parking took an age, and she uttered a silent prayer in celestial thanks that she wasn't a regular city commuter as she competed with the early-morning populace striding the pavements to their individual places of work.

A telephone call from her solicitor late the previous afternoon requesting her presence in his office as soon as possible was perplexing, to say the least, and a slight frown creased her brow as she entered the modern edifice of gleaming black marble and non-reflecting tinted glass that housed his professional suite.

Gaining the foyer, Alyse stepped briskly towards a cluster of people waiting for any one of three lifts to transport them to their designated floor. As she drew close her attention was caught by a tall, dark-suited man standing slightly apart from the rest, and her eyes lingered with brief curiosity.

Broad-chiselled facial bone-structure in profile provided an excellent foil for the patrician slope of

5

his nose and rugged sculptured jaw. Well-groomed thick dark hair was professionally shaped and worn fractionally longer than the current trend.

In his mid-thirties, she judged, aware there was something about his stance that portrayed an animalistic sense of power—a physical magnetism that was riveting.

As if he sensed her scrutiny, he turned slightly, and she was shaken by the intensity of piercing eyes that were neither blue nor grey but a curious mixture of both.

Suddenly she became supremely conscious of her projected image, aware that the fashionably tailored black suit worn with a demurely styled white silk blouse lent a professional air to her petite frame and shoulder-length strawberry-blonde hair, which, combined with delicate-boned features, reflected poise and dignity.

It took every ounce of control not to blink or lower her eyes beneath his slow analytical appraisal, and for some inexplicable reason she felt each separate nerve-ending tense as a primitive emotion stirred deep within her, alien and unguarded.

For a few timeless seconds her eyes seemed locked with his, and she could have sworn the quickening beat of her heart must sound loud enough for anyone standing close by to hear. A reaction, she decided shakily, that was related to nothing more than recognition of a devastatingly sexual alchemy.

No *one* man deserved to have such power at his command. Yet there was a lurking cynicism, a slight wariness apparent beneath the sophisticated veneer, almost as if he expected her to instigate an attempt at conversation, initiating a subtle invitation—to God knew what? Her *bed*?

Innate pride tinged with defiance lent her eyes a fiery sparkle and provided an infinitesimal tilt to her chin as she checked the hands of the clock positioned high on the marble-slabbed wall.

Two lifts reached the ground floor simultaneously, and she stood back, opting to enter the one closest her, aware too late that the man seemed intent on following in her wake.

The lift filled rapidly, and she determinedly fixed her attention on the instrument panel, all too aware of the man standing within touching distance. Despite her four-inch stiletto heels he towered head and shoulders above her, and this close she could sense the slight aroma of his cologne.

It was crazy to feel so positively *stifled*, yet she was supremely conscious of every single breath, every pulsebeat. It wasn't a sensation she enjoyed, and she was intensely relieved when the lift slid to a halt at her chosen floor.

Alyse's gratitude at being freed from his unsettling presence was short-lived when she discovered that he too had vacated the lift and was seemingly intent on entering the same suite of offices.

Moving towards Reception, she gave her name and that of the legal partner with whom she had an appointment, then selected a nearby chair. Reaching for a magazine, she flipped idly through the glossy pages with pretended interest, increasingly aware of the man standing negligently at ease on the edge of her peripheral vision.

With a hand thrust into the trouser pocket of his impeccably tailored suit he looked every inch the powerful potentate, portraying a dramatic mesh of blatant masculinity and elemental ruthlessness. Someone it would be infinitely wiser to have as a friend than an enemy, Alyse perceived wryly.

Something about him bothered her—an intrinsic familiarity she was unable to pinpoint. She knew they had never met, for he wasn't a man you would forget in a hurry!

'Miss Anderson? If you'd care to follow me, Mr Mannering will see you now.'

Alyse followed the elegantly attired secretary down a wide, spacious corridor into a modern office offering a magnificent view of the city. Acknowledging the solicitor's greeting, she selected one of three armchairs opposite his desk and graciously sank into its leather-cushioned depth.

'There seems to be some urgency in your need to see me,' she declared, taking time to cross one slim nylon-clad leg over the other as she looked askance at the faintly harassed-looking man viewing her with a degree of thoughtful speculation.

'Indeed. A most unexpected development,' Hugh Mannering conceded as he reached for a manilla folder and riffled through its contents. 'These papers were delivered by courier yesterday afternoon, and followed an hour later by a telephone call from the man who instigated their dispatch.'

A slight frown momentarily creased her brow. 'I thought Antonia's estate was quite straightforward.'

'Her estate—yes. Custody of your sister's son, however, is not.'

Alyse felt something squeeze painfully in the region of her heart. 'What do you mean?'

He bent his head, and his spectacles slid fractionally down his nose, allowing him the opportunity to view her over the top of the frame. 'I have copies of legal documentation by a delegate of the Stefanos family laying claim to Georg——' he paused to consult the name outlined within the documented text '—Georgiou. Infant son of Georgiou Stavro Stefanos, born to Antonia Grace Anderson at a disclosed maternity hospital in suburban Perth just over two months ago.'

Alyse paled with shock, her eyes large liquid pools mirroring disbelief as she looked at the solicitor with mounting horror. 'They can't do that!' she protested in a voice that betrayed shaky incredulity.

The man opposite appeared nonplussed. 'Antonia died intestate, without written authority delegating legal responsibility for her son. As her only surviving relative, you naturally assumed the role of surrogate mother and guardian.' He paused to clear his throat. 'However, technically, the child is an orphan, and a decision would, in the normal course of events, be made by the Department of Family Services as to the manner in which the child is to be cared for, having regard to all relevant circumstances with the welfare of the child as the paramount consideration. An application to adopt the child can be lodged with the Department by any interested party.' He paused to spare her a compassionate glance. 'A matter I had every intention of bringing to your attention.'

'Are you trying to say that my sister's lover's family have as much right to adopt her son as I do?' Alyse demanded in a fervent need to reduce reiterated legalese to its simplest form.

The solicitor's expression mirrored his spoken response. 'Yes.'

'But that's impossible! The clear facts of Georgiou's chosen dissociation from Antonia's letters would be a mark against him in any court of law.'

Tears welled unbidden as Alyse thought of her sister. Six years Alyse's junior, Antonia had been so carefree, so *young*. Too young at nineteen to suffer the consequences of a brief holiday romance abroad. Yet suffer she did, discovering within weeks of her return from an idyllic cruise of the Greek Islands that her capricious behaviour had resulted in pregnancy.

A letter dispatched at once to an address in Athens brought no response, nor, several weeks later, with the aid of a translator, did attempted telephone contact, for all that could be determined was that the number they sought was ex-directory and therefore unobtainable.

Truly a love-child, little Georgiou had survived by his mother's refusal to consider abortion, and he'd entered the world after a long struggle that had had the medics in attendance opting for surgical intervention via emergency Caesarian section. Fate, however, had delivered an incredibly cruel blow when complications which had plagued Antonia since giving birth had brought on a sudden collapse, followed within days by her tragic death.

Shattered beyond belief, Alyse had stoically attended to all the relevant arrangements, and employed a manageress for her childrenswear boutique during those first terrible weeks until she could arrange for a reliable babysitter.

Now, she had organised a satisfactory routine whereby a babysitter came in each morning, and the boutique was managed during the afternoon hours, thus ensuring that Alyse could spend as much time as possible with a young baby whose imposing Christian name had long since been affectionately shortened to Georg.

'I can understand your concern, Alyse. Mr Stefanos has offered to explain, personally, the reasons supporting his claim.'

Undisguised surprise widened her eyes, followed immediately by a degree of incredible anger. 'He's actually *dared* to come here in person, after all this time?'

Hugh Mannering regarded her carefully for several seconds, then offered slowly, 'It's in your own interest to at least listen to what he has to say.'

The solicitor depressed a button on the intercom console and issued his secretary with appropriate instructions.

Within a matter of seconds the door opened, and the tall compelling-looking man who had succeeded in shattering Alyse's composure only half an hour earlier entered the room.

She felt her stomach lurch, then contract in inexplicable apprehension. Who *was* he? She had seen sufficient of Antonia's holiday snapshots to be certain that the reflection depicted on celluloid and *this* man were not one and the same.

Hugh Mannering made the introduction with polite civility. 'Alyse Anderson—Aleksi Stefanos.'

'Miss Anderson.' The acknowledgment was voiced in a deep, faintly accented drawl, and an icy chill feathered across the surface of her skin. His eyes swept her features in raking appraisal, then locked with her startled gaze for a brief second before he directed his attention to the man opposite.

'I presume you have informed Miss Anderson of the relevant details?'

'Perhaps Mr Stefanos,' Alyse stressed carefully as he folded his lengthy frame into an adjacent chair, 'would care to reveal precisely his connection with the father of my sister's child?'

There could be no doubt she intended war, and it irked her incredibly that he was amused beneath the thin veneer of politeness evident.

'Forgive me, Miss Anderson.' He inclined his head cynically. 'I am Georgiou's elder brother— stepbrother, to be exact.'

'One presumes Georg,' she paused, deliberately refusing to give the name its correct pronunciation, 'dispatched you as his emissary?'

The pale eyes hardened until they resembled obsidian grey shards. 'Georgiou is dead. A horrific car accident last year left him a paraplegic, and complications took their final toll little more than a month ago.'

Alyse's mind reeled at the implication of a bizarre coincidence as Aleksi Stefanos went on to reveal in a voice devoid of any emotion,

'My family had no knowledge of your sister's existence, let alone her predicament, until several carefully concealed letters were discovered a week after Georgiou's death. Time was needed to verify certain facts before suitable arrangements could be made.'

'What arrangements?'

'The child will, of course, be brought up a Stefanos.'

Alyse's eyes blazed with brilliant fire. 'He most certainly will not!'

'You contest my right to do so?'

'*Your* right?' she retorted deliberately.

'Indeed. As he is the first male Stefanos grandchild, there can be no question of his rightful heritage.'

'Georg's birth is registered as Georgiou *Anderson*, Mr Stefanos. And as Antonia's closest relative *I* have accepted sole responsibility for her son.'

He appeared to be visibly unmoved, and her chin lifted fractionally as she held his glittering gaze.

'Verification of blood groupings has established beyond doubt that my brother is the father of your sister's child,' he revealed with chilling cynicism.

Alyse felt the rush of anger as it consumed her slim frame. How dared he even *suggest* otherwise! 'What did you imagine Antonia had in mind when she dispatched those letters begging for help, Mr Stefanos?' she managed in icy rage. 'Blackmail?'

'The thought did occur.'

'Why,' she breathed with barely controlled fury, 'you insulting, arrogant——'

'Please continue,' he invited as she faltered to a speechless halt.

'Bastard!' she threw with disdain, and glimpsed an inflexible hardness in the depths of his eyes.

'Antonia had no need of *money*—your brother's, or that of his family. As Mr Mannering will confirm, both my sister and I benefited financially when our parents died some years ago—sufficient to ensure we could afford a comfortable lifestyle without the need to supplement it in any way other than with a weekly wage. On leaving school, Antonia joined me in business.' She had never felt so positively *enraged* in her life. 'Your brother, Mr Stefanos,' she stressed, 'proposed *marriage* during their shared holiday, and promised to send for Antonia within a week of his return to Athens for the express purpose of meeting his family and announcing their engagement.' Her eyes clouded with pain as she vividly recalled the effect Georgiou's subsequent rejection had had on her sister.

'Georgiou's accident occurred the day after his return,' Aleksi Stefanos told her. 'He lay in hospital unconscious for weeks, and afterwards it was some time before he became fully aware of the extent of his injuries. By then it was doubtful if he could foresee a future for himself in the role of husband.'

'He could have written!' Alyse exclaimed in impassioned condemnation. 'His silence caused Antonia months of untold anguish. And you underestimate my sister, Mr Stefanos,' she continued bleakly, 'if you think she would have rejected Georgiou simply because of his injuries. She loved him.'

'And *love*, in your opinion, conquers all?'

Her eyes gleamed with hidden anger, sheer prisms of deep blue sapphire. 'Antonia deserved the chance to prove it,' she said with quiet vehemence. Her chin lifted, tilting at a proud angle.

His raking scrutiny was daunting, but she refused to break his gaze. 'And you, Miss Anderson?' he queried with deceptive softness. 'Would *you* have given a man such unswerving loyalty?'

Alyse didn't deign to answer, and the silence inside the room was such that it was almost possible to hear the sound of human breathing.

'Perhaps an attempt could be made to resolve the situation?' Alyse heard the mild intervention and turned slowly towards the bespectacled man seated behind his desk. For a while she had forgotten his existence, and she watched as his glance shifted from her to the hateful Aleksi Stefanos. 'I know I can speak for Alyse in saying that she intends lodging an adoption application immediately.'

'Legally, as a single woman, Miss Anderson lacks sufficient standing to supersede my right to my brother's child,' Aleksi Stefanos declared with dangerous silkiness.

'Only if you're married,' Alyse insisted, directing the solicitor a brief enquiring glance and feeling triumphant on receiving his nod in silent acquiescence. 'Are you married, Mr Stefanos?'

'No,' he answered with smooth detachment. 'Something I intend remedying without delay.'

'Really? You're *engaged* to be married?' She couldn't remember being so positively *bitchy*!

'My intended marital status is unimportant, Miss Anderson, and none of your business.'

'Oh, but it is, Mr Stefanos,' she insisted sweetly. 'You see, if *marriage* is a prerequisite in my battle to adopt Georg, then I too shall fight you in the marriage stakes by taking a husband as soon as possible.' She turned towards the solicitor. 'Would that strengthen my case?'

Hugh Mannering looked distinctly uncomfortable. 'I should warn you against the folly of marrying in haste, simply for the sole purpose of providing your nephew with a surrogate father. Mr Stefanos would undoubtedly contest the validity of your motive.'

'As I would contest *his* motive,' she insisted fiercely, 'if he were to marry immediately.'

'I'm almost inclined to venture that it's unfortunate you could not marry each other,' Mr Mannering opined, 'thus providing the child with a stable relationship, instead of engaging in lengthy proceedings with the Government's Family Services Department to determine *who* should succeed as legal adoptive parent.'

Alyse looked at him as if he had suddenly gone mad. 'You can't possibly be serious?'

The solicitor effected an imperceptible shrug. 'A marriage of convenience isn't an uncommon occurrence.'

'Maybe not,' she responded with undue asperity. 'But I doubt if Mr Stefanos would be prepared to compromise in such a manner.'

'Why so sure, Miss Anderson?' The drawled query grated her raw nerves like steel razing through silk.

'Oh, really,' Alyse dismissed, 'such a solution is the height of foolishness, and totally out of the question.'

'Indeed?' His smile made her feel like a dove about to be caught up in the deadly claws of a marauding hawk. 'I consider it has a degree of merit.'

'While *I* can't think of anything worse than being imprisoned in marriage with a man like you!'

If he could have shaken her within an inch of her life, he would have done so. It was there in his eyes, the curious stillness of his features, and she controlled the desire to shiver, choosing instead to clasp her hands together in an instinctive protective gesture.

Against *what*? a tiny voice taunted. He couldn't possibly pose a threat, for heaven's sake!

'There's nothing further to be gained by continuing with this conversation.' With graceful fluidity she rose to her feet. 'Good afternoon, Mr Mannering,' she said with distinct politeness before spearing her adversary with a dark, venomous glance. '*Goodbye*, Mr Stefanos.'

Uncaring of the solicitor's attempt to defuse the situation, she walked to the door, opened it, then quietly closed it behind her before making her way to the outer office.

It wasn't until she was in her car and intent on negotiating busy traffic that reaction began to set in.

Damn. *Damn* Aleksi Stefanos! Her hands clenched on the wheel until the knuckles showed white, and she was so consumed with silent rage that it was nothing short of a miracle that she reached the boutique without suffering a minor accident.

CHAPTER TWO

THE remainder of the morning flew by as Alyse conferred with the boutique's manageress, Miriam Stanford, checked stock and tended to customers. It was almost midday before she was able to leave, and she felt immensely relieved to reach the comfortable sanctuary of her home.

As soon as the babysitter left, Alyse put a load of laundry into the washing machine, completed a few household chores, and was ready for Georg at the sound of his first wakening cry.

After changing him, she gave him his bottle, then made everything ready for his afternoon walk—an outing he appeared to adore, for he offered a contented smile as she placed him in the pram and secured the patterned quilt.

The air was fresh and cool, the winter sun fingering the spreading branches of trees lining the wide suburban street, and Alyse walked briskly, her eyes bright with love as she watched every gesture, every fleeting expression on her young nephew's face. He was so active, so alive for his tender age, and growing visibly with every passing day.

A slight frown furrowed her brow, and her features assumed a serious bleakness as she mentally reviewed the morning's consultation in Hugh Mannering's office. Was there really any possibility that she might fail in a bid to adopt Georg? *Could* the hateful Aleksi Stefanos's adoption application succeed? It was clear she must phone the solicitor as soon as possible.

On returning home Alyse gave Georg his bath, laughing ruefully as she finally managed to get his wriggling slippery body washed and dry, then dusted with talc and dressed in clean clothes. She gave him his bottle and settled him into his cot.

Now for the call to Hugh Mannering.

'Can I lose Georg?' Alyse queried with stark disregard for the conversational niceties.

'Any permanent resolution will take considerable time,' the solicitor stressed carefully. 'Technically, the Family Services Department investigates each applicant's capability to adequately care for the child, and ultimately a decision is made.'

'Off the record,' she persisted, 'who has the best chance?'

'It's impossible to ignore facts, Alyse. I've studied indisputable records documenting Aleksi Stefanos's financial status, and the man has an impressive list of assets.'

A chill finger slithered the length of her spine, and she suppressed the desire to shiver. 'Assets which far outstrip mine, I imagine?'

'My dear, you are fortunate to enjoy financial security of a kind that would be the envy of most young women your age. However, it is only a small percentage in comparison.'

'Damn him!' The oath fell from her lips in husky condemnation.

'The child's welfare is of prime importance,' the solicitor reminded her quietly. 'I'll have the application ready for your signature tomorrow.'

The inclination to have a snack instead of preparing herself a meal was all too tempting, and Alyse settled for an omelette with an accompanying salad, then followed it with fresh fruit.

She should make an effort to do some sewing—at least attempt to hand-finish a number of tiny smocked dresses which had been delivered to the house by one of her outworkers this morning. Certainly the boutique could do with the extra supplies.

The dishes done and the washing folded, Alyse collected a bundle of garments from its enveloping plastic and settled herself comfortably in the lounge with her sewing basket. Working diligently, she applied neat stitches with precise care, clipped thread, then deftly rethreaded the needle and began on the next garment.

Damn! The soft curse disrupted the stillness of the room. The third in an hour, and no less vicious simply because it was quietly voiced.

Alyse looked at the tiny prick of blood the latest needle stab had wrought, and raised her eyes heavenward in mute supplication.

Just this one garment, and she'd pack it all away for the evening, she pleaded in a silent deal with her favourite saint. Although it would prove less vexing if she cast aside hand-finishing for the evening and relaxed in front of the television with a reviving cup of coffee. Yet tonight she needed to immerse herself totally in her work in an attempt to alleviate the build-up of nervous tension.

Specialising in exquisitely embroidered babywear sold under her own label, *Alyse*, she had by dint of hard work, she reflected, changed a successful hobby into a thriving business. Now there was a boutique in a modern upmarket shopping centre catering for babies and young children's clothes featuring her own exclusive label among several imported lines.

Five minutes later Alyse breathed a sigh of relief as the tiny garment was completed. Stretching her arms high, she flexed her shoulders in a bid to ease the knot of muscular tension.

Georg's wakening cry sounded loud in the stillness of the house, and she quickly heated his bottle, fed him, then settled him down for the night.

In the hallway she momentarily caught sight of her mirrored reflection, and paused, aware that it was hardly surprising that the combination of grief and lack of appetite had reduced her petite form to positive slenderness. There were dark smudges beneath solemn blue eyes, and the angles of her facial bone-structure appeared delicate and more clearly defined.

Minutes later she sank into a chair in the lounge nursing a mug of hot coffee, longing not for the first time for someone in whom she could confide.

If her parents were still alive, it might be different, she brooded, but both had died within months of each other only a year after she had finished school, and she had been too busy establishing a niche in the workforce as well as guiding Antonia through a vulnerable puberty to enjoy too close an empathy with friends.

The sudden peal of the doorbell shattered the quietness of the room, and she hurried quickly to answer it, vaguely apprehensive yet partly curious as to who could possibly be calling at this time of the evening.

Checking that the safety chain was in place, she queried cautiously, 'Who is it?'

'Aleksi Stefanos.'

Stefanos. The name seemed etched in her brain with the clarity of diamond-engraved marble, and she closed her eyes in a purely reflex action as undisguised anger replaced initial shock.

'How did you get my address?' she wanted to know.

'The telephone directory.' His voice held an infinite degree of cynicism.

'How *dare* you come here?' Alyse demanded, trying her best to ignore the prickle of fear steadily creating havoc with her nervous system.

'Surely eight-thirty isn't unacceptably late?' his drawling voice enquired through the thick wood-panelled door, and she drew in a deep angry breath, then released it slowly.

'I have absolutely nothing to say to you.'

'May I remind you that I have every right to visit my nephew?'

For some inexplicable reason his dry mocking tones sent an icy chill feathering the length of her spine. *Damn* him! Who did he think he was, for heaven's sake?

'Georg is asleep, Mr Stefanos.'

Her curt dismissing revelation was greeted with ominous silence, and she unconsciously held her breath, willing him to go away.

'Asleep or awake, Miss Anderson, it makes little difference.'

Alyse closed her eyes and released her breath in one drawn-out sigh of frustration. Without doubt, Aleksi Stefanos possessed sufficient steel-willed determination to be incredibly persistent. If she refused to let him see Georg tonight, he'd insist on a suitable time tomorrow. Either way, he would eventually succeed in his objective.

Without releasing the safety chain, she opened the door a fraction, noticing idly that he had exchanged his formal suit for light grey trousers and a sweater in fine dark wool. Even from within the protection of her home, he presented a disturbing factor she could only view with disfavour.

'Will you give me your word that you won't try to abduct Georg?' she asked him.

His eyes flared, then became hard and implacable, his facial muscles reassembling over sculptured bone to present a mask of silent anger.

'It isn't in my interests to resort to abduction,' he warned inflexibly. 'Perhaps you should be reminded that your failure to co-operate will be taken into consideration and assuredly used against you.'

The temptation to tell him precisely what he could do with his legal advisers was almost impossible to ignore, but common sense reared its logical head just in time, and Alyse released the safety chain, then stood back to permit him entry.

'Thank you.'

His cynicism was not lost on her, and it took considerable effort to remain civil. 'Georg's room is at the rear of the house.'

Without even glancing at him, she led the way, aware that he followed close behind her. She didn't consciously hurry, but her footsteps were quick, and consequently she felt slightly breathless when she reached the end of the hallway.

Carefully she opened the door, swinging it wide so the shaft of light illuminated the room. Large and airy, it had been converted to a nursery months before Georg's birth, the fresh white paint with its water-colour murals on each wall the perfect foil for various items of nursery furniture, and a number of colourful mobiles hung suspended from the ceiling.

Fiercely protective, Alyse glanced towards the man opposite for any sign that he might disturb her charge, and saw there was no visible change in his expression.

What had she expected? A softening of that hard exterior? Instead there was a curious bleakness, a sense of purpose that Alyse found distinctly chilling.

Almost as if Georg sensed he was the object of a silent battle, he stirred, moving his arms as he wriggled on to his back, his tiny legs kicking at the blanket until, with a faint murmur, he settled again.

Alyse wanted to cry out that Georg was *hers*, and nothing, *no one*, was going to take him away from her.

Perhaps some of her resolve showed in her expressive features, for she glimpsed a muscle tighten at the edge of Aleksi Stefanos's powerful jaw an instant before he moved back from the cot, and she followed him from the room, carefully closing the door behind her.

It appeared he was in no hurry to leave, for he entered the lounge without asking, and stood, a hand thrust into each trouser pocket.

'Perhaps we could talk?' he suggested, subjecting her to an analytical scrutiny which in no way enhanced her temper.

'I was under the impression we covered just about everything this morning.'

Chillingly bleak eyes riveted hers, trapping her in his gaze, and Alyse was prompted to comment, 'It's a pity Georgiou himself didn't accord his son's existence such reverent importance.'

'There were, I think you will have to agree, extenuating circumstances.'

'If he really did *love* my sister,' she stressed, 'he would have seen to it that someone—even *you*—answered any one of her letters. He had a responsibility which was ignored, no matter how bravely he grappled with his own disabilities.'

His gaze didn't waver. 'I imagine he was tortured by the thought of Antonia bearing a child he would never see.'

'The only bonus to come out of the entire débâcle is Georg.'

He looked at her hard and long before he finally spoke. 'You must understand, he cannot be raised other than as a Stefanos.'

Alyse saw the grim resolve apparent, and suddenly felt afraid. 'Why?' she queried baldly. 'A man without a wife could only offer the services of a nanny, which, even if it were a full-time live-in employment, can't compare with my love and attention.'

His shoulders shifted imperceptibly, almost as if he were reassembling a troublesome burden, and his features assumed an inscrutability she had no hope of penetrating.

'You too employ the part-time services of a nanny in the guise of babysitter. Is this not so?' An eyebrow slanted in silent query. 'By your own admission, you operate a successful business. With each subsequent month, my nephew will become more active, sleep less, and demand more attention. While you delegate, in part, your business duties, you will also be delegating the amount of time you can spend with Georg. I fail to see a significant difference between your brand of caring and mine.'

'On that presumption you imagine I'll concede defeat?' Alyse queried angrily.

'I would be prepared to settle an extremely large sum in your bank account for the privilege.'

She shook her head, unable to comprehend what she was hearing. 'Bribery, Mr Stefanos? No amount of money would persuade me to part with Antonia's son.' She cast him a look of such disdainful dislike, a lesser man would have withered beneath it. 'Now, will you please leave?'

'I haven't finished what I came to say.'

He must have a skin thicker than a rhinoceros! Alyse could feel the anger emanate through the pores of her skin until her whole body was consumed with it. 'If you don't leave *immediately*, I'll call the police!'

'Go ahead,' he directed with pitiless disregard.

'This is my home, dammit!' Alyse reiterated heatedly.

His eyes were dark and infinitely dangerous. 'You walked out on a legal consultation this morning, and now you refuse to discuss Georg's welfare.' It was his turn to subject her to a raking scrutiny, his smile wholly cynical as he glimpsed the tide of colour wash over her cheeks. 'I imagine the police will be sympathetic.'

'They'll also throw you out!'

'They'll suggest I leave,' he corrected. 'And conduct any further discussion with you via a legal representative.' He paused, and his eyes were hard and obdurate, reflecting inflexible masculine strength of will. 'My stepbrother's child has a legal right to his stake in the Stefanos heritage. It is what Georgiou would have wanted; what my father wants. If Antonia were still alive,' he paused deliberately, 'I believe *she* would have wanted her son to be acknowledged by her lover's family, and to receive the financial benefits and recognition that are his due.'

Alyse's eyes sharpened as their depths became clearly defined. 'I intend having you and your *family* fully investigated.'

As a possible threat, it failed dismally, for he merely acknowledged her words with a cynical smile.

'Allow me to give you the relevant information ahead of official confirmation.'

Beneath the edge of mockery was a degree of inimical anger that feathered fear down the length of her spine and raised all her fine body hairs in protective self-defence.

'My father and stepmother reside in Athens. *I*, however, left my native Greece at the relatively young age of twenty to settle in Australia. Initially Sydney—working as a builder's labourer seven days a week, contractual obligations and weather permitting. After three years I moved to the Gold

Coast, where I bought land and built houses before venturing into building construction. The ensuing thirteen years have escalated my company to a prestigious position within the building industry. Without doubt,' he continued drily, 'I possess sufficient independent wealth to garner instant approval with the Family Services Department, and there are no mythical skeletons in any one of my closets.'

'Hardly a complete résumé, Mr Stefanos,' Alyse discounted scathingly.

'How far back into the past do you wish to delve? Does the fact that my mother was Polish, hence my unusual Christian name, condemn me? That she died when I was very young? Is that sufficient, Miss Anderson?' One eyebrow slanted above dark eyes heavily opaque with the rigors of memory. 'Perhaps you'd like to hear that a sweet, gentle Englishwoman eased my father's pain, married him and bore a male child without displacing my position as the eldest Stefanos son or alienating my father's affection for me in any way. She became the mother I'd never known, and we keep in constant touch, exchanging visits at least once each year.'

'And now that Georgiou is dead, they want to play an integral part in Georg's life.' Alyse uttered the words in a curiously flat voice, and was unprepared for the whip-hard anger in *his*.

'Are you so impossibly selfish that you fail to understand what Georg's existence means to them?' he demanded.

'I know what it means to *me*,' she cried out, sorely tried. 'If Antonia hadn't written to Georgiou, if——'

'Don't colour facts with unfounded prejudice,' Aleksi Stefanos cut in harshly. 'The letters exist as irrefutable proof. *I* intend assuming the role of Georg's father,' he pursued, his voice assuming a deadly softness. 'Don't doubt it for a minute.'

'Whereas I insist on the role of *mother*!' she blazed.

'You're not prepared to compromise in any way?'

'*Compromise?* Are *you* prepared to compromise? Why should it be *me* who has to forgo the opportunity of happiness in a marriage of my choice?'

His eyes narrowed fractionally. 'Is there a contender waiting in the wings, Miss Anderson? Someone sufficiently foolish to think he can conquer your fiery spirit and win?'

'What makes you think *you* could?'

His eyes gleamed with latent humour, then dropped lazily to trace the full curve of her lips before slipping down to the swell of her breasts, assessing each feature with such diabolical ease that she found it impossible to still the faint flush of pink that coloured her cheeks.

'I possess sufficient experience with women to know you'd resent any form of male domination, yet conversely refuse to condone a spineless wimp who gave way to your every demand.' Alyse stood speechless as his gaze wandered back to meet hers and hold it with indolent amusement. A sensation not unlike excitement uncoiled deep within her, and spread throughout her body with the speed of liquid fire, turning all the highly sensitised nerve-endings into a state of sensual awareness so intense it made her feel exhilaratingly *alive*, yet at the same time terribly afraid.

'The man in my life most certainly won't be you, Mr Stefanos!' she snapped.

'One of the country's best legal brains has given me his assurance that my adoption application will succeed,' he revealed. 'This morning's consultation in Hugh Mannering's office was arranged because I felt honour-bound to personally present facts regarding my stepbrother's accident and subsequent death. As to Georg's future...' he paused significantly '...the only way you can have any part in it will be to opt for marriage—to me.'

'You alternately threaten, employ a form of emotional blackmail, attempt to buy me off, then offer a marriage convenient only to *you*?' The slow-boiling anger which had simmered long beneath the surface of her control finally bubbled over. 'Go to *hell*, Mr Stefanos!'

The atmosphere in the lounge was so highly charged, Alyse almost expected it to explode into combustible flame.

He looked at her for what seemed an age, then his voice sounded cold—as icy as an Arctic gale. 'Think carefully before you burn any figurative bridges,' he warned silkily.

Alyse glared at him balefully, hating him, abhorring what he represented. 'Get out of my house. *Now!*' Taut, incredibly angry words that bordered close on the edge of rage as she moved swiftly from the room.

In the foyer she reached for the catch securing the front door, then gasped out loud as Aleksi Stefanos caught hold of her shoulders and turned her towards him with galling ease.

One glance at those compelling features was sufficient to determine his intention, and she struggled fruitlessly against his sheer strength.

'The temptation to teach you the lesson I consider you deserve is almost irresistible,' he drawled.

His anger was clearly evident, and, hopelessly helpless, Alyse clenched her jaw tight as his head lowered in an attempt to avoid his mouth, only to cry out as he caught the soft inner tissue with his teeth, and she had no defence against the plundering force of a kiss so intense that the muscles of her throat, her jaw, screamed in silent agony as he completed a ravaging possession that violated her very soul.

Just as suddenly as it had begun, it was over, and she sank back against the wall, her eyes stricken with silent hatred.

At that precise moment a loud wailing cry erupted from the bedroom, and Alyse turned blindly towards the nursery. Crossing to Georg's cot, she leant forward and lifted his tiny body into her arms. He smelled of soap and talc, and his baby cheek was satin-smooth against her own as she cradled him close.

His cries subsided into muffled hiccups, bringing stupid tears to her own eyes, and she blinked rapidly to still their flow, aware within seconds that her efforts were in vain as they spilled and began trickling ignominiously down each cheek.

This morning life had been so simple. Yet within twelve hours Aleksi Stefanos had managed to turn it upside down.

She turned as the subject of her most dire thoughts followed her into the nursery.

'You bastard!' she berated him in a painful whisper. 'Have you no scruples?'

'None whatsoever where Georg is concerned,' Aleksi Stefanos drawled dispassionately.

'What you're suggesting amounts to emotional blackmail, damn you!' Her voice emerged as a vengeful undertone, and Georg gave a slight whimpering cry, then settled as she gently rocked his small body in her arms.

'What I'm suggesting,' Aleksi Stefanos declared hardily, 'is parents, a home, and a stable existence for Georg.'

'Where's the stability in two people who don't even *like* each other?' Damn him—who did he think he was, for heaven's sake?

An icy shiver shook her slim frame in the knowledge that he knew precisely who he was and the extent of his own power.

'The alternatives are specific,' he continued as if she hadn't spoken, 'the choice entirely your own. You have until tomorrow evening to give me your answer.'

She was dimly aware that he moved past her to open the door, and it was that final, almost silent click as he closed it behind him that made her frighteningly aware of his control.

CHAPTER THREE

ALYSE stood where she was for what seemed an age before settling Georg into his cot, then she moved slowly to the front of the house, secured the lock and made for her own room, where she undressed and slid wearily into bed.

Damn. *Damn* him, she cursed vengefully. Aleksi Stefanos had no right to place her in such an invidious position. For the first time she felt consumed with doubt, apprehensive to such a degree that it was impossible to relax.

Images flooded her mind, each one more painful than the last, and she closed her eyes tightly against the bitter knowledge that adoption was absolute, so *final*.

If Aleksi Stefanos was successful with his application, he would remove Georg several thousand kilometres away to the opposite side of the continent. To see him at all, she would have to rely on Aleksi Stefanos's generosity, and it would be difficult with her business interests, to be able to arrange a trip to Queensland's Gold Coast more than once a year.

The mere thought brought tears to her eyes, and she cursed afresh. At least divorced parents got to *share* custody of their children.

However, to become divorced, one first had to marry, Alyse mused in contemplative speculation. Maybe... No, it wasn't possible. Or was it? How long would the marriage have to last? A year? Surely no longer than two, she decided, her mind racing.

If she did opt for marriage, she could have a contract drawn up giving Miriam a percentage of the profits, thus providing an incentive ensuring that the boutique continued to trade at a premium. As far as the house was concerned, she could lease it out. Her car would have to be sold, but that wouldn't matter, for she could easily buy another on her return.

A calculating gleam darkened her blue eyes, and a tiny smile curved her generous mouth.

When Aleksi Stefanos contacted her tomorrow, he would discover that she was surprisingly amenable. It was infinitely worth a year or two out of her life if it meant she got to keep Georg.

For the first time in the six weeks since Antonia's funeral, Alyse slept without a care to disturb her subconscious, and woke refreshed, eager to start the new day.

With so much to attend to, she drew up a list, and simply crossed every item off as she dealt with it.

A call to Hugh Mannering determined that marriage to Aleksi Stefanos would reduce the adoption proceedings to a mere formality, and he expressed delight that she was taking such a sensible step.

Alyse responded with a tongue-in-cheek agreement, and chose not to alarm her legal adviser by revealing the true extent of her plans.

Miriam was delighted to be promoted, and proved more than willing to assume management of the boutique for as long as necessary.

By late afternoon Alyse was able to relax, sure that everything was in place.

A light evening meal of cold chicken and salad provided an easy alternative to cooking, and she followed it with fresh fruit.

The telephone rang twice between seven and eight o'clock, and neither call was from Aleksi Stefanos.

A cloud of doubt dulled her eyes as she pondered the irony of him not ringing at all, only to start visibly when the insistent burr of the phone sounded shortly before nine.

It had to be him, and she let it peal five times in a fit of sheer perversity before picking up the receiver.

'Alyse?' His slightly accented drawl was unmistakable, his use of her Christian name an impossible liberty, she decided as she attempted to still a sense of foreboding. 'Have you reached a decision?'

He certainly didn't believe in wasting words! A tinge of anger heightened her mood. Careful, a tiny voice cautioned. You don't want to blow it. 'Yes.'

There was silence for a few seconds as he waited for her to continue, and when she didn't he queried with ill-concealed mockery, 'Must I draw it from you like blood from a stone?'

If it wasn't for Georg she'd slam down the receiver without the slightest compunction. 'I've considered your proposition,' she said tightly, 'and I've decided to accept.' There, she'd actually said it.

'My parents arrive from Athens at the beginning of next week,' Aleksi Stefanos told her without preamble, and she would have given anything to ruffle that imperturbable composure. 'They're naturally eager to see Georg, and there's no reason why you both shouldn't fly back to Queensland with me on Friday.'

'I can't possibly be ready by then,' Alyse protested, visibly shaken at the way he was assuming control.

'Professional packers will ensure that everything in the house is satisfactorily dealt with,' he said matter-of-factly. 'Whatever you need can be airfreighted to the Coast, and the rest put into storage. The house can be put into the hands of a competent letting agent, and managerial control arranged at the boutique. I suggest you instruct Hugh Mannering to draw up a power of attorney and liaise with him. All it takes is a few phone calls. To satisfy the Family Services Department, it would be advisable if a civil marriage ceremony is held here in Perth—Thursday, if it can be arranged. Relevant documentation regarding Georg's adoption can then be signed ready for lodgement, leaving us free of any added complications in removing him from the State.'

'Dear heaven,' Alyse breathed unsteadily, 'you don't believe in wasting time!'

'I'll give you a contact number where I can be reached,' he continued as if she hadn't spoken, relaying a set of digits she had to ask him to repeat as she quickly wrote them down. 'Any questions?'

'At least *ten*,' she declared with unaccustomed sarcasm.

'They can wait until dinner tomorrow evening.'

'With everything I have to do, I won't have *time* for dinner!'

'I'll collect you at six.'

There was a click as he replaced the receiver, and Alyse felt like screaming in vexation. What had she expected—small talk? *Revenge*, she decided, would be very sweet!

Removing the receiver, she placed a call to Miriam Stanford and asked if the manageress could work the entire day tomorrow, informed her briefly of her intended plans and promised she would be in at some stage during the afternoon.

Alyse slept badly, and rose just after dawn determined to complete a host of household chores, allowing herself no respite as she conducted a thorough spring-clean of the large old home, stoically forcing herself to sort through Antonia's possessions—something she'd continually put off until now.

It was incredibly sad, for there were so many things to remind her of the happy young girl Antonia had been, the affection and laughter they had shared. Impossible to really believe she was no longer alive, when celluloid prints and vivid memories provided such a painful reminder.

Despite her resolve to push Aleksi Stefanos to the edge of her mind, it was impossible not to feel mildly apprehensive as she settled Georg with the babysitter before retiring to the bathroom to shower, then dress for the evening ahead.

Selecting an elegant slim-fitting off-the-shoulder gown in deep sapphire blue, she teamed it with black stiletto-heeled shoes, tended to her make-up with painstaking care, then brushed her shoulder-length strawberry-blonde hair into its customary smooth bell before adding a generous touch of Van Cleef & Arpels' *Gem* to several pulsebeats. Her only added jewellery was a diamond pendant, matching earstuds and bracelet.

At five minutes to six she checked last-minute details with the babysitter, brushed a fleeting kiss to Georg's forehead, then moved towards the lounge, aware of a gnawing nervousness in the pit of her stomach with every step she took.

Now that she was faced with seeing him again, she began to wonder if she was slightly mad to toy with a man of Aleksi Stefanos's calibre. He undoubtedly ate little girls for breakfast, and although she was no naïve nineteen-year-old, her experience with men had been pitifully limited to platonic friendships that had affection as their base rather than any degree of passion. It hardly equipped her to act a required part.

Yet act she must—at least until she had his wedding ring on her finger. Afterwards she could set the rules by which the marriage would continue, and for how long.

Punctuality was obviously one of his more admirable traits, for just as she reached the foyer there was the soft sound of car tyres on the gravel drive followed almost immediately by the muted clunk of a car door closing.

At once she was conscious of an elevated nervous tension, and it took every ounce of courage to move forward and open the door.

Standing in its aperture, Aleksi Stefanos looked the epitome of male sophistication attired in a formal dark suit. Exuding more than his fair share of dynamic masculinity, he had an element of tensile steel beneath the polite veneer, a formidableness and sense of purpose that was daunting.

'Alyse.' There was an edge of mockery apparent, and she met his gaze with fearless disregard, blindly ignoring the increased tempo of her heartbeat.

Just a glance at the sensual curve of his mouth was enough to remember how it felt to be positively *absorbed* by the man, for no one in their wildest imagination could term what he had subjected her to as merely a *kiss*.

Conscious of his narrowed gaze, Alyse stood aside to allow him entry, acknowledging politely, 'Mr Stefanos.'

'Surely you can force yourself to say Aleksi?' he chastised with ill-concealed mockery.

Alyse choked back a swift refusal. Steady, she cautioned—anger will get you precisely nowhere. Opting for the line of least resistance, she ventured evenly, 'If you insist.' Remembering her manners, she indicated the lounge. 'Please come in. Would you care for a drink?'

'Unless you'd prefer one, I suggest we leave,' he countered smoothly. 'I've booked a table for six-thirty.'

Without a further word she preceded him to the car, allowing him to reach forward and open the door, and she slid into the passenger seat, aware of his close proximity seconds later as he slipped in behind the wheel and set the large vehicle in motion.

'Where are we dining?' As a conversational gambit, it was sadly lacking in originality, but anything was better than silence, Alyse decided wildly as they joined the flow of traffic leading into the city.

'My hotel.'

She turned towards him in thinly veiled astonishment. 'I could have met you there.'

'Thus preserving feminine independence?' Aleksi mocked as he spared her a quick assessing appraisal before returning his attention to the computer-controlled intersection.

'I'll take a cab home.'

One eyebrow quirked in visible amusement as the lights changed, and he eased the car forward. 'Impossible,' he declared smoothly, and she felt like hitting him for appearing so damnably implacable.

'Would it dent your chauvinistic male ego?' she queried sweetly, and heard his soft laughter.

'Not in the least. However, as my fiancée and soon-to-be wife, you can't be permitted.'

She closed her eyes, then slowly opened them seconds later. It was the only defence she had in masking the incredible fury she harboured against him.

As if he sensed her inner battle, he slid a tape into the cassette-deck, and she leaned back against the headrest, her eyes fixed on the tall city buildings and the wide sweep of river.

Alyse was familiar with the hotel, if not the restaurant, and when they were seated she permitted Aleksi to fill an elegant flute with Dom Perignon, sipping the superb champagne in the hope that it might afford her a measure of courage to face the evening ahead.

Aleksi conferred with the waiter over the menu, asking her what she wanted before placing their order, then he leaned well back in his chair and subjected her to a veiled scrutiny.

'Aren't you in the least curious to learn what arrangements I've made?'

She lifted her glass and took a generous swallow before replacing it on the table. 'I have no doubt you'll reveal them soon enough.' Tiny aerated bubbles of alcohol set up a tingling warmth inside her stomach and began transporting them through every vein in her body.

'We have an eleven o'clock appointment with the register office on Thursday, followed by a consultation with Hugh Mannering at two, and at three we're due to present ourselves at the Family Services Department. On Friday we catch the late morning flight en route to the Coast,' he informed her cynically.

The enormity of what she was about to undertake seemed to assume gigantic proportions, and she suffered his raking scrutiny with unblinking solemnity.

'This is no time for second thoughts,' Aleksi stated in a voice that was silky-smooth and infinitely dangerous. 'The reason for a marriage between us is obvious,' he declared hardily, 'and will be accepted as such.'

'Am I supposed to get down on my knees and kiss your feet in sheer gratitude for the privilege?' Her voice dripped ice, and she saw his blue-grey eyes assume a chilling ruthlessness.

'Careful,' he warned dangerously. 'I insist we present a veneer of politeness in the company of others.' He directed her a swift calculated appraisal that sent shivers of fear scudding the length of her spine. 'In private you can fight me as much as you like.'

'In private,' she conceded with ill-concealed fury, 'I shall probably render you grievous bodily harm!'

'Don't expect me not to retaliate,' he drawled.

'Do that, and I'll have you up for assault!'

His eyes narrowed and assumed the hue of a dark storm-tossed sea. 'I wasn't aware I alluded to physical abuse.'

Her eyes widened into huge pools of incredulity as comprehension dawned, and she fought valiantly against an all-encompassing anger. 'Abuse is still an ugly word, whether it be mental or physical,' she said tightly.

'Then perhaps you would be advised to keep a rein on your temper.'

'I must have been mad to agree to *any* alliance with you!' she declared bitterly, sure she'd become a victim of temporary insanity.

'Georg is the crux,' Aleksi remarked cynically, and she cried out in vengeful disavowal,

'I don't have much choice, damn you!'

'I offered you the opportunity of assuming the role of Georg's mother.'

'The only problem is that *you* form part of the package!'

'Oh, it mightn't be too bad.' His smile was totally lacking in humour. 'I live in a beautiful home—a showcase to display my expertise within the building industry. I enjoy the company of a close circle of friends, and frequently entertain. The Gold Coast is far from dull. I'm sure you'll manage to amuse yourself.'

'When do you intend informing your parents of our impending marriage?' asked Alyse.

'I already have,' he drawled with hateful cynicism. 'They're delighted that we've chosen such a sensible solution.'

'Are your parents visiting for very long?'

'Question-and-answer time, Alyse? Or simply sheer curiosity?'

An angry flush crept over her cheeks, and her eyes sparked with brilliant blue fire. 'I imagined it was a legitimate query.' If they'd been alone, she would have thrown the contents of her glass in his face. 'Perhaps I should opt for silence.'

'Apparent subservience?' he queried sardonically. 'Somehow I can't perceive you acquiring that particular mantle.'

'No,' Alyse agreed coolly out of deference to the waiter, who deftly removed their plates and busied himself serving the main course.

The grilled fish with hollandaise sauce and accompanying assortment of vegetables was assembled with artistic flair and infinitely tempting to the most discerning palate. Yet she was so incredibly angry she was hard pressed to do the course the justice it deserved. Afterwards she declined dessert and the cheeseboard, and simply opted for coffee, noting with silent rage that Aleksi Stefanos's appetite appeared totally unaffected.

'Perhaps you could bring yourself to tell me what progress *you* have made?' he suggested.

Alyse met his gaze with fearless disregard. 'Everything is taken care of—the boutique, leasing the house. All that remains for me to do is *pack*.'

'And shop for a wedding dress,' he added with hateful ease, one eyebrow slanting with a degree of mocking humour, and a diabolical imp prompted her to query,

'Traditional white?' Her own eyebrow matched his in a deliberate arch.

'Do you have any objection?'

You're darned right I have! she felt like screaming. 'Surely a civil ceremony doesn't warrant such extravagance?'

'Humour me.'

'The hell I will! A classic-designed suit is adequate.' She paused, her eyes wide and startlingly direct. 'In black, or red. Something that makes a definite statement.'

He leaned further back in his chair, his posture portraying indolent ease. Yet there was a degree of tightly coiled strength apparent, and a prickle of apprehension feathered the surface of her skin.

'Flamboyant reluctance?' Aleksi queried with deceptive mildness. 'You choose to be recorded for posterity in a manner that will doubtless raise questions from our son, ten—fifteen years from now?'

Her lips parted to say that ten years down the track she would no longer be his wife. In fact, the requisite two would be two too many! Except that no sound escaped as she snapped her mouth firmly closed. 'I'll agree to a cream linen suit, matching accessories and a floral bouquet,' she told him.

'Adequate,' he drawled. 'But not precisely what I had in mind.'

'Well, isn't that just too damned bad?' Alyse snapped with scant attempt at politeness. 'Perhaps you've decided to compound the farce with formal tails and an elegant striped silk cravat?'

'Are you usually so quarrelsome, or is your behaviour merely an attempt to oppose me?'

Her eyes flashed pure crystalline sapphire. 'Oh, both. I'm no timid little dove.'

A lazy smile broadened the generous curve of his mouth. 'Even the wildest bird can be trained to enjoy captivity.'

A surge of anger rose to the surface, bringing a tinge of pink to her cheeks and sharpening her features. 'That's precisely the type of sexist remark I'd expect you to make!' She looked at him with increasing hostility. 'If you've finished your coffee, I'd like to leave.'

'So early, Alyse?' he mocked as he signalled the waiter to bring their bill. 'You've no desire to go on to a nightclub?'

'What would be the point? We're at daggers drawn now!' She tempered the remark with a totally false smile that almost felled the waiter, but didn't fool Aleksi in the slightest.

'We'll doubtless shatter every romantic illusion your babysitter possesses if I return you before the witching hour of midnight,' he remarked.

'As there's nothing in the least romantic about our alliance, it hardly matters, does it?' She stood to her feet and preceded him from the restaurant, uncaring that he followed close behind.

In the car she sat in silence, conscious of the faint swish of tyres on the wet bitumen. There was movement everywhere, people walking, colourful flashes of neon as the large vehicle purred through the city streets, and she became fascinated by the reflection caught in the still waters of the Swan River as they headed west towards Peppermint Grove.

'I'll arrange for a chauffeured limousine to collect you at ten-thirty on Thursday morning,' Aleksi declared as he brought the car to a halt in her driveway. 'You have the phone number of my hotel if you need to contact me.'

Polite, distant, and totally businesslike. It was almost as if he was deliberately playing an extremely shrewd game with every single manoeuvre carefully planned, Alyse brooded, aware of a chill shiver that owed nothing to the cool midwinter temperature.

'I doubt if there'll be the necessity,' she declared as she reached for the door-clasp, only to catch her breath in startled surprise as he slid out from behind the wheel and walked round to open her door.

Moving swiftly from the passenger seat, she stood still, unsure of his intention, her movements momentarily suspended as she prepared for a rapid flight into the safety of the house. If he *dared* to kiss her, she'd hit him!

His faint mocking smile was almost her undoing, and she drew a deep steadying breath before issuing a stilted, 'Goodnight.'

Without so much as a backward glance she walked to the front door, put her key in the lock, then closed the door carefully behind her.

Inside was warmth and light, the endearing familiarity of a home where there were no shadows, no insecurity.

Summoning a smile as she moved into the lounge, she checked with the babysitter and paid her before looking in on Georg, then she simply locked up and prepared for bed.

CHAPTER FOUR

THE civil ceremony was incredibly brief, and only the fleeting appearance of Hugh Mannering provided a familiar face as Alyse affixed 'Stefanos' after 'Alyse' on the marriage certificate.

There were photographs, several of them taken by a professional, followed by lunch in the elegant dining-room of an inner city hotel.

Their appearance attracted circumspect interest. Her pencil-slim skirt with a long-line jacket in pale cream linen and matching accessories portrayed designer elegance, while Aleksi's impeccably tailored silver-grey suit merely accentuated his magnetic masculine appeal. Together, they scarcely presented the image of loving newlyweds, and she wondered a trifle wryly if they looked married.

Food was the last thing on her mind, and she ate mechanically, totally unappreciative of the superb seafood starter or the equally splendid lobster thermidor that followed. Even the champagne, Dom Perignon, suffered the sacrilege of being sipped seemingly without taste, and she declined both dessert and the cheeseboard in favour of strong aromatic black coffee.

Conversation between them verged on the banal, and Alyse heaved a mental sigh of relief when Aleksi indicated that they should leave if they were to keep their appointment with Hugh Mannering and the Department of Social Services.

'We'll take a taxi,' he said as they stepped out on to the pavement.

Within minutes he managed to hail one, and Alyse sat in silence, her gaze caught by the twin fitted rings adorning her left hand. The prismatic facets of a large solitaire diamond sparked blue and green fire in a brilliant burst from reflected sunlight, providing a perfect setting for its matching diamond-set wedding-ring.

'They suit you.'

Alyse glanced towards the owner of that drawling voice, and met his gaze without any difficulty at all. 'A simple gold band would have been sufficient,' she acknowledged with utter seriousness.

'No, it wouldn't.' There was an edge of mockery apparent, and she summoned up a dazzling smile.

'I forgot the *image* factor.'

He deigned not to comment, and it was something of a relief when the taxi cruised to a halt outside the building housing the solicitor's offices.

Fifty minutes later they summoned yet another taxi and instructed the driver to take them to the Family Services Department.

Bureaucratic red tape had a tendency to be time-consuming, with appointments rarely running to schedule, and today appeared no different. Consequently it was late afternoon before they emerged into the cool winter sunlight.

'A celebratory drink?'

There was a wealth of satisfaction in knowing that the initial legalities surrounding Georg's pending adoption were now officially in place, and Alyse found herself tilting her head as she met Aleksi's penetrating gaze. Quite without reason she found herself feeling slightly breathless, and desperately in need of a few hours away from his disturbing presence.

'There are still quite a few things I have to do.' Nothing of drastic importance, but he didn't need to know that. 'Could we combine it with dinner?'

'I'll organise yours and Georg's combined luggage and have it sent to the hotel. I'm sure the babysitter won't object to a change of venue.'

Her eyes widened in surprise, then long lashes swept down to form a protective veil. 'Is that really necessary?' she managed with remarkable steadiness, and detected cynicism in his drawling response.

'For the purpose of convention, we'll begin our marriage together by sharing the same roof. It's the hotel, or your home. Choose.'

'Just as long as you understand it won't involve the same bed.'

'Did I suggest that it would?'

Alyse closed her eyes, then slowly opened them again. Careful, a tiny voice cautioned. 'In comparison, I'm sure your luggage is far less substantial than Georg's and mine combined,' she declared in stilted tones, and watched as he hailed a taxi and instructed the driver to take them to his hotel.

His suite was situated on the twelfth floor and offered a magnificent view of the river. Alyse crossed the deep-piled carpet to stand at the window, all too aware of the intimacy projected by the opulently spread king-size bed.

'Help yourself to a drink,' Aleksi directed. 'The bar-fridge is fully stocked, and there's tea and coffee.' Without waiting for her reply, he moved towards the bedside phone and lifted the receiver, stating his intention to check out.

Anything remotely alcoholic would go straight to her head. 'I'd prefer coffee,' she said as he replaced the receiver, and good manners were responsible for her asking, 'Will you have some?'

When it was made, she sipped the instant brew appreciatively while Aleksi emptied contents of drawers and wardrobe into a masculine-styled bag. It was a chore he executed with the deft ease of long practice, and when it was completed he drained his coffee in a few measured swallows.

'Shall we leave?'

Alyse stood to her feet at once and preceded him from the suite, aware of an increasing sense of trepidation as she walked at his side.

It couldn't be fear, she analysed as they rode the lift down to the ground floor, for she wasn't afraid of him. Yet in some strange way he presented a threat, for she was aware of an elemental quality apparent, a primeval recognition that raised all her fine body hairs in protective self-defence.

It was after five when they reached suburban Peppermint Grove, and Alyse was grateful for the babysitter's presence as she effected the necessary introductions before escorting Aleksi to one of the spare bedrooms.

'You can leave your bag here. I'll make up the bed later.'

She felt awkward and ill at ease, and her chin tilted slightly as she met his mocking gaze. Damn you, she longed to scream at him. I *hate* you!

'I'll check on Georg.' Without another word she turned and left the room, telling herself she didn't care whether he followed her or not.

Georg was fast asleep, and Alyse moved silently towards her own bedroom, where she quickly shed her shoes, then exchanged her suit for a towelling robe.

Despite the babysitter's being hired until late evening, Alyse wanted to bath and feed Georg herself before settling him down for the night. It was a ritual she adored, and tonight it held special meaning, for only due legal process separated Georg from being officially hers.

Almost on cue she heard his first wakening cry, and she reached him within seconds, loving the way his tears ceased the moment she picked him up.

Bathing and feeding took almost an hour, and Alyse was supremely conscious of Aleksi's presence during the latter thirty minutes.

'May I?'

With extreme care she placed Georg into the crook of Aleksi's arm, watching every movement with the eagle eye of a mother-hen.

'I won't drop him,' Aleksi drawled with hateful cynicism, and her eyes darkened to a deep cerulean blue.

'I never imagined you would,' she snapped, aware that the babysitter was in the kitchen preparing her own dinner and therefore happily in ignorance of their barbed exchange.

Alyse willed Georg to cry, thus signalling his displeasure at being placed in a stranger's care, but he failed to comply and merely lay still, his bright eyes wide and dark. One could be forgiven for imagining he was fascinated, and perhaps he was, she decided uncharitably, for there had to be an awareness of change from her own scent and body-softness in comparison with his uncle's muscularly hard male-contoured frame.

Aleksi's expression was inscrutably intent, and she watched as he placed a forefinger into Georg's baby palm, detecting a momentary flaring of triumph as tiny fingers closed around it.

'He's a beautiful child,' she said quietly, and suffered Aleksi's swift scrutiny.

'He's my brother's son.' He paused slightly, then added with soft emphasis, '*Our* son.'

For some reason a chill shiver feathered its way down her spine. His words sounded irrevocable, almost as if he was issuing a silent warning. Yet he could have no inkling of her intention to instigate a divorce and gain custody of Georg—could he?

Stop it, she bade silently. You're merely being fanciful.

'He really should go down for the night.' She purposely shifted her gaze to Georg, who in total contrariness looked as if he had every intention of remaining wide awake.

'Why don't you go and change?' Aleksi suggested. 'The babysitter can settle him into his cot, and you can check him before we leave.'

A slight frown momentarily furrowed Alyse's brow.

'Dinner,' he elaborated.

The thought of suffering through another meal in his sole company was the last thing she wanted, but the alternative of staying in was even worse.

'I'm not very hungry, and I still have to pack.' It was a token protest at best, and he knew it.

'We won't be late.'

Dammit, what she'd give to ruffle that implacable composure! A sobering thought occurred that she *had*, and the result wasn't something she'd willingly choose to repeat.

'In that case, I'll go and get ready.'

'Unequivocal compliance, Alyse?'

'Conditional accedence,' she corrected, and leaning forward she brushed her lips to Georg's forehead. 'Goodnight, darling,' she bade softly. 'Sleep well.'

The gesture brought her far too close to Aleksi, and she straightened at once, moving away without so much as a backward glance as she left the room.

Selecting something suitable to wear took scant minutes, and she chose to freshen her make-up, merely adding a light dusting of powder and re-applying lipstick before running a brush through her hair.

Slipping into shoes, she collected a clutch-purse, then took one quick glance at her mirrored reflection, uncaring that the tailored black dress and red jacket provided a striking foil for her attractive features and pale shining hair.

As she emerged from her room she almost collided with Aleksi, and she bore his scrutiny with equanimity.

'Georg is already fast asleep,' he enlightened her quietly as he walked at her side to the lounge.

'Aleksi has written down the name and telephone number of the restaurant in case of any emergency,' the babysitter revealed, her eyes sparkling as they moved from one to the other, and Alyse could have sworn there was a degree of wistful envy in the young girl's expression. 'Please enjoy yourselves, and stay as long as you want. I don't mind.'

One glance at Aleksi Stefanos had been sufficient for the romantic eighteen-year-old to weave an impossible imaginary fantasy that bore no similarity whatsoever to reality!

Alyse could only proffer a sweet smile and utter her thanks, although inwardly she felt like screaming in vexation.

'Save it until we're in the car,' murmured Aleksi as he stood aside for her to precede him from the house, and she turned towards him with the smile still firmly pinned in place.

'Thus preserving the required image, I suppose?'

His gaze was full of mockery. 'Of course.'

Her expression registered an entire gamut of emotions, and she struggled to contain them as she slid into the passenger seat. 'Oh, go to hell!'

'I would advise putting a curb on your tongue.' His voice was dangerously soft, and in the dim interior of the car it was impossible to determine his expression. Not that she cared, she assured herself. He could bring down the wrath of a veritable Nemesis on her head, and it wouldn't matter at all.

The restaurant Aleksi had chosen was intimate, and offered superb cuisine. As a perfect complement, he ordered a bottle of Cristal, and proposed a solemn toast to their future together.

It wasn't something Alyse coveted, and she merely sipped the excellent champagne and forked morsels of food into her mouth with seemingly mechanical regularity.

Consequently it was a relief when coffee was served, and she breathed a silent sigh as Aleksi summoned the waiter for their bill.

In the car she sat in silence, grateful that he made no attempt at idle conversation, and the moment they arrived home she moved indoors with indecent haste, paid the babysitter and presented her with a parting gift, forcing a smile as the girl gave her an impulsive hug and bestowed her best wishes on them both.

'I'll make up your bed,' Alyse declared minutes after Anna's departure, 'then finish packing.'

'If you retrieve the necessary bed-linen, I'm sure I can manage,' Aleksi drawled, and she retaliated with deliberate sarcasm,

'A domesticated husband—how nice! Can you cook too?'

'Adequately. I also iron.'

'It almost seems too much!'

'Me, or my—abilities?' Aleksi's emphasis was deliberate, and she directed him an arctic glare.

'As I haven't experienced any of your abilities, I'm hardly in a position to comment.'

'Is that an invitation?'

His sarcasm was the living end. 'You know damn well it's not!' She moved quickly past him into the hallway and flung open the linen closet. 'You should have stayed at the hotel,' she declared, and was utterly incensed when she glimpsed his silent humour.

'Alone?' Aleksi mocked.

Alyse closed her eyes, then opened them again in a gesture of pure exasperation. 'Take a clean towel with you if you want to shower. Goodnight,' she added pointedly. Without a further word she walked towards her bedroom, then went in and closed the door behind her.

If he dared to follow her, she'd do him a mortal injury, she determined vengefully as she set about filling a suitcase with the remainder of her clothes. When the chore was completed she looked in on Georg, then crept back to her room, undressed, and slipped into bed.

She was so tired she should have fallen asleep within minutes, except there were fragmented images torturing her subconscious mind, the most vivid of which was the compelling form of Aleksi Stefanos. He appeared as a dark, threatening force: compelling, and infinitely powerful.

She had married in haste, out of love and loyalty to her sister and baby Georg. Would she repent at leisure, transported several thousand kilometres to the opposite side of the continent, where Aleksi Stefanos was in command?

Alyse found it impossible not to feel apprehensive as she boarded the large Boeing jet the following morning, and as each aeronautical mile brought them steadily closer to their destination the anxiety intensified.

A stopover in Melbourne and change in aircraft was instrumental in the final leg of their flight, and Alyse followed Aleksi into the arrival lounge at Coolangatta, aware that Georg, who had travelled surprisingly well, was now wide awake and would soon require the bottle the airline stewardess had kindly heated prior to disembarking.

Aleksi gave every appearance of being a doting uncle—*father*, she corrected silently, incredibly aware that he exuded dynamic masculinity attired in dark casual-style trousers, pale shirt and impeccably designed jacket that served to emphasise his breadth of shoulder—and she mentally squared her own, tilting her chin fractionally as he moved forward to lift various items of their luggage from the carousel and load them on to a trolley.

'I arranged to have my car brought to the airport,' he told her as Georg broke into a fractious wail. 'Wait here while I collect it from the car park.'

Alyse nodded in silent acquiescence, her entire attention caught up by the baby in the carrycot, whose tiny legs began to kick in vigorous rejection of what she suspected was a freshly soiled nappy.

By the time Aleksi returned Georg was crying lustily, and she opted to care for the baby's needs while Aleksi dealt with the luggage.

'Forceful young fellow,' Aleksi drawled minutes later as he eased the large BMW away from the terminal.

'Who's obviously intent on continuing in the same domineering vein as his forefathers,' Alyse offered sweetly as she gave Georg his bottle.

'Of whom you know very little,' reproved Aleksi, shooting her a quick mocking glance via the rear-view mirror, and she was quick with a loaded response.

'Oh, I wouldn't say that. I'm learning more each day.' She deliberately focused her attention on Georg, pacing the baby's attempt to drain the contents of his bottle in record speed, then when he had finished she burped him and laid him down in the carrycot, watching anxiously until he lapsed into a fitful doze.

Alyse pretended an interest in the darkened scenery beyond the windscreen, viewing the clearly lit highway and abundance of neon signs with apparent absorption.

'Is this your first visit to the Gold Coast?' he asked.

She turned towards him, glimpsing strength of purpose in features made all the more arresting by reflected headlights in the dim interior of the car.

'My parents brought Antonia and me here for a holiday about ten years ago,' she revealed.

The tiny lines fanning out from his eyes became more pronounced and his mouth widened into a slight smile. 'You'll notice a lot of changes.'

'For the better, I hope?'

'That would depend on whether you prefer the relaxed, casual holiday atmosphere the locals enjoyed all year round with only the inconvenience of visiting tourists during peak season, or the bustling commercial centre Surfers' Paradise has now become.'

'I guess one has to admit it's progress,' Alyse opined as the luxurious vehicle purred swiftly north along the double-lane highway.

'There's been a massive injection of Japanese-controlled funds into the area—hotels, resorts, golf courses,' Aleksi told her. 'The flow-on has resulted in a building boom: houses, shopping centres, high-rise developments, offices.'

'As a builder, you must be very pleased with the increased business.' It was a non-committal comment, and not meant to be judgemental.

However, it earned her a quick piercing glance before the road reclaimed his attention.

'The Coast has a long history of boom-and-bust cycles in building and real estate. Only the foolish choose to disregard facts and fail to plan ahead.'

No one in their right mind could call Aleksi Stefanos a fool, Alyse thought wryly. Remembering the force of his kiss, the steel-like strength of his arms as they had held her immobile, provided a vivid reminder of what manner of man she intended playing against. Yet it was a game she must win.

As the BMW pulled into the outer lane and sped swiftly past a line of slower-moving vehicles with ease, Alyse could only wonder at its horsepower capacity. There were outlines of densely covered hills reaching into the distance as Aleksi veered inland from the coastal highway.

'Sovereign Islands comprises a number of bridge-linked residentially developed islands situated to the east of Paradise Point, less than an hour's drive from the airport,' he told her. 'It's a prestigious security-guarded estate, and accessible by road from the mainland via a private bridge. Every home site has deep-water anchorage.'

'A gilded prison for the fabulously wealthy, with a luxury vessel moored at the bottom of every garden?'

'The residents prefer to call it civilised protection, and are prepared to pay for the privilege.'

'Suitably cushioned from the harsh realities of life.' Alyse couldn't believe she was resorting to sarcasm. It simply wasn't her style. Yet for some unknown reason the man behind the wheel generated the most adverse feelings in her, making her want to lash out against him in every possible way.

He didn't bother to reply, and she sat in silence, aware of an increasing anxiety as the car sped steadily north. Her home in Perth seemed a million kilometres away; the relative ease of life as she'd known it equally distant.

Her marriage was one of necessity, and merely mutually convenient. So why was she as wound up as a tightly coiled spring?

'We're almost there,' Aleksi declared drily, and Alyse spared her surroundings a swift encompassing glance, noting the numerous brightly lit architect-designed homes and established well-kept grounds.

Aleksi had said his home was a showcase, and she silently agreed as he turned the car on to a tiled driveway fronting a magnificent double-storeyed residence that seemed far too large for one man alone.

Pale granite walls were reflected by the car's powerful headlights, their lines imposing and classically defined. At a touch of the remote control module the wide garage doors tilted upwards, and Aleksi brought the BMW to a smooth halt alongside a Patrol four-wheel-drive vehicle.

Minutes later Alyse followed him into a large entrance foyer featuring a vaulted ceiling of tinted glass. A magnificent chandelier hung suspended from its centre, lending spaciousness and an abundance of light reflected by off-white walls and deep-piled cream-textured carpet. The central focus was a wide double staircase leading to the upper floor.

Wide glass-panelled doors stood open revealing an enormous lounge furnished with delicately carved antique furniture, and there were several carefully placed oil paintings gracing the walls, providing essential colour.

'I suggest you settle Georg,' said Aleksi as he brought in the luggage. His expression was a inscrutable mask as he chose a passageway to his left, and Alyse had little option but to follow in his wake.

'The master suite has an adjoining sitting-room overlooking the canal——' with a wide sweep of his arm he indicated a door immediately opposite '—an en suite bathroom, and, to the left, a changing-room with two separate walk-in wardrobes.'

The décor had an elegance that was restful and visually pleasant, utilising a skilful mix of pale green and a soft shade of peach as a complement to the overall cream.

'There's the requisite nursery furniture in the sitting-room,' he continued, moving forward. 'And a spare bed which you can use until——'

'Until—*what*?' Alyse's eyes blazed blue fire in an unspoken challenge.

'You're ready to share mine,' he drawled with imperturbable calm.

She was so incredibly furious that she almost shook with anger, and she failed to feel Georg stir in her arms, nor did she register his slight whimper in sleepy protest. 'That will be *never*!'

Dark eyebrows slanted above eyes that held hers in deliberate mocking appraisal. 'My dear Alyse,' chided Aleksi with chilling softness, 'surely you expect the marriage to be consummated?'

Her eyes widened with angry incredulity. 'In a house this large, there have to be other adequate bedrooms from which I can choose.'

'Several,' Aleksi agreed. 'However, this is where you'll stay.'

Her chin tilted in a gesture of indignant mutiny. 'The hell I will!'

'Eventually you must fall asleep.' He gave a careless shrug as he indicated the large bed. 'When you do, I'll simply transfer you here.'

'You unspeakable fiend!' she lashed out. 'I won't let you do that.'

'How do you propose to stop me?'

His expression was resolute, and only an innocent would fail to detect tensile steel beneath the silky smoothness of his voice.

Alyse's heart lurched painfully, then skipped a beat. Only a wide aperture separated the sitting-room from the bedroom, with no door whatsoever to afford her any privacy.

'You're an unfeeling, insensitive——' She faltered to a furious halt, momentarily lost for adequate words in verbal description. *'Brute!'*

Something flickered in the depths of his eyes, then it was successfully masked. 'I suggest you settle Georg before he becomes confused and bewildered by the degree of anger you're projecting.' He turned towards the bedroom door. 'I'll be in the kitchen, making coffee.'

Alyse wanted to throw something at his departing back, and the only thing that stopped her was the fact that she held Georg in her arms.

Experiencing momentary defeat, she turned towards the sitting-room, seeing at a glance that it was sufficiently large to hold a pair of single chairs and a sofa, as well as a bed and nursery furniture.

Placing the baby down into the cot, she gently covered him, lingering long enough to see that he was asleep before moving back into the bedroom.

Defiance emanated from every pore in her body as she retrieved her nightwear from her bag. A shower would surely ease some of her tension, she decided as she made her way into the luxuriously fitted bathroom. Afterwards she'd beard Aleksi in the kitchen and reaffirm her determination for entirely separate sleeping quarters for herself and Georg.

It was heaven to stand beneath the jet of pulsating hot water, and she took her time before using one of several large fluffy bathtowels to dry the excess moisture from her body. Her toilette completed, she slipped on a nightgown and added a matching robe.

There were bottles to sterilise and formula to make up in case Georg should wake through the night, and, collecting the necessary carry-bag, she went in search of the kitchen.

She found it off a passageway on the opposite side of the lounge, and she studiously ignored the tall dark-haired man in the process of pouring black aromatic coffee from a percolator into one of two cups set out on the servery.

Luxuriously spacious, the kitchen was a delight featuring the latest in electronic equipment, and in normal circumstances she would have expressed pleasure in its design.

'I'm sure you'll find whatever you need in the cupboards,' Aleksi drawled as he added sugar and a splash of whisky.

'Thank you.' Her words were stilted and barely polite as she set about her task.

'A married couple come in daily to maintain the house and grounds,' he informed her matter-of-factly. 'And a catering firm is hired whenever I entertain.'

'With such splendid organisation, you hardly need a wife,' she retorted, impossibly angry with him—and herself, for imagining he might permit a celibate cohabitation.

'Don't sulk, Alyse,' he derided drily, and she rounded on him with ill-concealed fury.

'I am not *sulking*! I'm simply too damned angry to be bothered conducting any sort of civilised conversation with you!' With tense movements she put the newly made formula in the refrigerator.

'The bedroom arrangement stays,' Aleksi declared with hard inflexibility, and her eyes became brilliant blue pools as she stood looking at him, refusing to be intimidated by his powerful height and sheer indomitable strength.

'All hell will freeze over before I'll willingly share any bed you happen to occupy!'

A faint smile tugged the edges of his mouth, and the expression in his eyes was wholly cynical. 'Why not have some coffee?' he queried mildly, and Alyse was so incensed by his imperturbable calm that she refused just for the sheer hell of opposing him.

'I'd prefer water.'

He shrugged and drained the contents of his cup. 'I'll be out most of tomorrow, checking progress on a number of sites, consulting with project managers. I've written down the name and phone number of a highly reputable babysitter in case you need to go out, and I'll leave a set of keys for the house and the car, together with some money in case there's anything you need.'

'I have money of my own,' she declared fiercely, and saw one eyebrow lift in silent quizzical query.

'Call it a housekeeping allowance,' Aleksi insisted as he leaned against the servery. 'And don't argue,' he warned with dangerous softness.

Without a further word she turned and filled a glass with chilled water, then drank it. With head held high she crossed the kitchen, her expression one of icy aloofness. 'I'm going to bed.' It was after eleven, and she was weary almost beyond belief.

'I'll show you how to operate the security system,' he insisted, straightening to his full height.

Five minutes later she entered the master suite, aware that he followed in her wake. Her back was rigid with silent anger as she made her way through to the sitting-room, and once there she flung off her robe, slid into bed, closed her eyes and determinedly shut out the muted sound of the shower operating in the en suite bathroom.

Much to her annoyance she remained awake long after the adjoining bedroom light was extinguished, and lay staring into the darkness, incredibly aware of Aleksi's proximity.

She hated him, she denounced in angry silence. *Hated* him. Why, he had to be the most damnable man she'd ever had the misfortune to meet. Indomitable, inflexible, *impossible*!

She must have slept, for she came sharply awake feeling totally disorientated and unsure of her whereabouts for a brief few seconds before memory surfaced, and she lay still, willing conscious recognition for the sound which had alerted her subconscious mind.

Georg? Perhaps he was unsettled after the long flight and restless in new surroundings.

Slipping cautiously out of bed, she trod silently across the room to the cot, her eyes adjusting to the reflection of the low-burning nightlight as she anxiously inspected his still form.

Wide eyes stared at her with unblinking solemnity, and Alyse shook her head in smiling admonition. With practised ease she changed his nappy, then covered him, only to hear him emit a whimpering cry.

Within seconds it became an unrelenting wail, and, quickly flinging on a wrap, she picked him up, murmuring softly as she cradled him.

'Problems?'

Alyse turned in startled surprise at the sound of Aleksi's voice so close behind her. 'He's only very recently started missing a late-night feed,' she told him quietly. 'I think the flight may have unsettled him.'

'Give him to me while you heat his bottle.'

'I can easily take him into the kitchen, then you won't be disturbed.'

'Go and do it, Alyse,' drawled Aleksi, calmly lifting Georg from out of her arms.

Her chin tilted fractionally as she met his unequivocal gaze, then just as she was about to argue the baby began to cry in earnest and, defeated, she stepped past Aleksi and made her way from the bedroom, fumbling occasionally as she searched for elusive light switches.

The tap emitted hot water at a single touch. *Boiling* hot, she discovered, biting her lips hard against a shocked curse as she withdrew her scalded hand. Ignoring the stinging pain, she warmed a bottle of prepared formula, then hurried back to the bedroom.

Aleksi was sitting on the edge of the bed cradling the tiny infant, and Alyse experienced a shaft of elemental jealousy at his complete absorption.

She wanted to snatch Georg out of his arms and retreat from the implied intimacy of the lamplit room with its large bed and the dynamic man who seemed to dominate it without any effort at all.

'I'll take him now,' she declared firmly, and her hand brushed his as she retrieved the baby, sending an electric charge through her veins.

Sheer dislike, she dismissed as she tended to Georg's needs, and on the edge of sleep she took heart in the fact that she would have most of the day to herself. A prospect she found infinitely pleasing, for without Aleksi's disturbing presence she could explore the house at will, even swim in the pool while Georg slept. And attempt to come to terms with a lifestyle and a husband she neither needed nor coveted.

CHAPTER FIVE

ALYSE entertained no qualms whatsoever as she followed Georg's pre-dawn routine. If Aleksi insisted that she and Georg occupy the master suite, then he could darned well suffer the consequences of sleep interrupted by a baby's internal feeding clock, she determined as she settled Georg after his bottle. Gathering up jeans, a warm long-sleeved sweater and fresh underwear, she crossed to the en suite bathroom and took a leisurely shower.

When she re-entered the bedroom Aleksi was in the process of sliding out of bed, and she hastily averted her eyes from an expanse of muscular flesh barely protected from total nudity by a swirl of bedlinen.

'Good morning.'

His drawled amusement put her on an immediate defensive, and her eyes lit with ill-disguised antagonism as she uttered a perfunctory acknowledgment on her way to the sitting-room.

Damn him! she cursed as she quickly straightened her bed, tugging sheets with more than necessary force. He possessed an ability to raise her hackles to such a degree that she was in danger of completely losing her temper at the mere sight of him!

Aleksi was already in the kitchen when she entered it some five minutes later, and she cast his tall rangy jeans-clad, black-sweatered frame the briefest of glances as she took a cup and filled it with freshly brewed coffee, blithely ignoring the fact that he was in the process of breaking eggs into a pan.

'Breakfast?'

She met his dark gaze with equanimity. 'It's barely six. I'll get something later.'

A newspaper lay folded on the servery and she idly scanned the headlines as she sipped the contents of her cup.

'There's an electronic device connected to the intercom system that can be activated to ensure that Georg is heard from any room in the house,' Aleksi told her.

'You were very confident of succeeding, weren't you?' Alyse couldn't help saying bitterly. 'The abundance of nursery furniture, toys—everything organised before you left for Perth.'

He skilfully transferred the contents from the pan on to a plate, collected toast and coffee and took a seat at the breakfast table.

His silence angered her immeasurably, and some devilish imp urged her along a path to conflagration. 'No comment?' she demanded.

He looked up, and she nearly died at the ruthless intensity of his gaze. 'Why indulge in senseless fantasy?'

'Don't you mean fallacy? Somehow it seems more appropriate.'

'Are you usually this argumentative so early in the morning? Or is it simply an attempt to test the extent of my temper?'

There could be no doubt he possessed one, and she cursed herself for a fool for daring to probe the limit of his control. Yet beneath that innate recognition was a determined refusal to be intimidated in any way.

'Do you have a problem with women who dare to question your opinion?' she countered, permitting one eyebrow to lift in a delicate arch. 'Doubtless all your female *friends*,' she paused with faint emphasis, 'agree with everything you say to a point of being sickeningly obsequious. Whereas I couldn't give a damn.'

'That's a sweeping generalisation, when you know nothing about any of my friends.'

'Oh, I'm sure there's any number of gorgeous socialites willing to give their all at the merest indication of your interest,' she derided. 'I wonder how they'll accept the news that you've suddenly plunged into matrimony and legally adopted a son?'

Aleksi subjected her to a long level glance. 'I owe no one an explanation for any decision I choose to make.' He picked up his cup and drained the last of his coffee. 'The keys to the BMW are on the pedestal table beside my bed.' He rose from the table with catlike grace. 'Enjoy your day.'

'Thank you,' Alyse responded with ill-concealed mockery, watching as he crossed the kitchen before disappearing down the hallway.

She heard the slight snap of a door closing, followed by the muted sound of an engine being fired and a vehicle reversing, then silence.

Suddenly the whole day lay ahead of her, and with at least three hours before Georg was due to waken again, she hurriedly finished her coffee and made her way towards the foyer.

Mounting the staircase, she slowly explored the four bedrooms and adjoining bathrooms, plus a guest suite, all beautifully furnished and displaying impeccable taste.

Returning downstairs, she wandered at will through the lounge, formal dining-room, guest powder-room, and utilities, and merely stood at the door leading into an imposing study, noting the large executive desk, computer equipment, leather chairs and an impressive collection of filing cabinets. There were also several design awards in frames on the wall, witness to Aleksi's success.

From there she moved towards the kitchen, discovering another flight of stairs leading from an informal family room down to a third level comprising a large informal lounge, billiard-room, gymnasium, and sauna. Wide glass sliding doors from the lounge and billiard-room led out on to a large patio and free-form swimming-pool.

The colour-scheme utilised throughout the entire home was a combination of cream and varying shades of pale green and peach, presenting a visually pleasing effect that highlighted modern architecture without providing stereotyped sterility.

A thorough inspection of the pantry, refrigerator and freezer revealed that there was no need to replenish anything for several days, and a small sigh of relief escaped her lips as she emptied cereal and milk into a bowl and sat down at the breakfast table with the daily newspaper.

Afterwards there was time to tidy the dishes before Georg was due to waken, and with determined resolve she moved through the master suite to the sitting-room and quietly retrieved her bags. She was damned if she'd calmly accept Aleksi's dictum and share the same suite of rooms!

It was relatively simple to transfer everything upstairs, although as the day progressed a tiny seed of anxiety began to niggle at her subconscious.

Dismissing it, she set about preparing an evening meal of chunky minestrone, followed by chicken Kiev and an assortment of vegetables, with brandied pears for dessert.

It was almost six when Alyse heard Aleksi return, and her stomach began a series of nervous somersaults as he came into the kitchen, which was totally ridiculous, she derided silently.

'I hardly expected such wifely solicitude,' he drawled, viewing her slight frown of concentration with amusement.

Alyse glanced up from stirring the minestrone and felt her senses quicken. He looked strong and vital, and far too disturbingly male for any woman's peace of mind.

Her eyes flashed him a glance of deep sapphire-blue before she returned her attention to the saucepan. 'Is there any reason why I shouldn't prepare a meal?'

'Of course not,' Aleksi returned smoothly as he leaned against the edge of the servery.

She could sense the mockery in his voice, and hated him for it. 'Stop treating me like a naïve nineteen-year-old!' she flung with a degree of acerbity.

'How would you have me treat you, Alyse?'

'With some respect for my feelings,' she returned fiercely.

'Perhaps you'd care to elaborate?'

It was pointless evading the issue, and besides, it was only a matter of time before he'd discover Georg's absence from the nursery.

She drew a deep breath, then released it slowly. 'I've moved my belongings into an upstairs bedroom.'

The eyes that lanced hers were dark and unfathomable.

'I suggest you move them back down again,' he drawled with dangerous silkiness.

'*No*. I refuse to allow you to play cat to my mouse by dictating my sleeping arrangements.'

'Is that what I'm doing?'

Oh, she could *hit* him! 'Yes! I won't be coerced to conform by a display of sheer male dominance.'

'My dear Alyse, you sound almost afraid. Are you?'

Now she was really angry, and sheer bravado forced her to counter, 'Do I look afraid?'

'Perhaps you should be. I don't suffer fools gladly.'

'What's that supposed to mean?'

At that precise moment a loud wail emitted through the monitor, and Alyse threw Aleksi a totally exasperated look.

'It's time for his bottle.'

'I'll fetch him while you heat it.'

Momentarily defeated, she retrieved a fresh bottle from the refrigerator and filled a container with hot water.

Aleksi was a natural, she conceded several minutes later as he caught up the bottle, took a nearby chair and calmly proceeded to feed Georg.

'He should be changed first,' Alyse protested, meeting those dark challenging eyes, and heard him respond with quiet mockery,

'I already have.'

There was little she could do except give a seemingly careless shrug and return her attention to a variety of saucepans on the stove, although it rankled that he should display such an adeptness when she had so readily cast him into an entirely different mould.

Alyse settled Georg in his cot while Aleksi had a shower, and it was almost seven when they sat down to dinner.

'This is good,' he remarked.

Alyse inclined her head in silent acknowledgment. 'What would you have done if I hadn't prepared a meal?'

His gaze was startlingly direct. 'Organised a babysitter, and frequented a restaurant.'

'I mightn't have wanted to go.'

'Perversity, Alyse, simply for the hell of it?'

She couldn't remember arguing with anyone, not even Antonia at her most difficult. Yet something kept prompting her towards a confrontation with Aleksi at every turn, and deep within some devilish imp danced in sheer delight at the danger of it all.

'No comment?' he queried.

She met his gaze with equanimity. 'I have a feeling that anything I say will be used against me.'

'Perhaps we should opt for a partial truce?'

She was powerless to prevent the wry smile that tugged at the edges of her mouth. 'Would it last?'

'Probably not,' Aleksi agreed with a degree of cynicism. 'However, I'd prefer that we at least project an outward display of civility in the company of my parents.'

'Why? They know the reason for our marriage, and are aware it isn't an alliance made in heaven.' Alyse sipped from a glass of superb white wine. 'If you expect me to indulge in calculated displays of affection, forget it.'

He spooned the last of his minestrone, then waited for her to finish.

'I'd prefer to help myself,' Alyse said at once, knowing he'd serve her a far too generous portion. She wasn't very hungry, and merely selected a few vegetables, then toyed with dessert.

'There are numerous friends and business associates who will be anxious to meet you, and a party next Saturday evening will provide an excellent opportunity.' He leaned back in his chair and surveyed her with a veiled scrutiny. 'I'll organise the caterers.'

She got to her feet and began stacking plates, unable to prevent a flaring of resentment as he lent his assistance.

'I can manage,' she said stiffly, hating his close proximity within the large kitchen.

'I'll rinse, you can load the dishwasher,' Aleksi told her, and she gritted her teeth in the knowledge that his actions were deliberate.

'You now have a wife to take care of all this,' Alyse voiced sweetly. 'Why not relax in the lounge with an after-dinner port, or retire to your study?'

'So you can pretend I don't exist?'

Oh, he was too clever by far! '*Yes*, damn you.'

Dark eyes gleamed with ill-concealed humour. 'No one would guess a firebrand exists beneath that cool façade,' he mused cynically, causing her resentment to flare.

'I didn't possess a temper until you forced your way into my life!'

'*Forced*, Alyse?' he queried with soft emphasis. 'I've never had to coerce a woman into anything.'

His implication was intentional, and Alyse quite suddenly had had enough. Placing the plate she held carefully on to the bench, she turned and made to move past him.

'Since you obviously believe in equality, *you* finish the dishes. I'm going for a walk.'

'In the dark, and alone?'

Her eyes flared with brilliant blue fire. 'I need some fresh air, but most of all, I need a temporary escape from *you*!'

'No, Alyse.' His voice sounded like silk being razed by tensile steel, and she reacted without thought, hardly aware of her hand swinging in a swift arc until it connected with a resounding slap on the side of his jaw.

For a wild moment she thought he meant to strike her back, and she cried out as he caught hold of her hands and drew her inextricably close. Any attempt to struggle was defeated the instant it began, and after several futile minutes she simply stood in defiant silence.

Her pulse tripped its beat and measurably quickened at the degree of icy anger apparent. He possessed sufficient strength to break her wrists, and she flinched as he tightened his grasp. 'You're hurting me!'

'If you continue this kind of foolish behaviour, believe me, you *will* get hurt.'

His threat wasn't an idle one, yet she stood defiant beneath his compelling gaze. 'That's precisely the type of chauvinistic threat I'd expect you to make!'

With slow deliberation he released her wrists and slid his hands up to her shoulders, impelling her forward, then his mouth was on hers, hard and possessively demanding.

Alyse clenched her teeth against his intended invasion, and a silent scream rose and died in her throat beneath the relentless determined pressure. She began to struggle, flailing her fists against his arms, his ribs—anywhere she could connect in an effort to break free.

She gave a muffled moan of entreaty as he effortlessly caught hold of her hands and held them together behind her back—an action that brought her even closer against his hard masculine frame, and there was nothing she could do to prevent the hand that slid to her breast.

A soundless gasp escaped her lips as she felt his fingers slip the buttons on her blouse, then slide beneath the silk of her bra. She wanted to scream in outrage as his mouth forced open her own, and his tongue became a pillaging, destructive force that had her silently begging him to stop.

When he finally released her, she swayed and almost fell, and a husky oath burned her ears in explicit, softly explosive force.

Her lips felt numb and swollen, and she unconsciously began a tentative seeking exploration with the tip of her tongue, discovering ravaged tissues that had been heartlessly ground against her teeth.

Firm fingers lifted her chin, and her lashes swiftly lowered in automatic self-defence against the hurt and humiliation she knew to be evident in their depths.

Standing quite still, she bore his silent scrutiny until every nerve stretched to its furthest limitation.

'Let me go. Please.' She had to get away from him before the ache behind her eyes manifested itself in silent futile tears.

Without a word he released her, watching as she slowly turned and walked from the room.

The temptation to run was paramount, except where could she run to that he wouldn't follow? A hollow laugh choked in her throat as she ascended the stairs. Escape, even temporary, afforded her a necessary respite, and uncaring of Aleksi's objection to her move upstairs, she crept into Georg's room and silently undressed.

It wasn't fair—*nothing* was fair, she decided as she lay quietly in bed. Sleep was never more distant, and despite her resolve it was impossible not to dwell on the fact that the day after tomorrow Aleksi's parents would arrive. An event she wasn't sure whether to view with relief or despair.

A silent scream rose to the surface as she heard an imperceptible click, followed by the inward swing of the bedroom door. Anger replaced fright as she saw Aleksi's tall frame outlined against the aperture, and she unconsciously drew the covers more firmly about her shoulders.

She watched in horrified fascination as he crossed to the cot and carefully transferred Georg on to the bed beside her.

'What do you think you're doing?' she vented in a sibilant whisper.

'I imagine it's perfectly clear,' he drawled as he effortlessly picked up the cot and carried it from the room.

Within minutes he was back, and she stared in disbelief as he scooped the baby into his arms. At the door he turned slightly to face her.

'You can walk, or be carried,' he said quietly. 'The choice is yours.'

Then he was gone, and Alyse was left seething with helpless anger. *Choice?* What choice did she have, for heaven's sake! Yet she was damned if she'd meekly follow him downstairs and slip into bed, defeated.

With each passing second she was aware of her own foolishness; to thwart him was the height of folly, and would doubtless bring retribution of a kind she would be infinitely wise to avoid. Except that wisdom, at this precise moment, was not high on her list.

Fool, an inner voice cautioned. *Fool.* Haven't you suffered enough punishment already, without wilfully setting yourself up for more?

Even as she considered capitulation, Aleksi re-entered the room, and she held his narrowed gaze with undisguised defiance as he moved to the side of the bed.

Without a word he wrenched the covers from her grasp, then leant forward and lifted her into his arms.

Alyse struggled, hating the ease with which he held her. 'Put me down, you fiend!'

'I can only wonder when you'll learn that to oppose me is a totally useless exercise,' he said cynically, catching one flailing fist and restraining it with galling ease.

'If you're hoping for meek subservience, it will never happen!' Dear lord, he was strong; any movement she made was immediately rendered ineffectual.

'You'd have to be incredibly naïve not to realise there's a certain danger in continually offering resistance,' he drawled, and she momentarily froze as fear licked her veins.

'Sex, simply for the sake of it?' she queried, meeting his gaze with considerable bravery. 'How long did you allow me, Aleksi—two, three nights?'

She could feel his anger unfurl, emanating as finely tuned tension over which she had little indication of his measure of control. Her eyes blazed a brilliant clear blue, not crystalline sapphire but holding the coolness of lapis lazuli.

'Well, get it over and done with, damn you! Although I doubt if you'll gain much satisfaction from copulating with an uninterested block of ice!'

His eyes seemed incredibly dark, and his mouth assumed a cruelty that made her want to retract every foolish word. In seeming slow motion he released her down on to the floor in front of him, and she stood mesmerised as he subjected her to a slow, raking appraisal.

Her nightgown was satin-finished silk edged with lace and provided adequate cover, but beneath his studied gaze she felt positively naked. A delicate pink tinged her cheeks as his eyes lingered on the gentle swell of her breasts, then slid low to the shadowed cleft between her thighs before slowly returning to the soft curves beneath the revealing neckline.

Against her will, a curious warmth began somewhere in the centre of her being and slowly spread until it encompassed her entire body.

Reaching out, he brushed gentle fingers against her cheek, then let them drift to trace the contours of her mouth before slipping to the edge of her neck, where he trailed the delicate pulsing cord to examine with tactile sensuality the soft hollows beneath her throat.

Her eyes widened, but her gaze didn't falter as his hand slid to the soft curve of her breast and slowly outlined its shape between thumb and forefinger. When he reached the sensitive peak it was all she could do not to gasp out loud, and she suppressed a tiny shiver as he rendered a similar exploration to its twin.

Slowly and with infinite care, he slid his hand to the shoestring straps and slipped first one, then the other from her shoulders.

For what seemed an age he just looked at her, and she stood mesmerised, unable to gain anything from his expression. Then he lowered his head down to hers, and she tensed as his mouth took possession of her own.

Except that the hard, relentless pressure never eventuated, and in its place was a soft openmouthed kiss that was nothing less than a deliberate seduction of the senses.

His tongue began a subtle exploration, seeking out all the vulnerable ridges, the tender, sensitive indentations, before beginning a delicate tracery of the tissues inside her cheek.

He seemed to fill her mouth, coaxing something from her she felt afraid to give, and she released a silent groan of relief as his lips left hers to settle in one of the vulnerable hollows at the base of her throat.

Then she gave an audible gasp as she felt his lips slide down to her breast, and the gasp became a cry of outrage as he took the peak into his mouth and savoured it gently, letting his teeth graze the sensitised nub until she almost screamed against the myriad sensations he was able to evoke.

Oh, dear lord, what had she invited? To remain quiescent was madness, yet to twist out of his grasp would only prove that she was vulnerable to his potent brand of sensual sexuality.

Just when she thought she could stand it no longer, Aleksi shifted his attention to its twin, and she arched her neck, her whole body stretching like a finely tuned bow in the hands of a master virtuoso.

It wasn't until she felt his hand on her stomach that she realised her nightgown had slithered to a silken heap at her feet, and a despairing moan escaped her throat.

At that moment his head shifted, and his mouth resumed a provocative possession that took hold of her inhibitions and tossed them high, bringing a response that left her weak-willed and malleable.

Then it was over, and she could only look at him in helpless fascination as he slowly pushed her to arm's length.

His lips assumed a mocking curve as he taunted with dangerous softness. '*Ice*, Alyse?'

The sound of his voice acted like a cascade of chilled water, and her own eyes widened into deep blue pools, mirroring shame and humiliation. She crossed her arms in defence of her lack of attire, hating the warmth that coloured her cheeks, and there was nothing she could do to prevent the shiver that feathered its way across the surface of her skin.

Without a word he bent to retrieve her nightgown from the floor, slipped it over her head, then slid an arm beneath her knees.

She wanted to protest, except that there was a painful lump in her throat defying speech, and the will to fight had temporarily fled as each descending step down the elegant staircase brought her closer—*to what*? Sexual possession?

In the centre of the master bedroom he released her, setting her on her feet, and she stood hesitant, poised for flight like a frightened gazelle.

'Go to bed.'

Alyse reared her head in startled surprise, and her eyes felt huge in a face she knew to be waxen-pale.

'Yours,' Aleksi added with soft cynicism. 'Before I change my mind and put you in mine.'

Her lips parted, then slowly closed again. There wasn't a thing she could say that wouldn't compound the situation, so she didn't even try, choosing instead to walk away from him with as much dignity as she could muster.

Sleep proved an elusive entity, and she lay awake pondering whether his actions were motivated by cruelty or kindness. Somehow she couldn't imagine it to be the latter.

CHAPTER SIX

ALYSE chose to stay at home with Georg when Aleksi drove to collect his parents from Brisbane airport on the pretext that it would give them time alone together in which to talk. It would also give her the opportunity to prepare dinner.

As their expected arrival drew closer, Alyse became consumed with nerves, and even careful scrutiny of a family photograph did little to ease her apprehension.

Alexandros Stefanos was an older, more distinguished replica of his indomitable son, although less forbidding, and Rachel looked serene and dignified. Both were smiling, and Alyse wondered if they would regard her kindly.

She fervently hoped so, for she was infinitely more in need of an ally than an enemy.

After initial indecision over what to wear, Alyse selected a stylishly cut leather skirt and teamed it with a knitted jumper patterned in varying shades of soft blue and lilac.

It was late afternoon when the BMW pulled into the garage, and her stomach tightened into a painful knot at the sound of the door into the hall opening, followed by two deep voices mingling with a light feminine laugh.

Drawing in a deep breath, she released it slowly and made her way towards the foyer, where an attractive mature woman stood poised, looking every bit as apprehensive as Alyse felt.

Even as Alyse came to a hesitant halt, the older woman's mouth parted in a tentative smile, and her eyes filled with reflected warmth.

'Alyse,' she greeted quietly. 'How very nice to meet you.'

'Mrs Stefanos,' Alyse returned, unsure precisely how she should address her mother-in-law. The circumstances were unusual, to say the least!

'Oh, *Rachel*, please,' Aleksi's stepmother said at once, reaching forward to catch hold of both Alyse's hands. 'And Alexandros,' she added, shifting slightly to one side to allow her husband the opportunity to move forward.

It was going to be all right, Alyse decided as she submitted to Alexandros Stefanos's firm handshake. Perhaps some of her relief showed, for Aleksi spared her a reassuring smile that held surprising warmth.

'I'll take your luggage upstairs to the guest suite, then we'll have a drink,' he said.

'I'll give you a hand,' Alexandros indicated in a deeply accented voice, and Alyse turned towards Rachel.

'Come and sit down. Georg is due to wake soon.'

The older woman's eyes misted. 'Oh, my dear, you can't begin to know how much I want to see him!'

'He's beautiful,' Alyse accorded simply as she sank into a sofa close to the one Rachel had chosen.

'You love him very much.' It was a statement of fact, and Alyse's gaze was clear and unblinking.

'Enough not to be able to give him up. For Antonia's sake, as well as my own,' she added quietly.

An expression very much like sympathy softened Aleksi's stepmother's features—that, and a certain understanding. 'Aleksi is very much Alexandros's son,' she offered gently. 'Yet beneath the surface lies a wealth of caring. I know he'll be a dedicated father, and,' she paused, then added hesitantly, 'a protective husband.'

But I don't want a husband, Alyse felt like crying out in anguished rejection of the man who had placed a wedding band on her finger only days before. And if I did, I certainly wouldn't have chosen your diabolical stepson!

The sound of male voices and muted laughter reached their ears, and Alyse turned towards the men as they came into the lounge.

'A drink is called for,' declared Aleksi, moving across to the bar. 'Alexandros? Rachel?'

Somehow she had imagined an adherence to formality, and Aleksi's easy use of his parents' Christian names came as a surprise.

'Some of your Queensland beer,' Alexandros requested, taking a seat beside his wife. 'It's refreshingly light.'

'I'll have mineral water,' Rachel acknowledged with a faint smile. 'Anything stronger will put me to sleep.'

'Alyse?'

'Mineral water,' she told him, then turned to Rachel. 'Unless you'd prefer tea or coffee?'

'My dear, no,' the older woman refused gently. 'Something cold will be fine.'

Georg woke a few minutes later, his lusty wail sounding loud through the intercom system, and Alyse dispensed with her glass and hurriedly rose to her feet.

'I'll change him, then bring him out.' She met Rachel's anxious smile. 'Unless you'd like to come with me?'

'I'd love to,' the older woman said at once, and together they crossed the lounge to the hall.

By the time they reached the master bedroom Georg was in full cry, his small face red and angry.

'Oh, you little darling!' Rachel murmured softly as his cries subsided into a watery smile the instant he sighted them.

'He's very shrewd,' Alyse accorded, her movements deft as she removed his decidedly damp nappy and exchanged it for a dry one. 'There, sweetheart,' she crooned, nuzzling his baby cheek, 'all ready for your bottle.'

His feet kicked in silent acknowledgment, and Rachel gave a delighted laugh.

'Georgiou used to do that too.'

Alyse felt a pang of regret for the older woman's sorrow. 'Would you care to take him? I thought you might like to give him his bottle in the lounge.'

Rachel's eyes shimmered with unshed tears. 'Thank you.'

It was heart-wrenching to see the effect Georg had on his grandparents, and Alyse had to blink quickly more than once to dispel the suspicious dampness that momentarily blurred her vision.

An hour later the baby was resettled in his cot for the night, and Rachel retired upstairs to freshen up while Alyse put the finishing touches to dinner.

After much deliberation, she had elected to serve a chicken consommé, followed by roast chicken with a variety of vegetables, and settled on fresh fruit for dessert. Unsure of Alexandros's palate, she'd added a cheese platter decorated with stuffed olives and grapes.

The meal was a definite success, and with most of her nervousness gone Alyse was able to relax.

'Tomorrow you must rest,' Aleksi told his parents as they sipped coffee in the lounge. 'In the afternoon I'll drive you into town and settle you both into the apartment, then in the evening we'll dine out together.'

Startled, Alyse felt her eyes widen in surprise, and Rachel quickly intervened in explanation.

'Aleksi owns an apartment in the heart of Surfers Paradise. Alexandros and I will stay there until we leave for Sydney to visit with my sister, after which we'll return and spend the remainder of our holiday on the Coast.'

Her expression softened as Alyse was about to demur.

'*Yes*, my dear. We value our independence and respect yours. The circumstances regarding your marriage are unusual,' Rachel added gently. 'You and Aleksi need time together alone.'

Alyse wanted to protest that the marriage was only one of convenience, and would remain so for as long as it took for her to escape to Perth with Georg. Except that she wouldn't consider voicing the words.

'And now,' Rachel declared, standing to her feet, 'if you don't mind, we'll retire.' Her smile wavered slightly as it moved from her husband to her stepson. 'It's been a long trip, and I'm really very tired.'

Alyse rose at once. 'Of course.' Her heart softened at the older woman's obvious weariness. 'There's everything you need in your suite.'

'Thank you, my dear.'

It seemed good manners to walk at Aleksi's side as his parents made their way into the foyer, and it wasn't until Rachel and Alexandros were safely upstairs that she turned back towards the lounge.

'I'll make some more coffee,' Aleksi said smoothly. 'I have a few hours' work ahead of me in the study.'

'There's plenty left in the percolator,' Alyse said with a slight shrug. 'It will take a minute to reheat. I'll bring it in, if you like.'

With a curt nod he turned towards the study, and it was only a matter of minutes before she entered that masculine sanctum and set a cup of steaming aromatic brew on his desk.

He was seated, leaning well back into a comfortable leather executive chair, and he regarded her with eyes that were direct and faintly probing.

'What do you think of my parents?'

'I hardly know them,' she said stiffly, longing to escape. In the company of Rachel and Alexandros she had been able to tolerate his company without too much difficulty, but now they were alone she was acutely aware of a growing tension.

'You like Rachel.' It was a statement, rather than a query, which she didn't bother to deny. 'And my father?'

'He seems kind,' she offered politely, and saw his mouth curve to form a cynical smile.

'Far kinder than his son?'

Her polite façade snapped. 'Yes. *You* seem to delight in being an uncivilised tyrant!'

An eyebrow rose in sardonic query. 'Whatever will you come up with next?'

Her eyes flashed a brilliant blue. 'Oh, I'm sure I'll think of something!'

The creases at the corners of his eyes deepened. 'I have no doubt you will.'

The temptation to pick something up from his desk and throw it at him was almost irresistible, and her hands clenched at her sides in silent restraint as she turned towards the door.

'Goodnight, Alyse.'

His drawled, faintly mocking tones followed her into the hall, and she muttered dire threats beneath her breath all the way into the kitchen.

An hour later she lay silently seething in bed, plotting his figurative downfall in so many numerous ways that it carried her to the edge of sleep and beyond.

It was almost midday when Rachel and Alexandros came downstairs, coinciding with Aleksi's arrival home, and after a relaxing meal Rachel eagerly saw to her grandson's needs, gave him his bottle, then settled him down for the afternoon.

Over coffee there was an opportunity for Alyse to become better acquainted with Aleksi's stepmother, and it was relatively simple to fill in details of Antonia's life, although she was aware of Aleksi's seemingly detached regard throughout a number of amusing anecdotes.

'I have some photographs,' Alyse told her. 'Most of them are in albums which are somewhere in transit between here and Perth, but I brought a few snaps with me that you might like to see.'

They were pictures of Antonia laughing, beautiful and lissom with flowing blonde hair and a stunning smile.

'What about you, Alyse?' Aleksi asked quietly. 'Were all the snaps taken only of Antonia?'

'No. No, of course not,' she answered quickly. 'There didn't seem much point in bringing the others with me.'

His gaze was startlingly direct. 'Why not?' Humour tugged the edges of his mouth. 'I would have enjoyed seeing you as a child.'

'Perhaps I should insist that you drag out shots depicting your pubescent youth,' Alyse said sweetly, and heard Alexandros's deep laugh.

'He was all bones, so tall, and very intense. An exceptional student.'

'Yes, I'm sure he was,' Alyse agreed with a faint smile.

'At nineteen he filled out,' Rachel informed her, shooting Aleksi a faintly wicked grin, 'developing splendid muscles, a deep voice, and a certain attraction for the opposite sex. Girls utilised every excuse under the sun to practise their own blossoming feminine wiles on him.'

'With great success, I'm sure,' Alyse remarked drily, and heard his husky laugh.

'I managed to keep one step ahead of each of them.'

'Shattering dreams and breaking hearts, no doubt?' The words were lightly voiced and faintly bantering, but his eyes stilled for a second, then assumed a brooding mockery.

'What about your dreams, Alyse?' he countered, silently forcing her to hold his gaze.

She swallowed the lump that had somehow risen in her throat, aware that their amusing conversational gambit had undergone a subtle change. 'I was no different from other teenage girls,' she said quietly. 'Except that my vision was centred on a successful career.'

'In which young men didn't feature at all?'

How could she say that Antonia was a carefree spirit who unwittingly attracted men without the slightest effort, while Alyse was merely the older sister, a shadowy blueprint content to shoulder responsibility? Yet there had never been any feelings of resentment or jealousy, simply an acceptance of individual personalities.

'I enjoyed a social life,' she defended. 'Tennis, squash, sailing at weekends, and there was the cinema, theatre, dancing.' Her chin lifted fractionally as she summoned a brilliant smile. 'Now I have a wealthy husband who owns a beautiful home, and an adored adopted son.' Her eyes glittered, sheer sapphire. 'Most women would rate that as being the culmination of all their dreams.'

Aleksi's soft laugh was almost her undoing, and it was only his parents' presence that prevented her from launching into a lashing castigation.

'Shall I make afternoon tea?' It was amazing that her voice sounded so calm, and she deliberately schooled her expression into a polite mask as she rose to her feet.

In the kitchen she filled the percolator with water, selected a fresh filter, spooned in ground coffee and set it on the element. Her hands seemed to move of their own accord, opening cupboards, setting cups on to saucers, extracting sugar, milk and cream, then setting a cake she'd made that morning on to a plate ready to take into the lounge.

When the coffee was ready, she put everything on to a mobile trolley and wheeled it into the lounge, dispensing everything with an outward serenity that would, had she been an actress, have earned plaudits from her peers.

Conversation, as if by tacit agreement, touched on a variety of subjects but centred on none, and it was almost four o'clock when Aleksi rose to his feet with the expressed intention of driving Rachel and Alexandros into town.

'I'm looking forward to this evening, my dear,' Rachel declared as she slid into the rear seat of the car, and Alyse gave her a smile that was genuinely warm.

'So am I,' she assured her, then stood back as Aleksi reversed the BMW down the driveway.

Indoors, she quickly restored the lounge to order and then dispensed cups and saucers into the dishwasher before crossing to the bedroom for a quick shower. Georg would wake in an hour, and she'd prefer to settle him down for the night rather than leave him to the babysitter.

Selecting something suitable to wear was relatively simple, and she chose an elegant two-piece suit in brilliant red silk, opted against wearing a blouse, and decided on high-heeled black suede shoes and matching clutch-purse. Make-up was understated, with skilful attention to her eyes, then she blowdried her hair and slipped on a silk robe, confident that within five minutes of settling Georg she could be ready.

The sound of the front door closing alerted her attention, and seconds later Aleksi entered the room.

'The babysitter will be here at six,' he told her as he shed his jacket and tossed it on to the bed. 'We'll collect my parents at six-thirty, and our table is booked for an hour later.'

Alyse merely nodded as his fingers slid to the buttons on his shirt, and he paused, his eyes narrowing on her averted gaze.

'Is there some problem with that?'

'None at all,' she said stiffly.

'Don't indulge in a fit of the sulks,' Aleksi cautioned, and she rounded on him at once with all the pent-up fury she'd harboured over the past hour.

'I am not sulking!' she snapped angrily. 'I just don't care to be figuratively dissected, piece by piece, in the presence of your parents, simply as a means of amusement!'

One eyebrow arched, and his mouth assumed its customary cynicism. 'What, precisely, are you referring to?'

'I didn't sit at home while Antonia went out and had all the fun,' she told him, holding his gaze without any difficulty at all.

'But you assumed responsibility for her welfare, did you not?' Aleksi queried with deceptive mildness. 'And, as the eldest, shouldered burdens which had your parents been alive would have given you more freedom?'

'If you're suggesting I assumed the role of surrogate parent, you couldn't be more wrong!'

He stood regarding her in silence for what seemed an age. 'Then tell me what you did out of work hours, aside from keep house?'

Her eyes became stormy. 'I don't owe you any explanations.'

'Then why become defensive when I suggested you took the elder sister role so seriously?'

'Because you implied a denial of any social existence, which isn't true.'

'So you went out on dates, enjoyed the company of men?'

The desire to shock was paramount. 'Yes,' she said shortly, knowing it to be an extension of the truth. Her chin tilted slightly, and her eyes assumed a dangerous sparkle. 'What comes next, Aleksi? Do we each conduct a head-count of previous sexual partners?'

'Have there been so many?'

'I don't consider it bears any relevance to our relationship,' she said steadily, and saw his eyes narrow.

'Do you doubt my ability to please you?'

The conversation had shifted on to dangerous ground, and Alyse felt her stomach nerves tighten at the thought of that strong body bent over her own in pursuit of sexual pleasure.

'Are you suggesting we indulge in sex simply for the sake of it in a mutual claim for conjugal rights?'

His eyes gleamed with sardonic humour. 'My dear Alyse, do you perceive sex merely as a duty?'

He lifted a hand and cupped her jaw, letting his thumb brush her cheek. 'Either your experience is limited or your lovers have been selfishly insensitive.'

It was impossible to still the faint rush of colour to her cheeks, and her eyes silently warred with his as she sought to control her temper.

Slowly he lowered his head, and she stood in mesmerised fascination as his lips caressed her temple, then slid down to trace the outline of her mouth in a gentle exploration that was incredibly evocative.

A faint quiver of apprehension ran through her body, and her mouth trembled as his tongue probed its soft contours, then slid between her lips to wreak sweet havoc with the sensitised tissues.

It would be so easy to melt into his arms and deepen the kiss. For a few timeless seconds Alyse ignored the spasms of alarm racing to her brain in warning of the only possible conclusion such an action would have.

A soft hiccuping cry emerged from the adjoining sitting-room, and within seconds Georg was in full swing, demanding sustenance in no uncertain terms.

'Pity,' murmured Aleksi as he released her, and her eyes widened, then clouded with sudden realisation as she turned quickly away from him.

Crossing into the sitting-room, she picked Georg up from his cot and changed him, then made her way to the kitchen where she heated his bottle and fed him.

He sucked hungrily, and she slowed him down, talking gently as she always did, sure that he was able to understand simply by the tone of her voice that he was very much loved. He seemed to grow with each passing day, and her heart filled with pride as she leant forward to brush her lips against his tiny forehead.

He was worth everything, *anything* she had to endure as Aleksi Stefanos's wife. A truly beautiful child who deserved to be cherished, she decided wistfully as she settled him almost an hour later.

Swiftly discarding her robe, she quickly donned the silk evening suit and slipped her feet into the elegant high-heeled suede shoes. A brisk brush brought her hair into smooth order, and she sprayed a generous quantity of her favourite perfume to several pulsebeats before standing back to survey the result in the full-length mirror.

Muted chimes sounded through the intercom, and Aleksi emerged from his dressing-room.

'That will be Melanie. She's a dedicated law student, the eldest of five, and extremely capable. I'll let her in.'

The breath caught in Alyse's throat at the sight of him, and she rapidly schooled her expression as she took in his immaculate dark suit, thin-striped shirt and impeccably knotted tie.

Any feelings of unease at leaving Georg with a total stranger were dispelled within minutes of meeting the girl Aleksi introduced as the daughter of one of his associates.

'I've written down the phone number of the restaurant,' he told her, handing over a slip of paper. 'And the apartment, in case we stop for coffee when we drop off my parents. We'll be home around midnight. If it's going to be any later, I'll ring.'

'Georg is already asleep,' Alyse added. 'I doubt if he'll wake, but if he does it's probably because he needs changing. If he won't settle, give him a bottle. He's just started sleeping through the night, except for the occasional evening. If you'll come with me, I'll show you where everything is.'

Fifteen minutes later she was seated in the luxurious BMW as it purred along the ocean-front road that led into the heart of Surfers Paradise.

'Where are we dining?' she asked.

'The Sheraton-Mirage; it's located on the Spit.'

'Where anyone important is *seen*, no doubt.' She hadn't meant to sound cynical, and she suffered his swift analytical glance as a consequence.

'Rachel fell in love with the resort complex when she and my father were here last year. It's at her request that we're dining there tonight.'

She should apologise, she knew, but the words refused to emerge, and she sat in silence until the car pulled to a halt at the entrance to a prestigious multi-storey apartment block overlooking the ocean.

At attendant slid in behind the wheel as Alyse followed Aleksi into the elegant foyer, and seconds later a lift transported them swiftly to an upper floor.

The apartment was much larger than she had expected, with magnificent views through floor-to-ceiling plate glass of the north and southern coastline. Pinpricks of light sparkled from a multitude of high-rise towers lining the coastal tourist strip, and beneath the velvet evening skyline the scene resembled a magical fairyland that stretched as far as the eye could see.

'You look stunning, my dear,' Rachel complimented Alyse quietly.

'Yes, doesn't she?'

Alyse heard Aleksi's faintly mocking drawl, and opted to ignore it. 'Thank you.'

'Would you prefer to have a drink here, or wait until we're at the complex?'

'The complex, I think,' Rachel concurred. 'I'm sure Alyse will be as enchanted with it as I am.'

A correct deduction, Alyse decided on entering the wide lobby with its deep-piled blue carpets, cream marble tiles and exotic antiques. The central waterfall was spectacular, as was the tiled lagoon with its island bar.

'We must come out during the day,' Rachel declared with a smile. 'The marina shopping complex directly across the road is delightful. We could explore it together, and share a coffee and chat.'

'My wife adores to shop,' Alexandros informed Alyse with a deep drawl not unlike that of his son.

They took a seat in the lounge-bar and Alyse declined anything alcoholic, aware of Aleksi's faintly hooded appraisal as she voiced her preference for an order identical to his stepmother's request for mineral water spiked with fresh orange juice.

'My dear, don't feel you must abstain simply because I choose to do so.'

'I don't drink,' she revealed quietly. 'Except for champagne on special occasions.'

'Dom Perignon?' queried Rachel with hopeful conspiracy, and Alyse smiled in silent acquiescence.

'In that case, we'll indulge you both at dinner,' said Aleksi, giving the waiter their order, then he sat well back in his chair, looking infinitely relaxed and at ease.

Alyse would have given anything to be rid of the nervous tension that steadily created painful cramps in her stomach. It was madness to feel so intensely vulnerable; insane, to be so frighteningly aware of the man seated within touching distance.

The image of his kiss, so warm and infinitely evocative, rose up to taunt her, and she had to summon all her reserves of willpower to present a smiling, seemingly relaxed façade.

No matter what private aspirations Rachel and Alexandros held for their son's marriage, it was apparent that the union afforded them tremendous pleasure. Equally obvious was an approval of their daughter-in-law, and Alyse experienced a feeling of deep regret—not only for Antonia's loss, but for her own. If she could have selected ideal parents-in-law, it would be difficult to choose a nicer couple than Aleksi's father and stepmother.

Such introspection was dangerous, and it was a relief when they entered the restaurant and were shown to their table.

CHAPTER SEVEN

THE setting was superb, the food a gourmet's delight, presented with flair and artistry. Except that Alyse's appetite seemed to be non-existent as she selected cream of mushroom soup, then followed it with crumbed prawn cutlets.

After sipping half a flute of champagne she felt more at ease, but she was supremely conscious of Aleksi's solicitous attention, the accidental brush of his fingers against her own, and the acute sensation that he was instigating a deliberate seduction.

Consequently it was a relief when Alexandros asked if she'd care to join him on the dance floor.

Alyse spared Rachel an enquiring smile. 'Do you mind?'

'Of course not, my dear.' Rachel's features assumed a faintly mischievous expression. 'Aleksi and I will join you.'

Alexandros, as Aleksi's father insisted she call him, was every bit as commanding as his indomitable son, Alyse decided as she rose graciously from the table and allowed him to lead her on to the restaurant's small dance floor. There was the same vital, almost electric energy apparent, an awareness of male sensuality that had little to do with chronological age. Alexandros Stefanos was charming: polite, deferential, and genuine. The sort of man a woman could entrust with her life.

'You're light on your feet, like a feather,' he complimented her. 'So graceful.'

'You're an accomplished partner,' she returned with a faint smile.

'And you're very kind.'

Am I? she thought silently. I'm not at all kindly disposed towards your son. Out loud, she said, 'I hope you and Rachel are enjoying your holiday.'

'My dear, how can I explain the joy among the grief in discovering that Georgiou had fathered a son? He's very much loved, that child, his existence so precious to us all.'

Alyse couldn't think of a single thing to say, and she circled the floor in silence, hardly aware of the music or their fellow dancers on the floor.

'Shall we change partners?' a deep voice drawled from close by, and she missed her step, distinctly ill at ease that she was about to be relinquished into the waiting arms of her husband.

Aleksi's hold was far from conventional, and she wanted to scream with vexation.

'Must you?' she hissed, totally enraged at the proprietorial possessiveness of his grasp. She was all too aware of a subjugation so infinite, it was impossible not to feel afraid.

'Dance with my wife?'

His resort to mockery was deliberate, and momentarily defeated in the knowledge that self-assertion would only cause a scene, Alyse tilted her head and gave him a brilliant smile.

'This is *dancing*, Aleksi? You can't begin to know how much I'd like to slap your face!'

One eyebrow slanted in cynical amusement. 'Good heavens, whatever will you do when we make love? Kill me?'

'I'll have a darned good try!'

His eyes darkened with ill-concealed humour. 'Yes, I do believe you will.'

There was no doubt he'd enjoy the fight, and its aftermath, while instinctive self-preservation warned that if she dared submit she would never be the same again.

The music playing was one of those incredibly poignant songs that stirred at the heartstrings, with lyrics of such depth that just hearing them almost brought tears to her eyes.

You're mad, she told herself shakily. You hate him, remember? The strain of the past few days; meeting Georg's grandparents. It was all too much.

A slight shiver feathered its way across the surface of her skin. Any kind of emotional involvement was a luxury she couldn't afford if she were to instigate a divorce and return to Perth with Georg.

'I'd like to go back to our table.' The words came out as a slightly desperate plea, and she strained away from him in her anxiety to escape the intimacy of his hold.

'The band will take a break soon. Besides, my parents are still dancing. We should return together, don't you think?' His voice sounded mild close to her ear, and she felt his breath stir at her temple, teasing a few tendrils of hair.

'I have the beginnings of a headache,' she improvised, and felt immeasurably relieved as he led her to the edge of the dance floor, his gaze sharp and far too discerning for her peace of mind.

'Fact, or fiction?'

Her eyes blazed a brilliant blue. 'Does it really matter?' Angry beyond belief, she turned and moved quickly away from him.

On reaching the brightly lit powder-room she crossed to an empty space in front of the long mirror and pretended interest in her features.

She was far too pale, she decided in analytical appraisal, and her eyes bore a vaguely haunted look, reflecting an inner tension that was akin to a vulnerable animal confronted by a hunting predator.

A tiny bubble of derisive laughter rose and died in her throat at her illogical parallel. Dear lord, she'd have to get a hold on herself. Imaginative flights of fancy were of no help whatsoever in her resolve against Aleksi Stefanos.

The invention of a headache wasn't entirely an untruth, for a persistent niggle began to manifest itself behind one eye, and she attributed its cause directly to her husband.

Aware that her escape could only be a temporary respite, she resolutely withdrew a lipstick from her evening purse and tidied her hair to its smooth bell-like style before returning to their table.

'My dear, are you all right?' Rachel asked the moment Alyse was seated, and she countered the force of three pairs of apparently concerned eyes with a reassuring smile.

'Yes, thank you.'

'You're very pale. Are you sure?'

Obviously she wasn't succeeding very well in the acting stakes! 'Georg still wakes through the night,' she explained lightly, 'and is often difficult to settle.'

'Georgiou was the same at a similar age—an angel by day, yet restless at night.' Rachel offered a conciliatory smile. 'It will soon pass.'

'Meanwhile it's proving quite disruptive to our sleep,' drawled Aleksi, shooting Alyse a particularly intimate glance.

Damn him, had he no shame? she fumed, forced into silence out of deference to his parents' presence.

'Tell me about the party you've both planned,' Rachel began, in what Alyse decided was a sympathetic attempt to change the subject.

'A delayed wedding reception,' Aleksi elaborated with bland disregard for her barely contained surprise. 'Providing an opportunity for family and friends to share the celebration of our marriage.'

Alyse felt her stomach execute a few painful somersaults. How dared he propose something so ludicrous? It was only compounding a mockery, and she wanted no part in it.

'What a wonderful idea!' his stepmother enthused, while Alyse sought to dampen an increasing sense of anger for what remained of the evening.

In the car she sat tensely on edge as Aleksi brought the luxurious vehicle to a smooth halt in the wide bricked apron at the entrance to the tall apartment block.

'Will you join us for coffee?' asked Rachel, and Alyse held her breath as Aleksi issued a reluctant refusal.

'It's quite late, and we're both anxious to get home.' His smile appeared genuinely warm. 'The babysitter is extremely capable, but it's the first time we've left Georg in her care.'

That was true enough, although it was unlikely that there had been any problems, and Alyse managed to smile as they bade each other good-night, issuing a spontaneous invitation for the older woman to join her the next day.

However, the instant the car cleared the driveway Alyse burst into angry pent-up speech.

'You are impossible!'

'Why, specifically?' Aleksi countered cynically, and she was so incensed that if he hadn't been driving she would have hit him.

Spreading one hand, she ticked off each consecutive grudge. 'Deliberately implying that we share the same bed. And when you announced a party, I hardly imagined you'd expect me to give a repeat performance as a blushing bride.'

'My dear Alyse, do you still blush?'

She cast him a furious glare. 'I used the term in a purely figurative sense.'

'Of course.'

'Oh, don't be so damned *patronising*!'

'If you want to fight, at least wait until we reach home,' he cautioned cynically, and, momentarily defeated, Alyse turned her attention to the passing scenery beyond the windscreen.

The sky was an inky black as it merged with the shallow waters of the inner harbour, providing a startling background for brightly lit venues along the famed tourist strip. Outlines were crisp and sharp, and a pinprick sprinkling of stars lent promise of another day of sunshine in a sub-tropical winterless climate.

Aleksi chose the waterfront road, and Alyse wondered darkly if he was deliberately giving her temper an opportunity to cool.

Georg hadn't even murmured, Melanie reported, accepting the notes Aleksi placed in her hand before departing with a friendly smile.

'I'll check Georg,' said Alyse hastily.

'An excuse to escape, Alyse?'

'No, damn you!'

His eyes gleamed with latent mockery. 'I'll make coffee. Liqueur and cream?'

Resentment flared as she turned to face him. 'I'm going to bed—I've done my duty for the evening. Goodnight.'

There was a palpable pause. 'You consider an evening spent with Rachel and my father a duty?'

Alyse closed her eyes, then opened them again. 'They're both utterly charming. Their son, however, is not.'

'Indeed?' His voice sounded like velvet-encased steel. 'Perhaps you would care to clarify that?'

'You act as if I'm your wife!'

One eyebrow rose in cynical query. 'My dear Alyse, I have in my possession a marriage certificate stating clearly that you are.'

'You know very well what I mean!'

'Does it bother you that I accord you a measure of husbandly affection?'

'Courteous attention I can accept,' she acknowledged angrily. 'But intimate contact is totally unnecessary.'

His smile was peculiarly lacking in humour. 'I haven't even begun with intimacy.'

Her hand flew in an upward arc, only to be caught in a bonecrushing grip that left her gasping with pain.

'So eager to hit out, Alyse? Aren't you in the least concerned what form of punishment I might care to mete out?' he asked deliberately, pulling her inextricably close.

'Do you specialise in wife-beating, Aleksi?' she countered in defiance, and suffered momentary qualms at the anger beneath the surface of his control.

'I prefer something infinitely more subtle,' he drawled, and she retaliated without thought.

'I hardly dare ask!'

'Sheer bravado, or naïveté?'

'Oh, *both*,' she acknowledged, then gave a startled gasp as he slid an arm beneath her knees and lifted her into his arms. 'What do you think you're doing?'

The look he cast her cut right through to her soul. 'Taking you to bed. Mine,' he elaborated with icy intent.

Her eyes dilated with shock. 'Don't! Please,' she added as a genuine plea to his sensitivity, rather than as an afterthought.

'You sound almost afraid,' he derided silkily.

Afraid I'll never be the same again, Alyse qualified silently, hating the exigent sexual chemistry that drew her towards him like a moth to flame.

'I hate you!' she flung desperately as he carried her through the lounge, and she was absolutely incensed at the speculative amusement apparent in the depths of his eyes.

In the bedroom he let her slide to her feet, and she was powerless to do anything other than stand perfectly still beneath his dark penetrating gaze.

'You react like an agitated kitten, all bristling fur and unsheathed claws.' His smile was infinitely sensual, his eyes dark and slumbrous as he took her chin between thumb and forefinger to tilt it unmercifully high. 'It will be worth the scratches you'll undoubtedly inflict, just to hear you purr.'

'Egotist,' she accorded shakily. 'What makes you think I will?'

He didn't deign to answer, and there was nothing she could do to avoid his mouth as it took possession of hers in a deliberately sensual onslaught that plundered the very depths of her soul.

With shocking ease he dispensed with her clothes, then his own, and she gave an agonised gasp as he reached for the thin scrap of lace-edged satin covering her breasts.

'Aleksi——'

'Don't?' he taunted softly, releasing the clasp and letting the bra fall to the carpet.

It was impossible to come to terms with a mixture of elation and fear, so she didn't even try, aware even as she voiced the protest that there could be no turning back. 'You can't mean to do this,' she said in agonised despair.

His hands cupped the creamy fullness of her breasts with tactile expertise, and the breath locked in her throat when his head descended and his mouth closed over one vulnerable peak. Sensation spiralled from the central core of her being, radiating through her body until she was consumed by an emotion so fiery, so damnably erotic, that it was all she could do not to beg him to assuage the hunger within.

His tasting took on a new dimension as he began to suckle, using his teeth with such infinite delicacy that it frequently trod a fine edge between pleasure and pain.

Just when she thought she could bear it no more, he relinquished his possession and crossed to render a similar onslaught to its twin.

Unbidden, her fingers sought the thickness of his hair, raking its well-groomed length in barely controlled agitation that didn't cease when he shifted his attention to her mouth and began subjecting that sensitive cavern to a seeking exploration that gradually became an imitation of the sexual act itself.

Alyse was floating high on a cloud of sensuality so evocative that it was all she could do not to beg him to ease the ache that centred between her thighs, and, as if he was aware of her need, his hand slid down to gently probe the sweet moistness dewing there.

Like a finely tuned instrument her body leapt in response, and she became mindless, an insignificant craft caught in a swirling vortex beyond which she had no control.

It wasn't until she felt the soft mattress beneath her back that realisation forced its way through the mists of desire, and she could only stare, her eyes wide with slumbrous warmth, as Aleksi discarded his shirt, then his trousers and finally the dark hipster briefs that shielded his masculinity.

There was a potent beauty in his lean well-muscled frame, a virility that sent the blood coursing through her veins in fearful anticipation, and she unconsciously raised her gaze to his, silently pleading as he joined her on the bed.

Her lips parted tremulously as his eyes conducted a lingering appraisal of their softly swollen contours, before slipping down to the rose-tipped breasts that burgeoned beneath his gaze as if in silent recognition of his touch.

Her limbs seemed consumed by languorous inertia, and she made no protest as he began a light, trailing exploration of her waist, the soft indentation of her navel, then moved to the pale hair curling softly between her thighs.

A sharp intake of breath changed to shocked disbelief as his lips followed the path of his hand in a brazen degree of intimacy she found impossible to condone.

Liquid fire coursed through her body, arousing each separate sensory nerve-end until she moaned an entreaty for him to desist. Except that nothing she said made any difference, and in a desperate attempt to put an end to the havoc he was creating she sank her fingers into his hair and tugged—*hard*.

It had not the slightest effect, and her limbs threshed in violent rejection until he caught hold of her hands and pinned them to her sides, effectively using his elbows to still the wild movements of her legs.

For what seemed an age she lay helpless beneath his deliberate invasion, hating him with a fervour that was totally unmatched, until, shifting his body weight, he effected a deep penetrating thrust that brought an involuntary gasp from her lips as delicate tissues stretched, then filled with stinging pain.

She was so caught up with it she didn't register the brief explicit curse that husked from Aleksi's throat, and she tossed her head from side to side to escape his mouth before it settled over hers, gentle, coaxing, and inflexibly possessive as she strove to free herself.

Without thought she balled her hands into fists and hit out at him, striking anywhere she could, then she became impossibly angry when it had no effect whatsoever.

The only weapons she had left were her teeth and her nails, and she used both, shamelessly biting his tongue, at the same time raking her nails down his ribcage, achieving some satisfaction from his harsh intake of breath.

'Witch,' he growled, lifting his mouth fractionally, and she cried out in agonised rejection.

'*Bastard!* I hate you, *hate* you, do you understand?'

His hands caught hers in a punishing grip and held them immobile above her head, and she began to struggle in earnest, fear lending her unknown strength as she fought to be free of him.

'Stop it, little fool,' he chastised, holding her with ease. 'You're only making it worse for yourself.'

Angry dark blue eyes speared his as she vented furiously, 'Get away from me, damn you!'

'Not yet.'

'Haven't you done enough?' It was a tortured accusation dredged up from the depths of her soul, and yet it failed to have the desired effect. 'Aleksi!' She would have begged if she had to, and it didn't help that he knew.

'Be still, little wildcat,' he soothed, easily holding both her hands with one of his as he gently pushed stray tendrils of hair back behind her ear. Then his mouth brushed her temple, pressed each eyelid closed in turn, before trailing down to the edge of her lips. With a touch as light as a butterfly's wing he teased their curved outline before slipping to the hollow at the base of her neck.

'Please don't.'

'What a contrary plea!' he murmured against her throat, and she could sense the smile in his voice. 'Just relax, and trust me.'

'Why should I?' she cried in an impassioned entreaty, only wanting to be free of him.

'The hurting is over, I promise.'

'Then why won't you leave me alone?' Her eyes seared his, then became trapped beneath the latent sensuality, the sheer animal magnetism he exuded, and almost in primeval recognition an answering chord struck deep within, quivering into hesitant life.

'This is why,' husked Aleksi, covering her mouth gently with his own as he began to move, slowly at first, creating a throbbing ache that swelled until she became caught up in the deep rhythmic pattern of his possession.

Impossibly sensuous, he played her with the skilled mastery of a virtuoso, bringing forth without any difficulty at all the soft startled cries of her pleasure, and the hands that had raked his flesh now cajoled in silent supplication as she accepted everything he chose to give.

The climax, when it came, was unexpected and tumultuous, an entire gamut of emotions so exquisite it defied description in that first initial experience, and afterwards she was too spent to attempt an accurate analysis.

With a return to normality came a degree of self-loathing, and the re-emergence of hatred for the man who had instigated her emotional catalyst. She became aware of her own body, the soft bruising inside and out, and the increasing need to escape, albeit temporarily, from the large bed and the indomitable man who occupied it.

'Where do you think you're going?'

It was difficult to stand naked before his gaze, although innate dignity lifted her head to a proud angle as she turned at the sound of that quiet drawling voice.

'To have a bath,' she responded evenly, and saw his eyes narrow fractionally before she moved towards the en suite bathroom.

Once inside, she closed the door, then pressed the plug into position in the large spa-bath and released water from the taps.

Within minutes steam clouded the room, and she added plenty of bath-oil to the cascading water before stepping into its warm depth.

Aleksi walked into the room as Alyse was about to reach for a sponge, and she was so incensed at his intrusion she threw the sponge without thought, watching as it connected with his chest.

His soft husky laughter as he calmly stepped into the bath to sit facing her was the last straw, and she flew at him in a rage, flailing her fists against his shoulders, his arms, anywhere she could connect, until he caught hold of her wrists with a steel-like grip.

'Enough, Alyse.' His voice was hard and inflexible, and she looked at him with stormy eyes, ready to do further battle given the slightest opportunity.

'Can't you see I want to be alone?' It was a cry from the heart, and to her horror she felt her lower lip tremble with damnable reaction. She was physically and emotionally spent, and there was the very real threat of tears as she determined not to let him see the extent of her fragility.

Eyes that were dark and impossibly slumbrous held her own captive in mesmerised fascination, and helpless frustration welled up inside her as her chin tilted at an angry angle. 'Must you look at me like that?'

'We just made love,' he drawled with latent humour. 'How would you have me look at you?'

'I hated it!' Alyse flung incautiously.

One eyebrow rose with sardonic cynicism. 'You hated the fact that it was *I* who awakened you to the power of your own sensuality.' His lips moved to form a twisted smile. 'And you hate yourself for achieving sexual pleasure with someone you profess to dislike.'

The truth of his words was something she refused to concede. 'You behaved like a barbaric—*animal*!'

'Who took his own pleasure without any concern for yours?' he demanded with undisguised mockery.

Colour stained her cheeks, and her lashes fluttered down to form a protective veil against his discerning scrutiny. 'I'll never forgive you,' she declared with quiet vehemence. *'Never.'*

'Spoken like an innocent,' Aleksi declared with sardonic amusement, and her eyes flew open to reveal shards of brilliant sapphire.

'Not any more, thanks to you!'

Lifting a hand, he brushed his fingers along the edge of her jaw. 'I'm almost inclined to query why.'

Alyse reared back from that light teasing touch as if it was flame, wanting to scream and rage against his deliberate seduction, the sheer force of his sensual expertise. Except she was damned if she'd give him the satisfaction. Instead, she said bitterly, 'I would have preferred a less brutal initiation.'

'Yet after the pain came pleasure, did it not?'

Her eyes glittered in angry rejection. 'Never having experienced anything to compare it with, I can't comment.'

His soft husky laughter was almost her undoing, and she stood to her feet, reached for a towel, then stepped quickly out of the bath, uncaring that he followed her actions.

It was then she saw the long scratches scoring his ribcage, and she turned away, feeling sickened that she could have inflicted such physical injury.

In the bedroom she collected her nightgown and donned it, then turned hesitantly as Aleksi entered the room.

'You'll sleep here with me, Alyse. And don't argue,' he added with quiet emphasis as her lips parted to form a protest.

Before she had the opportunity to move more than a few steps towards the sitting-room he had reached her side, and her struggles were ineffectual as he calmly lifted her into his arms and carried her to the large bed.

'I don't want to sleep with you,' she said fiercely, pushing against him as he slid in between the covers.

'Maybe not,' he drawled, settling her easily into the curve of his body. 'But I insist you do.'

'You damned dictatorial tyrant!'

'My dear Alyse, I can think of a far more pleasurable way to deploy your energy than by merely wasting it in fighting me.'

She froze at his unmistakable implication. 'I won't be used and abused whenever you——'

'Feel the urge?' he completed sardonically. 'I have a twelve-hour day ahead of me, and right now all I have in mind is a few hours' sleep. Unless you have other ideas, which I'll gladly oblige, I suggest you simply relax.'

'Oh, go to hell!' she was stung into retorting as he reached out and switched off the bedside lamp.

Seconds later Alyse was aware of his warm breath against her temple, and she lay perfectly still, willing the nervous tautness in her body to ease, then slowly her eyelids flickered down as sheer exhaustion gradually took its toll and sleep provided blissful oblivion.

CHAPTER EIGHT

THE ensuing few days provided an opportunity for Alyse to become better acquainted with Rachel, for each morning Aleksi's stepmother arrived in time to help with Georg's bath, then they would each take it in turns to feed him his bottle before settling him back into his cot.

There was time for a leisurely morning tea and a chat before eating a light midday lunch, after which Georg was fed, resettled, and placed into Melanie's care for the afternoon while they explored one of the many shopping complexes scattered along the Gold Coast's tourist strip.

Alexandros joined his son in a daily round of building site inspections, meetings and consultations, from which they returned together each evening.

Dinner was inevitably an informal meal, with both women sharing the preparation, and Alyse felt faintly envious of the friendship Aleksi shared with his parents. It was genuine and uncontrived, and while part of her enjoyed sharing their company, another constantly warned against forming too close an attachment for two people who, after her intended separation and divorce from Aleksi, would no longer find it possible to regard her with any affection. Somehow such a thought caused her immeasurable pain.

The nights were something else, for in Aleksi's arms she became increasingly uninhibited, to such an extent that she began to hate her own traitorous body almost as much as she assured herself that she hated *him*.

Arrangements for the party Aleksi insisted they host to celebrate their marriage proved remarkably simple, with a series of telephone calls to a variety of guests, and the hiring of a reputable catering firm.

All that remained for Alyse to do was to arrange for Melanie to babysit, and select something suitable to wear.

While the former was remarkably simple, choosing a dress took considerable time and care, although Rachel's wholehearted approval proved invaluable, and the silk and lace ensemble in deep cream highlighted the texture of her skin and the brilliant sapphire-blue of her eyes. The bodice was demure with elbow-length sleeves, with a fitted waist that accentuated her small waist, and the skirt fell in graceful folds to a fashionable length.

The guests were due to begin arriving at eight, and Alyse settled Georg upstairs just after six, then she hastily showered, taking extreme care with her hair and make-up.

Nerves were hell and damnation, she decided silently, cursing softly at the unsteadiness of her hand, and she cleansed her eyelids and started all over again.

She wished fervently that the evening were over and done with. Aleksi's friends would be super-critical of his new wife, and she had little doubt she would be dissected piece by piece from the top of her head to the tips of her elegant designer shoes.

An hour later she stood back from the mirror and viewed her overall appearance with a tiny frown.

'Problems?'

She turned at once at the sound of that deep drawling voice, noting that Aleksi displayed an inherent sophistication attired in a dark suit, white shirt and sombre tie, and she envied him the air of relaxed calm he was able to exude without any seeming effort at all.

Her eyes clouded with anxiety. 'What do you think?'

He took his time answering, and she suffered his slow appraisal with increasing apprehension.

'Beautiful,' he told her, lifting a hand to tilt her chin fractionally. His smile held a mesmerising quality, and she ran the tip of her tongue along the edge of her lower lip in a gesture of nervousness. 'I'm almost sorry I have to share you with a room full of people.' His eyes gleamed darkly. 'An intimate evening *à deux* would be more appropriate.'

Her lashes swept up in a deliberate attempt at guile. 'And waste this dress? It cost a fortune.'

His mouth curved with humour. 'I'm impressed, believe me.' Releasing her chin, he caught hold of her hand. 'Melanie is already upstairs with Georg and an enviable collection of law books. Rachel and Alexandros have arrived. The caterers have everything under control, and there's time for a quiet drink before the first of our guests are due to arrive.'

Alyse wondered if it was too late to opt out, and some of her indecision must have been apparent in her expression, for he bent forward and brushed his lips against her temple.

'It's no big deal, Alyse. In any case, I'll be here.'

'Maybe that's what I'm afraid of,' she said with undue solemnity, and saw his smile widen with sardonic cynicism.

'Ah, this is the Alyse I know best.'

Suddenly flip, she responded, 'I wasn't aware there was more than one of me.'

His husky laughter brought a soft tinge of colour to her cheeks, and she made no demure as he led the way out into the lounge.

Everything appeared superb, Alyse decided a few hours later as she drifted politely from one group of guests to another. Background music filtered through a sophisticated electronic system, and hired staff circulated among the guests with professional ease, proffering trays of tastefully prepared morsels of food. Champagne flowed from a seemingly inexhaustible supply, and she had been introduced to so many people it was impossible to remember more than a few of their names. Beautiful, elegantly attired women, who seemed discreetly intent on discovering the latest in social gossip, while the man stood in segregated groups talking business— primarily their own as related to the state of the country's current economy.

'Darling, you really *must* come along,' a gorgeous blonde insisted, and Alyse brought her attention back to the small group of women who had commandeered her attention. 'It's a worthwhile charity. The models are superb and the clothes will be absolutely stunning.' Perfect white teeth gleamed between equally perfectly painted red lips, and the smile portrayed practised sincerity. 'Annabel will be there, Chrissie, Kate, and Marta. You'll sit with us, of course.'

'Can I let you know?' Alyse managed politely, and saw the ice-blue eyes narrow fractionally.

'Of course. Aleksi has my number.'

Within seconds she was alone again, but not for long.

'Do you need rescuing?'

A warm smile curved the edges of her mouth at the welcome intrusion of her mother-in-law. 'How did you guess?'

'Everything is going beautifully, my dear,' Rachel complimented. 'You're doing very well,' she added gently, and Alyse sobered slightly, although her smile didn't falter for a second.

'I'm the cynosure of all eyes. Circumspectly assessed, analysed, and neatly categorised—rather like a prize piece of merchandise. Will I pass muster, do you think?'

'With flying colours,' Rachel told her, and Alyse could have genuinely hugged her.

'Ah, an ally,' she breathed gratefully. 'It seems I should join numerous committees, play the requisite twice weekly game of tennis, frequent daily aerobic workouts, attend weekly classes in exotic flower arrangement, and become part of a circle who gather for social luncheons.' A wicked gleam lit her expressive eyes. 'What hours left free in the day are advisably spent visiting a beauty salon, shopping, or, importantly, organising the next luncheon, dinner party, or simply the informal get-together for Sunday brunch.'

'You don't aspire to joining the society treadmill?'

'Not to any great extent.' Her shoulders lifted slightly in an elegant shrug. 'A few luncheons might be fun. A stunning blonde whose name escapes me issued an invitation to a fashion parade held at Sanctuary Cove on Tuesday. Perhaps we could go together?'

'Lovely,' the older woman enthused. 'It will give Alexandros an opportunity to spend a day on the golf course.'

Alyse let her gaze wander round the large room, noting idly that the various guests gave every appearance of enjoying themselves. Although who wouldn't, she thought wryly, when provided with fine food and wine, and glittering company? The women dripped diamonds, and several wore mink, elegantly styled jackets slung with apparent carelessness over slim designer-clad shoulders.

'Do you know many of the people here?' she queried tentatively.

'Most of the men are business associates, with their various wives or girlfriends,' Rachel revealed with a sympathetic smile. 'The glamorous blonde who last engaged you in conversation is Serita Hubbard—her husband is a very successful property speculator. The brunette talking to Serita is Kate, the daughter of one of Aleksi's best friends—that's Paul, her father, deep in conversation with Aleksi and Alexandros.' Rachel paused, tactfully drawing Alyse's attention to a stunning couple on the far side of the room. 'Dominic Rochas, and his sister Solange. Together they represent a highly reputable firm of interior designers.'

Tall, slim and beautifully dressed, they could easily have passed as models for an exclusive fashion house, Alyse decided without envy. Somehow they didn't seem real, and instead were merely players portraying an expected part on the stage of life.

'Given time, I'm sure I'll get to know them all,' she ventured quietly.

'Aleksi and Georg are very fortunate to have you,' Rachel complimented softly.

With a hand that shook slightly Alyse picked up her glass and savoured its contents in the hope that the excellent champagne would calm her nerves. It was all too apparent that Rachel held fond hopes for the apparent affection between her stepson and his new bride to blossom and eventually bloom into love.

Something that Aleksi seemed to deliberately foster by ensuring his glance lingered a few seconds too long, augmenting it with the touch of his hand on her arm, at her waist, not to mention the lazy indulgence he accorded her on numerous occasions in the presence of his parents.

'Put several business friends together in the same room,' a familiar voice drawled at her elbow, 'and inevitably the conversation drifts away from social pleasantries.'

Talk of the devil! Alyse turned her head slowly towards Aleksi and gave him a brilliant smile. 'I hardly noticed your absence.'

'I think that could be termed an indirect admonition,' Alexandros declared with humour as he directed his wife a musing glance. 'Yes?'

'Alyse and I have been enjoying each other's company,' Rachel acknowledged with considerable diplomacy.

'Aleksi *darling*!' an incredibly warm voice gushed with the barest hint of an accent. 'We're impossibly late, but Tony got held up in Brisbane, and we simply *flew* down. Say you forgive us?'

Alyse sensed the effervescent laughter threatening to burst out from the large-framed woman whose entire bearing could only be described as *majestic*. A dark purple silk trouser-suit with voluminous matching knee-length jacket, long trailing scarves and an abundance of jewellery completed an ensemble that on anyone else would have looked ludicrous.

'Siobhan!' Aleksi's smile was genuinely warm as he accepted her embrace. 'Tony. Allow me to introduce my wife, Alyse.'

Alyse immediately became the focus of two pairs of eyes, one set of which was femininely shrewd yet totally lacking in calculation.

'She looks perfect, darling,' Siobhan pronounced softly, and Alyse had the uncanny feeling she had been subjected to some kind of test and had unwittingly passed. 'Is she?'

Aleksi's eyes gleamed with silent humour. 'Incredibly so.'

'Siobhan, you're outrageous,' her husband drawled in resignation. 'I imagine the poor girl is almost witless with nerves.'

Wonderfully warm dark eyes gleamed as they held hers. 'Are you?' asked Siobhan.

'Like a lamb in a den of lions,' Alyse admitted with a wry smile.

Mellifluous laughter flowed richly from Siobhan's throat. 'Several of the female gender present undoubtedly are, my dear. Especially where your gorgeous hunk of a husband is concerned.'

'I suppose there must be a certain fascination for his dark brooding charm,' Alyse considered with a devilish gleam, and Siobhan grinned, totally unabashed.

'He's a sexy beast, darling. To some, it's almost a fatal attraction.'

Alyse merely smiled, and Siobhan said softly, 'How delightful—you're shy!'

'A fascinating quality,' Aleksi agreed, taking hold of Alyse's hand and threading his fingers through her own.

She tried to tug her hand away, and felt his fingers tighten in silent warning. 'Perhaps we could get together for dinner soon? Now, if you'll excuse us, we really must circulate. Enjoy yourselves,' he bade genially.

It was impossible to protest, and Alyse allowed Aleksi to lead her from one group to another in the large room, pausing for five minutes, sometimes ten, as they engaged in conversation. Georg's existence had precipitated a marriage that had aroused speculative conjecture, and by the time they had come full circle her facial muscles felt tight from maintaining a constant smile, and her nerves were raw beneath an abundance of thinly veiled curiosity.

'Another drink?' asked Aleksi.

Dared she? Somehow it seemed essential to appear to be in total command, and she had merely picked a few morsels from each course during dinner and barely nibbled from the abundance of food constantly offered by hired staff throughout the evening. 'I'd love some coffee.'

An eyebrow slanted in quizzical query. 'I can't tempt you with champagne-spiked orange juice?' His gaze was direct and vaguely analytical, and Alyse was unable to suppress the faint quickening of her pulse.

He had the strangest effect on her equilibrium, making her aware of a primitive alchemy, a dramatic pull of the senses almost beyond her comprehension, for it didn't seem possible to be able to physically enjoy sex with someone she actively disliked. Hated, she amended, unwilling to accord him much favour. Yet he projected an enviable aura of power, a distinctive mesh of male charisma and sensuality that alerted the interest of women—a primeval recognition that made her feel uncommonly resentful.

'I'd prefer coffee,' she responded with forced lightness, and he laughed, a deep, husky sound that sent shivers scudding down the length of her spine.

'The need for a clear head?' His teeth gleamed white for an instant, then became hidden beneath the curve of his mouth.

'Yes,' she admitted without prevarication.

'Stay here, and I'll fetch some.'

'I'd rather come with you.'

He examined her features, assessing the bright eyes and pale cheeks with daunting scrutiny. 'No one here would dare harm so much as a hair on your beautiful head,' he alluded cynically.

'Forgive me if I don't believe you.' She hadn't meant to sound bitter, but the implication was there, and she felt immeasurably angry—with herself, for allowing him to catch a glimpse of her vulnerability.

Without a further word he led her towards a table where an attractively attired waitress was dispensing tea and coffee, and within seconds he had placed a cup between her nerveless fingers, watching as she sipped the hot aromatic brew appreciatively while her eyes skimmed the room.

'When you've finished, we'll dance,' he told her.

Alyse brought her gaze back to the indomitable man at her side. 'You've succeeded admirably at playing the perfect husband all evening. Dancing cheek-to-cheek might be overdoing it, don't you think?'

His eyes were dark and unfathomable. 'Inconceivable, of course, that I might want to?'

She suddenly felt as if she'd skated on to very thin ice, and she resorted to restrained anger in defence. 'I'm damned if I'll act out a charade!'

'Are you so sure it will be?'

This was an infinitely dangerous game, and she wasn't at all sure she wanted to play. Yet in a room full of people, what else could she do but comply?

Her eyes glittered as he removed the empty cup from her hand and put it down on the nearby table, and her smile was deliberately winsome as he drew her out on to the terrace and into his arms.

There were strategically placed lights casting a muted glow over landscaped gardens, and the air was fresh and cool.

'You have a large number of friends,' Alyse remarked in a desperate bid to break the silence.

'Business associates, acquaintances with whom I maintain social contact,' Aleksi corrected wryly.

She tilted her head slightly. 'How cynical!'

'You think so?'

He was amused, damn him! *'Yes.'*

'Careful, little cat,' he cautioned softly, controlling with ease her effort to put some distance between them. 'Your claws are showing.'

'If they are, it's because I detest what you're doing.'

'Dancing with my wife?'

'Oh, stop being so damned—*impossible*! You know very well what I mean.'

'This party was arranged specifically to give a number of important people the opportunity to meet you. The reason for our marriage is none of their business.'

'There are several women present who appear to think it is!'

'Their problem, not mine.' He sounded so clinical, so damned—detached, that she felt sickened.

'Let me go. I want to check on Georg.'

'Melanie is ensconced upstairs doing precisely that,' drawled Aleksi, refusing to relinquish his hold. 'In a minute we'll go back inside and mingle with our guests.'

'I hate you!'

'At least it's a healthy emotion.'

It didn't *feel* healthy! In fact, it razed her nerves and turned her into a seething ball of fury.

For what remained of the evening Alyse displayed the expected role of hostess with charm and dignity, so much so that she surely deserved a medal for perseverance, she decided as she stood at her husband's side and said goodbye to the last remaining clutch of guests.

Only when the tail-lights of the final car disappeared from sight and Aleksi had firmly closed the front door did she allow the mask to slip.

'I'll pay the babysitter, and activate Georg's electronic monitor,' Aleksi determined. 'There's no point in disturbing him simply to move him downstairs.'

The fact that he was right didn't preclude her need to oppose him, and she opened her mouth, only to close it again beneath the force of his forefinger.

'Don't argue.'

She drew back her head as if touched by flame, and her eyes flashed with anger. 'I'll do as I damn well please!'

His expression assumed a musing indolence. 'Go to bed.'

She was so angry, it almost consumed her. 'And wait dutifully for you to join me?'

Without a word he turned and made for the stairs, and she watched his ascent with impotent rage.

Damned if she'd obey and retire meekly to the bedroom! Although at several minutes past two in the morning it hardly made sense to think of anything else. And perversity, simply for the sheer hell of it, was infinitely unwise.

Except she didn't feel like taking a sensible course, and without pausing to give her actions further thought she crossed the lounge and made her way downstairs.

The caterers had been extremely efficient, for apart from a few glasses there was little evidence that a party had taken place.

A quick vacuum of the carpets and the room would be restored to its usual immaculate state, she decided, and, uncaring of the late hour, she retrieved the necessary cleaner and set it in motion.

She had almost finished when the motor came to a sudden stop, and she turned to see Aleksi standing a few feet distant with the disconnected cord held in his hand.

'This can surely wait?' His voice was deceptively mild, and didn't fool her in the slightest.

'It will only take another minute, then it's done.'

'In the morning, Alyse.'

'I'd prefer to do it now.' It was as if she was on a rollercoaster to self-destruction, able to see her ultimate destination yet powerless to stop.

'Obstinacy simply for the sheer hell of it is foolish, don't you think?' Aleksi queried, depressing the automatic cord rewind button, and Alyse glared at him balefully.

'Aren't you being equally stubborn?' she returned at once.

He spared the elegant gold watch at his wrist a cursory glance. 'Two-thirty in the morning isn't conducive to a definitive discussion.'

'So once again I must play the part of a subjugated wife!'

His eyes narrowed, assuming a daunting hardness that was at variance with the softness of his voice. 'Perhaps you'd care to clarify that remark?'

Alyse stood defiant. 'I don't like being continually dictated to,' she told him angrily. 'And I especially don't like being taken for granted.' She lifted a hand, then let it fall down to her side. 'I feel like a child, forced to conform. And I'm not,' she insisted, helpless in the face of her own anger.

'Aren't you?' Aleksi brushed his fingers across her heated cheeks. 'Most women would exult in my wealth and scheme to acquire all life's so-called luxuries.'

'Are you condemning me as a child because I'm unwilling to play the vamp in bed?'

'What a delightfully evocative phrase!'

'I hate you, do you understand? *Hate* you,' she said fiercely, then gave a startled cry as he calmly took hold of her arms and lifted her over his shoulder. 'What do you think you're doing?'

He turned and began walking towards the stairs. 'I would have thought it was obvious.'

'Put me down, damn you!' There was a terrible sense of indignity at being carried in such a manner, and she hit out at him, clenching her hands into fists as she railed them against his back. 'Bastard!' she accused as he reached the ground floor and crossed the lounge. *'Barbarian!'*

On entering their bedroom he pulled her down to stand facing him, and she looked at him through a mist of anger.

'This seems to be the only level on which we effectively communicate.' His eyes were hard and inflexible.

'Speak for yourself!' she flung incautiously.

His eyes lanced hers, their expression dark and forbidding. 'I'm tempted to make you beg for my possession.'

'What's stopping you?'

'Little fool,' Aleksi condemned with dangerous silkiness. 'Aren't you in the least afraid of my temper?'

'What would you do? Beat me?'

'Maybe I should, simply to teach you the lesson you deserve.'

'And what about the lesson I consider *you* deserve?' cried Alyse, tried almost beyond endurance. 'For forcing me into marriage, your bed...' She faltered to a shaky halt, hating him more than she thought it was possible to hate anyone.

'Your love for Antonia and Georg surpassed any minor considerations.'

'Minor!' An entire flood of words threatened to spill from her, except that his mouth covered hers with brutal possession, effectively stilling the flow.

'You don't hate me as much as you pretend,' Aleksi drawled as he lifted his head, and she flung heatedly,

'There's no pretence whatsoever in the way I feel about you!'

Placing a thumb and forefinger beneath her chin, he lifted it so that she had no option but to look at him.

'Perhaps you should query whether a proportion of anger doesn't originate with yourself for enjoying something you insist is merely physical lust,' he alluded silkily.

Did he know how impossible it was for her to come to terms with her own traitorous body? Even now, part of her wanted to melt into his arms, while another part urged her to pull away. It was crazy to feel like this, to be prey to a gamut of emotions so complex that understanding why seemed beyond comprehension.

'I don't enjoy it!' To admit, even to herself, that she did, was something she refused to concede.

'No?'

Aleksi sounded indolently amused, and she flinched away from the brush of his fingers as he trailed them along the edge of her jaw, then traced the throbbing cord at her neck before exploring the hollows at the base of her throat.

'Such a sweet mouth,' he mocked gently, lowering his own to within inches of her softly curved lips. 'And so very kissable.'

The breath seemed to catch in her throat. 'Stop it.' Her eyes clung to his, bright, angry, yet intensely vulnerable. 'Please.'

'Why?' Aleksi murmured as he touched the tip of his tongue against the sensual centre of her lower lip, then began to edge gently inwards in an evocative discovery of the sensitive moist tissues.

'Aleksi.' His name whispered from her lips with something akin to despair. 'No!'

A hand slid beneath her hair, cupping her nape, while the other slipped to her lower back, urging her close, and his mouth continued its light tasting; teasing, deliberately withholding the promise of passion until his touch became an exquisite torture.

She ached for him to deepen the kiss, and she gave a faint sigh as his mouth hardened in irrefutable possession, wiping out every vestige of conscious thought. A deep flame flared into pulsating life beneath his sensual mastery, and each separate nerve-end tingled alive with unbridled ardency as she gave the response he sought.

His clothes, hers, were a dispensable barrier, and she made no protest as he set about freeing them both of any material restriction.

Her body arched of its own accord as his mouth trailed her collarbone and began a downward movement to her breast, silently inviting the wicked ecstasy of his erotic touch, and she cried out as he caressed the delicate swelling bud, luxuriating in the waves of sensation pulsing through her body.

A faint cry of protest silvered the night air as he shifted slightly, then she gave a husky purr of pleasure as he trailed the valley to render a similar supplication to its aching twin.

With consummate skill his fingers traced an evocative path over her silky skin, playing each sensitive pleasure-spot to fever-pitch until she was filled with a deep, aching need that only physical release could assuage.

Alyse barely registered the silken sheets beneath her back, yet the relief she craved was withheld as his mouth feathered the path of his hand in a sensual tasting that was impossibly erotic, making the blood sing through her veins like wildfire until her very soul seemed *his*, and she began to plead, tiny guttural sounds that her conscious mind registered but refused to accept as remotely *hers*.

Hardly aware of her actions, she reached for his head, her fingers curling into the thickness of his hair as she attempted to divert his attention, wanting, *needing* to feel his mouth on hers in hard, hungry passion.

Like something wild and untamed, her body began to thresh beneath his in blatant invitation until at last he plunged deep into the silken core, creating a pulsating rhythmic pattern that took her to the heights and beyond in an explosion of sensual ecstasy that was undeniably his pleasure as well as her own.

For a long time afterwards she seemed encased in a hazy rosy glow, and as she drifted slowly back to reality she became aware of the featherlight touch of his fingers as they traced the moist contours of her body.

She didn't feel capable of moving, and a tiny bubble of laughter died in her throat scarcely before it began.

'What do you find so amusing?'

Alyse turned her head slowly to meet the deep slumbering passion still lurking in those gleaming eyes so close to her own. 'I think you'd better stop. There's a young baby upstairs who'll soon wake for his early morning bottle.'

Aleksi's lips curved warmly as he lifted a hand to her hair and tucked a few collective tendrils back behind her ear. 'I'll feed him, then come back to bed.'

She tried to inject a degree of condemnation into her voice, and failed miserably. 'You're insatiable!'

His lips touched her shoulder, then slid to the curve of her neck in an evocative caress. 'So, my sweet, are you.'

Remembering just how she had reacted in his arms brought a tide of telltale colour to her cheeks, and her eyes clouded with shame.

'Don't,' he bade softly, 'be embarrassed at losing yourself so completely in the sexual act.'

'I might have been faking,' she said unsteadily, and almost died at the degree of lazy humour evident in the gleaming eyes so close to her own.

'Liar,' he drawled. 'Your delight was totally spontaneous.'

'And you're the expert.' She hadn't meant to sound bitter, but it tinged her voice none the less, and her lashes descended to form a protective veil against his compelling scrutiny.

'Sufficiently experienced to give consideration to your pleasure as well as my own.'

'For that I should be grateful?'

'I would advise you against provoking me to demonstrate the difference.'

A faint chill feathered across the surface of her skin, and she shivered. 'I'm going to have a shower.'

She half expected him to stop her, and when he didn't she felt vaguely resentful, electing to take over-long beneath the warm jet of water and even longer attending to her toilette.

Emerging into the bedroom, she slipped carefully into bed and lay still, only to realise within seconds that Aleksi was already asleep, his breathing steady and uncontrived.

For several long minutes she studied his features, aware that even in repose there was an inherent strength apparent, a force that was slightly daunting. Relaxed, his mouth assumed a firm curve, and she experienced the almost irresistible desire to touch it with her own.

Are you *mad*? an inner voice taunted.

With a hand that shook slightly Alyse reached out and snapped off the bedside lamp, then laid her head on the pillow, allowing innate weariness to transport her into a deep, dreamless sleep.

CHAPTER NINE

SUNDAY showed promise of becoming one of those beautiful sunny days south-east Queensland was renowned for producing in the midst of a tropical winter. A slight breeze barely stirred the air, and the sea was a clear translucent blue with scarcely a ripple to disturb its surface.

'The weather is too good not to take the boat out,' Aleksi declared as Alyse entered the kitchen after bathing and feeding Georg. She smelled of baby talc, and her eyes were still soft with the sheer delight of his existence.

Crossing to the pantry, she extracted muesli, retrieved milk from the fridge, then poured generous portions of both into a bowl and carried it to the table.

'I'm sure Rachel and Alexandros will enjoy a day out on the Bay,' she said with studied politeness, and incurred Aleksi's sharp scrutiny.

'There can be no doubt you will come too.'

She forced herself to look at him carefully, noting the almost indecently broad shoulders, the firm sculptured features that portrayed inherent strength of will. He had finished his breakfast, and was seated opposite, a half-finished cup of coffee within easy reach.

'I'm not sure it's fair to expect Melanie to come at such short notice, especially on a Sunday, and

140

particularly when she babysat Georg last night.' Her gaze was remarkably level as she held his dark, faintly brooding gaze. 'Besides, I don't think Georg should be left too often in a babysitter's care. Young children need constancy in their lives, not a succession of minders their parents install merely as a delegation of responsibility to ensure the pursuit of their social existence.'

One eyebrow rose to form a cynical arch. 'My dear Alyse, I totally agree. However, Georg is so young, his major concern is being kept clean and dry, with sustenance available whenever he needs it. I doubt if being left in Melanie's care will damage his psyche. Besides, we'll be back before five.'

Her eyes grew stormy. 'Are you always so damnably persistent?'

'My parents like you,' drawled Aleksi. 'And I'm prepared to do anything that's in my power to please them during the length of their stay.'

'With that in mind,' she began heatedly, 'I would have thought they'd both want to spend as much time with their grandson as possible. Not socialise, or sail the high seas.'

He was silent for a few long minutes, then he said silkily. 'During the past year they've seen their son horrifically injured, and suffered the despair of knowing his life-span was severely limited. As soon as his condition stabilised, Rachel and Alexandros turned their home into a veritable clinic, hiring a team of highly qualified medical staff to care for Georgiou. They gave up everything to spend time with him, taking alternate shifts along with the staff so that either one was always at his side.' He paused, and his voice hardened slightly. 'Now they need to relax and begin to enjoy life again. If that entails socialising and sailing, then so be it.' His eyes assumed an inexorable bleakness. 'Have I made myself clear?'

Alyse pushed her bowl aside, her appetite gone. 'Painfully so.'

'Eat your breakfast.'

'I no longer feel hungry.'

'Maybe my absence will help it return,' Aleksi said drily as he rose to his feet. 'I'll be in the study, making a few calls.'

Within two hours they were on board a large luxuriously-fitted cruiser that lay moored to a jetty on the canal at the bottom of Aleksi's garden.

Alyse had elected to wear tailored white cotton trousers with a yellow sweater. Rachel was similarly attired, and both men wore jeans and casual dark sweaters.

'This is heaven!' Rachel breathed, turning towards her stepson.

Alyse almost gasped out loud at the warmth of his smile as it rested on Rachel's features.

'We'll berth at Sanctuary Cove for lunch. Afterwards, you and Alyse can wander among the boutiques while Alexandros and I sit lazily in the sun enjoying a beer.'

'You're spoiling her,' Alexandros chided his son in a teasing accented drawl, and Rachel laughed.

'All women adore being spoiled by men, don't they, Alyse?'

She was doomed no matter what she said, and, summoning a brilliant smile, she ventured sweetly. 'Definitely.'

Aleksi shot his father a mocking glance. 'I have a feeling the Cove could prove an expensive stopover.'

After a superb seafood lunch the two women strolled at will, visiting several exclusive shops where they purchased a variety of casual resort-styled ensembles, and Alyse fell in love with a pair of imported shoes which she recklessly added to a collection of brightly designed plastic carrier-bags already in her possession.

'What did I tell you?' drawled Aleksi with amusement as Alyse and Rachel joined them in the Yacht Club's lounge.

'Alyse had bought the most gorgeous outfit,' Rachel enthused, taking hold of her husband's out-stretched hand, and her sparkling smile softened as he lifted it to his lips in a gesture that made Alyse's heart execute an unaccustomed flip in silent acknowledgment of the love these two people shared. 'I've persuaded her to wear it to the fashion parade Serita Hubbard invited us to attend at the Cove on Tuesday.'

The cruiser traversed the Bay to reach Sovereign Islands just before five, and after relieving Melanie Alyse checked on Georg to find him stirring and almost ready for his bottle.

'Let me,' Rachel offered at his first wakening cry. 'I'm sure you'll want to shower and change.'

'Thanks,' Alyse acquiesced in gratitude. 'I won't be long.'

When she returned, Aleksi and Alexandros were in the kitchen, and Georg was seated on Rachel's knee, his eyes moving from one to the other, his tiny fists beating the air in undisguised delight.

'See?' beamed Alexandros with Greek pride. 'He is strong, this little one. Look at those legs, those hands! He will grow tall.' He shot his son a laughing glance. 'A good protector for his sisters, an example for his brothers. Yes?'

It was difficult for Alyse to keep her smile in place, but she managed it—just. Part of her wanted to cry out that brothers or sisters for Georgiou's son didn't form part of her plan. Yet she could hardly blame Alexandros for assuming his son's marriage would include other children in years to come.

And what of Aleksi? Was he content with a marriage of expediency which provided a woman in his bed and a mother for his children? Or would he eventually become bored and seek sexual gratification elsewhere?

Far better that she steel her heart against any emotional involvement. Two years wasn't a lifetime, and afterwards she could rebuild her future. A future for herself, for Georg.

Dinner was an impromptu meal of grilled steak and an assortment of salads, with fresh fruit, and followed by a leisurely coffee in the lounge.

Rachel and Alexandros took their leave at nine, declaring a need for an early night, and Alyse felt strangely tired herself from the combination of sea air and warm winter sunshine.

'I'll tidy the kitchen,' she declared as Aleksi closed the front door and set the security system.

'We'll do it together.'

She was already walking ahead of him. 'I can manage.' For some reason his presence swamped her, and she wanted to be alone.

There were only a few cups and saucers, glasses the men had used for a liqueur, and she quickly rinsed and stacked them in the dishwasher, all too aware of Aleksi's presence.

'All finished,' she announced, and made to step past him.

'I've opened a separate bank account with a balance sufficient to meet whatever cash you need,' he told her. 'The details are in the escritoire in your sitting-room, as well as a supplementary card accessing my charge account.'

Alyse felt a surge of resentment, and forced herself to take a deep calming breath. 'I'd prefer to use my own money, and I already have a charge account.'

His gaze focused on her features, noting the faint wariness in the set of her mouth, the proud tilt of her chin, and the determination apparent in those beautiful blue eyes. 'Why be so fiercely independent? It's surely a husband's right to support his wife?'

'The housekeeping, and anything Georg needs,' she agreed. 'But I'll pay for my own clothes.'

'And if I insist?'

'You can insist as much as you like,' she retaliated. 'I won't be cowed into submissive obedience simply out of deference to a marriage certificate.'

Aleksi's eyes hardened fractionally, and his mouth curved to form a mocking smile. 'An enlightened feminist?'

Now she was really angry! 'If you wanted a decorative doll whose sole pleasure was to acquire jewellery and designer clothes at your expense, then you made a mistake in choosing me!'

'I don't think so,' he drawled.

'You *enjoy* our parody of a marriage?' she demanded, and was incensed to hear his husky laughter.

Lifting a hand, he slid it beneath the curtain of her hair, threading his fingers to tug gently at its length, tilting her head.

'I enjoy *you*,' Aleksi accorded silkily. 'The way you continually oppose me, simply for the sheer hell of it.'

Alyse forced herself to hold his gaze, although she was unable to prevent the slight trembling movement of her lips, and she glimpsed the faint flaring evident in the depths of his eyes.

'Be warned, it's a fight you may not win.'

She wanted to lash out and hit him, and only the chill sense of purpose apparent in those dark features stopped her. 'Do you imagine I'll be swayed into becoming emotionally involved simply because you can——' She faltered, momentarily lost for words in the heat of her anger.

'Turn you on?'

'Oh!' she raged, gasping out loud as he drew her close against him, and her struggles were in vain as his head lowered to hers. His lips were firm and warm, caressing with evocative slowness, and she wanted to cry out against his flagrant seduction. It would be so easy to close her eyes and allow herself to be swept away by the magic of his lovemaking. Against her will, the blood began to sing in her veins and her bones turned to liquid as sheer sensation overtook sanity. She became lost, adrift without sense of direction until anger at her own treacherous emotions rose to the surface, and she forcibly broke free from his devastating mouth.

'Let me go, damn you,' she said shakily, straining against the strength of his arms, and her eyes were clouded with an inner struggle she had no intention of confessing—even to herself.

Aleksi held her effortlessly, his expression an inscrutable mask, and it seemed an age before he spoke.

'Go to bed. I have to go over some plans due to be submitted at a meeting tomorrow morning.'

Without a word she turned and moved away from him, her breathing becoming more ragged with every single step, and by the time she reached the bedroom she felt as if she'd run a mile.

Perversity demanded that she sleep in the adjoining sitting-room, but at the last moment common sense prevailed.

What was the point? she decided wearily as she slid in between the sheets on her side of the large bed. Aleksi would undoubtedly remove her, and she was too tired tonight to fight.

An hour later she was still awake, a victim of her own vivid imagination, and it seemed an age before she heard the soft almost imperceptible sound of his entry into the bedroom. In the reflected illumination of Georg's night-light she watched through lowered lashes as he discarded his clothes, and she unconsciously held her breath as he slid into bed. Minutes later she heard his breathing slow and assume a deep steady rhythm.

He had fallen asleep! For some unknown reason that angered her unbearably, and she cursed her own feminine contrariness for the slow-burning ache that gradually consumed her body until she was aflame with the need for physical assuagement.

Alyse glanced around the high-domed marquee with seeming interest. There were more than a hundred women present, each so elegantly attired she could only conclude that their main purpose was to catch the photographer's eye and thereby make the society pages.

Her vivid peacock-green silk suit teamed with black accessories was an attractive foil for Rachel's ensemble in cream and gold.

Champagne flowed, pressed eagerly upon them by handsome formally suited young men.

'Have they been hired by an agency especially for the occasion, do you think?' Alyse queried quietly of Rachel.

'Definitely. They're too much in awe of the cream of society's glitterati.'

'And hopeful of making a conquest?'

Rachel cast her a faintly wicked smile. 'Don't look round, but you've definitely caught one young man's eye.'

Alyse gave a negligent shrug in silent uninterest, and sipped at her champagne. 'Tell me about Greece. Do you like living there?'

Rachel's expression softened. 'We have several homes in various parts of the world. Some are splendid, but the one I love best is situated in the bay of a small island off the main coast. It's a fairy-tale—no cars, just peace and solitude with the only means of entry via boat or helicopter. It was there that Alexandros and Aleksi taught Georgiou to sail.'

Alyse sensed the older woman's sadness, and touched her hand in a gesture of silent sympathy.

'It's all right, my dear. As one gets older, one realises there is only *now*. Memories can't be changed, and I count myself fortunate that mine are many and such happy ones. Our two sons were a constant delight, although Georgiou was the friv-olous one, coveting the thrill of the moment behind the wheel of a high-powered motorboat or car. I lived in constant fear of the day he might make a misjudgment.'

Alyse had to ask. 'And Aleksi?'

'He was more serious, and despite the difference in age and character he and Georgiou were very close. During those awful months after the ac-cident, he flew back and forth to Athens countless times, and when he wasn't there he rang every second day.'

'Alyse! How wonderful of you to bring Rachel, darling,' a husky feminine voice enthused, and she turned her head to see Serita Hubbard in a vivid white ensemble that undoubtedly bore a Diane Fries label.

'Serita,' she returned politely.

'I've arranged for us to be seated together at lunch. If we do become separated during the fashion parade, just meet me in front of the marquee afterwards.' Serita's smile flashed friendly warmth. 'Must dash, there's a slight muddle with tickets supposed to be handed out by one of the committee members. She thought I'd collected them, and I was under the impression that *she* had. I need to show my list to the organiser. There are quite a few people here you've met, and Solange said she'd probably be running late. Do mingle, won't you?'

It was a brilliantly orchestrated parade, quite the best Alyse had attended, for the models were top-class professionals and the clothes not only superb, but many were available from the Cove boutiques.

'See anything you particularly like?' Rachel asked, then laughed as she glimpsed the appreciative gleam in her daughter-in-law's eyes.

'An hour with our marked catalogues after lunch?' Alyse suggested.

'Definitely,' Rachel agreed. 'And talking of lunch, we'd better head for the marquee entrance.'

The restaurant chosen for the venue was cantilevered out over the water, with splendid views of the harbour-front villas and a flotilla of luxury craft moored at an adjacent marina.

Solange was seated opposite, beside Serita, Marta, Chrissie, Kate and Annabel, and Alyse felt as if she was facing an inquisition committee.

The same impeccably suited young men who had so earnestly served champagne before the parade also waited on tables, and Alyse found it amusing to be the recipient of one particular man's attentive solicitude.

'Darling, you do seem to have made a hit,' Solange declared artlessly. 'Are you going to slip him your phone number?'

Without faltering, Alyse responded with an absence of guile. 'With a young baby to care for, I haven't the time or the inclination to foster the attention of a toy-boy.' She offered a brilliant smile. 'Besides, I doubt if Aleksi would be amused.'

Solange's eyes narrowed slightly. 'A little jealousy stimulates a marriage, surely?'

Oh, heavens, she was beginning to feel like a butterfly pinned to the wall, with numerous pairs of interested eyes waiting to see if she'd squirm! 'Do you think so?' she queried, then gave a light faintly husky laugh. 'Aleksi would probably beat me.'

Serita smiled in silent amusement, while Solange merely fixed Alyse with an unblinking glare. 'Dominic insists we host a dinner party on Saturday evening,' she drawled. 'I'll ring Aleksi with the details.' Her gaze rested on Rachel. 'You must come too, of course.'

'We leave for Sydney tomorrow to spend time with my sister, so we won't be here, I'm afraid,' Rachel declined graciously, and Solange gave a slight negligent shrug.

It was after two when Alyse and Rachel managed to slip away, and within an hour and a half they were heading towards Sovereign Islands with a few selected purchases reposing on the rear seat of the car.

Alyse had planned an informal dinner at home for Rachel and Alexandros's last evening on the Coast, and there was a certain sense of sadness apparent when it came time for them to leave, for she would miss Rachel's company.

'A week isn't long,' the older woman assured her as she gave her an affectionate hug. 'And I'll phone frequently to check on my grandson.'

'I shall probably have to restrain her from making at least three calls a day,' Alexandros declared with amusement as he slid into the rear seat of the car.

Alyse moved quickly indoors as soon as the BMW drew out of sight. The house seemed to envelop her, so large and strangely silent, and she was unable to suppress a feeling of acute vulnerability.

Georg was sleeping peacefully, and she quickly showered before slipping into bed, where she lay wide-eyed and reflective as a dozen conflicting thoughts vied for supremacy in a brain too emotionally fraught to make sense of any one of them.

When she heard Aleksi return she closed her eyes in the pretence of sleep, aware of a deep ache in the region of her heart. It would have been wonderful to seek the comfort of his arms, to have them enfold her close, and simply hold her. A few tender kisses, the soothing touch of his hands, so that she felt secure in the knowledge that she was infinitely cherished.

Except that such an image belonged in the realm of fantasy, and she gave up waiting for him to join her in bed as the minutes dragged on. The only feasible explanation seemed to be a wealth of paper-

work awaiting him in the study, and when she woke
the following morning it was to discover he was
already up and dressed.

In a way Alyse found it a relief to spend the following few days quietly at home. There were letters
to write, and she rang Miriam Stanford at the Perth
boutique to learn that everything was progressing
extremely smoothly—almost as if she had hardly
been missed, Alyse thought wryly.

During the afternoon she prepared their evening
meal, taking infinite care with a carefully selected
menu. Aleksi invariably arrived home just before
five, and after a quick shower he would insist on
changing and feeding Georg.

'He needs to recognise a male figure in his young
life,' Aleksi had said the day after Rachel and
Alexandros departed for Sydney. 'Besides, this is
the only time I have to give to him five nights out
of seven.'

It left Alyse free to set the table and make a last-
minute check on dinner. Just watching the tiny baby
in Aleksi's arms wrenched her emotions, for she
could imagine Aleksi being an integral part of
Georg's existence, playing ball, teaching him to
swim, simply being there throughout his formative
adolescent years. Each time the pull at her heartstrings became a little more painful, and she was
gripped with a terrifying fear that although removing Georg to Perth was right for her, it wouldn't
necessarily be right for Georg.

Conversation over dinner was restricted to their
individual daily activities, polite divertissements
that lasted until dessert had been consumed, then

Aleksi would invariably disappear into the study and not emerge until long after she had gone to bed.

The possibility that his actions might be deliberate angered her unbearably, and she found herself consciously plotting a subtle revenge.

The occasion of Solange and Dominic Rochas' dinner party seemed ideal, and on Friday morning Alyse rang Melanie and arranged for her to babysit Georg while she went shopping for something suitable to wear.

The desire to stun was uppermost, and she found exactly what she wanted in an exclusive boutique. In black, its bodice was strapless, exquisitely boned and patterned in black sequins, with a slim-fitting knee-length skirt that hugged her slender hips. A long floating silk scarf draped at her neck to flow down her back completed the outfit, and, ignoring the outrageously expensive price-tag, she simply charged it. Shoes came next, and she chose a perfume to match her new image.

As Saturday progressed it was impossible to quell her reservations, and after feeding and settling Georg into his cot she quickly showered, then settled down in front of the mirror with a variety of cosmetics.

It seemed to take an age to achieve the desired effect, but eventually she stood back, satisfied with the result. Her hair was brushed into its customary smooth bell-shape, and in a moment of indecision she caught its length and twisted it high into a knot on top of her head.

Yes? No? *'Damn,'* she muttered softly, beginning to view the evening ahead with a certain degree of dread.

Solange was someone with whom she doubted it was possible ever to share an empathy. Even on so short an acquaintance, it was impossible not to be aware that the interior decorator lusted after Aleksi, and the mere fact that Alyse was Aleksi's wife stacked the odds heavily against her from the start.

Her dynamic husband had a lot to answer for, she decided as she crossed to the large mirrored closet and slid back the door. Although to be fair, he couldn't help his dark good looks, nor his sexual appeal, for both were an inherent quality, and, while some men might deliberately exploit such assets, honesty forced her to concede that Aleksi did not.

A tiny frown of doubt momentarily creased her forehead as she extracted *the* dress from its hanger. Although it had been selected to shock, she suddenly developed reservations as to its suitability. Remembering precisely why she had purchased it deepened her frown, and her eyes clouded with indecision. What had seemed an excellent means of revenge at the time no longer held much appeal, and she was about to slip it back on to the hanger when she heard Aleksi move into the dressing-room.

'What time have you organised for Melanie to arrive?'

'Seven,' she answered, turning slightly towards him, watching as he discarded the towel knotted low at his hips, then he stepped into dark briefs and reached for a snowy white shirt.

His physique was splendid, emanating innate power and strength, and Alyse was unable to prevent the surge of sheer sexual pleasure at the sight of him.

Impossibly cross with herself, she slid down the zip fastener and stepped into the gown. Her fingers automatically slid the zip into place, then smoothed its sleek lines over her hips before settling on the gentle swell of her breasts, which were exposed to a greater degree than she remembered when originally trying on the gown.

'Did you select that with the intention of raising every red-blooded man's blood pressure at the party tonight, or simply mine?' Aleksi drawled from behind, and she slowly turned to face him.

'Why would I deliberately want to raise yours?' she queried sweetly.

'The result is stunning, but I may not be able to stand guard at your side every minute during the evening to fend off the attention you'll undoubtedly receive,' he warned with an edge of mockery, and her eyes acquired a fiery sparkle.

'Really? Are you suggesting I should change?' There was anger just beneath the surface, and a crazy desire to oppose him.

His expression darkened fractionally. 'Yes.'

'And if I choose not to?'

'The only choice you have, Alyse, is to remove the dress yourself or have me do it for you.' His voice was hard and inflexible, and her chin lifted in angry rejection, her eyes becoming stormy pools mirroring incredulous rage.

'Why, you chauvinistic domineering *pig*,' she re-iterated heatedly. 'How dare you?'

'Oh, I *dare*,' he drawled silkily, and a shiver slithered the length of her spine at his determined resolve.

'It's the latest fashion and cost a small fortune,' she flung angrily. 'And besides, I won't have you dictate what I can and can't wear!'

He reached out a hand and caught hold of her chin between thumb and forefinger, tightening his grasp when she moved to wrench it away. 'Stop arguing simply for the sake of it.'

'I'm *not*!' She was so incredibly furious, it was all she could do not to hit him.

'Surely you know me well enough by now to understand that you can't win,' he cautioned with deadly softness.

'You mean you won't allow me to!'

He was silent for a few seemingly long seconds, and she held his gaze fearlessly.

'A woman who deliberately flaunts her body indulges in subtle advertising of a kind which promises to deliver. Wear the dress when we're dining alone, and I'll be suitably appreciative.'

'Oh, for heavens's sake! I don't believe any of this!'

'Believe,' he said hardily. 'Now, change.'

'No.'

'Defiance, Alyse, simply for the sake of it? Aren't you being rather foolish?'

'If you derive a sadistic thrill from forcibly removing a woman's clothes, then go ahead and do it.'

His eyes assumed a chilling intensity, and she was suddenly filled with foreboding. Without a word his hands closed over her shoulders, propelling her forward, and her chin tilted in silent rebellion as he lowered his head.

His mouth took possession of hers, forcing her lips apart in a demanding assault that showed little mercy and she held back a silent groan of despair as he deliberately began a wreaking devastation.

When he relinquished his hold, her jaw ached, even her neck, and her eyes were bright with a mixture of anger and unshed tears.

His eyes bore an inscrutability she was unable to penetrate, and her mouth trembled slightly.

'Change, Alyse,' he directed inflexibly. 'Or I'll do it for you.'

She looked at him with scathing enmity. 'And if I refuse, you'll undoubtedly admininster some other form of diabolical punishment.'

'Take care,' he warned. 'My temper is on a tight rein as it is.'

'So I must conform, at whatever cost? That's almost akin to barbarism!'

An eyebrow lifted in sardonic cynicism. 'So far I've treated you with kid gloves.'

A disbelieving laugh emerged from her throat. 'You have to be joking!'

'Only an innocent would fail to appreciate the slow hand of a considerate lover intent on giving as much pleasure as he intends to take.' His expression became dark and forbidding. 'Continue opposing me, and I'll demonstrate the difference.'

Alyse looked at him with unblinking solemnity, frighteningly aware of his strength and sense of purpose. To continue waging this particular war was madness, yet some alien stubborn streak refused to allow her to capitulate.

'Don't threaten me,' she warned.

'Is that what you imagine I'm doing?' His voice held a hateful drawling quality that sent shivers of fear scudding down her spine.

'What other word would you choose?'

'Take off the dress, Alyse,' he warned softly, 'or I won't answer for the consequences.'

It was as if her limbs were frozen and entirely separate from the dictates of her brain, for she stood perfectly still, her eyes wide and unblinking as he swore softly beneath his breath.

Then she cried out as his fingers reached for the zip fastener and slid it down. Seconds later the exotic creation fell to her feet to lie in a heap of silk and heavy satin. All that remained between her and total nudity was a wisp of silky bikini briefs, and her hands rose in spontaneous reaction to cover her breasts.

With deliberate slowness Aleksi slid down the zip of his trousers, and it was only as he began to remove them that she became galvanised into action.

Except that it was far too late, and she struggled helplessly against him, hating the strength of the hands that moulded her slim curves against the hard muscular contours of his body. Her briefs were dispensed seconds after his own, and there was nothing she could do to avoid the relentless pressure of his mouth. He lifted her up against him, parting her thighs so they straddled his hips, and without any preliminaries he plunged deep inside, his powerful thrust stretching silken tissues to their furthest limitation.

Relinquishing her mouth, he lowered his head to her breast, and she cried out as he took possession of one roseate peak, savouring it with flagrant hunger before rendering several bites to the soft underside of the swollen peak.

Alyse balled her hands into fists and beat them against his shoulders then gave a startled cry of disbelief as his hands shifted down to grip her bottom, lifting her slightly as he plunged even deeper.

Then he stilled, and she felt him swell even further inside her, while the hand at her back slid to clasp her nape, urging her head back as he forced her to meet his gaze.

She wanted to vilify him for an act of savagery, yet among the outrage had been a degree of primitive enjoyment, and she hated herself almost as much as she hated him for it.

He knew; she glimpsed the knowledge in the depth of his eyes, and hated him even more for the faint mocking smile that curved his lips.

Hands that had been hard gentled as they cradled her, and he buried his mouth against the hollows at the base of her throat, teasing the rapidly beating pulse there with his tongue, then, just as she thought he was about to release her, he began a slow circling movement with his hips, taking her with him until, almost as a silent act of atonement, pleasure overtook discomfort and her senses became caught up with his, spiralling towards a mutual climax that made her cling to him in unashamed abandon.

Afterwards she showered, then dressed in a vivid emerald-green ruched satin gown with a demure neckline and fitted lines that accentuated her petite figure.

Keeping her make-up to an understated minimum, she accented her eyes and outlined her mouth in soft pink before checking on Georg.

Melanie had arrived and was comfortably settled in the lounge when Alyse emerged several minutes later, and she greeted the girl pleasantly, then accepted Aleksi's light clasp on her elbow as they took their leave and made their way to the garage.

'I rang Solange and told her not to hold dinner as we'd been unavoidably detained,' Aleksi told her as the BMW cleared the driveway. 'I've made a reservation at the Club's restaurant. We'll eat there.'

Alyse took a deep breath, then released it slowly. 'I'm not hungry.'

'You'll eat something, even if it's only *soupe du jour*,' he declared with unruffled ease.

The fact that she did owed nothing to his insistence, and seated opposite him in the well-patronised room she did justice to soup, declined a main course in favour of a second starter of sautéed prawns, refused sweets and settled for a Jamaican coffee.

It was almost ten when the BMW passed security and slid into a reserved car space in the spacious grounds adjoining a prestigious block of apart-

ments housing Solange and Dominic Rochas' penthouse apartment, and Alyse stood in meditative
silence as they rode the private lift to the uppermost floor.

CHAPTER TEN

'ALEKSI!' Solange purred, immediately embracing him in a manner that slipped over the edge from affection and bordered on blatant intimacy. She stepped back, her eyes shifting with glittering condescension to the woman at his side. 'Alyse.' She tucked a hand into the curve at Aleksi's elbow and drew him forward.

'Solange,' Alyse murmured in polite acknowledgment. 'How lovely to see you.'

Liar, a silent voice taunted. She felt about as well equipped to parry a verbal cut and thrust with the glamorous and very definitely bitchy Solange Rochas as flying over the moon! 'Charming' was the key-word, and she'd act her socks off—subtly, of course, with the innocuous innocence of an ingénue.

'Everyone is here,' Solange declared huskily. 'I was so disappointed you couldn't make dinner.'

'We were delayed,' drawled Aleksi, and Alyse merely proffered a sweet smile when Solange cast her a brief interrogatory glance.

Aleksi had sought to teach her a lesson, and it didn't bear thinking about the resultant passion that flared between them in the aftermath of anger.

'Unfortunately,' Alyse added with sweet regret, and almost died as Aleksi caught hold of her hand

and lifted it to his lips, deliberately kissing each finger in turn.

His eyes blazed with indefinable emotion for a brief few seconds, then became dark and faintly hooded as he threaded his fingers through her own and kept them there.

Liquid fire coursed through her veins, activating each separate nerve-ending as it centred deep within the vulnerable core of her femininity, and she ached, aware of bruised tissues still sensitive from his wounding invasion.

Almost as if he was aware of her thoughts his thumb brushed back and forth across the throbbing veins at her wrist, and her pulse leapt in recognition of his touch. If she hadn't retained such a vivid memory of his wrath, she could almost imagine the gesture was meant as a silent token of— what? Apology? Remorse?

'I'm sure you had a very good reason, darling,' Solange declared, her eyes narrowing with speculative interest as she drew them into the lounge. 'I'll get you a drink, then there's something we must discuss.' She gave a brittle laugh, then offered in throwaway explanation to Alyse, 'Business, I'm afraid.' Then she turned away, effectively shutting Alyse out. 'The Holmes residence. You absolutely *must* dissuade Anthea against the shade of pink she insists on having as the main theme. It really won't do at all.'

Alyse moved slightly, watching with detached fascination as Aleksi's mouth curved into a wry smile.

'If you're unable to exercise your professional influence, Solange, then you may have to accept that it's Anthea's house and she's paying the bills.'

'But it's *my* reputation.'

'Then relinquish the commission.'

The woman's eyes glittered as she made a moue of distaste. 'The problem with the nouveaux riches, darling,' she conceded, with a careless shrug, 'is their gauche taste.'

'Why not show her a visual example of one of your previous commissions?' ventured Alyse, thereby forcing Solange's attention. 'Magazine layouts and countless sample swatches can be confusing.'

Solange looked as if she had just been confronted with an unwanted dissident. 'Something that would be an impossible intrusion on a former client's privacy,' she dismissed with patronising hauteur.

'If I were really delighted with the décor of my home, I'd be only too pleased to share it,' Alyse qualified quietly.

At that precise moment Dominic came forward to greet them, and his deep smile was infinitely mocking.

'Ah, there you are,' he greeted, flicking his sister a brief questioning glance before acknowledging Aleksi, then his gaze settled on Alyse with musing indulgence. 'You look gorgeous, as always. What can I get you to drink?'

'Mineral water will be fine,' Alyse requested without guile, while Aleksi opted for soda with a splash of whisky.

Her glass was icy, its rim sugar-frosted, and she sipped the contents, silently applauding the dash of lime juice and twist of lemon.

'Aleksi,' a soft breathy voice intruded, and Alyse turned slightly and failed to recognise the owner of that husky feminine sound. The slight pause was deliberate, as was her deliberately sexy pout. 'Didn't the babysitter arrive on time?'

Alyse shifted slightly and summoned a brilliant smile. 'Aleksi is to blame. He didn't approve of what I'd chosen to wear, and...' She trailed to a halt, made an expressive shrug, then directed the man at her side a wicked smile. 'One thing led to another.'

The stunning brunette's scarlet-painted mouth parted slightly, then tightened into a thin, uncompromising line.

'How refreshingly honest, darling,' drawled Dominic, and his eyes gleamed devilishly. 'I presume it was worth missing dinner?'

'Really, Dominic,' Solange derided in a voice dripping with vitriol, 'must you be so crude?'

'My husband can be——' Alyse paused, deliberately effecting a carefully orchestrated smile, 'very persuasive.' There, let them make of it what they chose, and be damned! She was heartily sickened by the various snide comments, the none too subtle innuendo designed to shock or at least unsettle her. Timidity had no place in her demeanour if she were to succeed within Aleksi's sophisticated circle, and it would seem her only strength lay in presenting an imperturbable if faintly humorous exterior.

Aleksi's eyes narrowed faintly, but she really didn't care any more.

'I'm sure Dominic won't mind keeping me amused for a while if Solange would prefer you to confer with Anthea,' she said sweetly, and glimpsed Solange's smile of triumph.

'I'll speak to Anthea later,' Aleksi determined mildly, although there was nothing remotely mild about the warning pressure of the hand clasping her own. 'Shall we mingle?' he queried pleasantly. 'We can't monopolise our hosts' attention.'

Solange's expression clearly revealed that he, at least, could monopolise her attention any time he chose, and Alyse had little choice but to drift at Aleksi's side as he drew her among the glittering guests.

The penthouse apartment provided a brilliant advertisement for Solange and Dominic's interior decorating expertise. Perfection personified, Alyse thought, with the smallest detail adhered to from the exquisite floral arrangements to the attire of the hired staff. Even the music had been deliberately selected to blend with conversation rather than provide a cacophonous intrusion.

'Aren't you being a little careless?' Aleksi queried with deceptive calm as they paused near the edge of the room, and Alyse idly twirled the contents of her glass.

'Another guessing game, Aleksi?' she countered, deliberately meeting his gaze.

'I find it particularly unamusing to have my wife offer provocative comments to a known society playboy.'

'Dominic?' Her eyes widened measurably, then became startlingly direct. 'Really? When almost every woman in the room homes in on your presence like a prize bitch in heat?'

'Aren't you being overly dramatic?'

'No,' she said simply, and had to force herself to stand perfectly still as he lifted a hand and brushed his fingers across her cheek.

'Does it bother you?'

Yes, she wanted to cry out. It bothers me like hell. Yet if she acknowledged how she felt it would amount to an admission of sorts, and she wasn't ready to accord him any advantage. Instead, she held his gaze and returned evenly, 'Why should it?'

Something flared in his eyes, an infinitesimal flame that was quickly masked. 'We can always leave.'

Her surprise was undisguised. 'We've only just arrived.'

'Do you want to stay?'

What a loaded question! Whichever way she answered would be equally damning and, although she didn't particularly want to remain, she wasn't ready to go home.

'Aleksi! I'm so glad you're here.'

The intrusion was welcome, and Alyse glanced with interest towards the petite blonde hovering nearby as Aleksi effected an introduction.

'Anthea Holmes, my wife Alyse.'

'How nice to meet you,' she acknowledged with gracious charm before turning towards Aleksi. 'I'm almost at my wits' end!' Her pretty hazel eyes darkened with anxiety. 'The house is superb, but I can't help wondering when I'll be able to move in.'

'Solange mentioned a conflict of interest over the colour scheme,' Aleksi acknowledged. 'What seems to be the problem?'

'A shade of pink,' Anthea said at once. 'I originally chose an extremely delicate salmon shade to blend with cream, and utilising various apricot tones as the main theme. Solange insists on shell-pink to blend with mushroom and various tones of amethyst.' She turned towards Alyse. 'What do you think?'

Oh lord, Alyse groaned inwardly. Why drag me into it? 'I wouldn't presume to infringe on Solange's territory,' she ventured diplomatically. 'But surely it's a personal choice?' Solange was bound to feel insulted if she discovered Anthea had solicited another opinion, especially *hers*, and, while the woman could never be her friend, she didn't particularly want her as an enemy.

'I'd appreciate your viewpoint.'

'Whose viewpoint, darling?'

Alyse almost groaned aloud, and was somewhat startled to see that Anthea was not in the least perturbed that Solange had overheard part of their conversation.

'I've invited Alyse to see the house.'

It was clearly evident that the cat had been well and truly placed among the pigeons, for Solange cast her a sharp narrowed glance. 'Well, of course, if you value the opinion of an unqualified outsider over and above my own...' She let her voice trail to a deliberate halt.

'Alyse is naturally interested in my work,' Aleksi inserted smoothly. 'Aware, also, that I consider my individual clients' wishes are paramount.' His dark eyes encompassed Solange's features in silent warning before switching to Anthea. 'I'll ring my painting contractor tomorrow, then confirm with you and have him meet us at the house.'

Anthea's relief was instantly evident. 'Thank you.' She touched Alyse's hand. 'I'll be mailing invitations to a housewarming party just as soon as I've settled in. You will both come, won't you?'

'We'd be delighted,' Aleksi responded warmly, and Anthea looked quite overcome.

'Another conquest, darling?' Solange asked archly the instant Anthea had melted into the crowd.

'Anthea is a very pleasant woman,' he acknowledged coolly. 'And a valued client of mine.' But not necessarily of yours.

The words remained unspoken, yet Alyse was supremely conscious of the veiled threat. Aware also that Solange sensed his displeasure, for her features underwent a startling transformation.

'A figurative rap across the knuckles, Aleksi?' Solange queried provocatively. 'Dear little Anthea can have her salmon pink and cream with apricot, if that's what she wants. Why, when she has such rigid ideas, she should consult with an interior designer is beyond me.' Her exquisitely manicured hands fluttered through the air. 'One mustn't forget the newly rich consider it quite the thing to gather opinions without the slightest intention of applying one of them.'

'Perhaps because they prefer to impose something of their own personality,' said Alyse, and drew a raised eyebrow in response.

'Really, darling,' Solange gave a faint shudder, 'I hope this doesn't mean you intend making too many changes in Aleksi's home. It's total perfection just as it is.'

'An incredible compliment,' a drawling voice intervened, 'considering you had no part in it.'

'Dominic. Eavesdropping again?'

Alyse's glass was whisked out of her hand before she had an opportunity to protest, and she made no demur when Dominic took hold of her elbow.

'Come and let me show you the view from the window,' Dominic insisted. 'It's really spectacular.'

It was; beyond the wide expanse of plate-glass tiny pinpricks of light outlined countless high-rise buildings along the foreshore curving in an arc towards the ocean. The sky was a crisp cool indigo, meeting and merging on the horizon with a moon-dappled darkened sea.

'It's beautiful,' Alyse said softly, caught up in the thrall of man-made monoliths of concrete steel and glass blending with the stark simplicity of nature.

'I can pay you the same compliment.'

She stood quite still at the degree of warmth in his voice. 'I shall accept that in the context in which it should be given,' she said lightly, and heard his purring laugh.

'I'm shattered,' he remarked musingly. 'I imagined you to be an innocent in paradise.'

'Innocence belongs to the very young.'

'Cynicism too,' he mocked. 'From one whose air of fragility is positively intriguing. A mystery woman-child with clear eyes and a beautiful smile. I hope Aleksi appreciates you.'

Of its own accord her smile deepened, and she laughed, a light bubbly sound filled with genuine amusement.

'No comment?'

'May I choose not to?' Alyse countered, and her eyes flew wide as he took hold of her hand.

'Old-fashioned values?'

'I consider a respect for one's privacy is merely good manners,' she corrected solemnly, and saw his eyes lose their customary jaded expression in favour of what appeared to be genuine warmth.

'What a pity Aleksi saw you first.'

Even if he hadn't, she couldn't imagine herself being smitten by Dominic's superficial charm. Whereas Aleksi possessed depth and strength of character, the man at her side bore a shallow brittleness that was undoubtedly motivated by self-obsession.

She turned slightly, unconsciously seeking a familiar dark head across the crowded room, and her eyes widened as they encountered Aleksi's riveting gaze. He was engaged in conversation with a group of men she had met but vaguely remembered, and it was almost as if he knew she had conducted a mental comparison, for she saw one eyebrow lift in silent query.

For one crazy moment she felt as if everything faded away and there was no one else in the room. It was totally mad, but she wanted to be with him.

Not only by his side, but in his arms, held close, and loved with such incredible tenderness that she would probably cry from the sheer joy of it.

Her eyes widened and assumed an ethereal mistiness for an incredibly brief second, then she offered a slightly shaky smile and turned back towards Dominic, feeling completely disorientated as she launched into a conversational discourse that was unrelated to anything of particular interest.

It must have made sense, she thought vaguely, for Dominic responded with a flow of words she barely registered, let alone absorbed, and she gave a mental shake as if to clear her head.

What on earth was the matter with her?

'Dominic—you won't mind if I rescue my wife?'

Alyse heard Aleksi's deep drawling voice an instant before his arm curved round her waist, and she felt all her fine body hairs lift up in silent recognition of his presence.

'I assure you she isn't in the slightest danger.'

Never from Dominic. Aleksi, however, was an entirely different matter!

'Shall we leave?' Aleksi queried, bending his head down to hers, and she shrugged.

'If you like.'

'It's barely midnight!' protested Dominic, and Aleksi responded smoothly,

'We said before we left that we wouldn't be late.'

'But surely you can ring the babysitter?'

'I think not.'

In the car Alyse sat in silence, grateful for the light music emitting from stereo speakers, and she simply let her head fall back against the seat's headrest as the BMW purred through the darkened streets.

On reaching home Melanie reported that Georg hadn't even stirred, and Alyse checked his sleeping form while Aleksi saw the young girl into her car and then locked up.

Slipping out of her shoes, Alyse stepped through to the en suite bathroom and set about removing her make-up. Her features looked pale, and her eyes seemed much too large, she decided broodingly. Even her mouth bore a faintly bruised fullness, and she ran the tip of her tongue along the edge of her lower lip in unconscious exploration before lifting the brush to her hair.

She had only just begun when Aleksi entered the bathroom, and her hand faltered slightly as he moved close and took the brush from her nerveless fingers.

She knew she should protest, but no words left her lips, and she stood still beneath his touch, held as if enmeshed in some elusive sensual spell.

The temptation to close her eyes was irresistible, and when the brush strokes ceased she let her lashes flicker up as she met his gaze via mirrored reflection.

His hands moved to the zip fastening of her dress, and she made no effort to prevent its slithering folds slipping down to the floor, nor the thin scrap of satin and lace of her bra as he released the clasp.

Fingers traced the length of her spine, then spanned her waist before slipping up to cup her breasts. His breath fanned her nape, and she let her head fall forward in silent invitation, unable to suppress a shiver of sheer reaction as his lips sought a vulnerable pulsebeat and savoured it until tiny shockwaves of pleasure spiralled from deep within her central core.

It was almost as if he wanted her to see the effect of his touch on her body, and she moved back against him, arching slightly as his fingers teased the soft fullness of her breasts, then shaped them as the peaks tautened and became engorged with anticipatory pleasure. With detached fascination she glimpsed the soft smudges where hours earlier his mouth had wrought havoc as he had sought to punish, and her eyes clouded in remembered pain.

Hands slid to her shoulders and turned her round to face him, and she was powerless against the caressing softness of his lips as they brushed each bruise in turn before trailing up to settle on her trembling mouth.

His touch was an evocative supplication, teasing, tasting, *loving* in a manner that made her want to cry, and when he slid an arm beneath her knees and lifted her into his arms she could only bury her face against the hollow of his neck.

In bed she closed her eyes, grateful for the darkness as he led her with infinite slowness towards the sweet oblivion of sexual fulfilment, and she clung to him unashamedly, adrift in a sea of her own emotions.

A week ago, even yesterday, she had been so positive her planned escape to Perth was what she desperately wanted. Now, the thought of walking away from Aleksi caused doubt and indecision, and for the first time she was filled with despair.

If she stayed, it would have to be for all the right reasons, and she doubted if love formed any part of his rationale. The most she could hope for would be an affectionate loyalty, a bond founded by Georg's existence. Somehow it wasn't enough.

For what seemed like an hour Alyse lay awake staring at the shadowed ceiling, a hundred differing emotions clouding her mind in kaleidoscopic confusion.

Nothing was the same; *nothing*, Alyse decided sadly as she slid carefully out of bed, each movement in seeming slow motion so as not to disturb the man sleeping silently at her side.

How could she leave? Yet how could she stay? a tiny voice taunted as she crossed to the sitting-room and paused in front of Georg's cot. He was so dear, *everything*, she decided fiercely, unable to prevent her eyes misting with unshed tears.

Moonlight streamed through the opaque curtains, creating an area of shade and silvery light, while long shadowy fingers magnified everything beyond. The balustrading surrounding the pool resembled a grotesque caricature of angles that were unrelated to its original structure, and the pool itself appeared a deep, dark void.

Like her heart. Dear lord in heaven, was it too much to expect happiness? Was she being a fool to even hope it could be achieved?

She had no idea how long she stood there, and it was acute sensory perception rather than an actual sound that alerted her to Aleksi's presence.

'What are you doing here?' His voice was deep and husky, and she was unable to prevent the shiver that shook her slim frame.

Hands caught her shoulders in a light clasp, then slid down her arms, slipping beneath her elbows to curve round her waist as he pulled her gently back against him.

'You'll catch a chill,' he chided softly, burying his lips against the vulnerable hollow at the edge of her neck.

I am cold, so cold there should be ice instead of blood in my veins. As long as I live, I'll never be warm again.

'Come back to bed.'

No! a silent voice screamed out in silent agony. That was her downfall, the place where she fought countless battles and inevitably lost. Her eyes began to ache with barely suppressed tears, and her vision shimmered as two huge crystalline drops hovered, momentarily dammed by protective lower lashes.

'Alyse?'

Hands gently turned her towards him, and she was powerless to evade the strong fingers that took hold of her chin and tilted it upwards.

The movement released her tears, and there was nothing she could do to prevent their slow trickling descent.

It was impossible that they might escape his attention; too much to hope for that he might choose not to comment on their existence.

She looked at him, her head caught at a proud angle, its planes sharply defined, yet his profile was indistinct viewed through a watery mist that failed to dissipate no matter how often she blinked.

I'm caught in a trap, she thought, feeling incredibly sad. Bound within a silken web whose strands hold me prisoner as surely as if they were comprised of tensile steel.

'Tears?'

Amusement was sadly lacking, and in its place was a depth she was almost afraid to analyse.

A finger traced one rivulet, then followed the path of its twin. 'Why?'

For all the dreams, the love I have to give; hope, eternity.

'Alyse?'

His voice was as soft as velvet, his breath warm as it fanned her cheek, and she closed her eyes against the featherlight touch of his lips at her temples, on her eyelids, then finally her mouth.

It was seduction at its most dangerous, and she almost succumbed as he lifted her into his arms and carried her back into the bedroom. The only thing that stopped her was the degree of treachery involved; sexual pleasure without emotional commitment was no longer enough, and she couldn't pretend any more.

Gently he let her slide down to her feet.

'Suppose you tell me what's bothering you?'

Where could she begin? By saying she'd fallen in love with him? A slight tremor shook her thinly clad form at the thought of his cynicism on learning that she had joined a number of women who had fallen prey to his fatal brand of sexual sensuality.

'I'm almost afraid to insist.' There was an indefinable quality in his voice, a rawness that sent her lashes sweeping upward in swift disbelief.

Alyse was aware of him watching every visible flicker of emotion, and she forced herself to breathe steadily to deploy the deep thudding beat of her heart.

'Please,' Aleksi demanded gently, letting his hands slide up to cup her face.

Something she dared not begin to believe might be hope stirred deep within. 'I don't think I can.'

His lips touched hers with the lightness of a butterfly's wing. 'Try.'

Dared she? No matter how she voiced it, the words would sound calculatingly cold, and afterwards there could be no retraction, only expiation when mere explanation might not be enough.

'Georg deserves to have you as his father,' she faltered at last, unsure whether she had the courage to continue, and something she could have sworn was pain darkened his eyes.

There was a strained silence, then Aleksi drawled with dangerous silkiness, 'You don't consider Georg deserves to have you as his mother?'

Alyse felt as if she was treading on eggshells, yet now she'd started there was nothing else for her but to go on. 'I love him,' she burst out. 'How can you doubt that?'

'Your love for *him* isn't in question.'

The breath caught in her throat, then escaped in a ragged expulsion as her features paled, and she actually swayed, fearing she might fall. Somehow the thought that Aleksi might know the extent of

her emotions made her feel physically ill. She had
to get away from him, if only temporarily. 'Please—
let me go,' she begged.

'Never.'

There was an inflexibility apparent that made her
feel terribly afraid.

'I think you'll reconsider when you realise the
only reason I entered into marriage was the prospect
of obtaining a divorce and legal custody of Georg,'
she began shakily, glimpsing a muscle tense along
the edge of his jaw as she fought for the strength
to continue. 'Almost right from the beginning I
plotted the ultimate revenge,' she continued unsteadily, struggling to find the right words, aware
that now she'd started, she couldn't stop. 'Two
years, that's all I figured it would take before I
could return with Georg to Perth.'

His silence was enervating, and after what seemed
an interminable length of time she willed him to
say something—anything.

'And now?'

'What would you have me say?' she queried in
anguish.

'Try—honesty.'

She was weeping inside, drenched by her own
silent tears. 'So you can have *your* revenge, Aleksi?'

'Is that what you think?'

'Oh, why do you have to answer every question
with another?' she beseeched, sorely tried.

'Because I want it all.'

It was too soon to bare her soul. Much too soon.
Love was supposed to happen gradually, not all at

once. How was it possible to know if it *was* love in only a matter of weeks?

'I *can't*,' she denied in a tortured whisper.

Aleksi was silent for so long she felt almost afraid, then when he spoke his voice was edged with quiet determination.

'As soon as Rachel and Alexandros return to the Coast, we'll fly to Athens.'

A startled gasp left her lips, and he pressed a finger against them to still the words in protest.

'My parents will delight in having Georg to themselves for a while.'

'Do you always arrange things on the spur of the moment?' she questioned weakly, unable to argue.

'Are you saying you don't want to go?'

She stood hesitantly unsure for a few timeless seconds. 'No,' she whispered at last, aware with frightening certainty that her fate had been irreversibly sealed.

CHAPTER ELEVEN

THE days that followed assumed a dreamlike quality. There was a gentleness apparent, a sense of almost secret anticipation that was fuelled by the touch of the hand, the exquisiteness of their lovemaking.

They accepted few invitations, although when they did venture out Alyse was conscious of the overt, barely concealed glances, the thinly disguised speculative gossip as Aleksi rarely let her out of his sight. At home she took delight in arranging gourmet dinners, with candlelight and wine, loving the long, leisurely conversation shared as they talked about anything and everything.

Two days after Rachel and Alexandros arrived back from Sydney Alyse and Aleksi flew out to Athens, spending two days in that ancient city before chartering a helicopter to a small remote island set like a shimmering jewel in the midst of a translucent emerald sea.

There were grapevines, orange trees, olive groves, a few goats, a dog, all lovingly tended by an elderly couple who greeted Aleksi fondly before boarding the waiting helicopter that would take them to visit relatives on another island.

'It's beautiful,' Alyse breathed as Aleksi led her towards an old, concrete-plastered, whitewashed house set on high ground.

Built around an inner courtyard, the rooms were large and airy and filled with antique furniture. Rich Persian rugs covered highly polished floors, and there were several soft-cushioned sofas in the lounge.

'As a child, I spent most of my holidays here,' Aleksi revealed.

'Did you ever return to the island after you emigrated to Australia?' Alyse asked, wandering around the large lounge at will, pausing slightly now and then to study one of the several framed family photographs resting atop items of furniture.

'Several times.'

She turned to look at him, seeing the inherent strength apparent, the sheer physical attraction, and a shadow fleetingly darkened her eyes at the number of women who had surely formed part of his life.

'To join Rachel and Alexandros, and Georgiou,' he added softly. 'This island has always been a family retreat.'

She summoned a bright smile that hid a slight degree of pain. 'It's so warm. Shall we swim before dinner?'

He was silent for a brief second, then he crossed to where she stood and caught hold of her hand. 'Why not?'

The water was crystal-clear and deliciously cool. Alyse challenged Aleksi to a race across the width of the tiny bay, and he merely gave a tigerish laugh as he deliberately let her win. In retaliation she scooped up handfuls of water and threw them at his chest, then shrieked when he pulled her into his arms.

For a moment she struggled, caught up in a playful game, then she slowly stilled, her expression hesitantly serious.

There were so many things she wanted to say, words she needed to hear, yet she was strangely afraid to begin.

A faint edge of tension was evident beneath the surface of Aleksi's control, and she looked at him in silence, her eyes wide and unblinking.

Remembering his lovemaking, the tenderness, the passion . . . She was tired of fighting, and stubborn pride no longer seemed to matter any more.

'Please help me,' she implored in a husky whisper.

He lifted a hand to her lips and traced a finger across the generous lower curve. 'Why not start at the beginning?'

Her mouth quivered uncontrollably, and she hesitated, unsure now that she had instigated the moment of truth if she possessed the courage to continue. It would be terrible if he was merely amused by a confession of her emotions. Impossible, if he didn't return them to quite the same degree.

'You were everything I disliked in a man,' she ventured unsteadily, her eyes silently beseeching him to understand. 'Overbearing, demanding, and far too self-assured. I told myself I hated you, and at first I did. Then I began to hate myself for being caught up in the maelstrom of physical sensation you were able to arouse.' She drew a deep breath and released it shakily. 'I didn't want to *feel* like that, and I had to fight very hard not to fall in love with you.' A soft, tremulous smile parted her lips. 'It wasn't a very successful battle, for I lost miserably.'

The tension left him in one long shuddering sigh as he gathered her close, then his mouth possessed hers, gently and with such an incredibly sweet hunger she thought she might actually die from sheer sensation, and when at last he lifted his head she could only stand in silent bemusement.

'Repeat those last few words again,' he commanded quietly.

Her beautiful blue eyes misted, and her lips trembled fractionally as she whispered, 'I love you.'

'I had begun to despair that you'd ever admit it,' Aleksi said huskily as he bent low to bestow a lingering kiss to her mouth, then he caught her close, holding her as if he never intended to let her go.

'Can't you feel what you do to me?' His smile held a certain wryness he made no attempt to hide. 'I travelled to Perth with one plan firmly in mind,' he revealed slowly. 'To get Georg at whatever cost. Yet there you were; so fiercely protective of the baby I'd vowed to adopt as my son, adamantly refusing to give him up when I was so sure you would be only too eager to hand over responsibility and get on with your own life.' He brushed his lips across her cheek, then pressed each eyelid closed in turn before trailing a slow evocative path down to the edge of her mouth. 'There was no woman of my acquaintance that I could envisage assuming a motherly role to an orphan child, and faced with your blatant animosity it seemed almost poetic justice to take you as my wife and tame your splendid pride. What I didn't bargain for was the involvement of my emotions.' His smile held such incredible warmth, she felt treacherously weak. 'You were a pocket spitfire, opposing me at every turn. Yet you were so angelic with Rachel and my father, charming to my friends, and I found myself deliberately using every ploy I could engineer in an attempt to break down your defences.'

He paused, taking time to bestow a long, lingering kiss that melted her very bones. His arms held her close, yet she stood strangely still, waiting, wanting so desperately for him to say the words she longed to hear.

'There were times when I was tempted to kill you for being so blind. I love you. *Love*,' he reassured her with a gentle shake.

Joy unfurled itself and spread with tumultuous speed through her veins, and she reached up to lock her hands behind his neck, pulling his head down to hers as she initiated a kiss so incredibly sweet it took only seconds before he deepened it with passionate intensity.

When at last he lifted his head, she could only press her cheek into the curve of his shoulder as he slid an arm beneath her knees and lifted her high against his chest.

'Where are you taking me?' she whispered.

'Indoors.' Aleksi's eyes were warm. 'To bed.'

A soft laugh bubbled from her throat as he carried her into the bedroom, and her eyes sparkled with witching promise as he let her slide down to stand on her feet.

Unable to resist teasing him a little, she protested softly, 'I'm not in the least tired.' Linking her hands together at his nape, she reached up and touched her lips against the corner of his mouth.

He lifted a hand and brushed a stray tendril of hair back behind her ear with incredible gentleness. His smile was warm and infinitely seductive, and she stood looking at him, seeing the strength of purpose etched on those dark arresting features, the passion evident in the depth of his eyes.

A slight tremor shook her slender frame as she reached out and slowly removed his briefs, then her own before unfastening the clip of her bikini bra. Collecting a towel, she carefully blotted every trace of sea-water from his body, then she stood still as he took the towel from her hand and gently returned the favour before letting the towel fall to the floor.

Without a word she reached up and pulled his head down to hers, and her lips brushed across his own, trembling a little as she instigated a hesitant exploration, then she drew him towards the bed and pulled him down beside her.

'Please make love to me.' The plea left her lips as scarcely more than a whisper, and her mouth parted in welcome to his as he wrought a devastating assault on her senses, plundering until she clung to him unashamedly.

It seemed an age before he broke the kiss, and she almost died at the wealth of deep slumbrous passion evident.

'I intend to,' he told her gently. 'For the rest of my life.'

my VALENTINE 1992

Celebrate the most romantic day of the year with
MY VALENTINE 1992—a sexy new collection of four
romantic stories written by our famous Temptation
authors:

GINA WILKENS
KRISTINE ROLOFSON
JOANN ROSS
VICKI LEWIS THOMPSON

My Valentine 1992—an exquisite escape into a romantic
and sensuous world.

 Harlequin Books®

VAL-92

HARLEQUIN
PROUDLY PRESENTS
A DAZZLING NEW CONCEPT IN ROMANCE FICTION

One small town—twelve terrific love stories

Welcome to Tyler, Wisconsin—a town full of people
you'll enjoy getting to know, memorable friends and
unforgettable lovers, and a long-buried secret that
lurks beneath its serene surface....

JOIN US FOR A YEAR IN THE LIFE OF TYLER

Each book set in Tyler is a self-contained love story;
together, the twelve novels stitch the fabric of a
community.

LOSE YOUR HEART TO TYLER!

The excitement begins in March 1992, with
WHIRLWIND, by Nancy Martin. When lively, brash
Liza Baron arrives home unexpectedly, she moves
into the old family lodge, where the silent and
mysterious Cliff Forrester has been living in seclusion
for years....

WATCH FOR ALL TWELVE BOOKS OF THE TYLER SERIES
Available wherever Harlequin books are sold

TYLER-G

Back by Popular Demand

Janet Dailey
Americana

A romantic tour of America through fifty favorite
Harlequin Presents, each set in a different state
researched by Janet and her husband, Bill. A journey
of a lifetime in one cherished collection.

In January, don't miss the exciting states featured in:

Title #23 MINNESOTA
    Giant of Mesabi

#24 MISSISSIPPI
    A Tradition of Pride

Available wherever
Harlequin books are sold.

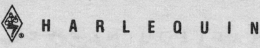

♦ HARLEQUIN

A Calendar of Romance

Be a part of American Romance's year-long celebration of love and the holidays of 1992. Experience all the passion of falling in love during the excitement of each month's holiday. Some of your favorite authors will help you celebrate those special times of the year, like the revelry of New Year's Eve, the romance of Valentine's Day, the magic of St. Patrick's Day.

Start counting down to the new year with

#421 HAPPY NEW YEAR, DARLING
by Margaret St. George

Read all the books in *A Calendar of Romance*, coming to you one each month, all year, from Harlequin American Romance.

American Romance®

COR1

HARLEQUIN Temptation

Rebels & Rogues

All men are not created equal. Some are rough around the edges. Tough-minded but tenderhearted. Incredibly sexy. The tempting fulfillment of every woman's fantasy.

When it's time to fight for what they believe in, to win that special woman, our Rebels and Rogues are heroes at heart.

Josh: He swore never to play the hero . . . unless the price was right.

THE PRIVATE EYE by Jayne Ann Krentz.
Temptation #377, January 1992.

Matt: A hard man to forget . . . and an even harder man not to love.

THE HOOD by Carin Rafferty.
Temptation #381, February 1992.

At Temptation, 1992 is the Year of Rebels and Rogues. Look for twelve exciting stories about bold and courageous men, one each month. Don't miss upcoming books from your favorite authors, including Candace Schuler, JoAnn Ross and Janice Kaiser.

Available wherever Harlequin books are sold. RR-1